VIKING
Mystery
Suspense

The Low End
of Nowhere

The Low End of Nowhere

A STREETER MYSTERY

Michael Stone

VIKING

VIKING
Published by the Penguin Group
Penguin Books USA Inc., 375 Hudson Street,
New York, New York 10014, U.S.A.
Penguin Books Ltd, 27 Wrights Lane,
London W8 5TZ, England
Penguin Books Australia Ltd, Ringwood,
Victoria, Australia
Penguin Books Canada Ltd, 10 Alcorn Avenue,
Toronto, Ontario, Canada M4V 3B2
Penguin Books (N.Z.) Ltd, 182–190 Wairau Road,
Auckland 10, New Zealand

Penguin Books Ltd, Registered Offices:
Harmondsworth, Middlesex, England

First published in 1996 by Viking Penguin,
a division of Penguin Books USA Inc.

10 9 8 7 6 5 4 3 2 1

PUBLISHER'S NOTE
This is a work of fiction. Names, characters, places, and incidents
either are the product of the author's imagination or are used fictitiously,
and any resemblance to actual persons, living or dead, events, or locales
is entirely coincidental.

LIBRARY OF CONGRESS CATALOGING-IN-PUBLICATION DATA
Stone, Michael.
The Low End of Nowhere: a Streeter mystery / Michael Stone.
    p. cm.
        ISBN 0-670-86154-5
        I. Title.
PS3569.T64144B8   1996
813'.54—dc20   95-21208

This book is printed on acid-free paper.
∞

Printed in the United States of America
Set in Minion
Designed by Virginia Norey

To Carla Madison,
for getting me going

The author would like to thank and acknowledge Rex Burns, Bob Diddlebock, Kitty Hirs, Irma Stone, and Danny and Shannon Dupler for their help and support. Also, a nod to Landmark Education.

The Low End
of Nowhere

1

Grundy Dopps, a sour-looking little pinch of white trash, waddled out of his trailer that morning somehow knowing it wasn't going to be his day. Unfortunately, this was one of those rare times that his intuition was right. His hay fever was killing him. An angry tumor of phlegm festered behind a nose that was rubbed so raw, it felt like he'd been wiping it with steel wool. The midday heat pushed the thermometer in his toolshed up past ninety-five. Everything was turned around. It wasn't supposed to be so hot this early in June, and the tree pollen wasn't supposed to be so thick this late in the season. Not in Colorado.

"Go figger it," he reasoned pitifully as he sneezed. "Very weird." More sneezes. "Everything's always so weird."

Then there was that call that woke him up earlier. The guy said he was an investigator for an attorney. Grundy had his doubts.

"My name is Soyko," the guy had informed him.

"You got a first name or is that it?" Grundy asked, holding a soggy handkerchief just inches in front of his nose.

"All you need to know is Soyko. We gotta talk, you and me."

It wasn't a request. "Man who hired me said we should go over your testimony. Make sure you get it right and all that."

Who does he think he is? Grundy wondered. Even Jesus Christ had two names. At least two. And what does he mean, "get it right and all that"? Grundy'd forgotten the attorney's name, but he had a good idea what was coming down.

"Is this about that maniac, what's his name?" he asked Soyko. "Fred Borders? Him and his murder trial?"

No answer at first and then a slow "That's it" slid out of the receiver.

"Ta-rrefic," Grundy mumbled and shook his head.

Tiny Fred Borders was a three-hundred-ten-pound bouncer at the Dangle, a biker-strip bar in Commerce City, just north of Denver. A sadistic lush who smelled like stale beef jerky, Tiny had all the charm of a buffalo with piles. One night a few months back, an investment banker wandered up to the Dangle for a little brush with life's underbelly and tested the big guy. He got stupid drunk and tried to stare down the bouncer.

"Nice bib overalls there, Gomer. Lose your way out of Green Acres or what?" the banker muttered in Tiny Fred's direction. Then he looked around the room, snickering at his own cleverness, and added in a loud voice, "What kind of loony breeding experiment produced a bloated moron like him?"

Truth, of course, was no defense in Tiny Fred's astoundingly limited mind. The bloated moron sucked in his enormous gut and simply went berserk. He threw the drunk, paisley tie and all, out into the parking lot. At that point, the banker shifted into some indignant mode and began cursing. The clown actually was going to put up a fight. Bad move. When Tiny Fred Borders decides to throw you a beating, about the best you can do is assume a fetal position until he gets winded or until his nominal attention span wanders. To call what happened next a fight is like calling what happens at a slaughterhouse a hunt. Still, when Fred finally stopped, the banker was able to totter to his feet, navigate to his BMW, and drive off. As he left the parking lot, he managed what proved to be the last gesture of a truly foolish man. He flipped off Tiny Fred.

Enraged, the bouncer jumped into his pickup and chased the doomed investment banker. About three miles to the south, he forced the BMW off the road and into a deserted parking lot. It was at that point that Tiny Fred, by virtue of one swift tire-iron blow to the head, made sure the uppity Yuppie would diss him no more. Grundy witnessed the fatal blow from the back porch of his welding shop, some thirty yards away. He recognized Tiny Fred standing in the headlights from his own numerous trips to the Dangle. Grundy saw the perspiring bouncer casually wipe blood from the tire iron onto the lifeless banker's pants and kick his stomach one final time. Then Borders farted passionately into the still night air, got back into the pickup, and drove away.

Wisely, Grundy shirked his civic duty and slipped out of town for a few days. He knew that calling the cops would put him on Tiny Fred's vast shit list. Just ask the banker what that felt like. But, alas, Grundy got drunk a couple of weeks later and started blabbing in a crowded bar. An undercover Denver cop overheard him and Tiny Fred was subsequently arrested.

"Listen up, you little turd," one of the investigating officers had admonished Grundy only the day before Soyko's call. "This trial starts in just four days, and if you even think of taking off again or if your memory goes lame on us, you'll walk into a shit storm so thick you'll never get out. You hear that, Dopps? We got us a dead white man here and we ain't gonna let nobody mess up our case. No way."

As he waited for Soyko, Grundy still wondered if he'd done the right thing by not splitting. Standing in the tepid shade of his shop awning, the welder idly ran one hand over his belly. He had an enormous gut and nose for such a short man with such a skinny face.

Suddenly a black El Camino in mint condition pulled up. The vehicle had a lone bumper sticker on the front proclaiming in green Day-Glo that "Disco Heals." It was Leo Soyko, with some guy in dark shades driving. They pulled around to the back, near the porch where Grundy stood when he saw the banker's murder and where he was now, more or less, poised. The car engine shut off, and the two men inside spoke to each other while staring straight ahead. Soyko then looked off as a narrow smile crimped his face. He had been at Tiny Fred's preliminary hearing. It was a joke. The welder up there on the witness stand all cotton-mouthed and twitchy, ratting out the big guy like that. Plain to see he'd rather be strung up by his toes than testifying.

Tiny's attorney knew that the state would have no case without Grundy but it had a virtual lock if a jury ever heard his story. Hence, Soyko was sent, cash in hand, to make sure that wouldn't happen. The lawyer specifically said he didn't want Grundy Dopps within a thousand miles of the courtroom come trial time.

"This is the damnedest thing I ever heard of," Soyko had told the attorney. "You want me to give this little punk three grand to cover his traveling expenses? Maybe I should kiss him good-bye, too."

The lawyer just glared and again told him to get Dopps out of town.

"You know, this screwing around makes no sense whatso-ever," Soyko now told his driver, Jacky Romp. "On three thou-sand like this, we could party serious. He wants me to just give it up like this guy's doing us a favor. It wasn't for him talking, Tiny wouldn't have all this grief. Just how do these jackoffs get through law school anyhow?"

"Beats me," Jacky Romp answered without actually moving his lips. He looked pained behind his shades. "No sense to it whatsoever, like you said. The whole thing makes me sick."

"This welder gives me any shit . . ." Soyko let the unfinished thought hang there in the midday heat. He sat for another min-ute, then got out of the car, still smiling.

What's so funny? Grundy wondered as Soyko moved toward him. Here the guy comes slouching up, dressed like James Dean just out of prison: blue jeans, white sleeveless T-shirt, dark motorcycle boots. His black hair was combed back in a casual pompadour, his sideburns were long and thick but closely trimmed. He was squinting into the sun. Too macho for shades, Grundy reasoned. When he got closer, Grundy noticed that his eyes were small and incredibly dark: deeply intense but flat. Even with the wide grin, there wasn't a sliver of warmth or humor in those eyes.

Two other things about Soyko stood out. First was his wide brown belt with the huge buckle. Second was his left arm. The muscles were impressive enough, like rubber stretched over chains. But high up on it there was a tattoo of a rattlesnake wrapped in barbed wire, coiled and ready to strike. Above the snake's head were two simple words: "Make Pain."

Damned Elvis impersonator on steroids, Grundy thought, then quickly said, "You must be Soyko." He tried to sound calm. "I'm the owner here. Grundy Dopps." He extended his hand.

Soyko kept coming slowly, looking around as he moved. He was still fuming at the lawyer's strategy and he didn't answer at first. Maybe he'd just handle this thing his way. Save the man some money and crank up his own fee. And look at this goof trying to act like he's in control of something. It was at that point that Soyko decided to free-lance.

Grundy neither expected the kick nor saw it coming. Soyko shot his right foot into the welder's unprotected groin so fast out of his casual stride, and Grundy fell so quickly, that it looked like the two men had rehearsed it. The air rushed from Grundy's lungs, so that when his knees hit the ground he was sucking hard. His hands instinctively shot downward to protect his aching balls, which had retreated inward in pain. He didn't fully understand what happened but a look of terror swept over his face. That was all Soyko needed to see. He swung his shoulders a bit to the right, and as he came back he let the welder have a solid backhand, two rings and all, to the side of his face. Grundy let out a scream and Soyko knew that somewhere behind him Jacky Romp was smiling.

"Let's us go over your testimony, pal," Soyko said. His thick smile remained despite what he'd just done. "We're not happy with it. Not at all. Guess you can understand that."

Tears gushed from Grundy's eyes as he struggled to get his breath back. The slap knocked him on his side on the filthy porch floor. He looked up at Soyko and squealed, "What the fuck you do that for?"

"If we're not happy, no way you're gonna be happy." Soyko waited a beat and then reached down and grabbed Grundy's neck with his left hand. "Let's get you up here."

There was just a trace of sympathy in his voice. His other hand snatched the front of Grundy's shirt as he guided him to a folding chair a few feet away. When Soyko got him situated on the chair, he stood over him. The smile was gone. His jaws clenched to indicate that maybe the worst was ahead.

Grundy felt blood rushing to his wounded crotch and he felt more blood flowing down his cheek. His nuts, along with the left side of his face, were swelling fast.

"I didn't want to tell them anything. Christ Awmighty, I didn't." Grundy's voice was shrill, tearful. His stomach was on fire. "They heard me say what I did about that Tiny guy and that was it. What am I supposed to do? Lie up there on the stand? They got me on record from that hearing. I change my story now, I'm totally screwed. Totally! They told me that already. You wouldn't believe the heat I'm getting from the cops. I can't lie up there on the stand."

The logic seemed highly reasonable to the welder as he spoke.

"No, we can't ask you to lie." Soyko sounded convinced, but he frowned. "You ain't getting up on no stand. That's guaranteed."

There was a finality in his voice that terrified Grundy even more. "I'm not?"

He was whimpering loudly now, and the sound infuriated Soyko. Little piece of garbage don't even know enough to protect his own balls and he thinks he's going to put Tiny Fred away, Soyko thought. Not in a million years.

"You're not. You're gonna be taking a long trip to somewhere very far away. Tomorrow night I'm coming back out here, and if you're still in this same time zone, I'll rip off your head and piss in your neck. You got that?"

A splinter of hope rushed through the man in the folding chair. Maybe there's a way out of this. He tried to focus. "I can't just leave, can I? I mean, I can't just . . ."

Soyko's jaw clenched harder. "You can if you want to keep your head attached to the rest of that lard-ass body. I'm not so sure I'm getting through to you. Take maybe two minutes to think about it. I'm going over to the car out there, and when I get back, let me know what you decide."

With that he turned and moved fluently back to the El Camino. He went to the driver's side and leaned in, his face close to Jacky's.

"I'm saving everybody three grand. This guy's so scared, he leaves town, it's with his own money."

"He giving you some grief?" Jacky never really moved his lips.

"A little. Probably too much. He's still asking all these stupid questions. Some guys're more dense than others. Maybe he's one of them."

"What next?" Jacky wanted to see if Soyko was done being nice.

"You're right." Soyko looked at Grundy as he spoke. He and Jacky had worked together for years and had been through enough jobs like this that they had their own shorthand down solid. "Done wasting my breath." Then he started back toward the porch.

Grundy was breathing almost normally, and his thoughts were clearing. Maybe this insane dude would let him go with just the warning. Could he leave town for the trial? The question rushed through him furiously. By now Soyko was again in front of him, and the welder didn't know what to say. He was about to learn that this was no time to improvise.

"You done with your travel plans yet?" Soyko was smiling again.

That alone made Grundy recoil slightly, his hands moving

automatically toward his groin. "I don't know. Those guys are gonna be really pissed when I get back. I miss the trial, they'll go ape shit on me."

The smile disappeared. "Let's us go inside and talk for a minute. You got any beer in there?" He nodded toward the shop door a few feet away.

Man wants a beer, Grundy thought. That's more reasonable. More like it. "Sure thing." He got up slowly and walked, huddled forward. When they got through the screen door, he turned to ask his visitor to sit down.

Soyko knew what had to be done, and he did it with few wasted motions. First, he grabbed the limping welder by the back of his neck. He squeezed so tight that Grundy couldn't see for a second and a harsh, gagging sound blurted from his throat. Soyko then reached down to his belt buckle and clutched it, moving his hand around. The welder was confused. Soyko shook his right hand, releasing the buckle head from the belt itself. It was a unique buckle, highly illegal. The head came loose from the leather, and when it did a four-inch blade slipped into view. Grundy could barely believe it. The blade must run behind the leather next to the buckle, hiding it.

Soyko lifted the blade to his chin level. Grundy felt warm urine flowing down his leg, but he had no idea where it came from. That was the last thing he ever felt, because Soyko thrust the pointed blade into his throat far too quickly for him to register any real pain. It cut his windpipe and slashed open an artery: either one could have killed him. A stream of blood shot out into the air for several inches, and Soyko knew Grundy was dead by the time he hit the floor. He'd seen it before.

"Tiny's trial is gonna go a whole lot easier from now on," he told Jacky Romp when he got back to the El Camino. "That's guaranteed."

2

Streeter knew that when you step into a lie, no matter whose lie, the same thing always sticks to your shoes. And what he was faced with now was nothing but pure, grade-A, designer crapola. From down the hall he could see the blonde take off her cervical collar and drop it next to her blood-burgundy, ever-so-stylish Prince gym bag. Then she grabbed her squash racquet and started bouncing it off her fingertips. Slow and relaxed, not even looking at it. Hot-shit boredom on her face, her hip cocked out like a naughty girl jock. She shot out her tongue for an instant, and the guy with her shook his head and laughed.

"Calvin, do you really want to beat up on a defenseless cripple like me?" She wore an innocent pout as she spoke. "But I guess I'm not supposed to say 'cripple' anymore, am I? Nowadays it's 'unabled' or 'differently capped' or 'structurally challenged.' Or whatever they call it so as not to make people feel like they're less than perfect. I can't even keep track of all the euphemisms we're supposed to call each other."

"Whatever they call it, I hardly think of the word 'defenseless' when I look at you," Calvin answered. "And that's even if you actually needed that collar."

With that, they both walked into the polished court.

Streeter touched the camera in his gym bag for assurance and headed down the hall. Clearly, the blonde hadn't seen him. The muffled smack of rubber balls on hardwood echoed around him. Subdued, almost eerie lighting engulfed the hallway. On both sides there were small doors with slit windows, like some kind of upscale prison in a Nike commercial.

He wanted to give the couple time to start their squash game, so he stopped in front of a tinted, one-way window looking into an empty aerobics room. Catching his reflection in the glass, he straightened his shoulders. Although he was pushing forty-two and he was just over six feet tall and weighed a solid two hundred ten pounds, Streeter still had the childhood habit of slouching. He also noticed that he should consider getting a trim. His thick brown hair was long and combed straight back. No sideburns. He kept his hair clean and combed. The ends fell nonchalantly far over the collar of his pale-blue Oxford shirt. He wore it long enough so as not to look corporate but still kept it neat. With his high, prominent cheekbones and clear, tan skin, he looked pleasantly rugged, but not pretty.

Hard digging and a little luck were about to pay off nicely. Streeter had been hired three weeks earlier by a nervous insurance-claims adjuster who asked him to dig up something on the little blonde.

"Show she ain't hurt nearly so bad, you know, like she claims in that bullshit lawsuit a hers," Swanson, the adjuster, had told him. "Do a real number on this chick—okay, Streeter? She's trying to make jerks out of us. No way in hell she got hurt with what happened to her." He opened a legal-sized file folder and read from it. "The jacket on her goes like this. Her name is Story Moffatt, if you can believe that. Looks great. Sort of beer-commercial cute." He pulled a photograph from the folder and slid it across his desk. "But she's savvy as hell in business. Runs her own successful ad agency, and she's all of maybe thirty-two."

He quit reading and looked up. "Then she gets into a two-car fender bender a few months ago. It's our guy's fault and now

she's suing for sixty grand. The old pain-and-suffering routine."
He emphasized his frustration with a prolonged shrug. "Claims
she's so bad off, most days she's lucky to hook up her damned
bra without screaming. Not much unusual about that, but our
guy was going all of four miles an hour when he hit her. More
like a burp than a collision. We fixed the damage with a tweezers
and nail polish, for Chrissake. Then she comes up with this crap.
Her lawyer knows a, shall we say, ethically limber orthopedic
surgeon, who diagnoses her: 'soft tissue injured, unspecified.' He
sends her to a chiropractor and pain clinic. Three treatments a
week at ninety bucks a pop, and now she's got enough medical
costs to sue."

Swanson had sniffed around on his own but came up empty.
So he called a friend who knew Streeter—a bounty hunter, of
all things. The adjuster didn't even know those guys still existed.
"Bounty hunter" sounded a tad theatrical, but Streeter made his
living tracking down people who posted bail and then couldn't
seem to find the courthouse at the appropriate time. He worked
alone, mostly for a bail bondsman with whom he shared a loose
business-and-housing arrangement. Because Colorado has no li-
censing for private eyes, from time to time Streeter also did related chores for lawyers and insurance companies. Chores like
witness interviewing and surveillances. Or skip tracing: locating
people who don't want to be found. As the bail bondsman put
it, "We're finders of lost assholes."

"You're gonna love this one, big man," Swanson said when
he gave Streeter the five-hundred-dollar retainer. "We're on the
righteous side here. No one gets hurt at that speed unless the
car runs over their head."

Streeter took the check and looked at the adjuster. Their mutual friend was a bookie Streeter had used for years. The bounty
hunter followed college football and basketball religiously and
wasn't above putting down a few bucks on games when he got
a stiff feeling about one of the teams. His feelings paid off with
remarkable frequency. Streeter had a keen eye for all manner of
team statistics and minute pregame detail. But that keen eye was

best utilized in his most passionate avocation: trivia. Annually, he fielded a team in The Knowledge Bowl, a trivia contest in Boulder, and Streeter had even made a two-day appearance on *Jeopardy* a couple of years ago. Pop culture and movies were his specialty. "I'll get right on it," he told Swanson as he stuffed the check in his shirt pocket.

It had started off badly, but Streeter didn't panic. He sat on Moffatt's house one Saturday morning and then tailed her late one Wednesday afternoon. Nothing. She was being careful, the cervical collar with her always. Story moved slowly, gingerly getting in and out of cars like she was wearing sandpaper panties. Strictly Oscar material. So much for deep distance and caution. The retainer was melting and his curiosity burned. That's when he decided to go face-to-face with the woman.

Getting people to talk was a strong suit. He had those safe, big brown eyes and that calm demeanor. He always listened intently, leaning in to people like nothing else in the whole world mattered except them. And usually he'd wait a few seconds after they spoke before responding. Just long enough to be noticed, but not so long as to be irritating. It let them know he was really considering what they just said. People responded to that, opened up. His size helped. Years of relentless weight lifting gave his shoulders mass without making him appear clumsy. Shoulders like a linebacker, which is what he was when he played the holy game of football in college. Linebacker intensity in the eyes, too.

People felt protected just being around him. Especially women. They liked Streeter and he liked them. Did he ever. Trouble was, his experiences in that department were consistently catastrophic. He'd already racked up four failed marriages, he'd been engaged another three times, and was at least nominally involved with more women than he could recall. They tended to own him. And it wasn't only that he couldn't say no to an attractive woman. Streeter couldn't say no to any woman with a pulse and at least a double-digit IQ. Take this Story Moffatt. He knew the first time he saw her smug beauty that she was trouble. Big trouble. If he ever fell for her, he'd be doing whatever it took to keep her around. Whatever. Good thing this was strictly business.

Story's advertising firm was located in Denver's eclectic Capitol Hill section, so named because it was a wide, low hill featuring the state capitol roughly in the middle of it. Her company consisted of five employees and a clientele that netted her nearly six figures annually. She was divorced, childless ("Who has time for a family?"), and overachieving in a business where nerve and style got you a hell of a lot further than an impressive résumé or real job skills. Streeter figured he could best get her attention by passing himself off as a prospective client. From his desk he dug out an old business card once belonging to Brad Tessmer, owner of the defunct Arapahoe Auto Body Shop. Then he set up an appointment with Story to get some four-color brochures made.

"That collar must really hurt you, Miss Moffatt," Streeter told her as they sat down in her office the following Tuesday afternoon. Collar or no, she looked sensational. Her hair, almost white-blond, was long but styled to accent the sensual roundness of her face. She wore a pinstriped pants suit, tailored to her body so closely that it easily avoided any trace of masculinity. "I bet that's slowing you up plenty, huh?"

"I manage," she said with little emotion and then flashed him a quick, obligatory grin. Even that forced, all-business smile had enough voltage to make Streeter blink. "But it certainly doesn't make life any easier. Please, call me Story."

"I had to wear something like that once. Hurt like a mother. How'd you get yours?"

"It's really not important." Her voice gave no openings. "Let's just say I earned it. A car accident, actually."

"Think that there might be a little payoff for you in all this? Hope you got yourself a good lawyer."

"Mr. Tessmer, I have a busy schedule this afternoon and I'm

sure a man like you has a million things to do as well. My neck will take care of itself, but this brochure will need our complete attention."

Her own deep-brown eyes—he had never seen such dark-brown eyes on a blonde before—returned his gaze. She used her best low-end client voice. A real pro. Not a trace of perfunctory flirting. She had a way of telling you to go pound sand that made it seem like it was your idea. Streeter pushed harder but got nowhere. Then, just as they were finishing up, she took a phone call. When she swiveled around in her chair to talk, he scanned everything on her desk. His prayers were answered in her open Daytimer. There it was, an entry for Friday morning. "Creekside SC—S. court. Match." Creekside Sports Club. It had to be. Combination meat market and high-tech gym, it was Denver's premier health club, located in fashionable Cherry Creek. "S. court. Match"—some kind of court game. Probably "S." for "squash."

When he left her office, he called the club to verify his hunch by pretending to be her confused opponent trying to nail down the correct time.

"Yeah," the guy at the front desk told him. "Story Moffatt. Eight-thirty on Friday morning. You got the date right. Court twelve." He said her name as though he knew her and liked her. That didn't surprise Streeter.

It put him just down the hall from court twelve at a little after eight. When Story and her friend had had time to get their game going, Streeter went to the court door and grabbed his camera. He let the gym bag slide to the floor. He noticed her cervical collar and he winced. Supposed to be for broken bodies, not for making quick cash. Streeter flashed on the man he'd killed long ago.

Killing someone with his bare hands drastically changed Streeter's life. It had a profound impact on Gary Van der Heyden as well. He was the twenty-year-old Streeter killed. It happened in the summer of 1974, between their sophomore and junior years at Western Michigan University. Streeter and Gary both played linebacker. The two never got along, and the animosity boiled over in a drunken fight at a preseason frat party. Insults were exchanged and they ended up on the frat house lawn, charging each other like a couple of demented rhinos. Finally, he gave Gary one good shot to the head. His massive forearm and elbow came up like a renegade piston, catching the smaller man just below the chin. Gary's head shot back, and his neck snapped like frozen vinyl. He died on the spot.

Streeter, who had been getting some attention from pro scouts after his standout sophomore year, never played football after that. He left Western Michigan without graduating. As close as he ever came to a four-year diploma was an associate accounting degree from a community college in his hometown of Denver. After that, he did bookkeeping by day and, because of his size and cool demeanor, he was a bouncer at country-and-western bars at night. That's where he met most of his wives and fiancées. That's also how he met Frank Dazzler. A veteran bail bondsman, Frank came to Mollie's Hitching Post back in the summer of 1985 looking for a jittery car thief who was partial to George Strait music and Old Milwaukee beer. He and Streeter got to talking about their respective jobs at the front door just before closing time.

"A bouncer and an accountant, huh? You like this kind of thing, big guy?" Frank asked, tossing his head to the side to indicate the bar. "You seem way too sharp to be checking IDs and throwing these phony cowboys around. Particularly at a shithole like Mollie's."

"Both jobs can get boring sometimes," Streeter conceded. "Especially keeping books. But this has its moments, if you can stand the music. It's really a pretty decent place."

Just then an announcement blared unceremoniously over the loudspeaker inside. "Last call for alcohol. Closing time. If you're not going to fuck the help, ya gotta leave."

Frank nodded thoughtfully. "Yeah, I see what you mean. Real classy. A regular Radio City Music Hall. But I'll bet it does have some payback, at that, what with the little cowgirlies and all. As for me, I'm way too old to chase these goofs around town day and night. Look, here's my card. You come by and see me sometime and I'll give you a job that's guaranteed never to bore you. You'll get to use your brains and your brawn. And there's some real money in it, too."

Three days later, Streeter walked into Frank's office and grabbed a pair of handcuffs, and he hadn't worked another bar or kept another book since.

Now, looking through the window slit into the squash court, he could see Story bent over, waiting for the serve. Bouncing easily up on the balls of her feet, she was ready. Kill-shot concentration. Her weight moved easily from cheek to cheek in a little round butt with dark shorts stretched over it tight as wallpaper. That butt had seen some serious gym time, Streeter noticed. Tanned legs flowed out of the bottom of the shorts without a sign of a wrinkle anywhere. The woman's entire life appeared to be so seamless. So smooth and nearly effortless.

He lifted the camera, and as he took the pictures, he knew he would be putting at least one major wrinkle in her day. He almost nodded to her out there on the court. You know: Good try, lady. She made a strong run at easy insurance money. But thanks to him she'd be coming up short. She had some real brass to her, still Streeter sensed that the line between brass and bitch was so slender, at times it almost disappeared. When he was done shooting, he took one last look as she scooped low to backhand a stinger off the front wall. Not a hint of pain or stiffness anywhere. He just wished he could be there when her lawyer showed her the pictures.

3

Max Herman sat squirming across the desk from his lawyer. Max had already had his shot in life. Clearly, he'd blown it. Here he was, all of forty-three, and he'd pissed away more than most men ever have. Ten years earlier, the American dream was his. A beautiful wife, two daughters, a plumbing-supply business that grossed him nearly a hundred and a half a year, and a cool one-ninety-four bowling average. Within a few years, it was sliding fast, and by the time he was forty it was gone. In its place was a cocaine Jones that cost over a grand a week, a twenty-three-year-old Mexican girlfriend with a prison teardrop tattoo, and his two daughters in therapy—neither of whom would talk to a daddy who was over a year behind in his support payments.

"Oh, hell yeah. I know I got troubles." Max bent forward to crush out yet another Camel Light. He coughed savagely, spraying ashes across the otherwise immaculate desktop. "That's obvious, counselor. Everybody seems to want a chunk oudda my tail. But there's gotta be a way oudda all this mess. There's always a way, ain't that the truth?"

"Of course there is," the lawyer offered unenthusiastically.

The attorney, Thomas Hardy Cooper, looked at his client and

wondered how well he was hiding his disgust. If it weren't for the twenty-two-thousand-dollar retainer, already cashed and spent, Cooper wouldn't give this guy the sweat off his socks. Cooper, who was five years older than Max, couldn't imagine ever looking that rough.

Amazingly, Max had managed to gain about fifty pounds of extra blubber while using cocaine daily. "I thought this shit's supposed to melt the fat off," he would tell himself angrily as his stomach grew larger by the week. Add in his chain-smoker's rasp and top it off with the thinning blond hair wilting sadly over his shoulders, and it was obvious that he'd torched his prime. Here he is talking about some "group of heavy hitters" he's putting together for a townhouse development in the foothills west of Denver, near Golden. Yeah, right. He's facing up to twenty years for possession of cocaine with intent to deliver, a few more tacked on for a weapons violation, and a whole bunch more thrown in for allegedly threatening a police officer. Top it all off with some forty-three thousand dollars in back child support and Max is basically screwed.

Only thing is, he was way too far gone to realize it. His brain was so incinerated from his many vicious habits that he'd become prone to monumental lapses from reality. Like three weeks ago, after he was served with a temporary restraining order to keep him away from his ex and the two girls. There was a ten-thirty court hearing set for a week later. Max showed up, all right. Made quite an appearance. He waltzed into court just out of bed, wearing a ratty plaid bathrobe and a vile-looking pair of slippers. But the real *coup de maître* was that he had an open plastic bottle of Aunt Jemima pancake syrup sticking out of one pocket.

Cooper thought how if he had half this yahoo's troubles he'd save the legal fees, make one more big coke run, and then take off for someplace warm and unknown. Instead, the lawyer focused on his assistant and unofficial paralegal. He couldn't forget the skirt she wore that morning. So tight, he recalled, he could practically count her pubic hairs. That is, if she didn't regularly shave "that particular stretch of paradise," as he referred to it. Streetwise, sexy beyond belief, and precisely half Cooper's age, Rhonda "Ronnie" Taggert was his sweetest dream come true.

Cooper was pretty much of a full-fledged dorker himself until law school and a rigid program of self-improvement made him presentable. With a clientele consisting of Max Herman types, he came off as almost classy. But he had never experienced anything like Ronnie. The first time she came into his office, she was with a guy who rivaled Max for sheer, brazen stupidity. She had these bee-stung lips and this porno-queen attitude the lawyer found irresistible. Cooper took on the guy's rather winnable auto-theft case, along with a seventeen-thousand-dollar retainer, and then did everything humanly possible to see that the poor schlep got double digits in the state prison at Cañon City.

Coincidentally, that left the precocious if pouty Ms. Taggert unencumbered, uncertain about her future, and open to all offers. The one Cooper made was that she come to work in his office, get her GED, and generally clean up her act to make herself palatable to the lower echelons of Denver's legal community.

"We get a little participation from the people up there on the Jefferson County Board and this project should come together real nice," Max was saying intensely. "I get the whole entire contract for pipes and fixtures, which makes me very well, thank you. Financially speaking, that is. We take care of this bullshit holding charge and all that other crap and get Charlene and the kids off my back, and things'll look just about right."

Christ, Cooper thought. The only pipe Max had touched since he lost his plumbing shop back about six years ago was loaded with crack cocaine. And where did he get this "bullshit holding charge" from? Even if Cooper gave it his best shot, which he certainly wouldn't, Mr. Herman would be spending what was left of his middle age—not to mention a good chunk of his golden years—behind bars.

"That's a fabulous attitude, Maxwell." Cooper beamed, but Max seemed puzzled by the use of his full first name. "I feel we have an excellent chance of getting most of their evidence disposed of at the suppression hearing. Actually, I was *exceedingly* amazed that we even got bound over for trial. I did not believe that the judge was too impressed with their evidence. It seems more of a political gesture, their continuing this travesty. I'm convinced that, once we get in front of a jury, we shall get the results we desire and so justly deserve."

Not too impressed? Cooper almost laughed. The judge nearly sentenced Max right at the preliminary hearing. And if any juror in his right mind takes one look at this pathetic load and the evidence against him, the DA gets a standing ovation.

"You know, I've been working overtime on this matter," he continued. "On all of your various troubles. You've had an incredible run of bad luck, Maxwell."

"Fuckin' A, I have." Max nodded wildly. "Incredible, like you said. Who could believe all this shit?"

"Taken individually, these matters are quite manageable. However, in the aggregate, they are indeed formidable. We have almost exhausted your retainer and secondary monies. I will require another payment of precisely fifteen thousand dollars by the weekend in order to proceed."

When Max heard the number he rolled his eyes and made a sour frown, like he was suppressing a fart. "Fuckin' A, fifteen large. What are you doing, burning the money I give you? Hell, Cooper, that might take some doing."

"I understand. But you have to understand that keeping you out of Cañon City for twenty years plus will take some doing as well." Cooper was getting irritated. This was the first time Max had even hesitated about coming up with money. "Trial preparation is no easy matter. There's expert-witness fees, process serving, a million details to work out. For God's sake, Maxwell, I and my staff will be holed up here for most of the weekend working on your suppression hearing."

Fat chance. Cooper and Ronnie had reservations at a bed-and-breakfast near Vail for the weekend. Neither he nor his "staff" would be within a hundred miles of the office or Max's files.

"I'm not saying I won't come up," Max said bitterly as he looked away. "Just it's a lot of money, is all. Okay. I want the best shot you got. You and your guys here. Balls to the wall on this one, counselor. Nothing less. You fuckin' hear me?"

Max had never seen anyone except, as he put it, "that sexy bimbo Cooper was always drooling over" and "that fat spade chick"—the former being Ronnie, and the latter being the receptionist, who snarled at him whenever he came to the office. But, based on Cooper's incessant pep talks, Max assumed that he had several partners and an eager support staff.

"But of course. That's precisely what you'll be getting, Maxwell." Cooper decided to tack on another hour just because of the hard time he was having. He reasoned that it was bad enough he had to go through this phony tap dance without having to hear a ton of shit in the bargain. "Right after this money situation is properly addressed."

Cooper, if not a class act from birth, was by no means stupid. He had worked himself up in life through basic determination, grit, and greed. First as a private investigator. After going back and finishing college at thirty, he created a résumé from sheer nerve and imagination that boasted of his "five years of experience as a trained legal investigator," and hunted up work. But he soon grew tired of chasing lawyers for forty dollars an hour in fees and decided to chase clients for one hundred forty dollars an hour. He went to the University of Denver Law School, where he realized that lawyering wasn't that hard. Not if you're willing to trim the edges. Life was simply too short for jumping through all those silly hoops. Like doing this tedious grunt work that Max's case required and actually logging all those hours he was billing. A man'd have to be totally insane to do that.

Cooper's way made sense. Stall his client for a few weeks and ignore the DA's offer. And a pretty good offer it was. Plead to the drug charges and they'd drop the threatening business, which was weak anyway. Also plead to the weapons charge and the two sentences would run concurrently. The DA would sit quietly at sentencing and Max would get maybe eight to ten years. He'd be out in four or five if he behaved himself and didn't get his throat slashed.

Cooper tabled the offer and told Max that the DA was being a real hard-nose. Then, after they got clobbered at the suppression hearing, he'd let the poor slug know how much trouble he was really in and how the judge was a total maniac on drug dealers. Scare the hell out of Max with the possibility of twenty years for sure. Finally, a couple of days before the trial, he'd lay out the DA's deal like he had just fought to the death for it. Max pleads out, thinking Cooper saved his ever-expanding butt. Everyone's happy. Especially Cooper.

"Awright, Chrissake, awright." Max wanted to end the discussion, too. "You'll have the fifteen by the weekend. I think I'll get trucking now, so you can get down to work. You give it your best there, counselor. Right?"

"You have my word." Cooper nodded and leaned forward with enough insincere humility to win office. "I will keep after the district attorney's office and see if we can get some concessions on these matters. However, judging by the way they're being so stubborn, I believe we will end up going to trial as scheduled. They simply do not want to bend. They're coming after you hard, Maxwell."

When Max left, Cooper focused on the problem that had nagged him since he read his morning newspaper. On the lower half of the metro page was a twelve-inch story about the murder of a Commerce City man, Merrill Dopps, aka Grundy. The story said that Dopps was the victim of an apparent robbery, because the cash drawer in his welding shop had been rifled. That sadistic bastard Soyko clearly had gone too far, the lawyer pondered as he read. Cooper had only wanted the welder out of town, not out of body. So this jerk goes and kills the guy. But, more important, what happened to that three grand he gave Soyko for traveling expenses? Cooper wanted answers and he wanted them now.

"Ronnie, get in here," he yelled toward the door.

He didn't have to wait long. When Ronnie saw Max leave, she

fluffed up her bleached hair and put on a seasoned pout that showed she was ready for business or pleasure. Cooper was no killer in the looks department, but, then, Ronnie never thought she'd have an attorney courting her. This guy would probably never make the Supreme Court. Still, he generated solid revenues and he paid his gold card on time. She'd be his secretary, his mistress, his *whatever*, until he produced a diamond and walked her down the aisle. She grabbed her notepad—not that she had ever taken one word of dictation. But she'd seen secretaries do that in a million old movies and so she'd acquired the habit.

When she walked into his office, Cooper looked up and tried to act serious. It was a real stretch, because just the sight of her in that red dress aroused him to giddy distraction. The longer he knew Ronnie, the more he realized that he was falling for her. Falling hard. At first, she was just this terrific lay. Given his luck with women, any lay was terrific, which put Ronnie completely off the charts. But as time went by, he noticed that he liked her for more than sex. She was really quite bright, and she came up with ways to work a client he never imagined.

For her part, Ronnie felt a certain fondness for the lawyer. With his choppy Beatle bangs, uneven, gaunt mustache, and doughy body, he had a certain harmless appeal. She'd had her fill of disturbed bad boys, thank you. All danger and excitement. All pain and disappointment. Like the cretin she married when she was sixteen. That crazy biker used to jam the barrel of his thirty-eight against her forehead and threaten her repeatedly. When he died in a motorcycle accident a year or so later, she was still so afraid she almost didn't go to the funeral.

"You see what that nut case Soyko did with our little problem in the Borders trial?" Cooper looked her over. He always felt the urge to impress her, let her know what a take-charge kind of man he was. He continually used the malicious and emotionally erratic duo of Soyko and Romp, in part just to show Ronnie that he could play hardball and hold his own with the two marginally psychotic "investigators." Cooper mistook her warnings against them for interest. "I better have a talk with that guy.

Tighten him up a few notches. Both he and his partner. This is really way the hell out there. Totally unacceptable."

He tried to sound cocky, but he couldn't pull it off. Actually, nobody on earth could tighten Soyko up. He was so toxic that even the criminal-justice system didn't want him. He'd been up on felony charges seven times, some of them serious. But except for periodic and brief county-jail time, he'd never seen the inside of a prison.

"I told you this guy could get out of control. I knew it the first time I ever met him." Ronnie casually smoothed out the front of her dress with one hand as she spoke. She never missed an opportunity to showcase her body to Cooper. "He reminds me of too many of those creeps I used to date. Mean as a snake with a hangover, and you never know what they'll do next."

"You mean 'the first time I met him,' honey," Cooper corrected her. "When you said 'the first time I ever met him,' it's redundant." He couldn't resist the constant urge to correct, improve, and refine Ronnie. It reinforced his notion that she needed him: that he was her best hope for a better life. He also knew the value of Soyko's services. "Look, your instincts were right about him, but don't forget the good work he's done for us. One conversation with that man gets more results than twenty restraining orders or depositions."

"Come on, Thomas Hardy. I know they've muscled some good results for you, but this is murder." She always called him that when she thought he was acting naïve or stupid. "I'd say that qualifies as something beyond 'totally unacceptable,' for God's sake. You just like all this heavy crap because it makes you feel like a regular gangsta. You better grow up if you plan on growing old."

Cooper leaned back in his chair and mustered all his nonchalance. "That is not correct, Rhonda." He used her formal name when he wanted to put her in her place and let her know the discussion was over. "Leo Soyko's propensity for violence and the so-called gangster mode do not factor into my hiring the man. He gets results. It's just that simple." He wished he believed it.

Jacky Romp picked up the phone on the first ring. "So talk," he said through clenched jaws.

Cooper was surprised by the rancor in his voice. "Uh, is Soyko there?"

Jacky knew it was Cooper, so he didn't say anything for a minute. Then, "Why?"

The attorney regained his composure and put some authority in his voice. "Because I asked you, that's why. Kindly put him on."

Kindly take a flying fuck, Romp thought. But he just smiled, knowing he had riled the man at the other end of the line. He waited before nodding to Soyko, who was sitting on the couch nearby.

Soyko guessed who it was by the way Jacky spoke. "Counselor," he said when he took the phone. He sounded relaxed, moderately amused. "What's to it?"

Cooper didn't like that. The crazy bastard ignores his orders, kills a man, and doesn't feel a bit defensive.

"I read about our welder this morning. That was not what I requested."

"The way I remember it, you just wanted to make sure the little prick didn't go to court," Soyko said slowly. "Even if they do get him there now, a corpse ain't gonna hurt you. Did my job, the way I see it."

Cooper had to admit Soyko took care of the Dopps problem. It would be just a matter of time before the charges against Tiny Fred would be dropped.

"Look, I'm not going to quibble over semantics. Suffice it to say that I did not order an execution. What about the three grand I gave you for his traveling money? I take it you'll return that to me."

"I don't know squat about semadics, but, the way I see it, you asked for this. You're the one sent me up there to deal with this crumb fuck. Do it your way, it's like he just won on *Wheel of Fortune*. The guy's ratting your client out and you want me to help him pack for a vacation. That three grand, the way I see it, I saved the money from being pissed down a rat hole. I should get it. That's just part of the cost of taking care of this particular piece of business."

Cooper could see there was no point in arguing about the killing. That was history. But the money definitely was not history.

"How about if we split it? Call it a misunderstanding or a tip or whatever. Fifteen hundred each." He could see Ronnie rolling her eyes slightly.

There was a pause on Soyko's end. Then, "That maybe sounds fair."

A done deal. Cooper moved on. "You can bring it by the next time we get together. I'd like to see you over the next couple of days. There's a certain woman I may need you to interview. Could be some money in it for both of us."

"I'm listening," Soyko said. "Who we talking about?"

Ronnie gave Cooper a hard look and mouthed, "No." It was way too soon to think about using this lunatic for Story Moffatt. Cooper just held up his hand, palm toward her, as if to indicate, "Don't worry."

"A nobody. But I might need you," he shot back to Soyko. Then his voice softened. "So how do you intend for us to split up the money you took from this Dopps' cash register?"

4

The red neon "Jesus Saves" cross that hung out over the front door hadn't worked in years, but it still demanded attention. "Jesus" ran horizontally and the "Saves" came down vertically. The first "S" in "Jesus" was the first "S" in "Saves," with a star above it to complete the cross. Streeter called it Bible Deco, and he kept it up there more as a novelty than as a statement of faith.

"They tell me that thing busted down about the same time Humphrey Bogart died, back in '57," Frank explained the cross to Streeter when they took possession of the brick church five years ago. "Could be some deeper meaning there. I'll tell you one thing, that man could eat up the screen. Bogey, that is. Not Jesus. No one like that around no more. Bogey, that is. At the time, this place was the Temple of Faith—a charismatic church, I'm told. That was the last religious go-round. It was St. Teresa Catholic Church when it opened back in the twenties and then, sometime right before the Korean War, it became Jesus the Redeemer. That's of the Methodist African Episcopal denomination. Whatever *that* is."

Streeter told Frank that he wasn't much interested and he just wanted help moving his furniture into the loft space above the rectory. Now that he and Frank owned the two-story church and his fourth divorce was just about final, he planned on living there.

"In good time, buddy," Frank told him. "You got to know what you're moving into first. Now, it stopped being a church in the early seventies. That's about when I moved my bail-bonds office into the old Sunday-school rooms. People told me I was nuts, being so far away from the jail downtown. But I told them, with all the housing projects sprouting up around here, I'd have more customers within spitting distance than I'd ever know what to do with. I was right, too."

Streeter and the aging Frank Dazzler took ownership of the place when the previous owner's son made an untimely run for the border, leaving behind a huge surety bond secured with the old church. Under a creative agreement with the father, Streeter went down to Mexico and brought the three-time armed robber back. He and Frank then took possession of the building. The robber's old man had plenty of property, and at the time an abandoned church in a then-decaying neighborhood wasn't seen as much of a prize.

Frank's office and small apartment shared the first floor with the garage and, later, a feminist survival-defense school forbiddingly named the Womyn's Workout Space. At first, Frank was delighted with the idea of his new tenants.

"I thought it'd be one of those aerobics places and they were just being cute with the name," he told Streeter when the gym first opened. "I expected some spandex jiggle show where the gals stretch wide, and sweat and bounce around to that loud music that's so popular nowadays. You know, that rap shit or whatever they call it. But then it turns out to be mostly a bunch of feminist maniacs in flannel shirts practicing kung fu so's they can castrate men. Gives me the creeps."

He was overstating the school's mission, but when they put signs in the window like "Mao was gender neutral, are you?"

Frank, a decorated Korean War infantryman and ex–sheriff's deputy, got more uneasy. Then, to everyone's utter amazement, the gym's normally stern founder took a shine to the gruff bondsman. The two of them had been carrying on a creaky romance in the nearly four years since.

The church was located on the fringes of Denver's rapidly Yuppifying "Lower Downtown." The Colorado Rockies' baseball stadium—Coors Field—was sprouting up a half-mile away, and the old warehouse district to the west was being converted into lofts and brew pubs to accommodate fans. To the north were the last remnants of the Old West, bucket-of-blood bars that had so excited Jack Kerouac when he passed through town some forty years earlier. Although the church was built without a steeple, its pitched, metal roof and dramatically arched stained-glass windows throughout gave it a definite cathedral look. But it also was as sturdy and defensible as a medieval fortress. Streeter— being in a business where angry and deranged bail jumpers came with the paycheck—particularly liked that. Actually, it looked a little like an armory, so he dubbed it Fort God.

Story Moffatt parked her Audi in front of the church and double-checked the address for Dazzler's Bail Bonds. Then she spotted the small "Bail Bonds" sign right below the nonfunctioning electric cross. When she and her lawyer saw the squash photos, they had no choice but to take the insurance company's offer of twenty-seven hundred dollars. The only concession she got from that weasel Swanson was that he told her the name and work address of the man who took the pictures.

She walked toward the church and noticed the Womyn's Workout Space. There was a window display featuring T-shirts imprinted, "Potential Rape Survivor," for fifteen dollars. Just to the right of the display, at the main church entrance, a man in a rumpled linen suit slouched against the wall genially taking in the neighborhood. She placed him just over sixty, but he had a quick smile and there was a hard liveliness in his blue eyes. This one had plenty of good years left in him, Story decided.

"Tell me you're not here to join the nutcracker sweets over there, darlin'." Frank straightened up and nodded toward the window display. "You look too tender for that crowd."

Story glanced back at the Womyn's gym. "Seems a little paranoid, and they could use a spelling lesson," she answered. The man appeared to be a borderline mouth-breather but he had a gentle lilt to his western twang that made him seem both smart and kind. His face had the warmth of age, like an old wooden desktop. Yet his features were sharp. She could tell he could be an ass kicker if he had to be. "You wouldn't happen to know where Mr. Streeter is by any chance, would you?"

He looked at her for a moment and then shook his head. "Who wants to know?"

"Obviously, I do."

"And you are?" His voice stayed gentle, even.

"Story Moffatt." She stepped forward and held out her hand.

He shook it carefully. "Frank Dazzler. Your friend in the bail-bonds business, darlin'."

At that moment, Streeter walked out the front door into the June sunshine. Story saw him come from behind Frank and immediately recognized him as Brad Tessmer. A smug grin took over her face, like she just stomped him at Yahtzee.

"And is this my friend in the bounty-hunting business or in the auto-body business?" she asked.

Streeter's eyes widened, but only for a second. "Well, well." He smiled broadly. "Squash, anyone?"

She was disappointed that he stayed so calm. She wanted to see some remorse, or at least a hint of surprise. Big guys always seem so cocky. "You work in a church. I suppose that makes you the insurance company's savior."

"You two kids know each other?" Frank moved away from the wall, looking back and forth at them. "Am I missing something here?"

Streeter looked at him and said, "It's a long story, Frank, but she's not about bonds. She's that deal I did for Swannie."

"Yeah, Frank." Story's face hardened. "I'm *that* deal. I don't know, maybe I came to the wrong place."

"That's possible," Streeter said. "Why are you here?"

"Is there somewhere we can talk in private?" she asked.

Frank shot both hands into his pants pockets and he rattled his car keys. "Use my office. I gotta head over to the jail. Go on and grab the office. It looks like you two kids got things to discuss."

Streeter shifted to the side of the church door and held out his left arm, indicating that Story should come inside. She walked up the steps and into the building. The large foyer for the main church had two doors inside. One went straight ahead, into the church itself, which was now used by the Womyn for their self-defense studio. The altar overlooked the workout gym and served as a combination lectern and reference library. The second foyer door, the one on the right, opened into a short hallway that led to the old Sunday school and assorted smaller rooms. That's where Frank's office was, with his apartment behind it farther down the hall in the old rectory. The office itself had the weird atmosphere of a combination holy place and government work space. There was thick, flowered carpeting, and rich mahogany cabinets and beams, yet the desk and the few other furnishings were strictly state-issued. Pale Formica and painted metal.

"I love what you've done with this room." Story glanced around. "It looks like a parochial mental hospital."

"Somehow, I knew you were the type to have opinions on everything." Streeter nodded for her to take a chair in front of the desk.

"I'm not a type, opinionated or otherwise." She sat down.

"What brings you to our humble little parish?" He moved slowly behind the desk and sat down in Frank's overstuffed chair.

"Mr. Dazzler is your partner?"

"Basically. It's a loose arrangement. Why?"

"He seems a little rough around the edges. All that darlin' stuff. Maybe a little patronizing to women."

"Astounding. You spend two minutes with the man and you've already got him pegged. Look, Frank's from the old school. He calls women darling because he always has and because he likes them. He's just trying to be friendly. And you'd be rough around the edges, too, if you ran a bail-bonds business. Frank Dazzler got me started in this racket and he's a decent man. Honest, beyond question. And he'll do anything for you once he likes you. Anything."

"I didn't mean to criticize, Streeter. By the way, what's your full name?"

"Streeter's full enough."

She just shrugged, obviously not amused. "Well, Streeter whatever, you caused me problems and you cost me money."

He hoped she hadn't come just to complain. "That's what they hired me to do. How'd you find out who I am and where to get a hold of me?"

"Your friend Mr. Swanson provided me with that. He told me you work with Frank Dazzler, so I just came here on a hunch. Do you live around here?"

He didn't answer and instead made a mental note not to work for the adjuster again. Streeter was highly secretive about where he lived. He was protective of his entire life. There were precious few ways to track him. No credit cards, no insurance of any kind. He subscribed to no magazines or newspapers, and belonged to no organizations. Streeter banked through Frank, so he had no accounts in his name; his two cars were registered and insured under Frank's name. His driver's license was under the name of someone he knew who more or less matched his description and had died years ago. Even his half-ownership of the church was a side arrangement with the bondsman, so his name appeared on no city property-tax rolls or utility records. Because he dealt almost exclusively in cash and barter, the IRS barely knew how to reach him. Streeter told no one his address and he never got mail. His friends got hold of him through Frank's business number, and his ex-wives never called. He had no children or siblings.

"So now you're here to tell me to go to hell or what?" he finally said. "If you want money, you're out of luck."

"Actually, I'm here to give you some money. You'll have to earn it, of course. But when someone does good work, I can appreciate that. Even if it causes me problems. You did good work, Mr. Streeter. As you know, I may have been somewhat less than totally candid with my insurance claim. I was pretty careful, but you got through all that. Now I want to see if you can help me. Show me that getting those pictures wasn't a fluke. I need someone like you, so I thought, rather than getting someone like you, I may as well get the real thing."

"I've been called worse, Ms. Moffatt." What's with this "fluke" crap?

"Please, you can call me Story. How would you like to get three thousand dollars up front for your time and have a chance to make a lot more down the road if we get what we're after? By the way, how much did you get for those squash pictures?"

"That sounds promising, in answer to your first question. None of your business, in answer to your second. Tell me about this three-thousand-dollar proposition."

"Fair enough." She settled back into her chair. "Basically, I want you to find money. Do you do that kind of work?"

"An assets search? You mean find out someone's net worth."

"Not exactly. I'm talking about finding money that I think exists. It's probably cash. It would have been left by someone who died a couple months ago. April 5 to be exact."

"An estate?" Streeter frowned.

"You might say. I just know that Doug—the man who died —left valuables around, and I want to find them. I've tried everything I could think of with no results, so now it's time to hire a professional. I'm told you do skip tracing. I figured if you can locate people then you can find things as well. I suppose I could get a private investigator, but, judging by what you did in my insurance case, I think you'll do just fine."

"I take it you were close enough to this Doug so you have a legal claim to his estate."

"Definitely. I'm really the only beneficiary in his will. We lived together for the better part of the past three years. We were even thinking about getting married. Actually, we were thinking about it less as time went by." She cocked her head to the side just a shade as she spoke. Cute but a little too affected. "We weren't very close at the end, but he didn't have any heirs and he was barely on speaking terms with his family."

"How much are we talking about?"

"I don't know. I never actually saw it but I'm estimating as high as six figures. Could be a couple hundred thousand. Maybe more. Certainly enough to make all this worthwhile." She waved her hand in the air to indicate her being there discussing it with him. "Doug was a realtor and he also used to dabble in selling cocaine. I think he made a ton of money at both in the eighties in Boulder. Being a realtor up there, he knew a lot of the fast-trackers. To be honest, I think he did better at real estate than at cocaine, but he made out fine with both commodities. He dealt drugs until things got too hot for him there. You know, police poking around, his suppliers making threats. Just hassles in general. So he bailed out of the business about four years ago. At least he said he did. He moved to Denver and sold real estate here. He did pretty well, and then, about seven months ago, he got popped for possession with intent to sell. Major trouble, and it was the last thing our relationship needed. I had no idea he was still dealing."

Streeter nodded like he believed her, but he kept thinking, Is she lying about not knowing or just stupid? Generally, drug dealers are about as subtle as a Madonna concert.

"Anyhow," she continued, "we were just about to come apart at the seams when he totaled his Porsche one night. He was very drunk and going about a hundred out on the I-25."

"And now he's dead," Streeter finished. "What makes you think he kept money around?"

"Well, for one thing, there were times when we needed quick cash and he always just went out and got it. And we're talking about a couple of grand each time. Sometimes quite a bit more.

He'd leave and then come back in an hour or less with the money."

"You never questioned that? I take it you're not a very inquisitive person."

She frowned but continued. "Never look a gift horse in the mouth, Streeter. As I was saying, he also told me that when he was dealing up in Boulder he used to keep a large amount of cash in his house in case of a robbery. Drug dealers are easy marks for robbers. He called it 'go-away money.' Ready cash to make the robbers just go away. He considered it part of his operating costs."

"If it was go-away money," Streeter said, "why didn't he keep it at your house? It wouldn't do any good if there was a robbery and the money was sitting in a bank somewhere."

"You're right." Story studied his face. "But I don't think he was afraid of being ripped off anymore. I think it was just force of habit that he liked to have cash on hand."

Streeter looked off for a moment. Then, "What about his personal belongings? I assume you went through all of them."

"Many times. I couldn't find anything, but you're welcome to look. I went through the car some. Checked the inside, the underside. There wasn't anything left of the engine compartment. Then I went through his office, the house. As I told you, he left everything to me. I get his half of the equity in our townhouse, some insurance money, and his personal belongings. He left this really nice clock, but not much else of value. I was thinking maybe he kept money in a safe-deposit box. Secure, but difficult to trace."

"That's possible," Streeter said. "Could be he kept the key on his key chain or in his glove box."

"Well, if he did, it won't do us any good." Story shifted in her seat. "That part of the car was demolished. The Porsche was very badly burned."

"I suppose I could do a sweep of every bank within, say, a ten-mile radius of your house for a safe-deposit box. Where do you live?"

"Cherry Creek. You know, Creekside."

"Yeah." He automatically flashed on her in her gym clothes at the Creekside. He'd done that more than once over the past couple of weeks. "I'd need a letter that gives me authorization to find out if Doug had a box. What was his last name?"

"Shelton. Doug Shelton."

"For three thousand, there's plenty I can do. But this could easily take a hell of a lot of time." His voice betrayed little, although he had raging doubts about this advertising woman who thought nothing of being "somewhat less than totally candid" with insurance companies and who so dispassionately hunted for a dead boyfriend's money. Still, if she had cash up front, there was a challenge to working for her that intrigued him. Streeter's last divorce had been final shortly after he moved into the church, and his last engagement was two years ago. He'd been keeping women at arm's length ever since. This would be a chance for him to see if he could hold his own with someone like Story without acting like a hormone-crazed teenager.

"You said something about me having a shot at making more money."

"It's a little treasure-hunt incentive. If you find whatever we're after, I'm willing to give you a quarter of it. That could add up if it's what I think it is."

"Why all the extra?"

"To keep you motivated. Do you think that'll keep you motivated?"

Streeter leaned forward, skeptical but interested. "This could end up being a total waste of time. I hate wasting my time, but more than that I hate not getting paid for wasting my time. Usually, I work just for Frank, bringing in bail jumpers. Sometimes I free-lance, like with Swanson. And sometimes I do skip traces for friends. Mostly, I deal in cash, and that's how it'd have to be with us. I'll need five thousand to get started and you'll just have to trust that I'm working for it. You don't get any invoices or written reports. If I think I've worked my way through the five grand, I'll ask for more and you can decide if you want to stay with me. And when we find this pot of gold, I get a third. Not a quarter. Your story has enough holes to read the newspaper through, and, if you'll pardon my bluntness, it's hard to believe anyone can be as dense about their boyfriend as you say you are about old Doug. But for five grand and a third of the action, I'm willing to work for someone that dense."

Story stared at him for a long time. "It's going to be a real pleasure working with you. I didn't know what to expect from a bounty hunter, but I guess good manners and class don't come with the territory."

"Lady, with some of the vicious clowns I track down, manners and class are not a plus. Besides, how much class does it take to fake a neck injury for insurance money? I do this work because I'm good at it and there's money to be made. And, to be absolutely honest, because my cooperative skills stink I have to work alone. Don't let the church fool you. This isn't missionary work. I get fed more horse manure in a week than most people hear in twenty years. But if the money's good enough I can live with the manure. Farmers do it all the time."

"My, aren't we the cynic." Her voice was as flat as her expression, but she had flushed visibly when he made the crack about the insurance fraud. "You're sweeping me off my feet, Streeter."

"Really? That wasn't my intent. You must be easily swept."

"As you get to know me better, you'll find out that I'm not easily anything. You don't think I'm telling the truth?"

"For three thousand, I'm not sure. For five thousand, it becomes less important. Listen, you'll tell me what you tell me. But the more you hold back, the longer it'll take me to find anything."

She finally nodded. "You'll do, Streeter. We've got a deal. I'll have your money for you in about two days."

"Then I'll start working in about three days. I can do the safe-deposit box check, but I have my doubts. I'll want to look through his personal belongings, talk to his family and friends, and then work my way out."

"You won't find zilch with his family. They hadn't talked to each other much in years. His mother's some sort of religious-fundamentalist nut up in Wyoming, and he has a retarded, I mean mentally disabled, brother who lives with her. The mother almost disowned Doug because of the drug arrest. She only briefly came to the funeral, and even then she treated me like I was trash."

"What did you expect? You're the jaded broad living with her son the coke dealer. Out of wedlock, no less. She probably figured you led him astray. It's easy for mothers to get into denial and blame other people for their children's problems. Maybe I'll save her for later. Did he have any hobbies?"

"He golfed some and played a little racquetball." She thought for a moment. "It was strange. Doug was pretty superficial for the most part. Certainly not an intellectual. But he did go to the Denver Art Museum from time to time. I guess he had an eye for beauty."

Streeter could see that, but at what cost? "Did you ever go with him?"

"No. I'm not big on art galleries. They seem so dead to me. He'd never talk about it, either. It was just kind of an interest of his. He liked to fix things, too. Or at least try. He liked to take things apart and see how they worked. Mechanical things, like toasters and VCRs. Trouble is, he wasn't very good at it. Half the time he'd take apart what was broken and then end up calling a repairman or we'd have to go get a new one. That happened with the disposal and the stereo."

Her eyes widened for just a second. "But not that Porsche of his. It was his baby. He put a lot of himself in that car. There was only one mechanic in town he'd let work on it. Hell, he'd barely let people ride in it with him, and he would never let anyone in the back seat. He was very tiresome about it."

"Some guys do that," Streeter said. He hesitated a moment. "There's one other thing. You said you two were on the outs. Is there any chance he had a girlfriend on the side?"

"Doug was a very good-looking man. He had this jet-black

hair. Great butt, great smile. Women liked being with him. He probably did have someone on the side. Our sex life was non-existent those last few months. It wouldn't surprise me if he had one or two tucked away. Men seemed drawn to him, too."

"Men? You mean he might go both ways?"

"I'm not sure which 'ways' he went. Let's just say that he had a lot of charisma and sex appeal and he said things sometimes that led me to believe bisexuality was a possibility. I didn't want to think about it, because of AIDS and all that."

"I'd say you two weren't close. I'm surprised you even noticed that he died."

Story stiffened. "You know, buster, you'll be getting a lot of money in your pocket soon. If you want it to stay there, you might keep in mind whose money it is. I don't need all these judgments."

"If it's in my pocket, I know whose money it is. Mine. And the name's not 'buster.'" Streeter leaned back. "But I'll certainly keep that in mind. Just remember, I warned you that my co-operative skills stink."

She gave one eyebrow an I-give-a-shit lift and moved on. "Look, I didn't press Doug about other women, *or men*, because secretly I hoped he had someone, and I just let it take its course. That would make it easier for us to break up. His car wreck did what neither of us had the energy or the strength to do."

"If he kept money with a girlfriend, we may as well kiss it goodbye," he said casually. "We'll never be able to pry it away."

"Probably not. But if you do find someone, I'll still want to talk to her."

"We'll see what we can work out. Let's not worry about girl-friends right now. Just get that letter for the banks ready and organize his stuff for me. There may be something you missed. I have to get going. Is there anything else?"

Story inhaled theatrically. Another gesture he didn't like. Why do so many attractive women have all these drama-queen man-nerisms?

"Doug had this attorney. I never liked the guy and I don't

trust him. He was at the funeral and he's called me a couple of times since then to see how I'm doing. The last time we talked, about a week ago, he hinted that Doug still owed him a lot of money. That's nonsense, because the guy hardly did any work. Hell, the charges against Doug were even dropped. There was some trouble with the evidence, and the case was thrown out shortly after the preliminary hearing. But this lawyer made it sound like I might be on the hook to pay him. Do you know about financial obligations Doug's estate might have if he owed money?"

Streeter shrugged. "Do you have a lawyer?"

"Of course. For my business."

"Ask him."

"Her."

"Ask her. I'll ask around, too. Who was Doug's lawyer? Maybe I know him. Assuming it was a him."

"His name is Tom Cooper."

Streeter knew the name. He had heard about Cooper and it wasn't flattering, but he couldn't remember what it was. Something in the paper a couple of years ago. The details were long-forgotten. He frowned.

"I take it you know him," Story said.

"Maybe. When you get my money you can just leave it with Frank if I'm not here."

5

Streeter glanced at his coffee maker and wondered why, no matter what type of expensive blend he put in the basket, the final product always tasted like ground water from Love Canal. He carried his cup into the living area of his loft. The place was enormous, taking up most of the entire second floor of the church. But it had an offbeat warmth to it thanks to huge throw rugs, overstuffed chairs and couches, and numerous bookshelves displaying more than a dozen sets of garage-sale encyclopedias and well over two hundred resource books. Twenty-seven framed movie posters helped give the room a light feel. His favorite was of the torrid beach scene from Lina Wertmuller's *Swept Away*. A tinny-sounding stereo, circa 1981, stood off to the side of the open kitchen area. He had little interest in music, since he was tired of sixties and seventies "Classic Rock" and anything remotely current struck him as redundant, not to mention aggravating, noise. "I can't tell U2 from R2-D2," as he put it.

He set down his cup and picked up a small address book containing the phone numbers of friends and professional contacts. He had his own network of sources scattered around the front range of Colorado, north up through Wyoming, and south into New Mexico. It was necessary. If he had to drive or fly everywhere to check out small leads and tips on bail jumpers or other people he was investigating, he couldn't get half his work done. Plus, many of his sources had access to information he couldn't touch. Before he did anything else, Streeter wanted to check out the cast of characters he was dealing with regarding Doug Shelton. He wanted more information on Doug as well as on Story Moffatt. While he was at it, he decided to find out about Thomas Cooper.

His first call was to a computer information source located in Castle Rock, a mall-and-golf community about twenty miles south of Denver. Stevey was the man's name and he was a world-class propeller head. Anything on record in any data bank was at his fingertips. He was invaluable for skip tracing and court searches, the latter of which Streeter ordered for Shelton, Moffatt, and Cooper. Stevey could do a statewide court sweep and get a printout of the case summaries. He got right on it, and about a half-hour later called the bounty hunter back.

"Let's see here." Stevey obviously was reading his screen while he talked. "Mr. Shelton was the plaintiff in a collections case in Boulder in 1983 and another one in 1986. He was awarded a small judgment both times. Then he got arrested for possession of a controlled substance in 1988 up there, too. Got probation. He was arrested again in 1993 in Denver for possession with intent to sell. The charges were dropped.

"Story Moffatt. Is that name for real? She likes to sue people, too. And she likes to win. I've got six collections cases where she was the plaintiff. All between 1987 and 1994. All in Denver. She won judgments in five. The sixth is still pending.

"And Thomas Hardy Cooper. He's either a lawyer or a doctor. Sounds like a real gem. He's been sued twice for malpractice. Both cases still pending. Looks like he was charged with assault in 1983 in Jefferson County. The case was later dismissed."

"Quite a crew, huh?" Streeter asked. "Thanks for the quick

turnaround, Stevey. Drop the printouts in the mail, okay? I want a closer look."

His next call was to a close friend, one of the few lawyers he would work for from time to time. "How you doing, Bill?"

The voice at the other end came back relaxed. "Not bad. Yourself?"

William Wesley McLean usually sounded relaxed. A former district attorney in Arapahoe County, just south of Denver, Bill McLean had a reputation for being cool but tough. The man would rather lose an eye than take an ounce of trash from anyone. He and Streeter had been tight since they had lived next door to each other during Streeter's last marriage. As with his first three marriages, Streeter and Beth lasted only two years. But during those two years, he and McLean got close, and their friendship continued to grow even after the divorce. He was one of the few people the bounty hunter let call him by the shorthand nickname of Street.

"How's Darcy?" he asked Bill.

"Excellent, as ever." Bill and Darcy had been married nineteen years. She was a successful psychologist. "She's working at the clinic. Thursdays she works family counseling. There's so much child abuse out there, it makes you sick."

"Tell me about child abuse. My father drank and my mother made me take accordion lessons."

"I'll bet you were a natural, Street." Bill, pushing sixty, was almost six feet six inches tall and had a full head of white hair. It gave him a distinguished credibility that helped greatly in court.

"Listen, I've got a quick legal question," Streeter said. "There's this lady I'm doing a little work for and it looks like she's going to be hassled by a lawyer. She's the executrix and main beneficiary of her boyfriend's estate and the lawyer claims the guy died owing him money. Does she have any legal obligation for his bills?"

"Depends. Did they ever tell people they were married? Were they engaged?"

"She says no."

"Then it's unlikely that his claim'll hold up. Who's the lawyer?"

"A spastic named Tom Cooper."

Bill grunted on the other end of the receiver.

"Guy with an office downtown? Yeah, I seem to remember him from back in my last days with the county. He was just getting into practice. Real nervous and tried to cover it up with a kind of swagger. Couldn't pull it off too well. Thought he was a real lady killer, too. But he couldn't pull that off, either."

"If he comes after her, will you represent her?"

"Sure. Who is she? You usually don't take private clients like this. Why the change for this one?"

"Interesting case, lots of cash up front, gorgeous client."

"Gorgeous, huh? Look, Street, you better be careful if you try to mix business with pleasure. What's that old saying about not slamming your dick in the cash register? You don't want to do that."

"That's very eloquent. And you're right, I don't. Catch you later."

Streeter hung up and then called Carl Shorts, a Boulder private investigator he used occasionally. A great many people in the Denver area knew Carl, if not for his legendary drinking habits and relentless womanizing, then at least for his nickname: Pokey. Try being ignored with Pokey Shorts for a handle. Rumor had it that he got the nickname because, as a newspaper reporter, he was slow at deadline time.

"How you doing, Poke man?" Streeter greeted him.

"Hey, Tarzan. Long time no see," Pokey shot back. Although just a shade past fifty and married with two sons, Pokey drank and caroused like he was just out of college. But when it came to investigating, he knew the secrets of every soul in Boulder County, and his drive for digging up dirt was even greater than his love of the bar scene.

"Too long. But this is more business than pleasure." Streeter told Pokey about Story Moffatt and her late boyfriend, emphasizing the part about his living in Boulder and dealing drugs.

"So now you need to find out about Mr. Shelton," Pokey said.

"You got it."

"The name sounds sort of familiar. I think he ran with Marcus Greenberg and that crowd over at Potter's and Quinn's. Some of those Pearl Street Mall watering holes. Let me look into it and I'll give you a holler back. I'm also thinking we should get together for a couple hundred beers one of these days."

"That sounds fine to me."

Streeter's last call was to Detective Bob Carey of the Denver Police Department. Carey was his only real source on the department, but one source like him was plenty. Carey had twenty-three years on the job and he played cards with Streeter and some friends every other week. They'd been doing it for just over ten years, and Carey had walked away a winner maybe five times.

"Robert, Streeter here."

"Robert?" There was a pause. "That means you want something."

"Right. Do you know anything about a Doug Shelton? A coke dealer who died in a car wreck a few months ago."

"Should I?"

"I'm just asking."

"Don't mean nothing to me. I'll check around, though."

"How about a drug lawyer named Tom Cooper?"

"Now, that name I do know. A regular certified shithead. You're not working for him, are you?"

"No. Against him probably."

"I don't think you want to work for him or against him. What you hear next, you didn't hear from me. We were looking into this Cooper jackass and so were the guys up in Adams County. Seems they had a homicide up there a while back. Some little welder who was supposed to testify in a murder trial ends up with his throat slit. Cooper was the defense lawyer in the aforementioned murder trial, and he has this investigator named Psycho or some damned thing that everyone is very interested in.

Psycho is right. Totally nasty fucker. Looks like the sergeant at arms at a Teamsters meeting, from what I hear. So far, he's clean. But Cooper and his friends are bad people. You be careful. You got half my pay for the last ten years at the poker table and I want a shot at winning it back."

"With all your stinking luck, you still never give up. I don't know if that's persistent or pathetic."

Carey coughed into the receiver. "Bad luck's like a marriage, Streeter. Sooner or later they both gotta end. You should know all about that."

6

As Jacky Romp watched Cooper walk across the parking lot, a
shadow of amusement twitched across his face. Actually, Jacky
never looked totally amused or totally happy or totally anything
you might call pleasant. His features were delicate, not unattrac-
tive, but at the same time he projected an overriding meanness.
There was a strange menace to his entire being, like barbed wire
covered with pale skin.

Watching Cooper shuffle toward the diner, he smiled and
looked across the table at Soyko, who was stirring his coffee.
Jacky glanced back out at the lot and muttered, "Goofy fuckwad," seemingly without moving his jaw.

Soyko nodded. He was so used to his partner's not using full
sentences that he just glanced at the scurrying lawyer and understood. Leo couldn't really disagree. Romp and Soyko had
done numerous jobs for Cooper over the years, making a good
chunk of change from the hard-assed collection shakedowns and
intimidating interviews. The work had increased in both volume
and scale lately—as Cooper's practice grew and intensified—to
a point where it was now Soyko and Romp's main source of
income. "That jerk's a regular cash cow," as he put it to Jacky

not long ago. But if anything, Leo's regard for the attorney decreased with time. Now, watching him in the lot, Soyko could only think, What a clown the lawyer is. Cooper always sort of shuffled along bent forward, as if he couldn't get where he was going fast enough. Or maybe he couldn't get away from where he'd just been fast enough. Either way, it appeared awkward and panicked to Leo.

Cooper had asked Soyko to meet him at The Full Belli Deli in the sprawling suburb of Aurora, immediately east of Denver. It was their usual spot. He didn't like Soyko coming to his office, and because he also lived downtown Cooper didn't want to meet in the city, where they could be recognized. The Full Belli was just fine. Soyko lived nearby and Cooper liked the coffee and the service. What he didn't like was Jacky Romp, and his features hardened as he entered the restaurant and saw him sitting there. Not that it surprised him. Soyko and Romp were inseparable. Still, the attorney's dislike for Jacky was monumental.

The feeling was eagerly reciprocated. Romp generally considered anyone who wore a suit to be "pure Yuppie rat shit," and Cooper specifically to be a phony stooge. The attorney sensed that hatred immediately and viewed Jacky as a highly repugnant loose cannon with the added liability of not being necessary. When he hired Soyko, he always felt like he was paying a little extra for Jacky even though Leo could do the job just as well by himself.

"There he is." Cooper smiled and approached the booth, looking straight at Soyko. "The most persuasive investigator in town. How you doing, my man?"

My man this, Soyko thought, looking back impassively. This jerk really thinks "my man" is some sort of hip street jive. "Yeah, my man." He looked over to Jacky and nodded. "Sit down, Mr. Cooper." There was no warmth in the invitation.

Cooper slid into the booth next to Soyko, still deliberately avoiding eye contact with the man across the table. Usually he barely acknowledged Jacky's presence and spoke to him only when necessary. For his part, Jacky seldom talked to anyone but

Soyko anyway, and the few words he directed at Cooper were mocking or vaguely obscene.

The waitress came and Cooper ordered coffee. Then, for the first time, he looked directly at Jacky, and his venom rekindled. Soyko had the blocky muscles and thick, strong hands of a foundry worker. Basically, he scared the hell out of Cooper. But Jacky Romp seemed too frail to be intimidating, so Cooper frequently took shots at him. The lawyer looked intently back at Soyko and in the deepest voice he could muster he asked, "Do you have to always bring this malignant piece of shit with you?"

Soyko had no idea what "malignant" meant, but the "piece of shit" part was clear. He rolled his eyes for a second and looked out the window. The constant friction between the two men bored him. "All right, ladies." He looked back with no emotion on his face. "Let's cut the 'malignant' bullshit here and get down to business." He glanced toward his lap and slid an envelope along the booth seat at Cooper. It contained fifteen hundred dollars in wrinkled bills. "Like we said on the phone, for the thing with Tiny. And now no more about it." His voice indicated that this was the end of the subject. Absolutely the end. "What's next? Something about a girl you want me to talk to?"

"That'll come in good time." Cooper looked down at the envelope and pushed it back at Soyko. "But first, I want you to gather information on a former client of mine. I'll want some real digging on this guy. Keep the money to cover your efforts."

"Who we talking about?" Soyko said in his slow, can-do tone.

Cooper lowered his voice slightly. "You know anyone named Doug Shelton? Greaseball handsome guy, always dressed to kill. Sort of a low-end player with the blow and the ladies. Hung around places like El Chapultepec, the jazz bar, and the Wynkoop poolroom."

The two investigators looked at each other for a long time, like they were having a telepathic conference. Then Jacky simply said, "Porsche prick," through his closed mouth.

Soyko nodded and looked back at Cooper. "I think I know who you mean. Guy about thirty-five maybe. Little older than me. Waved a lot of cash around but wouldn't even shoot you pool for fifty cents. I know he deals. Drives a red Porsche and acts like he's hot shit, too. Ain't seen him in a long time."

Cooper smiled, once again amazed at the broad range of people that his investigator knew. "Nor are you likely to see him in the future. He died a few months ago. He'd been arrested late last year for possession of several ounces of flake, excellent quality. Had a short rap sheet from here and there and he was facing some state time. Most judges have big erections for drug dealers these days. Like they think that putting them away for a few months to play tennis in medium security somehow protects society. It's a joke. But what the hell? It keeps me supplied with clients.

"At any rate, our Douglas was basically screwed because it was a hand-to-hand sale. Then something very unusual happened. A couple weeks after his preliminary hearing, I received a call from the prosecutor telling me they were going to dismiss everything. Seems the cocaine had inexplicably disappeared from the police-evidence locker. Other physical evidence disappeared as well. As we hadn't had a chance to test the coke yet, the charges were dropped and Douglas was free."

Soyko frowned. "Too bad he died." Then his face brightened slightly. "Normally, that means he's out of the picture, but I'm sure, if there's any way to get something out of a dead guy, you'll think of it. He owed you money?"

Cooper frowned in pained sincerity. Doug Shelton had paid him over nineteen thousand dollars in two quick cash installments. That basically covered his meager legal efforts about five times over. If anything, Cooper owed the estate a refund, but no one, least of all Soyko and his crazy partner, needed to know that. "A considerable sum, and I certainly don't intend to wipe out the debt without trying to collect," Cooper said severely. "I put in long hours on this man's case and I'm entitled to the appropriate payment."

Soyko studied his face. "I tell you this, it would break my heart to see you take it in the shorts like that. But don't you usually collect a shitload of money up front before you even budge on a case?"

Cooper inhaled deeply and spoke with a forced patience. "That is not at all an accurate characterization of my practice. Typically, I do like to get a decent retainer. That's just prudent business. But I provide all my clients with the best legal assistance possible regardless of their ability to pay in advance. I also do a considerable amount of work pro bono—that is, without receiving a penny. It's the least I can do."

Thomas Hardy Cooper was more likely to get pregnant and deliver twins than do one hour of pro-bono work and everyone at the table knew it. Jacky Romp spit out a laugh and turned away.

Soyko just shrugged. "Whatever you say. But if this guy was such a slow pay, what makes you think he had any money to go after?"

"I've handled a great many drug defenses these past few years and I can tell when a dealer has money. Theoretically, they all should have plenty, because their profit margin is so obscenely vast. Christ, just last month I had these two post-office guys, letter carriers, come to hire me. A couple of coons, no less. They had been arrested dealing eight balls to their fellow employees. They come to me and they're dressed about a notch above Goodwill. I tell them I'll need ten thousand in cash just for starters, figuring that would turn them away. One says to me, 'Okay, but I gotta get the money from the credit union.' He says it like it's hysterical. Then he reaches into one of his socks and pulls out a wad of cash the size of his dick and counts out the ten grand. I'm sitting there just about creaming my pants and thinking, Why didn't I ask for more?

"But drug dealers, like so many of us, fail to handle their money properly. Sadly, a good many of them are addicted themselves, so they piss their money away. Our Mr. Shelton was not like that. He also had a good real-estate income. He was always well turned out. You know, the car, the clothes. Plus, this evidence theft took some doing. It seems obvious to me that Douglas arranged it. He had to have someone on the inside, on the force. That costs plenty. He damned near told me that he arranged it, and he implied it was no big deal, money-wise. That man had assets, no doubt about it."

"He had a way of flashing it around, I'll give you that," Soyko interrupted. "Had a nice-looking blonde chick with him sometimes. Great ass and legs. His wife?"

"I'm not certain," Cooper answered, uncomfortable that Soyko knew about Story. "He implied that it might have been a common-law situation."

The three sat in silence for a couple of minutes. Finally, Jacky spoke up. "We supposed to be reading your mind or what?"

Cooper glanced at him for a second and then turned back to Soyko. "I want you to find out everything you can about Douglas. I think he kept women on the side, and I'm dead solid certain he stashed money. He used to brag about the financial reserves he kept hidden from his lady. Gentlemen, if this is anything like what Douglas led me to believe it is, there could be close to half a million in it for us. Or whoever has the balls to go get it. I'd say it's definitely worth a little looking into, wouldn't you?"

For the first time since he'd known them, Jacky and Soyko seemed impressed.

"And the girlfriend doesn't have it?" Soyko asked.

"Maybe a little sliver of it, but he used to brag about keeping her in the dark. We've got to dig into this. If I intend to collect from his wife or whatever she is, I'd like to know that she can pay. If he was keeping a woman, you may have to talk to her. But no more of that Grundy Dopps cowboy nonsense."

Anger flared across Soyko's face. "I don't want to hear about that."

Cooper backed off fast. "Well, just see what you can find out about Mr. Shelton." With that, the attorney stood up, pulled a twenty from his wallet, and dropped it on the table. He turned and walked out of the diner without another word.

Jacky Romp watched him leave and then, to no one in particular, he snarled again, "Goofy fuckwad."

Ronnie Taggert lived in a garden-level apartment on the city's predominantly Hispanic near West Side. The rent was a reasonable three hundred twenty-five dollars a month for a spacious two-bedroom, with a laundry next door and free cable. She had gotten used to living in that part of town from her days as a party-animal waitress at a rock-and-roll bar located there. Her apartment wasn't a prestige address, but the building was clean and she liked the nearby Mexican restaurants. Cooper hated visiting her there, because he intensely disliked all minorities. He always felt as though he were taking a giant step down the social ladder when he crossed the viaduct over the Valley Highway, just north of Mile High Stadium, into "their neighborhoods." Besides, in his book, "garden-level" was nothing more than a euphemism for "half-assed basement apartment."

He knocked on her door and smiled when she answered in just a silk slip. "Hi, baby," he said.

"Come on in." She kissed him on the cheek as he walked past her. "How did your meeting with those two deranged Nazis go?"

"You should stop referring to my investigative staff as Nazis. Even in jest."

"I'll keep that in mind." She lit a cigarette and turned her back to him.

"We had an interesting strategy discussion. You know I'm looking for a payoff from Doug Shelton's estate. This Story woman doesn't have a clue about what he paid me. She didn't know about his dealing coke, nor about his womanizing on the side. She's just some harmless, artificial advertising person."

"Yeah?" Ronnie turned to face him. "You sure?"

"Indeed. I've developed a twofold plan. First, I've retained Mr. Soyko to kick around under some rocks at the bars and hangouts that Doug frequented. If he had a girlfriend, I want to meet her. The second part calls for us to draw up one hell of a bill for

Story Moffatt. I'm figuring around forty thousand. This will have to be some of our best work, but if I can establish that they held themselves out as man and wife, I think I have a real shot at getting the court to order her to pay. Hell, I can probably just finesse it out of her without even having to go to court."

Ronnie thought in silence. "Developed a twofold plan." She hated the way he tried to make everything sound so formal. "Don't be so sure about his girlfriend. My hunch is that she's tougher than she looks. She held up pretty well at the funeral and she runs her own advertising agency. That's a tough racket, advertising. You really think you're going to stick a bill in her face, start screaming about court, and she'll just hand over forty thousand?"

Cooper walked to the kitchenette just off the living room where the refrigerator was and grabbed a beer. He knew it would be a long shot trying to talk Story out of money. She'd have to be nuts to just fold up and pay. But there was money for the taking, and he hated the condescending attitude she gave him at the funeral. Maybe she is tough, but she's never dealt with anyone like Soyko, he reasoned.

When he returned to the living room, he smiled at Ronnie. "Well, we shall just see what evolves. What's the worst that can happen?"

"Tom, with the way you practice law, damned near anything can happen."

7

Story sent Streeter an authorization letter, and the following week he hit a dozen banks during a two-day stretch. Doug Shelton had no accounts or safe-deposit boxes at any of them. Then the bounty hunter got bored. One of the reasons he never went into law enforcement is that he didn't have patience for repetitive, detail work. If the police were doing this search, they'd check every bank in the city. But Streeter liked to go on his instincts and his ability to read people and situations rather than relying on "procedures." Also, the more he thought about it, the less likely it seemed that Shelton kept a stash in a bank. As he told Frank after the two days, "Banks have short hours, which would be a definite drawback to a free-lance guy like Dougy."

"What about ATMs?" the bondsman asked. "They're open day and night."

"Yeah, they're always open, but you can only get a couple hundred dollars a day. That's nowhere near what we're talking about. Besides, ATMs and safe-deposit boxes can be traced."

He decided to check out Doug's court file. The criminal complaint would tell him a lot, like where he was arrested and if there were codefendants. He went to the basement of the Denver

Courthouse, room thirty-eight, and got the complete file on Douglas Lawrence Shelton's arrest of November 10: case number CR 94 1083. Although inactive, it was still over an inch thick.

Streeter copied every page and took it back to the church to read it. Most of it revealed nothing of value. The complaint and the arresting officer's report primarily interested him. There were no codefendants: Doug was arrested alone. He was popped selling almost one pound of cocaine to a Denver undercover officer behind a bar just off the touristy Larimer Square. That translated to close to sixty thousand dollars in street value, about half for Doug at wholesale. Tax-free.

The buy was made shortly before midnight, and the primary arresting officer's name was Detective Arthur Ernest Kovacs. Obviously, the name of the undercover narc who set up the buy did not appear. Doug apparently walked to the bar, because there was no mention of officers' finding or searching his Porsche. He also must have known the narc fairly well, because Doug was unarmed, and it mentioned several times that the two men had an ongoing relationship. There was a list of prospective witnesses, most of whom sounded like other Denver police officers or lab technicians. It appeared that no fewer than fourteen people were needed to bring down Douglas Shelton.

Streeter was disappointed when he finished. Nothing seemed to pertain to his search. He decided to call Detective Kovacs and fish around. Kovacs' work number was listed in the report, and the detective picked up on the second ring.

"Kovacs here," he answered abruptly, like he was just on his way to lunch or, more important to a man with his bowel miseries, to the restroom. Streeter explained who he was, that he was working for the estate of Doug Shelton, and that the survivors were curious about the arrest. Kovacs made it clear that Doug's estate was of no concern to him.

"No offense there—Mr. Streeter, was it? Yeah. But I give a good rat's ass if any of them ever find more money." Kovacs now sounded bored, like he was reading junk mail out loud. "This bum made his money from selling drugs, and in case you haven't heard, that's against the law. Hell, if we knew he had any cash laying around, we'd have grabbed it for the state. We can do that, you know. Your client's just lucky we didn't go after their house and stuff like that—attach all the assets from illegal activities. That's the way we used to do it in Detroit, back when I worked out there. Now, if that's it, I'll be saying goodbye. Maybe you should try the girl. You might have better luck with her than we did."

"His fiancée? That's who I'm working for. Story Moffatt."

"I ain't talking about any Story. Or any poem or any book, for that matter. I'm talking about the broad at the bar. The fuck's her name? It was on the witness list."

Streeter shuffled through the papers on his desk and found the last page of Kovacs' report, with the witness list. He started reading all of the women's names out loud.

"Nora Lewinski?"

"No, she's over at the lab. Keep going."

"Shannon Mays?"

"Bingo. There you go, Mike Hammer. She was the one that was waiting for him over at Marlowe's. He told our guy about her just before we popped him. We sent a couple uniforms over to talk to her after the arrest. We'd a loved to pop her, too. Smug little bitch."

"Why didn't you?"

"Possession of a wine spritzer ain't a crime in this state, ace. Least not that I ever heard of. Anyhow, we found her just sitting there having a drink. Happy as a pig in shit, if you pardon my French. A real cool customer. We tell her that her boyfriend just got nailed and she acts like we read her the weather report for Poland or something. But we had no cause for an arrest."

"Why wasn't she listed in the report itself?"

"Cause she didn't mean nothing to the investigation."

"Then why is she on the witness list?"

"No reason really. Just to bust her chops a little. Maybe shake her up some. Damned coke whore."

"Do you have an address on her? A phone number?"

Kovacs grunted something bitter-sounding at the other end but then said he'd check. A couple of minutes later, he came back on the line.

"I couldn't find no phone. She told us she lives at a joint, some high-rise, in Capitol Hill. Seven forty Pennsylvania. Number nine oh three. But I doubt she's going to be much help to you."

"Was she that uncooperative?"

"You might say so." Kovacs honked out a thick grunt indicating amusement. "I think you'll find her—how would I put it?—very tight-lipped. Anything else, ace?"

"No. That'll do it. And, Kovacs, it's been a real pleasure."

Former Detroit cop, Streeter thought as he hung up. An FBI agent he knew once told him that Detroit cops were world-class scammers and shakedown artists. He said that the Detroit FBI office was the only one in the entire country where the bureau specifically told its agents to share nothing with local police officers. He said so many of them were on the take there was no way of knowing whom to trust.

Just from his attitude, Streeter could picture Kovacs rutting around Motown, "kiting the coloreds out of a few bucks, ace," and generally being a useless imbecile. We'll see who's tight-lipped, the bounty hunter thought. Just because this Shannon Mays wouldn't talk to a clown like Kovacs didn't mean she wouldn't talk to him.

At his end, Kovacs could feel a decided twinge of activity in his lower intestine when he hung up. Pushing fifty-five, randomly flatulent, and constipated as a cement block, the detective was chugging into retirement some three months away. He subsisted primarily on cut-rate bourbon, Maalox, and your basic bran cereals smothered in prunes. Any inquiries into the whole Shelton business were about as welcome as another bowel obstruction. He decided to make a call up north for a little input on the matter. This bounty hunter probably didn't know his ass from a rearview mirror, but Kovacs had heard of Story Moffatt.

What he heard was, you don't want to underestimate her. He'd make the call later. First, he grabbed the *Sports Illustrated* off his desk and headed for the john, determined yet realistically glum. A weary veteran, he knew he was in for another long and at best moderately productive siege.

Shannon's building, imperiously named Penwood Heights, was a concrete high-rise built in the mid-1960s near the governor's mansion. The on-site manager was an aging, painted beauty who wore perfume so foul it could drop a wasp at ten feet. She was the kind of maintenance day drinker who was never really drunk, yet never fully sober. Streeter was surprised that a nice building would have such a rank manager. Fortunately, she was incredibly high-strung and talkative.

"My name is Nancy," she said when she buzzed him into her office just off the lobby. "Who did you say you're looking for, dear?"

She wore orange polyester slacks tight enough to render her childless and stood in the doorway with a cigarette in her right hand, the elbow braced against her side. Her left forearm ran across her waist in front, with that hand holding the right elbow for support. She looked fragile, like one solid belch would cause her to fall apart.

"Shannon Mays. I was told she lives in nine oh three, but the name on the register out there is Viveney. I buzzed up and they said Shannon doesn't live here anymore. I was wondering if you might have a forwarding address. She witnessed an accident and we need her help."

He'd used that witness story a thousand times. It made landlords feel safe in giving out forwarding addresses.

"Oh my." Nancy's ashen face flashed a sharp crimson. "Well, we don't have, I mean, there is no forwarding address. Shannon's dead. She died some, uhm, some, I don't know, maybe three months ago. Or so."

Streeter froze. His first lead and here she was dead. That bozo Kovacs knew it, too. Tight-lipped is right.

"Just a few months ago?" At first he asked it because he couldn't think of anything else to say, but then he realized the timing was curious.

"Yes, well, something like that, dear." Nancy seemed genuinely saddened by having to relate the grim news. Her erratic speech was due equally to Scoresby's Scotch and actual distress. "My goodness, yes. It was so sad. Such an attractive woman."

"Do you know what happened?" he asked.

"Car wreck. It was, oh my, a big car accident. Out on the freeway. Well, I don't mean there were big cars or anything." Nancy paused to suck in a deep breath. Then she hacked out a phlegmy cough that sounded like part of her throat came up with it. "It's just that, uhm, it was a big collision. Two people died. Shannon and her boyfriend, I think it was. Only one car, we heard later."

Doug died in a one-car accident. "Was the boyfriend's name Doug Shelton?"

"That was it. Yes. Very nice-looking young man."

Streeter felt his stomach twitch and his skin got suddenly warm. Obviously, Story knew about this. "Is Shannon buried here in Denver? Was her family from here?"

"I believe they were from, uh, let me see, California." Nancy took a deep drag from her cigarette and then looked around for her ashtray. "That other woman was here from, ah, from the lawyer, from the lawyer's office, asking a lot of questions, too. Maybe she's working on the same thing you are, dear."

"What woman? When?" He snapped the words out.

Nancy seemed upset by his tone—almost guilty, like she had done something wrong. "I'm sorry, dear. Let me, uh, think for a minute. I still have her card. No, it was the card for the lawyer. She, let's think, she had a very strange name. Like a man. She was just here about a week ago."

The manager's forehead went into spasms of concern. She pulled a stack of business cards out of a desk drawer and started rifling through it. The card she sought was near the top. She studied it and then handed it to him. That done, she appeared deeply relieved. It was Tom Cooper's card.

"Did the woman give you her title?"

Nancy frowned again. "She was a, uhm, what do they call it? Something legal."

"Paralegal?"

"That's it. Funny name she, uh, had. A man's name. Donnie. Ronnie. Something like that. I think, yes, it was Ronnie. Cute little thing. Very serious, though."

It figured that a greedy ambulance chaser like Cooper would be on the trail of the money, Streeter thought. And the lawyer easily would have known about Shannon. Streeter's only surprise was that it took Cooper a couple of months to get over here. The bounty hunter knew he had to get together with Story to talk about it. He was angry at her for not telling him about Shannon, but far more angry at himself for being so careless and not asking for details. Still, why the hell would she not let him know all about the accident? He had asked her if Doug had any girlfriends, and it was doubtful that Story believed Mays was just Doug's pal. It could turn out to be an insignificant detail, but it didn't do much for his trust level with his new client. He wondered what else Story neglected to tell him. He definitely wanted to talk to her, but for right now he mainly wanted a drink. That and to get out of range of Nancy's hideous perfume.

8

Story didn't liked Streeter's attitude on the phone when they set up the meeting. He sounded surly, sarcastic. She did not need grief from the hired help. However, she did want a progress report. Also, she wanted to talk to him about that dipshit Cooper's latest ploy. Sometimes Story wondered why men didn't simply shut up and get with the program. Just because they didn't menstruate, they seemed to think they ran everything.

And what was with this Thomas Cooper? He calls a meeting with her to discuss "Doug's outstanding balance," as if it were any of her concern. She didn't know specific numbers, but Doug had told her more than once that he dished out a huge amount of money to his attorney right after the arrest. Now Cooper was going to try and browbeat her into paying his phony bills. That kind of grief was something else she did not need. If he kept pushing her, he'd find out that hassling Story Moffatt could be about as pleasant as attempting foreplay with a cornered razorback.

But Mr. Streeter concerned her more right now. Even though he ruined her lawsuit and he was crabby on the phone, she liked the guy. He was probably no genius, but he was street smart and he had a gentle way about him without losing his masculine edge. As if someone with forearms and shoulders like his could ever lose his masculinity. They planned to meet at the Pearl Street Grill, an upscale, quasi-British pub in south-central Denver. She liked the Grill's secluded patio. The meeting was set for eight o'clock Friday night, and he was calmly nursing a Beck's Dark when she walked in a little before nine.

"Sorry to keep you waiting, Streeter." Her smile was barely noticeable as she walked to the back patio, where he was waiting for her at the far end, near the lighted garden. "Business, you know."

"It's okay with me. In my line of work you get used to waiting. Plus, it's your money we're pissing away here. I'll wait until closing time if you want to screw around like this."

She hesitated for an instant and then sat down. Streeter could tell he'd riled her. She had a way of letting you know she wasn't pleased with a quick, pinched-up smile. The waitress came and Story ordered a club soda. Then she turned back to the bounty hunter and gave him an intense stare. "So, how are we doing with our little search?"

"We?" He hesitated before continuing. "Nothing on the bank-vault idea. I've checked a bunch of them and come up with zip." He paused again. "Why didn't you tell me Doug wasn't alone when he died?"

So that was it, she thought. Poor little boy must feel excluded. The waitress brought the club soda, which gave Story a chance to think. She took a long sip and carefully put her glass down, deliberately wiping the corners her mouth with a linen napkin.

"Shannon doesn't have anything for us," she said as she settled back in the black cast-iron patio chair.

"That's really not the point." Streeter didn't like her lack of reaction. "If I'm going to do this job, you'll have to tell me everything that relates to the man. You had to know something like that was important, or at least it might be important. This hunt's going to be difficult enough. I don't have time to screw around. And how can you possibly know she doesn't have anything for us?"

"I spoke to her family and . . ." She shrugged, holding her palms out innocently.

"So what? You think they're going to come out and tell you. 'Hey, we found, oh, about seventy-five thousand bucks on top of Shannon's refrigerator. It must be yours. After all, she *was* screwing your fiancé. Here, take it.' Is that what you think?"

"If you'll let me finish. I also went through her apartment."

"How the hell did you manage that?" He leaned forward.

"Look, I may have been somewhat less than totally candid with you the other day. I knew about his affair with Shannon. All about it, including where she lived. Streeter, this hasn't been a picnic for me." Her voice softened and a trace of genuine pain spread over her eyes. It softened them nicely, he thought. "Telling you all about Doug's problems and the troubles he and I were having was very difficult for me. The drugs, the women, the lying. I just got tired of going into all the gory details." Then her voice stiffened slightly. "At any rate, I went over to Shannon's shortly after the accident and talked the weekend manager into letting me in. I told him I was her sister and he bought it. I went over every inch of the place and there was nothing."

Streeter didn't say anything for a moment and they sat in silence. Finally, he spoke. "You've got this annoying little habit of being 'somewhat less than totally candid.' Just keep it up and we'll be somewhat less than totally successful finding Doug's money. You're quite an operator there, Ms. Moffatt. Your fiancé isn't even cold in the ground yet and you're going through his mistress's apartment looking for his money. Sounds like an adult sitcom."

"Hell, our life together was a sitcom. Doug probably had several 'hobbies' like Shannon Mays. Let me tell you a little about us. I tried to make it work but he never really let me close. In public he could be very aloof and uncaring. And in private, well, let's just say Doug made love like he did everything else. Quickly.

To get done with it, and with as little hassle as possible. Half the time he was either so drunk or in such a big hurry, it was almost comical. We must have looked like the Special Olympics of sex, for God's sake. He'd put in a little showmanship along the way, but never with any real feeling. I endured a lot from him. If he left anything, I'm entitled to it and I'm going after it. It's my inheritance we're talking about. Maybe I should have told you about Shannon. I didn't and I apologize. But now let's get on with it."

Streeter shrugged. "You really don't have to tell me anything you don't want to, but if you keep holding back it'll just slow things up. I wasted a lot of my time, not to mention your money, finding out something you could have told me about last week. I got paid up front, so, if you want me to keep flushing it away, keep doing that."

They both sat in silence again until Streeter spoke. "Did you know that Tom Cooper is looking into this, too?"

Story blushed for a second. "I, uh . . . No, I didn't. Into what? How do you know?"

"I assume he's looking into Doug's affairs, if you'll pardon the pun. When I went to Shannon's apartment building, the day manager told me about it. It wasn't Cooper but some girl from his office. Ronnie or Donnie or something like that. She was there last week asking if Shannon had left any of her stuff."

"That jerk. That mother . . . I think I know who you're talking about. I met his secretary with him at Doug's funeral. She had some butch name like that. Kind of cheap-looking, and I got the impression Cooper and her had a thing together." She took a sip of her club soda. "He called me yesterday and we set up a meeting for next Wednesday. He wants to discuss a bill that Doug supposedly owed him. Can you believe the gonads on that schmuck? He's going to try and bully me into paying for what Doug already paid. I probably deserve a refund!"

"You have any invoices, receipts? Documentation?"

"No, but Doug told me he paid a bundle to Cooper right after his arrest and he was worried that Cooper wasn't doing much to earn it. I'm sure Doug didn't owe him anything. By the way, did you ever find out if I might be liable for his debts?"

"I talked to a lawyer friend of mine. He told me that, unless you two were calling yourselves husband and wife, telling everyone you were married, then Cooper probably doesn't have much of a chance. But he can still make the claim, and it could cost you a bundle to defend yourself."

"I've been thinking about that. When you start in with the lawyers, it always costs." She sat silent. "Will your friend work for me on this?"

"He said he would. His name is William McLean. He was the DA in Arapahoe County for a whole lot of years. Every lawyer in town knows him and knows how good he is."

Story nodded. She stared at her club soda, running her finger around the lip of the glass. The patio seemed almost dead except for some rustling in the trees that formed a green awning over part of it. At a nearby table, three androgynous Generation X'ers sat mumbling to each other, apparently lost in deep conversation. They all had the standard ponytails, baseball caps worn backward, pierced faces, and vacant, vaguely obtuse expressions. Story glanced at them for a moment. They seemed indistinguishable from one another. A warm breeze swept the whole area, causing the leaves to rustle much louder. Pronounced yet soothing, like soft, muffled chimes. She looked up, her face set like Charles Barkley's when he was charging the basket.

"Maybe I can cut Cooper off before he gets started," she said. "How's this for an idea? We'll draw up a demand letter saying that Doug told me he paid, hell, I don't know, thirty thousand dollars or something major like that for a retainer. We'll say he told me that only a small part of the money was earned by Cooper when the case was dismissed. I'll ask him for a breakdown of how the money was spent and demand about half of it back. We'll put it on McLean's letterhead. If his rep is as good as you say, Cooper might just fold up like a cheap telescope when he reads it."

Streeter considered the plan. "That'll sure give him something to think about. It couldn't hurt to put him on the defensive."

"Precisely. I'll run it all by McLean to make sure we don't cross the line. Nothing illegal. I just want to cut this guy off at the knees so hard and so clean that he'll go away for good. Plus, if he's tracking down Doug's money, this might get him off that trail. My hunch is he doesn't have the stomach for a fight."

Streeter thought about what Carey told him about Cooper's trial in Adams County, but he said nothing.

"It's important to show this joker that I'm no pushover," she concluded.

"That might do it, but don't underestimate Cooper. Is this how you run your business?"

"Advertising is like being at war half the time. You have to strike hard and fast. First impressions, appearances, they can mean everything. These guys I pitch to wouldn't take me seriously for a minute if I couldn't show right up front that I mean business. Don't tell me that in your line of work you never shovel a little crap or take a few shortcuts to fake someone out."

"True. I remember my first job for Frank. I found a bail jumper—a confidence man, of all things—up in Salt Lake City, staying at his sister's house. Frank wanted me to have him come back here on his own money so we could save the airfare cost. I sure as hell couldn't call him up and ask him politely to come home. So I decided to play on his greed. I sent him a cheap clock radio, like he's won a contest back here in Denver. I also sent with it a registered letter saying he's won the grand prize— a Town Car, I think it was; even put a Lincoln brochure in with the mailing. But the real clincher is, I sent him a one-way ticket to Denver. Told him he had to claim his prize in person. A lot cheaper than paying all that extra airfare for me and him. Course, I was taking a chance the guy didn't just keep the radio and cash out the plane ticket. Luckily, he was as greedy as I thought. Not to mention as stupid. I went out to the old Stapleton International the night his flight's due in, and sure enough the slob got off the plane looking every bit like he was expecting Vanna White to meet him. You should have seen his expression when I put the cuffs on him."

"You're kidding. That's fantastic. I knew there was something about you I liked."

"Coming from you, I'm not so sure that's a compliment."

Her smile stayed in place. "I suppose it's that kind of cleverness that got you on *Jeopardy*?"

The question surprised him. "How'd you find out about that?"

"When I gave your name to my secretary, she said she remembered seeing you on the show a couple of years ago. Memories of the big, bad bounty hunter from Denver stuck with her. She said you won the night she watched. You were pretty sharp with the facts, she told me. How'd you get interested in that?"

He shrugged. "It's all in the family. My parents and I used to toss trivia around while we ate dinner." Streeter didn't want to tell her the whole saga, but his parents—both pretty smart— liked to show off. They used their knowledge to outdo each other. Some families called it arguing, but his mother referred to it as a "lively exchange of ideas." "Trivia's a hard habit to break, I guess."

By now it was dark, and she asked him to walk her to her car. "I parked across the street, behind that office building. I know I'm not supposed to, but it's so hard to find an open spot around here. I'll show you my baby, too."

"Your baby?"

"Corky. He's my wheaten terrier. He's a good little dog but he's so cute, all white and fluffy, that I spoil him rotten."

They paid for their drinks and left. As they crossed the street they heard a faint jingling from down the block. Story seemed confused.

"That's Corky's bell collar. How'd he get out of the car?"

The sound grew louder as it came quickly toward them. Corky was about a half-block away when they spotted him in the streetlights. There was a bright-red streak along his side, and when Story saw that she screamed. "Corky!"

The dog didn't seem to be hurt as he ran toward his mistress. When he got to her, she and Streeter could see that someone had sprayed red paint on his back and down his right side. The dog was oblivious to the paint and clearly delighted to see Story. As she bent down to check him out, he jumped up and licked her face like it was smeared with lamb chops.

"Who did this to you, Corky?" Then she looked up at Streeter. "My car!"

They quickly walked around behind the two-story brick building to where she had parked. Corky had made out much better than the Audi did. Someone had slashed all four tires and sprayed red paint on the left side of the steel-gray sedan. The driver's door was jimmied open and they could see in the glow of the inside overhead light that someone had sprayed the dashboard with more of the paint.

"Oh my God," Story yelled when she saw the damage. "What the hell's going on, Streeter?"

He walked up to the car and noticed a crumpled piece of paper lying on the front seat. "Someone left a calling card." He picked up the paper and read it. The two simple words "back off" were scrawled in blue ink on the stiff white paper. He turned and showed it to Story. "Very subtle. It looks like someone wants you to stop doing something."

She took the paper between two fingers like Corky had just gone to the bathroom on it. "Who? What do they mean?"

Streeter again thought about his friend Detective Carey's warning on Cooper. "Maybe Doug's lawyer is sending you a message. Is there anything else you're doing that someone might want you to stop?"

"This is crazy." She dropped the note and walked slowly around the car, carrying her dog, who wiggled with excitement without knowing why. "They could have killed Corky. Is Cooper really that nuts?"

"Who knows? It's unlikely that he would pull something like this right after he sets up that meeting for Wednesday, but who the hell knows? Is there anyone else who might know about Doug and what we're doing?"

"It's hard to say." She was regaining her composure. "Doug knew so many people. So many nut cases. He probably dealt drugs with a lot of weirdos. Could be one of them found out about what we're up to."

"Well, it was either Cooper or someone else."

She stopped and looked right at him for the first time since they got to the car. "Now, that was profound, Streeter."

They inspected the damage for a minute and then she turned to him again. "Is there anything we can do before I call the police to make out a report?"

"Let's knock on a few doors across the alley and ask if anyone saw anything."

They talked to several neighbors. People in the first two houses noticed nothing, but at the third backyard from the entrance to the alley, they saw a man go into the back door. Streeter hurried up and knocked. A balding man maybe ten years younger than the bounty hunter answered. He was wearing just a pair of shorts and sandals and carried a half-empty quart bottle of Budweiser. Presumably, no one with such a swollen white stomach would leave his yard without a shirt.

"Excuse me," Streeter said. "My friend's car got vandalized sometime over the last hour and a half. It was parked in the lot of that office building." He nodded toward the end of the alley. "You didn't happen to see anything over there, did you?"

The man frowned in wild confusion as he listened, but when he answered he sounded basically lucid. "I thought I saw someone coming out of there about twenty minutes ago. I didn't get much of a look, but he left his car sitting still idling in the alley while he got out for a while and headed to the parking lot. Then he got in his car again and backed out and drove off. I couldn't see much of anything from my backyard and I didn't know what he was up to but I'll tell you this, he looked really pissed off. Major pissed off. I got a decent look at his license plate and I caught the three letters and the first number. B-J-J-3 something or other."

"That'll help. Thanks a lot." He walked back to Story and told her. They tried a few more neighbors, but no one else saw anything, so they went back to the car.

"I'll call the police," she told him when they got together again.

"Now, *that's* profound," Streeter said.

As they waited for the police, Streeter realized there was something familiar about the partial plate number, but he couldn't quite place it.

9

Soyko was all of eleven years old when his stepfather started kicking the hell out of him regularly. The old man, a bitter ex–professional middleweight, called each beating a "boxing lesson." They lived next to their junkyard on Chicago's near North Side, a couple of grimy miles from the city's Loop. Soyko, who seldom used his first name of Leo because he hated it, absorbed the beatings until he was big enough to fight back.

And finally, one day shortly after his seventeenth birthday, in the back lot of the junkyard, he put an end to it. Business at the yard had been going south lately, and the old man was in a particularly toxic mood. It was cold out, midwestern bitter-damp, with the sky so low you could scrape it with a pool cue, when the old man wanted to administer another lesson.

The fight was as short and violent as it was one-sided. Soyko got in the first punch and never really gave the old man a chance. He delivered the final blows with a ball-peen hammer. The coroner's report later said that the old man suffered massive internal bleeding and had seven cracked ribs, a splintered vertebra, four broken fingers, and several smashed facial bones. The kid even managed to break both bones in the elder Soyko's left forearm.

When it was over, Leo went back into the house, grabbed a few clothes, and left Chicago forever. Incredibly, the old man hung on for five days and then died without coming out of a deep coma. In the years that followed, Soyko often wondered if he'd actually meant to kill his stepfather. But he never wondered about his reaction to it. He was glad it happened.

"We'll divide this up," Soyko instructed Jacky in their search for Doug's money. "I'll take the strip joints and you check out the pool halls. The bars, places like that. I'll see if he had any girl-friends and you just try and get a handle on anyone at all who knew the guy."

He didn't want to let Jacky get too near women. Soyko was bad enough in that department, but Jacky was pretty much out of control. Neither man appeared to really like women, and they never had girlfriends. But Jacky seemed to genuinely hate the gender. Women knew it, too. The only ones he was ever with sexually were hookers, and even then he had to pay a premium for his bent desires. Not that Soyko was much better. His idea of romance consisted of a drunken, doggy-style roll on the couch with some dim-witted trailer-park bimbo. He'd usually keep his shirt and socks on, and he never spent the night. But at least he could talk to a woman without scaring the hell out of her.

He also wanted to work the strip joints because he sensed that Doug Shelton would have leaned toward that kind of thing. To a good-looking, fancy coke dealer, strip clubs would be a natural turf. Soyko started with the upscale strip bars, like the Diamond Cabaret and the Mile Hi Saloon. They were more like bizarre, X-rated aerobics classes with bars and restaurants attached. Horny professionals and free-spending construction workers couldn't seem to get enough of those places. Soyko talked to most of the dancers and waitresses at both bars and found nothing. He then went to the mid-range strip joints, like P.T.'s and Shotgun Willie's. Less flashy but still attracting a somewhat sane crowd. Again, no one remembered Doug Shelton, or at least admitted it.

But Soyko was not the type to get discouraged. He figured the further down the skin ladder he went the more he could relate to the dead realtor. And the bottom rung was a ragged joint near the city's Performing Arts Complex, appropriately named Art's Performing Complex. The dancers were mainly sad, sagging biker chicks with a blank toughness in their eyes. Their bodies were freckled with tattoos and laced with stretch marks. But the lighting was low enough and the show raunchy enough for the place to bring in a good buck. Art's was so murky that it didn't appear to have actual interior walls, but, rather, it was surrounded by a muddy darkness from which people drifted in and out.

Soyko hit paydirt when he talked to an off-duty waitress who said she'd "sort of dated" Shelton over the past couple of years. She told him her name was Chantel. She had naturally blond hair but her breasts stood at attention just a shade too well to be original equipment. Her face had broad, country-girl features, pretty if not overly distinctive.

"I'm not from here," she said. "Originally, I mean. I was born in Marshfield. That's a little-bitty town way up in the middle of Wisconsin." She was chewing gum, smoking, and drinking, all with a determined ferocity that let Soyko know she was pretty coked up. "It's the string-cheese capital of the world, you know," she added with a childish pride.

Of course, he thought. Who the hell doesn't know that? "That's really something. Lotta women up there named Chantel, are there?"

She stopped chewing for a minute and studied his face. Then she must have decided he was genuinely curious, because she started chewing again. "That's not my real name, actually. It's sort of a stage name I hung on to from when I danced here. It's not good to let these creeps know your real name."

"Can't be too careful, huh?"

"Boy, you said a mouthful right there." Her eyes widened. "You would not believe the maniacs we get in here sometimes.

Bikers, molesters, all sorts of weird ones. You look safe, though. I can always tell."

Soyko decided she must be a lot younger than she looked. "How'd you meet my buddy Doug? He a regular here?"

Chantel frowned. "You really friends with Doug? He never mentioned you."

He stared hard at her. "We ain't blood brothers or nothing, but we hang out together. I buy product from him, sometimes."

At that, her face lit up. A girl can never know enough men with cocaine. She looked around the room. "It's so noisy in here. You think you might be interested in maybe going somewhere to party a little?"

"Like where?"

"I could get us a room. There's a place I know out on Colfax that gives good rates."

"How much this party gonna cost me?"

"Well, you catch the room. Maybe thirty for that. Then"— she smiled and tried to twitch her shoulders like a little girl— "I'm thinking some nose candy for me would be a nice idea, too."

"And sex?"

"I'm not a pro. The sex is free." Then she lowered her voice, which was now anything but childlike. "But I practice safe sex and I keep skins in my purse. They'll cost you seventy-five each."

Seventy-five bucks for this clod, Soyko thought in disgust. "Those prices, maybe I bring my own rubbers."

"Not to my party you don't. You want me, you use my rubbers." There was a sudden edge in her voice that she didn't pick up in any string-cheese capital.

"Let's go." He stood up.

They drove to a dump on West Colfax Avenue with a name Soyko promptly forgot. It's the kind of place where they try to wash away the filth with industrial-strength antiseptic cleaners. It ends up smelling like a third-world hospital and has about the same overall charm as one, too. When they got to the room,

Chantel started bragging about how good she was in bed. It was supposed to turn him on, but it merely annoyed Soyko.

"I fuck like a Michael Jordan plays basketball," she said, "I mean, I get into some sort of hot zone and I'm a pure pleasure machine."

By now, Soyko was really losing his patience. Princess Condom here was getting dumber by the minute, and he had no intention of having sex with her. Not to mention that maybe she didn't know a thing about Doug. He decided to find out. He grabbed her in the middle of her left bicep and squeezed hard. Chantel's arm scrunched up like a water balloon. She let out a quick, shocked squeak, her eyes bulging in terror.

"Keep it down, Miss String Cheese," he snarled as he let go of her arm and shoved her into a chair with one hand. "I'm done listening to your bullshit and I wouldn't fuck you if you were paying me seventy-five a pop. Now, you're going to tell me everything you know about Dougy Shelton. If you convince me you're on the level, you might make it out of here."

Chantel just stared at him. Her eyes began to tear up at the corners. He pulled the dagger out of his belt, slammed the blade point down into the wooden dresser, and let it go. It sort of quivered there for a second and then stood still.

"Let's talk and maybe I don't have to use that."

She nodded her head so fast that she didn't even notice when her gum shot out of her mouth and dribbled down the front of her blouse.

"What do you want to find out?" Her voice was lifeless and hoarse.

"Mainly everything." He smiled back, knowing he was in complete control. "How long you known him?"

"Not quite two years. Maybe. He sold coke and I know he got busted for it last year. I remember that he got the living shit beat out of him right afterward. He said the cops did it. Who knows? Look, I only went out with him a few times. He'd come on like this big lady-killer and flash the money around. He had the car and all the good clothes. But he was different once you got to know him."

"Yeah? How?"

"Well, like he wasn't much of a stud. The way he looked, I expected him to jungle-fuck me into a coma, but with all the blow he put up his nose he couldn't cut it much. Half the time we went to bed, he'd get coke dick and we'd just sit around talking. Not that I was missing much anyhow. I mean, the guy was pretty small in the old pecker department. If you follow me. But it never seemed to bother him much. Sometimes I even thought he might be more into guys. Like maybe he was bi."

"You're kidding?" Soyko considered that. "Why'd he keep whoring around if he liked guys and he couldn't get his sorry little thing up?"

She thought for a second, getting a little more composed as the conversation went on. "Lots of reasons, I guess. He thought coke dealers were supposed to be lady-killers. It was all part of this front he was putting on. I think he was mostly just sad. He was living with some woman, but she couldn't do much for him."

Soyko thought about the blonde. "What was with them?"

Chantel shrugged and looked like she was going to cry. "He told me about her once." She shrugged again and smiled weakly. "But I was pretty wasted then, too, and I don't remember much. She was really kind of a bitch, from what he said. Looked good but had ice in her veins."

Figures. "He get coke dick with her, too?"

"How would I know? Probably. If I can't get 'em hard, who can?" She smiled, then glanced at the knife again, and the smile disappeared. "This is the same stuff that cop asked me when he came to Art's. He wanted to know all about Doug."

Soyko frowned. "Cop? When? What cop?"

"I don't remember the name. It was just a few days ago. All of a sudden everyone's so interested in Dougy."

"A uniform cop?"

"No, a detective. An old guy. He must have been over forty. A real meany, too. A bully. He scared me. I didn't tell him Jack shit. Course, he didn't pull any knife on me, either."

Soyko filed it away. "Did Doug ever talk about money much? You know, like he had a lot?"

She frowned. "Seems he told me a couple of times he was real rich. Sounded like more coke talk. He told me he was a good lover, too, but look what kind of shit that turned out to be."

Soyko pondered what she said, lit a cigarette, and didn't say anything for a while. Chantel kept quiet. He finally broke the silence. "Did he keep much cash on him?"

"He had it but he didn't spread it around much. If he went out for a night on the town with three hundred in his pocket, he'd go home with two ninety-five. You know what I mean? He was good about giving away coke sometimes, but the cash he held on to pretty much."

There was a whiny twang to her voice now that bugged him, so he slapped his open palm down on the dresser, next to his knife. It sounded like an explosion and Chantel jumped about four inches in her chair.

"Look," she said, "the guy was loud and showy and deep down he was cheap and scared or something. Maybe even a queer, I don't know. But just so he kept the coke coming, I didn't ask questions. I'll tell you this much. Whatever he did with his money, he didn't let it get too far out of his sight. He watched it closer than anyone I ever saw."

"He move much product?"

"Some, I guess. He could move a good amount of coke when he had to."

Soyko could see how scared she was. He believed her but, more to the point, he was tired of listening to her. He pulled his buckle blade out of the table and looked at it as he slowly turned it. Then he put it back in his belt.

That made Chantel feel more comfortable. She sat up for the first time. "Mind if I have a cigarette?"

"What do I care?"

She took a Kool out of her purse and lit it, studying his face as she did. "You think Dougy has money for you?"

"What do you care?"

"Maybe I can help you with something. I know a lot of people around town. I ain't seen Dougy in a long time, though."

"Neither have I. You know where I can maybe find him?"

She shrugged childishly, the string-cheese capital coming out again. "If I see him, should I let you know?"

"You and me friends now or something?"

"I just thought maybe I could give you a hand. And if I do you'd remember me if you got any money out of it."

Soyko had to smile at that. Coke whores. He shook his head. Here she is, scared for her life two minutes ago, and now she's trying to turn a buck.

"Just forget you ever saw me and I'll forget I ever saw you. No yakking to this detective about me. If anyone gives me grief about our little talk here, you'll be the one in trouble. I'll come looking right for you. You getting all this?"

Chantel thought about back at the bar, when she told him he looked safe. "I hear you. We'll never see each other again. I mean that."

"Nothing would make me happier. Or you. That's guaranteed. Have a nice walk home."

10

First thing Wednesday morning, Thomas Hardy Cooper put on his sharpest power suit. It was a double-breasted, deep-navy-blue number that cost him a ton.

"That faggot salesman at Neiman Marcus made it sound like only a blue-collar cretin would hesitate to spend eighteen hundred on a suit," he had told Ronnie the day before. "But I have to admit, I cut a pretty impressive figure in that thing. And I want you to wear something black. Something conservative. None of those thigh slits and come-fuck-me neckline plunges tomorrow."

He only hoped she owned such a garment. Then he called in Dwayne Koslaski, his part-time paralegal, short on experience and ambition, "but a beefy two hundred thirty pounds of ugly Polack," as he put it. He wanted Dwayne to attend the meeting with Story to help set the right mood. He hoped to present a united front, strong and solemn, when he hit her with a bill for unpaid for services in behalf of Douglas Shelton. He figured he'd sit at his desk with the large window behind him. He'd keep the shades wide open, so Story had to squint to see him. Cooper in his massive swivel chair, the enormous paralegal on his right, and a devoted Ronnie on his left.

Doug's invoice itself was a cleverly crafted bit of fiction totaling just over twenty-six thousand dollars. It was less than Cooper originally projected. But it had a more credible sound to it. He and Ronnie spent most of Tuesday afternoon creating it, and they were both justly proud. Unless Doug had been telling Story about his finances all along, the invoice should appear genuine. If she challenged it, Cooper could easily present it in court with a straight face.

"Straight face, hell," he told Ronnie when they finished. "I'm so impressed with this thing, I'm almost looking forward to showing it to a judge. All this legal research, pretrial motions, client conferences. Not to mention conferences with the district attorney, paralegal fees, and endless investigation by Soyko at sixty an hour. When I look at this I'm not so sure I didn't actually earn the money."

Ronnie, of course, was sure he hadn't. She said only, "You half-earned it just by making it up, honey."

"Here's the way we'll do it tomorrow," he told her. "I figure I'll hit her with the invoice before she even has time to settle into her chair. Feed her some crap about how much I hate to do it, seeing as how she must still be grieving over her loss and all. But I busted my hump for her Douglas and all I have to show for my Herculean efforts is that paltry thirty-five-hundred-dollar retainer. I've even dummied up a receipt copy for that amount. I dated it right after Doug's arrest.

"I want to shove this invoice into that flawless, condescending face and ask her how she'd like to arrange the payments. I expect she'll counter with a few tears and maybe bitch about not being liable for Doug's debts. But tears do not mean a thing. Not when we're pulling a number like this. We'll be in the red zone, Ronnie, with a nice piece of change just a couple of yards away. We get this close, we can't let a few tears sidetrack us.

"I figure that when she stops blubbering I'll hit her with the threat of a suit. Then I'll lighten up a little by offering to knock fifteen—no, make that ten—percent off if she pays within thirty days. Let her know I'm not heartless. But I don't want there to be any mistake by her about my intentions here. No bullshit. If she really puts up a fuss, I've got a little surprise waiting for her in the other room."

But the next day, before the meeting was two minutes old, Cooper sniffed the foul odor of calamity in the air. First of all, Story showed up almost forty minutes late. Second, she brought along this side of beef named Streeter who made Dwayne look like a puffy blob. Then things got worse.

"Please be seated, Miss Moffatt, Mr. Streeter," Cooper said, a little more quickly than he intended. "Traffic bad or something?"

Story didn't answer and Streeter just moved his eyes slowly between the lawyer and his two assistants.

"Streeter? May I call you by your first name?" Cooper continued, not liking the vibe he was getting from across his desk.

"Streeter's fine."

"I believe I have heard about you. You are a bounty hunter employed by Frank Dazzler, the bondsman, are you not?"

"I know Frank," was all Streeter would acknowledge.

Cooper went through the Rolodex in his mind, struggling to recall what he knew about Streeter. He had a solid reputation in the legal community as a savvy skip tracer and bounty hunter. He never abused the people he was tracking. But he never gave up or took any guff, either. Cooper could feel the desired mood slipping away. Even the sky was against him: the cloud cover all but erased any sun glare on Story.

"Why, may I ask, do you feel the need for this burly assistant?" Cooper turned his attention back to Story.

"Why, may I ask, do you feel the need to paint my car?" Story had decided to throw out one quick accusation about her Audi to see if he'd bite.

He didn't. In fact, he seemed genuinely puzzled. "Is that supposed to be a joke?"

"Forget it. What is it you wanted to see me about?"

"This is not a particularly pleasant subject," he began, holding out his hand for Ronnie to give him the invoice. She fumbled with her papers, so Story jumped in. He had barely finished his sentence when Story slid an angry-looking document across his desk, pushing it gingerly with one finger.

"Well, this is a particularly pleasant subject for me," she said. "I like it when people owe me money and they pay up. Doug kept me posted on the financial arrangements he made with you. According to my calculations, based on numbers he supplied me, his estate should be getting money back from you. It's all spelled out in there. Take your time. I'm sure you're familiar with demand letters. But there can be no dispute that you didn't earn all the money for that little work you did. I've retained William McLean, as you can see. If you have any problems with the numbers, I suggest you speak directly to Mr. McLean."

So much for her crying, Cooper thought. Now he could really feel his plan sliding into the toilet. McLean, of all people. Ronnie finally handed him his invoice. Suddenly it looked feeble next to the demand letter, which he started skimming. Story was looking for fifteen thousand and change, saying Doug had paid thirty thousand up front. The numbers were off, so he knew she was guessing. Still, she was in the ballpark and he was in for a fight.

Streeter kept looking at Cooper and his crew. The attorney had one of those chunky bodies that made even an expensive suit look like it came off the rack at Kmart. Story's letter apparently had had the desired effect. Cooper looked like he was reading a death threat from the Ayatollah. The blonde next to him wasn't quite as cheap-looking as Story had described. Sort of sexy, but with a definite air of intelligence. Quite sexy, actually, and obviously pissed. She was glaring at Cooper and she seemed to be shaking her head. And the bovine paralegal with the hideous posture merely seemed confused. He looked like all he wanted in the whole world was to leave the room.

Cooper looked up when he got the gist of the letter. "You're kidding," was about the best he could do. "You can't be serious. I've got an itemized invoice here documenting far more than the sum of this fictitious retainer to which you allude. Hell, all Doug came up with was thirty-five hundred. I've got the receipt right here."

He nodded to Ronnie, who didn't budge.

"Speaking of fictitious," Story said, glaring back, "I'd like to see that invoice. Talk about fairy tales. Listen, Cooper, you've got my letter. Give me your invoice. We'll let a judge settle this. There's no point in us arguing about it now."

That really hit Cooper. His final trump card was Jacky Romp waiting in the next room to serve her with a summons and complaint in a collections action. But if she had William McLean ready to go to court, the suit sure as hell wouldn't shake her. Chalk one up for Ronnie. She had read Story a lot better than he had. But he'd come this far, might as well play out the string. He leaned over to Ronnie and told her to get the process server. She was watching their two visitors across the desk, thinking what a bitch Story was and how the big bounty hunter had nice forearms and such a gentle face. He can hunt my bounty any day, flashed through Ronnie's mind. Then she turned and looked hard at Cooper and seemed about to speak. Instead, she merely got up and left the room.

"In anticipation of your response, I've formalized my grievance in the lawsuit that is forthcoming," Cooper said without much enthusiasm.

The door opened and Jacky Romp entered. His eyes darted around until he saw Story. He broke into his patented lizard smile and strolled toward her.

"This would be for you, lady," he said with his mouth shut. He looked over at Streeter and his smile faded. Then he turned and left the room.

Streeter shifted in his seat and pulled some sort of document from his back pocket. He looked at Story. She nodded. Then he leaned across the desk and chucked the papers toward Cooper.

"In anticipation of your chicken-shit response, Mr. McLean drew this up." Story smiled. "It's a summons and complaint all of your own. We'll see you in court. And another thing." She glanced at Ronnie, who had returned to her chair. "Tell Hot Stuff there to quit looking into Doug's past. I know she was over at Shannon Mays' place and I can only guess what else she's doing. And if anything more happens to my car, I'll hold you personally responsible."

Cooper's mouth dropped open in genuine shock. Papers flying at him from every direction and now all this cryptic talk about cars and Shannon somebody. Ronnie stayed cool, glaring at Story but not saying anything. "Shannon's? I don't . . ." Cooper quickly regained his composure. "The activities of my staff are none of your concern."

"From the looks of it, they're not much of your concern, either," Story shot back. "Just don't pry into Doug's life. A judge'll settle this."

With that, she and Streeter got up and left.

Soyko had just rounded the corner next to the elevators when he saw Doug Shelton's girlfriend and some guy coming out of Cooper's office. He was surprised, because Cooper had told him the meeting would be long over by then. The couple didn't seem to notice him as they passed in the hallway. When they walked by, he turned to admire Story, or more specifically her bottom, heading for the elevators. He also noticed the size of the guy with her and wondered if her new boyfriend had any fight in him. In Soyko's world, it was performance that counted. Bulging muscles without a killer instinct meant nothing. Just more meat to put down.

A frowning Dwayne Koslaski came out of Cooper's office, and Jacky was sitting in the waiting area. He was ignoring the receptionist, who was ignoring him. When Soyko walked in, she switched into high gear and ignored both of them. Jacky gave him a quick nod toward Cooper's office and rolled his eyes. Soyko walked slowly over and sat next to him.

"That clown gets more worthless all the time," Jacky fumed.

"Tried to lean on the little blonde, and I gather she handed him his ass. She had some meatball with her."

"I saw them out in the hallway. She wasn't going for any of his bullshit lawyer bills? Some move, huh?"

Jacky grunted through his teeth.

"How you know what happened in there?" Soyko asked.

"When the fat guy walked out of the office, he left the door open. Mr. Shit-for-Brains Lawyer was yelling at the broad that works for him, Mrs. Shit-for-Brains. Something about her sticking her nose into something or other. She looked like she wanted to kick his butt. Probably could. Anyhow, he started whining about how the other broad might be more trouble than she's worth. Looks like another Cooper fuckup in the making."

Soyko nodded. He stared at Cooper's office door. "Let's find out what's going on." When they walked into his office, the receptionist didn't even look up from her crossword puzzle.

"Jesus, all I need is you free-lancing," Cooper was yelling at Ronnie. They stood in the middle of the room, about a foot apart, glaring at each other. Neither seemed to notice when Soyko and Romp walked in. "Every idiot in town is looking for that money! What the hell were you doing, going over to her apartment like that?"

"Somebody better get real on finding that money," Ronnie hurled back. "If you think these two dildos are going to locate anything"—she threw her arm out in Soyko's direction—"maybe you should find another line of work. Like sorting apples."

Cooper noticed them for the first time. He straightened his tie, went behind his desk, and threw himself into his chair. "That will be all for now." He looked back at Ronnie, trying to put as much authority into his voice as he could. No one in the room bought it.

She studied him. "We'll talk later." With that she left.

"See what happens when you spoil a woman?" He looked at Soyko.

"I see. She nosing around in your business, counselor?"

Cooper's face got red. "Everyone's nosing around in my business. And it appears that everyone has the same idea about Mr. Shelton's cash reserves. That goddamned girlfriend of his is out looking for it. You're looking for it. I'm looking for it. That one out there is looking for it." He nodded toward the door. "What the hell is going on around here?"

"Looks like you're having one miserable morning."

"It would appear so." Cooper was now more reflective than depressed. "And then that Story woman practically accused me of trashing her car. I'm not sure I know what she was implying. Either of you two been screwing around with her?"

Soyko frowned. "Hell no. What for? Tell me what happened and we'll see what we can come up with." He sat down across from the attorney and Jacky flopped onto the couch.

Cooper stared at Soyko for a long time before he spoke. "My meeting with Moffatt went like shit. Not only is she contesting my invoices, but she's fighting back. Here I thought she'd be glad to take a discount just to make it right with me. That bastard Doug must have told her something about our arrangement, because she has a pretty good handle on the money end of it.

"As though that weren't enough, she's hired William McLean to represent her. Even getting her served"—he nodded quickly to Jacky—"didn't faze her. She brought some muscle-head with her to glare at me. That miserable Koslaski damn near wet his pants. He tells us his name is Streeter. So I asked his first name. He sits there like Buddha and says to me, 'Streeter's fine.'

"Then comes the grand finale." Cooper's eyes got wide as he scanned the room. "My own secretary is out there looking for Doug's money without even telling me. Jesus, who can you trust? This thing's beginning to look like one monumental foul-up. Maybe I should just dump the whole effort."

Soyko nodded. "Who can you trust, is right." He made a

mental note to have a little chat with Taggert. He wouldn't tell Cooper about that, because he would get all protective. The lawyer acted like Ronnie was the only woman on the face of the planet. He could never understand Cooper's loyalty toward her. Any woman of mine starts messing in my business, Soyko reasoned, she gets the belt.

"Don't get too discouraged," he advised the attorney. "Just give it a shot against this McLean guy. You already served the papers. Can't stop that train once it's left the station."

Cooper knew he was right. He doubted if Moffatt could get any money out of him. He might as well take his chances in court. See if he could squeeze something out of her in front of a judge. If she had money to hire McLean, she had money to pay for Doug.

"About the rest of it," Soyko continued, "just don't worry so much. I got an idea there's something to all this hunting around. I talked to a couple of people who knew Doug and it seems he did move a fair amount of blow. I just know that he had some serious money—of the six-figure variety, like you said. My own theory is that he wasn't hiding it with no girlfriend. This Story doesn't have it, why should some other broad? I'm thinking maybe he tucked it away somewhere else. And don't worry about her goon. He gives you too much grief, you let me know."

The prospect of Soyko's going up against Streeter intrigued Cooper. "I might just do that."

"Your little girlfriend there isn't the only surprise person nosing around into this business, either."

Cooper stiffened. "What do you mean. Who else?"

"Some cop's been sniffing around the last few days. My hunch is, this Story asked the cops some questions and that got them interested in Doug all over again. By the way, did Dougy get into a fight last fall? Maybe around the time he got busted?"

"I'd hardly call it a fight. Someone beat the snot out of him shortly after his incarceration. He wouldn't tell me who did it. I never understood all that happened last fall with him. The beating, the charges being dropped. Not that I was paying much attention. This cop worries me more. You really think Story got them worked up again?"

"Who knows. But this may not be bad news. It seems to me that, the more attention this guy's estate gets, the more likely it is he left some serious money behind. And we're the ones gonna find it. That's guaranteed."

11

"So, how did we make out with the opprobrious Mr. Cooper this morning?" Bill McLean asked. Streeter had called him when he got back to the church just before dark.

"I'll have to get back to you on the opprobrious part," Streeter answered, "but we sure put the fear of God into him. This guy's in a league of his own. I can understand trying to shave the corners a little to get a few extra bucks. But what corks me is that he acted indignant when we nailed him on it. Amazing. He tried to intimidate Story and she ended up crushing him. When he got that demand letter and then the complaint, I thought he was going to pass out. To top it off, his own secretary is out looking for Doug's money and he didn't even know about it."

"He may be a fool," McLean said, "but you have to admit that he has a pair a pumpkins on him. Serving Story like that. I'm looking forward to getting into court with this guy. I'd love to have seen his face when you served him. I bet they could hear his butt clamp shut all the way up and down 17th Avenue. Legally, I think we're in good shape, and I've got a few ideas how we can speed things up. I don't want this to drag out and let Cooper think he's got a shot."

"Story'll like that. Speaking of which, someone trashed out her car, spray-painted her dog, and left her a cute little message. They want her to back off. They apparently meant our treasure hunt. It could be one of Cooper's associates. I heard he has some dangerous friends."

"I've heard stories myself. Between his secretary and his investigators, he'll be spending half his time watching his own backside. We can assume that the secretary's looking for what you're looking for. And we can further assume that, if Mr. Cooper wasn't looking for that before today, he is now. That means you better be very careful. As Story's attorney, my main concern is keeping Tom Cooper's hands off whatever Doug left her that she already has. I'll try to get a quick hearing on this. Tell Story I'll call her when we have a court date."

When he hung up, Streeter called his client. He gave her McLean's message and then he filled her in on something else. "I've got a meeting tomorrow afternoon up in Boulder with a guy named Carl Shorts. He's plugged into the whole county up there and he's got a line on an old girlfriend of Doug's. It sounds like she might have something for us."

"Who is it? Do you have a name for the woman?"

"He didn't tell me on the phone. You think you might know some of his friends from when he lived up there?"

"No, but I might have heard the name before. Let me know what you find out."

"You got it."

Frank walked into the office shortly after Story hung up. "Working late, are we?" he asked.

"Just wrapping up some calls. What's to it, Frank?"

"Same old. I take it you're still busy with that lady from the other week."

"Busy with her problem. It's getting weirder all the time. Maybe you can give me a hand. Someone messed up her car last

Friday night. Spray-painted the side—along with her dog, if you can believe that. Left her a bad note that made me think it might be this lawyer we're dealing with. But the guy who lives across the alley from where she was parked got a partial on the plate of the car the painter was driving. I'm trying to think of why it rings a bell with me. The guy got B-J-J-3 clear but he couldn't see the rest. That mean anything to you?"

Frank frowned and flicked his thumb against his ear a couple of times. It was his way of letting you know he was thinking. "It means you might have a cop on your case. That's what it means to me. As I recall from my days with the Sheriff's Department, all the plates for Denver unmarked police cars start either with B-J-J or J-B-J. They're the only ones who get those prefixes. No wonder it sounded familiar. I probably told you that back when you started with me. If that's the car that did it, your friend's got at least one cop trying to tell her something. What the hell's this little lady done to make the police want to paint her doggy?"

"Beats me. Maybe she's got some unpaid parking tickets and they just wanted her attention. Maybe she wouldn't buy raffle tickets. You could write several long books on what I don't know about her."

"Well, we can sit here and crack wise all night, but if the cops are behind this you've got some serious trouble. I'm surprised, though. The Denver police may not be a bunch of geniuses or Eagle Scouts but this just ain't their style. I've dealt with these guys for thirty years and I know that's true. Listen, I'm hungry. Let's you and me go get pizza or some other big hit of garlic."

"Sounds good to me."

When they got back to the church after eating, Streeter read a little and then went to bed at eleven o'clock. But Frank's revelation about the police car wouldn't let him sleep. Finally, shortly after midnight, he got dressed and went to his weight room to think. Since he'd been a teenager, he had found solace and comfort in lifting weights. Growing up in a home with an alcoholic father, he used to retreat to the basement gym. It was his sanctuary where he could escape the endless arguments between his parents upstairs. He liked being alone with the cold iron, the smell of chalk dust and cold grease. There was a huge mirror on one wall, and a rusting bench dominated the middle. He would go through hours of repetitive sets, feeling strength and, more important, a sense of order in his chaotic and angry house. When he moved into the church, he immediately built a weight room off to one side of the garage.

He warmed up with five sets of fifty push-ups, his feet elevated a couple feet off the ground to give him more range and stretch. Then he did six fierce sets of bench presses, working up to two hundred forty-five pounds for a set of five. It was an easy weight for him. Next he moved on to curls, doing slow sets of six with a hefty one hundred eighty pounds. His biceps bulged and the veins shot out like someone had injected blue fluid in his arms.

Streeter knew he was biting into trouble when he and Story took on Cooper. But he never figured anyone else was in the picture. Much less a cop. Or cops. He had no idea how many there were, who they were, or what they were after. Nor did he know how far they'd go.

The most logical theory he'd been toying with was that the same cop who heisted the evidence against Shelton somehow heard that he and Story were looking into Doug's business. Obviously, that cop wouldn't want anyone nosing around. He was sure the cop thought that any possible problems died with Doug. All snooping now was to be discouraged. Before he and Frank went out to eat, Streeter had put in a call to Carey. He hadn't heard back yet. He'd ask his friend to sniff around the department and see if there ever were any suspects in that evidence theft.

His other theory was more disturbing. What if the cop or cops got wind that Doug left a bundle and they jumped into the hunt? Because of Doug's arrest, the police might have the inside track.

Who knows what Doug told them? He tried to think of who the renegade officer could be. Frank had a point. This isn't the way Denver cops usually behave. Still, you wave enough money in front of anyone and they can turn sour. Then he thought of Arthur Kovacs. This had to be the best suspect. The guy was right in the middle of Doug's case and he had been a Detroit cop. Streeter knew about them. Spray-painting foreign cars and dogs could be a hiring requirement in Detroit, for all he knew. Kovacs gave him that stupid tip about Shannon Mays and he made it clear what he thought of Story and Doug's family. He'd ask Carey specifically about Kovacs while he was at it.

Streeter got so deep into thought that his lifting was getting sloppy. He decided to call it a night at about one-thirty. No lights were on when he came out into the garage. His dumpy brown 1979 Buick Belvedere, a mule of a car that fit in with most of the neighborhoods he worked, sat illuminated by a streetlight through the huge stained-glass windows. Streeter's concern about how far the cops would go was about to get some illumination of its own.

The gunshots were loud but sounded distant. Streeter guessed a three fifty-seven or maybe a forty-four. He could almost swear that he saw the two bullets go through one of the high garage windows. He heard one of the bullets ricochet about twenty feet from him and it sounded like it ended up hitting the Buick.

He had dropped to his stomach when he first heard the rounds. After a minute or so, he got up and ran to the small side door. He opened it and stuck his head outside. No one was in sight. He figured that whoever did it was not firing at him. Not at that hour in the dark. Rather, they just wanted to send a couple more messages into the church.

One message was clear: I know where you live. The second was implied: Back way off.

Frank came slugging around the side of the building a couple minutes later. He held a large flashlight and he looked furious.

"That son of a bitch," he hissed. "I looked all over and he's gone. How the hell we gonna get a new window? Stained glass and all. I'm starting to wish that little lady friend of yours never found this place."

Streeter was thinking the same thing.

12

Rhonda Taggert, aka Ronnie, stubbed out yet another cigarette, then quickly grabbed the pack. Even though it was empty, she stirred her finger through it for quite a while. Then she crumpled it and tossed it on the table, wondering if she should go out for more. Better not. Her lungs already felt cooked and her warm breath was shallow. She'd gone through well over a pack that day, mostly since their ridiculous meeting with Story Moffatt.

The whole day was pretty much of a bust. The meeting soaked up most of the morning, and then she spent the rest of the day convincing Cooper that she'd done nothing wrong. Nothing disloyal. She'd never seen him that mad. It took a stream of tears and some quick sex on his desk to calm him down. But she had to admit the look on his face when Moffatt mentioned her being at Shannon's almost made it worthwhile. She thought he was going to blow breakfast right in his chair, and he looked pretty queasy for the rest of the day. Seeing the big bounty hunter helped make it worthwhile, too, she noted. He had an aura of competence about him and yet he wasn't pushy about it. He seemed stable but there was something unpredictable and exciting about him.

"Really, Tom, I wasn't actually looking for that money for myself," she had explained breathlessly to her employer. "All I was really trying to do is keep an eye on those two bozos you hired. I don't trust them, and you shouldn't, either. I think you're nuts to be using them all the time. Plus, honey, I wanted to surprise you. I wanted to show I've got a little initiative of my own. Maybe you can use me for some investigations from now on. Man, I can't believe you don't trust me after all we've been through. After all the love that's between us."

That seemed to satisfy him. Somewhat. Then, after he came off the ceiling from the blow job, she got down to some world-class ball busting.

"I told you this Story chick was no pushover," she laid into him. "She's got a pair of stones on her. A blind man can see that. You underestimated her and now you're looking down the barrel of a lawsuit. You could easily get your ass handed to you in court by this William McLean, whoever the hell he is. Keep going like you are and you'll end up paying her. Good day's work, Thomas Hardy. And you think I was a bimbo for snooping around into this mistress stuff. At least I didn't shove my tit into the old wringer like you did."

"You should have told me what you were doing," came his feeble response. Clearly, he was a beaten man. Overwhelmed on all sides. Then he added for emphasis, "You just should have told me, is all."

By the time she left, Cooper was so fed up with the whole pathetic soap opera he just wanted to go home, knock back some Scotch, and hit the rack. Pretend the day never happened. That was fine with Ronnie. She needed some downtime by herself to think of her next move. She knew the day could have gone worse. Much worse. What if, she pondered, Cooper had found out the truth about her and Doug Shelton? That was the kind of thing that got you tossed out of the job for starters and maybe netted you a conversation with Soyko and his lunatic partner. It would be a one-way conversation that might be your last.

Ronnie met Doug in the office a couple weeks after his drug

bust. He was feeling his old cocky self again and he was taken with Ronnie's street smarts, not to mention her MTV sexuality. For her part, Ronnie liked his looks and his constant patter. Too bad he couldn't produce in the bedroom. Like they say on the rodeo circuit back home, "Built like a Brahma, hung like a mama."

When Cooper started all this talk about the missing money, she thought she might have a little edge because of some of the things Doug had told her. She decided to give it a ride on her own. Hence, the trip to Shannon Mays' apartment. But so far she'd come up with nothing.

She walked to her desk and pulled out a small pad where she kept some rough notes about the deceased realtor. "Sex a D-minus. Definitely fucked up about women. Talked about himself and money constantly. Big surprise! Talked about his mother and darling brother up in Montana or somewhere. Acted like his car was made out of gold. He wouldn't let me stay in it alone when he went into liquor store. Said he didn't think I would be safe there by myself. Bullshit. Probably afraid the little whore would pee in the ashtray. Remember what Bobby said. Stingy with just about everything. Claimed to have tons of money but I never saw much. Lots of BS about how money sticks to him and he'll never worry about it again. Sure right about the 'sticks to him' part."

There was a knock on her door. Ronnie put the notebook back and went to answer it. Initially she hoped it wasn't Cooper, but when she opened it she instantly wished it was. Out in the hallway, leaning against her door frame, was a supremely relaxed Leo Soyko. His smile was thin and humorless. Ronnie sucked for air, startled but concealing it pretty well. How did this maniac find out where I live? She felt utterly unprotected, like when she was little and her mother's nameless lovers, with whisky and decay on their breath, would touch her all over. She was terrified, because she knew that the man at her door could do worse than that. His eyes, dead and furious at the same time, took in everything. Those eyes could see right through a concrete wall, she thought.

"I bet you're surprised I'm here." He widened his smile and thought how Ronnie didn't look nearly scared enough. "You're not going to ask me to come in?"

"Why would I want to do that?"

"That's not very nice." He pretended to be offended, something they both knew was impossible.

"All right. Why are you here? Did Cooper send you?"

"Don't I get to come in?" He said it with enough sting this time that she knew letting him in was her only move.

"So please do," she said as she stepped aside, giving him plenty of room. He had a faint body odor. Not dirty, more like he never used deodorant.

"You gonna offer me a drink?"

Ronnie hated the look of her place with him in it. She knew she couldn't force him out, but she doubted that he had come to hurt her. Her best shot was to hear what he wanted and get him out fast. Don't want him feeling at home here. Not ever. "You're not going to drink, you're not even going to sit down." She put as much spine in it as she could without sounding shrill. "Why don't you tell me why you're here, so then you don't have to be for very long."

Soyko studied her face. She kept even eye contact and didn't budge. His eyes said nothing, but when he spoke again his voice softened just a trace.

"Cooper could use your nerve, Goldilocks. Probably your brains, too. And, no, he didn't send me. The counselor doesn't know I'm here and I want it to stay like that. This visit's strictly my idea."

Ronnie acknowledged nothing. "What do you want?"

"What do I want?" he repeated as he leaned his butt against the dining-room table. His way of settling in. Show her he had all the time in the world. "I'm sitting there in Cooper's office today thinking, Why's Goldilocks out there looking for this money? And I'm wondering, What's she finding out? One thing's a dead-sure cinch. Perry Mason there won't be getting much out of you. I figure, you show him some snatch, he'll believe damned near anything you dish out. So whatever you told him today was either pure horseshit or only about a tenth of what you know."

Again there was silence. Then, finally, Ronnie spoke. "You figured that out, did you?"

"Yeah, I did. And here's what else I figured out. I figured I don't give a rip if someone beats me to that money. I'll just take it away from them and all they get out of it is hurt. But if someone was to help me get there first, why, hell, I'd be in a very generous mood. Wouldn't want to hurt a friend like that. Might even want to give them a little something for their trouble."

"You might, huh?"

"I might."

"Someone could get hurt, huh?"

"Oh yeah. That's guaranteed. Guy named Grundy Dopps would verify what I'm saying but he's not talking much these days."

Grundy's name drew blood. Ronnie looked away. This guy wasn't fooling around. He wouldn't mention Grundy if he wasn't certain she knew about that little number. This was his way of telling her to play ball or else end up in the same condition as the welder.

Ronnie'd been squeezed like this before and she had always worked her way out of it. When she was fifteen, a boyfriend had left her out in Ohio with these crazy drug dealers. She was the insurance on a big cocaine buy. If the boyfriend didn't produce the cocaine, Ronnie would get shot. Simple as that. The boyfriend didn't produce, but Ronnie came out okay. She had managed to get on the good side of one of the guys who were holding her. She was so young, but she could turn on the Marilyn Monroe so heavy the guy let her live. She became his sex slave for a couple weeks until she found an opening, and then she split.

But Soyko made those dealers look like Jerry's Kids. He

wouldn't get thrown off the track by a little action. No sir, this guy was after blood. Always. He never let up. That was her read. He was pure Robomaniac, with only maybe a nodding interest in sex and absolutely no interest in mercy. She decided to take the practical path. Feed him a little shit and stall him.

"I think you pegged Tom Cooper about right." Her voice softened but not too much. "He doesn't get it half the time. See, he's playing by some set of rules he must have learned at college or someplace weird like that."

"I'm not learning anything new here."

"Listen, I like your idea. There's no point in us both doing the same things without the other one knowing about it. I'll tell you what I know, which isn't all that much, and you tell me where we go from here."

"Then I tell you where we go from here," he repeated more to himself. "Say you don't know much, huh?"

"This is on the level. I didn't find nothing from the girlfriend's apartment. They wouldn't even let me in. But I'll tell you something you didn't know. I sort of went out with Dougy. Not really a date and no sex or nothing, but he met me for a drink one night. It was a few weeks after he got busted. We went over to some stupid theme bar in Aurora. The Jolly Douche Bag or something. Had a few beers and he loosened up a little. He told me that he wasn't close with his wife or whatever she was. Moffatt. You want my advice, you might look where he goes and no one else goes. I'd go through that car of his, maybe, for starters. He guarded that thing pretty damned close, if you ask me. It was really nuts."

"Didn't someone already do that?" Soyko sounded less sure of himself.

"I don't know. The man treated that thing like it was a woman, that's all I know. There must be other places to check, too. For instance, it might be nice to go through his townhouse. Another thing. There was something really strange about him and his mother. Seemed that way to me. She lives up in Wyoming or Utah or some damned place. Doug seemed really afraid of her but he talked a lot about her. Maybe they had some sort of deal going. He spent a lot of time talking about her—to me, of all people. Like I could give a rip."

"That sounds sick. What do you mean, some sort of deal going?"

"I'm not talking about sex. More like they had this connection that seemed important to him. It's hard to explain and I think it's a long shot. But you wanted to know what I know."

"I'll keep that in mind. Why didn't you do any of those things? Why didn't you try to check on all that?"

"I just got started. Plus, I've never done any of this before."

"Why'd you meet him out at that bar? You liked this guy?"

"He was kind of cute, but when we talked for a while he bored the hell out of me. About the only topic seemed to interest him was him. Boring with a capital B-O-R-E."

"What else do you know?"

"Nothing really. But I can be some good to you. You could use eyes and ears inside Cooper's office. My eyes and ears. You'd know what's going on everywhere."

"It could work, at that." Soyko sounded almost pleasant. "I just might like to know what's really up with that guy. Here's the deal, Goldilocks. You keep those eyes and ears open, let me know anything important. I get the money, I'll see you're taken care of. But if I find out you're holding back on me or you tell Cooper, then I come back here. And I bring Jacky. You know him, he's more than a little off the fucking wall. Like me. We come back out here, you wish you'd never heard of us."

She already wished that. "You won't ever have to come back here. You got my word on that."

13

Pokey Shorts stared at the woman across the table from him and thought, What a waste. What a horrible waste. Here she is, still relatively young, body by Hooters, and a face as sweet as sin. Susanne Skiles was built to party, and for most of her first three decades she did just that. Then, one week shy of her thirty-third birthday, everything changed. She woke up yet another morning when even her eyelashes ached from the previous night's indulgences. She looked in the mirror and her pretty face was puffy and contorted from toxins her liver could no longer process adequately and she could see how she would look at fifty. Sick and tired of being sick and tired, she made her way to a noon AA meeting. From then on it was twelve steps to happiness. She even quit smoking after a few months. Caffeine was her new drug of choice, celibacy the order of the day, and if she stayed out past ten she was living on the edge.

Susanne looked back at Carl Shorts and thought, What a waste. What a horrible waste. Look at him, she thought. We've been here all of a half-hour and he's slamming down his second beer and sizing up a shot of Jack Daniel's. And can't he give his lungs a rest? He must smoke at least three hundred cigarettes a day. He wouldn't be a bad-looking man if he'd quit trying to kill himself and act the fifty or however many years old he is.

"Yeah, Carl, those were the days," she said with little conviction. "Hot tubs, hash pipes, and dry red wine. I loved it. But times change and you start thinking about the future and what you might want to do with yourself. Hangovers can eat up a lot of precious time. Like we say in AA, 'Life is what happens to other people while you're waiting on a barstool.' "

"Tell me about it." Pokey's voice sounded sincere, but recovery talk bored him senseless, and her hot-tub comment set off a fantasy sequence that distracted him. He looked fondly at his beer. "I suppose I should taper off a little, but to be honest I've been at it so long I'm starting to enjoy the stuff."

Susanne pressed on. "Well, 'your ass was built for a barstool,' like we say in AA. That seems to be the case with you, all right. But if you ever give any serious thought to quitting, Carl, just let me know. Honestly. I can take you to a meeting. It's not that hard to quit. It totally changed my life, and I cherish my sobriety above everything else."

Pokey's eyes glazed over when she said "sobriety." The concept was unfathomable, but he appreciated her sincerity. "I'll keep that in mind. Yes, I will."

The sight of Streeter walking toward them gave Pokey a good reason to change the subject. They were sitting just off Boulder's Pearl Street Mall at a garden-level bar and restaurant called the Walrus. Pokey chose the place because it would have a mid-sized happy-hour crowd, perfect for secluded conversation. It was also one of the last places in town where he could have a cigarette without hearing a load of crap about the dubious hazards of secondary smoke.

About thirty freeway miles northwest of Denver and snuggled in the rolling foothills of the Rocky Mountains, Boulder was a place Streeter liked to visit. But not too often and not for long. The town itself was beautiful, but there were too many holistic fanatics who considered pyramid power to be perfectly reasonable and tie-dye to be hip and high art. It's a place where the local Birkenstockers dabbled in colonic irrigation and yet were mortified at the thought of eating red meat. He quickly tired of all the pious, new-age self-absorption and the naïve, Woodstock-driven politics.

"Street man, over here," Pokey yelled. Then, quietly to Susanne, "Here's the guy I told you about. He's a good man. You can trust him. I use him to track down people in Denver for me and he always comes through."

Susanne nodded serenely. In her sobriety, she relied so heavily on spirituality that human deception became almost irrelevant.

"When you trust your higher power, Carl, everything else falls into place. Like we say at the meetings, 'Let go and let God.' "

"I'll keep that in mind, Susanne." Why, he wondered, does she always have to talk like she's going for her black belt in recovery?

Pokey introduced her to Streeter. He thought she was attractive, but she seemed to work a little too hard at being relaxed. And he didn't like the look she gave him when he ordered a beer and bummed a cigarette off Pokey. Although Streeter stayed fit, he liked to kick back with a few beers and have a smoke from time to time. And there was something about doing it in Boulder, where he could tick off the sanctimonious locals, that made it even more inviting.

"How's my old friend William McLean?" Pokey asked.

"Great. He says hello," Streeter said. "You know he's helping me with this."

"So you said," Pokey responded. Then he turned to Susanne. "Bill's a lawyer down in Denver. Used to be a DA. Great guy. Intelligent. Excellent attorney. Harvard Law School and all that. But he's sort of crazy at the same time. He's always up to something provocative. Always slightly perverse. He's the type of guy who farts in a crowded elevator just to stir things up."

"He sounds charming," she said flatly.

Pokey stared off for a minute, smiling, as he contemplated Bill. "Well, let's get down to business. I know you have to leave soon, so why don't you tell Streeter what you told me."

She turned to the bounty hunter. "Carl tells me that you work for Doug's widow? Is that right?"

"Something like that."

"She's probably heavily codependent, what with Doug's substance-abuse problems. Tell her to call me if she's looking for a Codependents Anonymous group. I go to an excellent CODA session on Thursdays." Then, after some thought, "Carl tells me she's trying to find out if he salted some money away?"

"That's right." Streeter was put off slightly by the twelve-step talk. A few years ago, when he was concerned about his own increasing drinking, he went to a few AA meetings. He found that the concept of group support and confronting your problems was solid, but the relentless guilt, drama, and depression of the meetings, along with the religious overlay, put him off. He quit drinking for a few months. Then he decided he was tired of not having any fun, so he started nailing back a couple of beers from time to time and an occasional glass of wine with dinner.

"I didn't even know he was married. Actually, I haven't seen Doug for quite a while. Probably about four years or more. It was before I got sober, I know that. That poor man could have used some intervention and a spiritual program himself. He was wrestling with so many demons all the time. I understand he was very drunk when he died."

"I don't know about that. I hear different things about his partying."

"That's because he usually went through different phases," she said. "Sometimes he would hit the coke pretty hard, and then other times he would just drink. Sometimes both, sometimes neither. He would go through dry-drunk spells where he wouldn't do anything except sit around and be grouchy. Then he'd go off and become Captain Party for a while."

"When exactly were you with him?" Pokey asked. "I mean, how long?"

"Let's see. I met him in about '86. We lived together for a couple of years. Maybe more, maybe less."

"Was he dealing?" Streeter asked.

"Hell yes. He was dealing everything. The real-estate market was picking up, and he was moving a fair amount of coke, too. He bought a big house on Mapleton Hill. I think that's where a lot of his money went. He sold it a couple of years later and I think he lost some on that, if you can imagine losing money in the eighties."

"Tell him about the nickname," Pokey interrupted.

"I gave it to him back when we lived together. I called him Squirrel. Some of his friends used it, too. We came up with that because he had this habit of squirreling things away, all around town. Coke and cash, mostly."

"Did you ever see any of these places?" Streeter leaned in to her.

"No. Nobody else did, either."

"Did he ever talk about them?"

"No. But this happened a bunch of times. We would go out and someone who knew him would come up and ask to buy coke. It would just be kind of spontaneous, but Doug always managed to go score. He'd leave me at a party at midnight and go out for twenty minutes, maybe half an hour, and come back with flake. And usually it was a good-sized amount.

"I remember once he sold these bartenders at the old Pelican Pete's an ounce at closing time. The deal came up at the last minute and he had no way to know in advance that he would need it. No matter where we were in town, he could get cocaine or cash real quick. The only thing I could figure out was that he stashed it all over town. The guy was a genius that way."

Streeter thought about what she was telling him and tried to reconcile that with what Story had told him. It all fit. "Did you ever go with him?"

"He always went alone." She shook her head seriously. "I think he got a kick out of the squirrel thing. It was sort of his little specialty."

"Do you think he went to his supplier's place?" Pokey asked. "Maybe his source was close enough to handle all the last-minute orders."

"No. His supplier lived in the mountains somewhere. About an hour away. There wouldn't have been enough time. Plus, he couldn't count on his supplier being there all the time, and Doug never came back empty-handed. Listen, I have to take off in a second. I don't know if that helps you much. But I'd be real surprised if Doug left money or anything valuable with anyone. He didn't trust people. And if he was still hiding things, you'll have one tough job finding them. He was a very clever man who protected what he owned."

"Thanks." Streeter smiled. "Here's my card. If you remember anything else, give me a call at that number. A guy named Frank will probably answer, but he'll get a message to me. Anything. Patterns or similarities or information about how he did it. Will you do that?"

"Sure. By the way, I heard he got busted just a few months before he died. Is that true?"

"Something like that. He was arrested, and he was separating from my client. He got beat up around that time, too. Then the car wreck. He was on a real losing streak."

Susanne considered that for a moment. "Like we say in AA, 'Life doesn't come with any instructions and there's no guarantees. Shit happens.' "

14

Tom Cooper figured that day in his office with Story easily ranked as one of the five worst in his legal career. But what happened to him before District Court Judge Manuel Herrera eight days later went off the high end of the shit meter altogether. In addition to ruling against him, His Honor insulted him repeatedly from the bench. All Cooper could do was stand there and take it. That and watch Moffatt and McLean gloat, which royally tore his ass.

As usual, Cooper had no one to blame but himself. When he sued Story as administrator of the estate, he had the nerve to file an attachment on her and Doug's townhouse for the amount he sought. That enabled McLean to request a hearing and get a fast court date. That, in turn, meant both sides would go before a judge and be allowed to offer testimony on the merits of Cooper's claim. And that, finally, resulted in Judge Herrera's pitching his specious claim out the window. If only, Cooper chided himself later, he hadn't gone after the real estate. At least that way the case would have dragged on and given Story something to think about for a few months. Who knows, maybe she would have folded by then.

McLean and Story were delighted. They called Streeter from her office, not far from the courthouse, shortly after the hearing ended.

"I don't think Mr. Cooper will be much of a problem from now on," McLean told him. "Herrera spanked him and sent him home. You should have seen it. We couldn't have written a better script if we'd been on the bench with him. Cooper has his bookkeeper or whatever she was up there giving this convoluted BS about how they arrived at the numbers. And then Story takes the stand and relays everything Doug told her about the fees. The judge tied into Cooper like nothing I've ever seen before. Then, to top it all off, Herrera rather cordially invited us to request attorney's fees and court costs. He damned near came out and said if we file he'll sign the order. And that's not to mention we still have a claim in county court for a refund on Doug's retainer. All and all, it was not a bad day's work."

"That's great, Bill. I suppose your client's ecstatic."

"She sure is. I'm in her office right now. She wants you to come by here at—what? When did you want him here?" He put his hand over the receiver and looked at Story.

"One-thirty would be fine."

"She said one-thirty today. Can you make it?"

"Sure." Streeter wanted to talk to her about the unmarked police car, and the gunshots into the church the week before. He'd hoped to meet with Carey beforehand, but the detective was out of town for a few days' vacation. She needed to know about the new danger, and he couldn't wait to huddle up with her. "Tell her I'll be there. And good going, Bill."

"Thanks. I'd really like to be done with this Cooper jerk, but then something else came up yesterday."

"Yeah, what was that?"

"Out of the blue, I received a call from Max something-or-other. Max Herman. He's facing serious trouble on a cocaine charge, among other things. It seems his lawyer—or former lawyer—is none other than Mr. Thomas Hardy Cooper. Max did a little snooping around with people he knows in the DA's office and he finds out that he's been offered a pretty good deal. However, our man Cooper hasn't even told him about it yet, just so he can run up the legal fees. Well, now, Max is about ready to clobber his former legal team. He wants me to take his case and also wants to sue Cooper for malpractice."

"You going to do it?"

"I haven't decided yet. I'm meeting with him first thing Monday morning. In a way, it might be fun to keep after Cooper for a while."

"Sounds like you can make a decent living just beating up on him. Anyhow, I really appreciate what you did for Story."

"That's what I'm hired to do."

Story's offices suited her, Streeter remembered when he walked in that afternoon. Tasteful and impressive. She was on the second floor of an impeccably restored mansion that she shared with an architectural firm and two attorneys. The place was on the Denver tour of historic homes. Her suite had turn-of-the-century elegance with hardwood floors yet all the modern touches, including a built-in microwave.

"Sounds like you had a little fun this morning," he said as she showed him in.

"William was just phenomenal." She pointed for him to sit down across the desk from her. "He had that dope so confused and scared, I almost felt embarrassed for him. Almost. You should have seen Cooper. He stammered and stuttered and in the end he just took his beating from the judge. He looked like his diapers needed changing and he hoped no one noticed the smell. When we were leaving court, he just glared at me. I thought he'd explode."

"Are you going after a refund?"

"I considered it, but then I decided it would be such a hassle and I really don't know how much would be a fair amount to pursue. Doug never mentioned figures. I'll let it go, so we can concentrate on our work. We'll ask the judge to order him to pay legal fees, though. I'm just glad we've seen the last of this dork. I think it's best to leave Mr. Cooper to his little criminal practice so he can go back to short-changing his clients and chasing that tramp secretary of his around. Did you believe her? She looked about a notch above an East Colfax streetwalker."

Streeter thought about all that. On the one hand, he was glad she was going to drop the claim against Cooper. It showed she wasn't still looking for the easy score she didn't deserve. On the other hand, he felt a strange sense of protectiveness toward Ronnie.

"My, aren't we catty," he said. "She wasn't that bad. Scrape off a little of her eye makeup and she'd be kind of attractive."

"Oh, pull-ease, Streeter." Story rolled her eyes but was surprised that she felt a faint twinge of jealousy. "Attractive? You've *got* to be kidding."

He changed the subject. "At least we've seen the last of Cooper and his friends. I hope. He may not take this beating too well, you know. When Bill McLean goes for the jugular, he can really piss people off. There's something else we have to talk about. I gather you want to keep going with this treasure hunt."

"You're darned right. Look, if you're running out of money, just let me know. I'll get you more."

"No, it's not that. There's still money left."

"Did you hear anything in Boulder to make you want to stop?"

"No. As a matter of fact, the more I hear, the more I think we might be on to something."

He told her about Susanne and the Squirrel handle and how Doug had operated in Boulder. She listened intently to every word.

"And you asked if I wanted to stop now," she said when he finished. "Hell, we're just getting started. We've got the general layout and now we can focus in on specifics. Where do we go from here?"

"From here? Story, before we take another step, I have to tell you that this thing is getting dangerous and it could get even more twisted from now on. Your car and your dog were bad enough, but it's getting worse. Someone fired a couple of rounds into my house last week. At night after our meeting with Cooper."

"My God! Was anyone hurt?"

"No. It was the middle of the night and they just shot out a couple of windows."

"Do you know for sure it was connected to this business?"

"Not for sure. But I don't believe in coincidences, and now someone knows where I live. I hate that, especially if it's someone with a gun who doesn't mind firing it. And even worse, I think that someone has a badge."

She scowled. "A policeman? Where do you get that from?"

"The license number the guy got that night your car was trashed was for an unmarked police car. My hunch is it's the same cop who nailed Doug. I think he's the one that helped the cocaine disappear from the police-evidence room, and now he doesn't want any more attention. I suppose the shots could be Cooper just trying to scare us off the scent of the money, but my hunch is it's a cop."

"So go tell the cop we're not interested in him. Tell him we'll leave him alone."

"Now, why didn't I think of that? You want me to go accuse a cop of vandalism, tampering with evidence, and shooting at me and then tell him, 'Hey, but that's cool. We'll forget it if you will.' He'd blow me away on the spot, and I couldn't blame him."

"Look, Streeter." She stood up and came around the desk. Her face looked like it did that day in the squash court. "I don't care what you do or don't do about this cop or whoever it was that shot at your precious church. But I'm not giving up on this thing. If you want to, fine. I'll get someone else to help me. I'm simply not quitting."

Streeter stood up and faced her.

"You have no idea what you might be getting into, do you? You think this is just some other 'account' you might lose. You could lose a lot more than money if it's what I think it is. Cooper is capable of God knows what, and if it's a rogue cop, he could be worse. What's so damned important about this money?"

"It's mine. That's what's so important." Then she lowered her voice. "I don't want to argue with you. If you want out, I understand. Keep the money I gave you and no hard feelings. But I'm not stopping. If Cooper's behind this, that just makes me more convinced that I'm on the right track. Who knows what Doug may have told him? Or who knows what he told the cop who helped get him off? I'm going to keep looking, with or without you. For what it's worth, I hope it's with you."

Streeter laced his fingers behind his head and stretched back to give himself time to think. After a few seconds he said, "I'm not saying I want out. I'm just letting you know what we're in for. As far as I'm concerned, there's no way I'm going to let this asshole get away with shooting at my house. That's a bad precedent for someone in my line of work. I'm in, Story. I just wanted you to know the kind of people we're dealing with here."

"Okay. I'll consider myself warned."

"Do you own a gun?"

"I have a little thirty-eight. I usually keep it next to my bed."

"Do you know how to use it?"

"An old boyfriend showed me how. He's the one who gave it to me."

"Keep it close, just to be safe. And put it in your glove compartment when you go out. You never know when it might come in handy."

"I assume you have a gun."

"Several. I usually keep a three fifty-seven short-barrel under my car seat."

"Do you have a permit?" she asked.

"All of mine are registered, but I can't get a concealed-weapons permit. Practically no one can anymore. It seems that the cops hate to make the bad guys nervous by allowing honest citizens to carry a hidden piece or two. I doubt if we need them, but someone out there has a gun, and I'll feel better if you do, too."

"So where do we go from here?"

"I want to keep talking to Doug's friends, all the people he worked with. We know this money isn't in any bank, but it might be in a locker at the train station or a place like that. If Doug was as distrustful as I think, he wouldn't have told anyone about it. But maybe he left a spare key with someone for safe keeping without telling them what it's for. Maybe several spare keys, judging by what I heard up in Boulder."

"I'll make a list of anyone I know of who was close to Doug," she said, jotting something down in her Daytimer.

"Include even those people who weren't too close to him. He might have picked someone he wasn't tight with. And I'll want to go over everything he left at the house. We should do that together."

"Why don't you come over tomorrow night? I'll have it all ready and we can plow through it."

"Fine. And I'll want the address and phone number of his family up in wherever he's from. Wyoming, wasn't it?"

She frowned again.

"Some problem with that?"

"I'll have it for you," she said. "It's just that his mother is such a bitch."

"I don't want to move in with the woman. I just want to talk to her."

As Cooper slithered back to his office after court, he felt like he'd just paid a thousand dollars for a hooker and then couldn't perform. On top of that, she'd laughed at him. Why was that courtroom so packed? Rage and humiliation surged through him in giddy waves.

When he got to his office, Ronnie was in the lobby. "How did you make out?" she asked, even though she could tell from his expression.

"How'd Iraq make out in Desert Storm? I got totally hammered, that's how. Get me Soyko on the phone."

"No need to. He's waiting in your office," she said. "He got here about two minutes ago."

"How did he . . . Uh . . . Aw, who gives a shit? Come on. I want you in on this, too, seeing as how you're so interested in Doug Shelton."

Cooper walked into his office and saw Soyko sitting in front of his desk, with Jacky Romp sprawled out over the couch. Both men were smoking cigarettes, and they remained quiet when the attorney entered with Ronnie behind him.

"Do you two have to do that in here?" Cooper yelled as he sat down. He waved his hand like he was swatting invisible flies.

"Just a hunch, court sucked," Soyko said, crushing out his cigarette.

"Brilliant." Cooper looked off to the side. "That fucker had the judge in his hip pocket. Judge my ass. More like some affirmative-action appointment with an attitude. We got totally shot down."

We? Soyko was tempted to remind Cooper that he'd lost on his own. But he let it slide. Bust his chops and the lawyer might just self-destruct on the spot. Instead, he kept looking at Cooper, letting him blow off steam.

"That motherfucker . . ." Cooper muttered, too upset to finish. "And that bitch client of his. Both laughing at me. Rubbing my dick in the dirt. I don't know who I'd like to see dead first. They should both be tortured. Now she even has the option of coming after me for money. Judge José there practically told her to do it. I'd like to burn her for this. Her lawyer, too."

"That can be arranged, you know." Soyko's voice carried no emotion.

"Forget it. I just keep thinking of the stones on that broad. Lying in court under oath."

"Be a shame, someone'd try and get something they don't deserve like that," Soyko deadpanned. "There oughta be a law."

Jacky cackled at the irony.

Cooper looked from one man to the other. "Just keep yukking it up, you two. Big goddamned joke, isn't it? Let's us concentrate on what we have to do to get that money Doug hid. Okay? I don't suppose you have any good news for me on that score. You know, I don't even give a flying fuck about the money so much anymore." He lowered his voice, a thin trail of spit lacing off the side of his mouth. "I just want to stop this Story broad from getting it. What the hell kind of name is that anyway? Story. What is she, some princess from a fairy tale? I want you two to go balls to the wall on this thing. Take no prisoners and spare no expense. Find that money. I want all these bastards to bleed. Whatever it takes to screw them over."

"I hear you, counselor." Soyko got up. His partner got up, too. "We'll get right on it. You should maybe take the day off. Looks like you're about to blow wide open."

"Don't worry about me. Let's just deal with this fast and hard. Find that money, and no more Mr. Nice Guy bullshit."

When the two men left, Cooper leaned back in his swivel chair and began rocking quickly. Ronnie just stared at him for a while.

"You should have calmed down before you talked to them," she said.

"Yeah, why's that?"

"Because they might get the wrong idea about what you wanted. They might think you want them to hurt someone."

"Aw, Christ, Ronnie. Give it a rest. I just told them to find the money, whatever it takes."

"And you don't think they might take that to mean, mess somebody up? Really put the spurs to them?"

"Of course not. I made it perfectly clear. They won't get carried away."

She studied him for some time. Poor dope really didn't get it. Here he was with his coat on fire and he's busy looking for lint.

"Yeah, sure. Why would they?"

15

For someone who supposedly made a lot of money, Douglas Shelton had few belongings. Streeter discovered that the next night, when he and Story sifted through his so-called earthly possessions: clothes, papers, books, desk, golf bag, cabinets, knickknacks, ski equipment, and other items that belonged to the late realtor. They went through virtually every page of every document the man kept. They were at it for over three hours without finding anything the bounty hunter would say vaguely resembled a clue.

"He liked his cars and his clothes, but he never showed any real interest in accumulating much property," Story explained as they worked. "He'd hit the museums from time to time, like I told you before. But he never really collected things, from what I could see. Most of his spending was geared toward looking good. A lot of his money went to restaurants, too. We ate out almost every night. He bought some stuff for the house, but not much."

It was well after nine when Streeter noticed how hungry he was. "I'm starving. You want to call out for something?"

They were standing in the middle of what used to be Doug's study, surrounded by open boxes, open drawers, and stacks of papers. They were both wearing faded jeans, T-shirts, and sneakers. His was a white Broncos shirt, hers powder-blue, touting the name of a perfume he'd never heard of. Streeter appreciated the way her jeans so comfortably snuggled up to the contour of her legs and bottom without appearing like they'd been applied with a paint roller. But she kept her makeup and earrings on, which looked inappropriate to the task and to her clothes. Totally casual was not Story's style.

"I'll get the menu and we can call the Pagoda," she told him. "Great Szechuan, if you like it."

"Fine. I'll eat anything that's got duck in it."

He was sorting through a file marked "Taxes—1990 All." Apparently, Doug was fascinated by detailed and ultimately insignificant paperwork while at the same time he ignored obviously important things. For instance, Streeter found meaningless receipts and obscure reminder notices, yet no copy of Shelton's completed 1990 tax return. There was no discernible pattern to what he kept and what he threw away. It made Streeter's job more difficult. Luckily, Story had come up with a list of thirty-seven people—addresses and phone numbers included—who knew Doug, so he had more leads to explore.

"I don't know if this is doing us any good," he told her when they'd finished. "About all I can figure out is, he has a very strange sense of filing, and he doesn't know the correct name for the mayor of Denver."

"Mayor Webb. What makes you say that?" She came back into the study after calling for the Chinese food.

"There were some notes he kept with his bank slips where he wrote out 'W. Webb Wellington' instead of 'Wellington Webb.' He had to be referring to the mayor. Don't you think?"

"He must have written a check to Webb's reelection campaign. Who knows? Doug never was much on details. I could show you this letter he was writing to his mother. He wrote like a sixth-grader. All this melodramatic crap about how precious his time in Wyoming is. Doug was strange about his family. Especially his mother."

"So I gather. Like I said yesterday, I'm going to have to go up there and talk to her fairly soon."

"I suppose, but it won't be fun. She's really lonely and incredibly judgmental. Apparently, she's second-generation German. Real old-school and totally long-suffering with her religion. She thinks that if you smile too much you're not going to the Kingdom of God. In a strange way, Doug was sort of in awe of her. He'd complain about her, but when she was around he treated her like royalty. She was always criticizing him, yet he still tried to impress her. It was like he thought if he made enough money she would finally approve of him.

"Doug has this brother who's in and out of homes and hospitals. He's mentally and physically disabled. The mother, Gail, blames the world for that. She blames the world for everything miserable in her life. She blamed Doug's father until he died, and then she started blaming Doug. Now she's probably just sitting out there on the old family farm and blaming whoever's nearby."

"Doug was a farm boy?"

"Hell no. They lived on what was left of Gail's family's farm. They never worked the place. Gail was a schoolteacher and his father was a pharmacist."

"That would help explain Doug's interest in pharmaceuticals. You think she might know anything at all about what he left behind?"

"It's unlikely. They didn't see each other more than once a year in all the time I knew him."

Story had ordered a Happy Family combination and a gallon of hot-and-sour soup. They each drank a beer while they waited.

"Didn't you tell me he left you a clock?" Streeter asked.

"Yes he did. I took it to a good friend of mine who's an antique dealer and he knew of a buyer for it. I didn't particularly like the thing myself, but the guy paid twelve thousand five hundred dollars for it. I gave my friend a nice commission and I still kept over ten grand."

"I guess you *can* put a price on memories. That must have made your day. I didn't know there are clocks that expensive."

"Hell yes. My friend was telling me about ones that easily get two or three times that. This one was a Charles Gabrier or something like that. He threw a bunch of names at me. You wouldn't believe how pretentious the world of antique clocks is. I got a crash course on it."

"Twelve thousand's a lot of money. How'd he get such an expensive clock? He doesn't seem to be the type to go for high art."

"I wondered about that, too." Story frowned as she looked at him. "He told me it was given to him by a client once in return for Doug helping get her a great home-loan rate. But that's an awful lot of gratitude. Maybe he waived his commission to get the thing. It could be that all his trips to the museum gave him an idea of how valuable the clock is. Perhaps he had an appreciation for the finer things that he never shared with me. That's possible. Apparently, there was a lot that he didn't share with me, and Doug was no idiot. He had a good mind, when his head wasn't up his butt. That's a pretty conflicted metaphor, isn't it?"

Streeter nodded and said, "I've never had much interest in antiques. By the way, was Doug paranoid?"

"He was cautious but not particularly paranoid. Especially considering the line of work he was in. Why?"

"He has a flyer over there from a company called the Executive Protectors Inc., out in Indiana. It's only four pages, but it's got all this phone-debugging equipment. Scramblers, pen transmitters. All kinds of electronic equipment and home-security products. Did he ever actually buy any of that stuff?"

"Not ever. At least not that I know of. But some guys like to get product information and then never do anything with it. He'd get flyers for all sorts of different equipment and that was it. Doug hated to part with his money."

"Well, I'm not sure how all guys are, but Doug was one very

strange pack rat. Judging by what he kept in his files, he seemed to be a warehouse of useless personal information. Keep an eye out for anything like that. You know, electronic equipment, security stuff."

They both sat in silence for a minute, drinking their beers.

"Frank's been getting a lot of hang-up calls today," Streeter finally said. "That usually doesn't happen. One time the guy said 'Fuck off' and hung up. He said it so fast Frank wasn't sure he heard it right."

"Really? What time was that?"

"About five-thirty or so. Just before I left to come over here. Why?"

"I got a few hang-up calls last night, that's all. I wonder if this is from our friend the paint-spraying cop," she said.

"It sounds too juvenile even for him. Do you usually get many hang-up calls?"

"Once in a while. Never four or five in one night."

"Let me know if it keeps up. The guy didn't use my name, so it may have been just a random call." He tried to sound convincing. "I talked to a detective friend of mine who's on the Denver Police Department. I gave him the name of the cop I think helped Doug. Detective Arthur Kovacs. My friend's going to check him out. Evidently, Kovacs has been in Denver for about five years, and he's due to retire soon. He's got a rep as a world-class bully from back in his days as a Detroit cop."

Story just nodded. Since their discussion the day before, neither of them wanted to think much about possible danger. Streeter was concerned for Frank and Story. Their food came, and they set it out on the dining-room table and dug in. Streeter was famished and Story wasn't far behind, so they ate in near silence. When they were done eating, he started nosing into her past.

"Were you always interested in advertising, Story?"

"Always. Even in high school back in Omaha, I knew I wanted to run an ad agency somewhere. In a good-sized city. Then my family came out here for a vacation when I was a junior and I knew I wanted my agency to be here. I've never doubted my decision and I've never looked back."

"You're pretty headstrong."

"I believe if there's something you want you should go for it with all you've got. And if there's something in your life that doesn't contribute to that goal or holds you back, you get rid of it. No questions asked. Doug was the one sad exception to that rule. There's only one thing I want out of life. Everything. That may sound spoiled, but that's how I feel."

"You're right. It sounds spoiled. But at least you know what you want."

"And what do you want, Streeter?"

"I want to be left alone to do my own life my own way and never have to kiss anyone's ass. I want to know where I stand with people. I want the Broncos back in the Super Bowl, but I want them to win it this time. I want to know who's going to cover the spread for every college football game this fall. I want good food and I want good friends. And when I think about you in your little squash outfit that day, sometimes I even think I want you."

"You think you want me, but you're not sure."

"Not at all sure, is right. You make me nervous. For one thing, you're incredibly materialistic. Money-hungry, one might say." He was enjoying himself. Plain to see Story wasn't used to being spoken to like this. "Also, your whole relationship with Doug was pretty bizarre. You two never really connected. Physically or emotionally. Plus, you don't level with me. You're 'somewhat less than totally candid' way too often. If I can't trust you in our little working agreement, how could I trust you as a lover?"

"Oh yeah? And what fun is it if you trust your lover?"

"That seems terribly sophisticated, but I'm not sure I know what it means. I know I don't like the sound of it."

"About that second thing, I told you how little Doug and I had going for each other. He wasn't much for any kind of contact with me. Emotionally he was quite immature, and physically, let's just say he was self-conscious. Doug was about as well hung as a field mouse, if you get my drift."

Streeter grinned and raised his eyebrows, nodding slightly. "I thought organ size wasn't supposed to matter to you women."

"*Right.* And we women don't care about a man's income, either. Is that what you guys tell each other in the locker room to feel more adequate?"

"I don't usually have to tell myself anything to feel a hell of a lot more than just adequate." He leaned back in his chair. The conversation definitely was drifting into a dangerous area, but he was feeling warm and getting excited. He flashed on how it would be nice to kiss Story right then. "Our discussion's taken an interesting turn here. You want to keep going with it?"

The topic was making her nervous and moderately aroused, two feelings she didn't often experience. She was afraid of blushing, so she shifted back to his earlier comments. "You think I'm money-hungry, superficial, and dishonest. You make me sound terrific." Story stood up and started fussing with empty food containers.

"Actually, you make yourself seem terrific. I just make you sound real."

"I certainly doubt if I come across as pompous as you do."

"Believe me, you have that ability. Look, I don't want to start a fight, but you asked. I'm just trying to be honest."

She put down the food containers and smiled. "You're a real character, you know that? Mr. 'I Gotta Be Me.' That kind of crap's usually just a cover-up for being a loser. Not that Streeter—so much more than adequate as he may be—is a loser. Besides, regarding your crack about maybe wanting me, it's not really your call, is it?"

"Usually it's best if those decisions are mutual."

"I suppose. But for now, I have to get some sleep. I think we're through with our business for tonight, anyway. I've got a staff meeting scheduled for first thing in the morning and I'll need some sleep."

Streeter nodded, a vague trace of a smile on his face. "A Saturday staff meeting. You never let up, do you?"

On the way home, he felt wired and strangely anxious. He had hoped there would be more useful information in Doug's things. Also, he wondered if Story had shown him everything or if she was still holding back. Despite his attraction to her, he couldn't shake his doubts about her. Her bullheadedness troubled him. And what was that I-want-it-all crap? She sounded like a bad Volvo commercial.

When he got home he picked up his phone to check his voice mail. He had one call, a call that would change his mood for a long time. Actually, it would change his life.

"Streeter, it's me." It was Darcy McLean. She was sobbing. "Bill's in the hospital. He's hurt awfully bad. Someone beat him. Please call whenever you get in. I mean, I'm at Swedish Hospital. Please come."

He played it over several times, hoping it would change. When the message finally sank in, he froze for a minute, nauseous. He went to the bathroom, but nothing would come up. Then he got in his car and drove to the hospital.

16

William McLean was still unconscious when Streeter got to the hospital. He had suffered a severe concussion along with several broken ribs and numerous broken facial bones. His left arm, particularly at the elbow, was badly mangled. The doctors didn't know the full extent of his internal bleeding. He was in serious but stable condition, and word was that he would live. No one could tell if there would be any permanent brain damage, but, because of his age, the sooner he regained consciousness, the better.

Darcy was waiting in a television room down the hall from intensive care when Streeter arrived, shortly before three o'clock. She was so pale and tired that he barely recognized her. Stacy, her sister, was with her, and there were two cups of cold coffee sitting on the table coagulating silently in front of them. The television was off, and it seemed so quiet, like the entire hospital was empty. Streeter noticed that the two women didn't look like sisters. Darcy had dark features, ink-black hair streaked modestly with handsome gray, and lively hazel eyes. Her sister had washed-out, brown features and light hair that approached being blonde. The only common threads in their appearance were their height—both about five feet six inches—and their clothes: khaki shorts, sandals, and white polo shirts.

Stacy left to get fresh coffee.

"What happened, Darce?" Streeter asked. "Is he going to be all right?"

She looked up and smiled, but it barely creased the pain and fatigue in her face. "He's going to live, but they're not sure how he's going to come out of it."

Streeter stood there for a minute with his mouth open, vaguely aware of how foolish he must look. That was the best he was able to do: he couldn't focus his thoughts clearly. Finally, he mustered up a weak, "How're you doing?"

Darcy shook her head cautiously, as if it was fragile. "I'm sick to my stomach. My God, I was so scared. When they first called me it sounded like he was dying. I can't even imagine that. I got here about ten last night, while he was still in surgery. This is nothing but pure torture."

"What the hell happened?" Streeter sounded hoarse, as if he had just woken up.

"Somebody beat him. The police don't know who it is yet. They used bats or sticks or something. Can you believe that? It was still light outside. It must have happened last night, about six or so. It's all such a big mess that nobody knows for sure. To be honest, I didn't understand half of what the police told me. I was too upset. I felt like one of those hysterical bimbos from daytime TV. I just kept picturing Bill getting beaten. Maybe dying."

"It's going to be okay, Darce." He sat next to her and put his arm around her shoulder. Despite her fear, she felt solid and wasn't trembling. "Tell me what you can."

Stacy got back just then with the fresh coffee and gave a cup to each of them. "I ran into the floor nurse out there and she told me they don't expect any change for tonight," she said as she stood next to the couch looking down at them. "Are you going to stay here, Darcy? I'll stay with you."

Darcy stared at her for a long time, as though she had difficulty understanding what her sister said. Finally, she nodded. Then she looked back at Streeter. She took a sip of her coffee, and that gave her a boost.

"The officers said they found him down on South Santa Fe, behind one of those little sleazy hotels."

"What was he doing down there?"

"He was supposed to meet a client. Bill got a call about four, maybe four-thirty. It was from a brother of this man he represented last summer in a really bitter custody fight. The brother called and said the man got picked up for stealing—shoplifting, actually—and he's supposed to get bailed out of jail pretty soon. He asked if Billy would meet the both of them at his motel in a couple of hours, because the guy needed legal help. He pleaded, so Bill went. It turned out that the motel was closed and it was all a trap. Obviously."

She took another sip of her coffee and was quiet. Streeter felt a growing sense of guilt, and he couldn't understand why. Darcy's voice brought him back.

"What kind of animal would do this? Tell me, Streeter. You know all of these low-lifes."

"Thanks a lot." He thought of the most logical answer, but when he said it he didn't sound too convincing. "It could have been someone he put away back when he was the DA. Bill nailed a lot of sickos and made more than his share of enemies. Most likely this is a revenge deal. Some jailhouse brainstorm."

Darcy nodded solemnly, as if that made a great deal of sense, and then looked straight ahead. "I hope they catch the bastard and fry him." Suddenly she looked back up at him. "There's not much you can do here. Stacy'll stay with me. But I'd like you to do something for me over the weekend."

"Of course. Anything."

"Talk to the cops. I want to know everything they know, and I want to know it right away. Ride them hard, Streeter. I want to keep the pressure on to find this guy. Will you do that?"

"Sure. But I'll hang around here tonight. I can't sleep anyway."

Streeter didn't eat again until late Saturday afternoon. By mid-morning, he started smoking cigarettes. He hadn't smoked more than a couple of packs in the past ten years, but now it was steady Camels, no filters. Pure, high-octane self-punishment. He couldn't shake that guilty feeling. The only thing that made him feel better was hounding the police. McLean regained a shaky consciousness shortly before noon. For the rest of the day he didn't know where he was or much of what happened, but the worst was over. When he heard that, Streeter called Story and filled her in on the beating.

"Thank God he's not going to die," she said, obviously shaken. "This is terrible. You don't think it had anything to do with my suit against Cooper?"

"Could be. Like I told you, I don't believe in coincidences. I'm going to check around, and I'll let you know what I find out."

"When you talk to Bill, give him my love. I'd like to come to the hospital and visit him. Do you think that would be all right?"

"There's a lot of family there today and he's not really thinking too clearly yet," he told her. "Maybe you better wait a day or two, until things settle down."

In the early afternoon, Streeter drove to police headquarters, across the street from the Denver Mint. He went to the assaults division and talked to the sergeant heading the investigation. Because of McLean's high-profile DA career, his beating drew media coverage as well as a high priority with the police. Sergeant Stan Haney, a rubber-faced veteran with an obvious fashion impairment, told the bounty hunter that the beating looked like the work of at least two people.

"The doctors took wood splinters from Bill's skin," Haney said, his voice raspy from years of cigarette smoking. Although he was fifty, he still had the squat, stocky build of an old-time football player. A leather-helmet kind of guy. He was wearing a loud sport coat and a wide tie that indicated he hadn't been to a clothes store in well over a decade. "They found two different types of wood. One came from a baseball bat. The other was from a piece of raw oak. There was a deep cut on his right side, too. Looked like some sort of weird knife. They worked him over pretty hard, but I don't think they wanted to kill him."

"Why do you say that?"

"Well, for one thing, he was obviously still alive when they stopped. If they meant to kill him, they were pretty sloppy. He crawled about a hundred yards from where he was beaten. And it wasn't no robbery, either. They left his wallet and they didn't even bother to go through the car. We figure probably some assholes he sent down to Cañon City who wanted a little pay-back. Prison-style bullshit."

"Who found him?"

"Some guy that lives next to the motel. Checked out okay. He was working at the time it happened. When we found him, he was scared shitless, too."

"Did they leave anything at the scene that'll help you out?"

"Not much. We found tracks back there that look like they're from a big car. We're checking that out now. The weapons weren't there and, believe me, we scoured the whole place looking for them." Then Haney glanced off, smiling. "I think maybe Bill got in a lick or two himself."

"What makes you say that?"

"The doc told us the knuckles on Bill's right hand were badly bruised. One of them was broken. My guess is, he got a couple a punches in."

Streeter smiled. McLean boxed at Northwestern as an undergraduate. "I'm sure that whoever did this didn't expect the job to be quite as tough as it ended up. Anything else?"

"Nothing really." Haney paused. "We're doing all we can. Bill McLean has a lot of friends on the department. Give me a holler if you need anything else, and tell his missus we're all pulling for him."

When he got back to the church at about eight that night, Streeter went to Frank's apartment to kick around some ideas. The bondsman, who had known McLean longer than Streeter had, was badly shaken by the news. He looked terribly old and almost lost in his thick terry-cloth bathrobe. Frank had seen enough violence in his life to fill a Clint Eastwood film festival and he was sick to death of it.

"Jesus, big guy. I don't know what it's all coming to anymore." Frank grabbed a half-full bottle of Johnny Walker Red from the counter in the kitchen and then nodded for his partner to follow him to his office. That's where the two did most of their drinking together. When they sat down at his desk, Frank poured two tall ones—neat—and proposed a toast.

"To Wild Bill McLean." The bondsman held out his glass for a second and then took a long pull on the Scotch.

"To William." Streeter nodded and took a small sip. He noticed that he still was wearing the same jeans and T-shirt from the night before at Story's. Suddenly he felt grimy and wanted to take a shower. "This has got me thinking, Frank. That gunfire last week, and now this. Between Cooper and whatever cop is running around out there, I can't believe this attack was a con that McLean put away in the old days. I've got to believe it was tied in with Doug Shelton and that whole crew."

"You're probably right. But, hell, Bill won't be blaming you. That's not his style and he knew what he was getting into when he took on Cooper."

"That may be true, but I've got to put an end to all this junk. It's getting way out of hand. Shootings, beatings, vandalism." He lit another Camel and then crushed it out almost immediately. "I just met Carey for a few hoists down at Nalen's. He did some checking today and found out that Kovacs, the cop I think's behind this, was at a seminar Friday afternoon until way after six. Then he went to dinner with some of the boys. He couldn't have done Bill."

"He could have gotten some other cop to do it for him."

"Yeah, but then you have a conspiracy. A police conspiracy,

no less. That's not likely. Plus, that court hearing was just the day before, and Bill kicked the shit out of Cooper. He might want some quick revenge while he's still hurting."

"That makes sense. You find out where Cooper was last night?" Frank held up the bottle to see if Streeter wanted more.

Streeter shook his head. "Cooper didn't do this himself. Carey told me about a guy that works for Cooper. The guy's name is Psycho or something nutty like that. There was talk that Cooper sent him to slit the throat of a witness not long ago. Bill was cut by a knife, too. This nut has a sidekick, and I was told there were two people who beat Bill. Then there were all those hang-up calls last night. That sounds too chicken-shit for a cop but, who knows, a couple of these jerks that Cooper would hire might think it's pretty clever."

"Sounds very possible. Did you discuss all this with Carey?"

"Yeah, we ran over all the options together. For all we know, Cooper and half the police department are in on it together. I'm not sure why a cop would hassle Story or why someone shot at us. And I'm not sure why Bill's in the hospital. Neither is Carey. I tell you, Frank, this makes my little bail jumpers look halfway decent. Very sane and simple. All I know is, I have to do something. I have to talk to all these jerks and see what I can shake out of them. This Psycho and his playmate for starters. Carey said this was a message to Bill. There's been more messages flying around here than at a damned Western Union convention. Maybe it's time I start sending some messages of my own."

"I hear you, but be careful," Frank said with a dismal smile as he struggled to get up from the desk. The Scotch had taken its toll. "You're heading into the low end of nowhere with these people. They're poison, all of them. I don't want to have to break in a new skip tracer and get a new tenant for that loft of yours."

"That's a very warm thought, Frank. I'll hold it close to me in the days ahead."

17

"Will you relax, Ronnie? You don't even know for sure it was them." Cooper kept trying to grab her shoulders to steady her, but she was too agitated to be touched. Ever since they saw the news of McLean's beating on television Saturday night, Ronnie'd been hopping around like her shoes were on fire. She was furious and scared. It was now Sunday afternoon at Cooper's downtown loft, and she'd whipped herself into a state of inconsolable bitchiness that he'd never seen before.

"You had to make all those threats against him after the hearing," she said. "Right in front of those two freaks. I told you they'd see that as the green light for some kind of violent horseshit like this. And what the hell do you mean, you're not sure it was them? Get real, Thomas Hardy."

"Okay, it probably was them," he conceded. "I'll be more careful from now on. But why are you so upset? You didn't even know this damned McLean. And they said on the tube he's going to pull through. It's not like he was actually murdered."

Ronnie glared at him. Then she adjusted the front of her silk bathrobe and looked away. The hell you gonna do with this mutt?

"What a relief! He was only beaten half to death. And here I was starting to worry that you didn't have a conscience. You know, after that Commerce City stunt, we don't need more attention from the cops." Her voice rose as she spoke. "Even they can't be so stupid that they're not going to start putting this together fairly soon. It looks pretty obvious to me that you're the common denominator here. One might think that professional police detectives would notice that, too."

Cooper drew back, his forehead chopped deep in concentration; his words came more slowly now. "But they have nothing on me. Absolutely nothing concrete in nature. You must understand, Rhonda, that what seems 'pretty obvious' to you simply does not convict people in a court of law."

"Oh, right, Thomas Hardy." She spit the words out. "You're always right. For another thing"—she stopped to light a fresh cigarette off the one she was finishing—"these are very dangerous guys. They get an idea in their heads and someone gets hurt. What if they get the idea you're in their way? Or me? We might get something very 'concrete in nature' from those two, in the form of a baseball bat to the skull."

She thought of Soyko's visit to her apartment. She wouldn't tell Cooper about it, but the idea of him coming back for another visit was always with her, like ground glass under her fingernails.

"I'm their boss. They work for me." Cooper's voice was loud and shrill again. "They'll get back in line."

"Aw, Tom, you really don't get it." Her voice softened and she lowered her head a bit. He looked kind of pathetic, standing there in crisp new blue jeans with his pudgy stomach oozing out over his belt. *Pressed* jeans, for Chrissakes. "They work for themselves. You're just the guy that gives them stupid ideas and pays them. You like to have them on the payroll because it gives you a sense of power. Like you're suddenly above the law and you can reach out and hurt people any time you want. But you've got no power with them. No control. That should be obvious by now. Look at that little welder. Dopps. And now this. These two freaks are beyond you. They're beyond everything but their own crazy reality."

With that she walked into the kitchen area and poured herself another cup of coffee. Cooper's loft had twelve-foot ceilings and few interior walls. Ronnie didn't like it: it reminded her of a furniture-store showroom.

Fundamentally, Cooper knew she was right. He had been feeling a growing sense of fear since they heard about McLean. The beating bothered him more than the Dopps hit. At least with Dopps he'd instructed Soyko to go talk to the witness and get him to leave town. McLean was totally free-lance. All their own idea. But he had had enough of Ronnie's lip, and he couldn't bring himself to show her he made a mistake. To let her know she was right and he was powerless. He stalked after her.

"Listen, you." He was spitting lightly as he spoke. "They work for me and so do you. I'm sick of your whining about those guys. An arrogant son of a bitch like this McLean deserved everything he got, and more. So did that worthless punk up in Commerce City. I'm glad they did it and I'm glad I gave them the idea. And you let me worry about the cops. If they get within ten miles of me on this, I'll turn Soyko and that detestable little fuck Romp over to them in a second. I've got this thing under control, but I'm getting sick and tired of the way you talk to me. You were nothing before I met you, and I could turn you out any time. Now I've got to go to the office for a while. Just lighten up. I'll be back about five. In the meantime, why don't you make yourself useful and clean up around here!"

Cooper made a point of keeping hard eye contact with her until Ronnie looked away. He was furious and yet he knew he really didn't want her to leave him. "Look," he said with a gentler voice. "it's going to be all right. I'll have a talk with them when I get down to the office. You just shouldn't keep riding me like that."

Then he nodded and walked out of the condo without trying to touch her again. Anger and fear boiled inside Ronnie, forming a noxious burn in her stomach. I was nothing before I met you? She thought about leaving him, but that was so dramatic and final, not to mention fiscally unsound. First things first. Get those two "investigators" out of the picture. For good. She glanced at the phone, and the thought that had been percolating since she first heard the news about McLean suddenly erupted. She finished her coffee and had four more cigarettes—then she did the deed.

Her hands shook as she dialed the police number she had memorized the night before. It being Sunday, she had a little trouble getting through to the right department. Finally the right officer answered.

"Detective Lesley, may I help you?" The question came quickly through the line, and Ronnie almost hung up. The voice sounded so young.

"Are you working on the McLean case? The beating that I saw on the news last night?"

"Yes ma'am. Sergeant Haney is in charge, but he's not in today. Do you have any information regarding the attack?"

"You bet I do." She rolled her eyes at how loud her voice was.

"May I have your name, ma'am?"

"No, junior. I'll just tell you what I know and I'll tell you once. Try to get it all down. The same two men who did that Dopps guy up in Commerce City, the knife job, did McLean. I'd check out a couple of guys in Aurora. One of them's named Soyko. I think his first name is Leo. The other one is Jacky Romp. They live just east of Havana, near Iliff. They're the ones you're after. They'll give you a ton of crap, but be careful. They're trouble. And nobody asked them to do it. They did it on their own."

"Ma'am, how do you know this?" Lesley's words were coming quickly. "If I could just have your name and phone number."

"I told you, no, sonny boy. Look, just nail those guys. If you don't get them now, there'll be more trouble."

With that she slammed down the receiver. Seconds later, she

lit a cigarette and tried to remember exactly what she had just told Lesley. Her thoughts were clouded with fright. Soyko and Romp at her house. All anger had left her during the call, and it was replaced with fear.

Sergeant Haney had seen the look a thousand times. The same just-try-me sneer he got from damned near every dime-store hard-on he ever met. But this sneer wasn't forced or shaky like some of them. It was no pose. Haney could tell this guy meant what was carved on his face. His eyes gave up nothing and he smelled like he never showered. Contaminated. And Haney knew he had nothing on Soyko and his buddy, but he just wanted to shake the tree, see if anything fell out. That phone call to Lesley the day before was all he had to go on in McLean's case.

Soyko kept thinking how he could probably slap the hell out of this flabby old man before he could get his gun out. The guy looked like he could have been tough once, but that was about a hundred years ago, when he was young. Still, Soyko had never moved on a cop before, and he knew it would be a mistake. He also thought how Haney had squat to go on except for this one lame tip. He looked over and saw Jacky on the couch, twitching in rage and glaring at the detective.

"You two can have a lawyer if you want one," Haney said. "Course, then we all go downtown and make a big deal over this."

"I suppose we could just do that, but it don't matter," Soyko shot back. "We ain't talking to you about nothing, anyhow. Downtown, here. Don't matter. What's all this about? You come here talking about a guy dying up in Commerce City and some other guy getting beat up. We don't know squat. Last Friday, we were both over to the Drift Inn playing pool. All night. We can probably only get about twenty guys to back us up."

"I bet they're fine citizens, too." Haney was getting mad. "What about the afternoon of June fourth? I suppose you could get another twenty guys to back you up on that one?"

"That's guaranteed, pal. Look, I got no idea what you're talking about. Get my lawyer? Man, I work for lawyers. Jacky and me are private investigators. Like on the television."

Haney took in a deep breath and crushed out his cigarette. He thought how he'd like to kick some respect into this mouthy little punk. For twenty-seven years he'd been listening to all kinds of trash. White trash, black trash, brown trash. Whatever the color, trash was just trash. He had no idea who called with their names, but he was believing it more.

"What lawyers?"

"That's confidential." Soyko leaned back against the dining-room table, smiling. He didn't know if it was confidential or not, but he had heard it on enough lawyer shows and movies to use it.

Lesley had told Haney that the woman said something like no one ordered these two guys to do it either time. He said she sounded nervous about that part. Lesley didn't get a chance to ask her exactly what she meant.

"Could be it was one of your lawyers got you into this." He took a flyer. "The lady tells us you were on your own, but I'm not so sure."

Soyko felt his face flush for just an instant. "Unless you want us downtown, I don't have to say a word." Forty-five minutes is enough with this clown.

"Take it easy, slick." Haney leaned forward, obviously furious. His face looked soft, puffy from overuse, but even Soyko backed up a shade. Haney realized he had hit a nerve. "We've got some more checking to do on both you pukes. Maybe you might want to make sure you can get those twenty guys for the afternoon of the fourth and for Friday night. I'll be seeing you again. You can fucking bank on it."

When he left, Jacky got up and kicked the side of the sofa with a frightening amount of force for a thin man. "Son of a bitch," he screamed at Soyko. "Who did it?" His face was the color of blood.

"Got a pretty good idea. For one thing, he said it was a broad."

"How you know that wasn't a lot of crap?"

"Because that cop ain't ambitious enough to do no homework. Someone called on us or he would never have been here. If they had anything, they'd be building it into a case right now. To them, this is just an assault that'll blow over and a homicide out of their backyard. They were just squeezing our nuts to see if we'd fold."

Soyko was pulling his fingers individually, deliberately cracking each knuckle as he spoke. "When Cooper ordered this thing with McLean, he told us not to let it get back to Ronnie. Then yesterday, when he called, he told us how pissed she was. My bet is, he fed her some shit like it was all our doing. Not that I care. And she would tell the cops that it's our idea. Try and cover for her fat-ass boyfriend. My thinking is, she just got so mad she called the cops sometime yesterday or first thing this morning. Only two people know about us, and there's no way Cooper made that call. If it was him, he'd cut a deal, roll on us, and the first time we see the cops they'd have a warrant."

"That miserable little bitch," Jacky fumed, his jaws not moving.

"We gotta deal with this," Soyko said. "With both of them. And we gotta do it quick and hard. No fucking doubt about that."

18

Ronnie listened to the phone ring at the other end of the line. She had been trying to reach Cooper for well over an hour. He'd left work early that afternoon, and she needed to talk to him. Desperately. Her head pounded from nicotine and nervous fear as she paced her apartment. That call to the cops the day before was, in her own words, "making me mental." The more she thought about it, the more she realized that if they talked to Soyko he'd quickly figure out she dropped the dime on him. She tried to convince herself the police wouldn't move on him and Romp unless they had more evidence to go on. But how could she know that for sure?

She reached for her purse, containing her cigarettes, and glanced at the clock again. Almost seven. Cooper had to be getting home soon. She fumbled around inside the huge bag for a couple of minutes, looking for the pack. "Enough damned junk to fill a suitcase," she said furiously to no one. Inside there was the petite, off-white cellular phone that Cooper had given her for her birthday and an empty box of M&M's. There were nine half-full bottles of nail polish, along with her entire linty candy collection and an assortment of makeup far too extensive to itemize. There was her key chain, complete with attached hot-pepper spray designed to ward off dogs, and several checkbooks. There was a separate key chain for her personal safe-deposit box and a small coupon book. Finally, she found her pack and noticed that she had only one Marlboro left. She stuck the cigarette into her mouth angrily and lit it. Ronnie had a habit of turning fear or anxiety or sadness into anger. It never seemed to hurt as much. At that moment she'd rather be furious than feel the terror inside her.

"Screw it," she mumbled to herself and slipped her shoulder into the long strap from the black leather purse. If she had to sit around to wait for Cooper she'd jump out of her skin. Might as well go get some more smokes from the closest 7-Eleven. She figured he'd have to be home by the time she returned.

As she walked down the hall leading to the outer door, she felt more aggravation. Someone had parked in her usual spot that night, and the entire lot to the east was full. She'd had to park on the street that ran along the side of the building and past the lot. Definitely not my night, she noted.

When she got outside, she was surprised at how bright the sun still was. She put on her pink-rimmed sun glasses—"my hooker shades"—and took a couple steps toward her car, some fifty yards away. That was when she saw Jacky Romp get out of the driver's side of his El Camino. She looked farther and saw Leo Soyko get out of the passenger's side. They had parked the big vehicle between her usual lot and where her car was now parked in the street. Ronnie was absolutely amazed that her first thought was how nice Romp's car looked. Must be a new wax job: Just how the hell *does* my mind work? Her second thought was that she was thoroughly screwed. No chance to get to her car without them seeing her. And they'd be coming her way any second.

"Which one's hers?" Jacky asked his friend as they looked over the long white two-story apartment building.

Soyko lifted his arm and pointed to his left. "Over there. Sort of a basement apartment. Total shithole. I think that's her car on the street there. The maroon Tercel. Betcha Numb Nuts leased it for her. Spoiled bitch. Let's go get her, Jacky. She's done enough damage."

Ronnie saw Soyko point toward her building just before she ducked back into the hallway. She knew if they got her inside she'd be dead. Or wish she was. Instinctively, her right hand shot down into her purse and she grabbed the keys with the pepper spray. Lot of good that'll do, she thought as she fought back the panic. She glanced out the window and saw the two men walking slowly toward her. There was no other way out of the building, and she didn't have time to get to her apartment, way at the other end of the hall. She froze with fear and got ready to scream.

At that exact moment, the door to the nearest apartment swung open and three large men walked out. Two looked Hispanic, the third nondescript. Ronnie smelled a sticky blast of pot smoke trailing them into the hallway. She'd seen two of them before, and one, the shortest but stockiest, had flirted with her in the laundry once. They all were in their early twenties and dressed in Target grunge clothes. They smiled hazily at her.

"Hey, man. It's the blondie," the stocky flirter said. His voice was enthusiastic but syrupy, like he just woke up. Bad-ass pot voice. "Hey, blondie, man. How you doing, baby? You want to come in and party big-time? Party with Hector maybe?" His eyes got dreamy as he spoke but he definitely wasn't joking. His friends awkwardly nodded approval and flashed their stoned, shit-eating grins.

Hector wasn't much taller than Ronnie, but his arms looked thick as logs and his neck was the approximate size of his shoulders. She guessed his weight at well over two hundred pounds. His two friends were thinner and each was almost a foot taller. She instantly knew what she had to do.

"That sounds hot, Hector," she said in a breathy voice usually reserved for Cooper when she wanted something—a voice so laced with promise the lawyer never could turn it down. Her shorts were small and tight, and most of both smooth cheeks of her butt were exposed. The pink halter top added nicely to the effect. "Very hot. I've been wanting to do that ever since we talked that day."

"All right, man! *Amigos!*" Hector couldn't believe his good fortune. His friends shuffled their feet aimlessly and grunted. "Come inside, baby, for a little bong action. What you say?"

Ronnie took a step toward Hector, placed her left hand on his shoulder, and shot him a look that would stiffen a priest. They were eyeball to eyeball, and her words came out in a husky whisper. "One problem, big guy. My old boyfriend, the fucker that used to beat me silly, him and his buddy are right outside. He's pissed because I dumped him. If they get their hands on me, I'm history. Can you boys make them go away? Then we can party our asses off. Can you get rid of them?"

The large man on Hector's left fielded that one. "They beat you, little lady? That's pure horseshit." He sounded much more cowboy than Hispanic. "We're gonna tear both them bastards new assholes. You just watch this."

Hector nodded, his face twisted in concern. "We see who beats who now, baby. You let Hector take care of their shit." He pulled Ronnie around behind him so she was facing the doorway with the three heroes between her and the world outside.

The door swept open a second later and Jacky Romp and Leo Soyko strolled into the hall. The confidence on their faces waffled when they saw the three men waiting for them. They stopped about five feet from the men, and Soyko looked past them to Ronnie. "Hey, Goldilocks. You got bodyguards now?"

"Damned straight she does," the cowboy-sounding guy said as he glared down at the two. "Maybe you two shit buckets want to see how tough you are with men instead of girls. Maybe you come to the right place."

"Damnit," Jacky sputtered in rage. "You stupid cracker fucks don't know what you're doing. Just move on and you don't get hurt."

Hector took a step forward so he was a couple feet away from Soyko. "She stays and you go. Now. We not shittin' around here, man."

End of discussion, Soyko reasoned. His right fist snapped up and shot into Hector's mouth before anyone else could move. It wasn't a full punch, but that was usually more than enough to put someone down. Hector was stunned and he staggered back two steps. But he didn't come close to falling. Soyko knew they were in for a fight. The big cowboy rushed Jacky and threw him against the wall. Jacky screamed and started throwing punches, but he was clearly no match for the big man. The guy on Hector's right then rushed Soyko, and they both fell to the ground clawing each other. By this time Hector had recovered, and he jumped on top of Soyko.

Ronnie wasted no time. She slid along the wall closest to the door, past the fighting bodies, and grabbed the door handle. Then she looked back for just a second. Neither Soyko nor Romp noticed. She opened the door and was in a full run toward her car before she realized that in the excitement she'd squeezed her pepper spray down her leg. She figured the fight would last long enough for her to get to her car and drive at least a few miles. It didn't matter to her which side won. None of the five men would ever see her again.

19

"A lot of this crap seems to be coming back your way, Mr. Cooper." Sergeant Haney's voice was low and smoldering.

The lawyer looked up but didn't actually see the sergeant. He couldn't stop worrying about Ronnie, not to mention himself. She'd called him late last night and wouldn't say where she was staying. She was screaming with rage and crying from fear at the same time. Ronnie was mad because he had gotten them involved with Leo Soyko, and because Cooper hadn't been home for her call earlier in the night. Afraid, obviously, because the two hit men were still on the loose and still looking for her. Ronnie said she was "just outside of town" and she'd call him back this morning so they could make plans for getting together. He knew something drastic had to be done: Soyko and Romp were coming after both of them.

"What are you talking about?" Cooper said automatically. "What's coming back my way? My fiancée, the woman I love, has just been threatened in the most brutal and reprehensible fashion, and you're making it sound like I'm responsible. My God, she could have been killed."

They were standing in the hall outside Cooper's office along with a second detective, a chubby Hispanic man. He had the scarred complexion of a public golf fairway but wore an impeccable herringbone suit. The Hispanic cop didn't speak and Haney didn't introduce him. Cooper had returned to his office from a quick court appearance and found the two of them waiting. Although the sergeant wasn't smoking at the moment, his clothes reeked of tobacco and his breath smelled like a tiny reptile had died inside his mouth sometime ago.

"Oh, you could maybe convince me you didn't do that particular thing," Haney responded. "That brawl. She is your fiancée, like you said. All I'm saying is, a lot of crap seems to be headed your way. That guy up in Commerce City. Bill McLean. Now this."

"And just how am I connected to McLean, for God's sake? Or that witness in Commerce City?"

"We know you were in court against McLean last week and that he kicked the living shit out of you. And we know what happened to the case against your murder client, Borders, when the witness died."

Cooper looked at the detective like he just really noticed him for the first time. Haney had that all-over-bloated look that middle-aged men get from beer, fatty foods, and inactivity. The guy's heart was probably encased in sludge, like a filthy carburetor, and any beat could be its last, Cooper thought. To the attorney, Haney seemed utterly diseased and foul.

"I can account for my whereabouts at all of those times," he told the cop. "Are you really suggesting that I beat up a fellow attorney? You're not even as smart as you look, and *that* hardly seems possible. And what do I get out of attacking and possibly killing Ronnie? I love her."

"Yeah, yeah. I'm sure you do. And she's a real hot number, from what I hear. We got a tip from a woman on Sunday, two days ago. She tells us a guy named Soyko and someone named Romp were involved in McLean and Dopps. Turns out they both know you. So we go talk to those two first thing yesterday morning, and guess what? Your secretary or fiancée gets chased later by two guys matching the descriptions of Soyko and Romp. Several people get beaten like—how'd you put it?—'in the most brutal and reprehensible fashion.' All this happening right outside your fiancée's apartment. Incredible how it shook out like that."

The news about Ronnie talking to the police hit Cooper visibly. He looked away for a moment.

"Seems you didn't know about that call, did you?" Haney, seeing an opening, stepped closer. "I'll tell you the same thing I told that warped motherfucker Soyko. We're going to be looking long and hard at everything. We know those guys work for you. We'll put it all together, counselor. You got my word on that."

Cooper's stomach felt like Greg Norman was practicing his short irons off of it. So Ronnie called the cops on those two and this was their response. She never mentioned that call. Not Sunday or last night. He straightened up and returned Haney's glare.

"Sergeant, I resent this obvious attempt at intimidation. Believe me, your superiors will be hearing about how you have conducted yourself here. And I do not choose to continue this conversation without my lawyer present."

"That's probably not the dumbest idea you ever had." Haney nodded and looked at his partner. "Or will have."

When they left, Cooper stood in the hallway for several minutes considering what Haney had said. Then he went inside and told his receptionist to hold his calls unless it was Ronnie. He went into his office and sat down. He was sucking air in shallow blasts and his exhales sounded like a crippled accordion. Everything seemed beyond his control. He thought of how he wanted to call Ronnie into his office but couldn't. He opened his bottom drawer and pulled out the shiny Colt Python. He shifted it from one hand to the other, but the gun didn't give him any clarity. And it was options and clarity that he desperately needed. His life was unraveling laboriously around him. Soyko and Romp on a rampage, probably gunning for him. Ronnie terrified and in danger. And, hell, it would be just a matter of time before Haney would be back with a search warrant and then an arrest warrant.

He was pretty sure his investigators wouldn't roll on him. Certainly not out of loyalty, but they'd both rather get bone-marrow cancer than cooperate with the police. Still, they almost certainly would come after him themselves. They'd probably think he put Ronnie up to that call. They were so far out of control, who knew what they'd do next? What was it Ronnie had said? "They work for themselves. You're just the guy that gives them stupid ideas and pays them."

He thought of her. That woman always was far more perceptive than any three of his classmates in law school. Damn, she was right about a lot of things, but she must have been out of her mind to call the cops.

Got to do something, he told himself. If he went to the cops, he could finger the two men for Dopps and McLean. He could say he never asked them to do it but just paid them to go have a talk. Ronnie'd back him on all of that. It was almost true, and he knew Haney was drooling to clear those cases. He could say that, when he heard about what they did, he was too scared to call the police. But after the attack on his secretary, he knew they had to be locked up.

"Think again," he muttered to himself. How could he explain why he hired them to talk to McLean after he knew they killed Dopps? He was sure to get nailed for conspiracy, among other charges. Plus, he reasoned, as long as those two were alive, either in prison with him or on the street, eventually his sorry ass would get whacked. They'd have to be stopped with no chance of getting started again. Only one way to do that. He looked at the revolver for a long time.

Who was he kidding? He knew he could never shoot anyone.

He shifted to his next option. It was his only real option and he knew it: get far away and fast. Hook up with Ronnie and get them both out of Colorado by the next afternoon. It would take him that long to pull his money out of his accounts and sell his second car, the old Corvette, to that dealer on South Broadway who always was so hot to buy it. His quick calculations told him he could get maybe sixty-five or seventy thousand together that soon. Enough for a new start somewhere else. It would probably mean the end of his legal career. That certainly wasn't what he had in mind when he left law school, but it was better than getting shredded by Soyko, or spending the next fifteen years playing house with a three-hundred-pound ape in Cañon City. He'd like to do something to avenge the assault on Ronnie, but getting himself killed was in no way suitable. Better he should live, preferably out of jail, to keep her happy, he told himself. Leave all that Chuck Norris nonsense to those better suited for it.

"Someone here to see you, Mr. Cooper," the receptionist barked through the intercom. Her voice was drenched in satisfaction. "A police detective."

Cooper frowned. What did Haney want now? As he was reaching for the intercom button to tell her he'd be ready in a minute, his door swung open and in walked a man he hadn't seen since Doug Shelton's preliminary hearing.

"Looks like this ain't your week, counselor." Art Kovacs shut the door behind him and approached. "And here it is, only Tuesday."

"Well, come right in and make yourself comfortable," Cooper said with mock indignation. He paused. "You look familiar."

"We met on that Doug Shelton bust." Kovacs now stood at the desk.

"You're Korchak. No, wait. Kovacs, right? Arthur Kovacs, wasn't it?"

"It still is." The detective smiled quickly at his own cleverness. He dropped into the chair across from Cooper like he hadn't sat down in months. "I think we should have us a talk here. You look like you could use help. And I mean help from someone that's got a little pull."

"Let me guess. You just happen to have a little pull." Cooper was confused.

"Bingo." Kovacs pointed a finger at him like a pistol. "I don't want to waste a lot of time, so I'll just lay it all out. You'd be very mistaken to consider this a suggestion. We'll call it a mandate. That's a new buzzword we hear downtown. Now, I know for a fact that you're basically fucked with the department. It's just a matter of a day or two before that birdbrain Haney'll have something to go to the DA with. That means you'll be charged and they'll come down your throat with a meat cleaver, believe me. When Haney gets a hard-on for someone, he don't let up."

"I figured that one out for myself."

"I'll bet you did." Kovacs loosened his light-tan tie and rolled his neck like it was stiff. He was wearing a short-sleeved shirt the approximate color of prune juice, and his forearms were so hairy there was practically no skin visible. "Here's where your new friend could come in handy. I'm working on this investigation, too. I can make sure it drags out for a while, and I can give them enough troubles that maybe you don't burn. Maybe. They got a circumstantial case on this McLean thing, and that guy up in Commerce City—forget it. They got very little unless Soyko flips you. Is that possible?"

"Not likely."

"Well, then, with my help you might not be in such big trouble, after all. At the very least I can let you know what's coming down, and when and where. Think that might be helpful to you?"

"It might at that," Cooper acknowledged. "I just wonder what it is you want in return for all this magnanimous assistance?"

"I want you to stop chasing after Doug Shelton's estate. I want you to forget that guy ever existed."

"How did you know I'm chasing anything?" Cooper sat up straight in his chair.

"This coke whore what used to play with Shelton told me Soyko was trying to scare information out of her. He did a good job of it. I'll level with you, partner. That estate was located a long time ago. By me. Mr. Shelton told me a lot of interesting things about himself and his business ventures right after he was arrested."

"I gather that would have been about when you two hatched up a deal to steal the evidence against him."

"Basically. He took a fair amount of persuading, but he finally opened up."

Cooper broke into a smile of recognition. "So that explains who beat the snot out of him right after his arrest. How much did he leave?"

"There was some snot beating, all right." Kovacs grinned. "Dougy left enough to make me happy but not enough so's I'd want to share it with you or this Story what's-her-name. I don't need no interference from anyone. I'll deal with Story and her big, bad bounty hunter on my own. You just deal with those two jerkoffs that work for you. Pull them off the hunt. That sound like something you can handle?"

"It certainly does." Cooper sat back for a minute. He knew that if he told Kovacs how out of control Soyko was he'd get no help. "I'll be glad to do all that's within my power to keep my associates from making further inquiries into Mr. Shelton's estate."

"I don't give a shit what's within your power. Just call off those two mutts."

Cooper nodded. However, he had no intention of coming away from this Shelton search empty-handed now that he knew who had the money.

"You know, Kovacs, I put a lot of time and effort into looking for this money. If I were to suddenly cease my efforts, I feel as though I should be compensated in some fashion."

"No fuckin' way!" Kovacs yelled. He could feel his stomach churning. He'd been popping Pepto Bismol tablets like they were breath mints and still his intestines complained. No one ever cooperates. Everyone's always got their own angle. "You maybe keep from getting skinned alive on this thing. That should be compensation enough."

"I am not certain that it is." Cooper frowned thoughtfully. "But for, say, twenty thousand, my comfort level would increase dramatically."

"Oh, would it now?" The cop calmed down and studied the

attorney. "Let me get back to you on that one. I'd hate to do anything to disturb your fuckin' comfort level."

"Fair enough. Can I ask you one more question?"

"Would it matter if I said no?"

"How much did Douglas pay you for your help with his evidence?"

Kovacs stood up in disgust. His stomach was burning fiercely now, and he wondered where the restrooms were.

"Go to hell. Just get those two nut cases off my ass and away from my money and I'll let you know what's going on from our end."

He walked out of the office in determined search of the nearest "facilities." When the detective planted himself in the toilet stall on Cooper's floor, he was sweating from a gastric burn that gripped him like an enormous swamp slug. His insides were getting worse every day. His so-called partner had suggested this stupid talk with Cooper. Plain to see that the lawyer was more trouble than he was worth. No way he could control Soyko and Romp. Kovacs knew he'd have to do that himself. Turned out he had to do everything himself. And his partner was becoming as useless as Cooper. The stress of all these decisions was turning his stomach into a mini-Chernobyl. He just wanted to end the anguish, and it was becoming clear that that meant he was going to have to end several lives.

Streeter got information on Soyko from Cooper's receptionist on Monday. Without hesitation, she gave his and Romp's phone number and address. The bounty hunter had gone to their apartment a couple of times that day, but no one was home. Finally, about ten o'clock Tuesday night, he went back and saw a light in the window. Walking up to the third-floor unit, he could feel his nine-millimeter tucked into the small of his back. It was there strictly for self-defense.

From the outside walkway leading to the apartment, Streeter could see the shaky blue glow of Soyko's television dance off the curtains. He tried to look in the window, but the drapes were drawn too tight to give him much of a view. He rang the buzzer several times. No one answered. Then he pounded on the door. Still no answer. He rattled the handle, and was surprised to find it unlocked.

"Anybody here?" he asked calmly as he opened the door a couple of inches. Nothing. He pushed harder and repeated the question. "Anybody here?"

When he pushed the door open and stepped into the living room, he got his answer. There—draped over the couch, half on the floor—was the process server who had given Story her papers at Cooper's. The left side of his head was matted with blood, and there was a large spray of red over the couch and wall a few feet from him. This must be that Jacky Romp that Carey mentioned.

Streeter took out his handkerchief and covered his right hand. He walked to the couch and checked Romp for a pulse. There was none, but the skin was still mildly warm, indicating that he hadn't been dead for long. Streeter noticed that both of the man's wrists were cut and the marks looked fresh. Romp's face was twisted in rage, like he had died giving someone serious verbal grief. Judging by where the blood spray ended up on the wall, Streeter guessed that he was shot kneeling down and then sort of thrown onto the couch after he was dead. Streeter backed away from the body. He wiped his prints off the doorknob and left.

When he got back to the church, he went to Frank's room. Once again, the bondsman automatically grabbed his Scotch and they headed to his office.

"It's getting way out of hand, Street," Frank said when they sat down at his desk. Then he nodded to the Scotch bottle. "This is getting to be a regular event around here. You got to go to the police."

"I called 911 from a phone booth on the way back here."

"I assumed that. I mean you got to sit down with them and fill them in on all of this stuff."

"That would be nice, except that I think it's the police who's doing most of it. This Jacky business wasn't Cooper's work. And Soyko wouldn't do Romp. No motive, and Carey tells me these two guys were closer than brothers."

"You think Kovacs did it?"

"Romp had cuts on his wrists. My guess is handcuffs. Kovacs doesn't want anyone messing into Doug's business. This is his way of telling Cooper to back off. He probably figured he'd have to be a little more forceful with Cooper than he was with Story."

"So where's Soyko now?"

"I wouldn't mind knowing that myself. I'm meeting Carey tomorrow afternoon to see what I can find out. I also got a call today from Cooper's secretary. Seems she was attacked last night and she wants to get together with me tomorrow and talk about it. Ronnie Taggert. I may have mentioned her."

Frank was puzzled. "Why'd she call you?"

"I gather she can't go to the cops, because she's in over her head. And she doesn't think Cooper'll be much help." Streeter smiled. "I think maybe she's got a thing for me, too. For whatever reason, she trusts me."

"Great. You need to get messed up with someone like that. You got a real knack for hitching up with trouble all of a sudden."

"I'm not hitching up with anything," he said, dropping the smile, "but I'm dying to find out what she knows about all this. We're meeting first thing in the morning for breakfast."

Frank shook his head like he had a stiff neck and poured another drink. "Let me know if you need anything. And watch your ass, huh?"

20

Jacky Romp was one of the most dead-looking bodies Soyko had ever seen, and he'd seen maybe a dozen guys in that precise condition. He'd been standing in the middle of the living room smoking and looking down at Jacky for almost half an hour. It didn't take an orthopedic surgeon to figure out that Romp's condition wasn't brought on by natural causes. One side of his head looked like he'd stuck it in a blender. It had lolled off to his left and rested on the couch back. His legs shot straight out, like he was a puppet thrown down hard. It looked to Soyko like someone had used a cannon on his partner.

He had known Jacky for nearly ten years and roomed with him for most of that time. Jacky was not only Soyko's closest friend, he was the only real friend he ever had. But Soyko wasn't so much sad as puzzled about what to do next. Not about what to do with the killer. That was a definite no-brainer. No, he wondered about what to do in general without Jacky around.

Suddenly he turned to face the wall, let out a dull wail, and ran his fist through the cheap plaster. He did it twice more, then felt better. Jacky was history, but someone had to pay. Soyko would still leave town tomorrow, as they had planned, but he would be by himself. He knew he'd have to be careful until then. If the cops weren't on his tail before, this would certainly get them there.

Life could be very strange at times, he decided sadly.

He walked into his bedroom and stuffed his clothes into two suitcases. Exactly what happened to Jacky? It wasn't a burglary, because nothing was missing. It didn't seem likely the cops did it, either. The name Tom Cooper waltzed slowly through Soyko's noxious, if sparse, mind. So did the term "payback." The attack on Ronnie Taggert had to be avenged, so Cooper must have hired a couple of goons to turn Jacky out like that. Easy enough to find out. Go to his office in the morning and don't leave until you get some answers.

Forget Doug Shelton's money and that Moffatt broad, Soyko thought. He could feel pain and uncertainty sprouting around him. Time to take the two actions that always brought him relief: he had to lash out and then he had to split. This McLean beating had turned into one monumentally bad idea. He could see that now. Also taking Ronnie on brought too much heat, and maybe cost Jacky his life. Tomorrow, dealing with Cooper, that had to be done.

Then he would leave town.

He went back to the living room. When he reached in and cleaned out Jacky's wallet he noticed a foul odor. Jacky must have soiled himself as he died. He wondered how many guys Cooper had hired. Tiny Fred, maybe. He'd find out tomorrow. When he got Jacky's money, he left without saying a word. If Leo Soyko knew one thing for absolute certain, it was that there was no point in talking to a dead man.

He and Jacky lived in a wood-stained condo project, strictly low-end. It was the kind of prefab place where, when the real estate market goes sour like it did in the early eighties, fore-closure notices sprout on the windows like Christmas wreaths. Their unit opened directly into an outside stairwell that emptied into the parking lot.

Soyko had just gotten down one flight of stairs when the

woman from the unit below came staggering out. She was pushing fifty, which seemed ancient to him, and usually she was either asleep or in the process of drinking herself to sleep. She
smelled like the Dumpsters out back and slurred her words into
barely recognizable, choppy strings of syllables. And, clearly, she
was hot for the two men who lived above her. Just my luck, Leo
thought.

"How we tonight?" she asked. "Taking a little trip, are we?"

"*We* ain't doing nothing, you and me." He set his bags down
and looked at her.

She made a bitter face and drew her head back. "Why you
gotta talk to me like that? All the time. And where's your
roomie?"

"He's asleep."

"Your other friend leave? Where is he?"

Soyko perked up. "What friend is that?"

"The big guy in the Buick."

"Who you talking about? I was gone for a while."

The drunk, he never did know her name, could see that she
had his interest, so she played it to the hilt. "Maybe you could
come in and we can talk about it."

He didn't have the time or the patience for that. Even if he
had, the idea made him moderately sick. Instead, he reached out
with a gnarled right hand and grabbed her by the throat. Then
he squeezed hard. Her eyes widened in pain and terror and she
let out a thunderous, involuntary belch.

"Maybe not," he said. "Maybe I don't have time for your crap.
Now, what big guy you talking about?"

"Yuh, yech," escaped from her mouth.

He loosened his grip slightly. He noticed a series of dried
brown stains on the front of her flowered bathrobe, and for a
second he felt like gagging. "What did this big guy look like?"
He loosened his grip even further.

"Good-looking. Late thirties maybe." Her voice was tiny.
"Brown hair combed back some. Shoulders a mile wide."

He let the woman go. Then he thought of that muscle-head

boyfriend of Moffatt's. Streeter was the name Cooper mentioned. The bounty hunter who was with her that day at Cooper's. Against Soyko's advice, Jacky had made a bunch of hang-up calls to him last week. The guy was supposed to be tight with McLean, Cooper said. Had to be this Streeter that did Jacky, Soyko concluded.

"What kind of shit is this?" The drunk was rubbing her throat, which was turning red and felt like she'd swallowed a frozen tennis ball. "You're a regular asshole, you know that?"

"Relax. You'll live." Then, as an afterthought, "If you call what you do living."

He picked up his suitcases and headed toward the car. No need to squeeze Cooper about who did Jacky. It was that Streeter. To hell with Cooper. Soyko decided to follow Streeter for a while. Maybe he'd get lucky and the big guy would lead him to Moffatt, so he could take care of both of them. A two-for-one payback. Jacky deserved that much.

By the time he drove out of the lot, he was in a much better mood.

The drunk just stood out in front of her door for a long time after Soyko left. Her breathing was starting to get normal again. "Bastard," she mumbled to no one. She was glad she hadn't told Soyko about the other guy that went up there, before the big guy. That first visitor was not so nice-looking. He looked sick and ugly. And he had the look of a bully, just like Soyko. He had knocked on her door by mistake, looking for the men upstairs. The guy had to be a cop. Even a drunk could see that. She stood outside her door seething. Then she went inside and made a phone call, to 911.

21

Streeter was never much for breakfast. Particularly the cooked, restaurant kind. So he just ordered a large milk and looked out onto the half-full parking lot of Rudy's Ranch Buffet, the diner where he was to meet Ronnie in about ten minutes. The name notwithstanding, Rudy's was about as country as a subway. It was generic corporate schlock, with the grimly sterile atmosphere of a school cafeteria and Dwight Yokum softly piped in. Streeter figured they named it Ranch Buffet to sucker people into thinking they'd get a huge farm meal and then maybe not notice the glorified airplane food they were actually served.

Rudy's was located in the hideous maze of culs-de-sac, shopettes, and rambling streets with names like Briarwood Lane in Littleton, a far-south Denver suburb. With Ronnie staying at a trucker's motel out in rural Douglas County, about five miles farther south, she suggested Rudy's to Streeter because it was roughly halfway between her and the church. Also because Soyko would never think of looking for her there.

"Here's your milk," the waitress said, stating the obvious as she stood over his booth.

"Do you have a nonsmoking section somewhere?" Streeter had just noticed the swirl of cigarette smoke around him.

"Sure." The waitress clearly was bored. "Over there. Just sit anywhere you want." She threw her head listlessly toward a far wall and walked away.

Streeter worked his way into a booth on the back wall. He could no longer see the parking lot but now had a clear view of the entire restaurant and would be better able to see Ronnie come through the door. He still had a few minutes before she was set to arrive, so he sipped his milk and patiently looked around the room.

As Ronnie drove north toward Rudy's, she thought how all her plans of settling down with Cooper in Denver and leading a "normal" life with the attorney were dead. When she escaped Soyko on Monday, she'd headed south and checked into the motel. She finally called Cooper about midnight and told him what happened. The little worm uttered a few cursory words of concern and then went into a selfish tirade about her not caring about him.

"Did it ever occur to you, Rhonda, that I should have been apprised of this situation?" he'd sputtered indignantly into the phone. She could almost picture the wad of spit forming at each side of his mouth as he worked up his usual head of self-absorbed fear. "All this time with those guys running around out there. It's just fortunate I'm still in one piece. No thanks to you. What if they had come after me?"

"You lousy chicken shit," she'd screamed back. "I almost get killed and all you think about is what *might* have happened to you. How typical."

She wouldn't tell him where she was. Instead, they decided to meet in a couple of days at a motel just outside of Colorado Springs and leave for Mexico together. They'd get their hands on as much cash as they could before then. Most of that would come from Cooper selling his 'Vette and closing his bank accounts, with another portion from Ronnie taking out "ready cash" from their joint safe-deposit box.

But the more she thought about it the less thrilled she was. His reaction to her attack and his general inability to protect her made Ronnie reluctant to stay with the man. He wouldn't have that much money, and his earning power as an attorney probably was shot. And let's face it, she reasoned, his practical judgment grossly sucks. Look at how he misread that situation with Romp and Soyko. So she picked up just over twenty thousand dollars from their box. Now she had the Tercel, a fair amount of cash, plastic credit, and most of her clothes, which she'd retrieved from her apartment. The police would be after her as a witness against Cooper, and she could be facing charges. Leaving town definitely was the best move. By herself. Before then she wanted to straighten out a few things, and Streeter might help. He had a confidence that drew her to him. Not really showy, but a nice hint of cockiness. And he seemed trustworthy.

The bounty hunter was about half done with his milk when Ronnie came through Rudy's front door.

"I'm glad you made it," Ronnie said as she approached his booth.

"I said I'd be here." He liked the pale-pink summer sweater she had on. Short sleeves, like something a bratty teenage girl would have worn in a 1950s movie. "Eight-thirty Wednesday at Rudy's. You hungry?"

"I don't usually eat before noon. Coffee'll be fine."

The waitress came and took her order and they sat in silence until it came. Streeter spoke first. "This can't be easy on you. Are you all right?"

She nodded and stared directly at him. "You know the name Leo Soyko?"

"Cooper's flunky? I've heard rumors."

"Jacky Romp. You ever hear of him?"

Streeter flashed on Jacky's body on the couch. "Yeah. He's dead. Have you seen the morning papers?"

Ronnie looked stunned. "How? Yesterday?"

"The *Post* said his body was found about midnight at his apartment. Shot twice in the head at close range."

Ronnie didn't appear to be experiencing anything close to grief. "Maybe there is a God." She smiled quickly. "He and Soyko were the two boners that attacked me Monday night. If Romp had his way I'd be dead. Do they have any idea at all who did it?"

"No arrests, according to the paper. Do you think Soyko might have killed him?"

"I can't imagine why."

"Did they have any other enemies?"

Ronnie smiled and her head jerked in a knowing nod. "Only anyone who ever met either of them. But I can't think of anyone in particular. Tell me, Mr. Bounty Hunter, what's your hunch?"

Streeter's eyebrows shot up and he took a sip of his milk. "I have someone in mind but I doubt if you know him. Did Cooper have any friends or associates in the Denver Police Department?"

"Honey, you're looking at all the friends Thomas Cooper has in the world."

Again there was a brief silence.

"So, Ronnie," he said deliberately. "Why'd you call this meeting?"

"A couple of reasons. I'm leaving town soon and I hoped you could help me handle a little unfinished business. This news about Jacky takes care of part of it. Soyko's another part. Those two were scum and I'd like to see them both buried. Soyko's looking for that money Doug Shelton supposedly left behind. Cooper's looking, too, but I have a feeling he's out of the picture from now on. If you and that Story Moffatt chick are still going after it, you better be careful. I don't suppose you'd do me one little favor and shoot Soyko?"

Streeter could see she wasn't entirely joking. "You don't suppose right."

"Just a thought. If you won't shoot him, maybe you can help put him away. He killed a witness in a murder case up in Commerce City named Grundy Dopps. Tell the police that. Tell them Cooper paid Soyko to try and get Dopps out of town and then

Soyko decided to kill him instead. I've been involved with Tom Cooper for more than three years now and I know that whole bunch of jerks. I'm finished with all of them, but I'd hate to see Soyko get Doug's money. The thought of Leo Soyko getting any reward out of this makes me sick."

"Me, too."

"I'll bet 'you, too.' If I was a gambler I'd say you're the kind of guy who doesn't like to lose."

"Who does?"

"Right. Anyhow, I want to tell you what I know before I leave town. What you do with it is up to you."

"I'm listening." Streeter leaned forward.

"If it was me still looking for that money, I'd head over to wherever they're keeping what's left of Doug's Porsche. I used to date a guy who works at an import garage on South Downing. I ran into Bobby not too long ago and we went out for a few beers. As it turns out, he'd worked on Doug's car a couple years ago. Bobby told me it was customized special somehow."

"I thought the insurance people and Story did that."

"They might have, but Bobby led me to believe the car was very special. He was vague about it, but my instincts say check out the car."

Streeter nodded. "I was going to do that anyhow. But if my hunch is right, I don't think what Doug left could be stored in any car."

"Do what you want, Streeter. Just so you beat Soyko on this. Another thing. There was some cop that busted Doug on his last coke deal. I can't remember the guy's name anymore, but Doug was terrified of him. He beat almost the entire shit out of Doug right after the arrest. You ever come across the cop?"

Streeter nodded. "I've talked to him once." He paused briefly. "I think he might of had something to do with Jacky's situation."

"Then he can't be all bad," Ronnie said quickly. "I just wanted to warn you about him. Another hunch of mine is that this cop's looking for Doug's money, too. Doug said he was a real macho pig. Of course, so's everyone involved in this mess. Except for Tom Cooper. He isn't quite that evolved. He's what I'd call a macho pig wannabe. It's what he strives for."

"Yeah? Is that how he got hooked up with Soyko and Romp?"

"You got that right. Tom has this incredibly screwed-up notion of what's manly and cool. He's pretty insecure, and when he saw Soyko he saw a lot of the things he wanted to be. Lean, tough, decisive, always able to back up the talk with action. Tom could talk the talk but he could never walk the walk. Anyhow, between the cop on Doug's case and Soyko, this ain't going to be fun from now on."

"Like it's been a regular party up to now?"

"True."

"Look, Ronnie, I appreciate all this, but if you really want to stop these guys, why don't you go to the police?"

She rolled her eyes wildly and sat back in the booth. "I tried that once and it almost got me killed."

"How?"

"I blew the whistle on Soyko and Romp for beating up the lawyer. McLean. They damned near killed me for it."

"Are you sure they were the ones who went after Bill?"

Ronnie nodded. "For sure. You had some doubts?"

"Not really." He pulled out one of Frank's business cards and a pen and began writing on the blank backside. "Listen, Ronnie, here's the name of a cop. A friend of mine. Carey. A detective. Give him a call before you leave town and tell him what you know. Tell him about this conversation and that you know me. You can trust Carey." He finished writing and handed it to her. "At least think about it, okay?"

She took the card and studied both sides. "All right."

"Someone's been giving me and Story problems lately," he continued. "A few shots were fired at my house, and her car got vandalized. Could that have been Soyko and Romp?"

Ronnie frowned and thought for a few seconds. "Not that I know of. Moffatt mentioned something like that at the meeting with Tom and I asked him about it later. He didn't know what the hell she was talking about."

He nodded. That meant Kovacs did it.

Then her voice softened and she smiled. "So. Are you and this Moffatt an item, Streeter?"

"An item? No. I work for her. Why?"

"Just curious. Dougy used to talk about her a little. She sounds like a real live wire. Doug said she was so cold he thought maybe she had Freon sprayed all over her libido. You ever get that feeling about her?"

"I never gave it much thought," he said, hoping he sounded convincing. "Story can come across as somewhat shy of blood, and there's times I'd like to wring her neck. But Freon sprayed in that area sounds a little overstated." Ronnie was as catty about Story as the ad woman had sounded about *her*. "What difference is it to you whether she and I are an item or what's sprayed where on her?"

"I'm just curious, Streeter. I think you're an interesting man." She studied him with a scant smile on her face. "You're probably better than she deserves. That's all I was thinking."

There was a genuine sincerity to the remark that touched him. "Thanks. Listen, Ronnie, if I find whatever Doug left behind, maybe I can cut you in on a slice of it. For your help. In the meantime, you be careful, and think about calling Carey. He'll level with you, and we both know Soyko and Cooper belong in prison. Plus, that way maybe you could clear yourself from any trouble with the police."

"I might just do that. I'm curious. How are you going to find me to give me my 'slice'?"

"Where are you headed?"

"I haven't given it much thought. Maybe I'll find you some day and you can tell me how it all turned out."

22

"You look a little peaked there, kid." Detective Bob Carey was pouring cream into his coffee at the Newsstand Cafe, a coffee/ magazine shop on 6th Avenue, near the governor's mansion. He stared hard into Streeter's eyes while stirring his coffee. "You wouldn't happen to know anything about this peckerhead Jacky Romp, would you?"

As he stood there, Streeter felt his own coffee spilling on his hand, so he set it down. Then he pulled up a tall stool next to Carey at the long counter and sat down. It was sunny outside, and the post-lunch-hour traffic was heavy heading east on the one-way 6th Avenue.

"Not really. That's why I called you."

The detective nodded and said, "That's very good, because, like I told you, a person can get into a lot of trouble dancing around with people like attorney Thomas Cooper and his friends."

"It would seem so. Look, I'm just curious because of Bill and all. I met Cooper once. I don't really know any of the rest of them."

Streeter liked and trusted Carey, but he was a cop. No way he wanted any cop knowing he had been at Soyko's apartment the night before. Not yet, anyway. He also wondered if Ronnie Taggert would call Carey. That question was answered before he could settle into his seat.

"It's starting to look as though the whole situation is taking care of itself," Carey said. "These guys are like a bunch of inbred rats turning on each other. The rumble downtown is that Soyko must have flipped out yesterday, judging by the way they found Romp. Some woman who lived below them called in and said she saw Soyko leave about eleven last night and he was really steamed up. Everybody's out looking for Soyko today. I'm sure they'll get him pretty soon.

"It seems for sure these characters were in on the McLean thing and some other pretty heavy garbage. Over the weekend, one of the guys investigating McLean got a call from a lady saying Soyko and Romp did everything but shoot JFK. We sent someone out to talk to those two and, before you know it, Cooper's secretary nearly gets attacked by two guys exactly matching the descriptions of his two investigators. A woman named Ronnie Taggert. We figure she must have been the one who made the call.

"Then, just before lunch today, none other than Ms. Taggert herself—who's disappeared since her assault—calls me and asks if we can sit down and have a talk in the not-too-distant future. Seems there's this absolutely splendid bounty hunter exactly matching *your* description who gave her my name and number. She's got all sorts of information for me about this entire mess. I'm meeting her tomorrow morning—that is, assuming she's not dead or out of the state by then. I tried to get it sooner, but she wants to wait another day for some reason of her own. So now Romp's dead and his partner and Cooper should be in custody before long. With Ms. Taggert's help, we should be able to nail these two pricks to the wall and wrap up a whole lotta stuff."

Streeter smiled when he thought about Ronnie. "Listen to that lady, Robert. I had a good feeling about her from the time I met her at Cooper's. She's all right. One tough ball breaker, but my read is that she's honest. Do you really think Soyko turned on

Romp? And why would Cooper want to hurt Ronnie? Those two were dating. Or whatever it is that people like Cooper do."

"We got to sort all that out. The first thing we want to do is bring everybody in for questioning, especially Cooper. He had to be in the middle of all of it, but we're not sure how he fits. I heard he took that Ronnie thing pretty hard, so maybe that was just the two other guys playing around on their own.

"Anyhow, when we sent some people out to their apartment last night, we find old Jacky Romp laying on the carpet looking like he went bungee jumping off a fifty-foot bridge with a sixty-foot cord. Half his head was blown away. The woman who lives below them said she heard the two men fighting shortly before eleven and then Soyko went charging out like the place was on fire. We went through the El Camino that belonged to Romp and found a bat that they traced to McLean's beating. They got an arrest warrant for Soyko for assault on McLean and homicide for his friend. Or should I say ex-friend. Trouble is, no one knows what he's driving, and he could be halfway to Mexico or Canada or someplace like that by now. Do you think this fits in with what you're doing with Shelton's widow?"

"Hard to tell." Streeter didn't want to share much with Carey. "Who knows about that?"

Carey just looked at him for a few seconds. "I'd suggest that you lay low for a while. Just go back to chasing your bail jumpers until we sort out all the crap on this shooting and until we get Soyko and Cooper." Carey drained his coffee. "Will you do that simple thing for me?"

"I'll certainly give it some thought. Will you keep me posted on everything from your end of it?"

Carey grinned. "I'll certainly give it some thought."

When he left the Newsstand, Streeter got into his Buick and grabbed his cellular phone to call Story. He had resisted buying one for a long time, but finally he decided that since he spent so much time in his car he should have one. To someone in his line of work a car is like a portable office. Maps, phone, hand-cuffs, gun, camera, spare film, a change of clothes, and assorted surveillance and work tools, even a cup to urinate in, Streeter's Buick had them all.

He planned to spend the rest of the afternoon interviewing people on the list Story had given him. It would take his mind off Soyko. Let the cops deal with him from now on. When he got her on the phone, Story wanted to hear all about the unraveling of Cooper's empire. He told her most of what was happening, but not about his being at Romp's apartment or his meeting with Ronnie.

"It looks like things are coming together pretty well for us," she told him. "Your friend Bill's out of trouble, and Cooper and his crew should be way out of the picture before long. If that cop you think shot at your church leaves us alone for a while, that will free us up to work on Doug."

She had a way of saying "us" that always let him know she meant him.

"I'll let you know if *we* find anything," he said evenly. Then he hung up without saying goodbye.

He went to the church to talk to Frank and see if he had any messages. The bondsman was out, and there was nothing on the voice mail. Streeter glanced at the mail on Frank's desk. There always seemed to be a stack of junk solicitations and catalogues. One eight-and-a-half-by-eleven, two-color brochure caught his eye. It looked familiar. It was from the Executive Protectors Inc., the same company whose flyer was in Doug's files. Streeter leafed through it, wondering what Shelton wanted from the company. In the middle of page eight he found the answer. Not only did he find what Doug had bought from the Protectors, but if he was right, Streeter was one big step closer to finding whatever was hidden.

What he saw on page eight was called "The Movable Bank," a fireproof, bulletproof, solid-steel strongbox. "Ideal for keeping the things you value close to you at all times," the ad copy gloated. A photograph at the bottom of the page showed the twelve-by-twelve-inch-square box being inserted under the back seat of a nondescript car.

"Fits easily under car seats, in car trunks, engine compartments, or a thousand other places. Also good for home and office security. Regularly $179.95, now only $159.95. Locks extra."

Streeter reread the ad copy several times. He studied the picture, the box designed for small spaces in a car or truck. Story was adamant on how fussy Doug was about his Porsche: he wouldn't even let people in the back seat. That was probably where he'd kept the strongbox. Ronnie's mechanic friend said the car was customized, and this must have been what he meant.

And what was the common denominator in all his trips to get money and drugs, both in Boulder and Denver? The Porsche. A 1988 red 928. A nice car, but not valuable enough to deserve all the attention he gave it. Doug never was without cash or cocaine, because he never went anywhere without his car and the strongbox. Streeter had just been thinking about what a portable office his own car was. Doug's car was a portable safe and merchandise showroom: a drug dealer's portable office. Story said they'd looked through the car but then had given up because so much of it was burned or demolished. This "Movable Bank" could survive that. For the past few days, Streeter had been thinking that Doug had left valuable artwork hidden. Obviously, you can't store much of that in the back of a Porsche. So it must be money or something like money that he'd left behind when he headed off to the great unknown.

He picked up the phone and dialed Story's office number. "I'm coming over," he said. "I know where Doug left his money."

There was a long silence on her end of the phone. Finally, "Are you sure?" He couldn't decide if she sounded frightened or threatening.

"I'm not positive, but it'll be easy enough to find out. I want to move on this—now. I mean right now. I'm coming over."

"Please do."

With that, he hung up, grabbed the brochure, and went to his car. When he got there he looked inside his trunk to make sure he had all his tools, especially his crowbar. He slammed the trunk shut and got in the driver's seat. As he pulled away from the curb, he was driving much faster than usual. At Broadway, he turned south and zipped toward Capitol Hill.

Soyko wondered what all the hurry was about as he pulled out into traffic, about a block behind Streeter. The bounty hunter had been driving so slow and cautious all day. And what was so interesting in the trunk?

23

Story was pacing—marching, actually—in the downstairs foyer of her office building when Streeter arrived. She was wearing shorts, a plain white blouse, and flats. More casual than he had ever seen, but there was nothing casual about her demeanor. Her shoulders were rigid, her frown deep, like her squash pose that day at the gym. She'd had time to work up a good head of skepticism while he drove over. Story Moffatt was not the kind of woman who suffered false hopes or fools easily. Her pinched-up attitude instantly put him off.

"You know, Story, this is supposed to be good news," he said as he walked slowly toward her.

"Let's go upstairs and talk." Her voice was low and she didn't smile.

"Hello to you, too." He followed her up the stairs, the Executive Protectors brochure rolled up in his hand like a club.

When they got to her office, she nodded for him to go in and then told her secretary they were not to be disturbed. That finished, she came inside and closed the door. Streeter was standing in the middle of the room, watching her closely.

"Do you know for sure, Streeter?" There was a whiff of pleading in her voice. "I don't mean to act like a bitch, but I don't think I could stand it if you're wrong. Not after all that we've been through with this thing."

He nodded, his eyes nailed to hers. "It's the car. Doug left whatever we're looking for in his car." He held up his hand, palm toward her, as she grimaced. "I know you said you looked through part of it and that it was destroyed and all. But it's in there. Look at this."

He opened the brochure and held it out for her. She stared at it but wouldn't touch it.

"Does this look familiar?" he asked.

"I . . . Should it?" The bitchy edge returned.

"Read the name."

Story looked back to the catalogue and studied it. Her frown deepened.

"It's that booklet from Doug's stuff. I didn't know you took it with you."

"I didn't. Frank got this in the mail. He gets this kind of flyer all the time. We never read them very closely. I've never had much need for all these James Bond gadgets. But when I saw this today, and read the name of the company, the same one as Doug's flyer, I looked through every page to find out what he wanted from these guys."

He turned the booklet back to face him and stared at it for a moment. Then he flipped it open and went to page eight.

"I thought he was after the phone-sweeping equipment," he told her. "You know, home-security garbage, something like that. But this is what Doug wanted. I'll bet my life on it."

He turned the book around and gave it to her. This time she took it and read the open pages closely. Suddenly her head shot up and she looked at him.

"Fireproof. That's it, Streeter. We didn't look inside the Porsche because everything was burned. I figured that anything inside had to have been destroyed. But this"—she looked back at page eight—"this would take care of a fire. If he got one of these boxes it's in that precious back seat. No wonder he was so touchy about letting people back there. We have to get to that car."

"No kidding. Plus, I got some information this morning that Doug customized the damned thing. Almost from the start, I was thinking that if he left anything it was probably not cash. I assumed he invested in something like artwork or cars. Things that you can buy and they'll appreciate with time and then you can sell them without Uncle Sam finding out. But if this box is our answer, we're probably looking at cash. Do you know where the Porsche is kept?"

"When I saw it, they were keeping it at the police impound. They told me it would be there for a few days and then they'd ship it off to a junkyard. Oh, God, Streeter. You don't suppose they would have crushed it? We'll never get anything out of it."

"Relax, Story. Was there anything left intact? Any parts to salvage?"

"The back end was okay, I guess."

"Then they probably kept it for parts. Give me the phone book and I'll call the police yard to find out where they took it."

Streeter had dealt with the Denver police-impound people dozens of times in the past. Working for various lawyers suing insurance companies, he'd had to take photos of cars after they'd been in accidents. Luckily, the police had an excellent system of storing and disposing of vehicles, so if Doug's Porsche hadn't been crushed, the bounty hunter didn't anticipate any trouble finding it.

Story went behind her desk, fished out a phone book from her credenza, and handed it to him. He looked up the number for the police-impound lot and called. The clerk told him that all the cars shipped out last year would have gone to one of two lots. She gave the names and telephone numbers of both. Streeter hit paydirt at the second one, All-American Auto Salvage, just north of I-70 and northwest of the old Stapleton International Airport. That part of town is a run-down patchwork of tool shops, rusty salvage yards, ratty open fields, and an occasional convenience store or saloon.

"How late are you open?" he asked the man at All-American, who verified they had the Porsche. "Seven? We'll be out there before then. As a matter of fact, we're heading up now. What's that? Row thirty, slot twelve? Thanks. No, we're just going to take some pictures for the insurance claim. That's right."

When he hung up, Story asked, "What was all that about insurance-claim pictures?"

"This guy owns the car now. If I told them what we're after, he'd have it pulled apart by the time we got downstairs. This way, he'll leave us alone. Junkyard owners are used to people like me taking pictures of cars. He won't even watch us."

They had to fight rush-hour traffic, so they didn't make it to All-American until just before six. The sun was still high in the early-summer sky, and the view of Denver to the south and the Rockies to the west was spectacular, even if their immediate sur-roundings were not. The lot owner, an obese man with an ap-parent bathing dysfunction, steered them toward the Porsche.

"See that shed by those trucks there?" he asked without getting up from a filthy couch next to the office. "Car you want'll be right up next to it. How long you think you'll be?"

"Half hour, tops," Streeter answered.

The owner just nodded. Streeter kept his eye on the shabby wooden shed as he drove toward it. When they got into the main aisle, along the back row, Story suddenly got excited and jabbed an index finger toward the windshield.

"There it is. That black thing over there. You can see the red toward the back, where it wasn't burned."

Streeter pulled off to one side, so his Buick would sit between the Porsche and the office. The Porsche's burned front tires were curled up under the body like a begging dog's paws. All its win-dows were broken and he could see that the door on the pas-senger's side was badly buckled. There was a layer of hard black soot over everything but several feet in the rear. The car looked

like it had been dipped in licorice. Streeter got out of his Buick
and went to the trunk. He pulled out his camera and handed it
to Story, who was beside him.

"Keep an eye on the office. If that tub of lard comes out here,
pretend you're taking pictures."

He put on some work gloves and grabbed the crowbar. Then
he walked to the driver's side. The Porsche was nestled between
an old Celica on that side and the wooden shed on the other.
Streeter had to step carefully over broken glass that was scattered
in the aisle.

"I'll start here. It looks easier to get into, and he might have
been more likely to put the box right behind him."

The driver's door was buckled almost as badly as the passenger's, but it was cracked open a few inches near the top. Streeter
grabbed the edge firmly and gave it a hard pull. It groaned open.
Inside, it still smelled freshly burned in the warm air. When he
bent in, he could see why no one would bother looking too
closely. The seats were charred stretches of soot, and it was hard
to tell where anything started or stopped. He came back out and
looked at Story.

"Nothing destroys like fire," he said. "I'm going to just start
pulling everything apart and see what I find."

She walked over next to him and looked inside the car. "Can
you imagine dying in there?"

Streeter frowned and then bent back inside. He knew that his
chinos would be ruined by the soot. He pushed the front seat
forward and kneeled in, his knee resting on the transmission
hump in the back. The car was a liftback, and he had to push
the seat back upright. Then he took the straight end of the crowbar and poked around the front edge of the back seat. Horizontally, at about the point it touched the passengers' calves, there
was a slight lip where the top of the seat came over. He slipped
the crowbar under that and lifted. The seat came up, and he
could see that there was nothing but springs under it. He lifted
it higher, so that the crack ran partially to the seat on the other
side of the transmission hump. He poked around under that

side, and the crowbar clanked into something solid. No springs under there. He got out and walked around the car to where Story was waiting.

"I think it's on the other side," he said.

"Just hurry."

"Why? This isn't going anywhere."

He walked out onto the main aisle, behind the Porsche, and then around to the passenger's side, next to the shed. This time he had to use the crowbar to coax the door open. He bent inside. Then he put the claw of the crowbar under the seat opening he had created and gave a hard pull back. That forced the opening to smile all the way to the door and let him see the dusty, but highly functional, Portable Bank under the seat.

"Yes sir," he said quietly to himself. Now he could feel the beads of sweat rolling freely down his forehead. With the crowbar he reached under the seat and tapped the box. Then he leaned back and looked at Story. "I knew it was here."

She bent into the car like she was going to confession. "Bring it out."

Streeter bent down again and jiggled the strongbox. It was in tight, maybe even welded down. Then he looked more closely and he couldn't believe what he saw. There was a single eyehole-and-flap arrangement for a padlock, but no lock. Doug must have thought just having the box hidden like that was security enough.

"No need to. It's not locked."

"You're kidding. Open it."

Streeter slipped his gloves off and flipped the box top up. He looked inside and was mildly disappointed that it wasn't even full. On top was an eight-and-a-half-by-eleven manila envelope. He picked it up, squeezed it, and handed it to Story. It felt like money inside, but unless the bills all were thousands, there couldn't have been too much. Under the envelope were two other items. One was a plastic baggie with what appeared to be a chunk of white powder. Streeter quickly estimated it to be something just over ten ounces of cocaine. He left it there.

"There's a few ounces of coke in here, too," he said without looking up.

"Anything else?" Her voice was still expectant.

"There's another envelope. A smaller one." He picked it up as he spoke. It was white and unsealed. Before he could look inside, Story jabbed her hand back into the car, her palm up.

"That would be mine." Her voice left little doubt that she meant it.

Streeter looked up at her and then back down at the envelope. He handed it to her without a word. As he sifted through the strongbox one more time, he lifted out the cocaine. He got out of the car, stood up, tossed the baggie into the air a few inches, caught it, and studied it.

"You can keep that if you want," Story said as she stuffed the smaller envelope into her purse, with the larger, money envelope jammed in her armpit. She was looking at her purse as she spoke. "We'll call it a tip."

Streeter tossed the baggie in the air one more time and then bent back into the car. He replaced it in the box, shut it, and looked around. He pulled the seat over the box again. When he was done, he got out and brushed himself off.

"Let's go before the owner comes out."

A strange sadness fell over both of them. Here they were, standing in the middle of a wretched junkyard with these packets of drugs and paper. Bill McLean was in the hospital, Ronnie Taggert almost killed. Doug Shelton and Shannon Mays had died, probably trashed out on the cocaine from the back seat. The sun moved closer to the mountains and the air was still. Nothing seemed very important.

"Hardly appears to be worth it, does it?" he asked.

"It'll be more worthwhile when we find out what's inside. Don't you want to know how much money there is?" she asked as she pulled the big envelope out of her armpit. "A third of it's yours."

Streeter kicked the car door shut. "You can tell me on the way back to town. All I really want now is a shower."

Story turned and moved first. She walked with her head down. When she got to the back end of the car, she turned right, toward the Buick, and looked up. Streeter had the nagging feeling he was forgetting something, so he took one more look inside the car, through the window. Then he walked out to where Story had gone. He had just turned into the main aisle when he heard her scream. He looked first at her and then toward his car, the direction of whatever scared her.

There, leaning with his butt up on the trunk of the Buick and his legs crossed casually in front of him, was Leo Soyko. His face shivered in brutality but his voice was under control.

"Old Ronnie Taggert was right, after all," he said. "She told me to check out the car." Then he straightened up and gracefully shook the lethal belt buckle loose from his pants. The blade looked almost black in his shadow. He looked at Story as he moved toward her. "I believe you got something of mine there, darlin'. I'd strongly suggest you hand it over."

She was frozen, not sure who the man with the knife was but vaguely recalling his face from somewhere. The knife and his bloodshot eyes let her know she could easily lose everything.

"Let's have it, little lady." Soyko took another step.

"Streeter," Story yelled as she looked back for him over her shoulder.

The bounty hunter had been slowly coming forward as Soyko spoke. He was now at the back edge of the Porsche, just behind her, in the main aisle. "Back up, Story. Just back up." Then he directed his voice sharply at Soyko. "And you, hold it right there."

His words caused Soyko to stop and look at the man who spoke them. With that hesitation, Streeter repeated his instructions. "Back up, Story."

She started moving automatically heading in the direction of his voice. When she got to him, he reached out and grabbed her shoulder, gently but firmly. He pulled her back a few steps so she was behind him and he was between Soyko and her. All the while he kept steady eye contact with the man holding the knife.

"Just keep on going, Story. Get out of here." His voice stayed even; then suddenly he yelled to Soyko, "And you stay put!"

"I been waiting for this all day, shithead," Soyko responded. "I owe you big-time for Jacky. Getting whatever you found is gonna be a nice bonus. That and cutting up you and the lady." He was advancing as he spoke and there were only a few feet between them by now.

The blade looked short but thick. Soyko's hands looked equally thick around the base of the knife, and his shoulders quivered in anticipation. A sick feeling came over Streeter as he remembered what he'd forgotten inside of the Porsche—the crowbar. He wished he had either it or the gun he kept under his car seat.

"I had nothing to do with Jacky. I was at your place for a minute last night but he was dead when I got there. I'm pretty sure it was a cop named Kovacs who did it."

"Oh, a cop. Definitely. They run around killing people all the time. The lady below us made you for the guy."

"She's full of crap. She made you for the guy when she called the cops. They're looking for you right now."

"The cops, huh? The same ones that killed Jacky, I suppose. Shut up."

Soyko lashed out with the knife, shooting his right hand out at the bigger man like he was throwing a punch. Streeter quickly backpedaled and avoided the blade. Soyko lunged again and Streeter backpedaled again, the blade hitting only air. Trouble was, Streeter was stepping back into the space between the Porsche and the shed. It was a narrow space with no exit. Soyko could keep coming until there was no more room to back up. Streeter took a quick half-step forward to see if his attacker would give any ground. He didn't budge.

"Nowhere to run?"

At that Soyko made two more quick swipes with the blade. Both times Streeter had to give ground, forcing him closer to the back wall. He could hear Story yell something, but he couldn't make out the words.

He yelled back, "Get out of here. Get to the office."

Soyko straightened up, a smile crossing his face. "Saving the lady, huh? Now, that's sweet."

He then went back into his attack crouch, lifted the blade to shoulder level, growled, and moved forward. He intended this to be his last charge. It was.

Streeter saw it coming and, in the time it took Soyko to travel the last three feet, he turned slightly to his left, so he was facing the shed. As Soyko came, he deflected the blade hand by striking Soyko's wrist with his left forearm while, at the same time, grabbing him behind the head. He squeezed hard at a patch of hair and held Soyko upright for an instant. Then he turned the smaller man's head so that he was facing the shed from about two feet away.

He tried to ram Soyko's head into the shed to knock him unconscious. Instead, he rammed the head into the vacant cavity where a window used to be. All that was left was the jagged row of broken glass along the bottom of the ledge, which now smiled up like a row of uneven teeth. As Streeter shoved Soyko's head toward the building, his exposed neck was forced into the glass. The jagged edge cut through Soyko's throat like it was paper, and he died instantly. He died on his feet, leaning into the shed. Streeter held the head in place as Soyko gave one monumental kick back with both legs. When his feet again hit the ground, his whole body slumped.

Panting furiously, Streeter let go and took a step back. Out of the corner of his eye he could see Story walking toward him. She was pale and her mouth formed a gaping circle. Still, her voice was calm.

"Is he dead?"

Streeter kept staring at Soyko, breathing hard, his pulse racing. "No. I think he's just resting." Then he backed up and looked squarely at her. "Of course he's dead."

"Who the hell is that?" She was bent forward, and her breath seemed labored. "I've seen him before."

"His name is Leo Soyko. Cooper's muscle."

"His what?"

"His enforcer. He's one of the guys who beat up McLean for Cooper. He's also one of the guys who tried to attack Ronnie Taggert, Cooper's girl. He's killed people, too. The cops are looking for him right now."

Story stared at him, still breathing through her mouth. "I didn't know about this Ronnie thing. Why didn't you tell me?"

Streeter walked out from between the car and the shed. He was still shaking but starting to calm down. He looked at his pants and saw a trace of Soyko's blood painted on the side like a design. "I didn't have all the details until this morning."

"How did he find us?"

"I don't have a clue."

They were standing close now. Streeter could hear someone yell from the front of the lot. He looked toward the sound and saw the enormous lot-owner walking toward them. Actually, the guy looked like he was trying to run, but it came off absurdly slow and he appeared to be quivering as he moved.

"Who is Jacky and what did Kovacs do to him?" Story pressed on, much of her composure regained.

Streeter looked at her again. "It seems that Kovacs is getting more violent. Look, we better go call the police. I'll fill you in later."

"I've got my cellular in my purse."

As she called 911, Streeter went back for another look at Soyko. He appeared almost comical now, bent over the shed window, his body draped limply down the side. It was like he had been kneeling, looking inside, and he fell asleep. But there was nothing comical about the blood drooling down the side of the shed.

"They'll be here in a few minutes." Her voice brought him back. "What do we tell them about what we were doing?"

He thought for a minute. "Tell them we were going to take pictures and I started looking around inside and found the box."

"We're not giving them the money." She hugged her purse closer to her body.

"No need to. Hand them the coke and they'll be plenty happy."

That satisfied her. They could see the yard owner coming closer down the aisle, but they still couldn't make out what he was saying.

"Streeter, are you all right?"

"I'm not sure." His breath was getting back to normal, his thoughts were clearing. "I guess this had to be done. Like taking out the garbage."

The thick sadness they'd felt when they first found the money returned to both of them now, but much more pronounced this time.

24

"Jesus Christ, big guy. You must be eating your Wheaties." Sergeant Haney shook his head as the paramedics pulled the wilting body of Leo Soyko off the shed and placed it carefully on the gurney. "You just saved the taxpayers a ton of money. A trial, and then keeping that bug at Cañon City for the next hundred years or so, woulda cost a fortune."

Streeter said nothing as he watched them zip Soyko up in the body bag. He had had to defend himself, but he still felt a little sick watching the body being wheeled away. This should end the killings. Story was standing about twenty feet away talking to a young black uniformed officer. Streeter had difficulty making them out in the growing darkness. Haney crushed a cigarette with his shoe and squinted at the cocaine baggie in his hand. With a nod, he signaled to another uniformed officer. The officer walked over, took the baggie, and listened to the sergeant for a minute. He smiled at Haney like they were sharing a private joke and then he walked away with the cocaine.

Haney turned to Streeter again. "You sure that's all the flake you found in there?" His tone was more resigned than accusatory.

Streeter nodded. "I can tell you in all honesty that that's all the drugs I found in the car."

"The guy that runs this place is pretty pissed off at you for lying about what you were doing out here. He wants us to check out your car, to see if you found anything else. Says that whatever you found in the Porsche belongs to him and you should turn it over."

"You want to look in the Porsche, you don't need my permission. You want to check out my car, be my guest. And if you want to give that slob all the cocaine, that's entirely up to you."

Haney grinned and thought for a moment. Then he continued, "No need for that. You say that's all you found, then that's all you found."

Just then, the black officer and Story walked up to them. "All done with her, Sarge," he said.

"Give her a ride home," Haney responded.

"I came with Mr. Streeter. I'd prefer to go home with him." Story's voice was even, but she was anxious to leave.

"He's going downtown with us," Haney said without looking at her. "We'll need to get a statement from him, and that could take quite a while."

She nodded and looked at Streeter. He was standing with his shoulders slouched like he was tired. "I need to talk to you before I leave. Is that all right with you, Sergeant?"

"Fine by me." Haney was still looking at the shed.

Streeter walked her to the police patrol car. It was new and white, one of those nondescript, aerodynamic makes. It looked like a giant bullet in an unribbed condom. He hated its utter lack of style.

"You're not in any trouble, are you?" she asked.

"Probably not. They have to make out a report, is all."

"Give me a call when you get home tonight," she said. "I'll let you know how much money you have coming."

"There didn't seem to be that much cash in the envelope. I can't believe there's enough there to make all this killing worthwhile."

"Believe me, Streeter, I had no idea it was going to be this dangerous. But it'll be worth it. This cash is just the tip of the iceberg. There's a lot of money yet to be found, and now I think I know how to get it. I promised you a big payoff if we got what we're after. With what we found today, that payoff's getting very close. I know where the real money is."

"Something in that other envelope?"

"Exactly."

"Did you know all along that there were two parts to our little hunt?"

"Not really. I hope you believe me about this. I've leveled with you for the most part all along. I didn't tell you everything all the time but I didn't really lie to you." She reached out with her right hand and gently brushed at some soot that was smeared on his arm. "I know you must think I lack strong values. Or any values. But believe me, Streeter, I didn't want all the pain, and I never wanted to see you get hurt. I certainly never expected you'd have to do something like that." She nodded toward the shed.

"This gets more bizarre all the time," he said as he rubbed the bridge of his nose. "Knowing you has been . . . How would I put it? Let's just say it's been a very high-concept relationship, Story."

"We're close, believe me. If we're on to what I think we are, you'll feel better about all this. Just give me a call when you get home. Are you okay with not being there when I count out the money?"

"What choice do I have? These guys'll need me for a couple of hours and you'll be alone with the envelope. I doubt that you'll wait until I get there to open it. I have no choice but to trust you now. Just try not to be somewhat less than totally candid, okay?"

"I will. Call me later. We have to get together tomorrow. Good luck."

"I could be really late with them. If I am, I'll call first thing in the morning."

"Whatever you think is best." With that she turned and got into the police car. Streeter walked back to Haney.

"Nice-looking woman," the sergeant observed. "You two going at it?"

"Going at it? What the hell is that to you?"

"Just curious." Haney smiled. "Lighten up, for Chrissakes. By tomorrow morning, you'll be a local hero. You're the guy who took out the big bad man. Did it unarmed, no less. When word of this gets around town, you'll be handling more ass than a proctologist."

"Haney, I had no idea you're such a romantic."

25

By the time Max Herman had pulled in front of Cooper's building that afternoon, he'd reached a state of delirious equilibrium. He was toxic to the bone after drinking and pounding cocaine up his nose for three days straight. He hadn't slept for more than a couple of fitful hours since he started. Nor had he eaten much other than an occasional handful from the giant Fritos bag—large, dipping size—on his back seat. He hadn't bathed or brushed his teeth in nearly seventy hours. From time to time he went to the bathroom, and he smelled of queasy perspiration and warm malt liquor. He was wearing the same crumpled blue jeans, red-and-orange Hawaiian shirt, and sandals that he'd slipped into the previous Sunday afternoon. His hair was pulled back in a filthy ponytail, and a pair of expensive aviators hid two runny and narrowing eyes that looked more like fleshy little bags.

Still, despite the three days of ferocious abuse, he felt in control, coherent, and focused. He used to call it drinking himself sober during those vicious all-nighters with the bowling team, when he'd go right from the bars to his plumbing shop in the morning.

"I know what I got to do," he'd told one of his burned-out drug buddies as they sat drinking in a downtown bar earlier that afternoon. "No doubt about that. I got me a thirty-eight-caliber Smith Lady. Nice little five-shot number. That prick Cooper's got to pay. Ruined my life, is all he did."

Max's battered mind drifted back over the events of the last couple of weeks.

"I spent so much time and money paying this asshole that my business went down the tubes," he continued bitterly. "You know the drill. Fucking suppliers won't give me no more credit. No credit, no product. No product, obviously, no cash flow. Next thing you know, no girlfriend. Bitch left me Monday. Back to her husband, of all things.

"And then, to really make it worse, I find out that this shit-bucket attorney is holding out a truly fine plea bargain on me just so he can run up his bills. I can see doing a deuce or so in Cañon City if I can hop to it and get it over with. Maybe give up a couple customers to the cops and get just probation, for Chrissake. But thanks to this lawyer my case is all dragged out and costing me a ton. I figure I spent nearly fifty-five large just to get hosed by this cocksucker."

"It ain't fair," his friend said, shaking his head in painful wisdom. "I'd take care a his shit. Right quick."

"Fuckin' A. My life is crumbling around me and I got to watch this douche bag sitting comfortable in his cushy office with that little fuck-puppet secretary taking care of him. And using my money to foot the bill." Then he lowered his voice. "I bought me the Smith and some bullets from this jive ass at a spade joint up in Five Points. I plan to settle this guy's hash today."

Indeed, Max had scraped together what cash he could, loaded up a couple of grams of coke and his clothes into the ratty old Porsche, and made his decision. He would visit Cooper at home, shove the gun down his throat, rob the place, and then . . . And then what? Max had no qualms about stomping on the state's drug laws, and he even threatened people from time to time.

But he'd never physically hurt anyone and he certainly wasn't a killer.

He'd improvise, he told himself in the car. The word came to him from deep in his foggy stupor. He liked the sound of it. Make it up as you go along. That suited him just fine, and he smiled idiotically. Yes sir, hang loose and improvise. Once he had the little schmuck begging for his life, Max figured, he'd automatically know what to do. With that, he took one last pull from a warm can of Colt .45 Malt Liquor, tossed it on the floor in front of him, and belched triumphantly at his steering wheel. He shoved the gun into his belt, the handle resting between his sweating gut and his shirt.

It took him nearly a minute to find and properly activate the door handle. When he stepped out of the car, his left foot caught on the floorboard and he stumbled forward. He landed hard on the street on both palms and both knees, cutting the former and bruising the latter.

"Mothafucka!" he yelled at the pavement. He staggered to his feet, looked back at the car door, and kicked it shut. "Cock, suck-fuck!" he screamed at the offending equipment. Both palms ached as he brushed tiny bits of sharp gravel from each. "Mo-tha," he mumbled in conclusion.

Denver Police Detectives Petronilo Padilla and Art Kovacs watched the pathetic show from their unmarked car across the street. They both laughed.

"Is he ever fucked up or what?" said Padilla, the driver, with the horrible complexion and the expensive clothes. "I'd like to have me a little talk with that guy. Bet he'd blow a point three on the Breathalyzer."

"I'll get his plate number," Kovacs said. "You keep an eye on where he goes. He takes off again, we'll call it in to Traffic. We ain't got no time now to nurse that moron, Petro."

"You ever see a Porsche with that much primer on it?" Padilla asked. "That tub of shit can't be worth as much as my Nissan."

"That sounds about right. Look, he's heading into our guy's building. What the fuck?"

"Maybe he's the man's driver." Padilla smiled at the thought. "Be some fun following those two coconuts around, huh?"

"Yeah. Some fun."

The two detectives had been sitting on Tom Cooper's remodeled loft building for the past six hours. The attorney had been holed up there for the past couple of hours, and Padilla and Kovacs were instructed to "ride his tail like bikini underwear" if he tried to leave. Sergeant Haney would be bringing the arrest warrants sometime around six or seven, and they would all go up to pop Cooper together. That was the official plan. It was now almost five, and Kovacs instantly didn't like the intrusion from the drunk.

Kovacs had had to scramble to get on the detail with Padilla. He had no idea Haney was so close to an arrest, and the news caused him to drastically change his plans. He called Cooper early that morning and told him part of his revised plan. He said the bust was going to hit tonight, so Cooper better move up his travel arrangements. The lawyer better have his cash and clothes all packed and ready that day. Then he instructed him to meet him in the basement garage of his building at precisely five.

Finally, Kovacs told Cooper, purely as a safety precaution, to be sure and bring his gun with him. That was where the plan shifted, and Mr. Cooper wouldn't find out about it until about four minutes past five, when the detective would put a couple slugs from his service revolver into the attorney's head. No way Artie Kovacs was going to let Thomas Cooper get hauled in and use what he knew about Jacky Romp and Doug Shelton against him as a plea-bargain chit. And he just couldn't take the chance that Cooper would successfully escape. Kovacs would wait until a couple of minutes before five, tell Padilla to go and check the upper floors, and then slip down to the garage to meet Cooper. With the lawyer bringing his own gun, it would be easy enough for Kovacs to claim the shooting was self-defense.

"Maybe you should hop up there and see if this goof's going after our guy," Kovacs suggested.

Padilla thought for a minute. "Naw. I mean, why? If they're going to leave together, we'll see it. They have to come out this way. And if he's going up there to cause the man some trouble, let him. This lawyer's one major-league asshole, from what Haney tells me."

As Kovacs looked off, he felt his stomach churn laboriously. A hot lick of heartburn bubbled up behind his sternum. He reached into his shirt pocket and pulled out another antacid. Placing it carefully on his tongue, he decided to wait a few minutes and then order Padilla to go check the floor. His whole plan still could easily unravel.

Thomas Hardy Cooper kept the front pages of both the Rocky Mountain *News* and the Denver *Post* with him that entire day. The headlines and stories about Jacky Romp were the best news he'd received in weeks. His world may have turned utterly sour, but he was still better off than that punk Jacky Romp. At least he was breathing, and as long as that continued, Cooper knew he had a shot at making things right. Now, he thought, if only Leo Soyko would meet the same fate, he'd be a happy man. The attorney assumed it was Kovacs who'd disposed of Romp. He further assumed that the brutal cop would now be looking for Soyko. Now, *that* would be a battle he'd pay to see.

Cooper had spent the morning closing out all three bank accounts, including the one for his corporation. Then he sold his Corvette to that dealership on South Broadway. He even managed to unload some stereo equipment and a new set of Pings, although he wondered if he might not miss the high-line golf clubs when he hit Mexico.

Now he was finishing up his packing and he had almost fifty-five thousand in cash for the trip south. He had hoped for more but he was in no position to bargain, especially after that call from Kovacs first thing in the morning. He figured that amount, plus the cash Ronnie brought, would give them a running start on a new life. He only hoped she would make their rendezvous. She was furious on the phone Monday night, an anger he couldn't understand. Then, when she called the next morning, she still wouldn't tell him where she was staying. She sounded remote and indifferent to their plans. When she didn't call today, Wednesday, he started to worry.

Cooper had barely slept the night before and he had been stuffing his nose with blow all day. Normally, he never touched the stuff, but he needed it to stay alert, and he knew he would need more to get him through the next couple days of driving. He had just over nine grams of cocaine left. That should do the trick, unless Ronnie got greedy in the car. Once they were safely to Guadalajara, he would sell his BMW and they'd set up a new life. He'd chosen Guadalajara because it is an inland, mid-sized capital of a Mexican state. He figured it was populated enough to get lost in and yet would not be as obvious a hiding place as the seaside resort towns.

At precisely four-forty-seven, he was ready to load up the car, check in with Kovacs downstairs, and split. Kovacs said he'd have a few bucks for Cooper from Doug's stash. Nowhere near the twenty grand he'd hoped for, but enough to make meeting the obnoxious police detective worthwhile. He grabbed his two suitcases and the metal briefcase with his life savings.

As he closed his loft door, a winded Max Herman, bleeding palms and all, was tromping up the stairs. When Cooper turned from his door and reached for his bags, Max wheezed around a hallway corner and into view. At first, Cooper didn't recognize him: Max was the last person he expected to see, and he still had on his dark aviators. But the lawyer recovered quickly.

"Maxwell. What, may I ask, are you doing here?" Cooper stood there with his bags in hand, about six feet from his visitor.

Max paused for a second, surprised to see the attorney before him. "Where are you going, may I ask, Mr. Shit Bird?" The sentence seemed to puzzle him for a second: he frowned deeply from behind his shades. Then he remembered his gun and struggled to pull it from his belt.

Cooper saw the small revolver and, understanding the gravity of the situation, took a step back. He realized that his Colt Python was in the trunk of his car, where it did him no good.

"Hold it right there, Mr. Bird Shit," Max yelled. Then, in a quieter voice, he added, "It's judgment day. Time to pay the piper." He had no idea what that meant, but it was the best he could do.

Cooper watched the gun wobble in Herman's hands. He calculated his options. He could try to talk some sense into the man, talk him out of the gun. Or he could try to verbally bully him into surrendering the weapon. Or, if Max was as far gone as he appeared, he could simply walk past him. He decided to invest a couple of minutes in conversation.

"What seems to be bothering you, Maxwell?"

Max took a minute to gather his thoughts. He suddenly felt nauseous and disoriented.

"The fuck you think is bothering me?" Actually, by now he was curious himself. All he could remember for sure was that Cooper had done something bad to him. He must have, or else why would Max be standing out there in the hallway with a gun on the man?

"I'm certain I have no idea." Cooper sensed that Max was running out of steam. He assumed that somehow the idiot had found out about what little work he'd put into the case. However, it might be no more complicated than that the imbecile was so wasted he was beyond all logic and was simply lashing out.

"You're certain," Max repeated as if he were considering a language foreign to him. He noticed his gun was pointing to a spot just in front of Cooper's feet, so he pulled it back up to aim at his chest. Random thoughts from the car came back to him. "Improvise," he shouted. "You sold me out. I'll improvise."

Cooper now felt relatively safe. He thought that the only real danger was if the gun went off by accident. He decided to wait until the barrel sagged down again and then walk past Max.

"I would suggest that you go home and get some sleep," Cooper said in his most soothing voice. "Then come see me at my office first thing in the morning. I'm certain we can straighten out whatever it is that's troubling you."

Armed or not, Cooper believed that Max Herman by now was manageable.

Max considered what Cooper said. His legs twitched briefly. He was dying to take a leak. He felt he had lost control of the situation and he feared he would soon lose control of his bladder. He took a deep breath and yelled, "Not good enough, Mr. Screw-Over. We settle this now." Settle what? He struggled to remember.

This is nonsense, Cooper thought. "Maxwell, please lower your weapon and go home. We'll iron this all out in the morning."

At first, there was silence. Then, as the gun barrel slowly lowered again, the clotted, nasal sound of a snore came from Max's open mouth. He was, literally, asleep on his feet.

Cooper rolled his eyes and in an even tone inquired, "Maxwell?"

The snoring sound only grew, and by now the gun was pointed almost directly at Max's own feet. Cooper had wasted enough time. He adjusted the bags in his hands and took two steps forward. He was about three feet away and just off to the right when Max jolted awake. Instinctively, he lifted the gun. All he saw for certain was the gleam of light from Cooper's brushed-metal briefcase. He still was almost asleep when he actually squeezed the trigger. Twice. The gun went off like a little cannon in the narrow hallway. Cooper's face looked stunned as the two slugs burned into his upper chest. His tongue shot out and his eyes froze wide open as his head shot back. He fell dead to the floor with his bags still firmly in his grip.

Max looked down at the lawyer and slowly realized what he'd done. That realization sobered him up plenty. Immediately. He looked down the hall in both directions but he was unable to move. He could hear footsteps pounding up the open stairwell.

Even that couldn't prompt him to move. As the sounds came to the top of the stairs, he finally started to backpedal away from Cooper. By the time Kovacs and Padilla came off the stairs and got a full view of what happened, Max had turned and was running away.

"Freeze," Kovacs screamed.

Both he and Padilla had their guns aimed at the fleeing figure. Automatically, Max turned back toward them and squeezed off a quick round. The bullet landed harmlessly in the ceiling, almost immediately over his own head, but it caused both detectives to drop to their knees. They opened fire from about fifty feet away. Miraculously, Max was able to run a few more steps, to where the hallway took a sharp right. He was gone before the officers got back on their feet.

"Follow him," Kovacs commanded Padilla. "I'll go back to the lobby and cut him off when he gets there."

"Right," his partner yelled as he ran down the hall. When he got to the corner where Max had just disappeared, he stopped and leaned his back against the wall, his gun clutched immediately in front of him with both hands. He inched his head around the corner. When he didn't see anyone, he ran down that hall.

Kovacs leaned over and glanced at Cooper for a second. He bent down to verify what he already knew—that the lawyer was dead. Next, he picked up the metal briefcase and opened it. When he saw the cash, he whistled lightly to himself and smiled. He closed it and glanced around the hall. Then he spotted a utility closet and went to it. He opened it and put the case inside, under a small bench. He'd be back for it later. As he shut off the closet light and closed the door, he heard three shots being fired from the downstairs lobby. He ran down the stairwell to verify something else he already knew—namely, that Padilla had killed the drunk.

Kovacs couldn't believe his good fortune. First the wino takes care of Cooper, and now Padilla takes care of the wino. For the first time in weeks, his stomach didn't feel like it was about to explode.

When Streeter walked into his apartment that night, it was almost twelve-thirty. Too late to call Story, and he was too tired to care about what was in the envelopes he'd pulled from the Porsche. He had given his oral statement to three different detectives at police headquarters and then went through a long written statement. All the while he kept picturing Soyko's body slumped over the shed and hearing the grunt from the man's death kick. The bounty hunter thought he'd feel deeply guilty and make all sorts of connections between this death and the one at Western Michigan all those years ago. But, strangely, he didn't. Soyko was one useless piece of garbage who had hurt a lot of people. A little bit of death didn't look half bad on the guy.

Streeter almost was too tired to check his voice mail, but he grabbed the phone in Frank's office right before he headed upstairs. There was one message. It was from Ronnie Taggert.

"I was watching the news and it looks like you've had a busy day." Her voice sounded soft, and Streeter could picture her in her hotel bed getting ready to fall asleep. "My hero. You did a good job on Soyko.

"But you weren't the lead story tonight," she continued, sounding more tired. "I don't know if you saw it, but Tom Cooper's dead. They said on the television that it was a pissed-off client who shot him to death. Then a Mexican cop killed the client. There's been so much going on the last few days. Unbelievable. It happened late this afternoon, about the same time I gather you were taking care of Leo Soyko. I was supposed to meet your friend Carey tomorrow but I don't think that's necessary now. Everyone he wanted to talk about is dead. So I'm going to bed, and then I'm leaving Colorado first thing in the morning. I've got serious thinking to do. This is goodbye. Thanks for the help and—who knows?—maybe we'll run into each other somewhere down the road. I might end up coming back here eventually."

Streeter sat there and stared at the phone for a long time. Then he stood up and walked upstairs to his loft. So much to think about, and he was so damned tired. As far as Cooper was concerned, it didn't shock him. The only surprise was that it wasn't Kovacs who pulled the trigger. He'd sort it all out after he got some sleep.

26

"What in the hell were you doing this morning?" Frank asked Streeter as the two stood out on the front stoop of the church that Thursday afternoon. "It sounded like you were throwing them damn weights against the garage door."

Streeter only nodded. He woke up early and he felt so jazzed that he went to the weight room and pumped serious iron for almost two hours. Later, he called Story and they agreed to meet at the church at four o'clock. She told him that there was just over thirty-one thousand in the envelope but said not to worry. "Then we'll be taking a little drive this afternoon and get the real payoff," was how she put it.

"I didn't sleep all that terrifically well last night," Streeter explained to Frank as they waited for her.

"I don't doubt that." Frank shook his head. "I'm surprised you slept at all, for crying out loud, after that business yesterday at the junkyard. It was me, I'd still be smashed. You feeling any better?"

"It was no picnic. But maybe now it's all finally over. I talked to Carey a little while ago and he filled me in on that shootout at Cooper's apartment. This town's turning into another Tombstone. And I don't mean the pizza. It sounded like the damned O.K. Corral over at Cooper's yesterday. Enough's enough."

"You got that right. I see by the paper your friend Kovacs was involved. Another coincidence?"

"I can't figure that one out. Carey told me that Art Kovacs didn't fire a shot. And there's no way he could have set it up like that, to have the other guy, the client, do it. I don't know what to think. Carey said that the second cop, Padilla, killed the guy that shot Cooper. He said Kovacs is clear on the whole thing. But I still can't believe I've been barking up the wrong tree with him. Coincidence, my ass. I have a feeling we haven't seen the last of Artie boy."

"For your sake, I hope you're wrong. What's next between you and the little lady with the money?"

"That's what I'll find out when she gets here. She said we have one more stop and we're home free, whatever that means. We found a little bit of money in the car but she said there's a lot more waiting for us."

"This is her now." Frank nodded toward the street.

Story's Audi pulled up in front of the church. She parked and got out, wearing a flower-print dress and sunglasses. Streeter had never seen her look better. Or happier. She smiled at both of them as she approached. "Gentlemen. Out getting a little sun, are we? How're you feeling, Streeter?"

"Better than our old friend Tom Cooper."

"Isn't that something? It looks like yesterday took care of a lot of things. I hate to see anyone get hurt, but Cooper died like he lived. So did his two associates."

"That they did," Streeter said.

"I hope to hell you kids are finally out of the line of fire," Frank said.

"It looks that way," Story said. "Can we go inside and talk?"

Streeter nodded toward the door. "Mind if Frank sits in?"

"That's fine with me," she said.

"This place is turning into a damned war room," Frank said

as they settled into his office. He took his usual spot in the big chair behind the desk.

Story sat in front of the desk, next to Streeter, and pulled an envelope from her purse. It was the smaller package they took from the Porsche. She also pulled out a thick wad of cash and handed it to the bounty hunter.

"There's about ten thousand there. Your third of what we found."

"Not a bad day's work," Frank said.

Streeter set it on the table, barely looking at it. "What else do you have?" He nodded to the package in Story's hand.

"This is what we've been after all along. Maybe I should have guessed it, but that's hindsight. We've been looking for clocks."

"Great," Streeter said. "Another couple of clocks. Now, that definitely makes everything worthwhile. You're telling me Doug left a few more clocks?"

"A lot more. These are receipts for thirty-seven of the stupid things. They're all worth about the same as the one he left in the townhouse. Or more. If they're in good shape, I place the total value at close to half a million dollars."

Frank let out a loud whistle. "Holy moly. That much for some clocks? What are they made out of? Gold?"

She turned to face him across the desk. "You'd think so. When I sold that other one, I got a short course on how valuable these things are. I had a hunch Doug may have bought more, but I had no idea he bought this many or that some of them would be so valuable. A couple of them go for almost thirty thousand each.

"Judging from the receipts, he bought all but a couple of them when he lived in Boulder. Before I met him. Some of these purchases are ten years old. Clocks." She shook her head. "That would explain his interest in the art museum. They've had clock exhibits there. It also fits in with his interest in mechanical things. He may even have tried to repair or restore some of them. God, I hope not. Not with his mechanical abilities. But at least he would be able to tell what kind of shape they were in when he bought them."

She pulled out some of the receipts. "They're all named after clockmakers and such. Look, Streeter. Here's one that's a William Webb Wellington. That must have been that reference to Webb in his checkbook. We thought it was the mayor. This is where all Doug's extra cash must have gone. Judging from what he paid for them and what they're worth now, that man knew his clocks. I talked to my dealer friend this morning and ran some of these by him. He told me what they're worth now, and I'll tell you, Doug made out all right. The good part is that we can sell them through my friend, and even with his commission, we'll still end up with over four hundred thousand. Maybe more."

Streeter looked at the receipts in silence. Then he said, "I thought it was artwork. Collectibles like paintings and antiques are the perfect investment for a drug dealer. A great way to hide assets. Everything is cash and there's practically no way to trace it for taxes or by the police. That is, if you buy at the right price, tuck them safely away, and then know when to sell them. Clocks make sense."

"We've got it made," Story said.

"Yeah, right," Streeter interrupted. "I take it you have them in your trunk?"

"Of course I don't have them." Then her voice softened. "Not yet, anyhow."

"My next question is fairly obvious."

"Yes, it is. And the answer is, Wyoming. They're up in Wyoming."

"What the hell they doing up there?" Frank shot in.

Streeter sat up. "They're with his mother. I wanted to talk to her all along and you kept saying no."

"I didn't say no." Story narrowed her eyes. "I just said I didn't think she would have anything. But now that I know what we're after, it makes sense. Assuming Doug trusted her, which he must have, her farm would be the perfect place to keep them. She probably had them under her homeowner's insurance. No one would think of looking up there."

"You know for sure she has them?" Streeter asked.

"There were a couple of letters from her in with the receipts. She talked about the whole situation. She's been keeping them in her basement and in the barn. The last one was bought about four years ago, and the clocks were all safe and sound at that time."

"So now what?" Streeter asked. "We call her and let her know we're coming and then rent a U-Haul and go get them? You think she'll just hand them over like that?"

"Hardly. Gail Shelton is one tough, self-centered old broad. Like I told you, Doug was kind of afraid of her. When you meet her, you'll see why. Plus, she can't stand me. But I talked to my attorney this morning and she said that I have every legal right to them. Doug's will says I get everything he had. My guess is, it's his way of telling the old lady what he really thought of her—otherwise she would be a beneficiary. I've got the will in my car, and I figure with a big guy like you along she'll have no choice but to turn them over."

"Right." Streeter frowned at Frank. "She gives me any grief, I kick the hell out of her. I hate to be negative, but what if she's already sold them? That could leave us basically fornicated, if you pardon my language. She's had months to do it, and that would be the smart move."

"Then we've got problems. If they're gone, we'll have to take her to court for the money. That could drag on forever. Let's just keep our fingers crossed."

"And you want to go now?"

"No point in waiting."

"You two think it's safe?" Frank asked. "I mean, the way this thing is going, who knows what's waiting for you up there. Kovacs may not be the one, but someone spray-painted your little puppy and shot at this place."

Story stood up impatiently. "I can't worry about that now. That's my inheritance and I intend to go get it. I have every right to it and I'm not going to let anyone stop me. I'm going now. With or without you, Streeter."

He stood up, too. He took the cash she gave him and slid it across the desk at Frank. "Put that in a safe place for me." Then he turned to Story. "We'll take your car, but I'm going to bring my thirty-eight along, just in case. I don't know if we're out of danger yet or not, but I don't want to get caught without a gun ever again."

27

Detective Arthur Ernest Kovacs certainly had done more than his share of twisted and degrading things for money over the years. But he figured sleeping with Gail Shelton easily had to have been the worst. Just the thought of it made him blink as he drove. Gail might be only nine years older than him, but she always seemed more like a maiden aunt. Too much of that Lutheran Bible guilt, he reasoned, made her look ancient in the morning. Like a stack of dry firewood next to him in bed.

Every trip up Wyoming State Highway 211, just north of Cheyenne, felt more like a forced death march to Kovacs. Thank God, this is the last one. Payday, and then no more dealing with the farm hag. Since he first met her, at Doug's funeral, Kovacs had been sucking up to Gail and turning on what he passed off as charm. Between that and laying on plenty of the old baloney about how he'd see to it that no one grabbed her precious clocks, he was able to talk her into a nice chunk of the revenue from them.

Now Gail finally had received her last check for the clock sales from a broker in Salt Lake City. Kovacs figured his half to be about a quarter of a million. Throw in the fifty or sixty thousand from Cooper's metal briefcase, next to him on the car seat, and his pension, and the officer figured to hit retirement in the approximate vicinity of solid comfort. God knows, he had never saved more than a couple hundred bucks on his own.

After tonight, no more worrying about Moffatt, either. Once he got the cash in hand no one could touch it. The sun was sitting low in the west as he pulled up the driveway to Gail Shelton's ancient house. The dump always reminded him of Ma and Pa Kettle's farm. No more of her endless ramblings about how she grew up in this pile of bricks and boards, he thought. No more bullshit flattery. And maybe, finally, no more eruptions and fiery spasms from his tortured insides. With the money in hand, Kovacs figured, it was young broads and solid food from here on out.

"Gracious, Arthur, you look like you've been sleeping in a Dumpster for the past few weeks," Gail greeted him when he walked into the kitchen. "I suppose you'll want a drink. You always do. Well, you know where it's located." She nodded toward the cabinet over the sink. "You better make it a strong one. You and I have to talk about a few things."

Gail had been pacing the decrepit kitchen when Kovacs entered. The room hadn't been remodeled in over thirty years, and it always smelled stale, with a hint of cooked onions. Heavy black metal pots hung ominously on the wall like medieval bondage equipment.

Gail was grim this evening. She knew that the upcoming confrontation was going to take all of her resolve. But it had to be done. She desperately wanted this mulish, sadistic cop out of her life, and she had no intention of parting with the kind of money she knew he expected.

"Who shit in your oatmeal?" Kovacs saw no need to hide his thoughts. "Can't you try and be pleasant? Just once? We should be celebrating."

"Please, just get your drink. I think it's time we both cut all the malarkey and leveled with each other. What's in the briefcase?" she asked, pointing to Cooper's metal case, which he'd lugged in with him.

"This is something I picked up from Doug's attorney. It's a long story, but the bottom line is, I got a little something extra for my efforts down there to Denver. There's cash in here, but there's still enough room for what you owe me."

"That's what we have to talk about."

With that, she turned and headed into the adjoining living room to sit on the old couch. That room wasn't much more pleasant than the kitchen, but at least the onion smell was less pronounced.

Kovacs reached over the sink and grabbed the lone bottle of discount bourbon stored there. As he poured a double, neat, into a glass advertising a local gas station in loud colors, he wondered why Gail was in such an angry mood. She was never what you'd call cheerful, but this was the first time she'd actually insulted him. He took a long pull on his drink and then headed to the living room, where he sat down in a stuffed chair facing the couch.

"There some problem with your guy in Salt Lake?" he asked. "That what got you in this mood? Didn't you get the checks this week?"

"The checks are in and the transaction is complete," she answered formally. Gail ran a hand through her wiry gray hair and frowned. "But we have to talk about the finances. You see, Arthur, it's not going to be the way we decided originally. I've made some changes."

"You made changes, huh? I don't remember you asking me about that. What might those changes be?"

She looked at him for a moment and then reached over to the end table and grabbed a rumpled brown paper bag. After studying it, she tossed it to him. Kovacs caught it and looked inside. There were rolls of twenties and fifties, but it didn't look like it amounted to any two hundred fifty thousand dollars' worth.

"This looks a little light, Gail. How much did you get for the clocks? The final grand total, I mean."

"To be honest, something just under five hundred twenty thousand."

"So I should be looking at what in here? Maybe two hundred sixty. Is that what I'm looking at, Gail?"

"No, it is not. There is exactly one hundred and twenty-five thousand in there. And that's the change I referred to." She sat back as if to indicate that was the end of the discussion.

"You got any more bags around here for me, or is this your idea of being clever?" He shifted impatiently in his seat.

"Don't act like a child. That is a lot of money."

Kovacs put his drink down on the floor between his legs and set the money bag next to it. Then he got up and took a step toward Gail.

"Enough of the crap, you old cow. I put up with a lot from you these past few months, but I did it for half of what those clocks were worth. That was our agreement. I had to deal with a ton of shit down there in Denver to keep people away from this money and keep your saggy ass safe. I did things that you don't need to know about but I kept my word. And, as ugly as it got down there, it was nowhere near as bad as what I had to do up here. Sex with you, hell, it was like doing it with a pile of old newspapers."

"I'll just bet you know what that's like, too," she shot back. "Look who's complaining about sex, will you? I deserve a medal for getting a rise out of that alcoholic roll of blubber you call a body."

His eyes widened in rage, and he drew his hand back a few inches like he was going to hit her.

"That's just great," she screamed. "Go ahead and hit me. Is that how you prove you're a man? I can't believe I ever saw anything in you. Your little act about caring for me was so obviously false. Such a lie. And all that garbage about keeping our affair a secret. Like it was our own little world we were building here. You were ashamed of me, is all."

She was crying by the time she finished.

"You got that right!"

"Now that I've got the money"—she looked up—"I don't need your 'protection' anymore. So I'm cutting your commission in half to compensate me for all the humiliation you've caused. Men have never been much more than trouble in my life. First that useless husband of mine, and then those two sons. Philip, poor child of God, will need to be in a home for the rest of his life. And the other one was nothing more than some kind of homo drug dealer.

"But at least his money will pay for Philip's care. Poor Philip, he's so lost. God knows, he's so bad off. This is my chance to make sure he'll be taken care of, and I am certainly not about to give that money up to some broken-down booze hound. You can stand there and yell all you want to, but that money's in a trust for Philip, and there's no way on earth you'll touch a penny of it. Just take what's in the bag, guzzle your drink, and then leave. And if you ever come back on my property, I'll have you arrested for trespassing and assault. Don't think I can't do it, either. I've lived up here all my life and I've got plenty of clout with the local law."

Kovacs took a step back, stunned by what she said. Trust funds, no more money. He couldn't believe it.

"You gotta be shittin' me. That money's around here some-where and you better produce roughly a hundred thirty-five thousand, right now, or you'll regret it. Believe me. I ain't screwing around here."

"You 'ain't screwing around here.' What utter intelligence," Gail said as she rose from the couch to face him. "You're so coarse, Arthur. So dumb, too. Do I have to use puppets or some-thing to get through to you? There is no more money. It's gone. It's in a fund in Laramie. That's where Philip is. You can't get at it, I can't get at it. Now, take this money and leave. You're not making out so poorly. I'm sure it'll keep you in bourbon and pornography for the few miserable years you have left."

Rage gnawed at Kovacs' innards like a starving rat. He felt

wildly nauseous, and the burn in his chest seemed as though he was having a heart attack. He shot both hands out and caught Gail squarely on her shoulders. The push knocked her backward hard into the couch, and the momentum of that caused her to almost bounce back to her feet.

"You bitch," he hissed. "You spent my money on that retarded kid. Who the fuck do you think you're dealing with?"

There was genuine terror in Gail's eyes when he drew his forty-four from its shoulder holster under his sport coat. Before she could say another word, the detective balled up the heavy gun in his fist and drove it into her face. He did it three more times, smashing the left side of her head and face. As she lay there, Kovacs thought for sure she was dead. Not that he cared.

Slowly, he wiped the bloody gun on the couch next to Gail. Then he went into the bathroom and cleaned it off better. When he was finished he scrubbed his hands. Back in the living room, he grabbed the bag with the money. Gail moaned and turned slightly on the couch, but the policeman barely noticed. Instead, he went to the kitchen and put the bag on top of Cooper's briefcase on the table. He took a long pull straight from the bourbon bottle and decided to go through the entire house. That bitch had to have part of the money around here somewhere, he reasoned. Kovacs wasn't leaving until he found it. Then he would make sure the old lady never told the local law what happened.

28

"So, Streeter, how is it that a stallion like you never got married?" Story asked as they drove up State Highway 211 toward Gail Shelton's house.

He smiled. "Stallion? Never been married? If only you knew. You're looking at one of the most frequently married men in Colorado. I've made the trip down the aisle on numerous occasions, with a couple of near misses."

"Really?" She glanced at him for a second. "How many trips are we talking about?"

"More than I care to admit."

"Why not tell me?"

"We'll be at the farmhouse in less than fifteen minutes and it would take a lot longer than that to run down my matrimonial history. We'd need a cross-country trip." Then, after a short pause, "Okay, I've been married four times and I've been engaged twice, make that three more times."

"Very impressive. You could practically have your own segment on *Oprah* with that kind of numbers. I trust they weren't all as cheap as that blonde working for Tom Cooper you were so interested in. Honestly, what do men see in something like that, Streeter?"

He shrugged. "She had a lot of appeal, Story. I think there was more there than you realize. And that's the second time you've acted jealous of her. I'm going to start thinking you're interested in me if you're not careful."

"Eat your heart out, big boy." She was quiet for about a mile and then, "One question. How come you couldn't make it work with any of those women? It certainly couldn't have been the woman's fault every time."

"You're right about that. It wasn't always their fault. I'm not sure if there was one reason they all failed. Let's just say that I'm not particularly good at long-term projects. I'm better at starting the fire than at keeping it going. That and my selection process tends to be flawed."

"Does that bother you? I mean, wouldn't you like to go the distance with a woman eventually?"

"I don't give it too much thought anymore." After a pause, he added, "Yeah, it would be nice to make it work." He studied her profile. "Now I have one question for you. Why do you always have to run things and have everything your way?"

"Technically, that's two questions."

"I'm not particularly good at math, either. Look, I don't want to pick a fight, but at times you take being headstrong to a new level. Why?"

Story seemed to be genuinely considering his words. "I have a friend who's a psychologist and she thinks that being aggressive is my way of keeping people off balance and at a distance. She thinks I'm afraid that, if I give up even a little bit of control, then I feel like I won't have any control at all. She said that, deep underneath, I'm not very secure."

Streeter continued to study her face as she spoke. Sometimes, he noticed, when she wasn't giving orders, she had a soft vulnerability that gave him an excited little twitch in the pit of his stomach.

"What do you think about that?" he asked.

"It's more probable than I care to admit. I've always been like that. When I was little, I used to order everyone around so much that my dad would call me 'sir.' Just to tease me. He told me a while ago that he still doesn't like when I do that. Parents." She shrugged. "How do you get along with your parents?"

He didn't say anything at first. "They've both been dead for years. My mother died when I was a senior in high school. Cancer. My father died a couple of years later. Cancer, too, although he had other health problems. He was a heavy drinker. Very heavy. I never knew either of them when I was an adult."

"Look, here's the ancestral home of Douglas Shelton," Story said. "We're here. Time to meet the dragon lady."

Gail's house stood off to the right, about one hundred yards ahead, quietly drooping in the sunset.

"I take it Doug wasn't much for home improvements."

"He didn't do a thing up here since he moved out after high school."

As they pulled into the drive, they noticed a tan Ford station wagon, circa late 1970s, with Colorado plates, nestled up near the side of the building. There was also a new white pickup truck with Wyoming plates off to the left, away from the house. They pulled up behind the Ford and parked.

"Looks like she's got company," Streeter said as he pulled his thirty-eight out of the glove compartment. "I'll just take this in with us in case it's someone who doesn't like me."

"Do you think it could be Kovacs?"

"That would be a coincidence and you know I don't believe in coincidences. Probably just a friend or something like that. But I lugged this thing all the way up from Denver. I might as well take it another twenty feet."

Kovacs was digging through Gail's bedroom closet when he heard the back doorbell ring. The bedroom was the last room he had to check. It was becoming clear that Gail had meant it when she said there was no money around. At first, he thought of just ignoring the doorbell, but then he figured, if it was one of Gail's loopy farmer friends, they would know the old lady was home, and be suspicious if no one answered.

As he walked through the living room, he noticed that Gail had shifted on the couch. Still, she seemed to be asleep. Walking through the kitchen, he gave his forty-four Magnum a quick pat in its shoulder holster. He moved quietly to the back door. Through the thin lace curtains he could see at least one figure standing out in the near darkness of the enclosed sun porch. Then he saw another, larger figure next to the first.

The detective put one hand inside his jacket on his gun as he pressed the light switch. When the yellowish overhead light hit Streeter and Story, Kovacs didn't immediately recognize them. But as he opened the back door, he remembered who they were and pulled out his gun.

It was at about that moment that Streeter made out the detective as well. He automatically reached around to the small of his back, where he had jammed his pistol under his shirt, between his skin and his pants.

Kovacs pushed open the heavy metal screen door and stepped quickly out and down the one step onto the porch. His gun was drawn and aimed at Story, who was the closer of the two visitors. By now, Streeter had his gun out, and he focused the barrel squarely at the cop's profile. Both men were close enough to their targets—five feet away at the most—that they couldn't miss.

Story let out a crisp scream when she saw the gun aimed at her. She spoke first. "Put that damned thing down," she yelled at the man coming out of the house. Then, almost as an after-thought, she added, "Shoot him, Streeter. Do something."

"You shoot me, I shoot her," Kovacs said without taking his eyes off of Story.

"Just take it easy, Kovacs. Put the gun down. Don't even think of shooting. Put it down or you're dead."

"If I'm dead, so is she. I swear it."

The three of them stood under the dingy light in utter silence for a moment. Kovacs was directly in front of the screen door, holding his gun at about shoulder level, with both hands. Story was in front of the door as well but about six feet from it, and Streeter stood off to the right side, a few feet away. He was in the same firing stance as the detective. The porch had an organic smell to it, part old apples and part litter box. There didn't seem to be enough air for all three of them.

"Looks like we got us your basic Mexican standoff out here," Kovacs said with a fair amount of crude irony. His voice had that trained cop control in it. "There's got to be some way we can work this out without two people getting killed."

"What the hell are you doing here?" Streeter asked. "Where's the woman who lives in this house?"

"You mean Gail? Oh, she's taking a nap. I think it'll be a long one, too. So what the fuck are you doing here?"

"We're here to pick up something that belongs to her," Streeter nodded to Story, although Kovacs wasn't watching him.

"If you're looking for them old clocks, I'm afraid you're too late. They're all gone. Sold. Every one of them."

Story, who until now had remained pale and quiet, suddenly stiffened.

"You sold my clocks?" she demanded. "You can't do that. That was my inheritance. Shoot him, Streeter."

"Relax, sweetie." Kovacs smiled at her outburst. "You're quite a little firecracker, aren't you? The old lady sold them, I didn't."

"How'd you get into all this?" Streeter asked. He could feel his shoulders tiring from holding the big gun with both hands.

"None of your business." Kovacs thought he heard a faint rustle from the kitchen behind him and he shifted his eyes quickly. He wanted to turn around, but he knew if he did that he would lose his bead on Story, and Streeter could shoot him. "The real problem for you is, how are you going to get out of all this?"

The question hung in the thick night air for a just a few seconds. No one actually heard anything before the back door exploded open. But when it did, the door's heavy, sharp edge hit

Kovacs squarely in the middle of the back of his head. It pushed him forward, toward Story a couple of steps, and stunned him. Disoriented, he looked back at the door and saw Gail Shelton stalking out of it. The caked blood on the side of her head made her look like a zombie, but she was moving fast and spitting anger. One of the black cast-iron skillets from the kitchen wall was in her hands, and she was lifting it over her head and off to one side. Kovacs looked down at his gun in confusion, and before he could completely reorient himself Gail let out a scream.

"You rotten slime," she hollered as she brought the enormous skillet across the front of her, driving the edge of it deeply into the perplexed cop's cheek and crushing the bone. "You lousy son of a bitch."

Immediately after that, the stunned and by now badly bleeding detective felt Story's fist land on the left side of his head. She had walked around to that side, between him and Streeter, when Gail came flying out the door. Story let out a curse as she swung and landed another punch in almost the identical spot.

Because Story was in his line of fire, Streeter couldn't shoot. From somewhere in his fog, Kovacs knew that he was in trouble. Again, he looked down at the huge gun he was holding with his right hand at about waist level. He brought it up a few inches and when the barrel was aimed in Gail's general direction he pulled the trigger. Fortunately for her, she was just lifting the skillet across her chest for another swipe at the man in front of her. The gun went off like a rocket and a shrill flash of sparks exploded on the skillet as the bullet ricocheted off of it and out into the night air.

Gail's eyes narrowed in further rage at the effrontery of the shot and she lowered the skillet to waist level. She and Kovacs stared at each other for just an instant, and then the farm woman, with both hands firmly on the handle, brought the utensil up and out squarely at him. It struck the forty-four just as the detective was about to squeeze the trigger again. The momentum of the skillet forced the gun upward and eventually back, till the barrel was quickly moving toward Kovacs' chin.

Sadly for him, that was when he fired off another round. The gun was still moving up and back when the flash of the bullet hit Kovacs just below his lower lip. The simmering lead kept flying upward, through his brain and out the top of his head, taking a surprisingly large chunk of his balding scalp with it.

He fell into a fast heap at the feet of both Gail and Story. Streeter had moved forward by now, and he kept his gun on Kovacs even though half his head was blown away. Streeter then kicked the forty-four away from the body. Story instinctively backed off a step or two, but Gail held her ground.

"That man never gave me credit for nothing," Gail said as she stared at the body. "He tried to kill me in there. He always underestimated me."

"He'll never make that mistake again." Streeter looked up at her on the porch step. "Neither will we."

29

"He seems more sad than anything." Story finally defined Kovacs' gaze to no one in particular. "The top of his head's nearly blown off. You'd think he'd be more surprised or pained or something, wouldn't you? You'd think he'd look different than just sad."

Tears flowing down her checks, she turned to Streeter with the question. He grabbed her gently by her shoulder with one hand and pulled her toward him. Then he looked down at Gail Shelton, who had sat on the stoop immediately after dropping the skillet.

"Are you okay?" he asked. "What happened to your head?"

"Oh, don't worry about me. Just take care of that delicate little thing. After all, she's crying. I'm only bleeding." Gail turned away, obviously disgusted.

"I'll call for help in a minute," Streeter answered.

"That would be a good idea," Gail said. "I've got the headache of the century."

"What *was* he doing here?" Streeter nodded down to Kovacs. Story wiped at her cheeks with the back of one hand and looked over to Gail as well. Her tears had stopped.

"Prince Charming? He was my knight in shining armor." She looked down at the detective and said no more.

"What do you mean?" Story asked.

Gail looked up at her like she'd just asked for a handout. She still said nothing. Finally, Streeter repeated the question. "What you mean by Prince Charming?"

Gail shrugged. "He got to me right after the funeral and told me how he and Doug had become good friends. He told me so many things about Doug, personal things, that I believed him. He knew Doug left stuff with me that was valuable and that there could be people coming after it. He said they would want to take the things away from me. He said he would see to it that that didn't happen. I bought it all. Hook, line, and the whole enchilada."

"You mean people like me?" Story insisted. "The people who own the clocks? People who Doug left everything to in his will? People like that?"

Gail looked back at her and actually spoke to her this time. "I didn't know he had a will. I just assumed he didn't have anything much but the clocks. If they were yours, why didn't you come up for them sooner?"

Story blushed, and it was Streeter who answered. "We had no idea where they were until recently. Or even what they were. Listen, can we go inside and call the police? I wouldn't mind a drink of water, either."

Gail got up and took one last look at the dead cop. Then she nodded for them to follow her into the kitchen. When they got inside, Streeter went to the sink for a drink of water and the two women sat down at the kitchen table without looking at each other. Tension was as thick in the air as the cooked-onion smell.

"That fella out on the porch isn't going anywhere, and my little headache can keep," Gail said when Streeter sat down. "We should really have us a talk before any police get out here."

"That's a good idea," Story said. "Kovacs said that you already sold my clocks. Is that true?"

"Yes. They're all gone, and there's no way to get them back.

Sold to collectors here and all the way to England, I'm told."

"Then it would appear you owe me money." Story was looking directly into Gail's eyes, but the older woman didn't flinch. "A great deal of money. I've got receipts for thirty-seven of those precious clocks of his, and they showed Doug Shelton is the owner. And I have a will that gives me everything that belonged to him. That means those clocks. According to my calculations, you had better come up with several hundred thousand dollars or prepare to spend your twilight years in court."

Gail considered that for a moment and then leaned across the table toward Story. "Sweetie, you can take me to court or you can grab that gun of his out there and put it to my head. But I don't have anywhere near the kind of money you're looking for. It's come and gone and that's all there is to it."

Story practically jumped out of her chair. "How dare you? Those didn't belong to you. You know how Doug felt about you. He couldn't stand you. He never said a kind word about you."

"I sure as hell didn't know any of them belonged to you. I was his mother. His family needed that money and that's where it went. To take care of Philip. That poor child's treatment is more important than you getting new clothes and a few new toys. Besides, judging from those last few letters I got from him, he wasn't too fond of you, either."

Story's mouth was just opening in response when Streeter stood up himself, holding out his open hand.

"Enough. This guy didn't seem too nuts about either of you, and I can't say as I really blame him. Standing around here screaming at each other like a couple of spoiled kids isn't going to get us anywhere. And we've got to call somebody about Prince Charming out there pretty soon." He shook his head. "Maybe we can settle this fast and first." He turned to Gail. "Exactly where is the money now? Have you spent all of it?"

"In a manner of speaking. I set up a blind trust for Doug's brother, Philip, over in Laramie. He'll be in a home for the rest of his life. He can't take care of himself. The rest of it, just under thirty-five grand, well, I've ordered some remodeling for this old barn. I put most of it in a down payment to the contractor. I plan on fixing this place up and then selling. That takes care of all of it except for his share." She nodded toward the back sun porch.

Both of her guests looked in that direction in unison.

"His share?" Story asked.

"We had an agreement," Gail said. "He wasn't too thrilled with the payment. That's how I got this." She nodded the side of her head with the blood. "He wasn't much for negotiating and, like so many men, he hated changes."

"You had money for him? How much are we talking about?" Story sat down again.

Gail considered the questions for a long time. "If I give you a hundred and twenty-five thousand dollars cash money, will you go away and never come back? I was willing to pay that for him to disappear. It'd be worth that much—easy—never to see you again. And that would sure beat wrestling each other in court for the next few years with no one getting rich but the lawyers."

"How long would it take you to get it for me?"

"You could have it today."

Streeter and Story looked at each other.

"Sounds like that might be the way to go," he said.

Story looked back at Gail, while brushing some hair from her face. Then, slowly, "If I can have it today and you can prove that the money's in a trust, I'm willing to forget the rest. I don't want to take money from Doug's brother. But if I thought you were keeping it for yourself, I'd fight you in court forever."

"We'll call it Philip's reward," Gail said. She reached on top of the metal briefcase, off to the side of the table, and grabbed the ratty paper bag. "Here you go. Now, after the police are done here, our business is finished."

Story took the bag and looked inside. "Fair enough. After I count it."

"You can have this, too, if you want." Gail pulled the briefcase toward her and opened it. She turned it around so they could see the cash inside.

"What the hell is that?" Streeter bent forward.

"Mr. Kovacs brought that to show me, for some reason. He said he took it from Doug's attorney. He said he earned it, but I imagine that means he stole it. Or maybe worse."

"He probably took it off Cooper yesterday," Streeter speculated. "I knew he was dirty on that deal, too." He picked up a stack of fifties and fanned through it. "There must be—what? —forty, fifty thousand in here."

Story looked at the money and then took the stack out of Streeter's hands and threw it back in the case.

"This isn't ours." Then she turned to Gail. "And it's not yours, either. This goes to the police. Let them decide what to do with it. You better call."

Gail took one more quick look at the money and then closed the case. "You're right. Let them deal with it. I've seen enough money for one day."

Gail called the sheriff's office. As the three of them waited, Story actually went to the bathroom with the older woman and helped clean out her head injury. Streeter sat on the back-porch step and watched Kovacs. Detroit cop, he thought. Those FBI agents had it right.

When the paramedics and deputies finally arrived, they spent little time questioning everyone and gathering evidence. This may have been the first shooting death they'd seen in over a year, but they all knew Gail Shelton so well that they pretty much took her word for everything.

It was nearly ten-thirty when Story's Audi finally pulled out of the farm driveway and headed back south toward Cheyenne.

"I have to ask you something," Streeter said after a couple of miles. "When you said the money in the briefcase isn't ours and that the police should have it, isn't that a little out of character for you? I mean, we could have taken it and no one would have known."

"Don't think that hasn't crossed my mind. But I keep remembering when you asked me how much class it takes to try and screw an insurance company with a bogus neck injury. I feel bad about that little stunt. This is one way I can help make up for it."

They drove on in silence until they got to the outskirts of Cheyenne.

"I'll buy you a drink once we get to Denver," Streeter told her. "We deserve it after the last couple of days. Unless you want to hurry home and put that bag in a trunk under your bed for the night."

"I'm so drained, I'm not sure I can make it all the way back to Denver. And I know I can't get that far without a drink."

"You want me to drive?"

"I'm okay for now. They've got a decent little bar at the Marriott in Cheyenne. How does that sound?"

"A hotel bar." He looked at her face in the dashboard light. Her features seemed tired, which relaxed them nicely. He was glad their business arrangement was over, and he noticed that he still had the urge to kiss her. To hold her. Maybe more. "I'm game if you are. Look, if you just want to crash for the night, we can each get a room and then head back to Denver in the morning."

Story didn't say anything for a long time. Then she glanced at him. "Why don't we get that drink and you can tell me about those fires you're so good at starting. Who knows, maybe all we'll need is one room."

Now it was Streeter's turn to be quiet. Finally, he said, "It sure can't hurt to talk about it."

Today's American Jew

Books by Morris N. Kertzer

Today's American Jew

BY MORRIS N. KERTZER

McGraw-Hill Book Company
New York · Toronto · London · Sydney

Library of Congress Catalog Card Number: 67-25354
First Edition   34237

To My Children

"I believe in the survival of American Jewry. I believe in its organic membership in the pattern of American civilization. My perception leads me to the conclusion that American Jewry is not something grafted onto the existing structure of an American nation, but is simultaneous with its birth and growth, and totally inseparable from its destiny."

—ABBA EBAN

PREFACE

"Every Jew in America Speaks Arabic!"

A number of years ago, an Egyptian Jew whom I had known in France during World War II came to visit the United States for the first time. Arriving at Idlewild (now Kennedy) Airport, he was taken directly to Bensonhurst, Brooklyn, a section inhabited by many Syrian and Egyptian Jews. A week later, in the course of his sight-seeing, his friends took him to East 25th Street in Manhattan, where a sizable business community of Oriental Jews deals in silks, laces, cottons, and other imports from their native lands.

"How do you like our country?" was my unimaginative question when I met my wartime friend.

"A wonderful country!" he told me. "Every Jew in America speaks Arabic."

In the America he saw, of course, all Jews did speak Arabic. There are other observers who are certain that all American Jews spend their days basking in the Miami Beach sun and playing gin rummy on their hotel porches, while still others are convinced that Jews devote most of their time to praying and studying in the synagogue. A good case could be made for the proposition that American Jews devote most of their energies to fund raising, and an equally good case for the notion that they are to be found primarily in the professions or in academe. The image of Jewry, it is clear, is a subjective one, and, like beauty, lies in the eyes of the beholder.

The profile of the American Jew in these pages is the product of a single observer—myself. It is the sum of impressions developed over more than thirty years of life and travel in various parts of the country—impressions checked and re-examined during two and a half years of reading, of retracing steps, and twenty thousand miles, and of interviews with scores of people—social scientists and social workers, agency executives and businessmen, doctors, lawyers, rabbis, editors, university presidents, government officials, and others who were kind enough to share with me their perceptions of the American scene.

In my own thinking about this book and in all my conversations with others two questions came constantly to the fore: *In what way are Jews different because they happen to live in the United States? In what way is America different because of its Jews?* What I was most interested in learning and in recording was the interaction of American culture and the Jewish value system.

As anyone who has ever sought to pin down any valid generalizations about the American Jew, or about anything else, will attest, it is not an easy task. My problem was one of focus: how to take hold of the subject—the contemporary American Jew, all 5,600,000 of them—and hold him under scrutiny long enough to get something more than a blur.

I wish I could assure my readers that all the impressions I have set down have the stamp of scientific accuracy. Unfortunately I cannot, for mine is a strictly amateur sociology. And although I did make generous use of hundreds of books, community surveys, monographs, and magazine articles, the major source of my information was people, informed people in more than forty communities, representing almost every conceivable field of human endeavor.

Some readers may regard these generalities about American Jewry as little more than hunches. (A generalization, someone once pointed out, is a conclusion reached by someone else.) And those who, like Plato, feel that the noblest of all investigations is the study of what man *should* be will be disappointed by the relative absence of value judgments. It has been my goal simply to report what I have observed about the social, religious, economic, political, and cultural behavior of the American Jew, and to see what his life style can tell us about the impact of Jews and America on one another.

I did not accomplish all I set out to do. Lack of time and space forced me to cover far more superficially than it deserves the field of youth and youth activities. I had hoped to examine the distinctive patterns of house buying which a number of real-estate operators assure me exist among Jews. (One Westchester agent told me he shows entirely different houses to Jewish and non-Jewish customers.) I had also wanted to examine the identifiably Jewish pattern of investments which several accountants and lawyers insist they have discerned in the course of their tax and estate business. But tracking down the facts behind both of these subjects would have required more time and more digging than my duties as rabbi of a large congregation allowed. Unhappily, too, I have had to omit the Jewish press and the general area of Jewish literature.

Except for some passing references to suburban living, I have made no effort to isolate this important aspect of American Jewish experience, which Albert I. Gordon has covered so thoroughly in *Jews in Suburbia.*

I have also deliberately steered clear of the well-plowed soil of Jews in literature, which Alfred Kazin, Norman Podhoretz, Robert Alter, and a half-dozen other critics have covered in a depth far beyond my competence.

In point of time I have written only of the here and the now. American Jews of the 1960s are the subjects—and the heroes—of my tale. In the telling, I have tried to cast some light into those recesses which the historian, Marcus Hansen, has called "that dim continent of knowledge called social history." How deeply the light has penetrated remains for the reader to decide.

ACKNOWLEDGMENTS

I am indebted to Mrs. Sonya Kaufer for her inspired editorial aid, and to Mrs. Cynthia Fried for her devoted assistance in the preparation of this manuscript.

My everlasting gratefulness goes to my wife, Julia, and to my children for their critical examination of the thoughts developed in this book.

I wish to acknowledge the kind assistance of a number of people whose guidance was invaluable in the preparation of this book. Among them are: Mrs. Morris Adler, Rabbi Jacob Agus, William Avrunin, Jacob Aziz, Emanuel Batshaw, Rabbi Jack Bemporad, Leonard Benari, Philip Bernstein, Theodore Bikel, Julius Bisno, Lawrence Bloomgarden, Rabbi Balfour Brickner, Rabbi Armond Cohen, Iva Cohen, Jules Cohen, Dr. Moshe Davis, Rabbi Leonard Devine, Dr. Samuel Dinin, Rabbi Frederic Doppelt, Rabbi Israel Dresner, Dr. Maurice Eisendrath, Dr. Azriel Eisenberg, Benjamin Epstein, Rabbi Leon Feuer, Andrew Fier, Rabbi Jerome Folkman, Arnold Forster, Dr. Isaac Franck, Rabbi Solomon Freehof, Dr. Herbert A. Friedman, Martin Gang, Max Gettinger, Rabbi Roland Gittelsohn, Hannah L. Goldberg, Rabbi Daniel Goldberger, Rabbi Morris Goldstein, Prof. Sidney Goldstein, Rabbi Oscar Groner, Carl Grossberg, Murray Gunner, Benjamin Hanft, Rabbi Abraham Joshua Heschel, Robert I. Hiller, Milton Himmelfarb, Rabbi Richard

Hirsch, Don Hurwitz, Albert Hutler, Rabbi David Jacobson, Rabbi Alfred Jospe, Rabbi Robert Kahn, Dr. Louis Kaplan, Dr. Mordecai M. Kaplan, Charles Kaufman, Alfred Kazin, Rabbi Wolfe Kelman, Rabbi Israel Klavan, Philip Klutznick, Bernard Kozberg, Rabbi Leon Kronish, Rabbi Manuel Laderman, Dr. Maxwell Lehr, Charles S. Liebman, Dr. Edward Lew, Hon. Mose Lindau, Rabbi Eugene Lipman, Mrs. Albert List, Walter Lurie, Ben Maccabee, Dr. Jacob R. Marcus, Arnaud C. Marts, Will Maslow, Rabbi Israel Miller, Herbert Millman, Frieda Mohr, Emanuel Muravchik, Max Perlman, Dr. Judah Pilch, Rabbi Albert Plotkin, Rabbi David Polish, Bernard Postal, Rabbi Amram Prero, Rabbi Joachim Prinz, Rabbi Sidney Regner, Robert M. Robbins, Dr. Seymour Romney, A. Abbot Rosen, Dr. Ben Rosenberg, Arthur S. Rosichan, Rabbi Jacob Rothschild, Rabbi Martin B. Ryback, Dr. Abram Sachar, Dore Schary, Rabbi Harold M. Schulweis, Rabbi Jack Segal, Dr. Morris B. Seidelman, Manheim Shapiro, Irwin Shaw, Jacob Sheinkman, Dr. Samuel Sherman, Charles Silberman, Hon. Charles H. Silver, Jeremiah Simmons, Mrs. Rhoda Simon, Dr. John Slawson, Isidore Sobeloff, Sanford Solender, Louis Stein, Rabbi Malcolm Stern, Rabbi Earl Stone, Rabbi Hugo Stransky, Dr. Morton Teicher, Rabbi Isaac Trainin, Mrs. Baruch Treiger, Sidney Vincent, Albert Vorspan, Dr. Max Vorspan, Rabbi Jacob B. Weinstein, Louis Weintraub, David H. White, Rabbi Saul White, Joseph Willen, Dr. Gershon Winer, Rabbi Edward Zerin, Henry Zucker, Robert Gamzey, Harold Sherman Goldberg, and Albert I. Gordon.

CONTENTS

CONTENTS

Today's American Jew

CHAPTER 1

Under Sunny Skies

Bright is the name for American Jewry: close to six million Jews flourishing in a cloud-free atmosphere, liberated from the centuries-long nightmare of rootlessness, uncertainty, and the unpredictable whims of besotted hooligans, petty princes, and benighted religious fanatics.

The American Jewish teen-ager knows, because he has been told by his elders and has read it in history books, that in the lifetime of his parents millions of Jews in many lands lived out their lives in constant hunger; that his grandparents or those of his friends came to this country cooped up in the foul steerage sections of storm-tossed ships, walked the streets of a city where few spoke their language, and labored from seven in the morning until eight at night to earn enough for food and shelter and somehow managed to rear children and grandchildren fully at home in the world to which they came. Our teen-ager *knows* this, with his intellect, but he cannot really feel it or understand what it means. He cannot be persuaded to believe that the sixty-year-old lawyer, whose counsel is sought by mighty corporations and whose life style is the last word in elegance, began by delivering newspapers in the Bronx when he was ten years old, at six every morning seven mornings a week, his meager earnings the only family income for months on end.

A generation ago we spoke about the wide chasm between the

immigrant Jew and his native-born children; but it was minuscule compared to the vast separation between today's Jewish youth and their elders. From the desolate depression days to the affluent Jewish society of the 1960s is a psychological and spiritual distance almost beyond measure.

By oblique inference, the young man living under America's sunny skies sometimes becomes aware that the present has little in common with the past. He may discover, in the dictionary definition of the word *Jew*, such pejorative descriptions as "sharp practice," and ask in shocked surprise how such wild definitions could find their way into a respectable dictionary.

He may learn that Uncle Ed, who graduated from engineering school in 1933, tried for five years to find an engineering firm that would employ Jews before he gave up and went into the catering business.

He may visit the cemetery where his grandparents are buried and discover for the first time that his father had changed his name. "What made my parents' generation so uncomfortable about their name that they would want to be rid of it?" he may wonder; "Grandpa's name was easier to spell than Eisenhower!"

The radical change in the American Jewish psyche is perhaps illustrated by the difference in the reaction of a sixty-year-old and a twenty-year-old to President Johnson's appointment of his intimate friend and adviser, Arthur Goldberg, to represent the United States of America at the United Nations. The older Jew said: "Imagine that! Someone named *Goldberg* speaking for all of America!" It was not so long ago that President Wilson was regarded as a study in courage when he named Brandeis to the Supreme Court. Among those who fought the nomination were Jewish leaders who worried that an unpopular Supreme Court decision involving a Jewish judge might cause blood to flow in the streets of Boston, New York, and Atlanta.

The twenty-year-old, however, found neither exhilaration nor trepidation in Justice Goldberg's appointment. The fact that Arthur Goldberg was a Jew carried no emotional baggage along with it, and the young man took for granted that most Americans would think of the man and not of ethnic origins.

Half a century ago, too, such an announcement would have been accompanied with self-conscious declarations about the inspired liberalism of a land that would permit a person of the Jewish "race" (everyone used the term race—George Washington; Rabbi Isaac Wise, founder of Reform Judaism; Samuel Gompers, the father of the American labor movement) to rise to eminent station. Today it is considered bad manners and worse sociology to refer to the religion of a political appointee.

"The New American Jew" described by *Time* is a "kind of culture hero" for the intellectual and very much a part of the "in group" of national life.

To the sixty-year-old, the novelty is not so much in the Jew as in America. If his social, political, and economic status has taken on a sort of idyllic quality, the change is in the whole people and the whole culture, not in that segment of it which is Jewish.

For the many American Jews who have known bleaker days, well-being produces nervousness rather than euphoria. Deeply ingrained in the spirit is an inborn uneasiness in the presence of success. One mustn't boast of well-being, even to oneself, lest the smile of fortune freeze. *Kein ayin horo,* "May no evil eye befall us," is the magic formula invoked in such circumstances.

And to balance good fortune with humility, we hear the voice of the Ben Gurions, reinforced by the warnings of Jews who have fled from czarist or Hitler atrocities: "A minority group has only three possibilities: absorption by the dominant body, relegation to inferior status, or flight. *There are no other choices.*"

Yet the story of the American Jew in the 1960s, so far as we can observe, seems to suggest that a fourth choice is quite possible. Although the threat of erosion by marriage out of the faith, conversion to Christianity, or sheer apathy are ever present, few real danger signs are at hand. American culture, seductive in its benignity, and only in rare irrational phases during the past decades plagued by xenophobia, has settled down to a live-and-let-live placidity which permits the Jew to enjoy the best of two worlds—group identification and individuality, *and* group respectability.

In 1954, the American Jewish community commemorated the 300th anniversary of the landing of the first twenty-three Jews in New Amsterdam. The celebration started in the fall of 1953, and by the dawn of the new year most American Jews, blasé and suspicious of sentimentality, had had enough of Peter Stuyvesant and "those twenty-three intrepid Jewish pioneers" to last a lifetime.

Yet the historian, cool and detached, must agree with Jacob Rader Marcus, one of the outstanding authorities on American Jewish life, that the story of the Jew in America is "a fabulous history." There is so much of a congeniality of spirit between the American character and the Jewish character that the events of the past three centuries and the creation of the most vital Jewish community in Judaism's 4,000-year history were virtually predictable.

John Slawson, a most perceptive student of Jewish "integration" in the United States, used the sociological term "goodness of fit" to capture this extraordinary meshing of American and Jewish values. Dr. Slawson cites a number of important characteristics cherished in both traditions: "Seriousness, foresight, purposefulness (*tachlis*), commitment to social justice, love of learning and education—not a bowing acquaintance but an actual involvement."

Foreigners generally remark on the inordinate friendliness of Americans, their rather breezy style, the easy and intimate way they relate to strangers. Observers from De Toqueville to Geoffrey Gorer have searched for explanations for the open character of Americans; some have related it to the wide-open spaces of the New World. Indeed the farther west the visitor travels, the breezier and the friendlier the attitudes he encounters. Yet the same broad expanse of land in South America has not produced the same trait. And the easy informality of the Jews has developed despite generations of constriction within narrow ghetto confines.

This American—and Jewish—air of informality is often exasperating to those who do not share it: many Europeans, especially the English, feel uncomfortable in the presence of new acquaintances who are so quick to use first names, share confidences, and invade their privacy.

Echoes of this mood of informality are heard in the very fabric of the language used by Jews. I have tried in vain to find the Yiddish or Hebrew equivalent for the word "privacy." There are obscure, unused phrases covering the meaning, but privacy is not a much-sought-after quality in Jewish life. In the most concentrated Jewish communities in the world, Tel Aviv, or parts of Manhattan's Lower East Side, or Brooklyn's Flatbush, no one ever heard of privacy. A visitor on a bus in Israel who asks directions to a certain street will get his answer not only from the bus driver but from a score of passengers as well. Someone else will ask whose house the traveler is seeking. Another voice will announce that she knows the family well, and they are old and respected residents of the neighborhood And still others will offer loud assent.

Several years ago, on a hot, crowded bus going from Haifa to Acco, I felt a hand rubbing my shoulder. Turning around, I discovered a middle-aged woman gliding her fingers on my upper arm. In response to my quizzical look, she asked, in a most matter-of-fact way: "What kind of material is that shirt made of? Is it that new thing called nylon?" As the bus plunged along the overheated highway, a small crowd gathered around us, expressing delight at the wonders of the new fabric, and speculating on how long it would take for Israel to produce such excellent material. In Israel, privacy is the rarest of commodities.

America's most eminent rabbi of the twentieth century, Dr. Stephen S. Wise, once remarked that the world's greatest sin was not difference, but *in*difference. Instant intimacy, pronounced among Jews, and fairly typical of Americans, may have its drawbacks. But on the other hand, it reveals a people who care for other people.

Much has been written about American generosity. We are the most *giving* nation in the world. One can divide America into two classes of people—fund raisers and contributors—those who find fulfillment in approaching their friends and acquaintances for charity, and those who dispense it. (See Chapter 8.)

To the American Jew, philanthropy is part of ordinary life. A large dinner party at which no collection is taken somehow seems like a golden opportunity wasted. Fund raisers count on the Jewish conscience, which evokes guilt feelings in the midst of frivolity to allay irritation.

On a transatlantic liner, during the height of the summer season, a young crewman leaped overboard in a moment of suicidal despair and was drowned. The luxury ship, with orchestras playing on various dance floors, shuddered to a halt while the inevitably futile search was undertaken.

A few Jewish passengers inquired about the identity of the suicide and were told that he was a twenty-five-year-old medical student, a native of the Philippines, married, and the father of two children.

"Can we take up a collection?" The chief purser explained that only crewmen were permitted to raise funds within their own ranks. It was forbidden to solicit aid from passengers, since such collections were a jarring note for pleasure-bound voyagers. Nevertheless, several Jewish passengers quietly placed collection boxes next to the bingo and horse-racing games so that the winners could share their gains with the stricken family. It was a Pavlovian response to a situation of need.

One of my most vivid childhood recollections is a Yom Kippur service in an Orthodox synagogue when the late Reform rabbi, Barnett R. Brickner, pleaded on behalf of the orphans and widows of Poland. The year was 1921. The sight of men weeping was unfamiliar to the children in the congregation, and it struck terror to our hearts. We were also aware of the sharp doctrinal cleavage between the Orthodox and the Reform. The extraordinary circumstance which impelled the citadel of Orthodoxy—my congregation —to permit a rabbi who ordinarily preached and prayed with head uncovered to mount our sacred pulpit underscored in my childish mind the cementing force of crisis which overcame credal differences. A bleeding Israel was a united Jewry, and similar scenes took place in hundreds of synagogues throughout America.

The year of the creation of the state of Israel saw a similar upsurge in Jewish communal giving, and in the following ten years American Jewry gave more than two billion dollars for both overseas and domestic needs. A machinery of fund raising was refined to create a self-imposed tax which the average American Jew took for granted. The inexorability of the United Jewish Appeal's annual campaign was the heart of its genius. Just as automatically as the tax collector issues his call every April 15, so in a specific month each year, varying from community to community, the voice of the UJA is heard in the land. In neither case is there any escape. If a Jew makes handbags, the leading members of the handbag association will get him. One UJA gathering which I addressed consisted of members of the ladies' undergarment industry. The luncheon was held at a leading New York hotel and the mood was far from solemn despite the fact that we were brought together by the needs of the starving and the tempest tossed. These men who were locked in bitter competition in their offices on Seventh Avenue were transformed into a pleasant social group very much like a Lions Club luncheon meeting. Several were pointed out to me, not by their own names, but by the brands of a well-advertised brassière or foundation garment.

But they remained in competition—and no one dared *not* give, with the eyes of the whole industry upon them. Any suggestion of a decrease from last year's generous level would be regarded as a sign that their particular business was on the decline! Might as well tell Wall Street as inform the UJA that things were not going too well at Adorable Undergarments!

The backbone of American Jewish philanthropy is not, as some assume, the high-powered, highly paid fund raiser. These men and women are merely instruments in the hands of Jews who have cultivated the art of combining business and professional careers with the vocation of charitable endeavor. In some instances, where several brothers, or other family members, operate a successful business together, one partner may be designated to withdraw from active participation in the firm and devote all of his time to communal matters.

Kivie Kaplan of Boston

Almost every newspaper photograph of Dr. Martin Luther King leading a protest march—in Selma, Alabama, Jackson, Mississippi, or other crisis cities of the nation—also includes a number of white men in the front ranks alongside the Negro leader. And almost invariably one of these men is a retired Boston leather manufacturer, walking with a firm stride despite his sixty-three years. Some of the pictures include his son and teen-aged grandson who have flown from Boston to lend their moral support.

Kivie Kaplan retired at the age of fifty-eight to channel all his energies into acts of justice and mercy. The Selma trip for his grandson was arranged so that the lessons Kivie learned from his parents and grandparents about translating Judaism into action would continue to be handed down in the Kaplan family to the generations yet unborn.

I wondered what prompted Kivie, whose early benefactions had been limited to building hospitals and supporting synagogues, to concentrate his recent energies on civil rights for the Negroes. In 1955, the NAACP had made him national chairman for life memberships: in ten years he increased the number of life members from 221 to more than sixteen thousand—both white and Negro. In a single month, in 1965, Kivie Kaplan covered twenty-five communities in Florida, helping to organize NAACP branches. Each successful speech cost him money—for whenever a new chapter was formed, the first substantial contribution came from the speaker himself. In 1965, Kivie was elected national president of the organization.

His speeches often began with a reference to his own people. "If a shaggy mongrel dog were to be captured and placed on a burning stake, the whole community would rise in righteous rage. Yet 6 million human beings were incinerated virtually without protest. I know what suffering is—mine and yours."

A traumatic experience thirty-two years ago launched Kivie on his crusade for justice. Traveling near Miami Beach in his chauffeur-driven car, his attention was caught by a hotel sign that read, "No Jews or dogs allowed." His Negro driver remarked: "I know how you feel, Mr. Kaplan. Do you know all these beautiful beaches up and down the coast? Well, every inch of that Atlantic Ocean is closed to us Negroes." Since that moment the destiny of Jew and Negro has been unalterably intertwined in Kivie Kaplan's mind.

There is no bitterness in him: he has a permanent twinkle in his eyes, and there is a bubbling effervescence in everything he does. He carries hundreds of cards that say "Keep Smiling" in a score of languages, and he hands them out to every new person he meets, every waiter who serves him, every airplane stewardess, every cab-driver. The attic in his Boston home is choked with gifts which he dispenses to friends and associates at the slightest provocation.

Kivie's father had a favorite proverb which he constantly repeated to his son: "The only thing you own is what you give away." And the latter has refined the traditional Jewish *simcha shel mitzvah*— the delight in performing an act of kindness—to a fine art. Forty per cent of his income is spent on good causes—a wing of a hospital for crippled children, a new NAACP unit in Mississippi, a new temple.

Obviously, since his retirement, all these benefactions reduce the size of his estate. "Edward," Kivie once asked his son, "do you mind my diminishing the amount of your inheritance?"

His son asked him what he had been giving to lately, and when Kivie listed his various charities, his son assured him, "It's all right with me, Dad." It is hardly surprising that Edward has begun to follow in his father's path.

Writing a check is only one form of giving. Shopping in the small

Florida town where he vacations annually, Kivie made some purchases in a store where the saleswoman was a Negro.

"Your saleswoman is an unusually fine and competent person," Kivie told the owner.

"Thank you. She has been with us for eighteen years, the veteran of our sales staff."

"Good. But why don't you have more than one colored salesperson?"

And to the saleswoman, wreathed in smiles, Kivie directed another question: "Do you belong to the NAACP? Why not? They make it possible for you to have this job!"

Like many American Jews, Kivie belongs to and supports a half-dozen Orthodox, Conservative, and Reform congregations. The Religious Social Action Center of American Reform Judaism in Washington is called the Kivie and Emily Kaplan Center—in acknowledgment of a quarter-million-dollar gift from the couple.

Kivie and Emily, whose mothers were first cousins, decided at the age of eleven and ten that they would someday be married. The official proposal came when Kivie was thirteen. At fifteen he decided to be a rabbi—there were many in the family—but fourteen-year-old Emily announced, "I wouldn't make a good rabbi's wife."

He began working for his father and older brothers in the leather business seven days a week. His brothers parted ways with their father, and Kivie joined him in establishing a new and highly successful business. Very early in this enterprise he introduced a profit-sharing plan, for social justice is not an abstract thing to be applied in Georgia and Alabama but ignored in Massachusetts. Besides, Mother Kaplan always said that "you live to give."

Kivie has his own philosophy of friendship. "It's best to have few friends—of quality. Sometimes I jeopardize lifelong friendships because of my ideas. Once when I was invited to a sumptuous cocktail party I sent my regrets. 'Our Boston list of contributors shows that you give only $300 to the United Appeal. This affair will cost you at least a thousand dollars. I wouldn't be able to enjoy food taken away from the needy.'"

His host called him the next morning. "I couldn't sleep last night. Tell the Appeal to increase my gift to $3,000." But most people, Kivie assured me with that bright twinkle, have no trouble sleeping —and if he loses a friendship occasionally, it is no loss.

"What do you regard as man's biggest failure?" I asked him.

"The worst sin is bigotry. I used to think it was hypocrisy, because in my youth I attended a synagogue where I saw a great disparity between creed and deed. Now I realize that in my adolescent impatience I was unfair. We are all the same."

❖ ❖ ❖ ❖ ❖ ❖

To evaluate the position of the Jews in America today we must underscore a distinction between the *attitudes* of non-Jews and the *experience* of Jews. Conceivably, an opinion poll may reflect a considerable pocket of hostility in a community, but individual Jews may be unaware of it. In the first place, there is a world of difference between *felt* prejudice and *overt* expression of bigotry. One mentally disturbed person with a paintbrush can flood a town with anti-Jewish slogans that may unnerve Jewish citizens and concerned Gentiles. Much more destructive is the quiet dropping of a Jewish application into a wastebasket in the personnel office of a corporation. The happiness and security of Jews are hardly affected in the first instance; they are seriously jeopardized by the second, which is therefore of serious import.

Actually, the points of contact between the two religious groups are not so many as we might think. If we were to sketch a huge map of the United States, neighborhood by neighborhood, we would find thousands of residential districts without any Jews at all. Draw a line down the center of the vast metropolis of Cleveland, through the heart of the downtown district. To the left of that line live only a handful of Jewish residents; to the right close to 90,000. A similar map of Pittsburgh would reveal some areas with a 90 per cent Jewish population, others with none at all. Albert Vorspan and Eugene Lipman, in their book *Tale of Ten Cities*, report that in St. Paul, Minnesota, a speaker at one public school was asked: "What do Jews look like? What kind of government do they have? If, in that area of St. Paul, some observable anti-Jewish feeling existed, it would have little impact on the thousands of Jews in other parts of that city.

Of the three arenas of daily experience—economic, political, and social—only the last contains remnants of frustration. Many of the prestigious social clubs still bar Jewish members. But for the majority of Jews who have neither the means nor the aspiration to join a yacht club or a beach club that "keep out" sign is academic, a mild irritant at most. Those who need such social facilities have provided clubs of their own, separate but superior because they are newer. Members of ancient yacht clubs swelter in the summer heat while their Jewish neighbors across the inlet relax in air-conditioned comfort. Thus many of the Jews who join in drives for open-housing occupancy in their community, as a protest against racial discrimination, will not bother agitating against the social bars that still remain against themselves!

Politically, Jews are fairly well represented on all levels of government. If they tend to cluster in appointive rather than elective offices, the choice is theirs. Jews with political ambition have been elected mayors in towns and cities where there are no more than a score of Jewish families.

Economically, the American picture is spectacularly bright. Although the poor Jew is by no means a phenomenon of the past—any Jewish social-service agency in a large city can attest to thousands of such cases—the annual income of Jewish heads of households is $5,954, compared to $4,340 for the Catholics and $3,933 for the Protestants (the latter figure is explained in part by the large number of nonwhites among the Protestants). What is even more remarkable, I would guess that if we examined the income of Jews who came to this country in the wake of the Hitler holocaust, the figures would probably match those of the long-time residents, even of the third and fourth generation—a tribute both to the opportunities provided by the American economy and to the bootstrap-lifting quality of these people.

One important fact about the residential pattern must be noted. Twenty years ago, John Gunther, in his *Inside U.S.A.*, wrote:

> The situation of Jews in the Middle West, especially rich Jews, is peculiar. The plain fact of the matter is that they are, in effect, segregated. Near the University of Chicago when I went there, a handsome, dignified, stately residential district existed that was almost as Jewish as Tel Aviv; here lived a cluster of Rosenwalds, Adlers, and so on, almost as dynastically interlocked as Hapsburgs. In Chicago certainly, and in other big Middle Western cities to an extent, the Jews who could afford it were driven by goy prejudices and discriminations not only to establish their own clubs of various sorts

(downtown and country), schools, kindergartens, and college fraternities, but even neighborhoods.

That description does not apply in 1967. Although many thousands of Jews have moved to Westchester County, communities such as Scarsdale, Rye, Harrison, and my own Larchmont have no "Jewish streets" or neighborhoods. The pattern in Elkins Park, Pennsylvania, Highland Park, Illinois, and in the suburbs of Atlanta is similar.

If there are so-called "gilded ghettoes," they develop fortuitously rather than by design, the result of like-minded tastes in housing, or through reports of earlier Jewish residents who have found a favorable community climate. It seems to me that barriers fall in domino fashion: intimate association in the college dormitory and, with growing frequency, the college fraternity and sorority; mixing in the armed services; free association in the luncheon club (rare in the period depicted by Gunther); open housing; joint activity in PTA's and other communal enterprises; and, in the fresh ecumenical air of the past few years, happy association in church and temple activities.

Certainly there are vestiges of past fears and uncertainties. A few years ago, a Jewish neighbor of mine in Larchmont answered her doorbell one evening and found a husky policeman standing on her doorstep.

"Madam, would you mind answering this question for me? Are you Jewish?"

A slight sense of panic gripped her as she acknowledged that she was.

"Are your neighbors on both sides Jewish?"

This was a woman who had lived through the Nazi nightmare in Germany, and now she was really frightened. The memories of Gestapo "courtesy calls" engulfed her as she admitted that both neighbors were Jews.

"As a matter of fact, this entire block of eight houses is all Jewish." (Even this is no longer true today.)

"That's exactly what I want to know." The policeman broke into a broad grin. "I just won a bet with another Jewish cop on the Mount Vernon force. I told him there was one street in Larchmont that was 100 per cent Jewish, but he didn't believe me!"

CHAPTER 2

A New World for Jews

"The land was ours before we were the land's.
She was our land more than a hundred years
Before we were her people."

ROBERT FROST

"Good by, dear God, I'm going to America."

This not too humorous joke of Jewish emigrants in the early 1800s reflected their fear of religious extinction as they set off for the New World. Tradition-bound parents in Odessa, Warsaw, and Vilna mourned as they bade farewell to their children, certain they were lost to the faith forever.

Their fears were not unfounded. Even as late as the middle 1800s, American Judaism possessed few of the ingredients necessary for survival. The men far outnumbered the women, and finding a Jewish wife was extremely difficult; there were no English-speaking rabbis, no seminaries, no training schools for religious teachers—none of the requisites for perpetuating the Hebraic tradition.

Yet, at a time when tens of thousands of Jews were swarming to baptismal fonts in Berlin, Budapest, Vienna, and Rome, Jews of frontier America were little tempted to renounce their faith. Christianity's traditional evangelical thrust was almost totally absent in the New World. In the expansive West, where a large portion of the early Jews settled, only one in every five Americans was church affiliated. Saloons far outnumbered houses of worship. And those Jews who chose to cling to their credal loyalties were relatively free to do so. Some left the ancestral faith, but no pattern of mass conversion had been established in predominantly Christian America by the time Jews began to pour into the United States in the 1880s and 1890s. With numbers came vitality and a closing of the ranks.

Since those early days, speculation on the ultimate fate of American Jewry has provided the subject matter for sermons, seminars, late-into-the-night discussions, articles, books, dinner conversations, meetings, and debates here and abroad. In the 3,500 years of Jewish history there are no real parallels to the American experience, which may explain why Jews leading the good life here are plagued by the nagging question, "Can American Jewry survive as a separate entity?"

Half a century ago, the English writer, Israel Zangwill, wrote a popular play, *The Melting Pot,* describing a social process which he observed taking place in the United States. Under the benevolent skies of a free society, Zangwill prophesied, Jews were in danger of losing their group identity. Old-World habits and manners—and even values—ran the risk of being submerged in a new culture, a homogenized, uniform Americanism embracing all of its citizens, whatever their background, tradition, or ancestry.

For Jewish survivalists the "melting pot" loomed as a fearful threat, an invitation to cultural and religious suicide. Those who welcomed the notion of Jews *melting* into America were branded as assimilationists, escapists—and, worst of all, self-haters. They were excoriated from the pulpit and in the Jewish press for their lack of dignity and self-respect.

Some observers concerned with the sociology of American Jewry preferred to describe the intermeshing of Jewish and American culture in terms of integration rather than assimilation, evoking an image of a pluralistic national culture with room for distinctiveness, uniqueness, everything but absolute separatism. Prof. Horace M. Kallen popularized this idea in the 1930s, and survivalists continue to find much comfort in the Kallen doctrine of cultural pluralism. Nowadays most other Americans do not regard Jews as second-class citizens if they insist on retaining their distinctiveness. While a generation ago, public-opinion polls, investigating attitudes toward Jews, often dredged up charges of Jewish "clannishness." In more recent polls this indictment has all but disappeared.

Why, then, when it is possible to be both an American and a practicing Jew, has American Jewry experienced a new survival panic? One explanation is the nervous tendency of American Jews to endow the opinions of the non-Jew with far more weight than those of his coreligionists. Thus, when the national (non-Jewish) magazines began publishing articles about "the vanishing Jew," a mood of uneasiness bordering on consternation swept through the Jewish community.

Jeremiads on the same theme repeated over the years from synagogue pulpit and Jewish center platform were taken in stride. But a single article printed in *Look* evoked a virtual crisis of apprehension. Emergency conferences were convened and experts called in to offer their opinions and suggestions on meeting the "challenge" to Jewish survival.

In June, 1964, the annual meeting of the National Community Relations Advisory Council, which represents the broadest gathering of informed Jewish leadership in the nation, devoted a special session to "Prospects for Jewish Survival in an Open Society." Dr. Isaiah M. Minkoff, the executive head of the NCRAC, outlined the current picture.

We cannot "infer a permanent future for any culture from the fact that it has had a long past," he pointed out. Special dangers lurked in the growing social and economic mobility of the American people, urban concentration with its impersonality and anonymity, the weakening of family ties. While all of these forces reduce the chances for group survival, Dr. Minkoff acknowledged, there were a number of important forces working in its favor: the large number of active synagogues, temples, and centers; the involvement of Jews as Jews in social-action movements; and, *above all, the acceptance of group identification as normal on the part of most Americans.*

All in all, Isaiah Minkoff's prognosis was quite positive, but it found many dissenters. Sanford Solender, national director of the Jewish Welfare Board, and one of the most knowledgeable students of the American Jewish scene, noted a "widespread absence of Jewish literacy" and a general apathy to Jewish values: "Judaism lacks modern relevance to most Jews; it is not a living force which infuses their lives," he declared. Mr. Solender faulted those responsible for Jewish education. Another disturbing symptom which he pinpointed was "the fact that fund-raising achievements of Jewish welfare funds have risen only 16 per cent over the last decade, notwithstanding the 61 per cent in gross national product. . . ."

Time magazine (June 25, 1965) probably came closest to an

accurate appraisal of the present situation in a scintillaitng and perceptive profile of "The New American Jew": "What is happening to the Jews in pluralist America is not the rash of assimilation which characterized the liberal period of nineteenth- and early twentieth-century Germany. [One could have added Austria, Hungary, France, and Italy.] . . . The American process is what sociologists call 'acculturation.' "

Time listed four clearly defined factors favoring the perpetuation of Judaism: synagogue affiliation; a desire of Jews to transmit their heritage to their children; extraordinary identification with and support for Israel; and, finally, a strong resistance to marriage out of the faith.

Perhaps the true hazards that lurk in the unique American Jewish experience lie in the process that might be called *mutual accultura-tion.* If America has had its impact on the Jews who have settled here, their impact on America is no less clear. As a columnist in the *London Jewish Chronicle* so accurately observed, "*Where they [American Jews] assimilate they do so into a world which is partly of their own making.*" And the world which is America today is more "Jewish" than ever before!

The America of the 1920s offered little impetus for Jewish assimi-lation. It was a small-town America, dominated by what William Whyte called "the Protestant ethic." The Jews have always been part and parcel of the big city; it is where they gathered, settled, and made their deepest mark. The old clash between village and metropolis, as old as the Bible, found many echoes in this country, and Jews in America often experienced a sense of alienation, not because of the difference in their faith, but because their big-city ties separated them from the rural and semi-rural life that was typical of Protestant America. But that was almost half a century ago.

The America of the sixties is an urban culture, very different from the prevalent pattern of the early twentieth century. In his *Making of the President—1964*, Theodore H. White described the so-called Eastern Establishment as dominated by a power structure of men born in Hannibal, Missouri; Live Oak, Florida; Bowling Green, Kentucky, and Murfreesboro, Tennessee. The shift from the small towns of the nation to its large metropolitan nerve centers reflects a fantastic transformation within a single generation. Thus the growing influence of the city in itself decreases the differences between Christian and Jew.

Although the different faiths still tend to gather in informal enclaves in the suburbs to which they have transplanted themselves en masse, Christians in this generation have become neighbors in the profound sense of sharing the outlook and fulfillments, the problems and frustrations of metropolitan living.

The economic pattern of America, too, is becoming more and more like that which the Jews have always known. For a variety of involved historical and traditional reasons, Jews have always concentrated in the professions, in sales, in managerial roles. Today, for the first time in our history, the majority of our total national labor force is devoted to services rather than to production.

In the 1920s and 1930s, Jews who were barred from many fields of endeavor sought a livelihood in such peripheral fields as entertainment, leisure, and luxury service, communication. Today, these same areas engage the energies of an ever-increasing flow of Americans of every faith and background.

Even in the practice of charity, Jewish and Christian traditions are merging. Protestant tradition has always emphasized individual acts of giving, person-to-person benefaction, while the Jewish social system, although encouraging individual aid, evolved through the centuries an elaborate communal mechanism for aiding those in distress. Jews traditionally have considered their community as a whole responsible for feeding the hungry, assisting the widowed and the orphaned, ransoming the captured, burying the dead, even supplying poor brides with an adequate trousseau and dowry. And each member of the community was expected to contribute according to his ability toward these needs.

There was little debate in Jewish charitable tradition about such issues as the "laziness" of the have-nots. A human being, *because he was a human being*, was entitled to food, clothing, and shelter with no questions asked. That there were some unscrupulous and shiftless characters who took advantage of this social code was fully recognized. On the other hand, there is no Jewish word that means one who must *seek* alms by begging from his neighbors.

Of course, the highest form of philanthropy, outlined by the twelfth-century Maimonides, is that of "helping a man to help himself." It was this formula that Sargent Shriver quoted to a congressional committee in explaining the rationale for President Johnson's war on poverty. It was this same principle that prompted the establishment of the Hebrew Free Loan Society in New York, in 1892. Relying solely on the endorsement of merchants of standing, the Society made interest-free loans of from $10 to $200 to immigrants eager to set up independently in business. The chances are that some of the Jewish family fortunes of our century had their genesis in these modest communal acts of assistance.

There is little doubt that the historic assistance programs of the American Jewish community have served as the models for many current programs of social welfare, both public and private, national and local. Of course, much of the inspiration for free hospital care had its roots in Roman Catholic tradition. And the Salvation Army is only one illustration of Protestant concern for the disinherited. But the structuring of much of the American welfare program, as well as the insistence that giving is a matter not of choice but of obligation, derives a good deal of its impetus from the eleemosynary tradition of American Jewry.

When, as in America, the dominant socioeconomic structure reflects strong parallels to what was once distinctly Jewish, there is indeed a subtle threat to Jewish survival. And yet paradoxically today, at the same time that the United States of America has become the nerve center of the free world, the financial capital, the UN capital, the heart of culture, scientific and medical development, American Jewry has seized the center of the stage in world Jewish history.

Nassau County, Long Island, with its 374,000 Jews, contains more citizens of the Jewish faith than all of Poland, Austria, Hungary, Germany, Rumania, Greece, Algeria, and Iraq combined. Before World War II, these countries had Jewish populations ranging in size from 100,000 to 3,500,000. Six million Jews disappeared in the Nazi holocaust. A significant portion of their remnants are nestled in one area of Long Island that covers no more than 300 square miles. There are 10,000 Jews per square mile in Brooklyn compared to 575 per square mile in Israel.

Hartford, Connecticut, Jewry, numbering 26,000 of a total population of 160,000 matches the Jewish population of European countries with a population of 30 million. Brooklyn, New York, has more rabbis than all the rest of the world with the possible exception of Israel!

Although the survival of American Jewry should be a matter of personal concern to every Jew, the indications are strong that America and its Jews will continue to be good for each other!

CHAPTER 3

Share in the American Economy

"The only apparent genius [of the Jews] is an indomitable energy and resourcefulness that are concentrated on whatever opportunities are open to them."
HERBERT J. MULLER, *The Uses of the Past*

America's booming economy has carried its Jewish population along with it to an extraordinary degree. Together with Episcopalians and Presbyterians, Jews are included among the highest-income brackets of the nation, and relatively few are to be found in what Michael Harrington terms "the subculture of poverty"—although there *are* poor Jews. (The Jewish Family Service in Los Angeles aids a thousand families a month, and Miss Freda Mohr, its director, estimates that between four and five thousand Jews in the city are unemployed. Many of these are sick or old, and have come to California because of its long history of public relief.)

Jews are equally scarce in the other subculture of vast affluence. Not more than a half-dozen Jewish families rank with the Hersheys, the Harrimans, and the Mellons. None can compete with the Fords and the Du Ponts, or with such oil tycoons as the Gettys, the Pews, and the Hunts. The bulk of America's wealth remains in the hands of the old Anglo-Saxon Protestant families. Banking, heavy industry, insurance, the land itself, mining, the power that keeps America running, and such pervasive enterprises as the automobile and chemical industries remain largely closed to Jews.

Hundreds of thousands of Jews are to be found in America's predominant middle class. A Philadelphia rabbi estimates that in his congregation—made up of civil-service employees, small businessmen, and white-collar workers—the average income is between six and seven thousand dollars a year. Scattered through America's suburbia—in North Hollywood; all through Long Island, New York; Skokie, Illinois; Framingham, Massachusetts; and others—one finds Jewish communities made up entirely of families with modest incomes. In New York City alone the Jewish civil-service organizations total 80,000 members, of whom 16,000 are schoolteachers, many additional thousands are postal employees, policemen, firemen, sanitation workers, and so on.

By and large, however, extremes of poverty are virtually nonexistent among healthy American Jews. In the smaller cities I visited this was especially true. Morris B. Seidelman, director of Family Services of Greater Utica, New York, whose office serves 4,000 Jews, told me that in that area "there are few instances of economic want except for the aged and infirm."

What a transformation within our lifetime! A half-century ago 80 per cent of New York's Jews worked in sweatshops, earning less than fifteen dollars a week when they could find work. Even in terms of what the 1910 dollars could buy, most Jews lived in dire economic want. The princes among them were the 25,000 pushcart peddlers (the number cited in Moses Rischin's *The Promised City*) who were not under the constant shadow of "slack"—layoff from work in the factory or store.

In his *The Other America*, Michael Harrington ascribes the inexorable chain of misery through which the grandchildren of the poor are destined to be the grandparents of the poor to four recognizable ingredients: poor physical health, poor mental and emotional health, inadequate education, and weak family ties. These handicaps are singularly absent among American Jewry, a fact which helps to explain this group's phenomenal upward mobility.

Jews have far fewer problems of social dislocation. "In the entire history of welfare assistance in our office," the Los Angeles Family Service people told me, "we have never had a single Jewish alcoholic." The San Francisco office, in a seaport city which is host to a steady stream of transients, also reports that alcoholism is a rarity among Jews. Every study made in recent years corroborates the fact that excessive drinking is not a problem in the nationwide Jewish community.

As a result, several of the consequences of alcoholism—family abandonment, chronic unemployment, injury and death through accidents—are also relatively rare.

Jews are also less involved in conflict with the law. Of the 4,500 inmates in San Quentin and Folsom penitentiaries, the Jewish population never quite reaches forty-five—1 per cent of the total number of inmates in a state whose population is 8 per cent Jewish. New York's Sing Sing Prison, in April, 1966, had thirty-six Jewish prisoners out of 1,800 inmates—a bare 2 per cent in an area that is 25 per cent Jewish.

From the cradle to the grave, every social index among the Jews is more favorable. They have a lower infant and maternal mortality rate, less juvenile delinquency, fewer fatherless homes, and their children stay in school longer. They have a higher rate of marriage and of remarriage of the widowed, and a remarkable comprehensive program of old-age assistance. Above all, there is a family cohesiveness that permits few to fall by the wayside. For those who do have problems, the Jewish community has contrived a matchless machinery of assistance and counsel. Being born a Jew in America provides a "social security" without parallel in history.

Jews also seem to live longer and to care much less about retirement. A Providence, Rhode Island, study reports that "among those seventy-five or over, 36.5 per cent of the Jews in the labor force as opposed to only 13 per cent of the total population" resisted retirement. In my own community of Larchmont, the Presbyterian Church has a large group of retired men who meet regularly. We would be hard put to find five such men in the Jewish population.

Many Jews are self-employed, and are therefore not subject to compulsory plans. Nathan Glazer, in his lucid study, *Social Characteristics of American Jews,* offers some insights into the motives for self-employment:

> The Jews are largely still proprietors of their own businesses —whether they be pushcarts, junk yards, groceries, or factories—rather than managers and executives of enterprises they do not own . . . the American Jew tries to avoid getting into a situation where discrimination may seriously affect him. In a great bureaucracy, he is dependent on the impression he makes on his superiors and, increasingly in recent years, dependent on the degree to which he approximates a

certain "type" considered desirable in business. The Jew prefers a situation where his own merit receives objective confirmation, and he is not dependent on the good will or personal reaction of a person who may happen not to like Jews.

A study by the Harvard School of Business Administration, reported in the *Harvard Business Review* of March–April, 1965, compares employment patterns in four types of corporations—some that are all Protestant, others that are all Catholic, still others that are all Jewish, and those that are religiously mixed. The author of the study reports that Jews are "conspicuously absent in the management teams of banks, public utilities, insurance companies, and certain large companies in heavy industry," and points out that while "8 per cent of all college graduates and 25 per cent of Ivy League colleges are Jewish . . . less than 1 per cent of the executive personnel in heavy industry are Jews."

Managements of the old-line companies, the writer declares, look for personality traits quite different from those to be found among most Jewish aspirants to the executive suite. Jewish trainees tend to avoid companies that stress such features as "play it safe" or "one happy family." Instead, they tend to gravitate toward companies "where risk taking is not discouraged, [toward] smaller companies where individual effort is more likely to be recognized. They want companies where profits are important. One would guess that this represents a willingness to be judged in terms of objective criteria of performance rather than in terms of personal impressions . . . more by qualities of ability and skill, less of qualities of pleasant and bland personality." (Lawrence Bloomgarten, a leading authority on the subject of discrimination in the executive suite, reports that "the implicit controlling criterion of selection of the executive has been: Does he look like us?")

I have spoken with a number of Jews who have penetrated the barrier of the executive level, who occupy responsible upper-echelon posts in leading corporations, and they agree that a modest breakthrough is being made. Tough competition, smaller margins of profits, and a greater sophistication in top management are beginning to elbow out the traditional clubhouse fraternalism. Discrimination based on religion—or even race—is a luxury few corporations can now afford. John W. Gardner in his book *Excellence* predicts the emergence of a new aristocracy of the gifted and the trained, whatever their racial or ethnic background may be. "We are witnessing a revolution in society's atittude toward men and women of high ability and advanced training," he points out. "For the first time in history, such men and women are very much in demand on a very wide scale."

America's talented and well-trained young Jews are sharing in the fruits of this revolution. A few hundred have organized their own companies, in such frontier fields as plastics, electronics, data processing, and communications. Others, such as Sol Linowitz of Zerox; Emanuel Piore of I.B.M.; Edwin H. Land of Polaroid; Leonard Goldenson, Richard Salant, David Sarnoff, William Paley, and others in radio and television, head up some of the vital new industries of our century.

Real-estate syndication has captured the imagination of many Jewish businessmen (75 to 90 per cent of those listed in the New York *Law Journal* in this connection are Jewish); so have such disparate ventures as the search for new distribution methods for thousands of electronic products and the creation of musical television commercials.

The booming leisure industry of professional sports has also attracted many Jewish investors. The immigrant generation knew little about football, horse racing, and baseball. (Many years ago, in my native Canada, my Russian-born father attended a hockey game and made the mistake of sitting behind the goal. A flying puck left a lifelong mark over his eyebrow, and he insisted that hockey was "strictly for Gentiles!") The present generation of Jews not only indulges in every sport, it is intimately involved in the business end of many. Some purchase football teams such as the Baltimore Colts, the Cleveland Browns . . . and race tracks such as Hialeah. In 1965, the first three winners of the famous Flamingo race, second only to the Kentucky Derby, were owned by Jewish sportsmen.

The academic community is also undergoing a revolutionary change. A generation ago, a Jewish head of a department at a university was a *rara avis*. Today, many institutions of higher learning have Jewish deans, full professors, and heads of departments. (But the Jewish college president is still virtually nonexistent, according to a recent American Jewish Committee survey.) (See the following chapter.)

During my recent travels around the country I asked a number of people in close contact with men who have made spectacular economic rises how they would explain the remarkable upward mobility of the American Jew in the past half century. They offered a number of familiar theories, and a few that were novel and interesting.

At least part of the answer, most people agree, is pure chance— the fortuitous circumstance of being at the right place at the right time. Jews came into a mushrooming economy that was concentrated in those areas where they lived—the boom landed on them.

Historic circumstances have cultivated a gambling instinct in many Jews. They are willing to take chances. Over the ages, only those who took risks were able to survive. Our swelling economy has done well for the less timid among us.

Basic sociological facts cannot be overlooked. Jews have the smallest families of any group in America. In a primitive culture, large families are an economic asset; in our society they are not. A two-child home can provide more education and more support for a longer period of time. The small family is more mobile; it can pick up stakes more readily and explore more rewarding opportunities.

The life style of the Jewish family, on the other hand, offers not only greater stability, but also more interdependence. In the process of business expansion—the opening up of a branch store, for example—it is customary to employ a cousin or a nephew, who ostensibly will be more loyal and trustworthy than a stranger. And by the same token, a young man who needs money for medical or engineering school may find it less embarrassing to approach a relative for a loan than a bank officer.

The family clan is by no means the limit of mutual support. The Jewish welfare organization, which cultivates close associations and friendships, is often the spawning ground for a number of financial ventures. Just as the country club is a frequent locus for large corporate transactions, so the Jewish Federation committee meeting, which brings together men who work intensely on ambitious civic efforts, may also provide a setting for joint investment.

"Do you know that piece of property on the corner of Fourteen Mile Road and Acapulco?" a furniture store operator may say at the close of a discussion about an upcoming fund appeal, "It's a natural for a shopping center. With those high-rise apartments coming up, and the new plant just a mile away, you can't miss."

The other men at the meeting—a doctor, an insurance executive, a lawyer, and three businessmen, will argue with their friend. Other such discussions will follow, and perhaps four of them will eventually plunge into a joint venture. They have confidence in each other because they have worked together at close range on hospital boards, allocations committees, and many other endeavors.

How much thought goes into the choice of a career? What motivates a man to go into the business of sewing machines or soybeans? Often the decision stems from pure accident. An insurance man told me that forty years ago he had been a textile salesman. One day, after making a particularly good sale, his sales manager, instead of commending him, sarcastically intimated that it was about time he earned his keep. An hour later, he happened to meet an insurance man who asked him if he would be interested in a different job. Thus was a textile man transformed into an insurance representative.

For most American Jews, however, choice rather than chance is the governing factor in determining a life occupation. Deliberation in the choice of a career is fairly basic to the Jewish life style. A Jew, my parents used to say in Yiddish, must be *oisgerechent*—must plan carefully for the future. Career decisions are the subject of endless family discussions. And, because the family circle invariably includes a larger circle of friends, and even acquaintances who are not too reticent about free counsel, young people are subjected to much advice.

Prof. Albert J. Mayer, in his Wayne University study of the Detroit Jewish community, comments:

> The Detroit Jewish population seems to be in the process of entering new occupational fields, and at a very rapid rate. This is more than a continuation of a long trend of alertness toward career opportunities on the part of the Jewish male. They seem to have the capacity to discern new fields of occupational activity, and then act positively to prepare themselves to fill these occupational roles. It would seem to indicate a high degree of conscious rational planning.

In many cities, the Jewish community offers vocational guidance. B'nai B'rith has pioneered in setting up guidance offices throughout the country. Originally intended to pinpoint areas of employment where discrimination was not a problem, the B'nai B'rith counselor today is concerned with aptitudes as well as opportunities.

A generation ago, Jewish discussion groups often concerned themselves with what was called "the inverted triangle." Too many Jews were in the professions, not enough were in agriculture or the heavy industries. Today that bogey has disappeared. Anti-Semitism is too complex a problem to be blamed on such factors as economic distribution of Jews.

Bezalel Sherman reports a considerable decline in the proportion of Jewish students in some professional fields. The steepest decline has been in dentistry and law, and there has been a not insignificant drop in medicine as well. At the same time, Jewish engineering students have doubled during the past twenty years, and almost twice as many young Jewish men and women are enrolled in business administration.

The chart belows indicates the occupational distribution of Jews in a number of cities:

City	Professional	Managers, Proprietors	Clerical	Skilled
Providence	20 per cent	40 per cent	25 per cent	11 per cent
Rochester	26	29	24	17
South Bend	18	56	15	8
Des Moines	14	53	24	5
Detroit	23	54	13	10

Taking Detroit as an example, it is interesting to see how these figures differ from those for the general population. In the over-all figures, 12 per cent of the total are professionals, 10 per cent are managers or owners of businesses, 16 per cent white-collar workers and 62 per cent blue-collar workers.

Only 2.5 per cent of Jews in the labor market are unskilled, compared to 12.4 per cent in the total population. The American economy, geared to absorb most quickly those with education and training, has been kind to the Jews.

"Meet Me at Goldfarb"

Jack Goldfarb's story follows almost to the letter what is now the typical background story of the successful American Jewish businessman, from European poverty to philanthropy in the New World. Born in Poland, his family moved to Germany, where young Jack was left fatherless at the age of six months. When he was ten, Jack drove a horse and wagon in Berlin. He was only eleven years old when he arrived with his sisters in New York. A short time in school, then, like so many of his classmates, he plunged into the business world long before he began to use a razor.

Although he wanted desperately to continue his education, he didn't feel he could continue to lean on his sisters once it became possible for him to work. The world of business beckoned—Western Union paid him two cents for each telegram *delivered*. (No payment if there wasn't anyone in to receive the message.)

A short while later a friend, Hyman Rothbart, five years Jack's senior, took an interest in the young boy and found him a job at $9 a week as a machinist in a pajama factory. Soon he had made himself indispensable: he was the only one in the shop who knew where every piece of goods was located and what stage of progress each article had reached. He was promoted from machinist to presser to cutter, and, before too long, to superintendent of the shop.

Then came World World War I, and Jack Goldfarb joined the Army. When he returned home from France, he took a job in an underwear factory in Indianapolis. In 1926, when Jack was thirty-one years old, his employer died suddenly. Jack had saved some money and he decided to buy the business. Living modestly, he poured himself into every phase of operations: manufacturing, shipping, selling. Administratively, the Union Underwear Company was a one-man task force. Its product a universally recognized trade name, the Goldfarb firm became the largest of its kind in the world.

Jack Goldfarb's formula for success was the old Henry Ford recipe: produce a low-cost item at a uniform price for a mass market.

No mass psychology marked Goldfarb's relationships with his workers. There was a time when he knew every one of them by name, could discuss their family problems with them. With a work force of 5,000, such intimacy is no longer possible. But the chief still arrives at his office early ("Call me any day at 7:30 A.M.," he told me). Even when he had to commute to a plant in Frankfort, Kentucky, fifty miles from his Louisville home, he opened its doors at 7 A.M.

He speaks softly, deferentially. There is none of the bluster of the self-made man, none of the stereotyped pretentiousness one associates with the single-minded, high-geared executive.

The Goldfarb family life style is unostentatious—a single car, a Manhattan apartment that is simply but tastefully decorated. No suburban estate or country club beckons on weekends. He and his attractive wife, Bertha, have four children and eight grandchildren.

All work and no play would make Jack what the rhyme says it would. But the Goldfarb interests are varied. A national vice president of the American Jewish Committee and a board member of Temple Emanu-El, he is also a leader in national UJA and New York's Federation. And as is often the case with those who were unable to continue their own schooling, Jack Goldfarb's particular interest lies in education.

When two students at Brandeis University, in Waltham, Massachusetts, arrange to see each other after dinner, one is likely to say: "Meet me at Goldfarb." The Goldfarb Library is one of the showplaces of the young university. But few of the Brandeis students who walk under the name plate are aware that at their age the man who donated the library had been earning his own livelihood for half his lifetime.

I once heard Jack Goldfarb remark: "Every time I see Dr. Sachar I feel like kissing his hand." It is an odd kind of indebtedness. Abram Sachar, Brandeis' president, has persuaded the New York industrialist to write checks totaling 3 million dollars (a goodly portion of his wealth) for a variety of Brandeis projects. A score of other colleges—Sarah Lawrence, Chicago, and Columbia among them—have also known his benefaction.

Six decades separate the eager Western Union boy from the gentle-mannered man whose name is synonymous with the Brandeis University Library.

America has dealt kindly with the orphan boy from Poland. And, like many of his contemporaries, he has returned that kindness.

CHAPTER 4

American Culture and Jewish Values

"The life of culture depends less on those who inherit
it than on those who desire it."

ANDRÉ MALRAUX

"Jewish intellectuality and artistic appreciation give the city a
special *élan*," declared *Fortune* magazine in February, 1960. In what
ways has the United States been transformed by its large Jewish
population? In what respects are Jews different because they live in
America?

This question might be answered, Jewish fashion, with another
question: To what extent is it a matter of historic accident that two
out of three Jews in the free world are Americans? Or, looking back
in history: To what extent did Jews *select* their lands of sanctuary—
Babylonia, Rome, Alexandria, Holland, Poland?

The last question presupposes a high degree of rationality: *Ubi
bene, ibi domi.* Men in flight find a roost wherever they can, but
they are most strongly drawn to lands of freedom and prosperity.
The Berlin underground is a one-way passage.

Jews have historically established their permanent homes among
peoples of the most advanced civilization. In ancient times, when
they were forced to leave Palestine, they made their way, in large
numbers, to Alexandria, with its numerous scientific institutions,
sophisticated libraries, and institutes of higher learning; to highly
civilized Rome; to such centers of philosophy, science, and poetry as
Babylonia and Spain.

In the wake of the Nazi onslaught, European Jewry scattered to the four corners of the earth: to Ethiopia and Rhodesia, to the Dominican Republic and Shanghai. But these were pauses in the wilderness. Within a decade or more, often after circling the globe, most of them had arrived in the United States.

With all these historic wanderings and settlements it is difficult to determine to what degree Jews made a difference in the cultural level of their host country and to what extent they were the beneficiaries of the highly developed cultures which afforded them a welcome. The historian Solomon Grayzel observed that in lands of freedom Jews enhanced the intellectual climate of their host nation and in turn "were stimulated by their contacts." Modern Germany and Austria are perfect illustrations of this interaction. As Prof. Jacob R. Marcus has well documented, German Jewry, less than 1 per cent of a population of 60 million, provided an immense cultural ferment during the nineteenth and early twentieth centuries. Jewish physicists, chemists, and medical researchers brought the Nobel prize to Germany time and again; psychologists, electrical engineers, musical composers, novelists, and other creative spirits all helped make that country a cultural giant among nations.

Would the United States be much different if it did not include the world's largest Jewish community? Certainly, Jews have found a congeniality of spirit in this land. America's "this-worldliness," tempered by a respect for eternal values, meshes perfectly with the Hebraic *geist*. The late Robert Oppenheimer's portrait of our time— "we live longer, labor less brutally, more seldom suffer starvation, find frequent comfort and relief in illness, travel, communicate, and learn with undreamed-of ease; and we need no slave nor peon"— describes both the American and the Jewish ideal.

Twentieth-century America has been the very nub of the knowledge explosion, especially in nuclear, genetic, and electronic advances. Our educational level has leaped forward. In one generation the number of high-school graduates increased from 21 per cent of the population to 69 per cent. One out of every six Americans in his early twenties is still in school, compared to one in fifteen in 1940.

Europe, the homeland of most Jews at the dawn of the century, has yielded its pre-eminence in art, sculpture, music, and the theater to America. The so-called cultural explosion has suffused the land with little-theater groups and little symphonies. From the heart of

America's corn country, the University of Iowa has dispatched its student symphony orchestra to play, not only on the banks of the Rhine, but on the banks of the Volga.

Theology, long the private domain of European and Asian scholars, has also found a dynamic home in the New World. America's intellectual and spiritual resources are at long last beginning to be worthy of its boundless material resources.

There is little doubt that America's Jews have been in the vanguard of this cultural revolution—in some instances as culture initiators, in others as culture bearers, and everywhere as culture consumers. In Texas, in southern Florida, in Los Angeles, Philadelphia, and Houston, all forms of art and music have received special encouragement from Jewish patrons.

But the word *culture* has meaning beyond the aesthetic and intellectual sense. C. P. Snow defined it as the application of knowledge to human needs. Within this concept, how deep is the enhancement and enrichment of life which have grown out of our new perception of the universe?

The social and psychological sciences, which have come into their own during our lifetime, have only in recent decades been translated from theory into practice. We are trying desperately to extend our knowledge of the human mind, human relationships, and human needs.

American Jews have flocked to the fields of high-school and college teaching, social-welfare administration, mental health, and all the other areas concerned with man's humanity to man. Statistical surveys all bear out the fact that American Jews rank high in educational achievement. A recent study of Jews in Camden, New Jersey, found that "the Jewish population reporting at least four years of college training is more than five times that of the whole population." While only one Camden adult out of four was a high-school graduate, only one Jewish adult out of five had *not* completed four years of high-school training. In the twenty-five- to thirty-four-year age group, 70 per cent of the Jewish males had at least four years of university training, and 45 per cent had *more* than four years of college. A similar survey of San Francisco Jews indicated that more than 47 per cent of Jewish males in the thirty- to forty-four-year age group "have obtained a college degree or a postgraduate diploma."

Again and again, as I traveled around the country talking to Jews in many different walks of life, I asked, "What are your children doing?" And again and again I was told of children in college, in graduate work, or about to enter a profession. It can be safely projected that by the end of the century nine out of ten young adult Jews will have attended college, particularly if subsidized higher education is made increasingly available.

Lawrence Bloomgarden, who has specialized in the study of discrimination in higher education, reported in May, 1966, that approximately 10 per cent of all professors in 785 American senior colleges and universities were Jewish. From 15 to 20 per cent of the faculty at Princeton, Harvard, Columbia, Pennsylvania, California, and similar institutions are of the Jewish faith. Jewish professors of sociology, psychology, anthropology, and economics fill out the departments of leading universities all over the country. Of the forty-five Jewish college deans, six head schools of social work, and five lead schools of government.

Jewish students constitute one-quarter of all the student body at the Ivy League colleges. The high rate of Jewish college enrollment, combined with a very low dropout rate, results in the reason why the American Jewish community, which constitutes less than 3 per cent of the United States population, produces more than 8 per cent of all college graduating classes.

In terms of eventual cultural impact on the nation, it is also interesting to note that Jewish students tend to enroll in the quality schools, including the great state universities: Michigan, Wisconsin, Ohio State, Illinois. Concentrated in the large urban centers, they take advantage of a University of Chicago, UCLA, the outstanding colleges of New York City, and the vast complex of institutions in the Greater Boston area. In past generations, many of the nation's most prominent figures emerged from the smaller schools. But the demands of a highly technical age, with its quickly expanding frontiers of knowledge in the arts, sciences, and technology, have given the advantage to the larger, urban-centered institutions—and these are the schools to which Jewish students have come in large numbers.

But the policy-making bodies of the Ivy League schools, despite their huge Jewish enrollment, remain the private sanctum of Anglo-Saxon America. In June, 1965, William Horowitz, chairman of the Connecticut State Board of Education, became the first non-

Protestant to be elected a trustee of Yale University. As of May, 1966, the American Jewish Committee reported, there were only five Jewish college presidents among the 397 major non-denominational colleges and universities in the country and none at all in the 378 publicly controlled institutions.

The World of Science

In 1960, *Fortune* published a list of "Great American Scientists" who have contributed to "America's rise to the forefront of world science." The list includes such men as Joshua Lederberg, "the most eminent biologist of his generation" at the age of thirty-five; Arthur Kornberg, Nobel prize winner at forty-two, "a biochemist of rare virtuosity"; Jesse Greenstein, head of astronomy at California Tech, "best known for his precise chemical analysis of the stars"; Murray Gell-Mann, a Ph.D at MIT at the age of twenty-one and at thirty-one "the most brilliant of the younger theorists in physics"; and such other colossi of the twentieth century as I. I. Rabi and J. Robert Oppenheimer, who have helped catapult us into the nuclear age. Add to this constellation such names as Albert Rabin, Adrian Kantrowitz, Selman Waksman, and Jonas Salk and dozens of other top names in the medical sciences whose research has saved the lives of hundreds of thousands and made life more livable for millions, and we begin to have some measure of the contribution which American Jews have made to the advancement of human knowledge.

Religion and medicine have long been handmaidens. The Roman Catholic Church over the centuries has created a chain of hospitals that circle the globe. Protestant medical missionaries have brought healing to the most remote villages of Asia, Africa, and the lonely islands of the Pacific. The same urge to translate abstract principles into practice—to mate science with human values—is seen in some of the medical institutions that have been established by the American Jewish community.

Tailors and cutters in the sweatshops of New York were frequent victims of tuberculosis and other lung diseases. They went West in search of health, and in the early part of the twentieth century some remarkable medical centers were created for them. The Jewish community of Denver, a vigorous segment of the city's population, grew out of a concern for the health of the Jewish transplants from

New York and elsewhere. Today the hospitals founded for the Jewish sick are completely nonsectarian, and some of the nation's most gifted specialists in thoracic medicine have gathered at these medical centers.

In Houston, where modern medical miracles in heart and vascular surgery have been wrought, one building in the Houston Medical Center carries a Shield of David on its front wall and a sign that reads: *Jewish Medical Research Center.* It is Jewish in name and origin only. Houston Jews raised the funds for the institution and turned them over to the center. They have no controlling voice in the operation of the center, which was simply a gift of local Jewry to the cause of medical research.

The Albert Einstein College of Medicine in the Bronx was born in 1955, and in a single decade has become one of the foremost research centers in the world. But one of its faculty members was quick to tell me, "There is no such thing as a Jewish scalpel." Although founded by Yeshiva University, the administration has studiously avoided any sectarian philosophy in its operation. And Yeshiva's president, Dr. Samuel Belkin, explains: "Though I do not believe that there is such a thing as Jewish medicine or Jewish science, there is a moral necessity for the Jewish community to make a contribution to the scientific advancement of medicine and public health."

The Kennedy Foundation, created by the Joseph P. Kennedy family to further its long-standing interest in the causes and treatment of mental retardation, recently gave one and one-half million dollars to Einstein College, where frontier researchers such as Dr. Harry Gordon are grappling with this tragic problem. Other vital research on mental illness, heart disease, and cancer is also under way in this bustling medical complex.

Mount Sinai Hospital, Maimonides, Montefiore, Beth Israel, the Hospital for Joint Diseases are all part of the web of Jewish-sponsored hospital research centers scattered throughout the New York area. These institutions have brought together many of the most gifted medical minds in the world, and there have been some strange by-products of their creativity.

I asked Himan Brown, the producer of the Madison Square Garden "Night of Stars" for the Federation of Jewish Philanthropies and other such extravaganzas, how he managed to arrange for the free appearance of non-Jewish stars, such as Henry Fonda, Carol Burnett, Marlon Brando, and hundreds of others. Mr. Brown explained that many of these famous entertainers, who often command as much as 30 thousand dollars for an evening's performance, volunteer their talents without charge out of gratitude for the kind of treatment they had experienced in Jewish hospitals.

Closeness between religion and medicine has not traditionally extended to the world of the physical and natural sciences, but today, in American Jewish life, at least, there seems to be a new rapprochement between the two. In several parts of the country, which are centers of space and general aeronautical technology, new synagogues and temples attest to the interest of many young Jewish engineers and researchers. Three such congregations were founded in the North Hollywood section of Los Angeles, and a number of Jewish scientists are active in San Francisco Bay temples. Jewish welfare funds, which form subdivisions along occupational lines, now have a division of scientists for fund raising among the men in this new field.

In Cleveland, Prof. Simon Ostrach, an eminent authority in fluid dynamics and one of the space-program leaders at Case Institute of Technology, is vice president and chairman of the school board of the Park Synagogue, a Conservative congregation of more than 2,500 families.

In the southern suburb of Houston, where NASA headquarters is located, there is a new congregation made up largely of NASA scientists, as is the synagogue in Cocoa Beach, near the missile base at Cape Kennedy. They are modest congregations, and it is sometimes difficult to gather a *minyan* (a quorum of ten men) for a daily service. One engineer suggested that in the missile synagogue, the *minyan* countdown be reversed to 10-9-8-7-6 . . .

American music without Jews would also be much thinner than we know it. Besides the more serious muscianship of George Szell, Erich Leinsdorf, Leonard Bernstein, Lukas Foss, David Diamond, and the popular, lilting music of Rodgers and Hammerstein, Irving Berlin, George and Ira Gershwin, Alan Lerner, the roster of Jews in music includes such performing artists as Artur Rubenstein, Vladimir Horowitz, Yehudi Menuhin, Isaac Stern, Richard Tucker,

Jan Peerce, Risë Stevens, Gregor Piatigorsky, Benny Goodman, scores of others. A Jewish mother traditionally placed a fiddle in her son's hands as soon as he was old enough to hold it, and it has been estimated that nine of every ten members of the string sections in the finest symphonies of America are Jewish.

Jews have also done much to popularize good music in the United States. Sol Hurok has brought the music and ballet of the world to large and small communities throughout the land. Saturday night at the symphony is a tradition among many big-city Jews from Boston to San Francisco. A disproportionate number of them hold season tickets. Jewish music lovers in smaller cities have often taken the lead in bringing the best talent to areas which have long been limited primarily to Western folk songs and rock and roll. And cultural exchange, a new phenomenon in a land which has often tended toward the parochial, has unquestionably been expedited by many Jews, who have shared their cosmopolitan outlook with their fellow Americans.

Jan Peerce

"If God doesn't give a man a brain to match his talent," said Jan Peerce as we both looked out at the snow falling on the spacious grounds of his New Rochelle home, "he is out of luck."

Jan Peerce was reminiscing about his quarter of a century with the Metropolitan Opera Company.

"A vocal artist," he said, "must produce a combination of sound, depth, color, nuance, poetry, sense, and other qualities. He must have both sincerity and integrity."

As he spoke, I looked at his rather sharp features and his aquiline nose, and thought about the woman sitting next to me at a Peerce concert who whispered to her neighbor, "He's Norwegian, you know . . . the name, Peerce."

Born Jacob Perelmuth, Jan Peerce grew up on the Lower East Side of New York. Like many Jewish boys, he studied the violin, but his prime ambition was to be a singer, and he used the money he earned as a violinist to pay for vocal training. His first rendezvous with fame as a popular vocalist came at the old Roxy Theatre in New York City. It was his employer, Samuel (Roxy) Rothafel, who urged him to adopt a more euphonious name for show business—a practice common among those who hoped for an entertainment career. After some thought, they chose Jan Peerce, and it has been his name ever since.

Peerce's musical fame has held steadfast for a full generation. The tenor has often been compared favorably with Enrico Caruso, and Arturo Toscanini was so impressed with the lyric quality of his voice that he encouraged Peerce to become an operatic singer.

Jan cautiously avoided a premature debut. He had been singing before audiences since he was eleven. In his pre-violin days, he sang at High Holy Day services at the synagogue. The alumnus of Radio City Music Hall journeyed to Italy to immerse himself in the language and the style of Italian opera. Louis Biancolli, the music critic who rhapsodized about Peerce as "one of the seven wonders of music," called him "a United Nations of a tenor."

"From the way he pronounces Neapolitan," wrote Mr. Biancolli, hailing Peerce's twenty-five years at the Met, "I would deem him a fellow Neapolitan. . . . When he sings in Yiddish and Hebrew, he is the epitome of all the protest and pain of the Jew. . . . I have also heard Peerce sing Bach with an intensity of fervor that argued the Protestant way to divinity. When he sings the "Manzoni Requiem" of Verdi, one would swear this to be the soaring voice and aspiration of a confirmed Catholic piety."

Jan Peerce and I discussed his philosophy of music. He clung to the definition of art as communication, and as a source of pleasure. To the artist, he explained, there is the ultimate satisfaction of sensing an electric quality of joy in the audience. His relation to the audience is crucial: "I don't think you can separate the artist from the man."

"What about the many artists who lack these qualities you prize?" I asked.

"The great artists, by and large, have the capacity of humanity. Caruso was a great human being. Even the lowliest person mourned for a man who was capable of such great kindness. . . . You have to be a *mensch* [an authentic human being] to be able to communicate."

"But how, with so much adulation, can a star avoid being a prima donna?"

"Of course, you need ego to stand before a vast audience. But I don't believe what the promotion men say about me.

"I think that an important ingredient in an artist's life is good family relationships, normal family experience. I think I'm self-critical, and my wife is candidly critical, though never in a destructive way."

Alice Peerce, a small, dark, brightly dynamic woman, nodded approvingly. Mrs. Peerce has had her own public career in communal work. She has been a leader in Bonds for Israel for eleven years, and for six years the national president of its women's division. Their home is constantly open for fund-raising functions. Alice Peerce judges artists on two separate scales: their talent—and their willingness to give of themselves to worthy causes.

Peerce is a perfectionist. He is one of the few recording artists whose contract assures him the right to correct every wrong note.

"On the concert and opera stage I am always conscious of the fact that there is someone in the audience who knows more about music than I do. I respect my audience. . . . You have to be honest with yourself.

"I cannot be happy doing one thing, like opera. I enjoy the variety of the concert stage, television, radio, recordings, working abroad. I even like working in a gambling casino. It's always astonishing to find that men and women can be diverted from the gambling table long enough to listen to serious music."

Jan Peerce sees himself also as an educator. He loves to bring his audiences the best Jewish music of an age gone by.

I recall the excitement of a packed auditorium in Moscow, when the opera star sang three Yiddish songs before an audience that included several hundred Jews, most of them young. The walls shook with rhythmic applause. Speaking to him in his hotel room after the performance, it was obvious that this was a deep emotional experience. Against the advice of his U.S. Embassy advisors, he had reached out to the community that had for so long been deprived of Jewish contact.

On the previous Saturday morning, Peerce had stepped aside from his operatic role to act as cantor at the Great Synagogue in Moscow. He had been a cantor for seven years, and in his home congregation, Beth El, he ascends the pulpit every Yom Kippur afternoon to chant the *Neilah* (concluding) service.

Every weekday of his life, Jan Peerce dons his *tefillin* (phylacteries) to recite the daily prayers prescribed by tradition.

"I find great beauty in religion. There is beauty and peace in putting on my *tefillin*. I believe in *hiddur mitzvah*—embellishing a required religious act—and when I find an attractive *siddur* [prayer book] I purchase a dozen for my friends. No matter how full my concert schedule, I arrange to be with my family all eight days of Passover. When I turn down an engagement for that period, I get special satisfaction in letting my Christian associates know that I respect my faith."

The much-traveled tenor adheres to the kosher dietary laws—an accomplishment which often requires considerable ingenuity. On his Japanese tour his luggage included large packages of permissible foods. "Once I went six weeks without tasting meat."

The artist's love of tradition is linked with strong parental ties.

"My childhood years were in a matriarchal setting. It was Mother's insistence on practice and her hope for a career that led me to musical proficiency." (Many an East Side boy remembers more vividly than any other single admonition his mother's oft-repeated plea, "Practice!") "But my father was learned, and probably influenced me more than she did."

Not long ago, at a party marking his father's eightieth birthday, Jan offered a toast:

"Poppa, I would love you even if you were someone else's father, for the big man that you are!"

A few days later he received a call from Poppa.

"I just listened to the tape recording of the party. When you spoke, I didn't quite realize what you were saying. Jan, do you really think it's true about me?"

Man with a Mission—Dore Schary

I first met Dore Schary in 1951, when he escorted me on a tour of the Hollywood studios of Metro-Goldwyn-Mayer. Vice president in charge of production, he had risen to the summit of international film fame as the author of such films as *Young Tom Edison* and *Boys' Town*, and producer of a score of box-office favorites. But Schary was restless in the routine of success. He wanted to say something, to deal with such unpleasant subjects as intolerance and injustice, even if it made the movie-goer in Paducah or Poughkeepsie squirm a little.

Experts warned him that bigotry was no fare for the millions of people who came to the theater for relaxation. Problem films lacked commercial appeal. Besides, he was told, they were un-American, for a substantial number of Hollywood movies made their way to the foreign market, and exposure of the nation's blemishes would tarnish the American image.

Schary was not convinced, and in the years that followed he proceeded to produce a number of taboo films, among them such classics as *Crossfire,* dealing with anti-Semitism, and *Go for Broke,* on the sensitive theme of Japanese-Americans.

I met the author-director-producer again early in 1966, in his art-filled apartment in Manhattan. An elaborately decorated *mezuzah* adorned the Schary doorpost.

We spoke about the role of Jews in the American theater as creators and as patrons. He quoted the quip of Brendan Behan: "If there were two Yom Kippurs, Broadway would go broke."

Mr. Schary estimated that about half the ticket purchasers are Jewish, and, for some plays, over 70 per cent. He talked about the Jewish playwrights—Arthur Miller, George Kaufman, Kingsley, Burrows, Rice (he did not refer to his own works, such as *Sunrise at Campobello*). We discussed other fields, and he ventured the guess that half the film writers were Jewish, more than half of the directors and 75 per cent of the film producers. Fewer Jews had attained eminence in acting—Paul Muni, John Garfield, Edward G. Robinson, Tony Curtis, and several of the better-known comedians, among others.

When I asked Dore Schary what in his opinion had led Jews into the creative arts, he speculated that Jewish family life encouraged self-expression. "We stress individualism; we are somewhat less disciplined. We are great storytellers around the family hearth, like the Irish.

"We have a lot in common with the Irish. They suffered social and religious discrimination; they couldn't get into many areas of employment. That is why vaudeville was Jewish and Irish, with a mixture of Italians. And we went into the movie industry for the same reason that those among the underprivileged went into boxing. The theater, especially movies, was a 'bastard art.' "

I mentioned the artistic *mezuzah* on his door, and our conversation turned to his religious philosophy. The Scharys are Conservative Jews, and he has devoted some of his writing skills to devising special rituals for the festivals of Hanukah and Passover.

"I think we ought to use the holy day of Yom Kippur much more creatively than we do. In my home, we follow the old tradition, on Yom Kippur eve, of gathering the family in a self-scrutiny session, asking forgiveness from one another for any offenses we have committed in the past year. My children couldn't wait until they were thirteen so that they could fast for the full twenty-four-hour period.

"I want my children to know the sights, the sounds, the smells of Jewishness. I'm happy that my daughters know how to make a Jewish meal, that my son adheres to Jewish tradition. I'm a great believer in the folkways of Judaism."

Schary often speaks at religious services, and he complained that synagogues are not reaching their congregants. He believes in much more experimentation in worship—and in teaching more of the basics—the meaning of the Kaddish and such simple things as what is inside a *mezuzah*.

Dore Schary is currently the national chairman of the Anti-Defamation League of B'nai B'rith. He has been active in ADL since the middle 1930s.

"Though the problem of prejudice has diminished in America, I feel that anti-Semitism, in its vulgar and obscene forms, still exists. Our agency has established itself as the repository of information that is used by everyone concerned with human rights.

"I believe that I have helped the ADL to maintain its proper focus, emphasizing the positive aspects of Judaism as well as its purely defensive needs."

Schary is a man with a strong sense of mission, as a Jew and as an American. He believes that America has given Jews a sense of security and an attachment to a political system that is completely congenial to the Jewish ethos. Jews have a sense of well-being in the United States, the feeling that they have contributed to the creation of a culture. In other lands, Jews have joined an ongoing culture. America has imbued them with a unique sense of involvement and participation.

Looking back over his own life, which began in Newark, New Jersey, sixty years ago, Dore Schary once said:

"Thank God, mine has been a happy life. I have always had a

dual identity with no apologies, no complications. I am an American and a Jew. And I have had no trouble functioning in either capacity, whether in the movies, politics, or Jewish affairs."

The revolution of human relations which has taken place in our generation cannot be traced to a single social force. Such experts as Gordon Allport and Bruno Bettelheim have analyzed the dynamics of social changes, and have noted its many subtleties and complexities.

The U.S. Supreme Court decisions, beginning in 1954, and the series of legislative enactments of the past decade which have outlawed discrimination, reflected a shift in national mood. What produced the change? In their book, *Social Change and Prejudice*, Bruno Bettelheim and Morris Janowitz pinpoint such factors as education and mobility:

> The mass media, by making use of official and unofficial statements on race relations and linking racial equality to religious tolerance, have created a new "definition of the situation" for its mass audience . . . this revolution in content has had at least a powerful negative effect in repressing extreme prejudice and creating the conditions under which governmental agencies and voluntary associations can operate to bring about social change.

Dore Schary, a valorous pathfinder in one of the most pervasively potent of the mass media, can look back with satisfaction upon his part in the revolution.

Jews and the Art Explosion

"I would estimate that 80 per cent of all contemporary art in this country—especially those pieces that cost less than $2,500—is owned by American Jews."

The speaker was a professor of art appreciation at a California university. I have quoted this estimate to a number of people knowledgeable in the field of art, and have found few ready to contradict it.

The world's largest collection of twentieth-century artists— estimated to be worth between thirty and fifty million dollars— recently was donated to the U.S. government by Joseph H. Hirshhorn, an immigrant from Latvia, whose 5,000 paintings and 1,500 pieces of sculpture will be housed in a building to be erected by the government, in cooperation with the Smithsonian Institution. Mr. Hirshhorn will also provide a million dollars toward the cost of creating a suitable setting for his collection.

Mr. Hirshhorn is far from alone in his interest in the contemporary masters. Edward G. Robinson in Hollywood; Norton Simon in Los Angeles; Arnold Maremont in Chicago; the late Billy Rose, the Guggenheims and Albert List of New York; Dr. Leonard Rosen of Miami Beach, are other American Jews who have acquired a sizable collection of major works in all the art media.

But perhaps the most striking symbol of Jewish involvement in modern art is the Museum of the Jewish Theological Seminary in New York. Originally founded as a showcase for traditional synagogue ceremonial art—the Fifth Avenue building houses the world's largest collection of Torah adornments—the museum has also devoted itself to the encouragement of modern Jewish artistic expression. Adjacent to the mansion housing the ritual objects is the Albert List Museum, one of the outstanding exhibit halls for contemporary art in New York City.

What explains this strange juxtaposition—the eleventh-century illuminated manuscripts of Spanish Jewry side by side with the abstractionists, the expressionists, the post-expressionists, the surrealists, and the "experimenters with junk?"

The Jewish Theological Seminary, a Conservative institution, has historically attracted to its lay leadership many of the old Jewish aristocracy. In recent years, the new wealth has joined the ranks of the Lehmans, the Schiffs, and the Warburgs in supporting the "seminary." (In the shorthand vocabulary of American religious Jewry, "the seminary" refers to the headquarters of the Conservative movement, "the college" is the Hebrew Union College, heart of the Reform movement, and "the Yeshiva" is Yeshiva University, focal point of Orthodox loyalties.) The Albert List family and others have fused their two interests, contemporary art and the theological school, in one institution—the Jewish Museum.

I visited Mrs. List in their apartment overlooking Central Park, not far from the museum. The List home reflects the family enthusiasm for contemporary art.

"Although there are other museums of modern art in New York," said Mrs. List, "our museum has done the most to encourage the new artists and the new art forms."

I spoke with a veteran lawyer, an art enthusiast in Philadelphia, who observed that women were often the motivating force in family art involvement. "She attends classes at the Barnes Foundation," he explained, "and the family gradually begins its acquisitions. As their investment grows, it is no longer practical to rely solely on their own judgment, and they consult experts in New York or Chicago or Los Angeles. Soon they acquire the vocabulary of the art world, and a realm of discourse is established with other enthusiasts.

"What motivates the art collector? Social status is certainly a factor. For some, the element of investment adventure may be a consideration. A Prendergast that originally cost $3,000 may now be worth $50,000. Perhaps it's like real estate. Those Jews who acquire wealth are willing to take chances, especially because of the rising market."

The attorney-collector speculated that there might also be certain deeply rooted historic impulses behind the Jewish passion for art collecting. For many centuries, Jews were not permitted to own land. It had become a folk habit to transform wealth into portable forms, as security against the possible need for flight.

A Jewish sociologist, who is also an artist, offered his theories about the Jewish interest in contemporary creativity.

"The power elite in America is, by and large, Protestant. Jews have seized a good part of the culture elite, and they want to bypass the power elite who run the boards of museums, symphony orchestras, and the like. By organizing a modern museum of art, they are able to create a parallel aristocracy.

"I have an idea, too, that Jews have stayed away from the old masters because so much of it is Christological. They like the contemporary—everything that is new—including Scandinavian furniture and modern architectural design. The past reminds them of their alien status. It is not an American phenomenon alone. Jews in London and Paris and Vienna also have gone modern. Jewish interest in art is always future-oriented.

"Look at the idea of the art show, which has raised such large sums of money for charity. The National Council of Jewish Women,

Hadassah, and the temple Sisterhoods started the idea; now the Urban League, the Little Red School House, and other groups use the same device."

At a recent private showing of outstanding privately owned works in Chicago I was told by one local leader: "The organization didn't have a single Jew on its board, but in the ranks of the collectors it was hard to find a single Gentile."

He added: "You can't vote yourself a member of the Art Institute Board, but you can vote yourself a fine collector."

I visited the offices of the industrialist, Arnold Maremont, who made his fortune in auto-parts manufacturing. The lobby of his twelve-story building overlooking Lake Michigan contains some eye-catching art, including a sculptural assemblage by Lesar, consisting of shells of auto headlights and parts of fenders. Maremont's roof-garden office is hung with the best of Jackson Pollock, Turnbull, and others. A lively work by Marisol called "A Date" held my attention as we spoke.

Arnold Marmont has been a civic leader in Illinois for many years. He stirred up a good deal of controversy in fighting for urban renewal, and has been a national leader in the planned-parenthood movement. But contemporary art is obviously a primary interest in his life. He showed me paintings and sculpture he had acquired in the art capitals of the world. The Maremont Foundation financed America's participation in the Venice Festival.

We spoke about the interest of Jews in contemporary works, and Maremont was candid in his comments. "Art is to Jews what politics is to the Irish; the means of entrance into the power structure of America. The Establishment has pre-empted all other areas. One area it had overlooked was contemporary art. This became, for wealthy Jews, a way of achieving distinction and meeting people. This is as true of Jews in Paris and Brussels and London as it is of Americans. . . . At any opening night at the theater or symphony, half the audience is Jewish. We have no Museum of Modern Art here in Chicago, but if one were founded, it would be all Jewish."

A member of Artists' Equity in New York estimated that about three-quarters of its 800 members were Jews, and described the art world in all its phases—artist, entrepreneur, and patron—as predominantly Jewish.

"Part of the reason for Jewish interest in living art is that the best of the past is already owned. Where can you get an El Greco today, if you feel like buying it? Jews have no feeling for the works of earlier centuries. It comes from a milieu they don't know. And modern art appeals to them because of its vitality, its play of ideas, its fascinating color, its adventurousness, its play on the emotions."

Aesthetic passion is regarded by some as alien to the Hebraic spirit. Heinrich Heine insisted that a human being could be either a Greek or a Jew—a slave of beauty or of holiness—but never both. A modern Hebrew poet laureate, Saul Tchernichovski, somehow conveyed to his readers that he had abandoned the Jewish spirit for paganism when he wrote *At the Feet of Apollo.*

There are those who regard the modern Jew's interest in art as a substitute religion, with Apollo supplanting Jehovah. And it may be true that art has become the faith of some American Jews. But others find a kinship between religious and artistic expression. Mrs. List, for example, recalling her lifelong enthusiasm for works of art, told me that it was intimately linked with her Jewish experience— with childhood memories of the Sabbath table, the warmth of family love, the glow of Sabbath candles. Dore Schary, another art aficionado, also discusses a tie that, for him, binds the religious and aesthetic impulses.

Perhaps it is all summed up in the answer Joseph Hirshhorn gave some time ago to an interviewer who asked him, "Why do you collect?"

"Why do I collect? I love it. It gives me an inner joy. It's great. I get up in the morning and see these things and it's beautiful. . . . It has to do with the heart, the brain, and that's it."

CHAPTER 5

Life, Liberty, and the Pursuit of Health

"What can we know of the next world if we know so little about this one?" These words of Confucius reflect the attitude of suspended judgment which most Jews also have toward life after death. Although traditional vocabulary is sprinkled with allusions to "paradise," "the eternal Garden of Eden," and the rewards of the world to come, Jews have placed most of their emotional investment in the here and now. "Choose life," the Bible says. And in America, especially, life style is grounded in a this worldly religion.

This delight in the present is not to be equated with hedonism, with a preoccupation with the pleasures of the moment. Jews have clearly cultivated the middle-class quality of postponing today's satisfactions for tomorrow's benefit. But this readiness to project into the future is related to a foreseeable future: the medical student who invests long years in his career is hardly following a philosophy of "tomorrow we die"; his is clearly a concern for the good life.

Jews mourn the dead in a way that presupposes the finality of death. And the prolongation of life is a *summum bonum*, and health is virtually an object of worship.

An act of charity acquires a special dimension if it is concerned with healing. A speaker at a Hadassah luncheon can reduce the audience to tears—and larger checks—with a report of how the Youth Aliyah program saved a ten-year-old Moroccan child.

48

Even the Miami Beach–Catskill ritual is part of this involvement with health. The annual winter pilgrimage to southern Florida to drink in the sun, and the summer hegira to mountains are like the ancient Roman journey to the baths. The Romans emphasized decorativeness and a variety of diversions. But for the Jews the baths, especially if they were spas, have always been the "fountains of living waters," to use a Biblical phrase. Jewish pilgrims flock to any place on the map which has the word "springs" attached to it: Saratoga, Sharon, Mount Clemens, Hot Springs—all America's answer to Carlsbad and Marienbad, where European Jewry of an earlier era gathered.

Not only the life abundant, but the long life, is a dominant theme in Judaism. "May you live till one hundred and twenty!" is a toast heard frequently on happy occasions. As a young man I visited Palestine, and met a great-great-aunt who was one hundred and fourteen. She was in excellent health, needed no glasses, and still danced at weddings—one of the traditional ambitions of the Jewish elderly. In the round of toasts at the dinner table, her eighty-eight-year-old son-in-law rose to offer the traditional one-hundred-and-twenty-year toast. But this time he modified the formula: "Mama, till the Messiah comes!" As the saying goes, he didn't want to shorten her years.

Jewish dedication to the practice of medicine is an ancient tradition, and one to which American Jewry is deeply devoted. In the 1930s an Ohio study revealed that while the general public produced one doctor per 756 in the over-all population, the ratio for Jews was one out of 231. Today, in most of the country's large cities, the ratio of Jewish doctors to Jewish population is about one to 140. According to a 1964 report of the American Medical Association, the proportion of doctors to the entire population was one to 704.

But the large number of physicians is only one aspect of the Jewish passion for medicine. Bezalel Sherman, in his *The Jew within American Society*, points out that "it is well known that Jews seek medical advice more than do non-Jews."

I queried physicians in many parts of the country about their Jewish patients, and encountered a wide disparity of views. Several suggested that the reactions of people in a doctor's office were affected less by religious beliefs than by socioeconomic status. A Long Island physician found no difference among his patients between second-generation Jews than others in the general population. An Ohio doctor wrote, "I feel that on the whole reactions are better categorized on the basis of literacy than religion . . . the amount and type the patients read . . . ladies' magazines, *Reader's Digest*, literature dispensed by various fund drives are far more influential in determining how soon a patient sees a doctor."

But another physician wrote: "Jews are more concerned and perhaps better informed about different diseases, and their attitude toward terminal disease is certainly not so stable as the Catholic patients in my practice."

And a medical specialist contributed this concurring view: "In discussing their ailments, they [Jews] are more apt than not to ask detailed questions based upon reading. When serious disease threatens a member of a Jewish family, they are more inclined to ask for a consultation."

A New Haven psychiatrist told me that when an old-line Yankee entered his office, he usually came alone, whereas Jewish patients were often surrounded by relatives. But so were Italians and Negroes.

The powerful family tradition among Jews is a factor in the physician-patient relationship: "Jewish patients are inclined to shield their loved ones from the knowledge of terminal disease, but show no greater antipathy toward knowing it for themselves."

Those physicians who felt that there were certain definable characteristics among Jewish patients held that Jewish families are likely to call a doctor more quickly when puzzling symptoms develop, and to ask early specialist consultation. They are also more apt to question the doctor's judgment, and to switch doctors if their confidence is shaken, or if the rate of recovery appears slow.

Mark Zborowski, the sociologist whose delightful *Life Is with People* evoked memories of the East European Jewish community of the last century, analyzed the reaction of Jewish patients in his study of "Cultural Components in Response to Pain." Comparing the behavior of Italian and Jewish patients in a veterans' hospital, Dr. Zborowski tells us that "while the threshold of pain is the same regardless of race, color, or creed, the underlying attitude may be different. The Italian men concentrated on the pain itself, and their preoccupation was in alleviating the discomfort and misery. The Jewish patients were more interested in the *causes* of pain, and the long-range threat to health implied in its presence. Thus, the former directed their concern toward pain-relieving drugs, while the latter wanted reassurance regarding the source of their difficulties."

The Italian patient, reported Dr. Zborowski, "displays a more confident attitude toward the doctor . . . whereas the Jewish patient manifests a skeptical attitude." The Italian is present-oriented: "When will I get back to work? The Jew is future-oriented: "What's the basic illness?"

Both Jews and Italians were more emotional than the Anglo-Saxon patients. They spoke more about their illnesses and expected more sympathy from their relatives. The Italian patient did not complain at home—that's a female role—while the Jew was vocal at home but calmer in the hospital. Jewish culture, according to Dr. Zborowski, allows the patient to exploit his pain within his own family, but would regard it as improper among strangers.

Like members of other minority groups, Jewish doctors often wish that their practice was "less Jewish." Members of the "in group" generally evince more patience and tolerance with outsiders than with their own.

A Missouri doctor suggested that there might be regional differences in the behavior pattern of Jewish patients, and a Beverly Hills, California, internist and a University of Cincinnati professor of medicine both took me to task for what they regarded as dangerous generalizations. Should they read this chapter, I trust that they will accept these observations as merely impressionistic. I leave to the social scientists a study in depth of this fascinating subject.

What about Jewish Longevity?

The most ambitious study in this area was undertaken by Prof. Sidney Goldstein, head of the Sociology and Anthropology Department at Brown University. The over-all evidence, Dr. Goldstein informs us, is quite meager. A few surveys, in St. Louis, New York, Montreal, and London, offer some interesting clues but there is still no definitive information.

Dr. Goldstein's conclusions based on a careful survey of the mortality pattern of Providence Jewry are very guarded and tentative. But his research "suggests that differences exist between the age-specific death rates, life expectancy, and survival patterns of Jews and of the total white population of Greater Providence."

The St. Louis study showed that the Jewish mortality rate was 14 per cent lower than the rest of the resident white population. The rates were also lower for accidents, pneumonia, diseases of early infancy, syphilis, tuberculosis, and alcoholism, and substantially lower for infant mortality and stillbirths. A similar study in New York reported "a much lower death rate." And an analysis of Canadian Jews, a generation ago, indicated that Jewish males have a life expectancy 4.5 years greater than other males, while Jewish females were likely to live 3.6 years longer than women in the general population.

Dr. Goldstein's statistics reveal that of 1,000 Jewish males born, all but eleven were alive at age five, while in the general population, twenty-eight failed to survive. Sixteen Jewish males out of 1,000 died before age twenty-five, compared with thirty-nine in the total white population. Eighty-eight Jews succumbed by age fifty-five; in the general white community the figure was 157.

But at age sixty-five the pattern is reversed. In other words, the chance is better than average that a Jewish baby will live beyond age sixty, but the favorable odds level out in the later years.

In all of these studies the determining factors seem to be prenatal attention and early child care. The head of obstetrics at a leading medical school noted that Jewish women are much more likely to seek medical attention in pregnancy and pediatric care when the baby is born.

Death through accident among Jewish children is also lower, not only because of social class, but because of greater "parental anxiety," and hence close supervision. Even in the forty-five to sixty-four age group, the Jewish accident rate is less than half the general population, a reflection perhaps of more sedentary style of living. The fact that there is virtually no death caused by alcoholism among Jews may also be a factor in the lower death and accident rate, since intoxication is a leading contributory cause of accidental death.

At all events, we do know that mortality rates vary according to occupation. The standard mortality ratio—the index used in government reports—places professional men, managers, and proprietors far ahead of service workers and laborers, craftsmen and foremen. The teaching profession scores best. A review of these guidelines leaves little doubt that American Jews are concentrated in those economic endeavors which favor longevity.

A vivid illustration of the Jewish pursuit of health was cited by Dr. George James, dean of the newly organized medical school of Mount Sinai Hospital in New York. Dr. James, former Commissioner of Health of New York City, told me that when a cancer-detection clinic was opened in the Yorkville section of the city, 90 per cent of the women who used the facility were Jewish. The examinations turned up few cases of cancer of the cervix, because Jewish women are only one-sixth to one-eighth as prone to this disease as are other women. When the clinic was moved to East Harlem, Dr. James reported, the cancer rate was still below average. For 75 per cent of these patients, too, were Jewish. "They just stayed on the subway a bit longer," Dr. James explained.

I asked Dr. James what accounted for the rarity of cervical cancer among Jewish women. "Jewish women have fewer children; they tend to marry later, they have better medical care before and after birth, they have far less venereal disease and, though it hasn't been proved, male circumcision may be a factor," Dr. James theorized.

Only one disease, diabetes, is distinctly more prevalent among Jews than among their non-Jewish neighbors. A Detroit internist specializing in diabetes explained that the disease is most prevalent among those who overindulge in food. It is an affluent-society disease.

There is also a rare childhood disease that is found almost exclusively among Jews—Tay-Sacks disease—a neurological disorder that is invariably fatal. According to one authority, this may be due to inbreeding, but not enough is known about it to warrant definitive conclusions.

In a rather uncomplicated and frankly nonprofessional attempt to validate the findings of sociologists in St. Louis, New York, Providence, and Montreal, I analyzed some data made available to me by the Riverside Memorial Chapel in Manhattan, covering some 1,000 Jews who had died during the months of July and December, 1965.

The average age of the men at death was 69.5, and of the women, 73.6. Eighteen per cent of the men and 32 per cent of the women had lived to age eighty or older; 82.7 per cent of the married men predeceased their wives; 26.5 per cent of the women died before their husbands. Only one out of a hundred was under forty-five at the time of death and one out of 500 was younger than twenty-five.

Of course these figures represent solely that segment of New York Jewry which normally turns to the Riverside Chapel for burial services—a group which is almost entirely middle class. As Dr. Goldstein's studies noted, the death rate in the high and middle socioeconomic class is 20 per cent below that of lower socioeconomic classes.

Dr. C. L. Rose, in an analysis of *The Social Forces in Longevity* (1963), cited a number of environmental factors affecting longevity. In addition to the biological factor of parental longevity, they include a high degree of intelligence and education "which leads to a special position more favorable to health and the maintenance of longevity"; a higher occupational status; smaller families (more typical of the Jews than any other ethnic group in America), "which limits the stress, both economic and emotional, placed upon the breadwinner and parent"; "maintenance of 'with-spouse' status which assures better physical and emotional support" (as mentioned earlier, less than 2 per cent of Jews remain unmarried, compared with some 7 to 8 per cent of the total community); and finally, "maintenance of the occupational role or its surrogate into the elderly years, which bolsters feelings of esteem, usefulness, and creativity."

It would seem that the Jewish pattern of living—cultural, economic, and social—is a distinct factor in determining the length of their lives. Many social scientists caution, however, that the Jewish patterns thus described persist largely under momentum of past traditions. Should the Jews lose much of their cultural distinctiveness in years to come the distinctions stemming from such differences are also likely to diminish.

Jews and Mental Health

There is a waggish definition, harking back to days of Old Vienna, that describes a psychoanalyst as "a bright young Jewish doctor who can't stand the sight of blood." Although absolute statistics are lacking, most knowledgeable people I have spoken to agree that a very high number of Jewish medical students choose psychotherapy as their specialty. It has been estimated that 70 per cent of the older analysts—especially those born in Europe—are Jews, and 55 per cent of the younger men.

Leo Srole and Thomas Langner in *Mental Health in the Metropo-*

lis, touched on the "Jewish factor" in psychiatry in their study of midtown Manhattan. Among their many observations about Jews as patients, the two sociologists report the following:

"Jews exhibit a high level of acceptance of psychoanalytical psychiatry with a minimum of disturbance of their social values. Jews convey the most favorable group picture of mental health in the stratum having the highest concentration of mental morbidity."

The emotional stability of Jews "may conceivably be eugenic on balance, in the scientific sense that powerful homeostatic supports are brought to play at danger points of crisis and stress that in other groups may be unbalancing for the family and impairing for the individual."

One of the few objective studies of mental disease among Jews was conducted by Dr. Benjamin Malzberg, who investigated first admissions to New York State mental institutions in 1950. In Dr. Malzberg's survey, Jews rated much lower than the general population in the incidence of senile psychosis (12 per 100,000 compared to 17 per 100,000), general paresis (much less than half the average), alcoholic psychosis (one-eighteenth of average), and manic-depressive psychosis (two-thirds of average).

History may explain this stability, Dr. Malzberg wrote, "A group that for thousands of years has been beleaguered by chronic threats of destruction survives by developing internal processes of resistance, deep within the dynamics of the family itself, that counteract in some measure the more extreme kinds of exogenous crises and check the more extreme forms of pathological reaction."

Thousands of years of buffeting, it would seem, have winnowed out the emotionally more vulnerable among the Jews, leaving the survivors more able to cope with their anxieties. "Whom the gods would destroy they first make mad," declared the ancient Roman poet. It would seem that whom the gods would spare they make more immune to madness—or at least resilient enough to handle life's complex problems.

Yet there is no doubt that "mild anxiety" and more serious emotional problems bring many Jewish patients to the psychiatric couch. Leo Rosten, whose scintillating *Captain Newman, MD,* portrayed a Jewish psychiatrist applying Jewish values to his professional work, quotes Levinson on the "high rate of mild anxiety among Jews." All work and not enough play may be a source of

Jewish neurosis, Levinson speculates. "In overemphasis on academic success, the social, recreational, and personal life of the Jewish male students has been hindered."

The so-called "New Haven Study" by B. H. Roberts and J. K. Meyers contrasts Jews, Irish, and Italians with regard to mental disorders. Confronted with the stress of everyday living, the Irish often turn to alcohol for solace. Not so the Jews. "From the psychodynamic viewpoint, it is remarkable that the Irish find an outlet for many diverse forms of psychic conflict in this single form of escape. On the other hand, the Jews' disapproval of inebriety precludes this means for the Jewish neurotic."

Possibly the Jewish neurosis is translated into terms of food. Anyone who has been to a modern Jewish wedding or Bar Mitzvah party and has watched the guests consume more food than is served at a normal banquet *before* they sit down to the dinner table, has had ample clinical evidence of the gastronomic solution to life's tribulations.

Although the proportion of Jews in public institutions is far below the general average (many times), many more find their way to private mental hospitals—a proportion of three to one, according to a 1950 Manhattan study.

The "New Haven Study" found that "not a single patient of Irish birth was receiving psychotherapy," a situation traceable in part to the strong opposition of some Catholic prelates to the entire concept of psychoanalysis. It was an opposition that Jewish religious leaders never shared. When Bishop Fulton Sheen directed a pulpit and television blast against the analysts some years ago, scores of rabbis rushed to their defense. "Whatever the ultimate verdict of science, psychoanalysis is one of the great scientific discoveries of the century," declared the eminent and widely respected Rabbi Robert Gordis.

As Srole and Langner observed, Jews feel little compunction about seeking skilled help for emotional problems. In response to a questionnaire about whom they would consult in emotional difficulty, 49.2 per cent of the Jews questioned said that they would see a psychiatrist, compared to 23.8 per cent of the Catholics and 31.4 per cent of the Protestants. Dr. Malzberg, too, writes that Jews "are more prone to consult physicians in connection with mental ills than any other group."

An urban, well-educated group, American Jews are probably more familiar with the theories and goals of psychotherapy than is the general population. They are also likely to have relatives or friends in the medical profession, and to be more familiar with the world of medicine as a whole. And since "Get me a specialist" is the standard Jewish reaction to illness, there is little hesitancy in turning to the psychoanalyst when need be as the specialist of choice.

The Arena of Medicine

When I visited Prof. Jacob R. Marcus, outstanding historian of American Jewry, at his home in Cincinnati, we spoke about the different branches of Judaism.

"And then there is the 'hospital Jew,'" Dr. Marcus pointed out, referring to the thousands of Jews in the United States whose major, if not sole, form of Jewish expression lies in service to one of the country's sixty-two Jewish-sponsored hospitals.

Judaism in America is practiced very frequently without benefit of either clergy or formal religion. All faiths, of course, look on applied religion as the highest form of worship; but while a nonpracticing Christian is commonly regarded as unchurched, a nonpracticing Jew with a commitment to a Jewish hospital still views himself as a "good Jew."

Thus, the *American Examiner*, the largest Jewish weekly in the world's largest Jewish community, devotes half a page to synagogue news, and includes a regular full-page feature entitled, "Jewish Chronic Disease Hospital News," which details the fund-raising efforts in behalf of the 770-bed institution.

Society columns in *The New York Times* report elaborate parties on behalf of the national Jewish hospitals in far-off Denver. And one single hospital, Los Angeles' City of Hope, raises more money nationally than is collected for all the Jewish religious institutions of the United States!

Care of the sick is a cardinal element in Judaism, as it is in Christianity. Nineteenth-century German-Jewish immigrants brought the tradition of the *Krankenhaus* across the Atlantic. When Berlin's Jewish hospital was opened in 1753, the New World had but a single such facility—the Pennsylvania Hospital, founded two years earlier. Several decades elapsed before New York City had a Jewish hospital of its own.

It should be admitted that the healing instinct was not the sole motivation for the development of the Jewish hospital. Traditional Jews wanted a hospital which would provide kosher food, Jewish surroundings, and a staff that would understand both their language and their ways. Beth Israel was established in 1889 on New York's Lower East Side "for the relief of such that would go to no other hospital," and to take care of newly arrived immigrants who were denied admission to city hospitals because they had not been in the United States for a year.

But by the early part of the twentieth century, the strongest argument for the Jewish hospital stemmed from discrimination against Jewish doctors. A gifted surgeon, who received his M.D. in 1963, told me:

"We had a hard time getting into any medical school. But the big problem was training for a specialty. Pathology was not closed to us, but it was almost impossible to receive a residency in surgery. Even Bellevue had restrictions. After medical school I went into the Army; then I tried several hospitals. They all told me that they didn't like Jewish boys as interns. So I ended up at a Jewish hospital. Even today many of the great medical centers will not accept a Jew as head of a department."

Albert Einstein College of Medicine came into being a little more than ten years ago, and is now one of the world's great medical research centers. Its vast campus in the upper Bronx is so extensive that we traveled half a mile by auto from my host-professor's office to the new University Hospital for lunch.

Einstein has received millions of dollars in grants for its ambitious research program. I examined the list posted on the walls of the modernistic building of the staff members of the departments of Cellular and Molecular Biology.

"Very few medical schools have separate departments in these fields," my host explained. "But separating out the research in this way has made it possible to corral many of the finest medical brains in the nation."

The men who built this enterprise—Dr. Samuel Belkin, an Orthodox rabbi, now president of Einstein's mother institution, Yeshiva University; Dr. Leo Davidoff, a brilliant neurosurgeon turned administrator; and Dr. Marcus Kogel, dean of the medical school—have managed to generate enough interest in DNA and all the other mysteries of genetics among the clothing manufacturers, real-estate operators, and industrialists who constitute Einstein's large donors to secure more than half-a-million dollars for these projects.

The sixty-two Jewish hospitals have one common denominator: research. How is the quality of medical service to be raised? By the application of intelligence, intensive study, and long years of post-graduate training.

Montefiore Hospital, in the Bronx, originally devoted to the care of the ailing aged, has been transformed into one of the leading research centers in America, and is now linked with the first Jewish-sponsored medical school, the Albert Einstein College of Medicine. Montefiore has also pioneered in creating full-time chiefs of departments who devote all their time to training and research—a luxury ordinarily limited to the medical schools.

Jewish hospitals in the United States often enjoy an international reputation as pathfinders in expanding the horizons of modern medicine. Denver Jewish researchers have attacked the problems of asthma and other pulmonary disorders. Cancer studies occupy the attention of City of Hope in California, Beth Israel in Boston, and many others. Montefiore has pioneered in open-heart surgery and developed the first pacemaker.

Prof. Eli Ginzberg of Columbia, America's ablest authority in the uses of national manpower, and consultant to several presidents, questions the present-day rationale for Jewish-sponsored hospitals and medical schools. He feels that the original arguments in their favor are no longer applicable, now that discrimination against Jews is ebbing and the government is assuming an ever-increasing responsibility for health needs.

Yet there are distinctive elements in these Jewish health-service agencies. Dr. Martin Cherkasky, medical director of Montefiore, served as a technical consultant to the Kennedy administration and helped to lay the groundwork for Medicare. Several features of Medicare, such as the home-health program, were borrowed from the Montefiore plan. The hospital has the only Division of Social Medicine in the country, and the only Community Center integrated within its program. Its elaborate system of volunteer services—involving hundreds of local residents—also serves as a model for other hospitals.

Dr. Ginzberg may be right about the fading of the Jewish hospital's original reasons for existence. But the service and the excellence remain. And they are reason enough for the hundreds of thousands whose pain and suffering they have helped to ease.

Albert Sabin, Master Microbiologist

"Your desk looks much more messy than mine," I remarked as I entered Dr. Alber Sabin's study-laboratory at the Children's Hospital in Cincinnati and looked at the scattered papers and rows of test tubes that surrounded us. This was the workroom of one of the century's great virologists whose work has helped save thousands of lives and end the scourge of crippling polio for millions of children the world over.

The soft-spoken white-coated doctor greeted me warmly. His ruddy complexion belied his frequent round-the-clock dedication to his test tubes. Later, we rode in his convertible. The evening was chilly, but the top was down. "This is about the only fresh air I get; in the morning, from home to the lab, and now back again."

A documentary film produced by a Cincinnati television station best expresses Albert Sabin's place in contemporary history. The film is entitled *The Benefactor*.

The fifty-nine-year-old genius has spent the last twenty-seven years in Cincinnati, but his research has carried him to the remotest jungles and deserts, to the Sinai wilderness of Egypt, to the tropics of Panama, to a tent in Okinawa, to the Philippines, Korea, China, Japan, and Germany—wherever the challenge of disease and suffering has called.

Albert Sabin was born in 1906 in a Polish village near Bialystok. The Sabin family came to America when Albert was thirteen. His father was a weaver, and the family made its first home in Paterson, New Jersey.

The boy worked after school and weekends during his high-school days, but there was no money for college. An uncle, Dr. Sidney (father of the actress, Sylvia Sidney), offered to sponsor a dental career. Albert agreed, but after two years of dental school his heart was hopelessly ensnared by medical research.

"I left my bed and board," he told me, "because I had already acquired a taste for research. Even when I was a college student, at nineteen, I begged my professor of bacteriology for a corner of the lab to pursue questions that bothered me. Today if a student made the same request, we would turn him down and recommend patience. My first scientific paper was published before I was twenty-one."

Young Albert went to work as a medical technician in New York, "typing" the pneumococcus organism, in the midst of a severe pneumonia epidemic. The test in use at the time required twenty-four hours to read, and Albert Sabin was unhappy at the delay, which slowed treatment by the proper serum. After considerable experimentation, he developed a three-hour test which won world-wide acceptance. His research career was under way.

As a medical student at New York University, Albert Sabin became interested in poliomyelitis, a disease that was taking a heavy toll in New York City. There was a spectacular rise in the disease in 1931, the year Sabin received his doctorate. In 1930, the city had recorded seventy-eight cases of polio. In 1931, the figure jumped to 4,138!

Sabin was still an intern when he succeeded in isolating a new virus and turned his attention to the mechanism of immunity to viruses. First at the Lister Institute in London, and later at the Rockefeller Institute in New York, he laid the groundwork for the process that was to culminate in the now-celebrated Sabin vaccine for polio.

"I left Rockefeller Institute," he told me, "because it was purely a laboratory, and I wanted clinical work with patients. That's what brought me to the University of Cincinnati.

"A man can be a perfectly good scientist purely out of interest in new knowledge—for the pleasure of intellectual growth, without caring particularly how that knowledge is used. To me, knowledge is not only an achievement for its own sake; it must help make life freer of pain and suffering and provide a richer existence."

"What about teaching?"

"My main interest is the lab. But I enjoy creating a certain excitement in students about learning and its application, and bringing students to the horizons of the unknown.

"One reason I accept invitations to address high-school assemblies is to help give young people perspective."

His soft eyes kindled with excitement as he repeated the last word. "*Perspective makes all kinds of drudgery bearable.* You know that much of our work is sheer drudgery."

Although most famous for his live polio vaccine. Sabin's genius has also cast light on the causes of meningitis, of rheumatoid arthritis, encephalitis, and other diseases. In the past five years he has concentrated on the role of viruses in cancer. But his interests are not limited to medicine.

"My basic philosophy is to be involved in all human concerns. I want to keep up with our society and understand all its ills."

I asked him if the scientific community could not do the work which the statesmen failed to accomplish. Would he trust the scientists to solve the world's ills?

"No," he responded emphatically, "most of them have too narrow an outlook. They are too specialized."

Addressing an audience of government leaders in Rome, Dr. Sabin chided his listeners for failing to apply the knowledge of science and technology. The title of his talk was "The Chances for Survival in the Remaining Years of the Twentieth Century," and he argued that the population explosion was as much of a threat to mankind as nuclear war. Research on this problem, Dr. Sabin declared, may ultimately prove of greater importance to human survival than research in cancer and heart disease.

We discussed his philosophy as a Jew. "My father was not observant, and I was never a religious Jew. But the phrase *Eretz Yisroel* [Land of Israel] brings me back to my early childhood. My grandfather used to take me to the synagogue on a late Saturday afternoon, and I would hear an old man spin tales about *Eretz Yisroel*.

"I married a Christian girl, and our daughters, who came late in our marriage, occasionally attended Protestant Sunday schools and observed the Christian festivals. My older daughter, Debbie, had few Jewish friends until she was admitted to Walnut Hills High School. It is a school for superior students, and a great many of them, brought in from all parts of Cincinnati, were Jewish. She asked if she could be confirmed and we enrolled her in the Rockdale Temple."

During World War II, Dr. Sabin was a lieutenant colonel assigned to the Army's Preventive Medicine Division. He was dispatched to Egypt on a special mission to investigate the cause of certain epidemic diseases.

"I journeyed by army vehicle across Sinai, retracing Moses' steps, but in a shorter time—eight hours. [He had no jeep.] I only spent ten days in Palestine and did not return for sixteen years. In 1959, the Israeli government invited me to the new state to look into a polio epidemic that was raging there."

He was entranced by what he saw. "I realized that I was witnessing the enactment of the greatest chapter in the entire history of the Jewish people. I had never felt the need of being Jewish until then."

Dr. Sabin visits Israel two or three times a year. (He begins his conversation with the apology, *"L' daavoni ayneni mdaber ivrit—* I regret that I speak no Hebrew.") He is a member of the Board of Governors of Hebrew University, and in the past few years he has helped raise funds for the Haifa Technical Institute, the Weizmann Institute, and Bonds for Israel.

"Though the Hebrew Union College gave me an honorary degree, I don't feel that man's spiritual strivings need be articulated through symbolic observances. Intellectually and emotionally I'm a Jew, without the prescribed activities of organized religion.

"My Jewishness is expressed by the strong link that I feel to my heritage."

Dr. Sabin quoted an Israeli colonel who explained, when asked for a definition of a Jew, "You're a Jew when a Jew in Minsk is hurt and you feel the pain."

We talked a bit about the Jewish philosophy of living life fully. Dr. Sabin's handsome face broke into a grin. "There's a story I heard about three atomic scientists, a Frenchman, an Italian, and a Jew, who received a lethal dose of radiation in a laboratory accident at their plant. The doctors gave them only six months to live, and in a magnanimous gesture the company they worked for offered them anything their hearts desired during their final days on earth. The Frenchman asked to be returned to Paris for a final fling of wine and women. The Italian wanted Venice and a round of opera and song. The Jew said simply, 'Get me another specialist!' "

CHAPTER 6

Jews and Government

"Seek no intimacy with those who run the government."
RABBI OF THE FIRST CENTURY B.C.

American Jews, despite their increasingly secure economic, social, and intellectual position, have been singularly absent from the arena of national politics. (The economist, Nathaniel Weyl, in *The Creative Elite in America*, using what he called "a performance coefficient" as a measurement, found that Jews were not distinguished in politics: their index was 66 [100 was average] compared to 578 in psychiatry.) True, there have been a handful of Jewish governors and senators, and a number of mayors of small cities—Galveston has had three Jewish mayors, and Cincinnati has also elected a number of Jews to top city posts. But the large Northern metropolises—Boston, Los Angeles, Detroit, Cleveland, St. Louis, Pittsburgh, Buffalo, and even New York City with more than two million Jews—have never elected a Jew to their highest office.

Those Jews who have held public office in the United States have generally been elected by predominantly Jewish constituencies. (Sen. Abraham Ribicoff of Connecticut is an exception, as was Gov. Henry Horner of Illinois.) Yet other immigrant groups, such as the Italians and the Irish, have entered politics successfully. What accounts for the Jewish lag in this area?

Certainly historic experience has been one important factor. Centuries of living as "outsiders" have taught Jews that governments were seldom to be trusted. Political power, the rabbis of the Talmud

64

suggested, was an instrument that was likely to sear its wielder. Sometimes, as in Spain and Italy, Jews did serve as counselors to the court. But generally experience proved involvement with power was dangerous to members of a minority.

Even a generation ago, in this country, the nomination of Louis D. Brandeis to the U.S. Supreme Court unleashed a stream of anti-Semitic invective, and certain well-meaning Jewish leaders warned the Boston lawyer that if he accepted this high office his fellow Jews might have to bear the brunt of any unpopular decision he handed down.

Fortunately, Mr. Justice Brandeis chose to ignore this advice. Nor is it surprising that a people which have since antiquity placed so high a value on the law should turn so many of its finer minds to the judiciary. "My son, the judge" is probably the only appellation in the galaxy of maternal pride higher than "my son, the doctor."

Thus, Chicago Jewry points with pride to its thirty-five judges, all of whom sit on the advisory board of its Welfare Fund. Jews in Los Angeles, San Francisco, Boston, Detroit, and Cleveland have achieved equal distinction on the bench. Judge Simon Sobeloff, a former Solicitor General, presided over the Federal Circuit Court in Baltimore. Judge Horace Cohen presides over Pennsylvania's highest court, and Judge Stanley Fuld, regarded by many colleagues as another Benjamin Cardozo, occupies a similar position in New York State. Several of President Franklin D. Roosevelt's history-making addresses were written by New York State Supreme Court Justice Samuel Rosenman, now in private practice. Justice Bernard Botein heads the state's Appellate Division, and approximately 60 per cent of New York City's jurists are Jewish.

Of the three branches of government, the judicial offers the greatest degree of independence. Many of the offices are appointive: and even the elected judges engage in more dignified campaigning and enjoy a longer term of office between campaigns than most political figures.

I asked a highly informed Jewish editor why relatively few Jews ran for political office. He theorized that the business of politics was such a dirty one and subjected a man and his family to such degradation that many sensitive Americans were simply not willing to take it on. The British tradition of heckling is not easy on candidates, but it pales in comparison to the *ad hominem* attacks and the exploitation of group prejudices that so often mar American political debate. There is still, apparently, a considerable doubt in political circles that a Jewish candidate can run without facing a backlash of latent religious bigotry.

Whatever the complex reasons, there are no more than sixteen or eighteen Jewish members in the House of Representatives currently, and as of this writing, only two Jewish senators, Jacob Javits and Abraham Ribicoff. Yet, Jewish involvement in the political process and their interest in affairs of state are intense. Scores of Jewish legislative assistants serve in the offices of the nation's legislators and help to administer the countless agencies of government.

I visited the offices of the Security and Exchange Commission, headed by one of the ablest and most respected men in Washington, Manuel Cohen. The 1,400 civil servants on the staff of the SEC are responsible for regulating one of the most important phases of the nation's economy. Manuel Cohen sees himself as a missionary for law and order in the world of securities, charged by his government to raise the ethical level of business by improving its standards of operation.

One of the many men brought to Washington by President Franklin D. Roosevelt, the SEC chief regards his function as reconciling the principle of freedom and the doctrine of antitrust, the meshing of individual rights and public interest.

Commissioner Cohen grew up in a poor Brooklyn family. A brilliant college student, he was accepted by both Yale and Harvard Law schools, but could not afford tuition, and took his degree at Brooklyn Law School. Deeply interested in economic affairs, he worked as a student for the Twentieth Century Fund, researching the organization of a Securities and Exchange agency, and later continued his researches in Geneva and Ottawa. Many years later he was invited by the Israeli government to help draft regulatory economic laws for the new state.

Cohen's family was Orthodox. "At the age of six, I spoke only in Yiddish: I can still write my mother in Yiddish, and read a Yiddish paper when I can. I think that I bring something of my Judaism to my work: concern for the underdog, for the rights of the individual. I know that I represent the state, but I think it's better for a few guilty persons to escape punishment than for one innocent one, one poor 'shnook,' to suffer unfairly."

We spoke about Jews in government, and the handicaps which existed in the past. Not too many years ago, as I learned in interviewing a score of Jewish officials, most upper-echelon jobs were closed to Jews, especially in the State Department and other policy-making divisions of the government. The barriers have come down slowly over the years.

Commissioner Cohen is one of many Jews who came to Washington from New York, Chicago, Philadelphia, and other cities during the Depression, and have stayed through the administrations of Roosevelt, Truman, Eisenhower, Kennedy, and Johnson, to help build a new social order. Like Commissioner Cohen, most of them would find the financial pastures greener in the business world, for they are men of extraordinary competence. But they enjoy the adventure of working "where the action is," and they choose to remain in government.

On the desk of the Securities and Exchange Commission's head is a photograph of President Lyndon B. Johnson inducting Manuel Cohen into office. Across the bottom is the President's inscription: "A dedicated public servant."

Few Jews have represented the United States abroad, either as ambassadors or as lesser officials. The total number of Jewish ambassadors designated by the United States in the twentieth century would not exceed the fingers of one hand. The State Department's apparent allergy to Jews as career diplomats has reflected, in part, the close link that has always existed between diplomacy and the socially elite, and in part the historic American self-image as a Protestant country.

The Kennedy election, as many historians have observed, effected a radical change in our national self-image. In April, 1966, an article in *Esquire* could discuss the question, "Can Javits Be President?" A decade earlier, such a question would not even have been posed. Within the next ten years, Jews, who represent about 10 per cent of the nation's highly educated population, are likely to share more fully in the diplomatic representation of the United States of America.

The United Nations has opened up a new source for government service, and appointments to the international body are less hampered by tradition. Jacob Blaustein has served as a U.S. delegate to the UN; so has Philip Klutznick of Chicago. And Arthur Goldberg gave up the cherished position of Supreme Court Justice to succeed Adlai Stevenson in the sensitive international post of ambassador to the United Nations.

"I Believe in Tradition"

I asked a leading Jewish theologian if any contemporary American could match the late Sen. Herbert Lehman in eminence. Without hesitation he answered, "Arthur Goldberg."

The UN Ambassador is a particular favorite of those close to Jewish tradition, because he is so direct in acknowledging the Jewish sources of his philosophy.

Addressing the annual convention of the National Jewish Welfare Board early in 1966, Arthur Goldberg elaborated on a theme he has stressed frequently in recent years. He was concerned about "the danger of losing our identity as Jews, or seeing that identity so watered down that we forget who we are and whence we came." Christians and Jews must indeed meet as brothers, Arthur Goldberg believes, "but they needn't act like identical twins."

The man who holds the world stage as the nation's chief advocate in the United Nations is far from flamboyant and sparkling. Completely devoid of pretentiousness, he seems singularly unimpressed with the high offices he has held and now holds. And he is clearly at home in his Jewishness.

"As an American I am a passionate believer in pluralism. To me, like Justice Brandeis, the true test of an American is this: that he does not conceal but affirms his origin: he is proud of whatever it may be, he wears his difference not as a cause of offense to others but as a contribution to the wonderful richness of American life."

Those who have worked closely with Arthur Goldberg—whether during his many years as a labor lawyer or in his more recent careers as Secretary of Labor, Supreme Court Justice, or UN Ambassador, comment frequently on his unassuming manner and approachability. He has the winning quality of those who are able to preserve the sense of wonderment about their rise to distinction. Youngest of eight children, Arthur Goldberg was raised in the poorest section of Chicago. His father, a fruit-and-vegetable peddler, died when Arthur was three years old. During his high-school and college years, Arthur worked nights in the post office and summers as a construction worker. He was graduated *summa cum laude* from Northwestern Law School, and at the age of twenty-nine was admitted to practice before the U.S. Supreme Court.

Gen. William Donovan, chief of the Office of Strategic Services during World War II, has stated that Major Goldberg's intelligence work behind enemy lines helped hasten the end of the war. As an influential spokesman for organized labor and later as Labor Secretary, he had a voice in every significant labor-management decision during the late fifties and early sixties. But his greatest pleasure came with his appointment to the U.S. Supreme Court, and it was with great reluctance that he agreed to President Johnson's request that he step down from the Court and step into Adlai Stevenson's shoes at the UN.

"I don't think I would have accepted the post, despite the President's urging, if I were not a Jew," Ambassador Goldberg told me, as we sat in his sumptuous top-floor office overlooking the United Nations.

"My country needed me, and I felt an obligation to America—it has been good to me. And as a Jew whose heritage is peace, I could not turn down a duty to work for it. Our first priority is world peace."

We spoke at length about the immense satisfaction of his Supreme Court days. There is no precedent, the Ambassador noted, for a judge's return to the Court once he has left it. Only Charles Evans Hughes, who left the bench to run for President, had ever been reappointed, and then only as Chief Justice.

On the Ambassador's desk is a picture of Goldberg and President Johnson with the LBJ inscription, "To Arthur Goldberg, whose wisdom and experience, devotion and loyalty, will pull us through." I asked Ambassador Goldberg how it felt to carry such an immense responsibility for the nation and for mankind. The Talmud says, I reminded him, that "a judge must ever act as though a sword hung over his neck."

"I've never felt that burden," Goldberg replied. "On the bench, I studied a problem thoroughly and gave it my best thought. Once I made my decision, I rested easily."

My eyes fell on another picture, of Goldberg and Adlai Stevenson, taken in Copenhagen when they both attended Dag Hammerskjöld's funeral. Now Hammersjköld and Stevenson were both gone and the youngish white-haired man who sat before me had inherited their concerns.

Did he have any political ambitions? He answered, as he has stated frequently, that he had permanently abandoned all thought of public office when he received his call to the Supreme Court.

We talked for a while about Jews in politics. The Ambassador felt that the breakthrough had just begun and that the next generation of American Jews would participate fully in the political process.

For many years Arthur Goldberg and his wife, Dorothy, have immersed themselves in Jewish studies. They read aloud to each other, and take keen delight in books of Jewish philosophy and theology. A favorite text is the latest work of Rabbi Abraham Heschel. Once, when Dr. Heschel was scheduled to speak at a Washington temple, he received a call from the Supreme Court. The Justice and his wife hoped that he was free for dinner. He was met at the airport, and for two hours before Rabbi Heschel's lecture the author of *The Prophets* answered questions that his host and hostess had penned in the margins of his book.

A Passover Seder is a memorable event in the Goldberg menage. When Dorothy Goldberg was first shown their ambassadorial suite in the Waldorf Towers, she is reported to have commented: "But how can we fit everyone in for our Seder?"

Forty or more guests, Jewish and non-Jewish, attend their annual celebration of the Feast of Freedom. The Goldbergs print their own Haggadah, which relates the traditional account of the Exodus to modern problems of freedom, including those of the laboring man.

Relevance is a crucial word in Arthur Goldberg's vocabulary. I asked him about his deep attachment to the Jewish Theological Seminary, since it was a Conservative institution and he was a Reform Jew.

"I have Orthodox roots. My father, of blessed memory, was president of an Orthodox synagogue, and my grandfather and great-grandfather were rabbis. But I admire the way the seminary has made Jewish tradition, especially Jewish law, relevant to our contemporary needs."

Addressing a seminary audience on the subject of "Morals in American Society," Goldberg expounded on the relationship between the verse in Genesis which described man as created in God's image and his philosophy of trade unionism. Limited hours of work are necessary, Mr. Goldberg explained, to provide man with the leisure to fulfill himself as a child and a reflection of God.

Rabbi Jacob J. Weinstein of Chicago, a close friend of the Goldbergs for many years, told me:

"I think that Judaism gave Arthur Goldberg his social orientation. He would quote the Talmudic words, 'Separate thyself not from the congregation' to mean that while the Jew must remain an individualist, he must constantly ask himself what he can contribute to the total community.

"The word *halachah*, the heart of Talmudic law, has always been very meaningful to Arthur. [*Halachah*, meaning Jewish law, connotes a walking along, a finding of the road, a going—law must be dynamic, changing, growing.]

"There is a mystical streak in Arthur Goldberg, too. He regarded his robes of office in the Supreme Court with a kind of awe, and the swearing-in ceremony was, to him, a 'folk poetry.'

"Goldberg's genius lies in his tremendous vitality, and in his ability to see the larger cause. He has that peculiar quality of Jewish thinking, a mastery of detail, the gift of pulling out the thread of continuity in the midst of conflicting details. It is deductive rather than Platonic. That is what made him a master in arbitration."

The future of Judaism is a subject of ongoing concern to Arthur Goldberg.

"I'm afraid," he told me, "that with the new ecumenical spirit—which I welcome—we are likely to develop a bland religiosity."

Speaking at a National Jewish Welfare Board banquet the following night, the Ambassador complained about the neglect of Jewish education. "Our young people are allowed to grow up virtually as religious illiterates." He urged especially the involvement of the young Jewish intellectual.

"It is a sad truth," he concluded, "that ignorance about the Jewish heritage is by no means confined to young people. Instead of a 'Project Head Start' perhaps what our grown-up community leaders need is a 'Project Late Start.'"

Not only knowledge but pride and self-respect are basic ingredients in the Goldberg creed. At a dinner honoring the Papal Nuncio he began the meal by pronouncing the Hebrew words of the blessing over bread. Miniatures of a Jewish theological seminary newspaper ad entitled, "Choose Life," embroidered by Mrs. Goldberg, who is an accomplished artist, are the New Year greeting cards the Goldbergs send out to their friends in December. And a columnist, reporting on Justice Goldberg's visit to Pope Paul VI, wrote, "he was received not as an American official but as a leader of American Jewry."

One of Arthur Goldberg's close associates, Philip Klutznick, an ambassador at large to the UN, told me of the high regard which the Arab delegates entertain for the Ambassador. On one occasion, Goldberg had a conflict of engagements, and called the Egyptian ambassador to express his regrets.

"But, Mr. Goldberg, we are giving this dinner in *your* honor," the United Arab Republic envoy, El-Kony, exclaimed. Mr. Goldberg was there.

The Ambassador once confided to a small Washington group that he had sought a model for himself in the three Jewish Supreme Court Justices, Louis D. Brandeis, Benjamin Cardozo, and Felix Frankfurter. Cardozo and Frankfurter, he discovered, had favored the florid British style. He preferred the unadorned logic of Brandeis.

Some UN diplomats, noted Drew Middleton, in an evaluation of the Ambassador's work, have commented on the fact that Goldberg lacks the elegant prose of his predecessor. But "many colleagues, including some from the diplomatically sophisticated countries of Europe, now suggest that Mr. Goldberg, an urban lawyer for years deeply involved in the affairs of the great labor unions, is perhaps more representative of contemporary America than Stevenson."

Whatever role the Ambassador is destined to play in the future, I daresay that he would be most pleased with the description of himself as "Mr. Goldberg, the contemporary American."

"We cannot be impartial. We can only be intellectually honest . . . aware of our passions and on guard against them. Impartiality is a dream, and honesty, a duty."

Jews at the Polls

A value system nurtured over the centuries and experience under a variety of political systems have produced, in the modern Jew, a definite style of voting. It is based on the assumption that any political philosophy that is liberal and that stresses human rights and the extension of human freedom is good for the Jews and good for the country.

In the 1930s this attitude meant that Jews, with few exceptions, supported Franklin Roosevelt's New Deal. Indeed, many of the New Deal innovations were particularly appealing to Jewish Americans. Prof. Lawrence Fuchs, in his classic study, *The Political Behavior of American Jews*, explains, for example, that "The idea of professors in government did not seem incongruous to them as it did to many Gentiles." The traditional Jewish love of learning and reverence for intellectuality "assured their positive response to the Roosevelt 'brain trust.'"

The 1960s have seen Jews, as a group or class, move into the realm of conservatism and geographically into suburban Republican territory. Nevertheless, in every city I visited I found the Jews in the front ranks of the Reform Democrats. Not only have they resisted the normal Republican blandishments of the middle and upper-middle classes (an easy decision in 1964 when the choice was Barry Goldwater), but they continue to view with suspicion the big-city Democratic machines which count on their automatic support.

The traditional Republican city of Cincinnati, I was told, yielded to a Democratic administration, with strong Jewish support and leadership, not because it was Democratic but because it represented Reform government.

Tribal voting probably continues to be present to some degree among Jews, just as it does among Italians, Irish, Poles, and other ethnic groups. But studies indicate that the general Jewish voting behavior does not follow tribal lines. Lucy Dawidowicz and Leon Goldstein, in a careful survey, *Politics in a Pluralistic Democracy*, have amassed impressive evidence to prove that Jews will vote against a Jew if they find his political ideology uncongenial. In 1961, 63 per cent of the voters in a Jewish neighborhood of New York City supported Robert Wagner, a Catholic, in the primary campaign for mayor against Arthur Levitt, a Jew. Colonel Levitt has a well-earned reputation as a leader in the Jewish civic and religious affairs, but his eminence in sectarian fields failed to influence Jewish voters determined to reject the Democratic machine in favor of a candidate they regarded as an independent. Even the very popular Republican, Louis Lefkowitz, could not win Jewish support when he ran against Democrat Robert Wagner in the mayoralty elections.

Dawidowicz and Goldstein, in their analysis of the election pattern in Providence, Rhode Island, point out that "for the Italian voters an Italian name is a major attraction," and in Boston, "the prominent appearance of a Negro on the Republican ticket . . . had some effect on Negro voters." But the so-called Jewish vote, the authors contend, does not mean a vote for Jews, it means merely an attraction to liberal government. In Oak Park, Illinois, for example, the Catholic vote for John F. Kennedy in 1960 was 71 per cent; the Jewish vote, 93 per cent. In 1956, 49 per cent of the Catholics and 37 per cent of the Protestants supported Adlai Stevenson. The Jews of Oak Park gave Governor Stevenson 89 per cent of their votes.

All indications point to a continuation of the Jewish-Democratic tradition. Young Jews emulate their elders in few respects, but in politics we may expect father and son to pull the same levers. An Elmira, New York, study cited by Professor Fuchs suggested that "those Jews who expressed a strong commitment to Judaism were more Democratic than those with low ethnic involvement." So we can understand why only 4 per cent of Yeshiva University students, in a college poll, voted for Eisenhower. But what of the students at Brandeis University whose ties to tradition are less pronounced? Eighty-eight per cent supported Adlai Stevenson.

Thus, as many a politician has learned by experience, it is misleading to speak of a Jewish vote. It is predictable, as Prof. Gerhard Lensky has suggested, that Jews will express a certain point of view on behalf of the United Nations, human rights, civil liberties, and government intervention in the economy. But there is a significant difference between a *predictable* vote and a *deliverable* one, for a ballot cast on the basis of philosophy of life is hardly the same as unthinking bloc voting.

Jews also tend to use the franchise far more than the general population. Deprived for centuries of the right to vote, and limited in complete suffrage in some countries today, American Jews exercise their right to vote with special relish. In the 1964 elections, for example, 81 per cent of all eligible Jews went to the polls, compared to the record 62.8 per cent of the population as a whole. Over the years the Jewish community has taken a number of political personalities to its heart. Abraham Lincoln is one of American Jewry's folk heroes, so are both Roosevelts. Vice President Hubert Humphrey is a long-time favorite, as are Sen. Clifford Case and Sen.

Wayne Morse. Mayor Theodore R. McKeldin of Baltimore has virtually been adopted as an honorary Jew.

More recently, Mayor John V. Lindsay of New York has been embraced as a kindred spirit. The city's Jewish voters rejected Abraham Beame, hailed by the tribal press, on election eve, as "the city's first Jewish mayor," in favor of a man who held out the promise of quality government. And Sen. Eugene McCarthy of Minnesota is a popular personality among Jewish audiences, despite the handicap of an infamous namesake.

A score of United States senators commute regularly between Washington and the banquet halls of American Jewry from coast to coast. Every one is a liberal. No program chairman would think of scheduling an Ellender or an Eastland, or even the colorful—and occasionally liberal—Dirksen.

Dawidowicz and Goldstein comment on the somewhat mystifying appeal of Adlai Stevenson, who became a symbol of liberalism largely as a consequence of Sen. Joseph McCarthy's frequent attacks. Jews assumed that he was pro-Israel, although he was not, and that he sympathized strongly with labor, although there was little in his record to support that image. Basically, the authors point out, Stevenson's attraction for Jews lay in "the qualities of urbanity, education, and culture." But such attributes alone are clearly not enough. William Buckley's similar gifts are lost on Jews: A public figure must also have a heart.

Upward social and economic mobility has thinned the ranks of Jewish radicals, as has disillusionment with the Soviet Union, both in its treatment of Jews as well as in the imperialism reflected in its treatment of satellite nations. And the achievement of many social goals in the United States has dampened the enthusiasm of many intellectuals for moderate socialism.

But none of these shifts has brought American Jewry into the ranks of political conservatism. A Jewish Republican is likely to share the liberalism of a Javits. Annual reports of such liberal groups as Americans for Democratic Action on the voting pattern of representatives in Congress find Jewish legislators overwhelmingly on the side of human rights as opposed to property rights.

Peace activities, freedom marches (estimates of the number of Jewish Freedom marches ran as high as 50 per cent of the white total; of Peace Corps workers, 33 per cent), and rallies on behalf of migrant workers—all the popular causes in support of "the revolution of rising expectations"—evoke massive support from Jews, especially the younger generation. They may wonder, as they look around, why so many of their coreligionists march at their side. Their synagogues have not sounded the tocsin, and their ties to the ancestral faith may seem tenuous. Yet what they do is entirely in line with centuries of Jewish concern for the underdog, and the still firmly held convictions summarized by Albert Vorspan, director of Commission on Social Action of the Union of American Hebrew Congregations, "the destiny of the Jew is linked with the fate of all minorities, and Jews can flourish only in an atmosphere of equality and respect for human rights."

CHAPTER 7

Love, Honor and Cherish

"He who is without a wife dwells without blessing, life, joy, help, good and peace."

THE TALMUD

"A rabbi doesn't officiate at a wedding," I once told humorist Sam Levenson when we were discussing Jewish marriage rites. "He referees!"

As soon as a starry-eyed boy and girl inform their parents of their decision to marry, the parents make clear to the young people that weddings are too serious a business to be left to the bride and groom. Marriage is for the two who are in love; the wedding is a matter for wiser and more experienced heads.

The first get-acquainted dinner involving the two families is like a session of the UN Security Council. The opening volley is fired by the bride's side. Protocol calls for wedding expenses to be borne by the bride's family. The girl's father feels that an intimate affair is in order. But the guest list worked out in the minds of "the opposition" includes second and third cousins, the *mechutanim*—that is, the relatives of children previously married—at least the immediate family of "my partner," certainly some of the leading members of the United Infants' and Children's Wear Association, and surely the Senior Class of Michigan State!

As the dining-room temperature rises, the young couple is invited to take off for the nearest drive-in movie. By the time they return, a few of the basic discussion points will have been settled.

Debate begins with the nature of the procession. The groom's

77

family belongs to a Philadelphia temple that might be labeled "Classic Reform." They have never heard of a groom still being escorted down the aisle by his parents, in the old-fashioned way. The thought that they will stand "under the bridal canopy" during the ceremony is equally appalling. Even the canopy itself is somewhat foreign to their taste, but they are willing to make that concession to Conservative requirements.

None of the "litigants," of course, knows anything about the requirements of Jewish law or is capable of making a distinction between law, custom, and what is virtually superstition. Local custom involves traditions that were born centuries ago in Berlin, Warsaw, Frankfurt, Amsterdam, and Bucharest, with refinements developed in the Bronx, South Boston, and Chicago's West Side.

A rabbi called in to settle some of the more subtle points of dispute may sometimes open up the *Jewish Encyclopedia* under the heading, "Weddings," and show pictures of ceremonies in different communities that admit of an infinite variety. But such logic is unimpressive. What is sacred is what the family has been witnessing over the years. And the searing question, Who shall stand and who shall sit, takes on all the solemnity of Yom Kippur's "Who shall live and who shall die, who in the fullness of years and who not in the fullness of years." The bride's side insists that Grandma must walk down the aisle on the arm of an usher. The groom's side wants a modern wedding, with the couple alone as the center of attention.

Slowly, as the evening wears on, the Council of War settles one issue after another: flower girl and ring bearer, the size of the orchestra, whose rabbi shall be used, the length of the bridal gown, and the color of the groom's tuxedo jacket. Still to be resolved by the time that the bride and groom return from the double feature is the matter of catering arrangements. The bride's family has been to dozens of weddings and at every last one of them the hors d'oeuvres were served before the nuptial rites. The groom's parents are horrified. *They* have never been present at such a wedding!

Fortunate is the rabbi who can maintain a judicious neutrality in these negotiations. He may be called in as arbiter in what the disputants regard as points of Jewish law. In any case, he is interested in launching the marriage as harmoniously as possible.

My own advice to the young couple is to retain all the good

humor they can muster and to try to please the parents and old folks wherever possible—to let the family derive full *naches,* unmitigated happiness, from the joyous occasion.

Family ties are so strong in Jewish life that the emotional level of a wedding is invariably high. The hurts are magnified, the tears more free flowing, and the new ties more binding and enduring. Parents of the bride and groom feel a sense of kinship which is seldom found in the non-Jewish community. It is not enough to maintain a judicious and distant cordiality; there must be an intimacy, for good or ill. Indeed, more than one Jewish marriage has foundered, not because the couple has failed to make adjustments, but because the parents have been unable to achieve a proper rapport. The standard "in-law joke" is not common among Jews. The art of being a good in-law is too earnest a matter to be treated frivolously.

One of the high moments in family drama is the scene when the young couple, having changed to travel clothes after the wedding party, is about to embark on the honeymoon trip. The four parents hold on to one another as they wave farewell, lips quivering, throats dry, tears flowing. They, too, have been married that day. For through the wedding of their children they are knit together for the rest of their lives.

I haven't seen any statistics comparing the size of Jewish weddings with those of non-Jews, but I would guess they are generally considerably larger. Wedding lists of several hundred are not unusual.

Undoubtedly the roots of this tradition go back to ghetto days. In the medieval Jewish community, no formal invitations for family occasions were sent out. Everyone participated and was welcome. A world that knew so much misery made much of every opportunity that provided joy and gaiety.

All the divorce statistics indicate that the incidence of family breakdown is smaller among Jews than among Christians. I would hazard the guess that there is some correlation between the quality of a Jewish wedding and its durability. A marriage launched by a large and enthusiastic circle of friends and relatives is bound to have some impact on the couple's attitude toward married life and their willingness to find a formula for coping with the disappointments and frustrations that must inevitably come up. One of the most elaborate weddings at which I ever officiated, however, launched a marriage that lasted only six months!

What is American about an American Jewish wedding ceremony? All three groups, Orthodox, Conservative, and Reform, have absorbed much from their neighbors. The double-ring ritual, the formation of ushers—Hollywood style or otherwise—the procession itself, with the music of Mendelssohn (a renegade Jew) and Richard Wagner (an anti-Semite) are all cultural borrowings.

There are some liberal rabbis who ignore the Biblical precept that the bride shall stand "at his right hand." On many occasions I have flaunted the "authority" of an unbending maître d'hôtel by altering the arrangements, even after several elaborate rehearsals.

But an authentic Jewish wedding rite is different and unique. The cup of wine which the bride and groom sip together, the ritual of the ring in which the bridegroom declares, "Behold thou art holy unto me with this ring," the breaking of the glass after the benediction (universal for first marriages among the Orthodox and Conservative and used by most Reform rabbis as well), which symbolizes the bridal couple's awareness, in their moment of supreme joy, of the burdens of mankind—these are all distinctive religious acts.

The personal message of the rabbi, a touch often absent in High-Church ceremonies, lends a good deal of warmth to a Jewish wedding.

Occasionally, a Christian guest at a temple wedding will tell me: "It's a good deal like our ceremony, especially when you repeat our threefold benediction: "The Lord bless thee and keep thee. . . ." I can seldom resist the temptation to point out that the church is the borrower and the synagogue the lender of this beautiful blessing.

The setting for the Jewish marital rites ranges from the rabbi's study, with only the immediate family in attendance, to the extravaganzas of the large hotels and catering establishments. Several rabbinic associations have declared a ban on all weddings outside of the synagogue or home. Both the Philadelphia Board of Rabbis and the Minnesota Association have called on their members to refuse to officiate at hotel weddings, and a leading Washington rabbi also declines any request to take part in a wedding outside of a temple or the family residence.

The catering hall is a modern American phenomenon. In the more elaborate establishments, it is possible to hold a number of weddings simultaneously. The latest staging techniques are used to dramatize the entrance of the bride, silhouetted against a colorful background or materializing out of the darkness, in the best Hollywood fashion.

In several of the larger cities, some synagogues have met the competition of these "marriage parlors" by transforming a goodly part of their own facilities into catering establishments. But only in New York City, I believe is it possible to find a substantial number of synagogues listed under *catering* in the yellow pages.

The ultra-Orthodox and Hasidic Jews, numbering tens of thousands, go to special pains to make their wedding ceremonies truly gala affairs. Following the ancient tradition of "marriage under the skies," the actual rites are performed out-of-doors even on the coldest December day. One Christmas Eve, when the traffic at Herald Square was light, the few passers-by who crossed in front of Gimbel's Department Store were astonished to see a group of bearded Jews singing their traditional chants around a wedding canopy.

The bride marches around the groom seven times. A series of witnesses are called: one set authenticates the rabbi's touching a handkerchief of the groom, symbolizing his right to act on the groom's behalf; two witnesses examine the ring and vouch for its intrinsic worth; and two witnesses sign the marriage contract which spells out the young man's solemn promise to support and cherish his beloved bride "as befits a Jewish husband to do."

The February 19, 1965, issue of the *Jewish Press*, an ultra-Orthodox publication, devoted an entire page to a description of a wedding attended by over 1,500 guests at the very modern Americana Hotel.

> As their ancestors before them in days of old, the *Kallah* [bride] and the *Chasan* [groom] were united under the heavens of the cloudy chill night of February 10, in the ultra-modern setting of the Hotel Versailles Terrace [on the roof of the fifty-story hotel], in separate seating [men and women seated separately]. Israel's embassy was represented by the Consul General and other officials.

Eight rabbis officiated, with Rabbi Moses Feinstein, dean of the Yeshivah Tiffereth Jerusalem, reading the marriage contract. Other rabbis included the rabbis of Cincinnati, Chicago, Camden, New Jersey, New York, Cleveland, Clifton, New Jersey, and Dublin, Ireland.

An hour prior to the ceremony, seventeen-year-old Esther was led into the room, a fresh vision of Sabra (native Israeli) beauty in her American lace wedding gown. . . . The President of the Orthodox Congregation of Johannesburg, South Africa, flew in to represent his rabbi, a brother-in-law of the groom. . . .

(The next issue of the *Jewish Press* described an even more elaborate wedding in B'nai Brak, Israel, involving two distinguished rabbinic families. Thirty thousand guests were flown to Israel by jet planes from the United States, England, France, Switzerland, and other countries. A thousand buses brought them to B'nai Brak.)

The closer we come to the old patriarchal Jewish society, the larger the circle of family and friends. Canadian Jews, whose roots in Old-World Jewry are more immediate, regard a wedding list of 300 to 500 guests as quite average. Often, years of future earnings are mortgaged to make certain a daughter's wedding is carried out with appropriate pomp.

Another vestige of the patriarchal tradition can be seen in the attitudes of the young people themselves. Recently I asked a group of high-school seniors representing sixteen temples in the suburbs of Newark, New Jersey, whether they were likely to make a final decision about their choice of mate without consulting their parents. Virtually none believed that the decision was theirs alone. Although this seeming dependence may be, in part, a reflection of middle-class mores, I daresay that the strong Jewish tradition of family integrity was the major operative force.

Even when a marriage is contemplated out of the faith, it has been my experience that most young people bring their chosen one home to their parents and grandparents in the hope that either the depth of their love or the special charms of their beloved will be successful in winning their parental hearts. The notion of a runaway marriage seems alien to most young Jews, and even when there is family resistance, they are likely to delay a break with their parents whenever possible.

The outstanding authority on American Jewish demography, Ben B. Seligman, tells us that Jews marry later in life than any other elements in the population. Does this reveal a more deliberate and thoughtful approach to the seriousness of marriage? Is it merely a reflection of a higher educational level? (Sociologist Manheim S. Shapiro reports that according to a survey 61 per cent of the Jews were high-school graduates compared to 39 per cent of the Protestants and 38 per cent of the Catholics.) Or is the lag in age a result of more persuasive parental control, which imposes restraint on Jewish youth? I am inclined to believe that the silver cord is both tighter and firmer in the Jewish family.

Paradoxically, the American Jewish family, despite its tradition of integrity and devotion, is smaller than the general population. Much has been written about the failure of American Jews to perpetuate themselves. The normal sociological explanations tell part of the story. Being both an urban and an educated people, Jews belong to all the sociological groups that consistently have the lowest birth rate. "In the twenty years prior to 1940," reports Prof. Nathan Goldberg," the Jewish birth rate fell 37 per cent. This decline was more than double the 15 per cent fall in the birth rate of the native white population."

It would seem that, despite the process of acculturation which characterizes American Jews we can still find a distinctive pattern of American-Jewish family living.

The paradox of change and constancy—the yielding of the most stubborn custom to the mores of a host culture combined with an imperviousness to change of a centuries-long established tradition— is best revealed in a wedding invitation sent by an ultra-Orthodox family which conceded to the new as it retained the old.

The English part of the bilingual invitation was standard Tiffany, in both design and language. The Hebrew portion read (names altered):

> With the help of the Almighty
> Rejoice in Judea   Be Glad in Jerusalem
> Mr. and Mrs. Menachem Fine

Mr. and Mrs. Sholom Weinstein
request the honour of your presence
at the marriage of their beloved children
The outstanding young groom
Aryeh (may his light continue to shine)
to the lovely virginal bride, Feigel
(may her years be long)
which will take place, God willing, on the happy
blessed hour of seven in the evening
on the fifteenth day of Elul, 5725,
in the Auditorium of Avenue O Jewish Center
(corner West 9th Street), Brooklyn, New York
Should you be blessed with a similar joyous occasion,
we shall, without solemn promise, be delighted to reciprocate.

Please note: Ladies are asked to wear long sleeves,
no décolleté.

American Jewish Family

"Formerly the Jew was born in, married in, and was buried from the same house. Today he is born in a hospital, married in a social club, and buried from a funeral parlor."

This wry comment by an Atlanta rabbi, quoted in Marshall Sklare's excellent volume, *The Jews*, mirrors the story of the American family. Jews are no exception—or are they?

In a number of respects the pattern of Jewish family living, even in the United States, has its unique elements.

As we report elsewhere, bachelorhood and spinsterhood are anathema in Judaism. The Camden, New Jersey, studies found only 2 per cent of all Jewish males single by the time they reached their thirties, and only 3 per cent of the females in their late twenties.

"It is evident that the Jewish population is one in which almost everyone is married," writes Dr. Albert Mayer. Other Americans have begun to emulate Jews in this respect. Fifty years ago, one out of eight Americans remained unmarried; today that figure is less than one out of twenty.

Some regional differences are also apparent. The younger generation of Jewish men in Camden seems to marry earlier (at twenty-three and a half) than their counterparts in Detroit and Providence.

(The Camden age at marriage has declined, in one generation, from twenty-seven to twenty-three for men and from twenty-four to twenty-one for women.)

The Jewish family also begins later. While the national average age at first marriage is about twenty-two for men and twenty for women, Jewish men wait until their later twenties, and women till they are twenty-three or more. Dr. Mayer's study of Detroit Jewry reported that Jewish grooms were four and a half years older than their brides—an age difference almost twice that of non-Jewish husbands and wives.

It is generally agreed that marital stability is substantially enhanced if the couple is more mature and have known each other for some time. The highest incidence of divorce is to be found among teen-aged couples. (Only one out of thirty Jewish men in Providence married before twenty.) In addition, a newly married couple has a much better chance of success when there is economic security, and a husband at twenty-six is usually a better provider than a husband of twenty-one.

All these advantages notwithstanding, divorce is no longer a rarity in American Jewish life. Most rabbis report a steep rise in family disruption, although the incidence of broken homes remains far below the national average.

I discussed some of the problems of the Jewish family with Rabbi Jerome Folkman, of Columbus, Ohio, a trained psychologist who teaches marital counseling. Dr. Folkman saw a mixed blessing in the Jewish tradition against divorce. "It keeps some families together when they would be better off separated." On the other hand, he wondered whether marital conflict was necessarily bad. "I've had couples come to me, after thirty years of marriage, who were bored with each other. Their marriage lacked that cohesiveness that comes after an occasional scrap."

Dr. David Crystal, of the San Francisco Family Service, found little difference between Jews and other religious groups in matters of divorce. "Tradition—any tradition—requires carriers," he remarked, "and in the case of both Jews and Christians, when tradition is an active, vital influence, it tends to operate in the same way against divorce."

Desertion, not altogether uncommon in early immigrant days, is rare among American Jews today, and the syndrome of alcoholism, unemployment, and abandonment is equally infrequent. "We have handled no cases of alcoholism in our county," the director of Jewish Family Service in Los Angeles told me. A conference on the subject of alcoholism might attract a score of Protestant and Catholic clergymen, but I have yet to hear of any rabbinic conference allocating a minute of its time to this problem.

Aside from the opportunities for meeting people through family communal work and temple activity, traditional Jews still resort to the age-old institution of the *shadchan*, the marriage broker. The *Jewish Press*, a weekly Orthodox journal, lists a number of agencies in its classified ads, appealing to the "marriage-minded."

"Do you long to belong?" demands one advertisement, in boldface type. Another typical ad reads: "Beautiful widow of a professional family background wishes to meet a gentleman of the medical profession. Middle forties to sixty. No intermediaries."

Still others are even more specific: "Gentleman, intelligent, slim, nice-looking, seeking woman fifty or younger, under 150 pounds, over 5'4" with zest for life. I am neither rich nor well established in business. Write fully in strict confidence. Life is still worth living."

The young, too, judging by the pages of the *Jewish Press*, seek mates through the medium of advertising. Several of the ads have bounce: "Have car will travel"; "non-Orthodox with a sense of humor"; "young, ardent Zionist, twenty-one, wishes to meet girl with muscles—to help row canoe to Israel."

Juvenile delinquency, a sure barometer of domestic health, is another unfamiliar occurrence among Jews. Sophia M. Robison, in her 1952 study of Jewish delinquents in New York City, estimated that 3 per cent of juvenile offenses were committed by Jews, although they constituted more than 27.2 per cent of the city's population. But here, too, cultural changes were evident. In 1930, Mrs. Robison reported, the leading offense among Jewish delinquents was peddling or begging without a license; while the contemporary Jewish youthful delinquent "exhibited violent and aggressive behavior" much like that of his non-Jewish neighbor in trouble.

Widowhood is a growing phenomenon on the American scene. Given the average four-year age differential between Jewish husbands and wives and the six-year advantage in life expectancy enjoyed by women in general, the average Jewish congregation is likely to have an inordinate number of widowed women.

"After sixty years of age, half of the women are widowed," according to the Detroit study. Many in Detroit and elsewhere accept the permanence of widowhood. But others, especially those under sixty, will follow the good Jewish tradition of remarriage.

Rabbis in southern California and in Miami Beach report that their communities abound with unattached older women. A widow in Omaha or Indianapolis, after trying for several years to find a mate in her home community, is likely to pick up stakes and head for the balmier worlds of California and Florida. There she finds a lively competition among other widows and their new competitors, the divorcees.

The next step is, of course, the cruise. A number of travel agents have told me that more than half the passengers on Caribbean, European, and Pacific cruises—and the vastly expanding around-the-world cruises—are Jewish and a sizable percentage of them are widows.

A Good Name for the Baby

Selecting a name for the baby is an act of supreme cultural importance, for under certain circumstances it constitutes an act of separation of one subgroup from the larger society. Historians commenting on the factors that led to the creation of a division between Indian and Pakistan have mentioned the Moslem names given to children in Pakistan—such as Muhammad, Ali, and Ahmed—as helping to create a feeling of apartness. The practice helped maintain the cultural separatism that ultimately led to geographic cleavage.

The acculturation process within American Reform Judaism has militated, in times past, against giving a Jewish child a special Hebrew name even for ritual purposes. But more recently, as Reform has returned to traditional forms, the Hebrew name has come back into use. A Bar Mitzvah boy will have, and perhaps know, his religious name; his forty-five-year-old father, if he was brought up in a Reform family, will not have one. The Reuben of the 1910s will be transformed into Richard in the 1930s—and back to Reuben (at least for religious purposes, such as on the day of his Bar Mitzvah) in the 1960s. So, too, a Solomon will pass through a transmigration of a Stuart before being reincarnated as Solomon.

Among American Jews a number of names with no Hebraic significance have become commonplace, maintained their popularity for a decade or two, and then faded away. Earlier in the century, immigrant parents gave "American-sounding" names to their children. Examining the list of presidents of Reform congregations (men, for the most part, between forty and sixty years old), we find that the most popular names are Louis, Robert, Morris, Irving, Joseph, Sam, and Harry. Among the Reform rabbis, the names of David, Samuel, Joseph, Robert, Bernard, Abraham, and William recur frequently. On the other hand, the seven basic names of modern Orthodox rabbis seem to be the Biblical Abraham, Samuel, Jacob, Joseph, Isaac, David, and Benjamin in that order of popularity.

Rabbi Alfred Kolatch, who has devoted a lifetime to research in this field, indicated in the first edition of his *These Are the Names* (1948), that there was a striking contrast between the generations. For example, these names appeared in the following ratio in his sampling (the first figure represents children, the second, their parents): Ellen, 174–0; Jeffrey, 74–0; Linda, 74–0; Stephen, 105–2; Nancy, 77–1; Peter, 86–2; Andrew, 59–2.

In another generation, Sam, Irv, and Harry will be part of American Jewry's archaeological past, along with Shirley and Selma. A new set of names has already put in an appearance. In the year 2000, the best way to spot a Jew may be to look for the names now appearing in the first grade of many Jewish synagogue schools: Meredith, Hilary, Brad, Craig, Ian, Megan, Heather, and Roxanne.

Of course, among the Sephardic Jews, those who come from Mediterranean lands, an entirely different set of first names is used. Among the older generation, boys were most often called Nissim, Behor (first-born), Rachamin, and Sabbetai. But even among these proud descendants of Spanish Jewry who have been loath to part with symbols of a distinguished ancestry, assimilation is taking its toll. The rabbi of a Sephardic congregation told me that one of his teen-agers introduced herself as "Sandy."

"Come, now. That's not your real name."

"You're right, Rabbi," she confessed. "It's really Sultana."

The inimitable Gertrude Berg commented on the curious Jewish passion for name-changing:

"Every Tom, Dick, and Harry is called Ronald."

Bar Mitzvah, U.S.A.

"May I suggest that your son's Bar Mitzvah be on Saturday, March 1, 1969?"

The listeners, parents of an eleven-year-old boy, nod their heads in approval, and the temple-school principal notes it in the congregational calendar. The date, two years away, seems understandably remote, but such are the logistics of Jewish religious life in America that there is no quarreling with the assignment.

Bar Mitzvah rites, American style, combine two opposite impulses—that of the individual and that of the group. On the day itself, the boy stands before the congregation, starkly alone, chanting the blessings and the Prophetic Portion in a voice that hasn't quite made up its mind whether it is child or adult. Knees tremble, lips quiver, the throat is unaccountably dry, but somehow the performance is completed with such an inspired flair that the family bursts with pride.

Yet the Bar Mitzvah, American plan, is essentially a family enterprise. March 1, 1969, is D Day for the entire clan. Mother's brother, Ben, in Worcester, Massachusetts, will find someone to take over the store; Uncle Joe will see no patients that day; and Cousin Phil will cut short a buying trip to Europe to get an *Aliyah* (the honor of standing before the Torah scroll to repeat the blessings as a Biblical portion is read).

Once the long-range plans are organized, little remains during the first year but the boy's Hebrew preparation. Three days a week of lessons (for the suburban mother it also means chauffeuring to and from the temple, alone or in a car pool) become a normal routine of life.

In the fall of 1968, Mother will turn down the chairmanship of membership for the PTA, because she knows she will be too busy working out the details of her son's Bar Mitzvah celebration. The family luncheon, the reception, the children's party, hospitality for out-of-town guests—all of these require elaborate planning.

Customs vary from congregation to congregation, but at Temple Emanu-El, in a suburb of New York City, the Friday-evening services offer an overture to the first act.

The boy's mother opens the service by kindling the Sabbath candles, with the appropriate blessing.

The rabbi calls father and son to the Ark. Solemnly the father drapes the *tallit* (prayer shawl) over the young boy's shoulders and the Bar Mitzvah candidate recites the blessing.

On Saturday morning the street is lined with cars bearing Pennsylvania, New Jersey, and Connecticut license plates. The *Kiddush* (blessing over wine) is chanted by the Bar Mitzvah boy's ten-year-old brother, and an older sister recites the blessing over the bread.

All in all, twelve members of the family will have participated in the rituals of the weekend, not counting great-aunts and uncles and an assorted variety of relatives who sit back and *kvel*. (Another untranslatable Yiddish word for a kind of joyous internal combustion that older people experience in the presence of attainments of the younger generation. You *kvel* when the boy is elected to Phi Beta Kappa or wins a Merit scholarship, or shows up well in a television interview.)

On any given Saturday, a few thousand Christian boys and girls will be present at Jewish worship, attending the Bar Mitzvah of their friends or neighbors. It is a pleasant and auspicious introduction to Judaism: pleasant to enter a world in which "kids count," and excitingly meaningful to witness a family in the thralldom of intimate joy.

If the experience of Temple Emanu-El is typical, why are so many rabbis ready to join in a ban-the-Bar-Mitzvah movement? Because the Bar Mitzvah along with other religious ceremonies in America—and in Great Britain, too—is often used as an excuse for lavish and ostentatious celebration in which the ritual itself is consigned to the background. Yet, despite frequent breaches of good taste, the Bar Mitzvah is usually an experience that welds the Jewish family closer together and heightens the consciousness—and the pleasure—of being Jewish.

CHAPTER 8

Living is Giving

The scene is a private dining room in a downtown hotel in Miami. Fifty men, all lawyers, have just finished lunch. They light their cigars and relax while writer-producer Dore Schary talks to them about the work of the Anti-Defamation League of B'nai B'rith. The author of *Sunrise at Campobello* concludes his half-hour address with the story of a chicken who struck up a conversation with a salmon swimming up the river. After two hours of talk, the chicken suggested to the salmon that they pause at a nearby restaurant for lunch.

"Nothing doing," the salmon insisted. "When we get there, all they will want from you is a token contribution. From me they will demand total commitment."

The audience chuckles, and the men proceed to fill out pledge cards.

On any weekday of the year this lunchtime scene is duplicated in scores of cities throughout the country. The New York Federation of Jewish Philanthropies estimates that for their campaign alone 5,000 such meetings, conferences, fund-raising strategy sessions, fashion shows, and cocktail parties are held during a single year.

The Jewish community of Detroit numbers 84,600 men, women, and children. In 1964, their Allied Jewish Appeal received contributions from 10,776 men and 10,367 women—virtually every adult who could be reached! Six hundred and thirty-eight lawyers contributed a quarter of a million dollars; only ten failed to subscribe. Six hundred and eighteen physicians pledged almost as much. In all, 95 per cent of the Jewish business and professional men of Detroit had some share in the Appeal.

The sheer inevitability of Jewish philanthropy produces a kind of relaxation. The United Jewish Appeal, for overseas needs, is here to stay. So are the hospitals and the old folks' homes (since 1945, the population in homes for the aged has doubled), Brandeis University, and Hadassah. The American Jew, whose calendar psyche has become attuned to the tax calls of April 15 and the inescapable ritual of "withholding," assumes that, when "the voice of the turtle is heard in the land," the voice of the volunteer fund raiser will be heard on the telephone: "Joe, what can we expect from you this year? You and I both know that your business is up 20 per cent over last year."

If giving is inexorable, it is also well embroidered and softened with fun and entertainment. At a Los Angeles fund-raising banquet, soon after the pledges had been announced, I watched two of my dinner partners—a couple in their sixties—return again and again to the dance floor, executing the intricate modern dance steps with a proficiency that bespoke many Arthur Murray lessons. Teasingly, I asked how they could feel in the mood to rhumba when we had come there to hear about Jewish suffering.

"How many years of suffering can one take?" was the good-natured response as they rose to answer the strains of a cha-cha.

The Jewish labor movement a half-century ago devised another method of painless extraction—the theater party. Groups such as the fraternal orders and benevolent societies added a premium to the cost of the ticket, provided members with the exciting project of selling a specific Yiddish performance to their friends and shop acquaintances. Today the Broadway theater party is considered one of the chief mainstays of a show and guarantees some stability in an extremely volatile enterprise.

Arnauld C. Marts, in *Generosity of Americans*, tells us that Americans gave 11 billion dollars to charity in 1965. Under our tax-exemption structure, 975,000 private-service and cultural agencies may receive contributions. Forty million of us are to be found in the lists, and 30 million Americans serve as volunteers, either as workers or fund raisers! No other nation in the world can match that achievement. But Marts points out that the base of over-all American giving is generally not very broad. Citing a college that raised more than $650,000, for example, he reports that this sum included one gift of $400,000, a few others totaling $245,000, and the remaining $9,550 in small amounts.

The unique quality of Jewish philanthropy is the breadth of its base. Perhaps three out of every four contributions total between $10 and $100. The tradition is that everyone gives, and even those who can afford to give little are expected to bear their share of the communal burden. Thus, in a typical campaign—in Detroit—16,863 of the 23,778 gifts amounted to less than $50 each and another 4,500 donors pledged less than $100.

In the seventeen postwar years of 1946–1962, Jews raised $2,290,-000,000 for central Jewish community organizations. It has been conservatively estimated that more than one million people contribute to federated campaigns. Out of a population of a little more than five and a half million, the experts tell us that "this represents close to total coverage, at least in the smaller communities."

The fellowship of givers extends beyond the grave. One of New York City's peculiarly Jewish institutions is the obituary column of *The New York Times,* which carries, in addition to the family notices announcing the death and informing friends about funeral details, an outpouring of tribute from those organizations which have been beneficiaries of the deceased. (Jewish weeklies, such as the Denver *Intermountain Jewish News* and the Houston *Jewish Herald-Voice* also carry these notices.) Not infrequently, twenty or thirty organizations will express their gratitude to the man or woman whose labors—and donations—will be missed. Often, grateful individuals feel impelled to insert their own words of appreciation: "In tribute to Henry K.," read one such notice, "without whom I would have been one of the 6 million consigned to the Nazi gas chambers."

Despite the prodigious amounts they have raised for sectarian purposes, Jews have been ecumenical in their benefactions. Heading the annual Alfred Smith drive on behalf of New York Catholic Charities for many years has been Charles H. Silver, president of Congregation B'nai Jeshurun. Several of the $1,000 tables are occupied each year by Silver's Jewish associates in charities ("I'll take a table for your hospital if you'll take one for my orphanage").

Another interesting pattern of Jewish giving is the large number of causes which claim their support. Unlike the majority of non-Jewish philanthropists—and some German Jews—who donate to a few selected charities over a period of years, and possibly endow a single institution very generously, the general Jewish pattern is more diffuse: regularity is the keynote and benefactions are widely bestowed.

Dr. Mordecai M. Kaplan's phrase, "the education of the conscience," is probably the best explanation of Jewish giving. An embattled people, faced with annihilation, expulsion, harassment, and exploitation over the centuries, cultivated techniques of self-preservation which involved the closing of ranks, mutual assistance, and the responsibility of the privileged for those less fortunate. And impulse born out of Biblical and rabbinic teaching was reinforced by historic demands. "Though charity is a precept in all religions, it was a matter of rule in the Jewish religion," declares *Fortune* magazine in a comment on "The miracle of Jewish giving."

To the question, Why me?—why should few assume responsibility while many sit on the side lines?—Henry Zucker, of Cleveland, one of the ablest Jewish executives in the nation, has an eloquent answer: "If our work is to move forward, it will do so on the backs of the people who have the understanding and the heart and the ability to carry out its purposes. It will not progress by hoping to even out the burden. *The burden will always fall heaviest on those who have the sense of obligation and morality, not on the nonparticipating members of our society.*" (Italics mine.)

The Organization of American Jewish Philanthropy

"Whether we like it or not, ours is a money culture, and our culture heroes are drawn from the ranks of the affluent," veteran fund-raiser Joseph Willen, who has recently retired as executive vice president of the New York Federation of Jewish Philanthropies, remarked to me at a dinner meeting one evening. There was frustration in his voice. He would have wished it otherwise. Nevertheless, he and a handful of executives have raised the level of American Jewish philanthropy by several hundred per cent.

The "trade luncheon," which solicits funds through the machinery of a particular trade or industry, was the brain child of Joe Willen's fertile imagination. A good example was the optical industry luncheon I attended not long ago, on behalf of the New York United

Jewish Appeal. Competitors clustered together at the same table: opticians, optometrists, optical wholesalers, owners of optical laboratories, lens and frame manufacturers. The guest of honor who, aided by his wife and secretary, had made more than fifty phone calls to be certain everyone who was anyone would be on hand, was delighted when someone responded to the "card caller" with a 20 per cent increase in his pledge "in honor of Sam." (A card caller is the campaign chairman who reads the names of the guests, sometimes quoting their last year's contribution.) In a loud stage whisper, his voice up a few decibels thanks to three noontime martinis, Sam could be heard to explain, "Abe can afford it. Business is up 25 per cent this year." This with a meaningful look across the table to several others whose recent prosperity warranted a painless increment in giving.

Outside of New York City, many Jewish communities in the United States and Canada have pooled their fund raising in one or two central welfare funds—the only ties that bind together Jews of different synagogue branches as well as those with no formal religious affiliation at all. In a literal sense there is no American Jewish community, only a loose confederation of welfare bodies, serviced in New York City by the Council of Jewish Federations and Welfare Funds and by a subsidiary Large City Budgeting Conference, a consultative office.

Close to half of all the money raised among American Jewry is allocated for overseas needs, through the United Jewish Appeal and the Joint Distribution Committee. The formula varies: some cities, such as Atlanta, send close to 70 per cent; others, such as St. Louis, keep 60 per cent for local needs. A vast machinery has been set up to pass judgment on the relative merits of a hundred causes. Allocations committees, consisting of the leaders in each community, meet for months, listening to the advocates of a host of institutions.

I asked one prominent rabbi in Detroit how it happened that his city subsidized Jewish education and other cultural institutions so generously. He replied smilingly: "We have a *Litvak* power structure in our city." It was another way of saying that the largest and most influential contributors to the Allied Jewish Campaign were Lithuanian or Russian Jews, many of them products of homes with a high level of Jewish learning. Denver Jewry allocates an unusually larger percentage of its funds to the Anti-Defamation League of

B'nai B'rith. Since Colorado boasted of its fine interreligious spirit, I often wondered why the ADL is so successful in its Denver appeal.

One leader explained that the Ku Klux Klan had flourished in Colorado forty years ago, but another agency executive admitted that it was present-day pressure rather than ancient history that accounted for ADL's allotment. The B'nai B'rith is stronger in Denver than in many other parts of the country, and its views are vigorously articulated before the city's allocations tribunal.

However keen the jockeying for support among the various organizations, the fact is that the method works, and no one would turn the clock back, although a few major institutions—Brandeis University, the Hebrew University in Jerusalem, the Los Angeles City of Hope, and some theological seminaries—still prefer to conduct separate campaigns. They are exceptions. "The *American* genius in the Federation idea," explains Clevelander Henry Zucker, "is expressed in the emphasis on voluntary participation and capacity for organization. The *Jewish* genius is derived from the age-old ethical concepts of help for the needy and the ideal of social justice.

"The Federation idea . . . prospered, matured, and evolved . . . out of the simple notion that it is simpler, more efficient, and more effective to raise money for Jewish health and welfare agencies in one annual drive than to scatter time, energy, and money into a variety of campaigns."

It was a rabbi in Denver, Rabbi William Friedman, who first developed the idea of a Community Chest, in 1890, and enlisted the aid of a Roman Catholic priest and a Protestant minister in summoning the civic leaders of Denver to launch a federated nonsectarian campaign. Today more than 2,300 American communities have adopted the plan.

Campaign strategy is fairly uniform throughout the country. Volunteer workers are trained and infused with a special enthusiasm about the particular needs of the year. The theme is invariably: "The demands upon us this year are infinitely greater than last. We cannot be satisfied with *status quo*. We must have a 20 per cent increase in this year's pledges."

Then begin a round of advance gift luncheons, cocktail parties, dinners. A parlor meeting for the large contributors is a must. And nothing is so crucial as the pace setter. Each October Rabbi Herbert Friedman leads a group of 140 key community leaders in a flying visit to Europe and Israel (each at his own expense) to study problems of refugees at firsthand. On their return to Milwaukee, Kansas City, and Atlanta, they will speak with a new-found fervor about the plight of fellow Jews in Rumania and Morocco: their infectious spirit will raise the fever of giving one notch in the coming year.

Leadership is determined by one criterion alone: a passion for the cause. The campaign chairman must have all the qualities of a successful sales manager, and besides being fired with zeal for his product, he must be willing to thrust his own personal and business life into the background for a year. He need not have charismatic qualities on the public platform or a sweeping command of the English language, but he must be a genius of persuasion around the conference table.

Newsweek magazine (December 13, 1965) depicted "the arm-twisting technique" associated with Jewish philanthropy. But to explain the prodigious character of Jewish giving in terms of pressure is a vast oversimplification. Certainly the pressure is there. In Boston, a Jew who has achieved some material success may decide to join one of three Jewish country clubs—Belmont, Pinebrook, or Sidney Hill. The style of the three clubs differs: Belmont is a quiet, conservative club; Pinebrook is a little livelier, but still restrained; and Sidney Hill is a club that caters to the big spenders, the owners of flashy sports cars, and those who like to play for high stakes. But all three clubs will blackball the applicant whose name does not appear among the large contributors to the Combined Jewish Appeal. That principle is operative in almost every city in the country (Houston is an exception, and there are a few others). "Just as you have to act with a certain decorum," explains Solomon Sutker, in *The Jews, Social Patterns of an American Group,* "your charity behavior is subject to close scrutiny."

Many communities publish an annual list of contributors. The book, sometimes called an honor roll, is one of the best-read publications, for everyone is consumed with curiosity about the charity patterns of friends, colleagues, and business associates.

Undoubtedly the system admits of abuses. A manufacturer whose orders are backlogged may give priority to a retailer who "does the right thing" at the annual dinner. An accountant may receive a call for a pledge from his best client. But such practices are not part of a "standard order of procedure."

Social pressure is one of the devices society at large employs to impose certain norms of behavior. In an atmosphere where so many of these pressures are exerted to promote conspicuous consumption —luxury cars, fashionable clothes, a stable of horses—a community which compels its members to maintain a high level of concern for the afflicted, the homeless, and the innocent victims of injustice, can hardly be condemned for its social zeal.

The Mystery of the Buttonholer

Giving is a thoroughly understandable phenomenon, especially Jewish giving. As Dr. John Slawson, executive vice president of the American Jewish Committee, has observed, it is part of the heritage of the *shtetl*, the first law of the ghetto universe. But what motivates a man or a woman to enlist in the ranks of the "getters"—the fund raisers?

Most people are diffident about extracting money from others. "What right have I to set myself up as a judge over my friend's pocketbook?" Yet in every American city there are hundreds of volunteers who, without much hesitation, plunge into the ice-cold sea of soliciting, of persuading stranger or friend to write a check.

Men such as Samuel Leidesdorf of New York (the "Bernard Baruch" of Jewish fund raisers), Leonard Ratner of Cleveland, Daniel Koshland of San Francisco, (Mayor) Edward Schreiber of Galveston, all thrive on a day-long diet of phone calls, letter writing, and conferences devoted to philanthropic solicitation.

I asked a number of professional fund raisers what motivates the volunteer who undertakes this seemingly distasteful job. And what is the secret of successful campaigns? How does the Jewish community in Cleveland manage to raise close to $80 per capita in its centralized campaign, while another city can raise only $20? Is the difference attributable to the skill of the professional fund raiser? The relative wealth of a community? A particular communal tradition?

Most professionals believe that technical skill is only part of the answer. A more important variable, they maintain, is the devotion and ability of the volunteer leaders. But what impels a man to sacrifice thousands of hours which others spend on the golf course, at the bridge table, or under a Florida sun, in order to buttonhole people for charity? Nor is the expenditure of time the only sacrifice.

Fund raising is worse than a high cholesterol count in its drain upon the heart. Tension, irritation, and frustration are routine in the daily life of the solicitor. Many a stroke or coronary has been induced by the wear and tear of communal effort.

"As long as social good is achieved," one professional fund raiser told me, "I don't pry into motives. It is amazing to watch the zeal of some of the volunteers. When the name cards for direct contact are distributed, they will ask for certain cards, and you can see that they relish the idea of approaching those particular friends or business acquaintances. Sometimes one volunteer will protest to another, 'You're taking away *my* card!'"

Many find their business or professional lives dull and unfulfilling. In philanthropy there are human problems to grapple with—intellectually challenging problems. It is a welcome change from the daily routine of making shirts or adding up figures, or drilling teeth. And fund raising is a sure cure for loneliness. Money making is often impersonal, boring, and monotonous. Money raising is problem centered, an instrument for dealing with people as people.

Manheim Shapiro, the former director of American Jewish Committee's Jewish Communal Service, theorizes that fund raising may be a rewarding means of expressing Jewishness for many, particularly when religion is not a prime force in their lives. And certainly there is a certain amount of ego satisfaction and status seeking. The testimonial plaques that hang on their office walls mean a great deal to the men who have earned them.

But Baron de Hirsch Meyer, a Miami Beach banker who devotes three-quarters of his time to communal affairs, provided me with the simplest answer. During the hour we sat in his sumptuous Lincoln Road office discussing Jewish affairs, the interview was interrupted four times. The Jewish Home for the Aged had a problem; a friend phoned about his pledge to the University of Miami; a meeting was being planned by the local chapter of the American Jewish Committee; and there was to be a "topping" that afternoon for the new wing of the Mount Sinai Hospital.

His list of benefactions over the past twenty years amounted to 30 per cent of his income; at times, 40 per cent. In one year he had also given away a substantial portion of his capital. He was chairman of four campaigns—two Jewish and two general. Why? Because he believed in the causes, and he wanted them to succeed. They couldn't reach their goals unless he was willing to pitch in and get the funds. As simple as that. "If not I, who then?" the ancient rabbi asked.

One man's intoxication with good causes may be in the field of Jewish education. He worries about the future of Judaism, and he will devote every spare hour to the Jewish Education Committee, an all-day school, or a seminary. Another will find immense delight in aiding the expansion of a university. I walked through the Yale campus a few years ago with the late Louis Rabinowitz. He pointed to the library which he had given to the university.

"Did your children attend Yale?" I asked, knowing that he, himself, had never gone to college.

"No," he beamed. "But isn't it nice to see such a fine building in such a wonderful place like Yale?"

"What about the Yale Classics you endowed?" I knew that Louis Rabinowitz was not a scholar, he had made his fortune making fasteners—hooks and eyes—and had come under the spell of Rabbi Louis Finkelstein, head of the Jewish Theological Seminary, who had charmed him into an enthusiasm for Jewish scholarship.

"You know, it's worth $50,000 to get a good translation of Saadiah Gaon [a philosopher born in Upper Egypt in 892]."

By far the most emotional appeal is evoked by the homeless Jews of Europe, Asia, and North Africa. The walls of the Allied Jewish Appeal offices in Philadelphia are covered with large signs:

ANTICIPATE CHARITY BY PREVENTING POVERTY
—Maimonides
BUT ALL MANKIND'S CONCERN IS CHARITY
—Alexander Pope
CHARITY SAVES FROM DEATH —The Bible

One Philadelphia contributor told Don Hurwitz, the able director of the AJA, that he could never fully discharge his obligation. He had been in a concentration camp: how could he forget the meaning of suffering? And a friend who has devoted most of his professional career to fund raising told me, "The greatest motive in giving is the feeling that 'there but for the grace of God, go I.' We all feel a little guilty for having been spared, so there is expiation in giving. Besides, many Jews are part of the same social group. They may go into investments together. They don't hesitate to say, 'Look, Irving, you made a lot of money last year, you ought to double your gift.' "

The professionals call it "peer giving." Only a man who gives in the four figures can make the most effective appeal for pledges on the same level.

A New York Jewish leader who has been involved in a score of drives confessed to me that he had made a serious mistake in ordering his life. "I devoted so much time to philanthropy that I let my business go sour. I would have accomplished more for Jewish education had I maintained my ability to give fifty thousand a year so that I could buttonhole others to give in the five figures."

The realities of peer giving militate against the success of the rabbi in appeals for funds. Only a few spiritual leaders have the magic touch. Rabbi Joseph Lookstein, the dynamic leader of Orthodoxy in New York City, can elicit large contributions on behalf of his educational institutions. And the ultra-Orthodox Hasidic rabbis need none of the skills of the solicitor. Thousands of Hasidic Jews offer their worldly possessions for use by the *rebbe* (Hasidic rabbi) as a way of sanctifying their material goods.

The late Rabbis Stephen S. Wise and Abba Hillel Silver both had a genius for commanding large contributions. So high was their standing in the Jewish community that their requests for funds were heeded as a summons to duty. It was an honor to give what they asked for.

The Jewish community of Cleveland ranks highest in the country in its philanthropic collections not only because of its lay leadership and its unusually gifted professional staff, but because the temperamental Rabbi Silver and the eloquent Rabbi Brickner thundered out their mandate to the people in terms of "This thou must do."

Of course, the national director of United Jewish Appeal, Rabbi Herbert Friedman, has cultivated this fiscal *savoir-faire* into a fine art. He still gulps a little, he told me, before the words, "one hundred thousand dollars" emerge from his throat. But in his current campaign, which involved a special program, he managed to make clear to his prospects, "We are limiting this appeal [for secondary education in Israel] to those who will give us a minimum of one hundred thousand dollars."

Perhaps the clearest articulation of the impulses that move the volunteer fund raiser was given in an address by William Rosenwald before a group of UJA workers. Mr. Rosenwald is the son of Julius

Rosenwald, whose Sears-Roebuck fortune was devoted to Negro philanthropies. He has worked for many years as a leader in the American Joint Distribution Committee, which has salvaged more than a million lives in Europe, Asia, and Africa.

William Rosenwald spoke candidly of the personal dividends which one gathers in the process of being a fund raiser. When he started out he was a poor speaker, uncomfortable in the presence of others. "The first time I spoke, it was a catastrophe."

Now, like many thousands of Jewish men and women trained in addressing public gatherings, he is relaxed and at home with people. "I have been broadened by the circle of friends in communal work and it has given me the privilege of getting to know a great many individuals in my own community, throughout the United States and other countries. It has deepened my understanding of how peoples and governments function. . . ."

Buttonholing reached its zenith, according to Rabbi Irving Koslowe, Jewish chaplain of Sing Sing Prison, when his parishioners were asked to contribute to the United Jewish Appeal. He discovered that the prisoners, who earned five cents a day, were averaging donations of $2.50—fifty days' pay—and that 100 per cent of the inmates had contributed. When he pointed a suspicious finger at his Collection Committee, they defended themselves:

"Honestly, Rabbi, we didn't use any strong-arm tactics!"

Portrait of a Giving City

A European, innocent of the English language, is mystified by the exotic names of the states. Three of them are particularly confusing, since they involve variations on a theme of vowels. Put an I and an O and an A together and you have one state, world-famous for its corn. Put the same set of vowels together in a different order and you get a mountain state, Idaho. Mix them again, using O twice and I in the middle and you have a state which, for some incredible reason, attracted thousands of Jews away from the warm familiarity of the Northeast. Cincinnati, host to a wave of German immigrants in the 1840s and 1860s, beckoned to the Jews of Berlin, Frankfurt, Stuttgart, Breslau, and scores of lesser towns, and they created a community which coalesced the best of two possible worlds—that of Beethoven, Goethe, and Heine with the *Jüdische kultur* of the distinguished academies and institutes of the Rhineland.

From the banks of the Rhine to the banks of the Ohio scholars and rabbis transported the liberal Torah of German Enlightenment, and Cincinnati gave birth to American Reform Judaism.

But the spotlight of Jewish creativity shifted from southern Ohio to a city on Lake Erie which blossomed into an industrial and cultural center of the twentieth century. A map drawn by the Cleveland Chamber of Commerce depicts a series of concentric circles to prove that no center of American life is really very far from Euclid Avenue. There are Cleveland Jewish patriots who would draw a similar map of America which makes their city the hub of the Jewish universe.

Many of the leading rabbis and scholars of the United States were born and trained in Cleveland. Just as, in generations gone by, Jewish parents sent their children to the great seat of learning in Lithuania called Tels, so youngsters journey from all parts of the land to the Ohio fountain of learning that bears the same name—a New-World transplantation of the historic institution. On my last visit to Cleveland, our plane was crowded with Brooklyn and Bronx teen-agers wearing *yarmulkes* and reading comic books. Their animated conversation reflected their excitement at the prospect of a weekend pilgrimage to the Tels Yeshivah, which they were visiting to survey the prospects of spending the next few years there studying Talmud.

I learned that most of the outstanding Federation executives in the leading Jewish communities throughout the country had received at least part of their training in Cleveland. The pride and the permanence of the city's commitment to philanthropy are evident in the resplendent headquarters of the Jewish Community Federation, a brand-new $800,000 building in downtown Cleveland, offices, meeting rooms, dining facilities on a grand, though not lavish, style.

Its top administrators justify the investment in the quality of their facilities by pointing to the extraordinary quality of their staff and the enduring importance of their work. Every weekday, and often on Sundays, too, the meeting rooms are used for planning, strategy, and discussion of communal problems. The business and professional offices of lay leaders surpass those of Federation in luxury, but in its streamlined modernistic rooms a sense of well-being permeates the meetings. Jewish endeavor, all agree, is important enough to warrant this fine setting for their labors.

The business community has learned to accommodate itself to the city's philanthropic-cultural tone. Malcolm Forbes, in *Forbes* magazine (August 1, 1965), wrote about Cleveland, "The prime criterion for acceptance in this town is not purely power and pelf. It's what you're doing with those things to further the weal of the whole Cleveland community." Forbes quoted a transplanted New Yorker complaining, "If you're not working on the United Appeal drive, or one or more of the educational activities, or at least a half-dozen such things in this town, the men you want to know haven't any interest in knowing you."

The standards of giving in Cleveland surpass those of any other city in the nation. With a population of 1,788,000, its Community Chest reaches a goal of more than 13 million dollars. Chicago, with 3,800,000, raises a million and a half dollars less.

In 1965, the Jewish Community Federation of Cleveland collected 6 million dollars. It is illuminating to look at how that money was spent:

Three and a half million dollars was allocated for overseas agencies. More than $160,000 was distributed to community-relations organizations such as the American Jewish Committee and the Anti-Defamation League. Almost $38,000 was spent on Jewish cultural bodies. The city's Mount Sinai Hospital received $550,000; the Jewish Community Center, $365,000; and Jewish Family Service, almost $300,000.

The Cleveland Jewish Community Chest added more than a million dollars for local Jewish needs. Administrative costs were less than 10 per cent, a remarkable figure when one takes into account that the central office also fulfills a number of educational and community-relations functions.

Yet, singularly absent from the Cleveland fund-raising strategy are the various pressure techniques.

One of the executives told me that it was simply a matter of tradition. The pattern of expectation has been so firmly established that his secretary contributes more than top executives in the city where he had previously worked.

Henry I. Zucker, head of the professional staff, is a handsome man in his early fifties, a native Clevelander, soft-spoken, direct, easily approachable, and relaxed, who is hardly the stereotype of the high-powered fund raiser. Other cities often seek his counsel.

"Hank" Zucker does not see himself as a money raiser. He described himself as primarily an educator, a communal leader whose task was to evoke loyalties to values out of which financial support must inevitably flow. He is not a great believer in public relations; and there is grace, rather than cold efficiency, in the running of his office.

Zucker is far from satisfied with Cleveland's record—and even less so with the national level of Jewish giving. In 1950, he points out, our national personal income totaled 228 billion dollars, while today it is more than 675 billion. Our level of giving, he stresses, has not kept pace.

The late Rabbi Abba Hillel Silver is generally credited with setting the tone for generosity, and the late Rabbi Solomon Goldman, it is agreed, also played an important role in determining standards. But the key to current enthusiasm is a lumberman, Leonard Ratner, a Russian Jew who presides, patriarch fashion, over a large family who were all involved in civic work. The Ratner business had expanded successfully into the real-estate field, and the family wealth is channeled into scores of Jewish and civic causes. Leonard Ratner, in his early seventies, led the building campaign for the Conservative Park Synagogue, one of the showplaces of Cleveland, and has held his entire family close to Jewish traditions—often with a Biblical severity.

Wealth for Ratner is a means to one end—philanthropy. He finds no pleasure in the accumulation of money, only in its distribution for social good. He despises any ostentation. None of the Ratner clan is permitted to own a Cadillac. And it is he who determines the level of their benefactions.

One of his great loves is the Jewish Theological Seminary, and he has opened his home for many parlor meetings on its behalf. At one such meeting, the seminary's professor of mysticism, Dr. Abraham Heschel, presented a rather metaphysical talk. "Israel," declared the bearded scholar, "lives in the dimension of both time and space." Host Ratner capitalized on the sentence, and waxed enthusiastic: "As our learned Professor Heschel has told us, the seminary needs a lot more space!"

Leonard Ratner is, in a way, *sui generis*, but Cleveland Jewry has developed a large cadre of leaders whose talents have spilled over into the larger community. In Federation alone, the number of active participants has grown from 150 to more than a thousand in the past decade. Although most of Cleveland's Jews have moved from the center to the suburbs (Eugene Lipman and Albert Vorspan, in their study of Cleveland, reported that only six out of a thousand Jewish high-school graduates in 1961 received diplomas from city schools), the institutions of Cleveland—Western Reserve University, the Community Chest, the Cleveland Symphony Orchestra, and scores of social-welfare agencies—continue to feel the impact of active Jewish involvement.

Henry Zucker beams with pride as he shows the visitor the building over which he presides. It may be true, he admits, that some people come under the banner of Federation for self-serving reasons; but, an optimist by nature, he is convinced that most people are well motivated. And, as the Talmud suggests, there are those who come for ulterior reasons and continue on for pure reasons.

CHAPTER 9

A Galaxy of American Jews

Jacob Blaustein of Baltimore

With a handful of notable exceptions, the Jews of the United States are strangers to the basic industries of the nation. Steel production, heavy manufacturing, air and land transportation, the automobile industry, chemicals, drugs, and oil—all of these primary elements in the economic structure of America are controlled, both in ownership and management, by the so-called "Protestant establishment" (with modest Roman Catholic participation). One of the few Jewish exceptions is a man who made his way to the top in the oil industry.

I visited Jacob Blaustein, a native and lifelong resident of Baltimore, Maryland, in his expansive offices on the twenty-fourth floor of the thirty-story Blaustein building, perhaps the finest office building in downtown Baltimore. He looked out upon the city below us, and he spoke, with evident pride and affection. The harbor reminded him of his tankers which bring crude oil from all over the world to the many American Oil Company refineries and to Standard Oil Company (Indiana). The first is the company his father and he founded, which was later merged into, and is now part of, the second, on whose board he serves, and in which the Blaustein family has a substantial interest.

The Blaustein offices, occupying many floors of the skyscraper, are the focal point of his varied interests which include the Union Trust Company, second or third largest Maryland bank; insurance companies; electronics; real-estate development; and every aspect of the oil industry from production and distribution to research pipe-line and marine transportation—in addition to his broad interests in public affairs, particularly the United Nations.

The Blaustein success had its origins in his father's early employment by the Standard Oil Company of New Jersey. Louis Blaustein parted ways with the founder of Standard Oil (New Jersey) when Rockefeller tried to persuade him to go to Germany to start the Standard Oil there. Louis didn't want to go back to the Old World, with its many unpleasant memories for Jews. So, in 1910, father and son started the American Oil Company with one tank wagon and a horse.

Jacob's eyes kindle with excitement as he describes the many innovations that occurred to them. These included the first and original antiknock motor fuel that revolutionized the whole petroleum and automotive industries; the first drive-in service station, so motorists could drive in off the street to have their auto tanks filled; and the first visible gasoline pump, the forerunner of the meter pump, so motorists could see they were getting the quantity of gasoline for which they were paying.

Asked for the key to his success, Jacob Blaustein outlined five principles to which he adheres: first, using good ordinary common sense; second, establishing a reputation for integrity; third, a close application to what one is doing; fourth, keeping ahead of the times; and fifth, taking a broad view of the entire economy. An obvious sixth point, which he did not mention, is the maximum use of intelligence, what Jews call *sechel.*

Stewart Alsop, in an article in a national magazine, described a number of men who have accumulated large fortunes in recent years, outlining some of the personality traits that explained their success. The group he selected "turn out to be, on the whole, remarkably interesting human beings . . . they all have an excess of energy which has to be worked off somehow."

Those who know Jacob Blaustein can attest to both these characteristics. He is an exciting person to be with, and, like President Lyndon Johnson, he wears out those who try to keep up with him, either in his industrial work or in his communal activities.

It is not unusual for him to rise at 5 A.M. in Chicago, where he has flown for a board meeting, rush down to the airport to catch a company plane which will take him to a breakfast meeting of the American Jewish Committee, or some other group in New York, then to attend a conference in Washington and return to his farm near Baltimore the same night. He is an honorary president of the American Jewish Committee, is deeply interested in its work, and takes his duties seriously.

A friend of mine once called him at seven-thirty on a Saturday evening. The long-distance operator located him at his office desk.

"Jacob," my friend began, "if I had your worth I wouldn't be at my desk on a Saturday night!" Blaustein, whose schedule calls for a sixteen-hour day, did not think he was doing anything unusual and did not even bother with an explanation.

He has commuted between Baltimore, London, Geneva, Paris, and Bonn for the past fourteen years, and has flown back and forth to Israel numerous times since the birth of the state in 1948. Staff members of organizations he has worked with tell me that he sometimes calls them after midnight to "do a little brainstorming for tomorrow's meeting."

Early in 1951, Jacob Blaustein received a call from Germany, where his friend, John J. McCloy was U.S. High Commissioner in the Occupation, asking him to advise what could be done to help restore Germany to the family of nations. After several thoughtful days and nights, the Baltimore Jewish leader, then president of the American Jewish Committee, offered a number of suggestions, including the concrete proposal of financial restitution and individual compensation to help rehabilitate the surviving victims of the Hitler onslaught, and aid to the kin of those who died in Nazi concentration camps.

Of course, no moral atonement could be purchased by the dispensation of funds. But a formal program of restitution for material claims would at least bespeak Germany's recognition of moral culpability. This unprecedented action would represent a *beginning* in Germany's desire to achieve ethical rehabilitation.

Other leaders of world Jewry, including Dr. Nahum Goldman, president of both the World Jewish Congress and the World Zionist Congress, shared the Blaustein position. In meetings with Chancellor Adenauer and other German statesmen, and with the constant help of President Truman and John McCloy (and later with Chancellor Erhard and succeeding U.S. Presidents and Secretaries of State) formulae were evolved with the Conference on Jewish Material Claims against Germany, of which Blaustein is senior vice president. As a consequence, approximately eight billion dollars of West German funds will be distributed through the efforts of the Claims Conference. The State of Israel, which provided refuge for the majorities of the survivors, received large parts of this, which, added to world Jewish support, enabled the new nation to reach its present high level of economic stability although Israel still needs considerable outside financial help.

Yet, there is nothing parochial about the Baltimore philanthropist's interests. Perhaps his greatest satisfaction came as a member of the U.S. delegation to the United Nations (appointed by President Eisenhower) which led to his association with the late Secretary-General Dag Hammarskjöld.

At the entrance to the Blaustein Building, in Baltimore, there stands a half-size replica of the Barbara Hepworth sculpture, "Single Form," which adorns the entrance to the United Nations headquarters in New York.

A few weeks before he met his tragic end, Secretary-General Dag Hammerskjöld had a long luncheon session about world affairs with Blaustein, Andrew Cordier, and Ralph Bunche, and they then took a walk near the pool in front of the UN Building. Hammerskjöld mentioned to Dr. Bunche his desire to see a brilliant piece of sculpture on that spot. Beyond Blaustein's hearing, Dr. Bunche asked why Hammerskjöld had not suggested the idea to his Baltimore friend, to which the Secretary-General replied that it would be wrong to exploit their friendship. After Hammerskjöld's death, however, Dr. Bunche told Jacob Blaustein of the conversation and the latter commissioned the world-renowned British sculptress, whose work the Secretary-General admired, to execute the sculpture which Blaustein presented to the United Nations to commemorate Hammerskjöld's life.

At the dedication of the memorial, in June, 1964, the donor quoted Hammerskjöld's philosophy, "The question of peace and the question of human rights are closely related. Without recognition of human rights we shall never have peace." For the industrialist who has amassed a fortune by his inexhaustible business dealings has given an equal measure of his energies to his efforts on behalf of human rights. Active on the board of scores of Jewish philanthropic organizations and many nonsectarian ones as well, his heart lies with the exciting work of the United Nations. Among his many unrelated efforts, was his appointment by the King of Sweden to the Dag Hammerskjöld Foundation to train citizens of the newly developing nations for careers in public service. Jacob Blaustein loves an audience and likes nothing better than to carry his ideas to the public platform with carefully prepared texts and a vigorous delivery.

All the Blausteins—his wife Hilda and their three children, Morton, Barbara (Mrs. David Hirschhorn), and Elizabeth (Mrs. Arthur E. Roswell)—share virtually all of his enthusiasms—they are simple in their tastes and manner of living, and none has the standoffishness which so frequently clings to wealth. All the children and the in-laws feel that they must do a full day's work.

"I suppose that the explanation of that is in our daily conversation," Jacob Blaustein explains. "In addition to family news and events of the day, we talk about human problems, including those of Jews, and about things that have to be done to make a better world. I guess we have conveyed these values to our children."

In the color and the dynamism of the Blaustein formula for living there is a full integration of his Jewish experience, his American experience, and his human aspirations—best symbolized perhaps by that Hepworth work of art that adorns the United Nations and the lobby of his office building—"Single Form."

Abram Leon Sachar of Brandeis

In its brief nineteen years of existence, Brandeis University has raised 146 million dollars for capital expansion—a matchless success story in any field of philanthropy. It is the story of one man, the sixty-eight-year-old head of the institution, who is himself an institution in American Jewish life. The voice of Abram Leon Sachar has been heard by more American Jews than any other Jewish speaker in the country. He has lectured, during his career, to hundreds of thousands. His surveys of Jewish history were so popular that, in large cities such as Chicago, many of the same listeners filled the halls of forums all over the metropolitan area to hear him speak over and over again.

The creator of the remarkable university which has in a brief few years won international eminence—Phi Beta Kappa established a chapter there in a record thirteen years after its founding—now prefers to limit his addresses to small audiences, one person, or a small group of men and women. But Abe Sachar remains a gifted and eloquent salesman. His product is higher education—and the dignity of the American Jew.

Few people who come within conversational range of Abram Leon Sachar escape his net. How is he able to convince a potential philanthropist to write a check for a million dollars?

"I tell the Jews of America that Christians have created 900 colleges in this country. We Jews, who dispatch our children to the universities in the largest proportion, cannot be hitchhikers in higher education."

There are three strains in the Sachar character—Jewish, English, and American. The grandson of a distinguished Chicago rabbi, he is a *maskil*—a Hebrew scholar, loving learning for its own sake. His *History of the Jews* is a standard textbook, the most widely read of its kind.

Born in New York City in 1899, he grew up in St. Louis and attended Washington University, spending his junior year at Harvard. The Harvard Club of St. Louis provided a fellowship in Emanuel College at Cambridge so that young Sachar could work toward his doctorate in English history.

In the English countryside he was able to satisfy both his passion for the past and his lively desire to perfect his mastery of the English language. Not only the ideas of history intrigued him but the form as well. Macaulay and Carlyle, Trevelyan and Benjamin Disraeli became his models.

At the University of Illinois, where he taught English history, hundreds of students flocked to his lectures on Disraeli and Gladstone. Of the two statesmen, he preferred Disraeli, because he "never took himself too seriously." Nothing is less forgivable in Sachar's list of human weaknesses than a lack of humor about one's own limitations.

For many years, Sachar was national director of the B'nai B'rith Hillel Foundations—a movement which had grown from a half-dozen Jewish college student centers to more than one hundred. In 1947, he was called to head the first Jewish-sponsored university.

Brandeis' meteroic rise to a well-established place in the academic firmament is entirely attributable to the Sachar genius, and the American quality in Abram Sachar is his insistence on relevance to the contemporary spirit.

In less than two decades, the fledgling university attracted a faculty of international renown: eminent biologists and biochemists mirroring the Brandeis concern for "The Genetic Revolution": gifted sociologists, anthropologists, and psychologists—a Jewish-sponsored university would naturally lay much stress on the science of Man— poets and philosophers, historians and political scientists; scholars in a score of disciplines who were induced by the persuasive president to take up residence in Waltham.

"It wasn't too difficult," Dr. Sachar insisted. "Boston is a great magnet to anyone who wants to be in the company of some of the world's best minds."

"How did I conceive of Brandeis as a university?" Dr. Sachar explains: "I examined Harvard and Fordham and Swarthmore. Each had a special reason for coming into existence. Harvard's essential impulse was service to country; it had its roots in religion, and it sought to produce good clergymen. Roman Catholic Fordham stressed reverence, and Swarthmore—the Quaker institution— humility. Our very name, Brandeis, recalls the man—Justice Louis Brandeis—who combined two impulses, intellectual intensity and a passion for the underdog. These two principles inform all that we are doing. We like to emulate Swarthmore's concern for excellence —a small school like ourselves, and we intend to remain small. We never worry about costs. We bring the best brains of our nation to our campus.

"There is a disadvantage in being a small school: we can't lean on alumni support, we have neither tradition nor status. But we have one advantage. We can experiment. We are not held down by alumni and we can tool up for the end of the twentieth century."

New frontiers include an internationally famous center for the arts, especially the musical performing arts. Experimental theater, art, and sculpture have brought some of the most creative people in the world to Waltham, Massachusetts. When the brilliant Mendès-France stepped down from the premiership of France, he came to Brandeis as a visiting professor. Eleanor Roosevelt was intrigued by the forward-looking university and lent it active personal support.

Brandeis has launched many firsts in higher education. It recently created a department of undergraduate legal studies; and its social-welfare school is a pioneer in the field.

"I think of Brandeis as a perfect synthesis of commitment to the liberal tradition in America and the principles of prophetic justice," Dr. Sachar declared.

The university is not a place for ideas alone, but for the enhancement of human welfare. Brandeis has drawn to itself a number of great Americans: Chief Justice Warren, Dean Acheson, the late Adlai Stevenson, to whom its emphasis on humaneness as the heart of the American ethos has held a strong appeal.

In April, 1966, President Sachar presided over the 477th dedication of a Brandeis building or facility! The ritual on the handsome Waltham campus is as well established as a vespers service. Many of the students resent sharing their campus with a steady stream of visitors and honorary alumni, but it is the small price they pay for this new and dynamic university.

The Sachar enterprise is a family one. Thelma Sachar, a beautiful woman, who taught high-school French when they were married, not only fulfills the role of a president's wife, but is an eloquent speaker, and has enlisted support on the public platform for many Brandeis undertakings.

"Every man who is high up," Abe Sachar quotes J. M. Barrie, "loves to think he has done it all himself: and the wife smiles, and lets it go at that."

One son, Howard, is a historian; a second, Edward, is a practicing psychiatrist; David, their third son, is a physician who is investigating cholera in East Pakistan.

At sixty-eight, Abram Sachar has a youthful air, a buoyancy, a quick, easy responsiveness to people. Old age, he says, is an attitude of mind, a looking back, a tiresome reminiscence. The fun of life is to keep looking ahead. "That is why I insist on being a teaching president, and the course I teach is one that is ever changing, 'The Contemporary World' given in two semesters, first, 'The World up to Munich' and second, 'From Munich to the Present.'"

Nature seems to have packed into the Sachar constitution an inexhaustible store of energy. Tight schedules, the nightmare of all peripatetic lecturers, never daunted him. Once, he was due to fly from Dallas, where he had just finished a convention address, to Tulsa, where he was listed as the keynote speaker at the annual meeting of the Oklahoma Teachers' Association. Bad weather had grounded all planes, and the Oklahoma chairman offered to send a private plane to get through the storm.

The flight from Dallas to Tulsa followed an eerie pattern. Every twenty miles the Piper Cub suddenly swooped down, almost touching the ground. The anxious passenger shouted to the pilot to stop stunting, but his voice was lost in the engine's roar.

Landing safely at Tulsa, the shaken traveler asked the pilot just what he had been up to.

"Oh, I wasn't stunting, I just didn't know my way. Every time I saw a railway station, I dived down to read the name of the town."

Moments later, Dr. Abram Sachar regaled the thousands of educators in his audience with the story of his hectic escapade, and added, with a characteristic twinkle in his eye, "My dear friends, when I tell you I'm glad to be here, I really mean it: I'm glad to be here."

I asked Abram Sachar whether he felt that he had accomplished all that he had set out to do.

"In the words of Winston Churchill, I would like to have another twenty years to see how things turn out. I have had the great satisfaction of reaping two harvests, my work in Hillel and now Brandeis."

"As a historian, what is your philosophy of history?"

"I believe that there is a purpose in the world. The greatest evil is cynicism. That is the true atheism. My philosophy is no different than my rabbi grandfather's. Only the paraphernalia has changed.

"Human progress is made through leadership. I have always been a disciple of Carlyle. Events are shaped by leaders—even though there is some interaction. The accident of Woodrow Wilson's stroke kept America from international leadership. Had Eisenhower recognized China at a crucial juncture in our history, we might not have had the tragedy of Vietnam."

Dr. Sachar is not a formal religionist, but he observes the holy days and festivals, and belongs to a temple. The Sachar family observes two Seders on Passover.

"I accept the pageantry of the festival and its social idealism."

The glow of Abram Sachar's affirmation of life shines through the concluding words of his *Sufferance Is the Badge*, a historical survey of Jewish life in the dark 1930s. Written in the impassioned rhetoric of September, 1939, the month when World War II's outbreak presaged an acceleration of Hitler's onslaught on the Jews, the historian urged his fellow Jews to be

> resolute in courage, in optimism, in faith that mankind has the capacity to conquer the forces of darkness. . . . This calls for no manufactured Pollyanna buoyancy. History is on the side of the optimists. . . . Jews, above all, have no right to fly in the face of their own history by succumbing to the vapors of despondency. There have been other periods when the whole nation has been trapped between the Red Sea and the Egyptians. Only the names of the persecutors and the detractors have been different. . . . The Jew can wait for the return of sanity . . . because the very excesses of anti-Semitism have wakened the world to the dangers of barbarism. . . .
>
> It may be sentimental to glory in such a fate. The uprooted communities in Germany and Austria and Poland and Rumania find little comfort in the suggestion that they are playing the benefactor's role. Yet, there is historic satisfaction in the realization that a minority group, which has never given up its cultural and religious uniqueness, its ethical Protestantism, has survived, and that in its survival it has served, not only itself, but the cause of civilization. This realization is a pillar of cloud by day and a pillar of fire by night. It strengthens the faith that the Hitlers and the Mussolinis, the Cuzas and the Codreanus, are merely men of the moment who have pitted themselves against an enduring people.

Abraham Kaplan, Teacher

The cover of *Time* magazine for May 6, 1966, featured men selected by the editors as the nation's most outstanding college teachers. Nine out of ten teach either on the West Coast or the East. The rest of the country is represented by a single institution, the University of Michigan, and its colorful philosophy professor, Abraham Kaplan.

The *Time* photograph shows the bearded philosopher addressing a seminar at Ann Arbor. His white socks, sweater, and loafers contrast sharply with the more formally clad students before him, and as he leans forward to stress a point, a cigarette dangles loosely from the outstretched fingers of one hand, a beer can is firmly grasped in the other. He is wiry thin. His gray, black-streaked beard seems tailored to his personality: jutting angularly from his youthful face—he is under fifty—with a suggestion of defiant benevolence.

Dr. Kaplan told the *Time* reporter: "I am by training a positivist, by inclination a pragmatist, in temperament a mystic, my faith, Jewish. . . ." It is obvious to those who follow his lectures that he is a committed Jew.

"Our family marks the Sabbath in a traditional way," Dr. Kaplan told me. "We sing *zemirot* at the table, even conduct Havdalah service at Sabbath's end. We don't observe, we celebrate. Each Jew, as the saying goes, must make Shabbos for himself.

"The whole business reminds me of the story of a Jew giving testimony in a courtroom. He mentioned a *shofar*, and the judge asked him what that was.

"The Jew struggled to find the appropriate words to describe the instrument, and after some time he explained, 'It's a kind of horn.'

" 'Why didn't you say so in the first place?' the judge asked impatiently.

" 'Ah, because a *shofar* is *not* a horn,' the Jew replied."

Dr. Kaplan spoke of his religious philosophy. "I am not a philosophic thesist, but an experimental theist. If someone asks me what is my God, I give him the answer of the Zen Buddhist: 'If you do, I don't.' However you define it, I find it to be something else. My God is Spinoza's and Job's God—and Hosea's, too. He is the God of Abraham, Isaac, and Jacob—but mostly of this Abraham," and he pointed to himself. "To me He is a kind of continuous, intimate presence. My father addressed God as *Tatenyu*—dear Daddy. There was familiarity, not awe, in it.

"I have a simple philosophy. Life is worth living and people are worth knowing."

He interrupted his exposition to tell a story, one of the many tales with which Kaplan sprinkles his lectures.

"I love the story of the Berditchever [Rabbi Levi Isaac, the eighteenth-century Hasidic rabbi of Berditchev, Poland]. He invited guests to a wedding with the following announcement: 'You are cordially invited to our daughter's wedding which will take place at this and this date in the holy city of Jerusalem. P.S. If the Messiah doesn't come by that date, our daughter's wedding will take place in our residence in Berditchev.'"

He spoke of his indebtedness to Martin Buber, and his use of the dialogue.

"I was born in Odessa. When I was two years old, my eighteen-year-old sister went to Palestine, and we did not meet for twenty-seven years. When we did meet, she knew Hebrew, Russian, and other languages, and I knew English and German, but we had no language in common. At first we groped for words, and seemed at a loss. But after a short while she said, 'It's all right, Abashe (my Russian nickname) you and I understand each other.' There is an understanding without words."

Dr. Kaplan has an interesting hobby, kite flying. He also collects kites, importing them from various parts of the world.

"Is it true," I asked him, "that you once said that kite flying is a kind of tug toward heaven?"

"Oh, don't take that too literally. Skiing is also a tug toward heaven. Kite flying is an I-Thou relationship with the wind and the air. The best part about my hobby is that when you are through with it at the end of the day, you haven't spoiled anything."

I asked the noted philosopher whether he felt Jews have contributed much to philosophy in America.

He mentioned an article in the *National Observer,* written a few years ago, which discussed the outstanding teachers of philosophy in the United States. Most of them were Jewish. What they brought to their teaching, the writer maintained, was vigor, thrust, and a certain tartness.

Certainly this is true of Kaplan himself. There is an electricity in the air when he lectures. He is not only a master of the subject, he loves it, and he is eager to share his ideas with his audience.

"A philosophy which speaks only to philosophers is no philosophy at all," Abraham Kaplan has written. "For the business of philosophy, as I see it, always was—and remains—to articulate the principles by which a man can live; not just as a scientist, citizen, religionist, or whatever, but as the whole man that he is."

Comedian with a Mission

For most Americans, the color and the texture of Jewish family life have been revealed not by the rabbis—who reach relatively few non-Jews—or by the social scientists, but by the world of entertainment.

A Roman Catholic nun, interviewed on television, rhapsodized about *Fiddler on the Roof*, the musical based on the life of the Jews in nineteenth-century Eastern Europe, which she had seen repeatedly on the Broadway stage. When the interviewer asked how the play compared with *Going My Way*, she grimaced and dismissed the film as somewhat less than authentic.

The character of Mollie, portrayed for many years on radio and television by the late Gertrude Berg, has also become part of the folklore of America. The homey virtues, taken for granted by most Jewish listeners, and a source of embarrassment for those nervous Jews who were afraid that they were alien flavored, struck a responsive chord in many a Gentile listener.

For the past two decades, a Jewish schoolteacher turned television star has strengthened the popular image of the family-rooted Jews. Sam Levenson has expressed the philosophy underlying his entertainment career in a delightful autobiographical book, *Everything but Money*. His infectious humor does not obscure the seriousness of his objectives. Ever the teacher, he uses the inspiration of his own childhood experiences to expose the foibles of contemporary parent-child relationships in American life.

As we lunched together at Lindy's Restaurant in Times Square, Sam Levenson reminisced about his childhood in the slums of New York.

He was the youngest of ten children, nine of them boys. Two died before they reached adulthood. His parents observed all the religious traditions, especially the holy days and festivals, although not too rigidly.

"I never use dialect. I will do nothing that will hold my parents and their generation in contempt. Besides, it was only funny when it was familiar. Today, even the grandparents in my audience were born in this country. I have one constant theme in my routine: My wonderful parents. I never felt a moment of insecurity about them.

"I didn't change my name because I have to make it as Sam Levenson or it is no victory. My goal is to universalize the Jewish home. I never refer to Miami Beach or the Catskills. I avoid the theme of 'Jewish brains'—we are no brainier than any other people. But my talks about the Jewish home and all its values appeal to non-Jews, especially the Irish and the Italians. Catholic priests like my stress on family, respect for culture, sacrifice for education, dignity in poverty, and respect for teachers.

"I make a point of a casual reference to the fact that we didn't drink in our house—'My mother saved pennies because we had no liquor in our house'—to audiences who spend a lot on drink."

I asked him about the violin he carried with him. We gave it to the check girl, and I was tempted to tell her to watch it carefully, for it was a $40,000 Stradivarius Levenson had borrowed from Isaac Stern for a TV appearance on the *Tonight* show.

"Don't tell the girl," he warned me, "it will only make her nervous. My mother dreamed that her youngest child would become Sam the violinist and play in Carnegie Hall."

Levenson's book dwells on the theme of parental infallibility. His childhood was a well-anchored world.

"Papa and Mama could do no wrong," Sam said, "But a higher commandment than filial obedience was the absolute infallibility of the teacher. The teacher was Pope in our home.

"I brought home a note from my teacher: 'Your son, Samuel, shows signs of astigmatism.' My father smacked me. It sounded as if I had done something wrong to the teacher.

"I model myself after Sholom Aleichem, especially his methodology. But I never beat my parents. And I can't stand comedians who make fun of their wives and families. I talk about my Jewish mother, and I may tease about the way she wanted to be a wonderful mother but sometimes fell flat on her face. I like telling the audience about her Jewish concern for health, for wholesome foods.

"My goal in life is to make it better. I have a responsibility toward my town [he lives in Neponsit, a New York City suburb in the Rockaways]. We helped organize a concert series, to bring the best music to our community. A city without culture is no city. Either you lead or the storm troopers take over. You have to give something to society. You can't drain the well dry."

Levenson spoke of his dissatisfaction with American education. "We haven't produced a literate generation. They read comic books, listen to Westerns. Our schools have failed to cultivate values and critical judgment in our young people."

He described his "Friends of Music" project.

"The culturally disadvantaged children don't have the motivation toward music that was instilled in our generation. In my talks I tell how my mother saved on food, using bones instead of meat, to pay for violin lessons. Through the New York City Board of Education we have distributed instruments to 2,000 children."

Off stage, just as in front of the TV cameras, Sam Levenson's humor seems to bubble up deep within him. He approaches life with relish and everyone near him is infected by his expansive view of mankind. The Levenson humor is not that of the wisecrack, the pun, or clever repartee. It rests on irony, on the lack of logic in the human situation, and on pricking the balloon of pretentiousness.

Levenson began entertaining at parties, for five dollars a performance, in the 1930s, when he was a teacher. Later he raised his fee to fifteen dollars, and by the 1940s he was earning more after school than in the classroom. He took a five-year leave of absence, and never returned.

He plans his entertainment "line" like an academic researcher. "What can I do about the problem of divorce? I read sociological and psychological works. I give an imaginary talk under the wedding canopy. I was really not cut out to be a comedian. I'm too much of a critic of our culture, of its shabbiness, its superficiality."

Levenson is a frustrated preacher. Occasionally he takes over the West End Temple pulpit of his rabbi, Joseph Weiss.

"Always expect the worst," I tell them. "Expect to quarrel." He proceeds to a catalogue of the standard quarrels they may expect, and his audience loves every line.

Maurice Samuel—Modern Maggid

Maurice Samuel, a native of Rumania who was educated in Manchester, England, has been called "the most authentic voice of American Jewish literature." He is also the present-day personification of the *Maggid*—the itinerant preacher who traveled from village to village in Eastern Europe like a Chautauqua circuit rider, stopping for one-night stands in the Sheboygans and Paducahs of Poland, Lithuania, Rumania, and the Ukraine, evoking laughter and tears with tales that exhorted, cajoled, brought tearful news of "what's happening in our land of Israel," and wove stories within stories for the entertainment and edification of young and old.

Maurice Samuel has been one of the most popular Jewish lecturers in the United States, Canada, Great Britain, and South

Africa. I have watched him spellbind a large Detroit audience simply by reading a story, in Yiddish, by J. L. Peretz, and I have heard him in his less mellow days chide a group in Sioux City for their intellectual lethargy, cutting short a question period with a peremptory: "Go home now, you're half asleep anyway." Even his puns are part of the folklore of world Jewry. After sitting fretfully through an overlong introduction by the chairman of a South African meeting, whose name was Rabbi Rome, Maurice Samuel glared at the long-winded speaker and told his listeners: "While Rabbi Rome was fiddling, I was burning."

I visited Maurice Samuel in his apartment in Manhattan's West Side. His study was strewn with papers and manuscripts. He was soon to publish his most ambitious undertaking, a definitive study of the famous Beiliss trial (*Blood Accusation, The Strange History of the Beiliss Case*), involving a Russian Jew who had been falsely accused of killing a Christian child. We discussed some of his many well-known books: *The Professor and the Fossil,* a scholarly answer to Arnold Toynbee's contention that the Jews are a "fossil people"; *The Great Hatred,* a seminal book on the subject of anti-Semitism, expounding the novel thesis that dislike of the Jew is rooted not in religious doctrine—the Crucifixion theme—but in the anger of the world, pagan at heart, because the Jews gave to man the Christian ethic.

Samuel's eyes, a bit dimmed and myopic, brightened as we moved from one book to another. His greatest satisfaction, he confided, was in his readers all over the world who informed him how much he had influenced their thinking.

It was Samuel's *World of Sholem Aleichem* that first introduced the "Jewish Mark Twain" to contemporary audiences. *Fiddler on the Roof* would have been inconceivable were it not for Maurice Samuel. "Jews have become America's pet," he commented, "but the idea has been taken over on a vulgar level." He particularly deplored the "Yiddishization of America," referring to an *Esquire* article which highlighted the squalid side of Jewish culture.

Samuel talked about the profound changes that have taken place in American Jewish life in recent years. Partly as a reaction to the Hitler era and partly in response to the creation of Israel, Jews have developed a psychological attachment to their Jewishness rather than a spiritual bond. But the permanent values of Judaism, Samuel feels, will be preserved. "We are going through a period like that between Ezra and the Maccabees—nothing seems to be happening that is visible or memorable—yet Judaism is being formed at this time.

"We have gone a full circle. When I first started the lecture circuit, more than forty years ago, I was asked, 'Why be a Jew?' Later the question was, 'How be a Jew?' Now as affluence and comfort have set in, the old question, 'Why be a Jew?' is back again. Hitlerism is no longer remembered. Anti-Semitism is out of fashion."

I recalled that his lectures of a generation ago were far from optimistic. Samuel's mood has changed considerably.

"Yes, I used to be otherwise," he agreed. "Today, the Jewish *mode* [he stressed the word] is part of human experience. Size is a matter of no importance. If in the year 2000 there are two million Jews deeply rooted in the Jewish mould, I would be satisfied.

"The *Jewish idea* will not perish in fifty years. Beyond that I am not interested. Judaism has an uncanny way of rebirth. That's why I cannot understand the panic in the air, the excitement of Save Jews Now!"

The writer spoke sharply about Jewish Orthodoxy. He could not forgive their refusal to make peace with the twentieth century.

"How can a modern-trained rabbi like Joseph Soloveitchik [leader of modern Orthodoxy] tell his students that God may have created the fossils at the time of Creation just to confuse mankind and make them think?"

I asked him what Jewry has done for America. "We have livened it up. We have given it the liveliness of the Litvaks [Lithuanian Jews], with their keenness of intellect, and the *schmaltz,* the sentiment, of the Russian Jew."

As I left the room, I commented again on the huge volume of notes he had gathered for his latest book.

"I learned the Russian language from scratch in order to read the record of the Beiliss trial."

One complete side of his study was lined with wall files. The floor, too, was covered with neat piles of notes. I asked why they were scattered on the floor.

"These are my footnotes," Maurice Samuel explained.

Jacob Potofsky, Union Leader, Twentieth-Century Style

The president of the Amalgamated Clothing Workers of America, AFL-CIO, Jacob Samuel Potofsky, who leads 400,000 workers in the men's clothing realm, a successful bank, and a number of vast housing cooperatives, was describing the difficult days of his Chicago youth.

"Our family came from Poland to Chicago when I was eleven. I began to work as a floor boy, soon after, at Hart, Schaffner, and Marx. My father, brother, and sister worked there, too. I started at three dollars a week, went up to five as a loop turner and seven as an operator.

"In those days, Hart, Schaffner, and Marx paid slave wages. All three of the owners were German Jews, assimilated. They gave a lot of money to non-Jewish causes and universities, but wouldn't pay a living wage. When I was sixteen, in 1910, we began the fight for union recognition. That was the beginning of collective bargaining in America."

At sixteen, Jacob Potofsky was elected secretary of the Union. At nineteen, he became treasurer of Pants Maker Local 144.

The bearded head of one of the nation's most successful unions does not seem like a man in his seventies. He is six feet tall, and stands erect. He has the look of a person singularly free of conflict, and he speaks quietly and deliberately. A widower with two married daughters (an only son died of leukemia), he might easily be mistaken for a rabbi of the old school—benign, paternal, scholarly.

There were no echoes in his voice of the hundred bitter battles in Gloversville, Cincinnati, Minneapolis, Baltimore, and other cities where neckwear, glove, shirt, and men's suit workers had manned the picket lines to assert their rights.

Jacob Potofsky was reminiscing about the villainy of Hart, Schaffner, and Marx during the second decade of the twentieth century. His phone rang. Two Jacks engaged in an amiable conversation.

"Yes, Jack, I think you should go to the dinner. I've lined up some large contributions."

The "Jack" at the other end of the line was Jack Gray, the current president of Hart, Schaffner, and Marx.

"I'm proud of you, Jack," Potofsky told him. "Your company is the best in everything worth while. I'm proud of your achievements."

I commented on the cordiality between labor and management. "Yes, we are in a fine industry today. We don't have to fight, we don't even need arbitrators. That same firm that paid slave wages fifty years ago is now the leader in promoting industrial amity.

"When I was a kid, we had to fight for the right to be organized. The bosses, many of them Jewish, told us, 'We will decide your hours of work, your rate of pay.' They used to blacklist anyone who joined a union. When we asked them to arbitrate, they said there was nothing to arbitrate.

"Today all that has changed. Our unions—those that were largely Jewish—organized and pioneered the way of settling labor disputes by calling in impartial outsiders. We used Clarence Darrow back in 1911."

It was under the leadership of Sidney Hillman, one of Franklin Roosevelt's close associates, that the Amalgamated adopted the old Jewish idea of submitting disputes to arbitration. And it was Hillman who influenced Roosevelt to adopt the Blue Eagle—the symbol of the minimum wage. ("Clear it with Sidney" was a campaign chant of Roosevelt's enemies.)

"Do you know what the base pay was in the 1930s when the minimum wage was first written into law?" Potofsky asked. "Eleven dollars a week."

Jacob Potofsky, unlike most of his predecessors in union organization, is no stranger to synagogue life, and is a long-time member of the Stephen Wise Free Synagogue.

"A Jew has to belong," he explained. "I'm a better Jew than when I was a kid. I've lost some of my youthful misgivings about my faith."

The huge labor empire over which he presides, now predominantly Italian and Puerto Rican, is more than a union. It is a large family, and it is concerned with all the problems of living.

"Our industry is socially minded and philanthropically minded, too. It's a Jewish industry, you know, and we support every cause, including Israel. The pace is set by a group of men called 'the Philanthropic Fifty.' When they decide that this year they will each add 10 per cent, you can be sure that everyone else in the industry will give another 10 per cent."

For more than forty years the Amalgamated has sponsored cooperative housing. In Coney Island, on a site that was once Luna

Park, thirteen twenty-story apartment buildings house over 5,000 families at a modest cost, with nursery facilities, clubs for the elderly, a Credit Union, and an ambitious adult-education program.

In the Bronx, replacing the ill-starred Freedomland, the new Co-op City will provide high-quality middle-income housing for 15,000 families.

New York, declares Jacob Potofsky, has been fashioned in part by its Jewish-organized unions. The labor peace they have evolved has helped make the city the mercantile capital of the nation, if not the world.

Morris B. Abram

The spirit of the New South is exemplified by Congressman Charles Weltner, great-grandson of a Confederate general, who voted for the Civil Rights Act of 1954, and was returned to Congress in 1964 by a substantial majority. This remarkable victory, which Weltner describes in his autobiographical book, *Southerner* (1966), was made possible because Georgia's county Unit System of voting, which gave a tremendous advantage to the sparsely settled rural counties over the densely populated—and far more liberal—urban areas, had been overturned in a brilliant constitutional challenge.

The man responsible for this historic turn in Southern political affairs was Morris B. Abram, a native of Ben Hill County, Georgia, an honor graduate of the University of Georgia, and a Rhodes scholar. "He was clearly the most brilliant young mind in the legal profession," wrote Congressman Weltner, "and had already earned an enviable reputation for sagacity and eloquence."

In 1954, Morris Abram had, himself, made a futile attempt to win a seat in Congress. But although he swept Atlanta's Fulton County by a wide margin, he lost to Congressman James Davis, who managed to garner the crucial rural vote. Young Abram set himself the goal of abolishing the County Unit System, although he realized that this required a frontal attack on the political device which enabled Southern politicians to disenfranchise the Negroes of the big cities. His first U.S. Supreme Court plea lost by one vote, but Abram refused to give up. In 1962, the Court handed down its famous "one-man, one-vote" ruling. The battle for reapportionment was won.

Morris Berthold Abram has deep roots in America and in the South. His birthplace, Fitzgerald, Georgia, is a town of 8,781 situated eighty miles southeast of Macon, in the heart of cotton, corn, peanut, and tobacco country. His father, Sam, a native of Rumania, who ran a store in Fitzgerald, had married a local girl, the daughter of a Jewish doctor and granddaughter of Rabbi Elias Epstein, one of the first Reform rabbis in America.

Young Morris Abram followed his undergraduate studies at the University of Georgia and his Rhodes scholarship at Oxford with a stint in the Air Corps Intelligence. After World War II, he served on the staff of the International Military Tribunal—the famous Nuremberg trials—and later helped administer the Marshall Plan.

Returning to the South, he joined a prominent Atlanta law firm. Soft-spoken, yet a masterful orator, the young attorney soon became the spokesman for a number of liberal causes. A pamphlet he authored, entitled *How to Stop Violence in Your Community*, became the basis for anti-Klan laws in several states and in fifty cities. A stanch supporter of equal rights for Negroes, Morris Abram became a warm admirer and close friend of the Rev. Martin Luther King. In 1960, when the Negro leader was jailed, it was Abram who persuaded the Democratic leaders of Atlanta to seek the intervention of Sen. John F. Kennedy, the Democrats' presidential aspirant. Martin Luther King was released from jail and Abram's inspired suggestion, coupled with Kennedy's telephone call to Mrs. King, is regarded as an important factor in swinging the undecided Negro vote in Kennedy's favor.

In 1962, Morris Abram left Atlanta to join one of New York's great law firms. He told me that months of inner turmoil preceded his decision. He had accepted President Kennedy's appointment as the first legal counsel to the newly established Peace Corps and was interested in working in a wider arena of human affairs. For a while he had been seriously tempted by President Kennedy's offer to appoint him ambassador to Tanganyika. He was offered a federal judgeship, but he declined. "I'm not temperamentally suited to sitting on a bench. I want to be more active."

"While I was agonizing, a friend suggested that I had to make up my mind whether I wanted to play with the Atlanta Crackers or with the New York Yankees. That triggered my decision."

I remarked laughingly that Atlanta had just joined Big-League baseball, and Abram commented that the city had become part of the Big League in a number of ways.

Since moving to New York, Abram has served as U.S. delegate to the United Nations Human Rights Commission, traveling to many parts of the globe as a vigorous U.S. spokesman on his favorite theme, the restoration of dignity to every human being.

Abram is also president of the American Jewish Committee, and devotes a great deal of his time to the Committee's far-flung interests. Some months ago, he headed a delegation to Argentina to express concern about the abridgment of Jewish rights in that turbulent country.

Argentina's Foreign Minister Servalla Ortiz spoke to Abram about "the affection and esteem I have for our Jewish colony."

Morris Abram retorted, "That comment indicates your attitude toward Argentinian Jewry. Secretary Rusk would never speak about 'our Jewish colony!' Evidently you regard them as outsiders."

Now a resident of my own Westchester community of Larchmont, Morris Abram is a familiar figure riding down Larchmont Avenue on his bicycle with his youngest son, Joshua, in tow, playing tennis with one of his other children: there are three sons and two daughters in the Abram household. It is not unusual for his neighbors to read about a Morris Abram meeting with a foreign diplomat in this morning's newspaper while they watch him practicing a complicated routine on the trampoline in his back yard.

I asked Morris Abram how he viewed the position of American Jewry today.

"The Jew in this country is comfortably American—more so than the Jew of any other land. American history is his history, for we are a country of immigrants. The English Jew has *rights*, but there was an English history long before he came on the scene, and a French history, too. . . . Argentina is still a Catholic country, and although Jews may live in it, they are not completely a part of it. In other countries, we speak of Jewish contributions, but in America, nobody has any greater claim to the main stream of this country than Jews do, for America is the history of an amalgam."

"One difficulty," I interjected. "What happens to an amalgam? Don't all the individual elements disappear? What happens then to Judaism?"

"If you study Jewish history, you know that there were 3 million Jews, or more, in Roman times. If we had reproduced our kind, in a theological sense, we would number many hundreds of millions today. But adherence to Judaism has always been voluntary, and therefore of better quality. Our time is no different than any other age. I'm hopeful about the Jewish future in America. Those Jews who have pride in our great tradition will find that it offers many rewards.

"I once asked Ben Gurion which he thought was the more authentic bearer of Jewish tradition—Albert Einstein or one of the rabbis of Meah Shearim [the ultra-Orthodox section of Jerusalem].

"He answered, 'Without question, Einstein. He represents our universalism, our intellectual, prophetic tradition.' "

We discussed Zionism and Israel.

"I grew up in Atlanta, in an anti-Zionist tradition. Our rabbi, Dr. Marx, was a strong anti-Zionist. But I discounted his ideas when I realized how much they were based on self-hatred. One day we discussed the Leo Frank case [the New York Jew who was lynched by a Georgia mob]. Rabbi Marx insisted that the hysteria was stirred up by East European Jews; that there was no anti-Semitism in the United States until the East European Jews came along. I felt that not only was his diagnosis wrong, but that he was morally wrong.

"The generation I grew up in generally had one or two immigrant parents. The father couldn't or wouldn't play games with his children. It was not easy for American-born children to understand or appreciate immigrant parents, and the young people often associated Jewishness with something foreign. I am sure some Jews became apostates in order to flee from foreign parents. But that is a thing of the past. Today that alien experience is gone, and the Jewish family is much more cohesive. That is why I don't believe American Jews will vanish."

We returned to his Southern experiences. Abram had been a classmate of Sen. Herman Talmadge at the University of Georgia, and although they have become political enemies, they have remained close friends. The Senator has often expressed his affection and respect for his outspoken opponent, and on several occasions he has suggested Abram's name to the White House for a key appointment.

Abram told me of a conversation with a politician—a Christian—from a neighboring Southern state.

"Do you know Mr. F. of my state? I can't understand him. He's a

Jew—and a segregationist. I am a segregationist myself, and I'm proud of it. But I can't figure a *Jew* being one. After all that persecution, a segregationist Jew must be one of two things. Either he's insincere, or else he has a hard heart."

Abram wondered why he didn't apply the same yardstick to himself, but the Southerner evaded a direct answer. "It just doesn't figure. A *Jew*—and a *segregationist?!*"

CHAPTER 10

The Faith of New World Jewry

"There's nothing like unity to fight over."
MORDECAI M. KAPLAN

The Double Establishment

In the past three decades a profound though subtle change has been effected in the structure of American Jewry. Without a formal superstructure and without the drama of spotlighted personalities, American Jews established a kind of democratic central authority, based on common consent rather than sanctions. To further this end, the welded Jewish communities of America created such agencies as the Large Cities Budgeting Committee, which offer guidelines as to how funds shall be allocated—how much for overseas needs, how much for Jewish education, how much to combat anti-Semitism, and so on.

The debates are endless, and not without rancor. But each year the key professional and lay leaders of American Jewry converge on the city designated for the meeting of the CJFWF (Council of Jewish Federations and Welfare Funds, the coordinating body for more than 200 centralized agencies serving about 800 Jewish communities. Its current collective budget: 130 million dollars.) General Assembly, and for days and nights they discuss not merely how to raise money more effectively, but substantive issues that affect the welfare of Jews everywhere in the world. And to guide them in their deliberations, they bring the world's great Jewish figures to their council rooms.

The offices of CJFWF are modest: One floor of a building on Seventh Avenue in the Times Square area. Its rooms are modest, too: simple furniture, no carpeting or paintings. But this is one of the nerve centers for the administration of Jewish affairs in America.

The offices of the NCRAC are no less modest. Facing the New York Public Library on 42nd Street, the National Community Relations Advisory Council coordinates the program of more than eighty local Jewish Community Councils, as well as the national Jewish bodies dealing with what is called "community relations." Their concern is the status and security of Jews in America.

The three major bodies devoted primarily to community relations are the American Jewish Congress, the American Jewish Committee (recently returned to the NCRAC), and the Anti-Defamation League of B'nai B'rith. The oldest of the three is the American Jewish Committee, founded in 1906 in the wake of the Russian pogroms. The American Jewish Congress, whose flavor is distinctly Zionist, came into being as a protest against what its organizers regarded as a lack of militancy in American Jewish Committee strategy.

Each of the three organizations has broadened its focus over the years, within the framework of a rather consistent philosophy. In recent years, the American Jewish Congress has leaned heavily on the law, invoking the courts and the legislature in defense of minority rights, racial and religious. The law itself, AJ Congress leaders insist, is a powerful educational weapon.

The American Jewish Committee and the Anti-Defamation League have generally eschewed a frontal attack on bigotry, convinced that the bigot is not moved by pleas for justice.

"The bleating of the lamb only excites the tiger," quotes Dr. John Slawson, professional head of the committee. The Anti-Defamation League, with its pipe line to 150,000 B'nai B'rith members, is especially active on a grass-roots level, and believes strongly in the power of mass media to transform intergroup attitudes.

All three agencies use a variety of methods in their efforts to extend and safeguard human rights—education, law, the enlistment of support from like-minded groups, and the mass media. The major difference is one of emphasis. And on both the local and national level their leaders sit side by side exchanging ideas, battling on behalf of their own tactics.

This second Jewish Establishment often serves as the counterpart of the church—more often, indeed, than the three synagogue bodies, Orthodox, Conservative, and Reform.

Thousands of diagnostic sermons have been preached on the theme of fragmentized Judaism in America. Why can't we religious Jews band together? Why does the National Council of Churches seek the cooperation of the American Jewish Committee on a score of projects? Why do the national radio and TV networks turn to the Committee or the Anti-Defamation League for Jewish programs? Why do Catholic universities invite the ADL, the Congress, and the Committee to represent the Jewish position not only in civic matters but even on the nature of Jewish belief and practice? How is it that the National Jewish Welfare Board, and not the Synagogue Council, is authorized by the Pentagon to conduct the chaplaincy program?

In the dynamics of social function, organizations tend to find their own level. Catholic Charities deal with their counterparts, the Jewish Family Service and Jewish youth-serving agencies; Protestants handling problems of the aging seek their opposite numbers within Jewish welfare agencies. Of the fifty to sixty thousand "professional Jews" in the United States and Canada, at least four out of five are employed by lay organizations rather than religious institutions. (Hundreds of these professionals are ordained rabbis. Washington, D.C., alone has some fifty non-pulpit rabbis).

The voice of lament heard in the synagogues is based to some extent on the false premise that American Jews have been alienated from religion in the process of becoming secularized. Actually Jews have always been in the vanguard of those who, according to Harvey Cox, have fashioned *The Secular City*. (For an excellent elaboration of this theme, read the chapter entitled "Judaism Secularized" in Moses Rischin's *The Promised City—New York's Jews, 1870–1914.*) The original artificial separation of the sacred and the secular, as Professor Cox explains, was a Christian departure from the Hebraic spirit. For secularism in Judaism does not connote abandonment of faith. In the context of the American scene, it means a fresh approach to the problem of man's relationship with the church (or synagogue).

There are moral concerns in which organized religion has a vital interest; but the expression or acting out of those concerns can properly be channeled through secular means. Dr. Mordecai M. Kaplan's entire philosophy of Reconstructionism, the most authentically American movement within Judaism, hangs on this very premise. A Jew, said Professor Kaplan fifty years ago, can live his Judaism in many ways outside the synagogue and still be an authentic Jew.

Pragmatically, however, the American synagogue has some grounds for complaint concerning the inroads of the secularists and this involves the simple logistics of competition for the best minds and the most spiritually motivated in the community. For the past half-century there has been a "brain drain" away from congregational life. Men and women of enormous talent, although members of synagogues, have directed their gifts to the work of the committee, Congress, ADL, Hadassah, and the National Council of Jewish Women—to name but a few. The synagogue is understandably envious when people such as Louis Stern of the Center Movement, Rose Halprin of Hadassah, Pearl Willen of the National Council of Jewish Women, Morris Abram and Sol Linowitz (currently U.S. ambassador to the OAS) of the Committee, Philip Klutznick of B'nai B'rith, Abraham Feinberg of Israel Bonds, and many others contribute their matchless leadership to the non-synagogue institutions.

The "Double Establishment" in Jewish life also presents some problems for those who like things neat. Who speaks for American Jewry?

Actually, no unbridgeable chasm separates the two establishments. Church-state matters, for example, are handled by a joint Advisory Committee which unites religious and secular groups on such questions as religious intrusions into public education and the use of tax funds for parochial education. And ranks are loyally closed when the need arises. Reform Jews having little interest in the dietary laws or the Orthodox Sabbath battle with equal zeal to preserve the rights of the traditionalists when they are threatened— although I suspect, as Milton Himmelfarb points out in his *Commentary* article (July, 1966), that the unanimity of American Jews on a strict interpretation of the "separation" principle may be more apparent than real.

We shall see, too, in Chapter 16, how remarkably unified American Jews are in their support of Israel. The chief dissenters, the American Council for Judaism, reflect the views of fewer than one out of twenty.

But if there are two establishments, are there two American Jewish communities? To some extent, yes. The hub of most social endeavor for the actively committed Jews is the synagogue. A synagogue-centered Conservative Jew in Chicago finds his friends among his fellow congregants, attends Illinois State conventions of the United Synagogue Brotherhoods, reads United Synagogue journals, sends his children to a Ramah camp in Wisconsin, and takes a lively interest in the many activities of the Jewish Theological Seminary. His Judaism is inextricably bound up with the adjective Conservative. His wife, interested in work for the blind, transcribes Jewish books under the auspices of the Women's League of the United Synagogue.

His law partner belongs to the same congregation and attends services on the High Holy Days and Bar Mitzvahs, but his Jewish way of life takes him on different paths. He is an officer in the Chicago Chapter of the American Jewish Committee, and attends regional meetings in Cleveland, Milwaukee, or Detroit, as well as the four-day annual convention in New York or Washington. His wife also devotes several hours a day aiding the blind, but her efforts are channeled through the National Council of Jewish Women. Both husband and wife are active in the Urban League. Both consider themselves stanch Jews who are living up to Judaism's finest ethical teachings.

A major locus for the social life of Jews living outside New York is the Jewish Community Center. These centers are an outgrowth of the Young Men's Hebrew Association and the Young Women's Hebrew Association established in the nineteenth century. Today, there are 445 such centers, with a total membership of close to 750,000, and a variety of recreational and cultural activities that draw many times that number for individual classes, concerts, and other services. The 92nd Street YM-YWHA, in New York City, attracts more than a million people a year to its classes, art exhibits, dramatic productions, and lectures.

Are the Jewish centers religiously oriented? That question has provoked many a lively discussion within the Jewish community. Technically, they are not concerned with religion. Indeed, the synagogues much prefer that the centers do not engage in programs which compete with their own religious emphasis, and argue that the centers should restrict themselves to the *recreational* needs of Jews. But center leaders, led by Sanford Solender, the national director of the National Jewish Welfare Board, coordinating agency of the center movement, envision their mandate in much broader terms. They see the Jewish center as crucial to the survival of American Jewry, and maintain that because of its informal, voluntary, and communal character, it provides an ideal setting for the preservation of Jewish values.

Judging by attendance alone, the centers do as well as the synagogues—perhaps even better. Most rabbis insist that a single session at a synagogue religious school class does more for Jewish values than a dozen trips to the center's basketball court, but supporters of the center counter that their informal program can be more productive than the formal classroom in relating Jewish values to personal attitudes and conduct. The center can be especially effective, they believe, in winning back those alienated Jews who, under the impact of a growing secularism, recoil from any formal religious experience.

Despite their seeming competition, the synagogue and Jewish center establishments are not mutually exclusive. Ninety per cent of those who belong to the Jewish Community Centers of Louisville, Kentucky, and Allentown, Pennsylvania, for example, are synagogue members. A 1965 survey of the Wilkes-Barre, Pennsylvania, Jewish community of 5,400, conducted by the American Jewish Committee, found that more than 96 per cent of the high-school students affiliated with the Jewish center had received some formal religious training. Nevertheless, I would guess that most Louisville, Allentown, and Wilkes-Barre Jews enter the doors of the centers more frequently than they attend their houses of worship.

Will the two Jewish communities become stabilized in this form? Religious spokesmen do not believe it is possible. Lacking strong religious moorings, they argue, the children of one establishment tend to disappear—they marry out of the faith, join Ethical Culture, or drop their synagogue affiliation altogether. (Little statistical evidence is available to confirm or refute this assumption.) But even more crucial, the rabbis argue, the synagogue provides the impulse toward ethical expression; how long will men and women be motivated to the sacrificial effort involved in Jewish causes without the spiritual prodding which religious knowledge and commitment provide? How long can a secular Jewry survive, cut off from the original source of ethical energy, the Bible, the sacred literature, and similar sources of inspiration?

The so-called lay agencies also sense a threat to their own continuity. Federations and welfare agencies all over the country, and in Canada as well, have instituted New Leadership Divisions, aimed at the nineteen-to-thirty-year-olds. Their training program is geared less toward cultivating fund-raising techniques than toward imparting basic Jewish knowledge—the *why* as well as the *how* of Jewish philanthropic endeavor.

During the past decade the lay groups have made enormous contributions to Jewish adult education. B'nai B'rith has the most ambitious program: hundreds of retreats, some of the best books on modern Jewish thought, and a serious magazine, *Jewish Heritage*. The American Jewish Congress, especially its Women's Division, operates dozens of programs designed to enhance understanding of Judaism and Jewish values, and the Congress quarterly, *Judaism*, is the best journal devoted to Jewish theology published in America. The American Jewish Committee also sponsors a program dedicated to self-understanding and Jewish continuity, and through its American Jewish yearbook, *Commentary*, and scores of well-written publications, the committee has extended its philosophy far beyond defense of Jewish rights to the preservation of Jewish values and institutions.

Clearly, Jewish continuity is as precious to the lay organizations as it is to the religious groups. Whether the two will be able to continue their parallel and separate roads remains to be seen. At the time of this writing, 1966, it seems to me that the power structure of American Jewry leans rather markedly toward the Secular City.

The Religious Establishment

Unlike its European counterpart, American Judaism did not originate from an Orthodox base. The handful of tiny Colonial congregations could not provide a sufficient nucleus for a recognized Orthodox establishment. It was the Reform Jews of the nineteenth century, most of them German-born, who brought the organizational skills from the Old World needed to establish nationwide institutions. Both Orthodoxy and Conservative Judaism followed in their footsteps.

Thus, history conspired to fashion American Jewish religious life in the same pluralistic pattern which marked American Christianity. Prof. Monford Harris of Chicago writes of the blossoming of Jewish denominationalism "in all its exotic richness in America, the land par excellence of religious denominationalism."

In Great Britain Orthodox Judaism is the Established Synagogue, recognized by Crown and courts as the official expression of the faith of Israel. American Orthodoxy, on the contrary, feels none of the security of a dominant, though minority, synagogue. Will Herberg's description of the three religious options in America, each seeing itself as an embattled minority, apply equally to the three wings of Judaism. This may be the reason for the relative flexibility and permissiveness which characterize American adherents of Orthodoxy, Conservative, and Reform, and for the ease with which the followers of one group pass into the other.

Mortimer May, the veteran Zionist leader, told me that he belonged to five congregations, three in his home city, Nashville, Tennessee (one Orthodox, one Conservative, and one Reform), and two in Miami Beach, where he winters. Philanthropist Jack D. Weiler is a member of four Orthodox and two Conservative congregations. A friend of mine belongs to seven different synagogues: the stately Temple Emanu-El on New York's Fifth Avenue—a bow to social demand; a Conservative congregation, where his family worships on the High Holy Days and where his children were confirmed, two synagogues in the garment district, where he marks the *Yahrzeit* (death anniversary) of his parents, a Conservative congregation near his home in the country, and three Florida congregations!

Dogmatism with regard to labels is limited largely to the rabbis and some of the more hidebound traditionalists. Few American Jews would tolerate the authoritarian declaration of South African Orthodoxy in 1966 placing Reform synagogues off limits. Although some Orthodox rabbis have urged their members to boycott non-Orthodox Bar Mitzvah or wedding celebrations, few of their adherents pay much heed to such injunctions.

A few general statistics are in order at this point, although it should be kept in mind that synagogue figures, like church statistics, are notoriously inaccurate, and the figures cited can be little more than reasonable conjectures. Although American Jews' official spokesmen oppose a government religious census and have never troubled to count noses, either as to their over-all numbers or as to their preference for a particular religious philosophy, it is estimated that some 4 million Jews are likely to express a preference for one of the three forms of American Judaism. A majority—possibly as many as 2 million—would opt for Conservatism: their ancestral roots are traditional, and they are not willing to break with the past to the degree that Reform implies. Somewhat more than three-quarters of a million consider themselves Orthodox, and about one and a quarter lean toward the Reform. Almost one and three-quarter million American Jews express no religious preference or belief.

It is generally reported that three out of every five American Jews belong to a congregation. This figure is only valid for New York City and Los Angeles. In the rest of the country, a more accurate estimate would be close to three out of four: in Portland, Oregon, according to a survey made by Rabbi Jack Segal, it is 71 per cent; the Jews of suburban Detroit are nearly all religiously affiliated: only 2 per cent in Southfield, and 9 per cent in Huntington Woods, belong to no synagogue.

The quality of affiliation is a subject of endless debate. Many retain membership only while they have children of school age; a few do not attend even on the High Holy Days. But however tenuous their temple ties, American Jews assume that membership in a Jewish religious institution is a norm of communal behavior. Only in the obscurity of metropolitan apartment living do they withstand the pressures to affiliate.

In a previous book I discussed Judaism in terms of belonging, believing, and behaving. The first level—of affiliation and synagogue attendance—I pointed out is only one form of religious behavior, and offers only a partial clue to Jewish loyalties.

For Judaism, unlike Christianity, is home-centered rather than sanctuary-centered. Roman Catholicism would be inconceivable without the apparatus of the Church; Judaism, at least theoretically, could survive, however falteringly, were there no synagogues. Many ritual observances are based in the home.

This explains, at least in part, the sharp statistical contrast between Christian and Jewish attendance at worship. (Many of those who have studied the Jewish community feel that even the oft-cited figure of 15 per cent regular attendance at Sabbath worship is an exaggeration. One such study suggests that only one American Jew in twenty-five attends services every week.)

Yet, these same studies reflect a great deal of religious observance. Rabbi Segal's survey of synagogue-affiliated Jews in Portland reports that 98.4 per cent of the Orthodox, 98.7 per cent of the Conservative, and 97.4 per cent of the Reform Jews hold a Passover Seder annually in their homes. More than 90 per cent of the families keep their children out of school on Yom Kippur. In Providence, Rhode Island, and Camden, New Jersey, more than 80 per cent of the Jewish families celebrate Passover, and similar statistics are reported for cities across the nation—although the figures appear lower for the West than for the East.

Perhaps the greatest ritual casualty even among traditional Jews is the observance of *kashruth* (dietary laws). The Portland study indicated that only one out of four Orthodox Jews felt inhibited by dietary restrictions when eating out. Two strongholds of Orthodoxy, Baltimore and Boston, have no first-class kosher restaurants. Jews who eat out—and they do so much more than the general population—obviously do not follow the dietary laws.

One Jewish festival, the Feast of Hanukah, has found a remarkable rebirth in America. A minor festival in the Jewish calendar (one of the few in which there is no restriction as to work), Hanukah has been elevated to a new eminence, in competition to, or as a substitute for, Christmas. (Some Jewish families observe Christmas in a minimal way with Christmas trees and fireplace stockings, but the practice is declining.)

In Providence and in Portland, fifteen out of twenty families reported lighting Hanukah candles, and in Camden 78 per cent of the families say they always light Hanukah candles, while 13 per cent say they never do. (The Camden studies indicate that this practice is most common among the least Orthodox.)

Religious awareness is also reflected in a tiny object, the *mezuzah*, which is found on the doorpost of many Jewish homes. The Orthodox Jew will not move into a home before the word of God, inscribed on a miniature scroll, has been mounted on its entrance. And an increasing number of Reform and Conservative Jews now follow the same practice. A survey conducted by the National Federation of Temple Brotherhoods revealed that more than 85 per cent of Orthodox, 82 per cent of Conservative, and 53 per cent of Reform Jews affixed a *mezuzah* on their doors. Eastern Jews are less inhibited about the practice, and worry less about accentuating differences or inviting the ubiquitous charity collectors. The director of one of Manhattan's largest Reform congregations, Rodef Sholom, told me that most of its members have *mezuzoth* on their doorposts.

What does one do with a *mezuzah* when one moves? It is customary to remove it, unless the incoming family is Jewish and asks that it remain, but it is not unheard of for a non-Jewish buyer to ask that the *mezuzah* be left in place. ("Please don't remove the *mezuzah*. If it made your home holy, we want our home to be holy, too.")

Within a single generation the God of Israel has been naturalized. The first talking picture produced by Hollywood contained several scenes of a cantor chanting the synagogue ritual. I remember a line repeated several times in each scene in which the cantor appeared, "Listen, he's pouring out his heart to *his* God." Between 1929 and 1966 "*his*" God had become "*our*" God.

As I have pointed out elsewhere, the blandishments of Christianity are not a potent force in the religiously benign atmosphere of America. Fewer than two Jews out of a hundred when asked if they wished they had been born Christians said that they did. Synagogue member or not, the average American Jew accepts his Jewishness and is comfortable with it: It was good enough for Grandpa—and it's good enough for me!

What the mood of the next generation will be is not easy to determine. Jewish youth, now predominately in the orbit of university life, is generally nonconformist. Jewish leaders, both religious and secular, are much concerned with the problems of youth and the threat to Jewish survival implicit in its unwillingness to accept the norms of the past.

Those younger Jews who care are severe critics of the American synagogue. Rabbi Alfred Jospe, national program director for Hillel Foundation, a perceptive authority on the attitudes of contemporary Jewish youth who has devoted a quarter of a century to his work with college students, writes:

They do not reject the synagogue as a matter of principle; they reject what is going on in the synagogue, or, to be more precise, the synagogues they know. They abhor the synagogue as a social club; its soullessness; its frequent mediocrity and shallowness; the preoccupation with budgets, numbers, adherents, and campaigns rather than content; the Marjorie Morningstar weddings and the Bar Mitzvahs with the big bar and no mitzvah. . . .

Other students, Jospe points out, reject all organized religion, but they are relatively few.

American Jews allocate an extraordinary amount of their resources to the religious nurture of their young. Between 60 and 70 million dollars are spent annually on such education.

The late Rabbi Morris Adler of Detroit was inordinately proud of the fact that almost half his congregation's budget—more than $220,000—was allocated to children's education. "A congregation which doesn't have an annual deficit," he told his Budget Committee, "is neglecting the education of its children."

Thirty per cent of all congregational expenditures are earmarked for training the young. But Jewish religious education in the United States and Canada is a lay as well as a religious undertaking. Many of its top educators are not rabbis: Dr. Judah Pilch, head of the American Association of Jewish Education; Dr. Azriel Eisenberg, head of the Jewish Education Committee of New York; Dr. Louis Kaplan of Baltimore; Dr. Samuel Dinin, head of Jewish education in Los Angeles, are some of the men responsible for the high standards achieved in the United States during the past thirty years.

The opportunities for Jewish education today are infinitely greater than they were thirty years ago. The vast majority of children are exposed to some training, a condition which did not exist in the 1930s. However, the religious establishment has been remarkably self-critical and acutely aware of their failure to reach a great many children. Despite a vast educational apparatus, a substantial outlay of funds, the professionalization of staff, and the introduction to the utilization of modern methods of pedagogy, Jewish educators are painfully aware that much of their teaching has been superficial—"a mile wide and an inch deep," as Mark Twain said of the Mississippi.

Among the Orthodox, religious education is controlled by the rabbinate, and one man, Rabbi Joseph Kamenetsky, has almost singlehandedly transformed the entire character of Orthodox education.

Of the 600,000 Jewish children in the United States enrolled in Jewish schools, 50 per cent attend once a week, either on Saturday or Sunday, and 40 per cent attend additional weekday classes. The remaining 10 per cent are enrolled in the type of school developed by Rabbi Kamenetsky, the all-day school, in which children study religious subjects in the morning (when their minds are fresh) and the secular subjects in the afternoon.

Both Conservative and Reform Jewish leaders have invested much hope in the summer and all-year weekend camp movement. They have come to recognize, as the Protestants did before them, that two months of intensive activity can inject enough spirit into a teen-ager to effect a complete reorientation and a "transvaluation of values." Young people come away from the Ramah (Conservative) and the Great Barrington (Reform) camps with a zest for their faith which astonishes their parents. Many are inspired to enter the rabbinate or some phase of professional Jewish life.

A generation ago, Jewish children attended *communal* institutions of learning. The Talmud Torah of Minneapolis, for example, drew children from all three branches, as well as those of no affiliation. Its guiding genius, the late Dr. George Gordon, abandoned a medical career to devote himself to Jewish education. Under his guidance, a whole generation of well-informed Jews was trained. Just as the Midwest furnished the religious bread basket for American Protestantism, so such cities as Minneapolis and Baltimore have trained men and women who are rabbis, educators, social-work and Jewish center executives in key posts throughout the country.

Often an entire community has been transformed by a single individual whose pedagogic skills are meshed with a warm, charismatic personality and a fiery idealism toward youth, the Jewish faith, and America's hospitality to plural culture. Dr. Gordon was such a person. A generation ago, too, Kansas City Jews were able to develop an intensive program of religious training under the leadership of one man, Saul Kleiman.

Baltimore's 85,000 Jews have been welded together by a master builder, Dr. Louis Kaplan. One of the strongholds of Orthodoxy— more than a third of its Jews are in the traditional camp and more than forty out of sixty of its synagogues are Orthodox—Baltimore Jewry is a perfect illustration of clearly defined yet loose separateness.

It may be easier to be a Jew in New York, at least in terms of numbers, but it is much easier to be an informed Jew in Baltimore. For, despite a sharp cleavage between the Reform and the Orthodox—until quite recently there was no middle Conservative group—Baltimore Jewry is united in the religious nurture of its children.

Radiating out of the Baltimore Hebrew College and the Bureau of Jewish education, both presided over by Dr. Kaplan, is a complex of programs that cross denominational lines.

I visited the college on Park Heights Avenue, in the heart of a resplendent Jewish residential area. My taxicab driver pointed admiringly to the beautifully landscaped homes, apartment dwellings, and to a score of Jewish institutions. "Nine out of ten people here are Jews," he said in a matter-of-fact way.

All the buildings were spanking new, including one synagogue, whose membership is limited to strict Sabbath observers.

The 7,000 Baltimore children who attend the Sunday, weekday, or all-day Jewish schools entertain no doubts that their community and parents take religious training seriously. The parents, in their youth, had gathered in makeshift basement rooms to study Hebrew under unskilled tutors. Their children are picked up at their public-school doors and transported by buses that serve the travel needs of all the Jewish schools, regardless of label, to bright, modern classrooms presided over by teachers ably trained at the Baltimore Hebrew College.

I met with Dr. Kaplan, the educational genius who heads this ambitious effort. In the field for almost forty years, the Baltimore veteran supervises a program which begins with nursery school and continues through adulthood.

"I don't believe in pediatric Judaism. Adults have to study, too."

In the morning, while children are in school, there are classes for women; others are tailored for the men of the house. One course, for business and professional men, has continued for the past twenty years. Every Tuesday afternoon, at four-thirty, the men leave their offices and stores and stop at the Hebrew College on the way home. Thirty-five students sip a cocktail, eat a piece of herring—a Kaplan custom imported from Lithuania, I suspect—and sit at the feet of their instructor, listening to a discussion of some phase of Jewish thought.

Two hundred and fifty women, representing all three branches of Judaism, meet on Tuesday mornings, studying Hebrew, Jewish history, the Hasidic movement, Modern Jewish Responsa, Customs of Daily Living in Bible and Talmud times, and similar subjects. Dr. Kaplan's course on favorite passages from the Bible is perennially popular.

Obviously the program does not reach the entire Jewish community of Baltimore, but a majority of the children attend classes more than once a week. At the end of a six-year course they take uniform examinations, and the highest scorers are granted the privilege of going on to a high school and later a college level.

Baltimore's story, duplicated in scores of cities from coast to coast, attests to the determined efforts of American Jewry to stem the tide of religious illiteracy. But the final verdict is yet to come.

Reform officialdom refers to the million souls associated with the movement; Conservative Jewish organizations use a similar figure. A few of the less thoughtful Orthodox leaders suggest that, by a process of elimination, all the rest are in their camp. A more realistic estimate has been cited by Prof. Charles S. Liebman, who refers in his article on Jewish Orthodoxy in the *American Jewish Year Book* of 1965 to a "total of 205,640 men affiliated with the 1,603 known Orthodox synagogues in the United States." Many unaffiliated Jews are also served by congregations—possibly as many as one million, including women and children.

Synagogue membership, of course, does not necessarily follow along the exact lines of the figures cited earlier. A family with no particular Reform orientation may join a Reform synagogue for social reasons, or because of geographical convenience. When I taught at the University of Iowa, I was struck by the contrast between two states on either side of the Mississippi. In most of the Illinois towns there was only one congregation, and it was generally Reform. Iowa communities, such as Ottumwa, Muscatine, Clinton, Iowa City, Waterloo, and Mason City also had a single synagogue, invariably Orthodox.

Historically, German Jews founded the Illinois congregations in the nineteenth century, and they took on a Reform character. Iowa Jewry—at least in the smaller cities—was organized by Eastern

European Jews in the early part of the twentieth century, and they were Orthodox. Newcomers had the choice of being either Reform or nonaffiliated in Illinois and Orthodox or nonaffiliated in Iowa.

Marshall Sklare, one of the first sociologists to attempt a scientific approach to the religious affiliation of American Jews, points out in his *Conservative Judaism* that membership in Orthodox congregations is often a reflection of filial loyalty rather than adherence to "Torah-true" Judaism. As long as Jews lived in their original ghettos—Dr. Sklare refers to them as the "first areas of settlement" —they retained their Orthodox institutions. It was only when they reached the second and third areas of settlement that Conservative congregations were founded.

Both Conservative and Reform Judaism are products of the American experience. An Orthodox service, however, such as one might attend in Memphis, where there is a very large Orthodox congregation, could be transplanted intact to Tel Aviv or Buenos Aires or London and the worshipers would not be able to detect the difference.

Dr. Sklare depicts Conservative and Reform worship as pulpit-centered, and Orthodox service as worshiper-centered. In form and structure, Reform was the first to model itself after American Protestantism, modified by specific Jewish needs. The pulpit-centered worship led by the rabbi, responsive readings, a uniform prayer book, organ music, and mixed choirs, streamlined services, beginning and ending at a set hour, English prayers, family pews, Confirmation rites, administration by lay committees, and a number of other elements of modernization were established by nineteenth-century Reform Judaism. Conservative synagogues emulated many of these practices, but retained many of the traditional elements, such as the wearing of a head covering (Reform lost out, they said, at the drop of a hat), the dietary laws, the reading of the Torah in Hebrew, and a greater emphasis on Hebrew texts in education.

Reform, at least in its early days, stressed the idea that Judaism in the New World "must be Americanized and republicanized." At the very first convention of liberal rabbis, held in 1890 in Cleveland, the Reform rabbis agreed that "American Judaism was a new creation, the most recent phase in Israel's ever-progressive faith."

The logic of history would dictate that of the two indigenous American Jewish movements, Reform would be dominant. More than one hundred years ago there were Reform temples in such cities as Paducah, Kentucky, Knoxville, Tennessee, Lancaster, Pennsylvania, Athens, Georgia, and Goldsboro, North Carolina. Yet, Conservative Judaism, born in the last decade of the nineteenth century, has become the largest branch of American Judaism and, according to some projections I have read, is likely to become even stronger.

One reason is transparent. The 300,000 native-born children of German Jews had little in common with the 1,700,000 newcomers, virtually all of them from the Orthodox ghettos of Russia, Poland, and Rumania who came to America late in the nineteenth century. Reform leaders were not disposed to welcome the ghetto immigrants into their congregational ranks. Indeed they were happy to see the newcomers organize their own institutions and often lent them the necessary financial support. And the tradition-bound Russian and Polish Jews could not accept as Jewish a form of worship without head covering, and the almost total substitution of English for Hebrew in prayer.

Had Reform Judaism turned earlier onto its present path—its greater emphasis on traditional ceremonies such as the Bar Mitzvah, a more generous use of Hebrew, the optional head covering for both pulpit officials and congregants, and, above all, a recognition of the peoplehood of Israel—it might have become the dominant form of American-Jewish religious practice.

I asked Rabbi Jacob Agus of Baltimore, whose *Modern Philosophies of Judaism* and other works mark him as one of the foremost students of contemporary Judaism, why Reform did not succeed more than it might have. He theorized that while both Orthodox and Conservative Judaism have always sought as their target the whole of Jewry, Reform, especially in the present century, has seemed content to seek support largely among the already convinced, lacking the dynamism of the evangelist.

The weakness of Reform is the built-in weakness of all liberal movements. In the period of its gestation, a missionary zeal pervades those who are fired by the novel ideas of the faith. But the essence of liberalism is broadmindedness, a compelling sense of accommodation and tolerance. The Unitarians in 1966 are no stronger than the Unitarians of 1866; despite the nation's growth in the past century, liberal Protestantism has been almost static. So, too, Reform Judaism has abandoned its early evangelical zeal. By regarding itself as one of the *options* of Judaism, not as the absolute best for the contemporary American Jew, the liberal movement has been content to reach out only to those who evince an interest in its ideas.

The strategy of Conservative Judaism has been totally different. It has concentrated power, in terms of leadership, in a monolithic seminary: to be a good Conservative Jew is to bow in its direction. At the same time, it has aimed its sights at the entire Jewish community, not one segment of it. In the words of Mordecai Waxman, historian of the movement, "The Conservative movement has always clung to the position that it is not a denomination in the Jewish fold."

In an extended interview, Rabbi Wolfe Kelman, the executive vice president of the Rabbinical Assembly of America, spoke buoyantly about the prospects for the Conservative movement in the latter third of the twentieth century. "American Jews," he had told the 1966 convention of rabbis, "are eager to retain their identity."

The Conservative leader disputed the estimate generally given as to the number of American Jews—"I think there are 10 million in the United States"—and he declared that the strength of the middle branch of American Judaism derived from the spectacular rise in the status of the rabbi during the past fifteen years.

"It is a matter of supply and demand. We have 150 pulpits we cannot fill. By July of each year every member of the Rabbinical Assembly is placed, and we turn down further requests. In the standard contract drawn up, we affirm that 'the rabbi shall be the final authority in all matters of Jewish law.' Whenever there is a pulpit change, the rabbi decides what prayer book shall be used, and really determines forms of worship."

I asked him about the various wings within the Conservative movement. All three branches in the United States have their right wing, center, and so-called left wing.

Rabbi Kelman feels that the right and left wings have virtually disappeared. At the most, he estimates, there are no more than 5 per cent at either extreme.

Paradoxically, Conservative Jews have shifted from the right to the left in observance, but might well argue for a more traditional approach to such doctrines as immortality. (My own observations suggest that, among the rabbis, the reverse holds true. Theologically, I find Conservative rabbis close to their Reform colleagues on such doctrinal issues as Revelation, and more traditional in observance. A generation ago, few Conservative rabbis would wear a head covering indoors, except when engaged in ritual acts; today most of them, at least in the East, do so.)

The inconsistencies usually associated with Orthodoxy now are to be found among the Conservative Jews. During Sabbaths and holy days, synagogue parking lots are closed, suggesting that members walk to worship. (The adjoining supermarket parking lots, however, are packed with worshipers' cars, much to the consternation of both management and shoppers.)

Rabbi Kelman, who has made 1,500 placements of rabbis, told me that his colleagues seem happier in the rabbinate than they were a generation ago. Their morale is high (much has been written about demoralization among the American clergy in recent years) and by and large their positions are much more secure.

"There has been a significant change in the character of our seminary students. Thirty years ago, the rabbinate was sometimes a refuge for those who couldn't get into medical school. Today, candidates tell us that they were offered attractive graduate fellowships and selected the rabbinate instead."

A highly placed Episcopalian had recently said to Rabbi Kelman: "I'm worried about the vanishing American Episcopalian. What is your secret for survival? We Episcopalians have much to offer civilization. It would be a tragedy it we were to disappear."

The rabbi laughed. "It sounds like us," he explained.

A Day in the Life of a Congregation

The college student who voices his disapproval of organized Jewish religious life—"its preoccupation with budgets, numbers, adherents, and campaigns rather than content"—has only a meager grasp of the ongoing life of a congregation. If he were to spend one full day, for example, at Temple Sinai in Washington, he might be sharply impressed by the variety of creative activities, the intense desire for knowledge, and the spirit of healthy fellowship that are evident there.

The imaginative design of Temple Sinai's modernistic building has evoked a great deal of comment. Its architect, Nicholas Satterlee, invested a great deal of himself in the structure which blends the contemporary environment and the antiquity of the faith in recognition that Israel constitutes an ancient but self-renewing tradition.

To the right of the temple lobby is a bookshop, crowded with women on their way into Bible class. The shop sells over $6,000 worth of books annually, mostly paperbacks. When Rabbi Eugene Lipman discusses Martin Buber in a Friday-night sermon, there is a run on Buber books. Heschel and Rosenzweig are popular authors, as are Milton Steinberg and Isaac Bashevis Singer.

The rabbi joins thirty women in a two-hour session on the Book of Judges. The students have evidently done their homework, for their questions are perceptive and pointed. Later, they join a few hundred women for a Sisterhood luncheon while the rabbi meets with temple officers in their weekly conference.

In the late afternoon, the children arrive for Hebrew school. And in the evenings, adult classes and a half-dozen committee meetings lend to the temple lobby the same bustling air that pervades the national airport.

The Ad Hoc Committee on Size of the Congregation discusses the problem of limiting membership. They are torn between two valid principles. A congregation is not an exclusive country club and should be open to anyone who seeks membership. On the other hand, if a congregation gets to be too large, it becomes an impersonal corporation. No rabbi can relate personally to three or four thousand congregants. Yet, there are fifty Reform temples with over 1,000 families. Some of them restrict membership, create a waiting list, and urge applicants either to join a smaller congregation or help organize a new one.

Rabbis of mammoth congregations often cannot even recognize all of their members. (A rabbi I know, visiting in London, was warned that the street on which his hotel was located was frequented by prostitutes. Walking out of his hotel lobby one evening, he was stopped by a woman who commented on the loveliness of the city. He turned his back on her. A few weeks later, standing in line at the end of synagogue services, one of his members rebuked him.

"I said hello to you in London, Rabbi, and you completely ignored me").

The Committee on Hebrew has been discussing the content of the

Hebrew program. They have investigated the curricula of scores of congregations, and they will soon make a recommendation to the Temple Board about an enrichment program.

The Social Action Committee recommends to the Temple Board a strong position statement on open housing. Washington is a city with many racial tensions, and the board will grapple long with the problem. But ultimately the committee's recommendation will be adopted.

These are some of the visible activities of the temple but they do not tell the whole story. For they do not include the rabbi's frequent counseling sessions with congregants, the Mitzvah committee caring for the children or preparing a meal at a house of mourning, the numerous social-service activities of the Sisterhood.

Temple Sinai is a Reform synagogue. Is a day at a Conservative synagogue very much different? Actually, a casual visitor might find it difficult to distinguish the nonworship activities of Conservative and Reform.

Both strive to give these activities a Jewish meaning and a relevance to today's world. But both Reform and Conservative congregations will concede that much of what passes for religion is superficial, bland, and often far from spiritual. And ruefully they will admit that American Jews, except for the most Orthodox, have lost the art of prayer. It is a lament all too familiar to Americans of all faiths in this secular age.

A Portland, Oregon, rabbi sadly depicts the sight which meets the eye of many a colleague when he mounts the pulpit on a Friday evening:

This   is   the   way   the   Congregation
      sometimes   looks   to   the
          Rabbi   when   he   stands
in
                   the   pulpit

Thisishowitwouldlookifeverybodycameandbroughtafriend.

CHAPTER 11

The Orthodox Community

Coat of Many Colors: The Orthodox Community

If we were to select a banner to symbolize American religious Jewry, the flag would surely be a Joseph's coat. Nothing amuses anyone familiar with Jewish organization life more than the notion that it is united by firm bonds of authority, or at least by a singleness of purpose. Only a non-Jew mistakes the *Shema,* the central prayer in Judaism, "Hear, O Israel, . . . the Lord is One," to be: "Hear, O Lord, the *people* of Israel, the *people* are One!"

Paradoxically, divisiveness runs deepest in Orthodoxy. By definition, theoretically, Orthodox Judaism is unyielding and inflexible, bound to a single book (the Torah) and to a single code—the *Shulchan Aruch*—containing the 613 laws of Joseph Caro (a Spanish-born scholar of the sixteenth century). But even the unalterable laws of God are, of necessity, transmitted subjectively—by frail and fallible beings. And Jewish religious law is so ramified that there are literally thousands of problems which admit of divergency of viewpoint.

Thus, while most Orthodox Jews warmly support the State of Israel, others insist it must not be recognized, because it is a secular not a religious entity. While many Orthodox Jews are outstanding scientists, others feel that education in the sciences, especially on a university level, is forbidden by Jewish law. Some traditionalists are absolutely certain that the universe was created fifty-seven centuries ago; others are not quite so sure. A few Orthodox congregations permit the mingling of male and female worshipers, but most insist on a rigid separation of the sexes in the synagogue. And while some Orthodox groups maintain that the American doctrine of separation of church and state forbids use of state funds for religious purposes, others welcome government aid to parochial schools. Even the issue of ultimate doctrinal authority is open to debate. Some insist that it rests with the Chief Rabbinate of Israel, others hold firm to their own favorite candidates.

Unity remains a persistent theme at most Orthodox conferences, an ecumenical cry that bids fair to be repeated, vainly, for many, many years. For despite the challenges of the secular materialistic world, rifts within Orthodox Judaism give promise of considerable permanence.

In a letter to *The New York Times* dated July 30, 1965, the executive director of the Central Rabbinical Congress of the United States of America and Canada (there is a cosmic scope to the names of many of these organizations) criticized the newspaper for suggesting that Rabbi Joel Teitelbaum, the so-called Satmer Rabbi—born in Satmer, Hungary—is head only of the "ultra-Orthodox." "Grand Rabbi Teitelbaum is not just the head of a few thousand 'extremists,'" declared the writer. "Besides being the Orthodox Chief Rabbi of Jerusalem [he] is the president of the Central Rabbinical Congress. . . . Hundreds of thousands of Jews in all parts of the world look to Rabbi Teitelbaum as their spiritual leader." The bland reference to Rabbi Teitelbaum as "the Chief Rabbi of Jerusalem" is very interesting, considering that, to the followers of the Satmer Rabbi Israel as a state does not exist.

In all, there are a score or more of Orthodox rabbinical bodies— the Union of Orthodox Rabbis, the Rabbinical Council of America, the Rabbinical Alliance of America, Agudas Israel, and others. In addition, 3,000 Orthodox leaders in the United States and Canada submit their theological problems to individual rabbinical authorities whose prestige is universally recognized. For some, the last word rests with the opinions of Rabbi Joseph B. Soloveitchik, the world-famous Boston scholar who turned down an offer to become Chief Rabbi of Israel. Other rabbis consider Rabbi Moshe Fernstein the last court of appeal. The late Rabbi Aaron Kotler of Lakewood,

New Jersey, also had a massive following. The disciples of each of these men sit at their feet in rapt attention. When Rabbi Soloveitchik speaks, hundreds of rabbis journey many miles to hear his three-hour exposition of a point of Jewish law. Scores of young rabbis would hang on the words of the scholar-saint, Rabbi Kotler, while he expounded on an obscure reference in the Talmud.

Many of the doctrinal problems presented to the authorities are purely academic, an extension of ancient Talmudic debates. But most concern the accommodation of the law to real-life issues:

Should a rabbi enlist in the armed services, since it may involve violation of the Sabbath and the dietary laws? (The answer is clear-cut in case of war, but the U.S. government enmeshed Orthodox rabbis in an unprecedented problem when they called Korea a "police action.") Is a certain product kosher? May an Orthodox rabbi officiate at a wedding with a Conservative one? How is one to interpret the law requiring the lighting of Sabbath candles at sundown when one is stationed on an Alaskan island where the sun sets only once a year? And, what happens to the Sabbath on a Friday evening if one's ship crosses the international date line and it's suddenly Saturday night?

Orthodox Renascence

One of the curious anomalies of American religious life, Christian and Jewish alike, is the remarkable expansion of the more conservative and fundamentalist groups during the past quarter century. Our national culture is science-oriented, permissive rather than authoritarian, individualistic more than collective. By all logical expectations, a natural tug of war should have developed between our secular society and those religious groups which emphasize dogma and conformity. And indeed, religious leaders constantly warn against the beguilement of our culture, complaining that our public schools are, at best, neutral in matters of religious belief and commitment, while our universities conspire against the old orthodoxies.

Yet, it is the conservative religious bodies that are waxing large— the Southern Baptists, the Missouri Synod Lutherans, the Pentecostal and the Roman Catholic Church. Further, judging by statistics alone, Jewish Orthodoxy is faring equally well.

Sixty thousand children are enrolled in all-day schools, an increase of 100 per cent in the past decade. The kosher food industry has mushroomed enormously. Orthodox clubs have been formed at a number of universities. Rabbi Herschel Schacter, one of the leaders of the Rabbinical Council of America, reports that "well over 15,000 young Americans, in their teens and early adulthood . . . are learning Talmud daily." Many of them, Rabbi Schacter indicated, belong to the American Association of Orthodox Jewish Scientists, "brilliant, young, indigenously American men and women in all disciplines, behavioral, natural, physical, and medical sciences." The *yarmulka* (skullcap), Rabbi Schacter declares, is worn with pride "in the advanced scientific laboratories of the Navy Department, in MIT, in Harvard, in Princeton, and various industries." And a number of Orthodox communities, such as in Far Rockaway, Long Island, can boast several congregations, whose Saturday-morning attendance, fifty-two Sabbaths a year, is over a thousand in each synagogue.

Seen from another angle, however, the view is far less sanguine. A survey of any Conservative or Reform congregation will point up the fact that close to half were drawn from Orthodox synagogues.

The inconsistency is not hard to explain. Judaism in the 1920s was generally Orthodox, fragmentized into thousands of small congregations and informal groups, but Orthodox, nonetheless. By the 1940s, these congregations had declined in numbers and in influence. But the postwar years witnessed a spectacular resurgence, explained in part by the influx of tradition-minded refugees from Hitlerism and in part by improved methods of organization, the development of a native-born leadership, and the disappearance of the alien quality with which Orthodoxy had once been associated.

Today, at the plush kosher resort, Grossinger's, each week finds a good number of college students, young doctors, psychiatrists, physicists, and an equal number of girls from the sororities of Northwestern, Pennsylvania, and Ohio State, all with one thing in common: their Orthodoxy, and all with the common objective of meeting other young men and women who will keep kosher homes and rear their children in traditional fashion. These young traditionalists are products of all-day schools, children of well-to-do parents, whose quest for a mate is limited in spring and summer to the few select Northern hotels catering to a kosher clientele, and to the Sterling Hotel in Miami Beach in the winter! Thus American Orthodoxy perpetuates itself.

"Source of Living Waters"

The secret of Orthodoxy's vitality is twofold: conviction and communication. James Michener's historical novel, *The Source,* reminds his readers of a hundred generations of Jews who preferred death to a compromise of their faith in the face of Assyrian, Greek, Roman, or Christian pressures. The modern Orthodox Jew is invited to emulate his forefathers. Rabbi Schacter asks, "Can we inculcate in the hearts and minds of our children an abiding sense of kinship, a deep feeling of affinity with the Jewish people, unless we and they are convinced that Jews and Judaism are different, yes, better, loftier, precisely because our peoplehood is rooted in God and sanctioned by His will? Unless we do so, can we expect the young, contemporary Jew to pay the enormous price of Jewish identity in the modern world with all the social, intellectual, and even economic disabilities which such identity imposes upon him?"

Orthodoxy's criticism of more liberal interpretations of the faith centers on its subjectivity. "We maintain," declared Rabbi Schacter, "the absolute independence of God's existence, and not as the figment of the individual or collective genius of Man." One of Orthodoxy's most gifted spokesmen, Rabbi Immanuel Jacobovits of New York (now Chief Rabbi of Britain's United Synagogue), explains that the Jew who would change traditional practices to keep pace with the times is like a sailor on the high seas who tries to find his way by using a mark on his ship rather than in the skies for his guide.

Today's Orthodox leadership is well aware that conviction without communication is sterile. "Thou shalt teach them diligently unto thy children," our ancient wise men enjoined us. Therefore, the Orthodox Jewish establishment has created a network of outstanding schools combining secular and religious training which have become the norm for religious education from Boston to Los Angeles. In New York City alone 25 million dollars is expended on the all-day school program. (It is not accurate to call these schools "parochial," because they are not necessarily part of a synagogue program and are generally controlled by lay rather than rabbinic boards.)

One of the nation's most eminent Orthodox rabbis, Dr. Joseph Lookstein, spiritual leader of a fashionable Park Avenue congregation, a professor at Yeshiva University, and president of a university in Israel, channels much of his energies into the Ramaz School in Manhattan. Its well-rounded curriculum and its gifted faculty produce graduates with a solid grounding in religious and Hebraic studies who also win merit scholarships and earn their way into the nation's best universities.

It is these young men and women who represent the greatest achievement—and the greatest hope—of Orthodox Jewry in America.

CHAPTER 12

The Hasidim

"O Lord, if I could love the greatest saint as much as
You love the greatest sinner."

HASIDIC PRAYER

Prof. Marcus Bach, of the University of Iowa, has devoted a lifetime
to what he terms "the dominion of little-known religions"—the obscure and sometimes exotic beliefs of some fifteen million Americans. Paradoxically, he observes, although their way of life seems
totally alien to the spirit of modern America—their bizarre dress,
their separatism, and odd manner of speech—these sects are a
natural outgrowth of America, for they are the product of our
cherished "right to believe." We Americans decry our passion for
conformity, the pressures for uniformity. Yet we are infinitely less
intense than, say, the French or English. The constitutional guaran-
tee to worship God in any way we please has protected the rights of
those whose ways of life seem alien and uncongenial to our spirit.

Although the branch of Judaism known as Hasidism has found a
home in a number of lands, it has flourished most in the United
States. Thousands of Jews in the major cities—some are found in
Denver, in Milwaukee, and Memphis—wear the medieval costume
of Hasidism, long silk caftans, shoes without shoelaces, fur hat for
festive occasions, and the characteristic earlocks.

Unlike the faiths described by Dr. Bach, the Hasidim have a
following many times their own size. The American Hasidic movement has attracted perhaps no more than thirty or forty thousand
disciples, but another hundred thousand or more might be described
as fellow travelers, supporters who contribute generously to the

"Rebbes" (the Hasidic name for their rabbis—spiritual leaders who do not function in the same way an ordinary rabbi does). Many Orthodox Jews, and others not-quite Orthodox, do not accept the Hasidic creed and manner of life, but they sympathize with their spirit and borrow a few ideas from them, motivated nostalgically by dim memories, but more probably by the thought that these people, with their serenity and their sense of certainty about what they are doing, may have some of the answers which we of wavering faith don't have.

The word *hasidim* means simply "disciples." The Protestant denomination of disciples carries the same connotation, and although ultra-Orthodox Jews would be appalled by the suggested parallelism, there is a worlds-apart similarity. For a *Hasid* is a disciple of God only through the mediation of his Rebbe, the rabbi whose intercession offers him hope of spiritual and moral redemption.

So the American *Hasidim* are divided into a number of subsects, depending on the Rebbe to whom they owe allegiance. Two of the largest groups might be mentioned here, the Lubavitcher, by far the most numerous, and the Satmer, the most conservative. The former are of Polish origin, more sophisticated and worldly; the latter trace their beginnings to the hill country of Hungary, far removed from modern influences. The national headquarters are, naturally, in the homes of the Rebbes themselves, Rabbi Menachem M. Schneersohn and Rabbi Joel Teitelbaum, both in the Williamsburgh section of Brooklyn.

The Lubavitcher might almost be called the liberal wing of the Hasidic movement. The outreach of this sect is to the larger Jewish community: it actively seeks disciples, especially among young people on the college campus. The Lubavitcher Hasidim use the mimeograph machine and the printing press to popularize their ideas, and dispatch youthful zealots to the four corners of the earth "to spread the Torah."

Under the influence of a leader who has a Ph.D. the Lubavitcher Hasidim welcome association with those who do not agree with them. Rabbi Schneersohn himself has often welcomed Rabbi Herbert Weiner, of South Orange, New Jersey, a Reform rabbi (Rabbi Weiner's *Commentary* articles are by far the best study of the movement); and Rabbi Zalman Schachter of the University of Manitoba, one of Rabbi Schneersohn's most colorful followers, has regaled audiences throughout the United States and Canada with the wonders of his master.

The Satmer creed, on the other hand, would virtually create an enclave of Jews completely insulated from the twentieth century. No secular education is permitted, and virtually no contact with other Jews—let alone the alien Gentile world.

Rabbi Teitelbaum's influence is far from parochial. He is regarded as the spiritual advisor of the ultra-Orthodox Jerusalem group, the Netura Kartei (Defenders of the Holy City), who have long opposed recognition of the State of Israel. In 1965, when their leader in Jerusalem, Rabbi Amram Blau, decided to marry a convert, the group turned to the Satmer Rebbe for legal permission.

A number of years ago I officiated at a wedding in Rock Island, Illinois, and I was joined by a Hasidic rabbi from Milwaukee, Rabbi Twersky (the Twersky clan are to be found in a dozen cities, all descendants of an eighteenth-century Hasidic dynasty). The rabbi did not object to my sharing the rabbinical duties, for technically no one officiates at a Jewish wedding. The religious functionary is merely an expert witness. As a matter of fact, the Lubatvitcher Rebbe does not regard officiating at a wedding or a funeral as one of his functions, for the normal locale of his functioning is at his home or "court."

At the Rock Island wedding, Rabbi Twersky excused himself during the course of the processional. A woman soloist sang "O Promise Me," and it is against traditional Judaism for a man to listen to a female voice singing. "The voice of a woman is a nakedness. . . ."

The Lubavitcher Rebbe, as Rabbi Weiner told me, has found in America a fertile home for his movement, a land where one can "use a light instead of a stick" in converting Jews to Hasidism. "Israel is more exile than America." The Satmer Rebbe feels that he must create his own environment; the Lubavitcher takes a chance with inner resources that are built up in the favorable atmosphere of a hospitable land. America has taught the world the art of communication. So the Lubavitcher has encouraged the use of mass media. His textbook, the *Tanya*, appears in paperback; his Saturday-night radio lesson based on the text and his sales technique are all native products. Disciples are sent to Finland, to South America, to Morocco, to gather in the wandering flock. Undergraduates from

Harvard, Yale, and Princeton are invited to spend a weekend in Brooklyn, put up at the homes of Hasidim, and exposed to the enchantment of Hasidic teaching at the master's table.

The key word, according to Rabbi Weiner's exposition, is *Uv'-chen*, which the Hasidim translate "what comes out [of your idea]?" Enough of mere talk: what can be done pragmatically? The Rebbe asks his disciples, "Will you build a *mikvah* [ritual bath essential for what the Orthodox refer to as family purity]? Is the Released Time program for public schools a valuable tool for our educational purposes?" Such considerations as the First Amendment take a back seat in terms of *Uv'chen*. Rabbi Schneersohn parts company with the organized Jewish community in supporting the Roman Catholic position on federal aid to education. If religious nurture is strengthened, why worry about constitutional technicalities?

Classical Hasidism, in the eighteenth and nineteenth centuries, stressed spontaneity rather than structured religious observance. Spirit—motion—was preferred over intellect and abstract ideas. But this is not so among the Lubavitcher. Torah learning is at the heart of modern Hasidism, according to Rabbi Schneerson. And in the American style, it is not unstructured as it was in the old-fashioned Yeshivah. A highly structured day is planned, a scheduled hour for each activity.

Hasidim are expected to be "in this world." They may take up any legitimate business or profession so long as their labors are not carried out on Sabbaths and festivals. The hours of Wall Street are particularly suitable for the pious, and some are stockbrokers. They may consult the Rebbe on business deals, and follow his advice without question. They may even make him a silent partner, on a modest scale, and if their firm "goes public" he may receive stock certificate number one.

The Lubavitcher Rebbe is extremely public-relations conscious. Once, when Rabbi Weiner was scheduled to speak in Cleveland, he received a telephone call from the Rebbe's office. "We hope that you will present our Hasidic viewpoint in a favorable light." The Hasidim, too, would like a good image!

In 1964, following an extended outbreak of assaults and robberies in the Crown Heights section of Brooklyn, the Hasidim organized a self-defense unit called the Maccabees, reminiscent of the ancient defenders of the faith. Joining them were people of all ethnic backgrounds, white and colored. In typical Hasidic tradition, they were unarmed. This was no vigilante body to supplant an inadequate police force. Their only weapon was the short-wave radio equipment in their cars, which afforded them instantaneous communication with Brooklyn police precincts. Front-page newspaper pictures showed the bearded Rabbi Pruzansky, earphones draped over earlocks, on the alert for would-be violators of the peace.

In many ways detached from the main stream of American life, the Hasidim are yet very much a part of it. Theodore H. White's *Making of the President—1964* describes a Lyndon B. Johnson campaign parade through Brooklyn: "Hasidic Jews with soft black hats and side whiskers waved wildly. Little boys in their temple skullcaps ran after the cavalcade."

I visited the Williamsburgh YMHA, one of the most remarkable Jewish institutions in the United States. Murray Gunner, the amiable director, has developed a program ideally suited to the needs of the thousands of Hasidic youth in the neighborhood. Two thousand children were enrolled in the 1965 summer program. Mr. Gunner, a trained social worker, wore a skullcap in deference to the sensitivities of his neighborhood. He has succeeded in winning the confidence of the Hasidim even though it is sometimes nip and tuck as far as the Satmer Rebbe is concerned. One of the most amusing photographs I have ever seen is that of a Hasidic instructor, beard, skullcap, and all, dressed in a Japanese judo costume, with a lock hold on one of his nervous students, as he demonstrated the gentle art of Oriental self-defense. The best of three worlds! Not only judo, but weight lifting and basketball are taught at the Y, and a solemn, scholarly looking Hasidic rabbi instructs young women in a special art class. His long, full gray beard would make him an ideal model for his youthful students.

I watched a fourteen-year-old boy, with flaming red hair and earlocks covered with a bright *yarmulke,* leaning over a pool table studying a difficult shot.

Around the lunch table 100 girls chanted the Hebrew prayer of grace after meals: "When ye eat and are satisfied, ye shall bless the name of the Lord."

One of the Y directors in charge of the girls was a young woman in her early twenties. Kayla had a beautiful face, without make-up, blue eyes, brown hair. She ran the program with a rare kind of warmth and tenderness. Kayla had gone to college. She was engaged to a rabbinical student of twenty-four, and they planned to marry later in the year.

"What would he do for a living?"

"We're planning to live in Lakewood, New Jersey, where he will study Talmud."

"What will you live on?"

"Oh, I'll work. We can manage on eggs. Maybe he'll be a rabbi. But it's enough that he will study. The Almighty will take care of us."

"How do your parents feel about this?"

"They're not too happy. But they're very understanding."

I looked at her lovely hair.

"Will you shave it off just before marriage?" (Standard procedure among ultra-Orthodox brides.)

"Of course," Kayla answered in a matter-of-fact tone, without a hint of regret.

Around the corner from the Y is a shop called Martha's Wig Salon. There are many wig stores in the neighborhood, and they do a thriving business in the land of the Hasidim, for all the married women among the pious wear wigs.

It was summertime, and the Y Day Camp was in full swing, spilling over into a neighboring public school. I visited the school, and its classrooms buzzed with the sound of tiny voices reading Bible and Talmud in the singsong fashion of ancient academies.

The Y summer program was obviously a compromise. Hasidic children would be permitted to play volleyball and enjoy arts and crafts, but the boys were required to spend an equal amount of time on Torah learning. The six-year-olds were reading Genesis, the nine-year-olds were already immersed in the "sea of the Talmud," while boys of eleven studied the intricacies of the Talmudic laws of divorce.

The "yoke of learning" was placed only on the boys. While the girls continued their volleyball and archery, their brothers returned to their texts. Although they would rather play, they didn't resent the extra burden. Their masculine self-image naturally demanded this extra responsibility.

I listened to a six-year-old ask the question: "Wasn't Haman a descendant of Amalek?"

A Hasidic child would never utter God's name, even in an English sentence.

"What did Hashem [His Name] say to Eve?" one of them queried.

Separation of the sexes was complete. New York City provided an instructor in Driver's Education, and the teen-agers gathered in the auditorium. Would the instructor have to repeat his lecture, once for boys and again for girls? An improvised curtain down the center aisle provided an ingenious solution. Both groups would see the instructor, but they would have no visual contact with one another, and would leave the hall separately, so that they would not be tempted to talk to one another. Such intimacies are permitted only after the engagement.

Fifty children in the Y nursery were served luncheon, not an ordinary kosher luncheon, but what is called *glatt*-kosher, strictly and absolutely kosher, the milk and cheese coming from a special New Jersey dairy farm which supervised its cattle with much more zeal than an ordinary kosher farm.

The Satmer Hasidim were not as easily won over to this summer program as the Lubavitcher. A flier distributed by one of their leaders early in the season denounced the program in the sternest tones: "To our fellow Israelites who fear the Lord and live by His Name: We hereby warn you not to enroll your children at the Y Day Camp at 575 Bedford Avenue, Brooklyn, or at other such day camps. We have learned that such exposure of our tender-minded children may harm their spiritual well-being and, G-d forbid, threaten their faith. We caution parents whose hearts have been touched by the fear of the Lord not to permit these young holy sheep to fall into alien hands."

Later, Director Murray Gunner informed me, in the wake of representations to the Rebbe himself, the order was rescinded, and a Hasidic *aggiornamento* permitted the children to take their chances with the outside world.

Near the Y stands a number of new high-rise apartments. Hasidic families, with the exception of the more conservative Satmer (who prefer splendid isolation) occupy the lower floors. Jews, observant ones, but not Hasidic, live in the upper floors. I asked how they overcame the Sabbath prohibition against using electrical devices. American engineering ingenuity has fashioned a solution. Beginning before sundown on Friday, the elevator mechanism is adjusted so that the elevators operate with automatic stops continuously at all floor levels.

A smaller but dynamic group of Hasidim are followers of the Bobover Rebbe, Rabbi Solomon Halberstam. Its present headquarters in Brooklyn will soon be moved to an ambitious housing development costing 20 million dollars in the Whitestone section of Queens, New York. The community will be called Bobov City, and will contain attractive apartments, a headquarters building with room for a 2,000-seat sanctuary, a Yeshivah for the boys, and a girls' school. It is a counterpart of an Israeli community built by the Bobover Hasidim near Tel Aviv, Israel. The Bobover Rebbe announced at the ground-breaking ceremonies in June, 1965, that "this project was the fulfillment of a dream. Hundreds of families will live together with a common purpose—Torah study. We will provide our children with the finest education in surroundings conducive to learning. Our people will live in modest homes that will be among the most modern on Long Island, and we will have a number of stores that will cater to our people."

Hasidism has gone suburban, too. Near Monsey, New York, a new village has been created called Square Town. (The name is a county clerk's misspelling of Skvar, a Polish village which gave its name to the Skvarer Rebbe.) The village is the only community in America that can boast of two Yiddish-speaking high schools. A restrictive covenant (unenforceable in the courts) limits purchase of homes to Sabbath observers, and owners who will not permit television or send their children to secular schools.

Every weekday the Square Town commuters' bus makes its way across the George Washington Bridge and drops its passengers on West 47th Street, the diamond center where many of the Hasidim work. It is not an ordinary bus. A separating curtain down the aisle keeps the sexes apart; and a curtained-off partition behind the driver's seat holds an Ark for a Torah, to be used for prayer.

The Rebbe assumes responsibility for assuring the economic stability of his disciples. Ultimately, he hopes the town will develop its own industry and the trials of commuting will be at an end. One of my friends was approached by a spokesman for Square Town to help set up a knitting factory there.

Rabbi Herbert Weiner, in his *Commentary* articles, distinguishes between the Lubavitcher Hasidim and those of other rebbes. "The other rebbes," one Hasidic staff member told him, "are interested mainly in their own Hasidim, while the Lubavitcher Rebbe considers himself responsible for the spiritual and bodily welfare of every Jew no matter where he lives or what he believes."

Among Hasidim, the Zaddik ("the saintly one"), as he is called, "holds court" daily from nine o'clock in the evening until 2 to 5 A.M. I have been told by a number of writers that their appointments with Rabbi Schneersohn usually took place between one thirty and two thirty in the morning.

The traditional scene around the Lubavitcher Rebbe's table is a wondrous combination of the old and the new. At the head of the table, the Rebbe holds a microphone as he calls out by name to one of the disciples. The Hasid leaps up in a kind of ecstasy at the sound of his name, whiskycup in hand, and proposes a toast, "*l'chayim* Rebbe"—long life to our Rebbe.

Then the Rebbe begins his talk. This is the signal to rise. The disciples will not remain seated while their leader preaches. It is no mean task to stand on one's feet for ninety minutes, at two o'clock in the morning, listening to a complex discourse.

Beginning with a mystical reference, abstruse and involved, the Rebbe addresses himself to the human condition. Rabbi Weiner recalls a sermon in which the master spoke with compassion about man's needs: "When a baby cries, he has to be answered. . . . Sometimes a seventy-year-old man cries like a baby. . . ."

Faith in the Rebbe brings healing to the body and to the spirit. Not infrequently a couple come to him because they are childless, and he offers them a blessing and a formula of prayer and good works to promote fertility.

At a Hasidic wedding attended by a friend of mine, the guests were entertained by a dancer—a man in his thirties who danced with such frenzied ecstasy that he fell limp with exhaustion. He was not a professional. The Rebbe had told him that his wife's sterility would be ended if he undertook the *mitzvah* (good deed) of enhancing the joy of wedding celebrations—a *mitzvah* which ranks high in the Hasidic hierarchy of virtuous deeds. He was to use his talents for the glory of God and the joy of man. Yet, the Rebbe's own prayers in this area have gone unanswered. "For some reason the Master of the Universe has withheld his blessing from him."

The Rebbe's powers, according to his Hasidim, extend beyond the seas. During the Korean war, one tale has it, a soldier made a pilgrimage to 770 Eastern Parkway—the Lubavitcher Rebbe's head-quarters—to seek his blessing before going off to war. The Rebbe's last words were: "Before you eat, make sure that you wash your hands." Later, during an attack, the soldier moved out of his position to wash his hands before eating. A shell landed on his foxhole, and all his buddies were killed. Such stories are recounted by the faithful to prove the miraculous gifts of the righteous one.

Some of the Hasidic sects, as has been suggested, are more worldly than others. The Bobover Rebbe insists that his disciples receive a high-school education, and he encourages vocational training. The Satmer Rebbe, however, views all contact with the world outside the Hasidic orbit as tainted. In the summer of 1965, a boy of nine—a camper at a Hasidic camp—was lost in the woods while on a berry hunt. A vivid account in the ultra-Orthodox *Jewish Press* explained why the camper was not found for four days. National guardsmen who passed near him while he lay huddled in a blanket of leaves called out his name. But they were strangers and he was afraid to cry out.

Lee Avenue, in Brooklyn, is the business street where the Hasidim do their shopping. Grocery stores handle only *glatt*-kosher products. Restaurants carry a *glatt*-kosher label. Even the pizza establishment is *glatt*-kosher.

The Lee Avenue music store, too, is a Hasidic version of the twentieth century. The untidy window display features neither the Beatles nor Beethoven. Records by cantors and local talent fill most of the space, together with records to dance Hasidic dances by.

The only English-language study of the Brooklyn Hasidim is Solomon Poll's *The Hasidic Community of Williamsburgh* (Free Press). Mr. Poll draws a picture of great domestic stability. The problems of wayward youth are generally unheard of. "Youth does not have high status in the Hasidic community . . . except in those respects when they show initiative and promise of becoming good Hasidic Jews. . . . Boys and girls do not meet ambiguities and un-certainties concerning their expected behavior, since the role of youth is to obey their elders."

A social worker informed me that this idyllic portrayal is not uniformly accurate. The Lubavitcher children, he declared, present few problems, but the Satmer youngsters, reared in the austerity of the Hungarian Orthodox tradition, sometimes rebel.

By and large Hasidism is an adult world—a married adult world. Poll reported that "the community does not extend appreciable social recognition to unmarried people: the only real person is a married one!" Few are the families without nine or more children. The authors of *Fiddler on the Roof* consulted the Poll study when they were researching for their play. One vivid description of the role of romance in the Hasidic world was obviously the basis for the tender song, "Do You Love Me?"

A Hasid, asked if he was in love with his wife, replied, "You mean in love while one is already married?"

"Yes," responded the questioner.

"I don't understand how one is in love while married. He is already married. I can understand that one might have some romantic feeling during the negotiations of the match or while engaged, but how can one be in love while married?"

Love, American style, is associated with sin and lust. A momentary impulse during courtship—a few furtive glances while parents are discussing the proposed match—might be winked at. But marriage, Hasidic style, is too serious a business to be cluttered up by romantic foolishness. "After twenty-five years," sings Golde to her Tevye, "I've washed your clothes, cooked your meals, cleaned your house, given you children, milked the cow. After twenty-five years, why talk about love right now?"

Apparently the recipe works, for Dr. Poll could find only two incidents of divorce in the entire community.

Hasidic ties to the Holy Land are substantial. Spiritual descendants of the mystics who journeyed to Palestine despite hostility and persecution, Hasidim regard "the land of their fathers" as the ultimate home, come the Messiah, for all the children of Abraham, living or dead.

When a rebbe announces his departure on a pilgrimage, the New York police force goes into emergency session. The scenes at Kennedy Airport or at Pier 59 are sheer chaos. The uniformed sons of Erin are confronted with 10,000 Jewish dervishes, all intent on touching the hem of the rebbe's garb, so that he carries something of them to the Holy City. His disciples crush him out of love and devotion. What if a few dozen fur-brimmed hats are crushed and some ribs bruised? It is all *l'shem shmayim*—for the sake of Heaven.

Among the Hasidim and the ultra-Orthodox the last journey of the dead to Israel offers much spiritual comfort. Resurrection, they say, will begin in the land of Israel, and those who are buried there will enjoy some kind of mystical priority.

An advertisement which appears regularly in the *Jewish Press* announces that the Maalin Bakodesh Society of 101 Park Avenue, New York, offers the following privileges to its members: "You will have the opportunity 'after one hundred and twenty years' for burial, within twenty-four hours after demise in the Har Hamnuchot Cemetery in Jerusalem . . . to be received by a *minyan* of world-renowned Chevra Kadisha [burial] Society of Jerusalem which will escort the deceased from the airport in Lydda and personally participate in the complete funeral ceremonies in accordance with traditional Jerusalemite customs."

At the El-Al Airlines office on Fifth Avenue, a special department processes such requests. Orthodox Jewish law requires burial within twenty-four hours after death. The swift flight of a Boeing 707 jet from Kennedy airport nonstop to Tel Aviv makes it possible to fulfill the exigencies of the law as well as the apocalyptic hope of the true disciple.

Portrait of a Hasid

The long, straggly black beard and earlocks of Rabbi Ayin are the badge of the Hasidic Jew. But his speech is unaccented. Born in Lithuania, Rabbi Ayin came to America when he was thirteen, and is a disciple of the Lubavitcher Rebbe, whose teachings provide the Constitution and the daily guidelines of thousands of followers. Mrs. Ayin, American-born daughter of another Hasidic rabbi, wears a wig, the symbol of piety. Her husband tells his congregants that, in our day, a married woman who doesn't wear a wig is neither modern nor Orthodox.

There are seven children in the family, "only seven," he says. The oldest, a nineteen-year-old son, attends a Yeshivah in Montreal. Since they live in New Jersey, where school facilities for the ultra-Orthodox are unavailable, it is customary to send the boys away for training at the age of twelve and thirteen. One daughter works as a cashier in a Jewish hospital (she has no problems of Sabbath and holy day observance).

The rabbi's wife presides over a "Family Purity Society" which encourages Jewish women in rigid observance of ritual cleanliness (sexual separation twelve days in the month and regular attendance at the *mikvah*).

Rabbi Ayin has known his wife since childhood. Their parents were friends. But, in the manner of the Hasidim, they had not spoken to each other since early childhood, and their engagement was arranged by a marriage broker—a rather informal procedure in technical fulfillment of the requirement that it be a planned rather than a romantic union.

I asked Rabbi Ayin why he selected her. He chuckled. "You mean, did I love? Of course not. We Hasidim assume that love comes after marriage. What is falling in love but a realization that two people have much in common? Sharing common ideals is certainly more enduring than emotional attachment."

"Is there any chance that the children will wander from the straight-and-narrow path?"

"It rarely happens. Our children remain close to us, go to our kind of schools, and show no inclination to break away.

"They can listen to radio, but we don't permit television. We have no right to delegate the education of our children for three to four hours a day to a 'man in a box.'

"I read *The New York Times*, especially the Sunday paper, and *Time* magazine. I am interested in politics. I've never missed a primary. I think Senator Case is an unusually fine senator. We are part of our American culture, but I won't give up our values for the 'vast wasteland' (to use the expression of the former head of FCC) of the dominant American culture.

"That is why we discourage our children from attending college. Why turn over a young person in those years, seventeen to twenty-one, when young minds are most delicate, most impressionable?"

I interjected: "You need a dentist, at times, and a doctor. You Lubavitcher are engaged in a mission to convert every Jew to your philosophy. What will happen if we produce no medical men, no dentists?"

"*Nu*, and do I train any of my children to be garbage collectors? I know what would happen to my street if there were no sanitation men. But that doesn't mean I have to train garbage men in my family. Who says there have to be Jewish doctors? We can use non-Jews. In the meantime our young men will devote themselves to the works of the Almighty, to studying the Torah; that is why we were placed on this earth."

"Isn't there any accommodation you make to America?"

"Of course. Our way of life is different in some ways. My daughters wear lipstick, and so does my wife. She dresses neatly. As a matter of fact, our women are not like other American women who dress up for strangers and look like slobs at home. Our women feel they ought to look their best when their husbands come home from work."

"Why do you feel so strongly about television?"

"We don't object to using it. I have appeared on it often, to explain the teachings of Hasidism. And I have often appeared on radio. Our rebbe has a weekly radio program in which he teaches from our standard text, the *Tanya*. It is only the waste of its use that we deplore. My wife and children go to the movies once in a long while. But there are better things to do with one's time."

"Better things" means study. Rabbi Ayin attends worship twice a day and twice a day he conducts a study group. He is a hospital chaplain, and also teaches at a girls' school—an Orthodox one, naturally. The rabbi has little time for any diversions.

What does he do for excitement? The most satisfying activity is *hidur mitzvah*—fulfilling the will of God in an extra-special way.

For example, a Hasid doesn't buy an ordinary ceremonial object. He searches out and purchases an especially beautiful one—a perfect one: "What is a Bar Mitzvah?—the occasion to don *tefillin* [phylacteries—special prayer boxes which contain the texts of divine commandments]. The average Jew spends ten dollars on his son's phylacteries. I paid a hundred dollars for my son's. So let him have less of a Bar Mitzvah party. It's a thrill to have these absolutely perfect phylacteries. It tells him how much we care.

"On Passover, most people buy ordinary manufactured matzoths. We pay five times as much for our specially baked matzoths."

The Ayin family live on a modest income, without frills. Their only luxuries are religious ones.

"What is so extraordinary about our matzoths? They are carefully baked by hand, and watched much more thoroughly than in a big factory.

"Incidentally, most people don't realize that there is little that is new in the world that wasn't thought of in our Torah and our Talmud. Do you know that the problem of automation is discussed in ancient Jewish law? The Talmud mentions that if you *manufac-*

ture matzoth instead of producing them by hand, a lot of poor workers will lose their jobs.

"Do you think that air pollution is a recent problem? The Talmud says that no smoke-belching manufacturing plants may be built within twenty-five miles of the Holy City of Jerusalem. The nearest one was at Modin, the scene of the Maccabean victory. So you see that the modern world doesn't have so much to teach us. The Torah covers everything."

I raised the question about the difference between his sect, the largest in America, and some of the others.

"The others are isolated from irreligious Jewry, from the less observant. They are worried about being tainted by contact, by exposure to corrupting influence. We have no such fears. We believe in the power of the soul. The *yetzer tov*—the impulse toward good—is in all of us, and it is a challenge to us to bring back the unbelievers into the ranks of the faithful. That is why we storm the college campuses, to save our youth by exposing them to our redeeming ideas. They are not happy people, as we are. They, too, can find happiness."

"How do you feel about Israel?"

"We certainly don't believe that it represents the ultimate solution of the problem of Judaism. Our faith is in the coming of the Messiah. He will surely come!"

I turned and stared straight into the eyes of Rabbi Ayin who, despite his beard and old-fashioned garb, was very much a child of the twentieth century— a reader of *Time* and *The Times*, an admirer of the liberal Senator Case, a man who drove an automobile, flew in a jet plane, and was comfortable in front of a television camera.

"Is this mere theological rhetoric, or do you really believe that someday the Messiah will come down to earth to redeem the children of Israel?"

Rabbi Ayin's eyes lit up, and he said cheerfully, with a tolerant smile, "What kind of question is that?"

CHAPTER 13

Rabbis and Other Religious Functionaries

"Nothing would give me greater satisfaction than to
die while preaching a sermon. But preferably at the
end."

RABBI STEPHEN S. WISE

A number of years ago, when I was teaching some courses at the
Hillel Foundation of the University of Illinois, I drove my car along
a bumpy country road and accidentally ran over a chicken. Brooding over the accident, several days later I mentioned the mishap to
one of my students.

"Last Sunday I killed a chicken."

"That's the only thing I don't like about your profession, rabbi—
having to kill chickens."

My student's cloudy conception of a rabbi's work has its roots in
the complex nature of Jewish life. For the Christian, the locus of
virtually all ritual and ceremonial life lies in the church, and the
Christian clergyman has a clearly defined sacerdotal role: to preach
and conduct worship services. But Jewish tradition calls for a
number of ritual functions unrelated to those of the rabbi.

The cantor (*hazzan* in Hebrew) is, in the structure of American
Jewish life, a clergyman (although the Social Security Administration is still trying to make up its mind if this is so). Historically, he is
the only one who actually conducts services. The rabbi teaches and
preaches, but he does not read or chant the prayers. Only in modern
Reform and Conservative synagogues does the rabbi take over the
duties traditionally assigned to the cantor. In American and Canadian practice, a cantor is generally accorded the title of reverend.

Orthodox and Conservative congregations, and some Reform Temples as well, retain the services of a full-time cantor at annual salaries ranging from $2,500 to $25,000. All three branches maintain cantorial training schools.

Among the Orthodox, some cantors have achieved great eminence with avid fans who buy all their records and fill the synagogues with which they are connected. A generation ago, the names of Yosselle Rosenblatt, Schlisky, Kwartin were American Jewish folk heroes, invited to "perform" in the leading synagogues of Europe and North and South America.

A few cantors, such as Richard Tucker and Jan Peerce, have gone from cantorial singing to distinguished operatic careers. Often these stars will be booked by resort hotels for cantorial services during Passover or the High Holy Days, at fees comparable to the top figures of the entertainment world.

But most cantors, Orthodox, Conservative, and Reform, have a variety of responsibilities in addition to their role in worship. They train Bar Mitzvah children, organize adult and youth choirs, assist in the religious school, and occasionally help the youth program.

Large Orthodox and Conservative congregations also retain the services of a reader (a *Baal Koreh*—one who chants the Torah reading) who serves as a second cantor, and may also bear the title of reverend.

The tradition of circumcision, a rigid requirement of all three branches of Judaism, is the responsibility of another religious functionary, known as a *mohel*. New York's Board of Rabbis, for example, has a *Milah* Board (Circumcision), a highly organized professional body, with an elaborate program of certification. Only a registered *mohel*, approved by this board, may enter the operating rooms of a hospital.

In a small city which has no *mohel* of its own the birth of a boy may entail importing one from a distant community. San Antonio, Texas, for example, calls in the *mohel* of Corpus Christi, some one hundred and forty miles away.

What does one call the circumcizer? Because there is no differential title assigned him, many people refer to him as "rabbi." So, too, the men engaged in kosher slaughtering, and other aspects of the kosher food industry. Some time ago, on a plane flying to Chicago, I saw a group of men traveling together clustered around a bearded gentleman wearing a skullcap whom they referred to as "the rabbi." From their conversation it was obvious that the group was en route to an important business conference—and that the "rabbi" was the only Jew among them. I learned that they were headed for a meeting of soybean dealers (the animated discussion concerned futures, the commodity exchange and the weather). The deferential manner in which these soybean experts looked up to the "rabbi" whenever he offered an opinion reminded me of a bevy of disciples encircling a learned Hasid.

But much more typical are the hundreds of rabbis who earn their living by supervising the "kosher business," described by *The Wall Street Journal* as one of the nation's "growth" industries. Packing houses use a *shochet* for slaughtering, and laymen refer to him as a rabbi—an easier word than *shochet*. In addition, many regularly ordained rabbis are retained by the meat companies, soap manufacturers, makers of processed foods, manufacturers of wax paper (to assure that no pork products are found in the wax), kosher jelly, and clothing (to uphold the Biblical law against mixing wool and cotton).

The original meaning of the word "rabbi" is teacher. Comparable to the Christian minister-educator is the rabbi-educator, engaged in the religious nurture of young and old. Hundreds of American rabbis are engaged in Jewish academic work—in all-day schools, in the Hillel Foundations of university campuses, and in the writing and preparation of religious textbooks and related teaching materials.

I would estimate that there are more Jews in the United States bearing the title "rabbi" who are not serving in pulpits than there are in congregational life. Indeed, many young Orthodox Jews enter seminaries with no intention of ever occupying a pulpit. These graduates of a yeshiva have generally received their early training in a religious all-day school, where they were strongly motivated to master more of Jewish learning, whatever their long-range professional or commercial aims may be. The backbone of the Young Israel movement, connecting a string of Orthodox synagogues in the larger cities, consists of business and professional men who have received their ordination in one of the yeshivas.

To confuse the picture still further, classic Judaism recognizes no doctrinal distinction between clergy and laity. Any competent Jew may officiate at a wedding or funeral, or at Sabbath or daily services. (Walk inside a traditional synagogue on any weekday at 7 A.M. or 7 P.M. and the likelihood is that the man leading the service is a lay member of the congregation.) If by "clergyman" we mean a person who officially performs a religious rite, any learned Jew may serve as a clergyman.

Several small communities, notably in the South and the Southwest, lacking an ordained spiritual leader, have enlisted the services of a layman. In Brownsville, Texas, Sam Pearl, haberdasher, is the local rabbi. Mr. Pearl, a fine-looking man in his late sixties, conducts well-attended Friday-evening services; he preaches sermons regularly (he confessed to me that he borrows heavily from published sermon material) and even officiates at weddings and funerals. Authorized by a Texas judge, he solemnized the wedding of his own daughter. "Rabbi" Pearl takes his pastoral work seriously. When a Mexican couple came across the Rio Grande and asked him to officiate at their wedding, he learned that the bride was not Jewish. "You'd better keep on going to Houston, where you will find one of those liberal rabbis who will marry you. I refuse to officiate unless both bride and groom are of our faith!"

Only among Jews, I would suspect, can we find a Brooklyn congregation made up of ordained laymen and a Texas congregation whose preacher is an unordained, but highly revered, clothing merchant!

Even rules of ordination are most unrigid—and state officials can hardly be blamed for the fog of uncertainty that hovers over the definition of a rabbi. Technically, in Jewish law, a rabbi may receive his ordination from another rabbi who is satisfied that he has met certain intellectual and spiritual requirements. Dr. Stephen S. Wise, unquestionably the most gifted rabbi of the century, was ordained, not by a seminary, but by his rabbi father.

When I was stationed at Fort Dix, New Jersey, as a World War II chaplain, I was summoned by a military court-martial to serve as an expert witness in the trial of a soldier who had been absent without leave for more than a year. The soldier claimed he was a rabbi, and as such should not have been drafted as an enlisted man.

"What is a rabbi?" the presiding military judge asked me. "Who determines the authenticity of the title?" I had to confess that there is no single standard.

The so-called "free-lance rabbi" is one who calls himself a rabbi, and is so regarded by his followers. In times past, such men have filled distinguished pulpits, often with much luster. The state of New York recognizes anyone who can produce the stationery of a synagogue with his name listed as a rabbi. When I first moved to New York City, I had difficulty getting permission from the Marriage Bureau to officiate at a wedding, because my congregation had not yet printed new stationery listing my name!

Jewish religious officialdom—the Synagogue Council of America, the New York Board of Rabbis, and similar organizations—recognize only those rabbis who have been ordained by a duly recognized theological school. But even these bodies have made exceptions for unordained rabbis who have occupied pulpits and have served as military chaplains.

The Pulpit Rabbi

Much has been written about the contemporary clergyman, his frustrations, his neuroses, his flights from church work, the meagerness of his compensation, the disturbing gap between himself and his congregants, his wrestling with theological dogmas. Altogether the picture is rather bleak, and provides an explanation for the reported decline in the number of candidates for theological training.

No comparable study has been made of the American rabbi. He probably shares both the griefs and the satisfactions of his Christian colleague, but there are profound differences in their experience, as we shall see.

The candidate for Jewish seminary entrance in the 1960s, unlike his counterpart of the 1930s, was most likely born in the United States, and may be a third- or fourth-generation American. His college training—indispensable for admission to a modern Jewish theological school—was science oriented, or in the field of literature. He knows that the preparatory course is equal to that of a medical education: five to six years of postgraduate training, followed by two or three years in the military chaplaincy. He will be close to thirty before he takes a pulpit. Possibly, he may have been a sergeant in Korea, who came under the influence of an Army chaplain —his first real contact with a rabbi—and became enamored with the ministry. A third-generation Reform Jew, he had decided to be a Conservative rabbi. Lack of preparation did not daunt him. The normal six-year after-college seminary training was gladly stretched to eight or nine years. Marriage and a family offered little handicap.

Once ordained, the new rabbi can move immediately into a position which pays nine to ten thousand dollars annually, in a Reform or Conservative congregation, and somewhat less in an Orthodox one. As of this writing, at least 150 Conservative congregations are without a rabbi for their pulpits, and according to Rabbi Kelman, only one rabbi in more than 800 is unemployed. Indeed the demand so exceeds the supply that even a student rabbi receives over $5,000 a year. In 1935, the married seminary student was a rarity. In 1965, there were few bachelors on ordination day, and graduation took on all the aspects of a family picnic.

Although exact figures are not available, it is estimated that there are 3,272 rabbis and 3,037 Jewish congregations in the United States and Canada.

The size of congregations varies to a degree which the average student never suspected. Reform temples affiliated with the Union of American Hebrew Congregations, for example, include 50 congregations with over 1,000 families and almost 150 congregations with fewer than 50 families. In between are congregations which average about 250 families, more or less.

Some Rabbinical Profiles

Authorities on the subject of rabbis like to divide them into neat categories. There is the social-action rabbi, the rabbi-scholar, the outstanding pastor, the Zionist.

Rabbi Aleph, who guides the spiritual life of a Reform congregation of 300 families, just beyond commuting distance of New York City, is a husky, sandy-haired, blue-eyed man in his middle thirties who sees himself as a synthesis of all these neat characterizations. When Martin Luther King leads a civil-rights march, Rabbi Aleph is frequently among the marchers. He has dined at the King home, and with the Abernethys. With sixteen other rabbis, he ate the baby-food rations provided by St. Augustine jailers, and he has seen the inside of a dozen Southern jails.

Rabbi Aleph's journeys on behalf of racial justice are not always applauded by his people. After some initial misgivings they were ready to approve his participation in the massive March on Washington. It turned out to be a respectable undertaking, involving 200,000 Americans. Several congregants pumped his hand vigorously at Sabbath services: "You represented us all. I wish I could have been with you."

As his jail days increased and the cost of travel and bail mounted, a few of his social action-minded supporters gave him financial assistance over and above the $2,000 of his own money spent in civil-rights pursuits. But when he began directing some of his energies to local problems, and joined a Protestant minister and a Catholic priest in picketing a neighborhood building project which employed no Negroes, the enthusiasm of his followers waned markedly. At one turbulent Temple Board meeting, which lasted well past midnight, one of the congregational officers shouted: "It's all right for the Protestants and the Catholics to get involved in this race business, but we Jews should keep our noses clean." Arriving home that night, he found his wife awake. A midnight caller had threatened to drop a bomb on their doorstep.

"Now I have a real working congregation," he explains, "half working for me and half against me."

The opposition to a rabbi is never one-dimensioned. Rabbi Aleph, who grew up in a Conservative environment, attended an Orthodox Yeshivah, and lived in Israel for a year after his ordination, found equally strong resistance to his ideas about religious education. But within two years after his arrival at the Beth Am Temple, Rabbi Aleph had completely revised the school curriculum. In addition to attendance at the Sunday-school program, almost all the children were enrolled in the midweek program. A few families resigned in protest.

Even the worship service underwent drastic changes. Half the male worshipers—many of them "refugees" from Conservative congregations—wore head coverings, and more Hebrew was added to the Sabbath ritual.

Rabbi Aleph has managed to hold criticism within bounds. "I still have the upper hand," he told me, "but one more crisis, and I'd really be in trouble." He was especially disturbed when the chief of police of a Southern city called his local chief to ask about his "criminal record." Another crisis arose when the parent of a member died, and the rabbi was away at a civil-rights march, unavailable for the funeral.

Rabbi Aleph pictures himself primarily as a student. Every spare penny is spent on books. His salary is $10,000 a year, plus a house: he neither asks for nor expects an increase. He finds preaching a joy and an excellent medium of teaching. He prepares his messages thoroughly: "I believe a rabbi should respect the intelligence of his congregants."

This rabbi is content with his lot. His life is full and varied, the adventure of the rabbinate is exciting, and, on occasion, rewarding. Once a week he joins his Conservative colleague in a study session; they read Hebrew books and journals together. He looks forward to the day when his family can spend a year in Israel. "If there were an all-day school nearby, I would give our children a more intensive Jewish education. If we don't have a corps of young Jews with solid training—learning the Bible in Hebrew and the Mishnah and the commentaries—American Jewry will have no cadre of religious leaders, rabbis, and teachers." And so, when some of his younger couples begin to read Jewish books, join social-action committees, and talk about Jewish commitment, Rabbi Aleph feels "all's right in God's world."

Rabbi Beth, parish rabbi

Like a fireman who appears at the scene of a blaze moments after the first alarm is sounded, Rabbi Beth is at the door of a household which has just lost a loved one moments after the temple is notified. For the rabbi takes his role as comforter seriously: indeed he takes himself very seriously. He once told a friend: "When I look into a mirror, I don't see Philip, but Rabbi Beth." He doesn't even call himself by his first name!

Many congregants appreciate this solicitous outpouring by their rabbi in their hour of bereavement. The special attention he lavishes raises their estimate of themselves and of him. A few complain that he doesn't allow them sufficient opportunity for private grief. Some of his critics wish he would spend more time preparing his sermons, taking part in civic enterprise, or become involved in outside affairs.

Rabbi Beth is essentially a "parish rabbi," content to channel all his talents into his congregational family. His few out-of-town expeditions are either speaking engagements at neighboring colleges under the auspices of the Jewish Chautauqua Society, or annual dinner meetings with young congregants away at school. The center of his world, all of his friendships, all of his associations in work and at play, is the congregational family of 1,500 souls (about four hundred and fifty families) of Temple Israel.

Temple Israel has done well by Rabbi Beth. For his twentieth anniversary, he was given an automobile, and for his silver jubilee, the rabbi, his wife, and their child spent three months in Europe and Israel, a gift of the Men's Club and Sisterhood. He is paid $15,000 a year, plus a housing allowance, and he accepts no fees for weddings or funerals.

Although on the short side, Rabbi Beth is striking in appearance. His iron-gray hair is worn long, in the fashion of a movie actor, and his tanned features bespeak good health and a strong sense of confidence. Mrs. Beth adores her husband, and congregants like to watch her face kindle with unabashed admiration as the rabbi preaches. But there are less ardent admirers as well. His affected accent, pleasing to the elderly Sisterhood members, is grating to the ears of the young marrieds, as is his penchant for such overworked phrases as "it is our sacred duty," "a crescendo of prophetic wrath," and "we shall never forget his sacrificial devotion." Perhaps his greatest weakness is his basic lack of humor—a failing many of his congregants find most difficult to accept.

Rabbi Beth's religious philosophy is uncomplicated. He accepts what is commonly called "classic Reform"—old-line liberal Judaism. The new winds of social change blow far over his head. Although he is tolerant of colleagues who sign petitions, demand American withdrawal from Vietnam, and press for extension of collective-bargaining rights for hospital workers, Rabbi Beth confines his own social idealism to works of charity. The world will improve only when the individuals in it are better, he explains. "Our job is to change hearts, not alter society."

If he finds any shortcomings in himself, it is in his role as a preacher. Early on Friday he dictates a vague outline of his sermon to his secretary, who finishes late in the afternoon. He would like to find more time, but two full days are devoted to hospital and other sick calls, at least three days to pastoral counseling, and one to the religious school. It is a seven-day, seven-night treadmill. Only during the summer months at Cape Cod, or occasionally abroad, does he enjoy the luxury of thinking.

Sharing intimacies with hundreds, perhaps thousands, of people over the years, his own intimates are few. No one but his wife calls him by his first name.

Rabbi Beth has some regrets about congregants who have slipped away because of his failure to deal with current social issues, as the nearby Conservative rabbi does. He realizes that his pulpit messages are confined to ethical generalities. But he finds immense gratification in the knowledge that his temple members love him as part of their family circle, and that he is held in high regard by the Christian community.

Like his fighting colleague, Rabbi Aleph, in the East, Rabbi Beth would not exchange his profession for any other.

Rabbi Gimel, the ecumenical rabbi

"I feel more like a stockholder in a large corporation than a member of a congregation. It's not like the old days when you knew everyone at services by name."

The complainant was a veteran member of Dr. Gimel's temple, whose 1,700 families are served by a senior rabbi, an associate rabbi, and an assistant rabbi. The complaint was not aired in the presence of the senior rabbi, for he is seldom accessible to the congregant. A private secretary, whose earlier training was obviously in the office of some outstanding celebrity, maintains an impenetrable wall between the doctor and the ordinary run of members, and an unlisted phone number makes his home a similar fortress against intrusion.

"We have two other rabbis to take care of your problems," the executive secretary explains soothingly.

Rabbi Gimel, ordained more than thirty years ago in Cincinnati, came from an Orthodox background. The quizzical expression he affected when he heard a Yiddish phrase belied the fact that his parents had rarely spoken to him in English when he was a young boy. But even before he married the daughter of a millionaire, he had cultivated the posture of the affluent. His reddish-brown hair was tinged with white, and his quip, "I've grown gray in the temple," accompanied by an eloquent stroking of his cheek with carefully manicured fingers, never failed to evoke a chuckle.

Dr. Gimel's face is familiar to the entire metropolitan community: his frequent appearances with the Methodist and Roman Catholic bishops on three television stations, and his monthly column in a leading newspaper, accompanied by a picture of him in doctoral garb (two honorary degrees), assure his place in the city's power structure.

Dr. Gimel's congregants talk glowingly about their spiritual leader's first-name friendship with the local Catholic prelate, but the Catholic leader privately refers to him as a stuffed shirt. By far his most successful endeavor is his biweekly book review. Fifteen hundred women, of all faiths and colors, swarm into his temple's auditorium in the fall and the spring. He has written on how to achieve "happiness," and he likes nothing better than to be cited as the Jewish Norman Vincent Peale.

Rabbi Gimel's religious philosophy is somewhat obscure. His series on "Judaism and Psychiatry," his Friday-night sermon-lectures on "My talk with Pope John XXIII," and "An Evening with Martin Buber" reveal only dimly the outlines of his personal creed. One must assume, however, that the unchanging character of worship services at his temple reflects the rabbi's inclination to avoid liturgical innovation.

The two other occupants of the pulpit face a number of problems. Every associate and assistant clergyman, if he assumes the mantle of preacher, is faced with an insurmountable dilemma. If he agrees with his senior on all the great issues—Zionism, civil rights, etc.—he is seen simply as a rubber stamp of his chief. If he disagrees, he is likely to be tagged a troublemaker.

Technology is also an enemy. For the senior rabbi, seated on a kind of throne to the right of the altar which reaches sixty resplendent feet toward the heavens, has two sets of volume control, one at the pulpit and one at his seat. Both men are convinced that colleague lowers the volume when they read the service and deliver their spoken message. But when Dr. Gimel walks slowly to the pulpit and raises both hands in a spine-tingling benediction, the rich Oxford-accented voice fills the temple to the forty-eighth row.

Mrs. Gimel takes little interest in temple affairs. She adorns the head table at the annual Sisterhood installation luncheon, and on occasion she is seen at the book review. The League of Women Voters and a dramatic group take up most of her free time, and she doesn't hesitate to tell the wives of board members that the temple has only one member of the family on its salary rolls. The women of the Sisterhood have long made peace with the arrangement. After all, there are two other *rebbetzins* to call on for invocations.

Classmates of Rabbi Gimel speak somewhat sadly of the young

man they knew thirty years ago. He had been fired with a passion to persuade the world that Judaism was the faith of the future. During his undergraduate days he immersed himself in Midrash, Biblical research, and medieval Jewish literature. Equipped with a first-class mind, he grappled with the intricacies of Aramaic and Hebrew grammar, and tried his hand at Arabic. But at some juncture in his career he fell victim to the intoxication of public acclaim. And after several years of hearing devoted followers proclaim, "Rabbi, you were simply wonderful," Dr. Gimel could no longer deny the judgment of humanity.

Rabbi Dalet, Southern style

Of quite another stripe is the sixty-one-year-old rabbi of a sleepy Southern community we will call Rabbi Dalet. A few years ago, Rabbi Dalet received a telephone call from the editor of his local newspaper.

"Doc, can you tell me what this European Common Market is all about?"

One of the few townspeople who subscribes to the Sunday edition of *The New York Times* and reads *Newsweek* regularly, the rabbi is considered an authority on any matter that concerns the outside world. In seminary days, he was considered a fairly good scholar. But after thirty-eight years in Southern pulpits, his Hebrew and Aramaic rusty, he has fallen into a pattern of mental relaxation.

Rabbi Dalet—more often Doctor or just plain Doc—serves forty-two families at Temple Sinai (the "Jewish church") in a city of 28,000. He also conducts worship and supervises Sunday school for fifteen Jewish families in a neighboring city. Actually his rabbinic territory measures some ten thousand square miles. A dozen towns, each with one or two Jewish families, have seen the rotund, bald, ever-smiling rabbi, and responded warmly to his pleasant "Hey, brother." Every Rotary, Kiwanis, Lions, and Exchange Club has enjoyed his easygoing wit, and many of the churches look forward to his lectures on the prophets and the ideals of Judaism.

No other clergyman has preached in as many Negro churches, or spent more of himself in finding jobs for the unemployed, bail for those who run afoul of the law.

Rabbi Dalet's region of the South has been the scene of much racial strife, and has played reluctant host to Northern visitors on missions of voter registration and education. His position on the race issue is well known to whites and Negroes alike. He was among the first to urge the mayor, an old friend, to organize a biracial committee to consider Negro grievances, and he has frequently denounced the bigots in his state. Often he drops into the newspaper office to chat with the editor about the need for a more balanced reporting of racial news.

Recent tensions have beclouded Rabbi Dalet's popularity among white citizens. Some of the townsmen wish he were less concrete in his teaching and preaching. A few members of his temple who are also members of the White Citizens' Council (they are worried about a boycott of their stores) have been approached about silencing the old doctor

But Rabbi Dalet's armor contains at least two layers. As a born Southerner, he cannot be accused of being "an outsider who doesn't understand our problems." And his long-standing popularity renders him fairly invulnerable to attack. A past president of Kiwanis, a state officeholder in the Masonic order, a former president of the Ministerial Association and of the United Fund, he mixes socially with every family in the power structure of both cities.

The three Dalet children, now grown and married, have left the South. They cannot understand why their father has never taken a pulpit in the more Jewish-populated cities of the North. But Rabbi Dalet realizes that there are imponderable rewards in a Southern congregation. The dignity of office, carrying a degree of respect largely unknown in the big cities, means a great deal to him. When he leaves a meeting without his automobile, one of his members will ask, "May I carry you home, Rabbi?" and in the ensuing days will point with pride to the seat occupied by his rabbi.

Mrs. Dalet is like the rabbi's twin sister, good-natured, generous-minded, sharing his talent for relating with people. She is an ideal homemaker and has occupied every office in the Sisterhood. After many years of Sunday-school teaching, she now aids the rabbi in training the volunteer staff.

Unlike his Northern and Western colleagues, Rabbi Dalet rarely preaches about general problems of world Jewry, Israel, or Zionism. He deals with religious and personal problems, citing Biblical authority rather than Talmudic sources. When he returns from a national meeting of rabbis, he confesses to his family that he finds little rapport with his big-city colleagues, especially with the fast-paced New Yorkers. He is more at home with his fellow Southerners, with their mode of thought and expression.

The prayer that concludes every Jewish worship service, describing man's ultimate unity, is very much a reality for the kindly Rabbi Dalet. He foresees the day when white and black men will live harmoniously with one another in the South he dearly loves.

Comment on the Profile of a Reform Rabbi

Examining the image projected by these four sketches of an American Reform rabbi, I realize the picture remains incomplete.

Some of the frustration of being an American clergyman is missing. There is much unhappiness in the rabbinate, as there is among the Christian clergy. The gap between what a rabbi expects of his fellow humans and the existential facts of life; his inability to evoke the best in his fellow man; the limits of his powers in relating Judaism to daily living—these are some of the reasons the pulpit rabbi decides he "would rather practice than preach." Recent magazine articles report an exodus of Protestant ministers from the life of the Church. I know one rabbi who, every day for the past twenty-five years, has studied the "business opportunities" column of his newspaper. He will plod on till retirement, but he will also dream on.

Limiting my portraits to four has caused me to neglect some fine rabbis. I have in mind one extremely sensitive and thoughtful leader of an Illinois congregation, a lover of Zion and the Hebrew language, a weaver of visions of a society transformed by the insights of liberal Judaism. The perfect pastor, in my judgment, is a rabbi in Ohio who introduced me, after I had preached in his pulpit, to over 400 members of his congregation, mentioning the first names of each, and the names of children in their families, and offering congratulations to those with birthdays and anniversaries that week! I have also neglected the scholar-rabbi, or the theologian, the neo-traditionalist who locks horns with Reform humanists who, in his light, have abandoned the God of Abraham. Nor have I done justice to the younger men, the fourth-generation Americans fresh from the military chaplaincy, utterly out of sympathy with the "social action" rabbis. In this view, pressure for social change must come from outside the synagogue—from groups such as the American Civil

Liberties Union or the American Jewish Congress. "A rabbi's work," they argue, "is in the realm of the spiritual. Our job is to make better Jews of our people."

Rabbi Lamed, Conservative

The Talmud tells us: "A man, no matter how tall, should lean down to listen to his wife, no matter how short." Rabbi Lamed has taken the wisdom of the sages earnestly: the *rebbetzin* has fashioned him largely in her own Jewish image.

When he was ordained at the seminary eleven years ago, he wore a *kipah* (a skullcap, or what old-fashioned Jews calls a *yarmulka*) only in acts of prayer or while reading a sacred text. Today, thanks to his wife's influence, the head covering is an integral part of his clothing.

Rabbi Lamed's congregation in Pennsylvania is completely in line with his theological tastes, not by accident, but as a result of masterly matchmaking. The Rabbinical Assembly Placement Commission, which exercises an iron control over all Conservative pulpits, is careful to place its "left-wing" men in liberal-Conservative congregations, its center-oriented men in middle-of-the-road pulpits, and "right-wing" rabbis, such as Rabbi Lamed, in synagogues close to Orthodoxy. A story has it that one chairman of a pulpit committee, whose knowledge of English was limited, approached the placement director with the plea: "Please don't send us an Orthodox-type rabbi, and we don't want one too liberal. Just send us a mediocre rabbi!"

Rabbi Lamed is close to six feet tall, with a thin ascetic face over which only an electric razor has passed. (The Leviticus injunction "thou shalt not mar the corners of thy beard" does not apply, according to rabbinic interpretation to use of an electric instrument.) Mrs. Lamed, a graduate of the seminary's Teachers' Institute, the happy hunting ground of many "rabbi-minded" girls, speaks Hebrew fluently. The two older children attend an all-day school where they have acquired a fairly extensive command of conversational Hebrew, and all three children address their parents in Hebrew.

The rabbi's duties sometimes occupy him seventeen hours a day. He attends the morning *Minyan* (7 A.M. services) every weekday; and not infrequently an evening meeting can last until midnight. Many of his congregants, especially those under the age of fifty, are not observant. Seen in a downtown restaurant at lunchtime enjoying their lobster and other forbidden sea foods, they would be hard to place as part of Rabbi Lamed's flock. With two or three exceptions, the Lameds will not dine at the homes of their synagogue members—a source of considerable resentment for those who do feel that their kitchens are kosher.

The rabbi's tenacious adherence to Orthodox practice has not always spared him criticism from "the right." A few old-timers complain about the intrusion of an English responsive reading of a single psalm at Sabbath morning services—the one departure from tradition. The late Friday-evening services also constitute to them a radical break with the past. Rabbi Lamed might well argue that they ought to join an Orthodox congregation, but he hesitates to do so. Not only is he a "disciple of Aaron"—a man of peace—but in his heart he is not certain he can justify the changes, since he accepts the same principle of *halachah* (the eternal law) that they do.

Indeed the Conservative rabbi sometimes finds himself standing "on the right" of his neighboring Orthodox colleague. His Orthodox colleague has been known to make some mild compromises, for example in the reading of the full Aramaic text of the marriage contract. Rabbi Lamed will not attend a dinner sponsored by a Jewish organization that is not kosher; the Orthodox rabbi will attend and eat a fruit salad. Rabbi Lamed will not even officiate jointly with a Reform rabbi unless he can lay down all of the ground rules.

The requirements of the pulpit are secondary for Rabbi Lamed. His congregants make modest demands on his preaching, and he measures up to those demands. His sermons are generally exhortatory, a plea for Sabbath observance, an appeal for support of the Religious School program, a request that the children be kept from public-school classes on all four days of a festival. But teaching, *Talmud Torah*, is what counts—teaching the young and old.

The Lamed circle of friendship is entirely Jewish. It is a small circle, for their hearts are back home in Brooklyn, with their parents, brothers, and sisters. Whenever there is a break in their grinding schedule, the family packs the car for a journey "home." Summers are spent, of course, with the *mishpachah* (the family clan) in their mountain resort home.

A salary of $11,000 a year, in addition to a rent-free home, may seem adequate. But were it not for Mrs. Lamed's part-time teaching salary, they would not be able to manage their finances. All-day school for the two older children involves about $1,600 in tuition (in addition to a partial scholarship), and Ramah camp for the two costs more than a thousand dollars. Books and charity amount to more then $900. After eleven years of marriage, the Lameds have yet to acquire a savings account.

The Lamed family plans to spend another five years in the United States and then settle permanently in Israel. Many seasons of summer camp, first as youngsters at a Zionist damp in the Poconos, and more recently as counselors in the Hebrew-speaking Camp Ramah, sponsored by the United Synagogue of America—the lay arm of Conservative Judaism—have profoundly affected the Lameds' thinking. To live a full, uncomplicated Jewish life, they are convinced, one must settle in Israel. They see the tensions among congregants with older children as parents plead with their high-school sons not to attend a basketball game on Friday night and students away at residence colleges waver about eating non-kosher food. The annual Christmas crisis, when the little ones are asked to sing carols or take part in nativity pageants, is part of the price Jews pay for living in a Christian world. And the Lameds feel certain that none of these problems will plague them in a land where culture and religion are integrated.

Rabbi Shin, traditionalist

The faculty of Chicago's Hebrew Theological College—at least in the 1920s—was just as Old Worldly and other-worldly as their colleagues in the East. But geography has done something to the young men who were trained in the Illinois school. Their style of speech is less redolent of parental Yiddish; their clothes somewhat less formal, in the manner of the Midwest, and their interests broad-gauged.

Rabbi Shin, a graduate of the class of 1930, was, in his Yeshivah days, like his classmates, a fervent rooter for the Chicago Cubs. The White Sox seemed to be a Gentile-type baseball team, and it was natural for Yeshivah boys to support the Cubs. Their teachers, fresh from Poland and Lithuania, could not quite grasp this alien cult of baseball. Somehow it evoked imagery of Canaanite and Amorite pagan rites. Who were these gladiators from Pittsburgh and from Cincinnati whom the Talmudic students regarded as mortal enemies? And what kind of name was that for a grown man—Babe

Ruth? Eliezer Shin, who had been enrolled as a student since he was eleven—separated from his parents in down-state Illinois so that he might receive a thorough Jewish education—knew his teachers intimately.

One day he hazarded the task of explaining the rules of baseball to his Talmud instructor. At the end of his exposition, the bearded teacher asked, "But tell me, my American young man, just one thing—is it good or bad for the Jews?"

Rabbi Shin has the build of an athlete. Now his physical exertions are limited to golf, but he enjoyed baseball and football in his high-school days, and he still walks with a vigorous gait. There were times when his home was located more than two miles from his synagogue and, of course, he does not use a vehicle either on Sabbaths or holy days. The five-mile walk did not bother him, even in inclement weather. Perhaps that explains the rabbi's ruddy complexion and the robust quality of his handsome face.

Today, as rabbi of an Orthodox congregation of a thousand families in a large Western city, Rabbi Shin's concerns are far from parochial. He and his wife are leaders of the Symphony Society, and have helped bring the world's finest musical artists to their city.

He serves on the board of a dozen civic enterprises. The governor appointed the Orthodox leader to the first Human Rights Commission established in the Midwest. Reform Jews point to Rabbi Shin with a proprietary pride. He has added immense dignity to the Jewish position and they are relaxed when he serves as their spokesman. Rabbi Shin states the viewpoint of the Jewish community, even when it runs counter to prevailing custom, as in the matter of Christmas celebration in the public schools, with graceful tact, and with no rancor.

Like all his traditional colleagues, no cause excites him as much as the education of children. An all-day school, called the Akiba Academy, now enrolls 150 students. But the most influential Jews in the city regard the academy as a threat to Jewish security, a persistent reminder of alien antecedents, of the eternal outsider.

Rabbi Shin's crusade on behalf of non-public school education would ordinarily infuriate the liberal Jews. Yet they cannot summon up any real animosity toward the rabbi. For his is a zeal that is moderated by good humor. There is a passion in the Orthodox leader, but it is warmth rather than heat. His sermonic addresses are for causes, not against those who do not share his views. On Rosh Hashanah, he tells the congregation why he believes that vital Judaism must be Orthodox, but he is never heard to castigate Reform and Conservative Judaism in the manner of most of his traditional colleagues.

Over the past three and a half decades Rabbi Shin often joins his liberal colleagues in presiding over a marriage ceremony. Making no demands, and always communicating the feeling of accommodation, he discovers that non-Orthodox rabbis are willing to meet him more than halfway in arranging the rites so that traditional requirements are fulfilled.

What was the happiest moment in his life? Was it the day he was invited (and declined) to become president of a distinguished Jewish seminary? The day he received an honorary doctorate from a Christian college? The time his congregation offered him a year's round-the-world travel for his entire family?

Rabbi Shin recalls, most of all, the excitement of the recent moment when he installed their son as a rabbi in a Chicago suburban synagogue. Six generations of rabbinic leadership, having its origins in a small Lithuanian town which has ceased to exist, went into the making of the twenty-five-year-old spiritual head of the modest Illinois congregation.

The miracle of Israel's persistence was climaxed in the simple event of a rabbi's induction. Back in 1940, the year the young Rabbi Shin was born, the ground on which the suburban synagogue stood was a cornfield, many miles from the nearest Jewish inhabitant. A realistic prognosis for an embattled Jewry would have offered the slimmest hope for the survival of Orthodox Judaism. Among the Jewish communities which Hitler was in the process of liquidating, tiny Lithuania contained more academies of higher learning than were to be found in all of America, Great Britain, and Western Europe combined. In 1965, the younger Rabbi Shin guided the destiny of a community of more than a thousand souls, which accepted the discipline of classic Orthodoxy, observed the dietary laws, made use of a *mikvah,* offered all-day school training to hundreds of children, and sent youngsters to nearby Hebrew Theological College—now gone suburban like the rest of Chicago Jewry.

How prodigious, then, was the satisfaction of the senior Rabbi Shin as he invoked a blessing on his son. When he began his preach-

ing, he found the words about Israel's eternity somewhat hollow—
and almost mocking. Today, a vital Orthodox congregation of young
Jewish doctors, attorneys, scientists, and business executives, led by
a bright-eyed rabbi in the fresh first-year bloom of ministry, offers
assurance that the tradition will long endure.

Rabbi Zadik, Torah-true rabbi

"I am convinced that any rabbi who cooperates with or is associated in any way with the sinful RCA is undermining the very
foundations of Torah-true Judaism."

The "sinful RCA" is not a reference to the colossus of communication whose president is David Sarnoff. The object of attack is the
Rabbinical Council of America, the largest body of Orthodox rabbis
in the world. Rabbi Zadik, forty-year-old leader of a large traditional congregation in Brooklyn, sounds the alarm for his Orthodox
associates.

To maintain the pristine purity of the historic faith, immutable
from Sinai to the present and for all time to come, those who hold
the burden of leadership must see in every divergence—whether it
calls itself Conservative, Liberal, Reconstructionist, Reform—a lethal threat to the true Judaism. There can be only one authentic
Judaism—that ordained by God through revelation—and those who
preach other versions, or collaborate with them, are worse than
sinners. They are what is called in the vocabulary of the ancient ex-
communicators—the most egregious of transgressors—"causers of
sin by others."

"I am especially worried," Rabbi Zadik wrote in his synagogue
bulletin, "over the effect which our joint efforts with the non-
Orthodox membership in the New York Board of Rabbis has on un-
informed Jews who will come to regard Reform and Jewish ministers as much rabbis as their Orthodox counterparts. Who knows
how many good Jews have wandered unsuspectingly into the Conservative camp because of this ignorance?"

After receiving his semichah (ordination) from a Brooklyn yeshivah (seminary) Rabbi Zadik has held three pulpits, all in the New
York area. He has been offered pulpits in the Midwest and in California, but he cannot conceive of living too far from the heart of
Jewish traditionalism. Even Israel has little allure. He has many ties
to Jerusalem institutions, but "his heart is in the West" where he can

live up to the most minute demands of the Torah. God be thanked, America boasts of more than three hundred seminaries, having supplanted Poland and Lithuania as the mainspring of Judaism.

Rabbi Zadik wears a beard, a small black one, a rather recent acquisition. Like many American-born rabbis, he felt no compunction about being clean-shaven. But his early use of a depilatory has left its mark on his complexion, and he has followed a fairly common new trend among the more pious to let his beard grow.

A traditional rabbi's walk has a character of its own. Custom dictates that a Jew walk humbly in the presence of the Lord, as the prophet Micah taught. A bold, energetic gait is unseemly, and lowered eyes a sign of dignified thoughtfulness. In his younger days, Rabbi Zadik enjoyed some sports. He played softball in high-school days, and was a fairly proficient tennis player while studying for the rabbinate. One day, during his student years, while walking down a wide Brooklyn avenue wearing tennis sneakers and carrying a racket, he spied his *Rosh Yeshivah* (seminary dean). He hurriedly crossed the mall in order to avoid being seen. Sports were a frivolity unbecoming a child of God. After that traumatic event, the *yeshivah* student gradually drifted away from all athletic activity, and, except for a subdued attraction to the Brooklyn Dodgers (completely dissipated when they moved West), the rabbi's world had no room for sports.

Echoes of a Lower East Side New York childhood can be heard in the rabbi's speech. He hasn't what one might call an accent, but the timbre of his voice and the cadence of his words betray a non-Anglo-Saxon origin. Generously interspersed in his speech are Yiddish phrases, Talmudic allusions, Biblical references, literal translations from the vocabulary of the ghetto. "He first came home today" (the Yiddish word for *first* and *just* are the same); "strictly from hunger," "I'm eating dairy," "give me a for instance" fall from his tongue as though they were part of universal Americanese.

Rabbi Zadik's absorbing interests are focused on three enthusiasms: a flourishing all-day school, in which more than a thousand children are enrolled; the observance of *Kashruth* (he has roundly condemned Jewish hospitals that don't have an all-kosher kitchen), and what the rabbis call family purity. He takes pride in the growing number of observers who use the *mikvah* and notes with satisfaction that hundreds of them have been erected in the past decade in Brooklyn alone. Rabbi Zadik unhesitatingly blames the burgeoning amount of divorce, parent-child conflict, juvenile delinquency on American Jewry's abandonment of this pillar of traditional piety—the separation of the sexes during periods of female "uncleanness." In the catalogue of sins listed during a Yom Kippur sermon, inevitably, the Jew's falling away from family purity leads all the rest.

Rabbi Zadik has few regrets about the choice of his career. "He who pursues honor finds that honor flees from him," said the ancient rabbis. He appreciates the high regard in which the community holds him. On occasion, his congregants wish he would not push them so hard, but they admire his persistence, and assume that "it's the rabbi's job to hold us in line."

The Orthodox leader once declared "we have very little in common with Reform rabbis in faith and in practice." He might also have had in mind the level of rabbinic compensation. For the officers of his congregation, in determining Rabbi Zadik's salary, take two things for granted. A rabbi must not reap the benefits of "this world" in abundance lest it jeopardize his "other-worldly" rewards. And, practically, they know that their rabbi serves a larger congregation of the unaffiliated, and he retains fees obtained at weddings, funerals, and unveilings.

CHAPTER 14

Yiddish Devotees

"Yiddish is a language of refuge, intimacy, domesticity, and affection. It has a warm religious colouring, but it is free from cant."

MAURICE SAMUEL

Most Americans categorize Jews with other religions—Catholic, Protestant, Methodist, Lutheran, etc. The American Council for Judaism considers its major objective to be the reinforcement of that notion. But even they, I suspect, are uneasily aware of the fact that it isn't quite so—and so are the countless non-Jews who number among their friends and acquaintances Jews with no attachments whatsoever to synagogue life. Have these nonpracticing nonbelievers ceased to be Jews? When an Israeli cabinet minister declares that he hasn't been inside a house of worship since his Bar Mitzvah, how is it that he still considers himself Jewish?

There are hundreds of thousands of American Jews, in scores of American cities, who are neither Orthodox, Reform, Conservative, nor Reconstructionist but who would take a back seat to no one in their claim to Jewishness: "We are part of the *Yiddishe Volk*, the Jewish people. We are at least as Jewish as devout members of a temple. At least our language is Jewish, and, what is more important, our *steiger* is Jewish."

I discovered that the word *steiger* looms large in the vocabulary of the Yiddishist world. *Steiger* means life style—the particular way of doing things, of looking at life. This attitude is not a matter of Jewish religious law, handed down from Sinai. An anthropologist would simply call it culture pattern. Much of this tradition has its roots in religious practice of the past. When one of the giants of the Yiddish world, Leibush Lehrer, died, all the mourners wore a head covering. Not out of a sense of piety; but only because it's a Jewish *steiger*. At a wedding of the Yiddishists it would be in bad taste to sing "O Promise Me"; proper *steiger* would demand a Yiddish folk song. Secularists though they are, the Yiddishists would look upon the highly individualistic recitation, even mumbling, of Hebrew prayers as suitably Jewish, and the responsive reading of psalms in English as too "churchy."

Jewish secularists use a rabbi for weddings, but not for funerals. But a Yiddish funeral is Jewish nonetheless. Leibush Lehrer left detailed instructions about his funeral service: readings from Yiddish poetry, certain Yiddish songs, the recitation of one of the Psalms—in Yiddish.

The *El Moleh*—the traditional memorial prayer—was chanted, but it was not a cantor who chanted it.

The Yiddishist defines Judaism as the expression of Jewish creativity, reflected in the ethical spirit, the intellectual experience and folkways of the Jewish people.

I visited a Yiddishist summer camp on a Friday evening. Although there are no religious services, Friday night is still Sabbath, and many of the elements of Sabbath are present: white clothes, special Sabbath readings, the recitation of a Yiddish poem about the Sabbath readings.

In the Yiddishist summer camps for children (a chain of such camps were founded by Leibush Lehrer), there are usually some kind of Sabbath services, and smoking is prohibited on Friday night and Saturday. Sabbath morning is generally devoted to a lecture on the spirit of the Sabbath.

Irving Howe and Eliezer Greenberg, in their *Treasury of Yiddish Stories,* comment sadly that "America has now become the last stronghold of Yiddish culture; her poets and novelists work without impediment and sometimes, alas, without an audience." The only sturdy vestige of Yiddish literature in the United States, the authors note, is in poetry—poets such as Glatstein and H. Leivich and Moishe Halpern still have their readers.

Most Yiddish prose deals with the past—in Eastern Europe, and in the shadow of the Nazi holocaust. Novelists of the caliber of Isaac Bashevis Singer, and Sholem Asch before him, reach out to larger audiences through gifted translators. *The Nazarene* and *The Apostle* made the best-seller list, thanks in part to the skillful rendition of Maurice Samuel. A reader of Singer's story, *Gimpel the Fool,* may note with surprise the fact that it was translated by Saul Bellow.

The seminaries that prepare teachers for the Yiddishist schools stress the social, communal, and intellectual aspects of Jewish tradition. The Jewish Teachers' Seminary, on Park Avenue in New York City, is trilingual. Teachers are trained in Yiddish, Hebrew, and English. The seminary is supported by the three groups, despite their different traditions, who have pooled their resources in recent years as interest in the Yiddish language has ebbed in the United States.

The *Farband*—the Labor Zionists—is probably the strongest of the three. The schools operated by the *Farband* are called Volkshule—people's schools. Their emphasis is socialistic, along the lines of the British Labour party or Israel's dominant political group, Mapai.

The Workmen's Circle—or *Arbeiter Ring*—also socialist in orientation, was born of a non-Zionist, if not anti-Zionist, philosophy. The dream of mankind was a universal brotherhood of man, sans nationalism and sans capitalism. Yiddish was the language in which they preached the doctrine of One World.

The third group, named after the most famous of Yiddish writers, Sholom Aleichem, established what they called Folk Institutes, that are neither Zionist nor socialist, but concentrate on the cultural aspects of Judaism. (A Communist-oriented group, the Jewish People's Fraternal Order, also at one time commanded a small following. In cities such as Detroit they attempted to become involved in the Jewish Community Council, but after some debate Jewish community leaders read them out of the fold.)

The summer camp has loomed large as an instrument for evoking the loyalty of the young. For years, the Labor Zionists beckoned youth to Camp Kinderweld, and the Workmen's Circle operated several attractive camps under the name of Kinderring. The Sholom Aleichem movement called its summer places *Boiberick*—the little Russian *shtetl* that was featured in many Sholom Aleichem stories

Camp Hemshekh, in the northern Catskills, serves for the most part the children of Nazi concentration camps. The name itself is an affirmation of faith: "We will continue." In a visit to Camp

Hemshekh I was told that parents of the campers stemmed from eighteen different countries. The director informed me that more than 40 per cent of the youngsters came from working-class homes, 18 per cent from white-collar families, and 24 per cent had parents who were professional. A few were attending a *yeshivah*.

Ideology is strong. The doctrine of the camp is grounded in the philosophy of Dr. Simon Dubnow, a Lithuanian Jewish historian who was liquidated by the Nazis. Dubnow had established a "party," the *Volkspartei*, whose central theme was the mission of Israel to bring the message of freedom to the world.

The camp's spiritual roots are in an organization called the Jewish Labor Bund, a movement that declares that the problem of anti-Semitism can be eliminated only by "the improvement of the lot of humanity as a whole. . . . Instead of fear and suspicion of non-Jews inculcated by Zionism, the Bund offers faith in mankind and in the brotherhood of all men."

The heart of the program is in the principle of self-government. The youngsters are encouraged to organize their own affairs as much as possible. (A model United Nations General Assembly was a big event of the season.)

I noted little Jewish chauvinism. Unlike other camps which fly their own flag alongside the Stars and Stripes, only the American flag was flown. True, the names of the teams for the model Olympic games were those of two Jewish writers, Peretz and Mendele, but the camp had evidently also celebrated the Shakespeare centennial, for a large poster with the Bard's portrait still stood, with the tender words, "Happy Birthday, Willie!"

At the same time, the children observed Warsaw Ghetto Day, and a huge tableau had been erected, based on the theme of John Hersey's *The Wall*. A mosaic of scenes from the ghetto had brought out the artistic talents of the youngsters.

Another day had been set aside as Soviet Jewry Day, to express concern at the suppression of Jewish rights in Russia.

The cottages bore names and pictures of Jewish cultural heroes: famous names such as Anne Frank, and unfamiliar names such as Dr. Yanush Korchak, a Warsaw doctor who gave up a lucrative medical practice to take care of Polish orphans, and who died with his wards in the ghetto.

The children are taught to celebrate four festivals, Passover,

Succoth (Tabernacles), Shevuot (Pentecost), and Hanukah, but they are holidays of the Jewish people rather than of a faith. Announcements over the public-address system are made in Yiddish, and most of the discussions are in Yiddish, too. But there is no question that English is the native language, and the most their leaders can hope for is to have the children truly bilingual.

An Old-World atmosphere pervaded the camp. In every classroom and in the library pictures of Yiddish authors adorned the walls. They were old plates of an age gone by, and I wondered how the children were able to relate to them.

What will happen in the next generation, when even the oldest Jews would have no personal reminiscences of Poland and Russia?

Dr. Gershon Winer, dean of the Jewish Teachers' Seminary, admitted that there is a wide gap between the generations. The young people are outright secularists, without even a nostalgic feeling for religious traditions.

The characteristic *steiger* of the Old Guard is also evaporating. Their style is out of fashion: the exaggerated politeness, the formalism which they attached to refinement. A generation ago, Yiddishists invariably referred to one another, and addressed one another, as *Chaver*. Technically a *chaver* is a comrade (shades of the Second International). But our English word, colleague, comes closer and even more accurately, a dear colleague. First names are taboo in the world of the old Yiddishists. Even after forty years of intimate association they address one another as Chaver Bernstein or Chaver Pincus. A program invariably lists their first names by initial only—a standard practice in Russia, birthplace of so many Jewish immigrants. Among the cultural elite, speech and writing tend to be florid and self-conscious—a Yiddish version of Disraeli or Macaulay. Their choice of words is assiduously rich, with many literary allusions. A few words are never used when a few paragraphs will do as well.

But pure, literary Yiddish is rare today. The *Jewish Hour* on New York's radio station WEVD (named in honor of Eugene V. Debs) offers a mixture of Yiddish and English in a potpourri that blanches the hair of the purists.

At the Jewish Teachers' Seminary I was shown a Yiddish typewriter used in a course on Yiddish typing and stenography. I was surprised to learn that it is very rare. There are many Hebrew typewriters whose carriages move from right to left and which use the same letters, but the letters occur with different frequency in the two languages, and the typewriter companies produce, or used to produce, two kinds of machines. Even in the world of technology, everything has its *steiger*.

A Future for Yiddish?

Where is Yiddish spoken today in the United States? Fraternal orders, or *landsmanschaften*, whose members were born in Eastern Europe, still conduct their meetings in the ancestral tongue. I participated in a meeting in which I was one of ten speakers, and the only one who spoke in English. The audience understood me without difficulty, but they appreciated an occasional Yiddish phrase. Among the working masses—and there are thousands still in the needle trades—Yiddish is frequently heard. Labor leaders such as David Dubinsky, Jacob Potofsky, Louis Stulberg, and most of the "old-timers" militantly espouse the cause of Yiddish culture and language and allocate funds liberally to a variety of cultural causes.

Emanuel Muravchik, the director of the Jewish Labor Committee, questions the value of some of the efforts expended on behalf of a language which has failed to make much dent in the lives of younger American Jews including those brought up in the Yiddish schools. He has recently challenged some of his leaders: "You have spent millions in perpetuating the language, have graduated a hundred thousand from your schools in the past generation. Can you produce ten who read the language regularly?"

But he conceded that young Jews nurtured in the tradition retained at least an emotional attachment to the language.

And there is clearly a resurgence of Yiddish schools. One project announced by a New York university called for a projected expenditure of more than a million dollars for the next seven years to publish a ten-volume dictionary. According to Joseph Landis, there are approximately one hundred and eighty thousand Yiddish words, of which more than twelve thousand have their genesis in Hebrew. And according to *Webster's Unabridged Dictionary,* at least five hundred Yiddish words have insinuated themselves into the American language.

Actually, Yiddish has two distinct faces in America. It is both a vehicle for piety and the instrument of secularism. For the Orthodox, especially the ultra-Orthodox, Yiddish has donned the mantle of sanctity. A four-year-old Hasidic child in Brooklyn learns the language as his mother tongue. His first introduction into the Bible comes with the words, "God created the heavens and the earth," translated into Yiddish. One authority reported that more than half the sermons preached in traditional New York congregations are in Yiddish—an estimate I would regard as exaggerated. Yet even such well-integrated American-born rabbis as Rabbi Israel Miller of the Bronx, who is most at home in the English language, will offer a commentary on the Bible every Saturday afternoon, in Yiddish, for older members of his congregation.

At the same time, Yiddish has provided much of the dynamism of Jewish anticlericalism in the Old World and the new. But neither the virulent antiecclesiastical Yiddish writings of the past, nor the benign outpourings of Peretz and Sholom Aleichem, were ever directed toward a break with the Jewish *people* or with Jewishness. The revolt was against the organized faith, never against the Jewish life way and traditions.

Manheim Shapiro has observed that for many Jews secular messianism and humanism, including a kind of aesthetic liberalism, became a substitute for religion. One of the major philosophers of the Yiddish labor movement, Prof. Israel Knox, reflects this spirit in his writings. Writing on "The Jewish Labor Movement in America" he declares:

> To be a Jew is to be the bearer of a great hope—the Messianic expectancy. To be a Jew is to believe with all your heart and all your soul and all your mind that this Messianic hope has not yet been fulfilled, but somehow it will be fulfilled. You can be a Jew whether you *daven* [pray] or not, whether you observe the dietary laws or not, but you cannot be a Jew unless you cherish and hold on with all your might to the Messianic expectancy.

Dr. Knox argues that such institutions as the Workmen's Circle, the United Hebrew Trades, and the International Ladies' Garment Workers' Union came into being, not simply to seek shorter hours and higher wages, but "out of a sense of dignity and human worth. That is why it was easier to organize the Jewish immigrants than it was the Poles or Italians."

Some of the Jewish labor unions, Dr. Knox noted, held their charter meetings in synagogue vestry rooms. Today, however, they are far removed from tradition. A David Dubinsky will call a luncheon meeting on Yom Kippur, and his Jewish lieutenants will not hesitate to attend, even on the holy fast day.

Whether impulse to perpetuate the language of the Eastern European Jew be pietistic or secularistic, those devoted to this cause are convinced that Yiddish is one of the keys to Jewish survival. Often called "the mirror of a people," it carries a built-in value system: to use its vocabulary meaningfully is to share in the ideas and ideals attached to its words and phrases.

But Yiddish is not only a language of ideals and ethics. Prof. A. A. Roback, one of the foremost authorities on the history of Yiddish, has detailed some of the earthy quality of the language: "Yiddish possesses a rich inventory of oaths, imprecations, and vulgarisms. . . . The imagination, ingenuity, and incision of Yiddish curses . . . almost come within the realm of art."

To speak in Yiddish is also to accept a certain realm of discourse without regard to the subject of health. "When a Jew will brag about his health," wrote Professor Roback, "you may be sure he is assimilated." For such bragging is not only considered in poor taste, but an invitation to disaster. Hovering over the language is an element of superstition deeply ingrained in Jewish folkways. One does not tempt the fates. You may not believe in "the evil eye," but why take chances? Thus, the proper response to "How are you? is not "fine," or "first-rate," but the more noncommittal "not bad," or "can't complain."

Unhappily, as Prof. Robert Alter of Columbia pointed out in a brilliant *Commentary* article (September, 1965), most American readers have only been exposed to the seamy side of Yiddishism. The so-called American Jewish literary renaissance is the product largely of American writers of Jewish descent who "utilize Jewish experience of which they are largely ignorant." What emerges, according to Dr. Alter, is a "sentimental myth" about Jews that has little relation to reality:

> The typical involvement in Jewish culture consists of an acquaintance with *gefülte* fish and crass Bar Mitzvahs, a degree of familiarity with overstuffed Jewish matriarchs, and a mastery of several Yiddish synonyms for the male organ.

Israel Knox voices the fear that the decline of the Jewish labor movement and a concomitant ebbing away of Yiddish literacy may result in a complete break with the past, "a failure to understand and acknowledge an indebtedness to a preceding generation." Jewish youth, he observes, shares with its contemporaries a discontinuity with history. Describing the college students he has known, Dr. Knox writes, "The impression is frequently compelling that their parents were born in a desert, in a no-man's land, or still worse, that they have no parents at all, except for payment of tuition."

Which is cause and which effect we cannot easily determine. But the alienation of native-born Jews from the language which gave a distinctive quality and life style to their grandparents seems, to many observers, to spell *mene, mene* for American Jewry.

Two of the nation's most gifted writers on Jewish themes, however—Maurice Samuel and Isaac Bashevis Singer—are not yet ready to accept the handwriting on the wall.

Isaac Bashevis Singer, "Last of the Yiddish Novelists"

"One thing I don't understand, Mr. Singer. When you talk, you're full of optimism about human nature. But your writings are uniformly pessimistic. Gimpel the Fool is always put upon, and most of the people he has to do with are malicious. *The Slave* is a tender love story, but it's peopled by bigots, and so are the characters in your short stories."

Isaac Bashevis Singer laughed as he sipped his coffee. There was a pixie quality in his smile.

"Every one of us is a split personality. We believe in contradictions."

Singer, who writes only in Yiddish (all of his widely read books are translated into English), has reached millions of Americans who had never heard of a *shtetl*, a *pogromtchick*, or a *Beth Din*. Describing the Polish-Jewish writer as "one of the most remarkable American authors who has ever lived," Kenneth Rexroth added, "If he were the only one left writing Yiddish, it would still be an important literary language."

As the waiter in the upper-Broadway dairy restaurant added more coffee to Isaac Singer's cup, I plied him with questions about some of his characters.

"Is Gimpel the Fool a symbolic figure for the Jew? And how do you account for his remarkable success?"

"The Jew never gives up. He feels there is always a way out, whatever the handicap or stumbling block. He has much to succeed for: a home, sons, daughters. Above all, he has a will to succeed—a success complex. The tailor's son wants to be a Harvard professor."

Singer looked up at our impatient waiter whose squirming made it evident that he would like the table cleared.

"Why is our waiter so obnoxious, like everyone else who works in a Jewish restaurant? Because he thinks he is really good enough to be prime minister of Israel, and here he is waiting on us. He's going to see that his children get the kind of education so that they won't wait on tables."

"In what way do you think we Jews are distinctive?"

"Both men and women are home sitters. Only among Jews do the men keep the home fires burning. We're not hunters or adventurers."

I told Singer that one of my pet peeves was the lack of privacy among our people. A few years ago, at the same restaurant, I had discussed a serious problem with a couple about to terminate their engagement. We spoke in low voices, but apparantly not low enough. A man who had been sitting at the next table walked up to us, check in hand, and asked, "Do you want my advice?"

"I agree with you. Once, at the Writers' Club, I was involved in a confidential conversation when another writer walked up to our table. I told him that what we were discussing was secret. His response was, 'With me, I have no secrets.' "

Isaac Bashevis Singer came to the United States in 1935 from Poland. The son and grandson of rabbis, he, too, had studied for the rabbinate, and his stories are saturated with religious references. But the mood he creates is mystical, and his world filled with an incredible assortment of devils, angels, and their farfetched offspring. And suffusing it all is an indescribable deep compassion.

Singer's genius is that of an artist who evokes interest with a few strokes of the brush. Read the opening paragraph of a story and you can't wait to find out how the plot unfolds. His conversation, too, is sprinkled with illustrative anecdotes.

I mentioned some of the research I had come upon concerning the attitudes of Jews as medical patients.

"Of course, what you say is true. Do you know the story of a Jew who came to the office of a famous professor? His arm had turned black. The specialist said, 'All you have to do is wash it with soap and water.'

" 'That's what our family doctor said,' the patient explained, 'but I wanted to hear it from a professor.' "

We spoke about his work.

"Writing involves painful effort, but the reader mustn't be aware of this. Otherwise the writing appears contrived. I love writing. The conscious is not very creative. Most of the mind's creativity stems from the unconscious or subconscious."

Singer's library shelves are lined with books about psychic phenomena, extrasensory perception.

"You need a sixth sense. Do you know why lovers quarrel? Because lovers use telepathy. Their quarrels are not based on words spoken, but on thoughts unspoken. I'm a firm believer in the hereafter. There are too many unsolved problems here on earth. We couldn't call God a just God if there were not a later reckoning. Marxism has misled the world in this respect. We here on earth are part of a larger drama, begun before birth and continuing in the hereafter."

He warmed up to his favorite theme, sexual love.

"Character is revealed most in the man-woman relationship. That is why a novel must be a love story. A man can build ten skyscrapers superbly and still be a henpecked husband. That is the key to his character: what he really is in relation to his wife."

Isaac Bashevis Singer has a lusty lack of inhibition, characteristic of the creative writer. Speaking from the pulpit of the Larchmont Temple, he startled the Sabbath-eve congregation with the following story:

"Once there was a Jew who asked his rabbi, 'Why are we forbidden to eat matzoth for a whole month before Passover?'

" 'Because we are supposed to whet our appetites for unleavened bread. Eating matzoth on Passover is like spending the night with one's bride the night before the wedding.'

" 'Ah,' protested the congregant. 'I've tried them both, and there's no comparison.' "

We flitted from one subject to another—from the currently popular James Michener's *The Source* ("He's not a great artist, but he certainly is a *best-sellernick*"), to his notions about America ("We are good industrially, but saturated with misery").

The author of *The Spinoza of Market Street* is very much at home in the streets of the New World. "For the first time in history," he explained, "the Jewish spirit and the non-Jewish spirit have met in an ideal kinship. Americans love the good life; we Jews like the abundant life. Of course a Gentile's idea of a vacation is to 'rough it.' A Jew wants the comfort of both country and city. That's why he built Miami Beach, which has everything—including a Wall Street ticker tape."

Singer is frequently questioned about writing in Yiddish, the language of the past. He explains, tongue in cheek, that he likes to write ghost stories, and "nothing fits a ghost better than a dying language. The deader the language, the more alive the ghost. Ghosts love Yiddish, and as far as I know they all speak it. I also believe in resurrection. I am sure Yiddish-speaking corpses will arise from their graves one day, and their first question will be: 'Is there any new book in Yiddish to read?'

"This is not the time to snub the dying. The way things are going in the world today, we may all soon belong to the dying. The chances of Yiddish are no worse than those of Russian or English.

"Besides," he concludes, "Yiddish is the only language I know really well . . . my mother language. Those who are near to us are never dead."

We returned to the inconsistency of his philosophy.

"You must admit that most of your writings reflect a gloomy estimate of mankind."

"I do have a low estimate of humanity as a whole. But when it comes to one single human being, my heart goes out to him. He seems so helpless, so willing to try hard. How can I have a dim view of *one* human being?"

Isaac Bashevis Singer is still somewhat startled by the worldwide acceptance of his creative work. *The Slave* has been translated into more than a dozen languages, and publishers are competing for as much as he can produce in the distant future. He wishes other Yiddish writers could find an audience, especially his idol, the poet Aaron Zeitlin. Unhappily, this is not the age of poetry.

Speaking about success, I wondered if the artist was able to esteem his own work—especially a Jewish artist whose Biblical tradition enjoined him from "worshiping the work of his hands."

"When you admire your own work, you admire God, Who kindled

it within you. What a man does is really not done by him, but by the powers that move in his spirit."

A number of critics have attacked Singer for his preoccupation with the bizarre, the benighted, and the offbeat faces of ghetto Jewry. Why not write about the sweet, kind, and noble side of Jewish living? I don't agree. The endearing quality of the world's most gifted Yiddish writer is his persistent faith in his people and its values. Singer's favorite character in his autobiography is Asher the Dairyman. One line in his portrait, it seems to me, is self-descriptive:

"His entire life was one great yes."

CHAPTER 15

American Jews and the Christian Church

"Half of the people in the world
Love the other half;
Half of the people of the world
Hate the other half.
And where is my place
Between the halves . . . ?"

YEHUDA AMIHAI (MODERN ISRAEL POET)

The American Jew's experience with the Christian has been full of contradictions. Christianity has displayed two faces to the children of the mother faith—friendship for the descendants of "God's chosen people" and hostility toward those stubborn souls who persist in rejecting Christ.

Hundreds of Jewish congregations have known Christian charity. In most communities, an announcement of a temple building project is met with great enthusiasm by the churches—often, indeed, with more relish than that with which one Protestant denomination has been known to welcome the establishment of another competing Protestant group. Individual clergymen, Roman Catholic, Greek Orthodox, and Protestant have extended helping hands, urged the lifting of zoning restrictions, and issued welcoming statements to the press. Even financial assistance is frequently forthcoming—especially when it is apparent that a small number of Jews are extending themselves to establish a Jewish house of worship. Many temples in Mississippi, South Carolina, and other Southern states could never have been built without Christian aid and benefaction.

Interfaith friendship has sometimes been welded in the crucible of fire. A congregation that suffers any kind of natural disaster usually finds a temporary home in a matter of hours as guests of another faith. Christian and Jewish congregations have served both as hosts and as guests in days of crisis and during periods of building construction.

Such interfaith cooperation is more evident in the United States, perhaps, than in any other country. Rabbis and ministers often become fast friends, and many a Protestant clergyman will confide to his rabbinic colleague: "I feel closer to you than to any of my colleagues in the ministerial association. We seem to have a lot more in common."

Not long ago a Protestant candidate for a distinguished pulpit asked a rabbi friend to write a letter of recommendation. It was the rabbi's letter, members of the church congregation later confided, that most impressed the pulpit committee.

Religion, as Will Herberg observed, is almost an object of religion in America. Despite sectarian tensions and deep-rooted, often bitter institutional rivalries, most Americans apparently believe that subscribing to some religion is better than having no religion at all. The result has been the emergence of a widely accepted interfaith civility—a spirit of live and help live among America's many churches and synagogues.

The fact remains, however, that Jews are concentrated in the large urban areas. There are thousands of small American communities whose residents have never met a Jew.

A letter I recently received from a girl in Forest City, North Carolina, is typical of mail I receive from Kansas, North Dakota, New Mexico, and a number of other states:

> My name is Jean H———. My eleventh-grade American History class has been studying the various religions. We have had ministers from the various religions come to speak to us. Because of the closeness of our community, we find ourselves lacking in Jews and therefore couldn't get a rabbi. We're mostly Methodists and Baptists with a few Presbyterians mixed in. We don't even have any Catholics.
>
> Anyway, I read your book *What Is a Jew?* . . . I like reading about Jews but I could never understand why everybody is always picking on them. I liked your book and no longer consider a synagogue a place of mystery. I always wondered what went on in them and now I think I know.

Christian ambivalence toward the Jew shines through such letters. To the devout, Jews are God's anointed, a holy people. But a Jewish neighbor is something else again. A Sunday-school teacher in Colorado Springs sees in the Jew a portion of a divine mystery, but he's not at all sure he wants him sharing a locker at the Kissing Camels Country Club, or buying one of the houses in the new development. The puzzled youngster who wrote me had good reason to feel confused by the anti-Jewish animus she sensed. If a Christian dislike of Jews is the reason for rejection of the true faith, why is there no comparable hostility against fellow Gentiles who are alienated from the church? And what explains the apparent correlation between Christian fervor and Christian anti-Jewish sentiment?

For many religious Christians there would seem to be a kinship between feelings of the holy and feelings of taboo. Visitors to Spain often remarked about the pervasive Jewish presence which clings to that country as a kind of mystical reminiscence. Monuments of the Jewish past are enshrined, but there is much uneasiness about a Jewish spiritual present.

Many a Christian preacher, teacher, and editorialist has found himself equally puzzled by the inconsistency within the church family. A religion of love obviously cannot breed hatred. Yet it has. A faith fashioned by Jews—and for Jews—cannot logically be anti-Jewish. Yet centuries of history have underscored the equation: The stronger the Christianity, the deeper has been its hatred of the Jew.

In the past decade, enlightened Christian leadership has accepted the challenge inherent in this equation. Two massive studies, the first sponsored by the Yale Divinity School, in cooperation with the American Jewish Committee, and the second by the University of California under a grant by the Anti-Defamation League, analyzed the effects of religious teachings on interfaith attitudes. A similar survey was conducted by Catholic scholars at St. Louis University.

The Yale study, with which I was associated, was reported by Dr. Bernhard Olson, director of the survey, in a comprehensive volume entitled *Faith and Prejudice*. A second book, by Prof. Charles Glock and Rodney Stark, entitled *Christian Beliefs and Anti-Semitism*, summarized the findings of the California investigations.

The Yale and the California studies, and the St. Louis University survey as well, concerned themselves primarily with the Sunday-school textbooks and lesson materials used by more than thirty million Protestant children and more than five million Catholic parochial-school students. Did these lessons, written to evoke loyalty and commitment to one faith, deliberately or unconsciously denigrate other religions in the process? Does the impressionable child exposed to negative teachings about other faiths tend to develop hostile attitudes toward the followers of those religions?

The Yale study, unlike that of the University of California, was designed largely as a self-study and had the support and help of much of the religious community. Dr. Olson involved the leading Protestant editors and lesson writers in every step of his investigation, and they helped develop the criteria by which their own publications were examined. The failure of the California study to elicit the participation of Protestant leaders in the study process was, I think, an important shortcoming. Self-indictment is much more palatable than an accusing finger which stamps one as a bigot.

Many Christians argue that the American church cannot be blamed for anti-Jewish prejudice. A Catholic monsignor, addressing a temple Men's Club, insisted that in the Bronx neighborhood where he had grown up—a community that was half Jewish and half Irish—he had never neard anyone refer to Jews as Christ killers.

Some years ago, in a discussion with two Jesuit priests, I cited some derogatory references to Jews in church literature. Both insisted they had never heard a disparaging remark about Jews. Somehow, I was reminded of the prize fighter who returned to his corner, round after round, groggy with pummeling, only to hear his trainer assure him, "Don't worry, he hasn't laid a glove on you." The weary boxer finally sighed, "Then you'd better keep an eye on that blasted referee, because somebody's beating the daylights out of me."

The truth is that many American Jews *do* have childhood memories of being taunted as "Christ killers" by parochial-school youngsters, and that not infrequently the Catholic youths expressed their zeal for their Lord by beating up those Jewish boys who happened by their school or street.

My Jesuit friends argued that I was drawing the wrong inferences. It was not the Catholic in the youngster that promoted bias, they said, but other influences which the church had been unable to overcome. The church school, they pointed out, teaches that anti-Semitism is a sin against God. But, just as religion is not always successful in eradicating other kinds of immorality, so it cannot wholly combat the baggage of bigotry which the Irish and the Poles and others brought over from the old country.

I'm afraid I find this an oversimplification. Enlightened prelates notwithstanding, there has been much subtle and not-so-subtle anti-Jewish overtone in Catholic teachings in the New World as well as the Old. The really marked change has come about only in the past decade or less. Few Jews today would deny that the spirit of American Roman Catholicism in the 1960s, as expressed by such spokesmen as Richard Cardinal Cushing and Francis Cardinal Spellman —and especially by such prelates as Bishop John Wright of Pittsburgh—is warmly ecumenical.

For many American Jews, Catholic means Irish, for in New York, Boston, and a number of other big cities these two groups were most frequently thrown together. There are many paradoxes in Irish-Jewish relations in the United States. Although most Jews are distinctly cool toward the Catholic *Church*—group memories persist over the centuries—there are strong bonds of shared social and political experiences between Jews and Catholics.

"I always feel at home in Jewish circles," Monsignor Francis Lally, editor of the Boston *Pilot*, the archdiocesan paper, told me. "You have a feeling that you are welcome. In the first place, we shared neighborhood experiences, the tribulations of immigrant status. And the Jews and the Irish in Boston, especially, share a *joie de vivre* in contrast to Yankee austerity. We love fun. We are outgoing and sociable by nature. We Irish are the only Nordics with that temperament, but, like the Jews, we are given a lot to introspection as well. And of course Cardinal Cushing has done a great deal to bring Jews and Catholics closer together."

The Monsignor admitted that religious groups in Boston tended to wall themselves in separate enclaves. Newton was a Jewish enclave, and its New High School was commonly referred to as "Jew High School," and Wayland was a Roman Catholic ghetto.

Realtors, following a line of least resistance, often created religious ghettoes. Yet, despite geographical isolation, the tensions of ten years ago are gone. Editor Lally was certain that some of the old battles, such as the adoption issue (In 1955, Boston was torn by interreligious strife over the adoption of a Catholic child by a Jewish couple, Mr. and Mrs. Melvin Ellis. A State Supreme Judicial Court decision, in favor of the natural mother, caused the Ellises to flee to Florida in order to retain custody of their adopted child.) and the controversy over religion in the schools, could not be repeated in Boston today. Lines of communication are so much better, and the magic word "dialogue" is an antidote to interreligious friction.

Yet Catholic-Jewish rapport still involves many subtleties. Such sensitive subjects as planned parenthood, censorship, "softness" or "hysteria" about communism continue to evoke a considerable degree of tension.

Sometimes an increased familiarity brings surprises of its own. Most Catholics have a tremendous admiration for Jewish family life, and generally assume that all Jews are deeply religious. They are often disappointed when they meet Jews who are not only irreligious, but quite ignorant of the elementary facts about Judaism.

There is an awe of rabbis among many Catholics which does not seem to exist in their feelings about Protestant clergymen. I remember the Irish motorcycle policeman who pulled up beside my car, gruff and angry because I had missed a stop sign. As he read my driver's license, his mood changed from severity to deference. "Please be careful, Rabbi. You not only might hurt someone, you might get hurt yourself."

At no time since the Middle Ages have events in Rome kindled such emotion among Jews as the Vatican Council discussion which took place from 1963 to 1965 in preparation for its official *Declaration on the Relations of the Church to the Non-Christian Religions,* promulgated on October 28, 1965.

American Jews were far from unanimous concerning the merits of the Declaration. Rabbi Joseph B. Soloveitchik, the eminent Orthodox leader, spoke for many of the traditionalists when he urged his fellow Jews to pay little attention to it. The problem of religious anti-Semitism, of assigning guilt in the Crucifixion episode, he argued, was a source of concern to Christians, not to Jews. Rabbi Soloveitchik also belittled the value of "dialogue" between Jews and Christians beyond that involving purely civic issues. Jews, he insisted, shared no common realm of theological discourse with Christianity that would render discussion fruitful.

On the other hand, Rabbi Marc Tanenbaum, of the American

Jewish Committee, discerned in the Catholic spirit of rapprochement and in the comparable approaches of the Protestant World Council of Churches a new Magna Carta for Christian-Jewish rapport.

It is hardly surprising that the debates in Rome engendered such mixed emotions among Jews. In medieval times, meetings of the church fathers often gave rise to some of the most vicious anti-Jewish pronouncements in history. It was just such conferences that were the forerunners of the infamous yellow badge, and the enforced ghettoization of Jews. Word that a council meeting in Rome was in the offing was enough to send the rabbis of the Middle Ages hurriedly to the synagogues, for fasting, prayer, and appeals for divine intercession.

During the sessions of the Vatican Council, the Jewish news coverage of the proceedings in Rome added much to the Jewish confusion about what was taking place. Although the meeting itself made no such mention, the reporters who covered the event made frequent reference to "absolving the Jews of the crime of deicide." No one wants to be *absolved* of a sin which he did not commit. Actually, the Church spoke not of absolution, but of its own misreading of history. Although, in the view of many Jews, the final language of the Vatican declaration did not adequately stress the Church's own sins, the act of inferential confession, such as emerged at St. Peter's, represented a giant step toward interreligious understanding.

Most Jews, conditioned by centuries of church-sanctioned anti-Semitism, look on Catholicism as more anti-Jewish than the Protestant religions. On the other hand, most Jewish interreligious experts acknowledge that the major bastions of discrimination against Jews in America have been Protestant in origin—the White Anglo-Saxon Protestant resistance to Jewish "newcomers."

But even these barriers are now crumbling. Middle-class status has brought Jews respectability and made Judaism fashionable. A generation ago, the religion of the peddler and the pants presser held little attraction for the non-Jewish American. But the religion of the clothing manufacturer, the surgeon, and the electronic engineer is something else again.

Prof. Richard Niebuhr's *The Social Sources of Denominationalism* has demonstrated how the religious groupings within American Protestantism were molded by socioeconomic factors. The most affluent and the best educated cluster within the Episcopalian and Presbyterian churches. In some regions, such as the South and Southwest, it is the Methodist and Baptist churches that attract the power structure. In other words, religious loyalties are very often a product of class rather than credal conviction.

The relationships between Jews and Christians are similarly influenced by noncredal factors. Forty years ago, if a Jewish salesman from a poor Brooklyn home fell in love with the daughter of a department-store owner in Richmond, Virginia, he was likely to settle in Virginia, join his father-in-law's Rotary Club, the family country club, *and* the family church. Intermarriage for the Jew in the twenties almost invariably meant that he was lost to the Presbyterians.

Today, if a Jewish neurosurgeon marries a non-Jewish nurse, his Gentile wife will, in all likelihood, move into *his* social circle and if there is religious conversion, she is very likely to join *his* temple as well.

In the past thirty years, as American Jews have moved steeply up the socioeconomic ladder, they have also become religious joiners. Synagogue affiliation has increased from 20 per cent to well over 50 per cent, and in the suburbs to 75 per cent or more.

Jews lost by default through the absence of organized religious life are now returning to the fold. In one Georgia city, the Jewish members of the Unitarian Church joined the temple as soon as it was established.

The transition from one faith to another is rarely ever direct. A Jew moves from commitment to no-faith, and then to an adopted one. Similarly, Gentiles who fall in love with Jews were generally lost to the religion of their parents before they made a decision about marriage.

Most of the available information on the effects of intermarriage is furnished by rabbis and congregational leaders. Little is known about the unaffiliated who, as a Los Angeles rabbi remarked, "don't stop to say good-by on their way out."

I would conjecture, in the absence of verifying statistics, that religious mobility has favored the Jews in the postwar years, in contrast to the prewar period, when Jews, an embattled minority, lost some of their numbers (according to one study, 19 out of 1,000) to the dominant faith. In other words, Christians who were born Jews (many of whom were born in Germany and Austria) are likely to be more than forty years old. Jews who were former Christians are, in all probability, under forty.

Like the Amish, traditional Jews resist the efforts of interested Gentiles to join the synagogue. Any young woman who has attempted to become an Orthodox Jew can testify to the stumbling blocks that have been placed in her way.

But American liberal Judaism has inducted thousands of Gentiles into the synagogue, many of them better informed and more devout than Jews born into the faith. The Central Conference of American Rabbis, at its 1957 convention, created a special committee with the authority to prepare suitable literature, conduct radio and television programs, and establish special congregational preaching missions for "those persons of Jewish and non-Jewish birth who are in accord, spiritually and intellectually, with the religious teachings of Judaism."

Formal courses leading to conversion to Judaism are found in a number of major cities. St. Paul, Minnesota, enrolls close to two hundred applicants a year. It is estimated that between two and three thousand converts find their way into Reform Judaism every year.

A Chicago layman, Ben Maccabee, a survivor of Nazi persecution, who adopted the militant name as a reaction to his experiences in Germany, has founded a Jewish Information Society of America, which sponsored a booth at the 1964 New York World's Fair. A few Conservative rabbis, notably Robert Gordis of New York and Jacob Agus of Baltimore, have also urged their fellow Jews to be zealous in promoting the teachings of Judaism. For a time it was believed that the Japanese people were searching for a faith, and excitement was kindled about the possibility of duplicating the historic conversion to Judaism of an entire people, such as took place among the Khazars of southern Russia in the eighth century.

Several years ago, when I addressed the Tokyo congregation, I met a few Japanese interested in Judaism. One young lady of nineteen attended worship regularly.

"I've met a lot of American Jews here in Japan," she explained.

"All of them were very nice. There must be something about your religion that makes people nice."

Prof. Abraham Kotsuji, a convert first to Christianity and later to Judaism, declares in his autobiography, *From Tokyo to Jerusalem,* that his conversion was self-generated. On the other hand, scholars such as Prof. Masayuki Kobayashi, a historian, have fostered an interest in Judaism as a result of exposure to American Jews. Occasionally an army chaplain has provided the spark of enthusiasm. One young man, Hiroshi Okamoto, came to Cincinnati with his vivacious wife, Kyoko, and infant son, Shemaya (named for a famed Talmudic rabbi, but not un-Japanese in sound). All three had embraced Judaism. I sat on the floor of their home at a sukiyaki dinner, which was followed by the traditional *benschen*—the grace after meals, using an Orthodox *siddur* (prayer book) while my host, sitting with crossed legs, Oriental fashion, rocked back and forth like a Hasid intoning the Hebrew prayers with a "Polish" accent.

Today the Okamotos run the Tokyo Jewish Seminar, not as an aggressive center for evangelism, but simply to teach the essence of Judaism, in the hope that others may find their way to the faith of Moses.

Born Jews—particularly those whose attachment to the faith is more a matter of condition than conviction—are astounded by the unalloyed rapture felt by some converts to Judaism. Albert Memmi, in his remarkable *Portrait of a Jew,* describes, autobiographically, his own malaise. "I do not believe I have ever rejoiced in being a Jew."

An articulate newcomer to Judaism, Margaret Ruth Jacques, expressed her joy in Jewishness to David Max Eichhorn, quoted in his recent study, *Conversions to Judaism:*

> I do not believe that any man or woman who has accepted Judaism out of a belief in its beautiful truths, out of love for its reservoir of strength and inspiration and courage to face life's problems, has ever wasted much time worrying about whether or not he has been "accepted."
>
> Judaism is the greatest gift that God has ever bestowed upon me. It is my sight, my ability to hear, my capacity to feel joy and pain, the guage by which I measure the value of every living thing. And being a Jew is its own reward . . .

because I firmly believe that the true nature of Judaism is such that the spiritual benefits of Judaism come only to him who earns and deserves them.

Despite the mild flurry about reaching out to the religiously unaffiliated and those in search of a faith, only one out of ten enrolled in courses leading to conversion do so without thought of marriage to a Jew. Now and then a young lady will offer herself as a candidate, hoping to meet a suitable Jewish mate. (In addition to the proverbial Jewish mother, there is also the proverbial Jewish husband, who is reputed to be especially considerate and attentive to his mate.)

The next decades are unlikely to produce a spectacular upsurge of "new Jews." The founder of American Reform Judaism, Dr. Isaac M. Wise, envisioned the time when the universalistic, rational appeal of modern Judaism would appeal to average Americans. And some Jews have entertained the idea that, in a "post-Christian" era, the ancient appeal of Judaism might reassert itself.

But I am mindful to the caveat of the eighteenth-century German theologian, *wie es sich Chriselt, so Judelt es sich*—when Christians are good Christians, Jews are good Jews. One might coin the thought that *wie es sich post-Christelt, so post-Judelt es sich*. Americans are likely to be attracted to the faith of Israel only in the context of general religious stirrings.

Will Herberg popularized the phrase "triple melting pot," first coined by Ruby Jo Kennedy in 1944, in referring to the essentially American quality of religious pluralism. But neither Mrs. Kennedy nor Dr. Herberg noted the tight geographical compartments into which the three faith groups are distributed. I used the term "triple ghetto" in a lecture describing this sociological fact, and Albert Vorspan and Eugene Lipman in their book, *Tale of Ten Cities*, documented the validity of the phrase.

Although neither the railroad nor its passengers view it that way, the fact is that every weekday morning a Long Island Railroad commuter train picks up its Protestant passengers at 6:42 A.M. somewhere east of Babylon, pauses at seven twenty-two to add its Jewish commuters living east of Freeport, and a half-hour later stops long enough to take on the more rested Catholics in the Valley Stream area. If the process continues, by 1984 our typical megalopolis will have three concentric circles, with the Protestants encircling the area in a hundred-mile radius, the Jews in the middle circle, the Catholics nearest the inner core.

"Real-estate agents accept as a perfectly normal part of their daily operations that Catholics will want to settle near their new suburban parochial schools, Jews around the many new institutions they have built, and Protestants in 'their neighborhoods,'" Vorspan and Lipman report.

I know of one Eastern suburban community, virtually all Protestant prior to World War II, that witnessed a flood of Jewish newcomers in the 1940s. As the Jews moved in, the Protestants headed gradually for exurbia. Some years later, the village became the headquarters for a new Catholic diocese, and Catholic parents competing for limited space in parochial schools were eager to find homes in the village. In a relatively short period, most of the Jews moved out of the village, and it became largely Roman Catholic in make-up.

Religious mobility is nationwide. San Francisco, the most religiously integrated city in the country, has experienced it, as have Boston, Baltimore, Detroit, Cleveland, Houston, and many other cities.

"Evidently," writes Prof. Albert Mayer, author of an informative survey of the Detroit Jewish community, "this process of almost constant movement is not too burdensome for it shows no sign of ceasing." Nor does it seem too much of a sacrifice to construct new centers, synagogues, and communal offices in the "Seven-Mile" area only to abandon them for the "Ten-Mile" road. Dr. Mayer details the creation of brand-new suburban ghettos in a decade's time, each having "the potential of containing a higher proportion of Jews than the central city." One extraordinary fact is the appearance of sub-ghettos: the Orthodox remaining back in the Northwest section, the Reform flocking to Huntington Woods (68 per cent Reform, 23 per cent Conservative, 0 per cent Orthodox) and Southfield blossoming into a Conservative stronghold (61 per cent Conservative, 18 per cent Reform, 11 per cent Orthodox) drawn, as Marion Sanders has vividly described in an article in *Harper's*, 1966, entitled "The Several Worlds of American Jews," by the magnetic force of the late Rabbi Morris Adler and Mrs. Adler.

Leo Pfeffer—Guardian of the "Wall of Separation"

One of the most colorful personalities in the world of Christian-Jewish relations is Leo Pfeffer, who directs the legal work of the American Jewish Congress. An expert on constitutional law, which he teaches at Long Island University, Dr. Pfeffer has participated directly in virtually every Supreme Court case dealing with church-state problems, beginning with the controversial McCollum case of 1948 which outlawed use of public-school facilities for so-called released-time classes.

For two decades, Leo Pfeffer has fought to prevent the use of public funds for any religious purpose, direct or indirect. If Pfeffer had his way, American churches and synagogues would pay taxes. They would not be permitted to receive state funds for school buses, school lunches, or textbooks, and they would not even be allowed the use of public-school facilities for after-school meetings.

Yet the scholarly legal authority, with his dark horn-rimmed glasses, sharp features, and bald head, is as familiar on the campuses of a score of Catholic universities as he is in the courtrooms of the country.

We spoke about this anomaly. Leo Pfeffer cited the philosophy expressed in his book *Creeds in Competition.* He is convinced that litigation between Jews, Protestants, and Catholics on constitutional issues does not jeopardize good relationships. On the contrary, he argues, it clears the air. If Jews and Christians disagree on the meaning of the law, what better resolution of their differences than to let the courts decide? Americans have faith, he believes, in the inherent justice of both our Constitution and its judicial interpreters.

Dr. Pfeffer pointed to the Miami case, which dealt with a number of sectarian practices that had crept into public-school classes, as an illustration that his contention is sound.

"I was very pleased by the outcome of this case, because it proved that those who predicted a rise in anti-Jewish feelings were wrong. Once the decision was rendered, we began to work together even more closely. Perhaps the greatest satisfaction in this work is to lose a case before the U.S. Supreme Court only to find it reversed ten years later by the same Court and to have *my* language quoted by the judges as the basis for reversal almost word for word. The Bible-reading case is a perfect example of that."

The American Catholic world recognizes Dr. Pfeffer as a spokesman for the Jewish community on church-state issues. They are aware that his is an "absolutist" position, an extreme one among Jews, but they respect his profound grasp of his subject as well as his genuine religious commitment. Pfeffer is, in one sense of the word, a secularist. But he's the kind who "keeps kosher," sends his children to Jewish all-day schools, worships regularly as a member of a Brooklyn Orthodox synagogue, devotes his spare hours to Biblical research, and writes articles on obscure Bible themes. His secularism consists in maintaining that the wall of separation, which the Founding Fathers of America decreed, must forever divide the state from the church (or synagogue) in a democracy. And in the view of those who oppose him as well as those who agree with him, his comprehensive 725-page volume *Church, State and Freedom* is the most definitive book ever written in the field.

Asked why such Catholic universities as Villanova, Fordham, and Notre Dame invite him back to speak, year after year, Pfeffer smiled.

"They know I'm not venal. They reject my viewpoint totally, but in this new Catholic era of reaching out into the world, they want to break through their isolation by hearing viewpoints such as mine."

Leo Pfeffer speaks in a rather high-pitched voice which gets away from him as his ideas cascade faster than his speech, especially in debate. He somehow combines an intensity of feeling that verges on the dogmatic with a completely benign tolerance of another's viewpoint.

"We dialogue with the Catholics but act with the Protestants. I have found Christian-Jewish relations are healthiest in the Northwest states. Where religion is most intense, prejudice against Jews is strongest. Often it is the German and the Irish Catholic who provide the base for it. But things change. Minneapolis, the Lutheran city, once a stronghold of anti-Semitism, is now liberal."

The many bitter—and sometimes ugly—controversies about Bible reading, prayers, Christmas carols, and a host of other practices involving religions in public education have in no way dimmed Dr. Pfeffer's vision of Jewish security in America. "I think that there is a greater ideological conflict between the Church and Americanism than there is between Judaism and the American spirit. Our ethos is much more permissive, less authoritarian. I am not at all pessimistic about the future of our faith in this country. I foresee a return, even of the intellectuals, to our tradition."

The Judaism produced by America, explains Dr. Pfeffer in the conclusion of his book, *Creeds in Competition*, is a new species of the ancient creed, the result of intimate, friendly, and competitive contact with other religious traditions.

"Judaism, too, has experienced much change in outlook and way of life as a consequence of cultural competition. Of all the groups it has adjusted itself most completely and most happily to the values of secular humanism. When one compares the Judaism of mid-twentieth-century America with the Judaism of mid-nineteenth-century Eastern Europe, one can see the radical changes effected by this alliance."

The warp of traditionalism and the woof of humanism are thus interwoven to form a novel pattern that is the raiment of the New American Jew.

Interfaith Marriage and Interfaith Homes

The price a minority group pays for living in a free society is the fear of being swallowed up in it—of losing its own identity. This is a fear that haunts American Jewry today. For ironically, *the easier it is to be a Jew, the easier it is to cease being one.*

Most Jewish community leaders are convinced that the number-one Jewish problem in Amerca is not anti-Semitism but group survival. The growth of ecumenicism in religious life is an important step in the direction of healthier intergroup understanding, but it also poses the threat that in the process of relating positively with one another each faith may be watered down, its integrity imperiled.

The half-decade of religious reconciliation, denominational mergers, pronouncements of mutual respect and rejection of interfaith bigotry has also produced a wave of uneasiness within American Jewry, at least within that segment of Jewry concerned with group survival.

A number of recent studies, particularly those of Albert I. Gordon and Alfred Jospe, point up the readiness of many young Jews to marry out of their faith. But no single monograph stirred as much uneasiness within the organized Jewish community as Erich Rosenthal's "Studies of Jewish Intermarriage in the United States," published in the *American Jewish Year Book* in 1963. For Dr. Rosenthal depicted a dark cloud on the horizon: the smaller Jewish communities, he indicated, could not long survive the growing trend toward intermarriage. And, if it was true that there was less resistance to intermarriage with succeeding generations, how long could American Jewry maintain its group identity, even in the great cities?

Conferences, on both local and national levels, were convened to examine the "perils of intermarriage." In December, 1964, New York's Federation of Jewish Philanthropies, under the leadership of its Commission on Synagogue Relations, brought together a group of outstanding social scientists and religious leaders to consider "Intermarriage and the Future of the American Jew."

Yet the actual effects of intermarriage on Jewish survival are not at all uniform.

Regional differences regarding the effects of intermarriage on the integrity of the group are striking. A New Orleans study in the 1950s indicated that more than 90 per cent of Jews who had intermarried were native born. Dual-faith families seem to have few ties to Judaism in the suburban areas of San Francisco, yet Rabbi Martin Ryback of Downey, California, informed me that he has had many converts to Judaism—most of them Catholic—as a result of intermarriage. A 1964 study of the Jews in Providence, Rhode Island, reported that "a majority of the children born of mixed marriages are actually being raised as Jews."

In Camden, New Jersey, a survey found a substantial difference between those interfaith families where the non-Jewish partner had converted to Judaism and where no conversion had taken place. In the first instance, all the children were being reared as Jews. Where there had been no conversion, only one-third of the families retained their Jewish identity.

All three branches of Judaism have been formally opposed to marriages across faith lines unless the non-Jewish partner is brought into the faith before the ceremony. The past decade, however, has seen a startling shift among Reform rabbis. As late as the 1950s it was difficult to find a Reform rabbi who would participate in such a wedding. Today, perhaps one out of three would officiate, as long as the couple undertook to rear their children in the Jewish faith.

Debating the issue at the 1962 convention of the Central Conference of American Rabbis, one Reform leader, Prof. Eugene Mihaly, argued that a rabbi's refusal was tantamount to a "harsh rejection which alienates the couple" and loses both to the cause of Judaism. But Rabbi Joseph Klein, of Worcester, Massachusetts, echoing the sentiments of the majority, countered that those rabbis who have not insisted on prior conversion "have opened the floodgates for mixed marriage on a large scale."

Probably the most experienced rabbi in the world in the field of conversion relating to marriage is Rabbi William Kramer, of Los Angeles, religious mentor to such famous converts as Elizabeth Taylor and Sammy Davis, Jr. Rabbi Kramer through the years has prepared thousands of Californians for entrance into the Jewish faith. I interviewed him at the University of Judaism on Sunset Boulevard, where he teaches. Only in Hollywood could a Reform rabbi sport such a full beard. But it suited his mirthful countenance. He punctuated every observation with a humorous anecdote.

"A Jewish boy who 'wants out' marries a Gentile girl who 'wants in.' You never go from one religion to another, but from no religion to religion. A Gentile girl is attracted to Jewishness. The attraction often comes because the girl (or boy) already has a conviction which, she discovers, is part of an already existing value system. The appeal of Judaism is its simplicity, its practically, its humanism. And that is what they are searching for. The typical convert is from a broken home. Judaism is family-centered. She is not only marrying the boy, but also adopting a set of parents. Eighty per cent of my converts used to be Protestants. Now, half are Catholic. In the past, most of the girls were from a social class above that of the Jewish boy. Now it is reversed."

Rabbi Jack Segal, who served a congregation in Portland, Oregon, made a recent analysis of the attitudes of Jews in his city toward intermarriage. In response to the question, "Would you be opposed to intermarriage if there was no conversion?" 81 per cent of the Orthodox, 50 per cent of the Conservative, and 34.7 per cent of the Reform answered in the affirmative. Dr. Segal discovered a great disparity between Reform and Orthodox attitudes toward the advisability of intermarriage even when conversion was involved. Only one of six Reform Jews saw any objection in such a marriage while two out of three Orthodox Jews were not convinced that the Gentile partner fully appreciated all the requirements entailed in embracing the faith of Israel.

My own feeling is that the danger of Jewish disappearance through intermarriage is still remote. The positive "environmental factors of conservation," to use Dr. Mordecai M. Kaplan's phrase, are still operative. Despite Christianity's avowed hospitality to Jewish candidates, it is less than aggressive in its evangelistic effort. Many church leaders share the view of Dr. Reinhold Niebuhr that it is somehow a breach of good taste to seek adherents from the mother faith. Some Christian theologians even argue that the persistence of the Jewish religion is a theological necessity, as an eternal witness.

Another "factor for conservation" is the fact that Jews find it hard to get lost in the church. A Centerville, Texas, church member whose great-grandparents were Jewish finds himself introduced as "our Jewish member." I have met a number of Protestant ministers who have referred beamingly to "the large number of Jewish members in our congregation." A friend of mine, walking down the main street of a Louisiana city, saw a long, solemn funeral cortege led by a number of nuns and the Archbishop of New Orleans.

"Who died?" he asked a passer-by.

"A Jew by the name of Frank."

"Why all these Catholic dignitaries?"

"Oh, Frank came to our town forty years ago, made a lot of money, and joined the Catholic Church. He was a very generous man, and gave generously to help build our parochial schools and hospital. That's why the Archbishop came to pay his respects."

Small-town Judaism, as we shall see elsewhere, may well disappear by the century's end. But suburban ghettos, less geographic than psychological, will persist.

Young American Jews are not unmindful of the elements that make for group preservation. A study by David Caplovitz and Harry Levy, "Interreligious Dating among College Students," pointed up an ambivalence among Jewish undergraduates. While 96 per cent disagreed with the statement "Intermarriage is morally wrong," a considerable proportion also rejected the statement "If two people are in love, nothing else matters." Nor were they unaware of the barriers to success in marriages between the faiths. In answer to the question "Do you foresee difficulties in interfaith marriages?" 87 per cent predicted difficulties in Catholic-Jewish matches, and 48 per cent for marriages between Protestants and Jews.

All the gloomy predictions notwithstanding, I am convinced that in the coming decades the winds of ecumenism are not likely to dislodge Judaism from its firm pedestal as one of the major religious forces in the nation.

The elder statesman of Jewish sociology, Prof. Horace M. Kallen, participating in a panel discussion of Jewish group life in the free plural society argued: "The prevailing Jewish view that intermarriage tends to take Jews away from Jewishness is traceable to the historical fact that membership in the Jewish community has been a disability. Once this disability has been removed, and being Jewish is regarded as equal with being anything else, intermarriage will come to be viewed as marriage *into* the Jewish community rather than out of it; and it will be found that those who marry into the Jewish community become more Judaistic than born Jews."

Christian and Jew in the Last Third of the Century

Prof. Moshe Davis of the Hebrew University in Jerusalem has devoted the past ten years to an examination of Jewish life throughout the world, and has specialized in the task of informing the Israelis about American Jewish life. Dr. Davis' *Jewish Communities in Perspective* is not too sanguine about the diminution of anti-Jewish prejudice in the United States: "I agree with those who interpret modern anti-Semitism as a continuing war against the Jews precisely because they are the living legacy and transmitters of a tradition which Western traditions and ideologies condemned or repudiated. Until mankind is prepared to accept the Jewish tradition and its legitimate role within civilization as a permanent fact, hatred and violence will continue to be manifest."

Viewed in this light, the conflict between the faiths is more than a "Christian-Jewish tragedy," to use the phrase of Prof. H. Conrad Moehlman—a falling out among kindred spirits. Rather it is a kind of religious *kultur-kampf*, destined to endure until a mutual recognition pact is signed.

Possibly Dr. Davis is wrong. America may become not so much a crucible in which the two religious traditions blend, but an amiable host that will keep both traditions alive, interacting but separate. The host culture may be the one delineated in Harvey Cox's *The Secular City*, for in a sense America is one of the few great nations which is neither truly religious nor antireligious.

Harvey Cox writes:

We need as our theological starting-point a Jesus who is neither the ecclesiastical nor the existentialist Jesus, but the Jewish Jesus. . . . Christians, as Kristar Stendahl rightly says, are really only honorary Jews. . . . All Jesus does for Israel's hope is to universalize it, to make it available even to us goyim.

The American masses, as Glock and Stark show in *Christian Beliefs and Anti-Semitism,* may be conservative theologically, accepting the reality of the devil, literal belief in Biblical miracles and other forms of orthodoxy, but that other America—the intellectuals, the ever-mushrooming academic community, the opinion makers, the business executives, as well as the younger clergy of all faiths— seems to be prepared to re-examine the ancient dogmas if not to reject them outright.

To my mind the "opening of the windows" in contemporary Roman Catholicism was an invitation to a hazardous journey. The sharp blades which cut through the weeds of credal bigotry are likely to cut down some cherished doctrines as well. The National Council of Catholic Men and the National Council of Catholic Women recently published a *Grass Roots Ecumenism Kit.* In describing the "common bonds between Christianity and Judaism," the booklet states, "Christians worship a Jew. And Jesus was not some lukewarm or deracinated Jew. . . . He certainly was squarely in the center of the Jewish tradition of prophets."

Attendances at Jewish religious functions are often eye openers to Christians, Catholics and Protestants alike. Some return again and again. They are moved by the ancient rites, affected by the informality (one young Catholic child remarked, after attending a service at my temple: "Everyone kisses everyone else after the benediction" —a reference to family exchange as they greet one another, "Good Sabbath") and touched by such emotional family occasions as the Bar Mitzvah.

American Christendom has come to learn a great deal about the Judaic tradition. During the past fifteen years the Jewish Theological Seminary has brought together thousands of clergymen, scientists, editors, jurists, statesmen, and industrialists to examine the relation of religion to science and to American culture. And in scores of small colleges which have virtually no Jewish enrollment, students have flocked to hear expositions of Judaism by spokesmen of the Jewish Chautauqua Society, sponsored by the Reform National Federation of Temple Brotherhoods.

Many of the national magazines have featured articles on the fundamentals of the Jewish faith. Radio programs such as *The Eternal Light* and *The Message of Israel* and comparable television presentations have brought synagogue and home rituals into millions of non-Jewish living rooms.

All of this is not likely to stimulate a mass flight toward Judaism, but it has normalized the *fact* of Judaism, and underscored its living reality. Whether or not Christians view themselves as "honorary Jews," America in the latter part of our century is far less likely to regard good Jews as "honorary Christians."

Jewish Community Relations

American Jewry's organized life is as initial conscious as Washington's. Visit the communal headquarters in any major city—590 Vermont Avenue in Los Angeles, the Fellowship House in Philadelphia, or 72 Franklin Street, facing the archdiocesan offices in Boston—and you will hear a language spoken that is neither Yiddish nor English. The air is filled with initials—CRC, NCRAC, AJC, ADL, and the like.

"To refer a problem to the CRC" is to summon a meeting of the local Community Relations Council, a democratically formed body of organization representatives which handles all matters relating to the general community.

I spent a day with the professional and lay leaders of the Philadelphia Jewish Community Relations Council and watched them in operation. Its director, Jules Cohen, has a well-earned national reputation in this special field. Since coming to the Friendly City from the NCRAC (the National Community Relations Advisory Council, the coordinating body of all the CRC's in New York), Cohen has enlivened the activities of Philadelphia Jewry.

The imaginative and energetic director decided that the local Jewish community was not doing enough to help alleviate the religious and social disabilities of fellow Jews in the Soviet Union.

To rectify this neglect, the CRC organized a Committee on the Local Implications of Anti-Semitism Overseas. Jules Cohen proposed to the Philadelphia Council, whose board alone consists of eighty men and women from thirty-four organizations, that a picketing campaign be organized, climaxed by a rally at Independence Square. In a three-week period, more than one thousand individuals from forty city-wide organizations and synagogues traveled to Washington in chartered busses to picket the Soviet Embassy, meeting with State Department officials and with senators and congressmen from Pennsylvania to express their concern.

The key to success in social action is to involve groups other than one's own. The Rev. Henry H. Nichols, a past president of the Council of Churches, offered a prayer outside the Fellowship House before joining rabbis and congregational leaders in one of the Washington-bound buses. A police escort at designated points not only expedited the trip, but helped attract public attention to the journey of protest.

Anatoli Myshkov, secretary of the Russian Embassy, who greeted the delegation headed by Rabbi Theodore Gordon, was, despite his courteous demeanor, obviously angry with the Jews of Philadelphia. Why had they libeled his country? Why had they called a rally at Independence Square? He implied that the Philadelphians were busybodies looking for some program activity. Nevertheless, their point had apparently struck home, for he knew the exact number of pickets, the contents of each sign, and the active involvement of non-Jews.

The "Save Soviet Jewry" program was only one of dozens of campaigns on behalf of various human-rights issues in which Philadelphia has engaged.

The approach is generally the same—not to make the problem a Jewish one, but to look for the natural allies in the community: Who besides us, in Philadelphia, is interested in our cause (civil rights, desegregation, elimination of sectarian practices in the schools, Arab propaganda in the United States, interfaith dialogue)? Whom can we count on to do the necessary spadework? What are the goals we want to achieve?

Volunteer workers are readily available. A postcard, mailed out to the eighty members of the board, will usually bring fifty-five out to a meeting.

Once a project is launched, volunteers will reach people they work with in other areas—planned parenthood, voter education, and soon Mr. A. will get in touch with Senator Scott. Mr. B. will contact the Bar Association. Others will solicit the support of church groups, labor, the college world.

When riots broke out in the Negro community in 1964, the CRC called a series of meetings to work out techniques of easing the tensions. Like many other organizations created to defend Jewish rights, much of CRC's efforts today are directed toward race problems, for Jews have come to the inescapable conclusion that their rights are inextricably tied to the democratic rights of all minorities.

There were times when Jewish agencies which concerned themselves with the race issue, such as the American Jewish Committee and the Anti-Defamation League, were criticized for meddling in outside affairs, on the theory that their sole job was to defend Jews. But today that debate is over and little is heard on this score, even from Jews in the South.

The last third of the twentieth century has been ushered in with the sweet, if not saccharine, tone of interreligious harmony. Every day is St. Valentine's Day; every week, Brotherhood Week. The respectability that once was attached to religious discrimination has long since evaporated: it simply isn't nice, any more, to make disparaging remarks about someone's faith, and even the private social club—last citadel of snobbish bigotry—is no longer altogether secure against the inroads of equalitarian democracy.

The Roman Catholic Church, ever the master of the pageant, captured the world's stage by renouncing religious intolerance with a blare of ecumenical trumpets. And the same theme has been played, if more quietly, by Protestant church leaders and educators in hundreds of conferences, workshops, and seminars the world over.

The dialogue—Martin Buber's gift to the twentieth century—dominates the interfaith arena. Not to be confused with the "duologue" (which has been described as two people talking oblivious to one another), dialogue between Christian and Jew, between Protestant and Catholic, demands a maximum acceptance of the other man's premises: Say not what you can do for *my* faith, but what I can do for *yours*.

Not many decades ago, Indiana was a hotbed of the Ku Klux Klan. Catholics were regarded with suspicion by Protestants, but both were united in their frequent, almost automatic rebuffs of the

Jews. These were the relationships as the authors of *Middletown* saw them in 1937. But by 1960, a great deal had changed; and at St. Mary of the Woods College, not far from Terre Haute, the Catholic Sisters of Providence initiated a series of interfaith student dialogues. Rabbi Bernard Cohen, a lecturer in history, and Rev. Paul Jones, a Methodist, are among eight non-Catholic clergy who have served on the panel during the past six years.

Residents of Niles Township, outside Chicago, Illinois, shared in a "service of worship and witness" to celebrate the high-school graduations of both schools of the class of 1966. The Interfaith Baccalaureate Service was held at the St. John Brebeuf Catholic Church. A Lutheran choir sang, Rabbi Sidney Jacobs offered a prayer of invocation, Cantor Lionel Godow chanted a passage from the Talmud, and a Presbyterian minister read a litany.

Only since the final pronouncement of the Vatican Council in 1965 have acts of worship been performed by non-Catholics under Roman Catholic auspices. I was invited to offer a benediction at the installation of a new president at Fairfield University, Connecticut, a Catholic institution. Although I had frequently *addressed* such audiences in the past, I had never before been called on to *bless* them, and the experience was equally unfamiliar to the students, professors, and visiting presidents who were gathered for the occasion. As I reached my closing sentence, they automatically raised their right hands for the sign of the Trinity, lowering them with some puzzlement when I failed to follow through with the expected ritual.

A historic and profound evolution has taken place. Twenty years ago, the very word "interfaith" was abandoned in deference to Roman Catholic sensibilities. For believers in *the* faith could not properly speak of *inter*faith. But the new Vatican vocabulary includes frank talk about a "deference to *other* faiths," and even such Oriental religious traditions as Buddhism and Hinduism, which had been categorized as pagan until 1965, are now ranked among the praiseworthy religions.

No longer is Judaism to be studied only through the filter of Catholic editorship. Across the border, in Canada, the Paulist Fathers have published a basic textbook on Judaism for use in Catholic parochial schools, written at their request by Rabbi Stuart Rosenberg of Toronto.

None can doubt the sincerity of the new effort to translate religious pluralism from an unhappy fact of life into a happy goal. On the Pakistan–Indian border, religion continues to be a *casus belli;* in Nicosia, Cyprus, the barricades erected under the banner of clashing faiths still stand. The Holy Land itself, with its infinite variety of churches, offers the vivid proof that nothing can launch a battle faster than the firing of a dogma. But America may nevertheless provide a crucial testing ground for the novel hypothesis that all men are God's children.

CHAPTER 16

Longing for Zion

"When I see the name of Israel high in print
The fences crumble in my flesh; I sink
Deep in a Western chair and rest my soul.
I look the stranger clear to the blue depths
Of his unclouded eye. I say my name
Aloud for the first time unconsciously."

KARL SHAPIRO

Zionism—the Jewish dream of a national homeland in Palestine—is directly related to the pain of being Jewish. American Jewry, which has felt little of this anguish, has not produced the breed of Zionism familiar in other parts of the world.

Fifty communities were represented at the Fifth Assembly of the World Jewish Congress which met in Brussels in August, 1966. Included were Jews from India, New Zealand, Hungary, Rumania, the Congo, South Africa, Uruguay, and virtually all of the larger countries of the Western world. Dr. Nahum Goldmann, president of a dozen international Jewish bodies who presided over the meetings in the Palais des Congrès, is a household name among the Jews of Liverpool, Bucharest, and Johannesburg. But it is unlikely that more than one American Jew in twenty can tell who he is.

There is a story—perhaps apocryphal—about the chief rabbi of one of the Iron Curtain countries who attended the previous World Jewish Congress Assembly in Stockholm in 1959. He had inadvertently been caught up in a guided tour of the Royal Palace of Sweden, and was unable to follow the remarks of the guide, who spoke in Swedish and English. When the group entered the Throne Room of the palace, the rabbi turned to one of the delegates, pointed to the throne, and asked,

"When is Dr. Goldmann scheduled to speak?"

Dr. Goldmann, president of the World Jewish Congress and the World Zionist Congress, is a citizen of the United States, although it was rumored some years ago that he was about to abandon his citizenship in order to assume a top government post in Israel. He is often looked upon as something of a Crown Prince of World Jewry, but American Jews, by and large, neither follow his leadership nor accept his major thesis that Jews the world over are united by *national* ties.

Dr. Goldmann voiced his concern about America in his presidential address at Brussels:

"The larger and the wealthier Jewish communities become, the more dynamic they are in their own community life, the more they develop tendencies to become independent of other parts of the Jewish people . . . and to forget the great truth of our history, that no isolated Jewish community, however strong and numerous it was, has ever survived, but disappeared once it had lost its consciousness as being part of the Jewish people."

As I listened to the various speakers at the Brussels Assembly and spoke with the delegates the difference in the psychology and outlook between American Jews and their coreligionists elsewhere was sharply highlighted. A Louisville Jew, unlike his Liverpool coreligionist, has little interest in events affecting Jews abroad except in terms of their *needs*. Virtually every Liverpool Jewish family subscribes to the *London Jewish Chronicle,* and follows with great interest the arrival of a new rabbi at the synagogue in Christ Church, New Zealand, or the dedication of a Jewish facility in Surinam. The oneness of the Jewish people is a simple fact of life for the Liverpool Jew. The Jew of Louisville is disturbed by threats against the security of Jews in Argentina and by the suppression of religious freedom for Soviet Jewry, but he is relatively unconcerned about the ongoing life of his fellow Jews in the far-flung corners of the world.

There are discernible differences in outlook even between the Jews of Canada and those of the United States. At a Canadian Jewish Congress banquet in Montreal which I attended—at which Canada's Prime Minister was one of the honored guests—the chairman, Samuel Bronfman, followed the traditional toast "To the Queen" with a second toast: "Ladies and gentlemen, the President of Israel!"

No one, so far as I could see, questioned the propriety of the second toast. It is offered at every Jewish banquet in Canada, and the many government officials present apparently see no incongruity in the fact that citizens of Canada recognize, even subtly, a special attachment to another country. Yet, no such toast would be proposed at the annual banquet of the American Jewish Congress. Indeed, a toast to the head of any other nation would be deemed most inappropriate, except perhaps at an Anglo-American Union dinner, or a banquet specifically marking Irish or Israeli independence.

The average American Jew wishes Israel well. He can be counted upon to support it financially and to defend the legitimacy of its aspirations. But he does not consider himself a Zionist. Membership in Zionist organizations is probably only a fifth of what it was in the 1940s. Leadership is largely in the hands of Jews who were not born in the United States.

I discussed the unique character of the American Jewish community with Philip Bernstein, executive director of the powerful Council of Jewish Federations and Welfare Funds. Dr. Bernstein, who has been a perceptive leader in Jewish life for more than thirty years, agreed that official Zionist organizations have lost their hold over American Jews. But he cautioned me not to underestimate the extent to which American Jews have moved toward a feeling of peoplehood. The sense of relationship with the rest of the Jews of the world which binds together Jewish communities in other lands, he declared, is just beginning to take shape here. "Organized Jewish communal life is new in America—really little more than thirty years old. European Jewries have been communally oriented for centuries. It is just beginning to take form in the United States."

I asked him how he would define this spirit. He quoted a definition proposed by Prof. Moshe Davis, of the Hebrew University: "It is a sense of interdependence of independent Jewish communities."

Dr. Bernstein also warned against judging American Jewry by what one sees in New York. "We should not be misled by numbers. New York is unorganized. The *organized* Jewish community of America consists of scores of 'smaller' communities—Cleveland, Detroit, Baltimore, Los Angeles, St. Louis, Philadelphia, and so on. This spirit of interdependence is already evident in these cities. And they are beginning to relate to the rest of world Jewry, not merely in terms of 'What can we do for you?' but rather 'What can we learn from each other?' "

Despite the waning of Zionist influence, there is no doubt that

American Jewry is staunchly pro-Israel. A Roper poll taken in 1945 indicated that 80.1 per cent of American Jews were in favor of establishing Palestine as a Jewish state, and only 10.5 per cent were opposed. The outpouring of financial support for the reborn state, in 1948, was one miracle among many that made a viable Israel possible. One hundred and seventy million dollars was contributed in one year—seventeen times the total raised in the entire decade of the twenties. In the same year, a quarter of a million American Jews enrolled in the Zionist Organization of America, and more than 20,000 leading non-Jews became members of the American Palestine Committee. Both houses of Congress have passed resolutions on behalf of the Zionist principle, and supporting resolutions and manifestos were adopted by many of this country's leading labor and professional associations. In April, 1966, the steelworkers of America sponsored a dinner at which more than $900,000 worth of Israel bonds were bought by labor and management in an industry that has few Jews!

Those who read history through conspiratorial eyes, including a few in government circles, whisper charges of a pro-Israel political lobby, past and present. The simple truth is that American Jews entertain a warm sympathy for Israel. The events of the past two decades have probably diminished the opposition considerably. Enthusiasm for Israel, like support for the Irish Free State, is a normal part of life for a "nation of immigrants."

In a 1959 survey of a large Southern community, one of the questions asked was, "Should we raise money for Israel?" Eighty-nine per cent of the respondents were in favor; only 8 per cent expressed disapproval. "Should we belong to a Zionist group?" The approvals fell to 45 per cent and the disapprovals rose to 50 per cent. And only 4 per cent favored the idea of American Jews becoming citizens of Israel.

There is a whimsical definition of American Zionism as "one Jew giving money to send a second Jew to Palestine." Indeed, the number of immigrants from Israel to the New World is considerably greater than the number who leave this county for Zion. Yet, the two Jewries are intimately linked in dozens of vital ways.

Hundreds of thousands of American Jews journey to the land of Israel, stake out claims in its economic life, attend its universities, dispatch their children to work on its land for a period of time. All three religious branches have established deep roots in the new state: seminarians receive credit for a year's undergraduate study, return again for postgraduate work. Dr. Nelson Glueck, the arch-aeologist-theologian, regards himself as a son of both America and Israel, and spends half a year in each country. Uneasiness about "dual loyalty"—a favorite bugaboo of the American Council for Judaism in the 1950s—has virtually evaporated.

The Zionist spirit persists most vigorously among Jews born in Eastern Europe. Arthur Hertzberg, the most scholarly of American Zionist historians, recalls in his *Zionist Idea* that in the early part of the twentieth century "The bulk of the growing Zionist body in the West, and especially in America, were not true Westerners. They were, as Chaim Weizmann remarked, East Europeans, kneaded from the same dough as himself, who brought their Zionist emotions with them as they joined the stream of migration."

Today, their ties to Israel follow political lines that seem rather alien to the American born. Like their European and Latin-American counterparts, their loyalties are channeled along party lines— the political parties of Israel. They are Labor Zionists, with firm ties to the dominant Mapai party in Israel; Revisionists, who sympathize with the militantly conservative Herut group; Religious Zionists, who support the hegemony of the Chief Rabbinate in Jerusalem; or followers of Mapam, the left-wing Socialists.

The ever-diminishing Zionist Organization of America considers itself linked with the General Zionist party, consisting largely of Israel's business and professional community. The largest American Zionist group is Hadassah, the Women's Zionist Organization, which seeks the difficult role of neutrality in the internal affairs of Israel. Its 300,000 members regard themselves as a service organization, concentrating on the medical welfare of the new state. But its leadership finds it no easy task to steer clear of the pulls and pushes of Israel's political maelstrom. A decision by the cabinet in Jerusalem to grant retroactive pay to hospital employees, for example, means that Hadassah must either raise additional funds to meet the increased cost of running its hospitals and clinics in Israel or cut back the services these facilities supply. Thus, there is frequent contact between Hadassah's leadership and Israel's officialdom.

Each year, more than a thousand young Americans spend a few months or a year in the Holy Land under the sponsorship of the

Jewish Agency for Israel. A major objective of the program is to encourage the young people to settle in Israel, but few take the ultimate leap. Most of them do, however, become lifelong devotees of the new state, and continue some association with it.

By far the strongest link between the Jews of Israel and America is cultural. The American Jewish academic and scientific community, which numbers many tens of thousands, feels a strong sense of rapport with the Israeli intellectual world. The Hebrew University at Jerusalem, the Technion of Haifa (Israel's MIT), and the famed Weizmann Institute at Rehoboth all have a great attraction for American Jews. The American Friends of the Hebrew University has an enthusiastic following. Miami Jews endow a humanities building, Baltimore Jews make possible a chair in special education, a Jewish family in Columbus, Ohio, endows a chair in secondary education, a Los Angeles sponsor gives half a million dollars for a biochemistry building.

The National Council of Jewish Women, with well over 100,000 members in virtually every community in the United States, has no Zionist political orientation. Its membership is "old-line" American, and its primary interest lies in American social problems. Recently, however, these women have undertaken a major Israeli project: to help modernize the education of children from backward countries —more than half the school population in Israel—so that more of them will be encouraged to continue their secondary schooling.

The character of American Jewish religious life has been transformed by modern Israel. In most traditional synagogues, Orthodox and Conservative, a special prayer is recited each Sabbath morning for the well-being of the land of Israel.

Of the three major groups, Conservative Judaism has reacted most completely to "the Zionist idea." Its religious educational program is focused on the *Hebrew* School rather than the *Religious* School. Critics such as Rabbi Jacob Agus of Baltimore deplore what they consider the nationalist spirit in the emphasis on the Hebrew language and a curricular concentration on matters Israeli. But the stress on the spoken language of Israel, in school and especially in summer camp, has not militated against an ever-increasing accent on ritual observance and social concerns.

Reform Judaism, which in the early years of Zionism rejected the "peoplehood" concept, has shared the enthusiasm of other Jews about Israel and is especially proud of the role played by two of its most eminent rabbis, Stephen S. Wise and Abba Hillel Silver, in bringing the new state into being. Dr. Maurice N. Eisendrath, the leading spirit of contemporary American Reform Judaism, has observed that Zionism is no longer a debatable issue. "To argue Zionism is an academic exercise," he explains.

The profoundest impact of Israel on American Jewry has been among the youth, the generation which "knew not Hitler." Alienated or committed in matters religious, informed or ignorant about details of faith, young Jews in the United States feel at home in their Jewishness not only because of the position of respect and security which Jews enjoy in their own country, but also because of the heroic posture of the new Jewish state. Whatever the literary inadequacies of Leon Uris' *Exodus*, its tale of young courageous Jews forging their nation's destiny won more hearts than a thousand sermons.

Dr. Abraham G. Duker, in a revealing essay, "The Impact of Zionism on American Jewish Life," writes:

The expression of Jewish identification through Zionism has many facets. They range from the introducton of regular prayers for Israel in the Orthodox synagogues to the normalcy of the appearance of the Zionist or Israeli flags at Jewish gatherings whose participants cannot imagine that their Americanism thereby becomes suspect. They are seen in the little synagogue art shops, in the Israeli Seder plates and pictures in homes committed to Judaism, in the substitution of the *hora* (Israeli dance) for the *sher* (East European dance) at weddings and other celebrations where notions of middle-class dignity do not inhibit Jews from expressing joy in Jewish dance forms. It is to be noted in the Yeshivah youth that does not hide its *yarmulke* (skullcap) in the subways.

Despite these influences, however, the words Zionism and Zionist carry none of the emotional overtones of a generation ago for most American Jews and especially the young.

I spoke recently to a youngster who had just returned from an extended tour of Israel, where he had celebrated his Bar Mitzvah. He spoke glowingly of everything he saw there and could not wait to return again. But when I asked him to define Zionism he hesitated.

"A Zionist is one who believes in Israel as the home of the Jewish people. A Zionist believes in moving to Israel permanently."

"Are you a Zionist?"

He shook his head thoughtfully. "No, of course not!"

The attachments were there: he wanted to know the Hebrew language better, to return often to Israel for short or long visits, and to help it prosper in any way he could. But that was the full extent of his commitment—no more, no less.

The boy is an accurate reflection of American Jewry's attitude toward Israel today. There is pride, and there is love. It is a warm love. But it is distant.

Charlotte Jacobson of Hadassah

In the complex of American voluntary organizational life, women's groups, numbering many thousands, have far outstripped their male counterparts in effectiveness. The male organizations whose members' workaday lives are busy with business or the professions rely heavily on professional staff, while the women's groups enjoy their members' consistent, nearly full-time involvement. Within the American Jewish community, both religious and secular women's organizations have attracted top-leadership people of immense talent.

The Zionist women have fashioned three lively groups: Mizrachi Women, the hub of interest for the Orthodox; Pioneer Women, backbone of the Labor Zionists; and Hadassah, whose membership of more than 300,000 makes it the largest Jewish organization in the world.

Created more than sixty years ago to bring medical care to Palestine, Hadassah's program today includes medical education and service in Israel, *Youth Aliyah*—the bringing of young people, mostly from lands of persecution, to the new state, the cultivation of Jewish values through education, as well as participation in the social concerns of the United States.

Hadassah membership is drawn largely from women affiliated with synagogues and temples. Half the members are college-trained, and a quarter have gone on to graduate school. They are also well traveled: almost a quarter of them have spent a holiday abroad.

Hadassah's gifted president, Charlotte (Mrs. Mortimer) Jacobson, of New York, is an attractive blond woman with dark-brown eyes, younger looking than her fifty years, quiet-spoken, somewhat introverted, with little of the overt intensity one associates with women leaders.

Half of Mrs. Jacobson's life has been devoted to Hadassah. She was one of three sisters (their maiden name was Stone, and they were dubbed "the three pebbles") who grew up in an Orthodox Bronx family. Their paternal grandfather imbued all three girls with a love for Judaism in both its religious and national expression. Charlotte met her husband, a manufacturer of restaurant supplies, through Young Israel, an Orthodox religious group; they are both active members of the Mosholu Jewish Center, a traditional congregation.

An avid debater since her high-school days, Charlotte became president of a Hadassah chapter at twenty-eight and a member of its national board in 1948. She has held every office in the organization, finding time to serve also in local Red Cross, American Cancer Society, and Civil Defense groups.

As guardian of a budget of more than ten million dollars annually, Mrs. Jacobson commutes frequently to Europe, North Africa, and Israel, keeping tabs on the great medical center in Jerusalem and the varied communal services Hadassah makes possible in Israel and in countries from which Jews immigrate to the Holy Land. In 1956, she journeyed to Morocco to help round up Jewish youngsters for the transport ships waiting on the Mediterranean. In 1966, she led a group of American women on a tour of the Soviet Union, conferred with Israeli government officials on medical budget problems, and attended the World Jewish Congress Assembly in Brussels.

For Charlotte Jacobson the importance of Hadassah is not limited to its obligations to Jews of other lands. She is equally concerned with the impact of her organization's work on its own members. "You ask me what I think Hadassah is all about? As I see it, Hadassah entails a continuing sense of responsibility, the need to change Jewish life."

"It is part of the Hadassah creed and program," she told the national convention that elected her to the presidency, "to help preserve and strengthen Jewish life. This must be an era of Jewish renaissance. Scientific, educational, and cultural achievements have always been part of Jewish tradition; and it is part of Hadassah's special role to help modern Israel to live up to the brilliance of that tradition."

"I'm optimistic by nature," Mrs. Jacobson told me, "but I think I'm a practical optimist. I think that the best way to strengthen an organization is to give members a sense of their importance, and to encourage them to experiment."

"What would you do if you had another 10 million dollars?"

"I would spend it mostly on youth. We can reach the parents through our young people. I would build housing for American Jewish youth who come to Israel in a variety of programs, for a summer or for a year."

For tens of thousands of Jewish women, Hadassah is a passion which absorbs much of their lives. The national office on East 52nd Street, next door to CBS, is manned almost completely by volunteer executives who arrive at nine in the morning, spend an entire day in administrative work, rush out to address a meeting or to fly to Duluth, San Antonio, or Atlanta to confer with regional leaders. One Hadassah officer I know, grieving deeply for her husband whom she had lost the previous month, flew to Anchorage, Alaska, to organize a Hadassah chapter of the group. Several of the top executives are forty- or fifty-year veterans. In their late sixties or seventies, their pace does not slacken, and they cover tens of thousands of miles a year. Many are masterful orators. They and the younger women they have trained can sway large audiences as well as inspire local leaders to equal commitment.

"What about the 'Hadassah widowers and orphans,' " I asked her, "the families who wait at home while their women work long and late at Hadassah?"

Charlotte Jacobson admitted that some children are resentful. "But most of our husbands take pride in our accomplishments, and they share our aims. And many of our daughters come into Hadassah. We now have third- and fourth-generation Hadassah members and leaders. Thirty-six out of a hundred members, according to a survey, are daughters of members."

I asked her about the pro-Israel passion of Hadassahniks that sometimes borders on "Israel can do no wrong."

"We believe in tolerance and patience. It's a new country. We know its faults best. We have many problems with the government. It is Mapai, labor-controlled, and for some reason they don't regard the Ministry of Health as important. Invariably the portfolio is given to the Orthodox party, which is not sympathetic to us.

"But what we have done in Israel has interesting repercussions here in America. We have been working for years with under-privileged children in Israel, and we are proud of our role in the American Head Start programs which are very similar to the Israel model. We've also provided a model for community-health pro-grams. Not long ago, an AID official in Washington consulted with us about setting up communal health stations in South Vietnam."

We talked about Mrs. Jacobson's appearance before a congres-sional committee in support of a Hadassah request for federal funds. It was an uphill battle, according to those present, for the head of AID, Mr. William Gaud, argued that Israel had graduated from the status of an underdeveloped country, and was no longer entitled to U.S. grants.

"I have been to Israel," he declared, "and I don't think we should provide funds on a grant basis."

The quiet-spoken Mrs. Jacobson responded firmly, "Your personal views don't count here. The law says grants, not loans. So it's only a question of eligibility."

"Is this the last year you are making this request?" the chairman asked her.

"Oh, no. I intend to come back every year, as long as the law pro-vides for American sponsorship of institutions of higher learning abroad."

After hearings before two congressional committees, Hadassah was voted the sum of 1 million dollars in foreign currency (taken from excess Israeli currency credited to the United States in Israel). The grant will be used for a doctors' residence at the University Hospital and for the expansion of nurses' education.

Such was Mrs. Jacobson's impact on her listeners that Senator Pell arose on the Senate floor, and on behalf of fourteen other senators from New Hampshire, North Dakota, and a dozen other states, hailed Hadassah for its humanitarian enterprise, and called on AID to cooperate with the women in "maintaining an institution which serves the highest objectives of our foreign-aid program."

Prospect

A leading Zionist writer, Judd L. Teller, has commented that "since movements and organisms can outlive their usefulness, it would be absurd to predict the longevity of the American Zionist movement." The women's organizations, "because they have retained their relevance through their social-welfare projects in Israel," Teller predicted, "are certain to outlive all the others."

The Zionist outlook for the immediate future, it would appear, is for tighter religious ties with Israel, on the part of the Orthodox, Conservative, and Reform institutions, continued tourism, and a growing bridge between the scientific and philosophic communities of Israel and the United States as a college-trained generation in America reinforces the cultural communication launched during the past decade. As Israel moves swiftly into the ranks of the privileged nations, the common concern expressed by their parallel Peace Corps enterprises is also likely to breed an enlivened sense of kinship among the youth of the two nations.

Abba Eban, on the eve of his departure after a twelve-year tour of duty as Israel's ambassador to the United States, spoke feelingly about the new nation's stake in American Jewry. "The florescence of American Jewish institutions is not something alien to Israel's destiny. . . . I cannot imagine any circumstances in which weakness and disaster could come to American Jewry without weakness and disaster coming to Israel as well. This is the covenant we have with each other—mutual and parallel growth and strength, together with the establishment of bridges of interaction and fraternal sentiment."

CHAPTER 17

New York, New York Is a Wonderful Town— for Jews Too

"There is Israel. There are the Jews of the Diaspora. And then there is New York!"

NAHUM GOLDMANN

Most Gentiles in New York are part Jewish by osmosis. A non-Jew may begin the day by buying his *Times* at a Jewish-owned stationery store (the Yiddish *Daily Forward* may be on the same counter), and he may be discommoded when he discovers the store is closed on an ordinary Wednesday morning because of Yom Kippur. On another morning, the news reports on the radio will tell him that alternate-side-of-the-street parking restrictions have been lifted for the day because of the Jewish Feast of Tabernacles. (That particular police custom reflects an amusing ignorance of Jewish practice. Observant Jews have no use for a car on a festival—they walk—and the less traditional Jews treat the holiday lightly, but New York nods its head in recognition when its two and a quarter million Jews observe anything.)

The eyes and the ears of the New Yorker are assailed with Hebrew letters, Hebrew words, Jewish foods and wines. And a delightful series of "ads" in the buses and subways assure the non-Jew "you don't have to be Jewish" to enjoy these pleasures.

Rabbis alternate with priests and ministers on Sunday radio and television religious discourses. And the newspapers and other media cover news of Jewish interest in depth. I wonder whether Gentile eyes have developed an automatic skipping response to those columns that tell about Zionist conventions, the views of

245

various rabbis, and how the Jewish War Veterans react to American Nazis. The New York *Post*—despite its growing Gentile readership —has long been viewed as New York Jewry's own daily. The *Post* contains many pages of ads clearly intended to entice a Jewish clientele to mountains and seashore resorts. Now, as New York's only evening newspaper, its gentile readers' Jewish exposure will be enlarged.

Only in New York State will a thousand Irishmen, Scotsmen, Italians, Germans, and a handful of Jews attend a Catskill hotel convention of Philco dealers or Rotarians, where the diet is limited to kosher food, and a "No Smoking on the Sabbath" sign graces the dining room.

So pervasive is the influence of Jews on the non-Jewish New Yorker's consciousness—and perhaps his subconscious as well —that the language of the ghetto often colors his vocabulary. An editor of *Commonweal*, the leading Catholic lay weekly, searching for an apt description of an article in *National Review*, decides that *chutzpah* is the most apt description of William Buckley's brashness and temerity. The editors of *America*, another Catholic journal, criticize the American press for its inept handling of news under the headline, "A Real *Schemozzle*" (a Jesuit variant of the Yiddish *schlimazzel*).

The cultural fallout from the Jewish community over the larger one is an excellent barometer of the amicable interfaith relations in the vast city. Individual neighbors may quarrel, as neighbors often will, but the three major faiths rarely permit their differences on such issues as religion in the schools, censorship, or tax support for non-public education to shatter the general sense of harmony. Since neither church nor synagogue is a primary force in the lives of most New Yorkers as it is in Dallas or upstate Kingston, sectarian positions on public issues do not necessarily determine personal attitudes.

If America is, on the whole, a live-and-let-live land, New York is a fairly much an I-don't-know-or-care-how-you-live society. Its size and passion for anonymity make it possible for people with strong but differing convictions to live side by side, without feeling threatened by those who disagree with them. They wrap themselves in an enclave of like-minded people, oblivious to the streams of thought and feeling that whirl outside themselves.

New York Jews even seem a little strange to other American Jews, and in years past there was little rapport between them. Travel and communication have to some extent corrected the New Yorker's distorted notion that no Jewish life worthy of mention exists west of Hoboken. And Jews from Illinois and Tennessee and Louisiana no longer regard their coreligionists from Manhattan, Brooklyn, and the Bronx as abrasive relatives they would prefer to shield from public notice.

One word spells the difference in the psychology between New York Jews and others—the word *minority*. New Yorkers tend to be natural in their Jewishness. It is not that they wear the label with particular grace, but rather that they are indifferent to its minority connotation. If some people don't like Jews, they are to be pitied. Americans feel little personal anxiety about the Yankee hatred reported in the press, and rare is the Englishman who is driven to self-denigration by a flare-up of anti-British sentiment. So, too, the average New York Jew possesses enough self-assurance to take in stride any animosity directed toward his group. He contributes to the American Jewish Committee or the Anti-Defamation League not as a Jew in Omaha would, because he is part of an embattled minority, but because he is worried that the virus "out there"—Birchites in California, the anti-Jewish hotel in Bermuda—will spread closer to home. And if the disease should appear at his doorstep—a rally of Rockwell's American Nazi party or the rantings of an Arab propagandist—his defense is on an eyeball-to-eyeball level, for psychologically New York's Jews are on a level of parity with Protestants and Roman Catholics.

Only in New York can one find organizations 100 per cent Jewish in membership which haven't the trace of an ethnic *raison d'être*. A wit has suggested that the only thing which some groups of Jews have in common is that they will have nothing to do with other Jews!

In New York, one can organize enthusiastic supporters for any cause, however limited. A few of the disease-combating organizations, especially of the rare-disease variety, are virtually all Jewish. I once addressed a group of Park Avenue Jewish women gathered at a $100-a-plate luncheon at the Waldorf. The Guardian Matrons League (not its real name) had not yet decided on a purpose for their club, but they already had more than one hundred thousand dollars in their treasury. They enjoyed luncheons, fund raising, and one another's hats.

From the viewpoint of organized religion, this sense of at-homeness is hardly a blessing. For a New York Jew preserves his Jewishness like breathing, without doing anything about it. His cousin in Pittsburgh or Providence has to join a temple, at least a B'nai B'rith lodge, to feel an ongoing sense of "belonging." But the resident of Flatbush or Forest Hills is a Jew *faute de mieux,* automatically.

Ask a New York cabdriver about his Jewishness—60 per cent of the city's cabbies are Jewish—and he will answer, "Of course I am."

"What do you do about it?"

"What kind of nonsense is that? I am because I am. That's enough for me."

"I'll tell you what makes me one," one outspoken cabby explained. "If someone called me a dirty Jew, I'd knock his block off."

New Yorkitis

Nathan Glazer and Daniel Moynihan, in *Beyond the Melting Pot,* refer to the New York Jewish community as "the greatest that has existed in thousands of years of Jewish history." Not only does nearly half of American Jewry now live in its immediate vicinity, "almost all the rest have once lived in the city, will at some time live there, or have parents or children who live there."

If it is true that a New Yorker's image of America extends not much farther than the Alleghenies, it is even truer that the New York Jew has a difficult time imagining that much worth while (Jewishly) exists beyond Manhattan's Eighth Avenue. West of that axis are the neighborhoods of the Irish, the Greek, the Germans— but not the Jews.

Every Jewish religious national office is located in Manhattan or Brooklyn. One of the reasons Reform Judaism failed to fulfill its nineteenth-century promise of becoming *the* American Judaism was that its influence radiated out of Ohio for one hundred years, far removed from where the action was. Conservative Judaism captured the majority of Americans—every survey I have examined indicated that it is a steadily growing majority in the religious community— because it used New York as its staging ground.

From Manhattan the Conservative movement launched the attention-getting *Eternal Light* radio and *Frontiers of Faith* television series, its Institutes of Science and Religion, and a number of key projects that elicited the support of the power structure among both Jews and Christians. Conversely, B'nai B'rith, by locating its national offices in Washington, removed itself slightly from the main stream of Jewish life.

One of the national organizations used to issue a report of its activities under two headings, "I. New York; II. Out of Town." If a Jewish cemetery is desecrated in Michigan, it is an irritation—something to be watched. But if it takes place in the New York area, it becomes a serious crisis. Especially if *The New York Times* sees fit to print it.

I am not suggesting that there are no attractions elsewhere for New York Jews. Thousands of college-bound young people look to out-of-town schools for their education, and many never return. Los Angeles is the home of many more ex-New York Jews than Long Beach has Iowans. But for Jews who want their Judaism—or Jewishness—in large doses, there is no place like New York.

As I observed in an earlier chapter, New York Jewry, of course, itself consists of hundreds of sub-enclaves, each only dimly aware of the others. At a Passover service in a Young Israel synagogue of Flatbush, hundreds of young men and women gathered in worship will assume that theirs is the norm of Jewish behavior in Brooklyn. At the same time, a block or two away, a line of would-be diners—all Jewish—will be clogging the street in front of a Chinese restaurant, waiting to eat a meal forbidden by traditional Jewish law at any time, and especially on Passover.

I have mentioned in Chapter 12 the Hasidic and ultra-Orthodox Jews who commute from Williamsburgh and Square Town to the diamond center on West 47th Street in Manhattan. Walking one single block, from Fifth Avenue to Sixth Avenue, one may come upon scores of people, many in the beard, earlocks, and gabardine of the Hasidim, engaged in an animated conversation punctuated by Talmudic allusions.

Touring a diamond factory, one sees a dozen skullcapped workers bent over their precious products. The polishers may pause at four o'clock to *daven Minchah,* recite the traditional afternoon prayers. In Antwerp, the home base of the industry, 75 per cent of the thousands of workers are Jews. Virtually all the cleavers are Jewish. A cleaver has the nerve-racking responsibility of deciding how to cut a rough diamond expertly.

But for the most part, the men on West 47th Street are dealers, specializing in different weights and shapes of the stones.

One element is not visible to the casual visitor. Nearly all of these Jews are knit together in formal association. Two Diamond Clubs, with a total of 2,200 members, are federated with clubs in Antwerp, Amsterdam, and Tel Aviv. They are subject to rigid club discipline, and abide by its decisions.

Dominating the clubs are the Arbitration Committee and the Conciliation Committee. The former consists of eight chairmen and twenty-four arbitrators who receive complaints and call members to account. The city's district attorneys and courts generally advise the diamond people to bring their legal problems to the clubs: "You have the machinery for resolving differences, for determining the true value of merchandise, for handling nonpayment, and the termination of partnership."

In the diamond world, a deal is consummated by Jews and the few Gentile strays alike with a handshake and the words *mazel and brochoh* (good luck and blessing). The elaborate machinery of arbitration stems from the nature of the business. Diamonds vary greatly in quality, and involve large sums of money. An honest mistake in judging the quality of a handful of gems can cause a miscalculation entailing a loss of thousands of dollars. A clerk may send a wrong shipment to Minneapolis, and the misshipped gems may be sold at the wrong price. If the arbitrators are persuaded that it was an honest error, they will suggest a compromise to seller and buyer: "Pay him what it cost him." The principle of *caveat emptor* is not operative. *Yosher*—equity—the principle of Talmudic law is invoked.

I heard of one case with complex historical and international implications. Shortly before *Anschluss*, a merchant in Vienna had received $2,000 from a fellow merchant in Antwerp for diamonds that were to be shipped to Belgium. Before the shipment could be made, Hitler's army overran Austria; the Viennese merchant fled, leaving behind all his possessions. Years later both met on West 47th Street. The Antwerp diamond buyer was in difficult financial straits; the Viennese dealer had prospered. The issue was brought before the

Arbitration Committee for judgment and the arbitrators ruled that the two men must split the difference. The Viennese dealer paid his Belgian buyer of two decades earlier $1,000.

The obligation was imposed by a court with no authority other than the ancient law of the Babylonian Talmud. But no one who hopes to remain in the good graces of his fellow diamond dealers would risk flouting this tribunal's decisions.

Some measure of the authority of the Diamond Dealers' Club (one of the two) may be gleaned from the articles of its constitution:

> Article XI. Section 12.
> The Arbitration Committee shall have the authority to:
> a. Investigate the facts charged in the complaint;
> b. Summon litigants and witnesses;
> c. Compel production of books and documents and records essential to the facts. . . .
> d. Impose fines in the event of a refusal of a witness to appear and testify or produce records;
> e. To punish litigants or witnesses for contemptuous behavior during the process of a hearing, by imposing a fine up to the sum of $100.

Nothing in the bylaws restricts membership to those of the Jewish faith. All that is necessary, beyond the usual preliminaries, is for the photograph of the candidate to be posted "in a conspicuous place within the clubrooms for a period of at least ten days."

The only Jewish flavor in the entire fifty-seven-page document lurks in Article XVI, "Trade Rules":

Sec. 1. Any oral offer is binding among dealers, when agreement is expressed by the accepted words, "*Mazel and brochoh!*"

The Sephardim: New York's Iberian Jews

Is it possible to be a traditional Jew, observant of all the demands of Orthodoxy, yet feel lost when a Yiddish word is spoken, regard chicken soup and gefülte fish as alien to your palate, and wax nervous when your daughter starts going steady with a boy named Finkelstein?

It is, if you are a Sephardi (pluralized by adding the letter m).

For that means that you are one of 100,000 Americans who trace their ancestry to the Jews who were expelled from Spain in 1492 and from Portugal in 1497.

The Sephardim came to America from the Mediterranean area. The forebears of Sephardic congregations in Montgomery, Alabama, and Seattle, Washington, came from the Island of Rhodes and a number of other Mediterranean cities. The new Sephardim, who immigrated in the first decades of the twentieth century, originated in Turkey, Greece, Italy, and Yugoslavia.

Fifty to sixty thousand Sephardic Jews live in the Greater New York area. Some of their ancestors settled on Manhattan Island one hundred and twenty-two years before the Declaration of Independence. The late Justice Benjamin Cardozo of the U.S. Supreme Court, and the late Justice Edgar Nathan, Jr., of the New York Supreme Court were both descendants of the original twenty-three Portuguese Jews who found their way to New Amsterdam via northern Brazil.

The historic Temple Shearith Israel facing Central Park—commonly known as the Spanish-Portuguese Synagogue—represents the Old Sephardim, the blue-blooded aristocracy of New York Jewish life.

I visited a synagogue in the Bronx whose members are Turkish and Greek Jews. A Jew whose background is the world of Sholom Aleichem would feel strange in this setting. Even the family names in the congregation have an unfamiliar ring: Matza, Amira, Haquel, Halfon, Coffino, Coumeri, Cabouli, and Piparno. . . .

Their rabbi, Asher Murciano, was born in Tangiers and ordained in one of its seminaries. I was surprised to learn that Tangiers had a training school for rabbis, and Rabbi Murciano complained that Ashkenazic Jews like myself deliberately ignored such communities as Tangiers, downgraded its spiritual and intellectual achievements, and were completely ignorant of the creative works produced by the Jews of Tangiers and North Africa.

The Bronx congregation is an outgrowth of the original Sephardic community of New Lots, in Brooklyn, which took shape at the turn of the century. A vivid description of these Levantine Jews appears in an article by Leonard Plotnik in *Commentary* (January, 1958).

Mr. Plotnik depicts a late Friday evening service in the capacity-filled sanctuary of the Congregation of Peace and Brotherhood of

Monastir (Turkey), one of the few new synagogues which have made a slight gesture toward Conservative Judaism:

> The service features Spanish hymns and music of Turkish origin, freely adapted from the songs of the Mahlavaneh or Dervish houses where the high-ranking Jewish officials of the old sultans went on Friday nights to pay their respects to Moslem colleagues.
>
> The congregation is young, made up of men and women in their twenties, thirties, and forties. They might easily be taken for ordinary middle-class Americans as they sit in their well-cut clothes, prosperous and at peace. And yet there is still something exotic about them, with their swarthy complexions, their aquiline noses, their large smoldering eyes.

In Rabbi Murciano's study I met with the author of the *Commentary* article and an "elder statesman" of the Sephardim, a native of Smyrna, Turkey. We spoke about the fragmented Sephardic community: although superficially united in the Central Sephardic Community of America, they are really quite segregated according to their countries of origin. Thus Syrian Jews, for example, who speak Arabic, have little to do with other Oriental Jews, and are isolated in the Bensonhurst section of Brooklyn.

The Sephardim have an inordinate pride in their ancestry, and tradition and custom play a large part in their lives. Family life is close knit; they rarely marry out of the community—and when they do, social pressure brings the Ashkenazic son-in-law or daughter-in-law into the small but dominant group.

Vestiges of a patriarchal society persist. Three generations often live in one household; women, especially young women, defer to the men. A young wife bows to the wishes of her mother-in-law, or to her older brother. Social life is built around the club, or the coffee house, Levantine fashion. Their foods are Oriental or Spanish. Breakfast often consists of *queso blanca,* a special kind of white cheese, and grapes, and favorite dishes—quite unfamiliar to a Grossinger menu—include *borekas,* a mixture of cheese, spinach, and eggs baked in a pie; *fila,* a thin dough filled with cheese or eggplant, *baklava,* a pastry. Pot roast or lamb is the main Sabbath dish, and chicken, the mainstay of the more familiar ghetto, is a rarity.

As we sat talking, the elder Sephardi discussed at some length the glorious traditions of his people. But his younger compatriots cautioned him also to remember their deficiencies. It was a community with a brilliant past, but the luster of medieval Spanish and North African poets, philosophers, medical geniuses, and religious writers had been dimmed by a singular lack of energy in transmitting the heritage. The majority of religious schools were third-rate; many of the children received little training.

The rabbi and the younger Sephardi depicted the day-by-day life of his people, bewailing the men's preoccupation with social life. The wives remain at home, they explained, while the men play cards and backgammon at their "societies." One of the most popular forms of entertainment, said the rabbi, is to watch belly dancing.

"Of course, we don't permit it in the synagogue vestry rooms," Rabbi Murciano pointed out. "But there are few social affairs without the dancers."

As we spoke, the elder Sephardi suddenly excused himself. His two friends explained that he was on the verge of tears and had left the room to compose himself. The honor of the Sephardim had been tarnished by this revelation of their feelings to an outsider.

We discussed other Sephardic customs. At family parties, the dancing is Turkish style. One popular dance is the *debka*, somewhat reminiscent of the Israeli *hora*, but slower. The men and women dance together, but are separated by holding opposite corners of a handkerchief. Older Sephardim still speak Ladino, a Spanish equivalent of Yiddish; grandparents often address the children in Ladino and the youngsters respond in English.

I sneezed, and my hosts responded, not with the traditional *gesundheit*, but with *salut* and *chayim tovim* (a good life!).

Passover is the favorite festival among the Sephardim, but many of them, especially the Egyptians, also celebrate Purim with special gusto. A considerable number of Sephardim are descended from Marranos—Jews who had survived the Inquisition by accepting baptism while secretly continuing to practice Judaism. Therefore, the Sephardim have a special place in their hearts for the Biblical Esther, who was a Marrano in the ancient Persian palace.

Although most of the prayers differ only slightly from those of other Jews, Sephardic worship, too, has its own style. Formality—unknown to the *shtetl* Jew—is the keynote. The Torah and the Ark are treated with special deference. As the worshiper enters a Sephardic synagogue he offers a half bow in the direction of the altar. And on leaving, a similar gesture is in order. A solemn dignity pervades the sanctuary, a quality rare among the more effervescent Ashkenazim.

Reform and even Conservative influences are virtually unknown. Wedding rites are the same as they were hundreds of years ago in Salonika or Istanbul. During the entire ceremony, the four parents of the couple stand under the wedding canopy, each holding one corner of a *tallit* (prayer shawl) over the heads of the bride and groom.

At the same time, some of the ultra-Orthodox Ashkenazic customs—such as the wig worn by the married women—are unknown. These practices—which had their origin in medieval Europe rather than ancient Israel—are looked upon with derision by the Sephardim as flaws unthinkable among "pure Jews." Leonard Plotnik, in his *Commentary* article, underscores the preoccupation with ethnic purity among the Sephardim. The wearing of the Star of David, he points out, a common custom, "signifies separateness not only from the world of the Gentiles but from the world of other Jews as well." Jews with blond hair and high cheekbones, who speak a European language (Yiddish) and are given to a "strange pronunciation of Hebrew," are viewed with suspicion—by Sephardic criteria they are unlikely to be considered of a pure breed.

The Meshed Jews who live in the Kew Gardens section of Queens are an outstanding example of the tenacity of tradition. Not more than a dozen families make up this tight-knit group—the remnants of a vigorous community of Persian Jews who settled two hundred years ago in the capital of Khorassan, a northeast province of what is now Iran. Tortured by a fanatic sect of Moslems, the settlers continued their adherence to their faith as Marranos. Ultimately they found their way to London, as well as Israel, and the United States. The Meshed Jews of Kew Gardens practice their Judaism as members of an Orthodox congregation whose rabbi, Gershon Appel, is an Ashkenazi. But, like other Sephardim, they retain their home life as though they were still in northeast Persia.

Some acculturation has set in. Overwhelmed by the Ashkenazic majority, they accept some of its customs. But the patriarchal pattern continues. Divorces are rare; the average family consists of four or more children. They have erected a beautiful old folks' home in Brooklyn, but it is still considered bad taste to have a parent living away from home.

Many have prospered. They deal in laces, linens, rugs, and novelties. One family, the Roussos, began a generation ago with a tiny shop, and now are among the nation's leading manufacturers of sportswear, the widely advertised Russ Togs. They have helped to build a $2 million Sephardic synagogue in Cedarhurst, Long Island, an architectural showplace with windows executed by Marc Chagall.

Dr. David de Sola Pool, rabbi emeritus of the Spanish-Portuguese Synagogue, is the scion of an old family, revered as a scholar and teacher. During World War II he headed the Jewish Welfare Board military chaplaincy program. Several of his books are classics.

I interviewed the president of the Central Sephardic Community, Rabbi Isaac Alcalay. (He retired in 1967.) The white-bearded patriarch of American Spanish Jewry was born in Sofia, Bulgaria, but was brought to Belgrade as a child. In the pre-Nazi days, he not only served as chief rabbi but also sat in the Yugoslav Senate, and was a close friend of King Alexander. Now in his early eighties, he has lost much of the vitality which enabled him to stand up to the Nazis. But an inner kindliness lights his face and he bears a striking resemblance to Rembrandt's "Rabbi." He is one of those rare human beings who evokes in others a feeling that they are in the presence of unblemished sainthood.

There is a wistful quality about the Sephardim, an intimation of the grandeur and nobility of the past. Not long ago, the Daughters of the American Revolution dedicated one of the historic Sephardic buildings as a shrine. But shrines offer little comfort about the future. And the future does not promise much continuity for the fiercely proud but rapidly dwindling Sephardic community. "Living in a self-contained world," Leonard Plotnik, one of their loyal sons writes sorrowfully, "they lack the Ashkenazic drive and initiative which mold Jewish life in America."

The New German-Austrian Jewry

In the summer of 1936, I traveled by ship from Haifa, Palestine, to Trieste, Italy, in the company of several hundred Jewish passengers from Austria and a few from Germany all of whom had come for a summer's visit with relatives in the Holy Land.

Why were they returning to Hitler's Europe? Didn't the Viennese realize that *Anschluss* was not far off, and that Austria would be overrun by the Nazi juggernaut? The answer—almost to a man— was a scornful assurance that Austria would resist the Germans. These Austrian Jews were too deeply rooted in the soil of their homeland to read the handwriting on the wall. Our tablemate, a Frau Katz from Hamburg, was equally indignant about our concern for her future. The Nazi plan for the Jews, she explained, was directed toward the *Ost-Juden*, the East European Jews. Her family was too bound up with the history of Hamburg to feel imperiled.

I often wonder how many of my fellow passengers survived the holocaust.

New York today is the home of more than 100,000 German, Austrian, and Czech Jews who managed to escape the death chambers. A whole area of Manhattan's Upper West Side, from 150th Street to 193rd Street, is peopled by Jews who fled from Frankfurt, Berlin, Düsseldorf, Mannheim, Vienna, and hundreds of other German and Austrian cities.

One can only speculate about the factors that determined "who shall live and who shall die." For some it was the fortuitous circumstance of having relatives in the United States who had established themselves earlier—although many others in the same position did not make it. Pure chance obviously played a significant role—the visa that came through in time, the bus, just caught, that proved the last link to life and freedom.

Luck rode with the rootless more often than with the comfortable. Newcomers to Vienna had less to lose, fewer bags to pack for a chancy trip across the ocean.

One perceptive member of this group, now established in America, offered his own theories. "Who got out? The politically astute. Those who could understand the nature of our politics. When the Austrian chancellor announced a plebiscite to be held in ten days, most of us were sure that the Nazis would never make it by ballot. But some of us knew enough about history and about Hitler to know that he would jump the gun and march on Austria. So we packed and fled.

"Then there were the young people. They had mobility, few impedimenta. And they saw no future in Austria in any case. But the owners of apartments and stores hesitated—fatally.

"And Vienna was full of émigrés. They were used to flight, and they made for the borders. The mountainous borders had no guards. It wasn't so hard."

Resourcefulness, always a self-preservative, provided a key to life. In Vienna, some Jews with their backs to the wall scanned the columns of the New York City telephone directory, selecting the Jewish-sounding names or those names which corresponded with theirs. They wrote thousands of letters in the dim hope that someone would respond with a "visa," a letter guaranteeing financial support. A surprising number of these letters were answered—and their writers rescued.

Although one cannot generalize about large masses of people, some pattern does emerge. The tender-hearted—those who could not conceive of man's depravity—remained behind. The tough-minded, by and large, had at least a chance.

The German-Austrian postwar Jewish community in New York can be characterized in a number of ways:

1. They have achieved a level of upward economic mobility even greater than that of the general Jewish community.

2. They suffered fewer of the traumas of emigration—unemployment, family instability, lack of parental control—than the East Europeans who escaped Hitler's Final Solution.

3. Once here, they demonstrated considerably less geographic mobility. About 54 per cent remained in New York City.

On the whole, it can be said that the German newcomers of 1935–1950 met with much more hospitality on the part of the established Eastern European Jews than was afforded their hosts at the hands of an earlier German-Jewish community.

Arriving almost as penniless as the earlier wave, they began life anew as workers in factories and as salesmen. A young, well-educated couple might take jobs as custodians in a Jewish institution and work evenings and off-hours making Viennese candy, selling handbags, peddling trinkets from door to door.

It was a collective Operation Bootstrap, following the Talmudic dictum, originally ascribed to King Solomon. When the people cried: "How shall we support ourselves?" the wise King replied, "Buy and sell from one another." In the same fashion, the German and Austrian émigrés moved from destitution in the forties to prosperity in the sixties.

One key word helps explain the comparative success of the new immigrants: organization. First they established the American Federation of Jews from Central Europe. No one was left uncared for. By 1955, they had established United Help, Inc., to meet the needs of Nazi victims now resident in the United States. Because of their systematic and well-ordered method of operation, they were able to obtain funds from the Jewish Restitution Successor Organization and other agencies responsible for channeling funds and the resources gathered from heirless and unclaimed property in Germany to those who needed help in re-establishing themselves in the New World. Thanks to the same methodical organization, there were child-care centers to aid working mothers, retraining opportunities for the oldsters, and scholarships for the more gifted children, workshops for senior citizens, and elaborate recreation programs to soften the blows of transplantation.

Rabbi Hugo Stransky, one of the spiritual leaders of Washington Heights, escorted me through his synagogue, Congregation Beth Hillel, in the heart of what used to be called "the Fourth Reich."

Beth Hillel, an Orthodox congregation of some seven hundred families, was organized in 1940 to serve the new German Jews. Even today, Dr. Stransky, a native of Prague, alternates on Saturday mornings between an English sermon and a sermon in German.

"Do they all understand both languages?" I asked.

"A few of them sleep peacefully when they can't follow."

The large sanctuary is a far cry from the ornate Synagogue of Munich, as few of whose remnants are enshrined in the American congregation. The Munich edifice was destroyed in the spring of 1938, half a year before the nightmarish Kristall-Nacht when most of Germany's synagogues went up in flames.

In 1938, the building that now houses the Beth Hillel Synagogue had been a U.S. post office. Despite imaginative efforts by the House Committee, some of the drabness lingers, and the shadow of the somber past falls over the sanctuary. On the wall, in a glass frame, hangs a yellow badge, imposed upon the Jews by Hitler as a mark of shame, but now a mark of honor.

The Ark is simple, graceful, without elegance. The Holy Scrolls and the Torah ornaments are all immigrants, salvaged, as were the worshipers, from the tragedy. Rabbi Stransky pointed out the unusually beautiful silver ornaments, precious museum pieces, and the work of gifted artists.

Worship service is Orthodox—"Conservative along the lines of continental Conservatism," Rabbi Stransky said—but German Jews lay great stress on dignity and formality. East European traditional worship is more exuberant and individualistic. Decorum is difficult to maintain in a three-and-a-half-hour free-wheeling Sabbath morning service in which many worshipers proceed at their own pace and children mingle with the adults.

Not so the Germans. Not only is the service itself somewhat streamlined; the German pattern is quiet prayer. "If you must whisper," a sign near the back reads, "whisper a prayer!"

"And we don't shake the way the other Orthodox do," Rabbi Stransky explained.

The German language, the formalistic style, and a host of common memories weld this group together and separate them from other New York Jews. Few of the young people marry out of the faith, and half of them marry within their own group. (Less so the ex-G.I.'s who have become Americanized more rapidly.)

The gap between the generations is not so perceptible as it is among other immigrant groups. The older people, who flock to Golden Age Clubs—euphemistically called Family Clubs—are highly literate. They will quote long passages from Goethe and Schiller in a way the younger generation cannot do in any language. Reverence for parents and grandparents is a deeply ingrained tradition. It is not unusual, Rabbi Stransky told me, for a teen-aged grandson to shepherd his old and infirm grandmother to the synagogue each week for worship.

More than a dozen German-Austrian synagogues dot the Washington Heights neighborhood. One of them dubbed the Breuer Synagogue (after Rabbi Breuer) attracts those Jews who came from the Jewishly aristocratic city of Frankfurt-am-Main. "The Breuer Jews," I was told by several of the Germans, talk to no one but themselves. They are the "nose-in-the air" Germans. Yet they are bound together by strong common memories, kept alive by their societies, as well as by *Aufbau*, the widely read German weekly.

On the sanctuary wall of the Beth Hillel Synagogue hangs an altar cloth, frayed and worn, and especially dear to this particular congregation. It is the handiwork of an eighteenth-century German convert to Judaism, symbolic of both the continuity and the spiritual power and tenacity of this people.

What Color is a Jew?

There are twelve congregations of Negro Jews in the New York area. Numbering over ten thousand members, most of whom live in Harlem, they present a serious theological problem to the city's rabbinic authorities. Are they authentic Jews?

It is a problem similar to that which confronted the Jerusalem Chief Rabbinate with regard to immigrants from India. Is a self-made Jew a member in good standing? Is it enough to observe all the commandments of the Torah, including circumcision, meticulous observance of the Sabbath, and the dietary laws?

These Black Jews of New York are Orthodox. One is enrolled at the Teachers' Institute of Yeshiva University; another was graduated from the Adult Education program of the Jewish Theological Seminary; and a number of youngsters attend all-day schools. Yet a synagogue membership committee consisting of men who may know few words of Hebrew, who eat bacon and shrimp, and themselves ignore the restrictions of the traditional Sabbath, pass judgment on the Jewishness of candidates who read Hebrew fluently, attend worship faithfully, and observe the minutiae of the kosher laws— and determine that they are not Jews—or at least not yet.

The problem hinges on the traditional process of admission to the faith. A cloud of doubt hovers over the origins of the Negro Jews. Rabbi Wentworth Matthews, their founder, has ordained a number of men as rabbis, and they now serve the Harlem synagogues. But whence came his own authority? Is he a descendant of the Falasha Jews of Ethiopia or, as one scholar insists, a self-converted Jew who learned Judaism as a synagogue employee?

Thus far, the organized Jewish community of New York has made no definitive effort to resolve the question. Most Jews who are aware of the problem—and few are—wonder at the temerity and tenacity of a people who are willing to endure the disability of being both a racial *and* a religious minority. On the other hand, a number of rabbis and Jewish laymen, who have made contact with the Harlem Jews, have been impressed with their seriousness, the fervor of their worship, and their high level of religious literacy. They helped organize a group called *Tzaad Harishon* (the First Step) to enlist support and understanding of their desire to be accepted into the main stream of American Jewish life. It is a young group, with all the zeal of youth. Its energetic members reach out to young people on the college campuses, telling their story, singing synagogue and Israeli melodies with an inspired beauty, and defending their status with passion.

"How far back do you go in your Jewish family identification?" one of the girls was asked at a campus forum.

"How far back do you go?" she answered crisply. "Show me *your* Jewish identification."

Only in New York

Sectarianism takes on some rather strange forms in New York City. The labels, Jewish, Catholic, and occasionally Protestant, are attached to organizations that haven't the remotest connection with religion. Which group is responsible for the fragmentizing of the faith groups is not clear. I have been given to understand that the Jewish Teachers' Association, whose membership consists of teachers in the city's public schools, was organized when the Catholic Teachers' Association was established, and the Protestants, willy-nilly, followed suit.

On more than one occasion I have addressed the annual breakfast of the Star of David Society of Macy's stores. About a thousand people were present in the grand ballroom of a large hotel, and the atmosphere suggested a Communion breakfast (but in these circumstances called a Community breakfast) such as Roman Catholics sponsor. The Star of David Society was the Jewish answer to the Lady of Fatima League, made up of Catholic employees of Macy's department stores, and is the largest of the three clubs. The third is the St. George's Association, Protestantism's answer to the other two. Well over two thousand of Macy's 16,483 employees are members of these three associations.

It is strictly a New York phenomenon. In other cities such groups would be regarded as divisive. Apparently, the Macy management looks favorably on the societies, as the top officers attend all three annual community breakfasts. An excellent spirit of fellowship permeates the triple-faith societies. Their officers attend each other's affairs freely, and with obvious relish.

The Manhattan phone book offers some clue to the extent of this type of organization peculiar to New York. Two columns are devoted to agencies with Jewish labels, one and a half to Catholic agencies, and about an eighth of a column to Protestant agencies. Among the less obvious listings are the Jewish Legion, whose members are, I presume, the veterans of World War I who fought with General Allenby in Palestine; the Catholic Daughters of

America, probably a Colonial America group; and the Protestant Defense League, which in the light of the paucity of listings in the telephone book seems highly warranted.

A perusal of these lists brings to light an institution uniquely New Yorkish: civic employees banding together along religious lines. The federal employees, too, have their religious divisions, especially the postal clerks, who are divided into three large groups, and I once addressed a gathering of 600 Jewish United States customs inspectors, who operate on the piers and in air terminals of New York City.

Although most New Yorkers think of their police force as overwhelmingly Irish, there are well over two thousand Jewish police officers, a larger force than the one which controls the city of Cleveland. Jewish civil-service groups prefer Hebrew names. The police society is called *Shomrim*—the Biblical word for watchman ("Watchman, what of the night?"). The firemen are members of the *Ner Tamid* (Eternal Light) Society. Each of these organizations has its own chaplain and carries on an active program.

The Morim, Jewish Teachers' Association, enlists almost half the 18,000 Jewish teachers in the New York public-school system. Its spirited program welds together teachers of the Jewish faith in a number of cultural enterprises.

I unearthed one group with a most impressive name, the Hebrew Spiritual Society, and discovered that they represent the Jewish employees of the city Sanitation Department! Finding no suitable Biblical name for garbage disposal, they borrowed their organization's title from the Negro Spiritual Society, exclusively made up of Negro sanitation workers.

It would be misleading to regard these religiously fragmentized groups as necessarily an outgrowth of a passion for parochialism. True, some of them do regard themselves as a kind of protective league. The Jewish Postal Workers' Welfare League is able to make representations to the government to enable those who wish to work on Sunday instead of Saturday to do so without penalty. Indeed, since the faith groups are organized, they are able to effect a smooth exchange of Christmas time off for Yom Kippur time off, and everyone is happy.

And, of course, history as well as philosophy plays a role in the birth of these faith groups. Both Judaism and Catholicism, as we have observed elsewhere, are not only ecclesiastical institutions, they are cultures. Their institutions, therefore, run the gamut of sociocultural life. A Jewish social worker is more than a social worker who happens to be Jewish. He is, presumably, equipped to cope with problems growing out of the Jewish milieu, and, in addition, he is trained to apply particular Jewish values in handling his problems.

Nineteenth-century New York Jewry was primarily built along nonreligious sectarian lines. No agency was as powerful as the United Hebrew Trades. The first city-wide strikes, which made possible the creation of strong garment workers' unions, were convoked by groups with Jewish labels. The Hebrew Hatters' Union marched side by side with the AFL Jewish Actors' Union to demand the right of collective bargaining. According to historian Moses Rischin, "Only the Hebrew-American Newsboys Union, ages six to twelve . . . evaded the United Hebrew Trades."

Upward economic mobility has changed the face of the Jewish labor movement. According to Emanuel Muravchik, director of the Jewish Labor Committee, 50,000 Jewish workers remain in the field of women's garments, but their numbers are declining rapidly. Jewish unionism of the last century, which provided part of labor's left wing, with its emphasis on social progress, has now shifted to the middle of the road, and is occasionally conservative. Under the banner of the Jewish Labor Committee, union leaders now join with other Jewish and civic agencies in the broad field of human rights.

But unionism is still a dominant theme in these Jewish circles. No longer pressers or trimmers, they have doffed their blue collars, and joined the white-collar unions of teachers or department-store workers.

The majority of Jews in New York City are to be found in their ranks. Their income is modest, but there is virtually no chronic unemployment among the able-bodied in their midst.

CHAPTER 18

"Magnolia Judaism"

"The South is full of people whose only profession is to be southerners."

JOHN GUNTHER

Southern Jews are like all Southerners, but less so. If there are ten kinds of American Jews, there are twenty types of Southern Jews.

The Southwestern Jew shares one fact of life with the Southerner: he is, unlike his Northern coreligionist, an alien element in a homogeneous, Anglo-Saxon, Baptist-Methodist society, which has not quite made peace with the idea that a person who worships God either as a Catholic or a Jew can be authentically American.

Yet the Southern Jew, while less integrated in the religio-cultural life of the community is, paradoxically, more at home socially.

In the late 1930s I spent three delightful years in Tuscaloosa, Alabama, where I taught at the university. It is easy for a white man to be shielded from the built-in cruelty of the South's racial pattern, for neighbors are kind, gentle, and genteel people. Even when they find difficulty in pronouncing such "foreign" names as Goldstein and Schwartzman, or insist on calling the temple a church and speak of the rabbi as a minister of the gospel, no malice lurks in their soft, well-modulated voices.

Jews are spread sparsely over the entire South. Except for a few big cities, not more than five out of a thousand residents are non-Christian. Perhaps for this very reason Southern Jewry is one large, fairly homogeneous family. A sociological study by Theodore Lowi describes the Jews of "Iron City," a city of 60,000 in "the hilly north of the Deep South":

"When they visit another Southern town, the Jews of Iron City are expected to stay with or look up Aunt Sophie or Cousin Abe. . . . Wherever they go in the South, particularly the old Jews whose roots are deep, they almost never leave the family."

Mobility is the word for Jews young and old south of the Mason and Dixon line. A girl in Charlotte, North Carolina, flies down to Montgomery for a picnic; the Jubilee in Birmingham attracts scores of young people from New Orleans, Atlanta, and Memphis. A social gathering in Mobile will have two distinctive qualities: the presence of a number of non-Jews and of friends and kinfolk from Georgia, Louisiana, and Tennessee, and occasionally a stray from Fort Worth or Little Rock. Part of the conversation will consist of the game of "Jewish geography." "You're from ——. I guess you know the Weils or the Blocks or the Hirsches." Chances are the names mentioned will turn out to be "kissin' cousins" of both questioner and listerner.

The old Jewish families are third or fourth generation, with few ties to the North. Their children are graduates of the state universities, or Tulane. If, as Alfred O. Hero suggests in an article in *Jewish Social Studies* (October, 1965) they attend an Ivy League school, some of the "purity" is diminished, and even graduation from such liberal colleges as Duke, Vanderbilt, and North Carolina effects a change.

A new Jew, reports Lowi, is regarded as "too pushy," too willing to stand out, and acceptance does not come easily. "Over the years, differences have congealed." In Iron City, presidency of the temple alternates between the old and the new. Larger cities, such as Baton Rouge, can afford the luxury of two Reform temples to accommodate both. One is likely to be slightly Zionist oriented; the other will insist that Judaism is nothing more than a religion.

Lowi dramatizes the wide chasm that separates the "old Jew" and the new in a vivid description of a controversy that ripped the Jewish community of Iron City apart in 1958.

The bombing of Temple Beth El in Birmingham had greatly agitated two brothers named Kahn. They appeared before a meeting of their congregation with the forthright suggestion that the congregation send a gift of $250 to be donated by the Kahn brothers to Beth El as an expression of sympathy. The older members strongly opposed the idea. They recalled that back in the twenties the Ku Klux Klan had whipped several Catholics and Jews in Iron City. Today, thank God, Jews had free access to the country clubs, the high-school football teams, and other social activities. Why borrow trouble by sticking their necks out? At the end of a stormy meeting, the Kahn brothers quietly withdrew their offer.

Two years after the debate, bombers struck right in their own back yard. While a new temple wing was being dedicated, in the presence of the mayor, the Christian clergy, and the city commissioners, a bomb was thrown, and the younger Kahn, who pursued the culprits, was hit by rifle fire. "The injured Kahn insisted that there be no pictures, no wide press coverage." Apparently subdued by the events of 1958, he ruefully remarked: "Magazine coverage has already done the South enough harm."

Paradox suffuses the entire panorama of Southern Jewry. There is timidity—and boldness as well. Harry Golden will address a small-town South Carolina church audience on racial justice and receive a standing ovation. Rabbi Jack Rothschild of Atlanta will embrace Martin Luther King in public and declare his support before a nationwide audience, and his Atlanta congregation will hold back any criticism.

On the other hand, Alfred Hero discovered, in a sampling of Jewish opinion, that "Southern traditions about the Negro had exerted significant effects on most Southern-born informants." They were less inclined to express segregationist, and particularly racist, ideology, and few Jews, even in Alabama or Mississippi, supported the Dixiecrats in 1948 or voted for the Independent Electors in 1960. The overwhelming majority vote Democratic in all elections. Yet, two out of five deemed the Supreme Court rulings on race as "unfortunate," and more than half concurred with the statement that "desegregation was proceeding too fast."

Lowi found that "practically all Jews in Iron City are publicly conservative, but easily a majority are privately conservative as well. . . . The new Jew can be pushed to concede the inevitability of desegregation; the old Jew, regardless of age, will use the rhetoric of states' rights, of *Plessy* versus *Ferguson* and, if pushed, of race superiority and Biblical sanction. The new Jew will not."

Dr. Hero discovered that former Jews, those who "had disappeared into the genteel Episcopalian group" as had the early Jewish communities of New Orleans, Greensboro, North Carolina, and Charleston, South Carolina, were extremely conservative, and he theorized that their reactionary views were based on "insecurity about acceptance by the Gentile elite." They had been lost not only to Judaism, but to the Jewish value system as well.

But even those small-town residents who retained their Jewish identity, Lowi found, "played poker with the sheriff, fished with the local judge, hunted with the planters."

Is Iron City a true image of Jewish status in the South? Is it anything like Birmingham, or Meridian, or Knoxville, or Little Rock? Is there anything common in the experiences of Jews in San Antonio and in Charlotte? The answers are not always clear. What about cities such as Norfolk, which are an integral part of the South, yet are influenced by the influx of many Northerners, and the steady intrusion of newcomers as a result of the military establishment?

One of Norfolk's best-liked Jewish citizens is not even a native Southerner. Charles Kaufman, born in Bellefontaine, Ohio, settled in Norfolk after World War I. Although he has never held public office, he is highly esteemed for his civic leadership and has been cited as the city's First Citizen. He is a past president of Temple Ohef Sholom, and his sons, too, are actively involved in Jewish affairs.

The Jew in the Ten-Gallon Yarmulke

David White, publisher of the Texas *Jewish Herald,* told me of a woman who came into his plant—which includes a small shop that turns out religious books and sacred objects—to order a *mezuzah* for the front doorpost of her home.

"I want a *mezuzah* that is not too Jewish," she explained.

The Southern and Southwestern Jew today seeks no flight from Judaism, but he wants it in a quiet, unobtrusive way.

Many obscure Texas towns have one or two Jewish families—often the operators of the local furniture store: Gonzales, Lockhardt, New Braunfeld, Luling, Seguin, Pharr, and Edinburgh. They organize into B'nai B'rith lodges, and meet socially. Religious training for the children may involve a driving stint of seventy miles, not only on Sunday, but twice during the week—especially when there is a Bar Mitzvah coming up. The greatest boon to Bar Mitzvah training is the tape recorder. The teacher records the chant of the blessings and the prophetic portion, and Amos and Jeremiah are kept alive by the miracle of electronics.

Rosenberg, Texas—named for a Jew—gets twenty worshipers at its Sabbath services, despite the fact that it now has only seven Jewish residents. The other thirteen temple habitués are Christians, showing true Christian spirit by augmenting the *minyan*.

What keeps the small-town Jew "down on the farm"? Simply, economic opportunity. Owners of successful business establishments, with real-estate investments to enhance their security, they maintain as much as possible their contacts with other Jews and Judaism. Unlike many of their Northern coreligionists, they close their stores on the holy days. They dispatch their children to college, not only to get an education, but, they will tell you, to meet "a nice Jewish boy or girl." Sometimes the young people never return, but frequently their daughter marries a boy who is willing to enter the family business. I have seen more three-generation homes in Texas than in New York.

A remarkably large number marry within the faith. Although the historic Sephardic community of Charleston has disappeared, the present generation seems inclined to preserve its identity. Being Jewish in the South and Southwest today is no longer exotic. At a B'nai B'rith convention held in McAllen, Texas, in 1965, the glee club and orchestra of Pan American College presented a program which included several Hebrew songs, among them *artza alinu* and *naaleh l'artzeinu*. As the words "let us go up to the Land of Israel in joy" came from the throats of the small-town Texas boys and girls, all of whom were Baptists, Methodists, or Episcopalians, the Jewish audience beamed with delight. "Don't you think it's wonderful," one of them exclaimed to me, "that a small town can present something as good as this, with a deliberate attempt to create a Jewish spirit?"

Something of Texas has left its mark on its 64,305 Jewish residents (only 0.61 per cent of the Lone Star State's population). A visitor to an Orthodox service on Saturday afternoon in Dallas is likely to see a worshiper sitting down to the traditional between-afternoon-and-evening Sabbath snack of herring, rye bread, and brandy wearing a huge Western hat. Jews ride herd in the pampas of the Argentine, on the slopes of modern Galilee—and also on the Texas range.

Of course, Texas is unique in that its city people affect the mannerisms, the drawling speech, and, on occasion, the costume of the rancher. I sat in a barbershop next to a circuit courthouse in a large Texas city. Several judges were having haircuts. Each seemed to vie with the others in prolonging his Southwestern drawl and amiable manner of speech.

Alex Miller of the Anti-Defamation League, who supervises seven Southern offices for his organization, detects a new spirit among the younger Southern Jews of the third and fourth generation. They are, he reports, more self-assured in their Jewishness, and more likely to go out on a limb on the issue of civil rights.

But the Old South remains slow in absorbing newcomers. The story is told of an Orange, New Jersey, businessman who settled in Selma, Alabama, more than a quarter of a century ago, and established a reputation for his collection of memorabilia on the "War Between the States." He has lectured to the Daughters of the Confederacy and other groups all over the South. Recently, when he was introduced to a Jewish visitor to Selma, one of the old-timers put his arm around his shoulders: "We're awfully fond of Art. Pretty soon we're thinking of naturalizing him."

Charles Bloch of Macon, Georgia
"Our Constitution affirms white superiority, not *supremacy*, but inferiority of the black race."

We were in the office of the senior member of an old and reputable Macon law firm. My host, who would be perfectly cast in the movie role of a venerable U.S. senator, spoke with fervor as he uttered the words, "our Constitution."

"Our leaders in Washington are playing politics, are ignoring the very fundamentals of our American Constitution."

There was restraint in his voice despite his strong feelings. He sensed that I did not share his enthusiasm, and he wanted to be a good host.

Charles Bloch's walls were lined with symbols of public recognition. He has practiced before the U.S. Supreme Court since 1918, traveling to Washington at least once a month. And he generally looked up his friend, Sen. George Russell whom he had nominated for the presidency as a States' Righter at the Philadelphia convention of 1960.

I was presented with a copy of his book, *States' Rights: The Law of the Land*. It was written with passion and dedicated to his grand-

sons "with the hope that constitutional government may survive."
The two Georgia senators both contributed approving prefaces to
the book. Herman E. Talmadge found "the genius of this great
Georgian in every facet of his work," noting that Bloch's writings
were "a devastating indictment of those Supreme Court justices who
are pursuing a cynical and calculated course to transform that
tribunal into a super legislature." Russell similarly applauded Bloch
for "clearly depicting the ominous trend to centralization and 'one
big government' which threatens the work of the Founders."

Charles Bloch was born in Baton Rouge and educated there. He
spoke with pride about his religious confirmation in the Baton
Rouge temple. "My religious philosophy is distilled in the words of
Micah, 'to do justly, love mercy, and walk humbly.'"

I mentioned that Lincoln had once pointed to the same verse as
the essence of his faith.

"I'm glad I'm in such distinguished company," Bloch responded.
"My grandfather was a first lieutenant in the Confederate Army,
Fourth Louisiana Infantry. He married a French girl. His second
wife, my grandmother, was a German-Jewish girl named Blum—
we're related to the golf pro, Arnold Blum. I attended school at LSU
and the University of Georgia, and served in the Georgia state
legislature in the thirties."

The university had accorded him many honors, and he sits on its
board of regents.

"In Atlanta, in those days, I was conscious of the fact that many
of my fellow legislators were Klansmen. We were keenly aware of
the Leo Frank case."

I mentioned a fellow Georgian, now a New York resident, Morris
B. Abram, a native of Fitzgerald, who successfully fought the
Georgia reapportionment case before the Supreme Court.

"I respect Morris; a fine young man. But he's in error, especially in
his 'one-man, one-vote' idea, which is unconstitutional." He spoke
benignly, without a trace of rancor against those who didn't see
things his way. There was more hurt and disappointment than anger
in his face.

"I have held every office in a temple: board member, treasurer,
secretary, vice president, president. I'm proud of my Jewish heritage, I want my grandchildren to remain loyal Jews and marry
within the faith. I would never leave it. I wouldn't want my Jewish

critics to say: 'We always knew Charlie wanted to leave his faith.' Although I'm not sympathetic with Israel, I support the United Jewish Appeal."

"What do you want most out of life, Mr. Bloch?"

"The health and happiness of my family, and"—his voice rose with emotion—"the restoration of harmony to our nation."

A number of Southern Jewish leaders, and national leaders who work in the South, insist that Charles Bloch is not typical. He and others have forcefully opposed public pronouncements by national Jewish bodies, lay and religious, on issues of civil rights, and have threatened to withdraw their financial support. But at conventions of the Union of American Hebrew Congregations, representatives from several Deep South cities rose to express what they called "the sentiments of the New South," and supported resolutions condemning racial bigotry.

Atlanta Profile—The New South

Atlanta, Georgia, has been called the New York of the South. While some Georgians disown the city as part of the Southland, most Atlantans see themselves as an integral part of Dixie.

Religiously it is unique. Virtually every Jewish family in Atlanta is affiliated with some congregation. More than 1,600 families belong to Conservative congregations; more than 1,100 to Reform, and close to 900 families are members of Orthodox synagogues.

Philanthropically, the Jewish community ranks high. Nearly every adult Jew contributes to the combined campaign. In 1965, Atlanta Jewry raised more than $850,000.

Economically, Jews are prosperous. No more than twenty families a year apply for assistance. The median income of Jewish families is estimated at $10,000, which is substantially above that of the general white population.

The skyline of the city, which gives it its "New York look," is due at least in part to the efforts of a Jewish builder. Culturally, Jews are prominent in art, music, and the theater. Although they represent less than a fiftieth of the city's population, they provide a quarter or a third of its theater audiences, and are very much in the forefront as culture consumers. Atlanta is a city of colleges, and there are many Jews on university faculties, especially in the sciences. A famous Israeli archaeologist is a visiting professor.

Socially, Jews are denied membership in the old-line clubs and have sumptuous city and country clubs of their own. On the other hand, the liberal city offers few signs of overt anti-Semitism. As in many other American cities, few Jews are to be found in government—there are no Jewish judges—and they are not in politics. The director of the Jewish Welfare Fund, who had once held a comparable post in Albany, New York, pointed out that while a quarter of the Jewish population of Albany is employed by the state of New York, he could not recall a single Jewish employee of the state of Georgia. An old-timer explained that the salary scale of state employees was so low, until recently, that few ambitious people were attracted to government work.

The racial convulsions of the past decade have found Atlanta in the vortex of the struggle, but Jewish leaders have refrained from assuming a leadership role. When liberal Mayor Allen convinced a meeting of the clergy to help lay the groundwork for racial change, Rabbi Jack Rothschild told him, "Without Protestant leadership you are a dead duck," and the Mayor agreed.

Some Jews are nervous. They still call to mind the Leo Frank lynching in Marietta a half-century ago, and the memories were revived by Harry Golden's recent book on the subject. On the other hand, when Rabbi Rothschild served as chairman of the Martin Luther King dinner, which attracted a national spotlight, the trustees of his influential congregation—many of whom wished he were more conservative—endorsed his right to follow the dictates of his conscience.

A Tale of Two Cities

Houston and Galveston, a large city and a small one, offer contrasting experiences to their Jews. Houston is a city with few moorings; 75 per cent of its population were born elsewhere. The Jewish community has not kept pace with the city's mushrooming growth. And despite their general prosperity and their quite opulent synagogues, the 6,000 Jewish families have not become fully integrated in the large community of a million, although Houston Jews insist that they are better off, in this respect, than their Dallas coreligionists.

The wide-open spaces of Texas are not always open to Jews who want to buy good homes—at least in Houston. River Oaks, a fashionable residential area for oil people and others, is restricted to Gentiles. I spoke to a prominent lawyer whose clients include some of Houston's great industrial establishments.

"Would you run for public office—for the post of judge, for example?"

He shook his head thoughtfully. "I wouldn't. I don't think that with my Jewish name I'd get elected here, and certainly not in Dallas.

"One of my clients once invited me to go on a hunting trip. We are old friends. When I learned that he had invited three other couples—oil people—I advised him to check with them. I was right; he called me back, very embarrassed."

In suburban Bel-Air a high-school assembly sponsored a revival talk by a zealous Protestant missionary urging students to return to Christ. It apparently never occurred to the principal that non-Christians might take offense at this assault on their religious convictions.

Yet there are Texas towns with only one Jewish family which have a Jewish mayor.

The city of Galveston has a long history of liberalism both racial and religious. Its schools were racially integrated long before other cities in the Southwest. When I visited Texas, the acting governor of the state was Babe Schwartz, state senator from Galveston. (Austin has a curious custom of delegating one of its senators to occupy the governor's seat when he is out of Texas.)

The present mayor of Galveston (1966), and the third Jewish mayor of the Gulf Coast city, is Edward Schreiber, who is also president of the local Orthodox synagogue. Jews have been county judges and chairmen of the school board. Several public schools bear Jewish names. Ed Schreiber, an expansive, easygoing Texan, is a successful businessman, a former president of the Texas Retail Merchants' Association. A man who knows how to mix work and play, he has entertained hundreds of organizations as a song-and-dance minstrel, and has been president of Kiwanis and a host of other organizations, including the Texas Shrine Chanters Association.

Mayor Schreiber has no hesitation in declaring his Jewishness or in taking a partisan public stand in support of Israel. He uses Talmudic quotations to add spice to his speeches.

The second Jewish mayor, in 1937, was Adrian Levy; and Ike Kempner, still erect and in good health at ninety-four, was the pioneer, first as treasurer and later as mayor. I. H. Kempner is a Galveston institution. The street on which he lived as a child is now Kempner Street, and nearby is Kempner Park.

I visited the Kempner old-fashioned elegant home just a few blocks away from his birthplace. Mrs. Kempner, handsome and beautifully groomed, and amazingly young after sixty-two years of marriage, showed me some of the mementos of early Galveston, including an iron crest of the original U.S.S. *Texas* given to them by the commanding admiral.

On his eighty-eighth birthday, the city of Galveston had tendered a banquet in honor of I. H., and soon thereafter Kempner wrote his memoirs. He offered me a copy of his *Recalled Recollections*, a delightful recounting of early Texas life, and inscribed his autograph "with the author's plea for mercy."

Ike Kempner spent his early childhood "in a home across from the Artillery Club, scene of coming-out balls for all Texas debutantes, next to the Baptist Church and the synagogue—and adjacent to Galveston's most exclusive house of prostitution." He became one of the state's richest men, first with a successful cotton brokerage business, later in export banking, and ultimately by introducing a sugar crop in South Texas. The town of Sugarland, not far from Houston, was founded by the Kempners.

The Kempner family became a part of Texas society in the late nineteenth century. His book contains many whimsical comments on this achievement. He recalled that once, at a social gathering, a banker's daughter appeared in a strapless gown. His father whispered to Ike, "Don't extend that loan of $80,000. His credit is no good."

Some time later the banker absconded to South America. Ike asked his father how he had known about the man's reputation.

"I had no inside information. I figured that a man who couldn't control his daughter couldn't control his business."

Ike's father felt that his son could not have a well-rounded education in the Southwest. A friend told him that Germany had great universities, and in the late 1880s Ike was sent to Göttingen for a year. Then he was enrolled at Washington and Lee University. Father Kempner, in the last year of his life, kept writing the university president, General George Washington Custis Lee, a descendant of Washington and brother of Robert E. Lee, asking, "Is Ikey an educated man?"

"My father had great faith in Texas and Texas land. He came from the agricultural section of Poland and knew that land was treasured there. But those of his religion were not permitted to acquire it."

The tribute by the entire community of Galveston was sincerely offered. I. H. Kempner had helped set the city on its feet during a series of crises. After the tragic flood of 1900, he organized for its rebuilding, as he also did after the great fire. A silver bowl gracing one of the mantelpieces is inscribed with the words: "From Galveston to its most distinguished citizen."

The years have not dimmed his wit. Tempted to reply at length to all the accolades of the banquet speakers, he cut short his remarks with a story:

"Many years ago, when we had a coachman instead of a chauffeur, our coachman came to me for advice. 'I want to divorce my wife. She talks and she talks and she talks. I can't stand it.'

" 'What does she talk about?'

" 'She don't say.' "

Another prominent Jewish citizen helped give Galveston its character: Rabbi Henry Cohen, the remarkable "man who stayed in Texas," serving as rabbi in one congregation for sixty-two years. The sugar grower and the Jewish preacher labored side by side in a score of civic causes. The Kempner family honored the rabbi's memory by providing a home for the temple's rabbi. The "parsonage" is known as the "rabbinage" in Galveston.

Kempner attributes the secure status of Jews in Galveston to the towering personality of Rabbi Cohen. When Rabbi Cohen marked his fiftieth anniversary as a Texas rabbi, 5,000 people filled the city auditorium for the celebration. Albert Vorspan, in his *Giants of Justice*, tells of the Episcopalian minister who declared, "In my church it is a high honor when a minister becomes a bishop. . . . To me, Rabbi Cohen always is Right Reverend, and, in all sincerity, my Father in God."

I am not convinced that the impact of the two personalities alone created the atmosphere of acceptance. Galveston, like San Antonio, and unlike the Texas cities to the north, has always been a heterogeneous community, with many Roman Catholics and many Mexicans. Both cities have been hospitable to their Jewish citizens, and have provided them with full economic and political opportunity. As I have already noted, it is homogeneity that has so often proved the enemy of Jewish status. Dr. Mordecai Kaplan has contended that the best thing that ever happened to the Jews of America, in terms of security, was "the presence in the body politic of a large and powerful group that insists upon remaining unassimilable"—the Roman Catholics.

Miami Beach: Love of This World

Miami Beach is a symbol in the vocabulary of the contemporary Jew. Jews in Jerusalem or Copenhagen or Buenos Aires think of Miami Beach the way New York Irishmen think of Killarney. There is a joke told about a dying Jew whose last request was, "I want to join *my people*." His friends and relatives thought he was asking to be buried in the ancestral plot in Israel; actually, it turned out he wanted to be sent to Miami Beach. Southern Florida, with its ever-mild climate and graceful palm trees, is "paradise regained" for hundreds of thousands of American and Canadian Jews.

The pattern of ghettoization is probably more pronounced in this part of the United States than in most parts of America. Originally a citadel of bigotry—Rabbi Leon Kronish recalled that when he arrived in Miami Beach twenty-two years ago there were still a few signs, "No Jews or dogs allowed"—some of the downtown areas around Lincoln Road today have all the characteristics of Tel Aviv's Allenby Road.

Fort Lauderdale and the beaches to the north are still Gentile territory. Occasionally a southbound Jewish tourist will get off the highway one exit too soon, but usually, after a day or two, he will join his coreligionists in southern Dade County.

Most of the permanent residents are past retirement. One hears much discussion about health, including some vivid details of gastric problems. "Bring me a large order of prunes," I heard one not too elderly woman say to the waiter, and her companion added: "Some farina, please. Make sure it's not oatmeal; that's so irritating."

The language of street, restaurant, and park bench is Yiddish-English.

"Are you going downtown today, Sadie?"

"It's all according."

Of the 175,000 tourists who arrive in Miami Beach in February, nine out of ten are Jewish. In July, the tourist crowds are dense, but they are Gentile.

Why don't the two mix? One old-timer explained it as a difference in style of enjoyment. "At the Standard Club, which is 70 per cent Jewish, the bar is deserted; at the American Club, which has few Jews, the bar is packed." But if Jews are absent from the bistros they are very present at the race tracks. Gambling, an ancient Jewish disease, seems almost endemic to Florida. Manufacturers and salesmen rush almost directly from the airport to Hialeah and the many dogtracks.

I discussed the pattern of Jewish tourist behavior with Jerry Sussman, one of the owners of the swank Carillon Hotel. The Sussman family represents five generations of Jewish hotelkeeping. His great-grandparents operated their first Catskill inn in 1880. His grandparents and parents owned the Tamarack Lodge. Sussman's nineteen-year-old son is a student at Florida State College, majoring in hotel management.

Grandpa Sussman asked his children to continue the tradition of keeping the hotel kosher, and most of the mountain hotels followed suit. On the other hand, Sussman declared, many Jews coming to the tropics feel they are in a different world. Even those who expect to observe the dietary laws in the "borsht belt" somehow imagine that tradition doesn't operate in the tropics.

The Carillon is Jerry Sussman's sixth Miami hotel. When he realized that the demand for kosher food was declining, he spent several hundred thousand dollars in an extensive advertising campaign to attract the non-kosher trade. "I couldn't be too blunt, so our first ads read, 'featuring international cuisine,' or, 'delicious shrimp and lobster salads.' It didn't always work. Some people said: 'What will they think of next? Kosher lobster!'

"We cater to a Jewish clientele, but from May to December half our guests are Gentile.

"What do our Jewish guests look for? Comfort and familiar foods of top quality. You'd be amazed how orderly most of them are. At our Burgundy Room they consume less than one drink per person a whole evening. Even when we offer free drinks, at some programs, there is no rush. No hotel here needs a bouncer. We never have a boisterous crowd. In the winter we serve roast beef to the Jews and in the summer, steak to the Gentiles.

"Entertainment has to be the very best. The more nostalgic, the better. The late Sophie Tucker, George Jessel, Danny Thomas, a Lebanese with Jewish memories, all play to standing-room-only audiences. Professor Backward packs in the summer crowd; Jews stay away in droves from such programs.

"Our people like familiarity. Forty per cent of our guests are repeats three or four times. They time their trip to coincide with others they have played cards with before. Fellowship is the big thing.

"Our Passover crowds are enormous. They long for the flavor rather than ritual observance. We pay Jan Peerce $15,000 for the two Seder dinners. But even with Peerce they don't stay till the end of the ritual.

"What they want most, I suspect, in addition to quality service and entertainment, is warmth. The big thing is to be remembered. They appreciate being called by name."

Jerry Sussman, tanned, handsome, relaxed despite the tensions of his work, looks young enough to be a graduate student. I asked him how he managed to preserve his youthful appearance.

"I love the hotel business, as my family did. What better work is there than to deal with people when they are in a happy frame of mind, looking for the delights of life in a good way?"

The backbone of Miami Jewry (not the Beach) is, of course, not the transient pleasure-seeking population—although they provide a livelihood for many—but those who have settled in the South, for reasons of health, because of Northern winters, or for other attractions.

Home building is a Jewish industry: 300 of the 400 Miami members of the National Association of Home Builders are Jewish. Of the ninety members of the Association of General Contractors, half are Jews.

One builder told me that because of their traditional emphasis on comfort, Jewish contractors pioneered in the use of air conditioning, which has by now become an essential element of life in the warm climate.

Miami has developed culturally in the wake of the Jewish influx.

Symphony music, a good library, a well-rounded university, top-grade medical facilities, great art—all of these have come to the Miami area with the spectacular rise of its Jewish population.

Religious life, too, has deepened as roots have been dug. The synagogues, especially Reform and Conservative, in Miami and Miami Beach have full and active programs. Temple Menorah attracts a thousand worshipers on Friday evening. The Hebrew Academy, an all-day school on Pine Tree Drive which caters to the children of executives like Jerry Sussman, is housed in an exquisitely beautiful building.

The Beach's showplace is the Miami Beach Jewish Center, a Conservative congregation whose rabbi, Irving Lehrman, is one of the most colorful and dynamic preachers in the country. During "the season," worshipers must come an hour early to be sure of a seat for Sabbath services, and often admission to the vast, resplendent temple is by ticket only.

CHAPTER 19

Jews of the Golden West

In San Francisco

The San Francisco telephone directory lists sixty subscribers whose last name is "Jew." Not one of them is Jewish.

But Jews are, or recently have been, heads of the Arts Commission and the Parks and Recreation Commission, president of the Police Commission, chairman of Public Utilities, president of the Chamber of Commerce, the Better Business Bureau, Community Chest, United Crusade, Salvation Army, and the board of Santa Clara University. Individual Jews have given their names to the city zoo, the aquarium, the civic swimming pool (world's largest outdoor), the musical amphitheater, and to one of the hills which surround the beautiful city.

If, from the Jewish viewpoint, San Francisco is the most thoroughly integrated city in the Western world, one simple fact of history must be borne in mind: In the first year of its birth, one hundred Jews were among its residents. In every other city, the Gentiles were already there, and settled, when the first Jews trickled in.

Mid-nineteenth-century San Francisco, rowdy and brash, attracted the more intrepid spirits among Jewish pioneers. Piety and intellectuality were not among its early endowments: no one adventured to the Far West to find spiritual sanctuary or stimulation of the mind. Even today the standard *Tourist Guide* contains scores of pages about the scenic attractions, fine restaurants, historic reminiscences of bawdy days, but hardly a line about cathedrals, and none about synagogues.

A century ago, the author of *Land of Gold*, Hinton R. Helper, contended that "California can and does furnish the best bad things that are obtainable in America." San Francisco has matured, in the present century, into one of the most cultivated cities in the nation. (There are those who would contend it has no peers.) The cultural tone of the Pacific Coast city can be credited, at least in part, to the ferment given it by Jewish leaders from its early days. If in the words of one writer San Francisco is a literary city, with probably a larger percentage of authors, bookstores, and readers per capita than most cities, "the presence of Jews offers some explanation."

The story of the Levi Strauss family, as Harry Golden has described it, is symbolic of the impact of Jews on the city. Levi Strauss noted that gold prospectors tore their pants too readily, because they kept the pockets full of heavy metals. He designed sturdy trousers with pockets reinforced with metal instead of thread. Levi Strauss' levis—the original blue jeans—spread throughout the land, and the family prospered.

Today, the families representing the original firm are part of the backbone of everything cultural in San Francisco art, music, the theater, social service. Walter Haas, the firm president, is the energetic and imaginative head of the Parks and Recreation Commission. I visited with his brother-in-law, Daniel Koshland, one of the top company officials, a handsome, gray-mustached man in his early seventies whom one of the city's leaders called "the Bernard Baruch of San Francisco."

Dan Koshland's parents were both born in San Francisco, his father in 1865. Both the Koshland and Haas families have preserved their Jewish loyalties, and Dan Koshland described the deeply ingrained family tradition of inculcating in their children and grandchildren a sense of communal responsibility. "Our whole circle of friends is involved in social service rather than social activity. We work for United Nations' causes, and especially for human rights."

Twenty years ago Dan Koshland organized the Council for Civic Unity, and became its first president. The council served as the instrument for bringing together the varied faith and civic groups in the broad area of human relations. Last year he chaired the city's United Crusade.

San Francisco Jewry is one of the few in America in which German Jews are still predominant today (the story has changed in one generation) and it is probably also the richest. Many of its downtown buildings are owned by men such as Louis Lurie and Ben Swig. Banking, mining, and lumber have brought prosperity to the long-settled Jewish community. The Zellerbach family owns forests the size of Rhode Island. There was a time when 90 per cent of the funds raised by the Jewish Welfare Federation was provided by eighty families. Today, the burden of raising more than two million dollars is more evenly distributed among the Bay area's 71,000 Jews.

Apparently there is little Gentile backlash to Jewish affluence. Some Negro leaders complain about the large number of Jews in positions of authority in the civil-rights movement, but the religious groups seem to work together harmoniously. Some of the Jewish community spokesmen explained the spirit of amity as a reflection of the city's cosmopolitanism; a mixture of French and Latin-American as well as Anglo-Saxon peoples. San Francisco, one of them suggested, is probably the only metropolitan area in the country whose power structure is not specifically WASP (White Anglo-Saxon Protestant). Religious groups tend to operate on a live-and-let-live basis. Little of the religious extremism of southern California is to be found in the amiable climate of the north.

Rabbi Morris Goldstein, one of the three veteran rabbis whose combined years of service to San Francisco congregations total more than one hundred and twenty years, spoke to me about the community's stability. "Our children tend to remain in our area. Those who marry outsiders and move away ultimately find their way back. Jews are, on the whole, accepted in a natural way. Minor pockets of discrimination still exist: the Pacific Union Club is closed to us, and the Bohemian Club takes in only a few. Our own Jewish club, the Concordia-Argonaut, has opened its membership to Gentiles, on principle." (Not a common practice elsewhere in the country.) Willie Mays, the Negro baseball star, was elected as a member. He was sponsored by a banker, Jacob Shemano, who had rescued the Giant star from fiscal chaos.

"We have had remarkable continuity of religious traditions. Incidentally, our Reform temples preserve some of the traditional forms. The new temples in San Mateo and Oakland follow our custom of wearing a head covering and *tallith!"*

He mentioned two families, the Borboys and the Monashes, whose children's confirmation represented five generations in one congregation (hardly duplicated anywhere in the New World).

Dr. Goldstein described a Bar Mitzvah in his congregation. The mother of the boy was Japanese, and a hundred Japanese attended services for the occasion. She is active in the Sisterhood, and her youngster sings in the temple choir. (Marriage with Japanese is not unknown among Jews on the West Coast. The wife of a young rabbi in Los Angeles is a Japanese convert to Judaism. On visiting his temple, I found that she was accepted readily by its members.)

"Originally Jews lived 'south of the Slot' [a local reference to Market Street], but now they have spread throughout the whole Bay area, to the Peninsula area and Marin County [beyond the Golden Gate Bridge], and we have a serious problem with inter-marriage. Many such marriages leave the families in limbo; only a few join churches and quite a number join synagogues."

Dr. Fred Massarik's 1959 survey of the Jewish population in the area revealed a much higher incidence of intermarriage than in other parts of the country: more than 17 per cent in San Francisco, 20 per cent in the Peninsula area, and 37 per cent in Marin County. Obviously, a Jew who takes a non-Jewish mate very frequently moves across the Golden Gate Bridge.

One institution in San Francisco has no parallel anywhere else in the country. It is a vestige of an ancient tradition, the *Chevra Kadisha,* a ritual institution for burial of the dead. Since one of the most prized acts of piety in Judaism was to attend and give honor to the dead, a kind of volunteer organization was developed, not unlike the tradition of the American volunteer firemen, which combined civic responsibility with a good deal of sociability. San Francisco has preserved this custom through its Sinai Memorial Chapel. Its director, Louis Freehof, a distinguished veteran of the community, described the operation of the unique institution. The chapel conducts about six hundred and fifty burials a year. For the destitute, services are arranged without charge, and since there are many transients in the port city, there are occasions when the chapel flies in a member of the family from other parts of the country for the funeral or ships the remains to Israel. Some one hundred and ten poor families are taken care of annually.

Despite these demands, the rates are fixed to provide a surplus (in consonance with the tradition that "charity redeemeth from death") and each year more than two hundred thousand dollars is distributed from the surplus to Jewish charities.

One final footnote to the story of San Franciscan Jewry. While the nineteenth-century Jewish newcomer to the Coast was generally part of the adventurous pursuers after the pot of gold, his twentieth-century counterpart is likely to be an electronics engineer, a nuclear physicist, or a biochemist, associated with the frontiersmen of science who have flocked to the academic and industrial institutions of California. Among the scientific talent concentrated in the San Francisco Bay area no less than eight are Jewish Nobel prize winners.

Southern California

Jews should feel at home in Los Angeles County in a basic historic way. The Israeli student enrolled at UCLA—and there are hundreds of them in California colleges—must feel comfortable with its climate; it is so much like Israel. The striking contrast between the sizzling valleys and the cool plains calls to mind the heat of the foothills near Jerusalem and the balmy comfort of the Old City. No wonder the Jews of the East—Eastern America and Eastern Europe—were drawn to sunny southern California. A century ago there were eight Jewish residents. Today, over a half-million have settled there—every tenth American Jew in the country.

Not many decades ago, Hollywood beckoned to the Jews of New York and Chicago, and they created the film industry—both its artistry and its tawdriness. Today it is the Rand Corporation which sends out its clarion call, and Jewish political and social scientists are among those who respond.

Beverly Hills, more than half Jewish, like Westwood and other Los Angeles suburbs, is flashy and full of Lincoln Continentals. (One of the faculty members at a college for Jewish studies told me, "Even I drive a Continental—secondhand.") A prominent temple on Wilshire Boulevard raffled off a race horse, and interest was intensified by the knowledge that last year's temple bazaar horse won a race at Santa Anita.

In Los Angeles' most distant suburb, Las Vegas, the outgoing president of the Synagogue Sisterhood was presented with a ring in the shape of dice, inscribed with the numbers 5 and 2—an expressive way for Las Vegas congregants to say *mazal tov*. When the son of the owner of the Tropicana had his Bar Mitzvah, the caterer wheeled in a cake baked in an exact replica of the twelve-story gambling casino.

But the tinsel quality of some aspects of Los Angeles living seems far removed from 590 Vermont Avenue, the headquarters for the entire Jewish community. Overlooking the Freeway to Hollywood and the Pacific Ocean is a magnificent building housing 400 different Jewish organizations in Greater Los Angeles.

I attended a meeting of the Executive Committee of the Jewish Welfare Federation. The two-hour luncheon session brought together some of the top people in the Jewish community: an attorney for many of the Hollywood stars; the owner of a large savings and loan bank; a distinguished physician. At the head table sat the executive Director, Isidore Soboloff, regarded as one of the ablest fund raisers in America, who had recently come from Detroit to give Los Angeles a shot in the arm. The diffuse southern California Jewish community has never really mustered its forces; only 55,000 make regular contributions to Federation.

Soboloff is a handsome man, with bushy, iron-gray hair, black eyebrows, and very light blue eyes. He is obviously an authority figure in Los Angeles Jewry.

Presiding over the sixty participants was Mrs. Leo Hirsch, vice chairman of Federation, and representative of Hadassah. The men responded to the authority of the chair as if they were used to being presided over by a woman. Other women who spoke were also fluent, precise, and obviously at home on a public platform.

Among other items, the agenda included a discussion of the Émigré Service report. In light of new U.S. immigration laws, Los Angeles would be required to handle at least twenty-five new families. The committee chairman asked for an allocation of $10,000. The treasurer, traditional watchdog of funds, urged caution about overspending. It was a standing joke, and everyone laughed as approval was granted.

Mrs. Hirsch told of a family she had interviewed which had made its way from behind the Iron Curtain. Their pride, their dignity, and their gratitude for liberation, she said, "made all our efforts worth while." The leaders nodded their heads in assent as they turned to a consideration of the problems raised by the recent Watts racial explosion.

The meeting duplicated similar Federation meetings throughout the country. Rumania and Iraq and Israel were 7,000 more miles away, but human imagination and compassion had not been diminished by distance.

A few elements in the picture were different, however. A report was given about courses offered on such subjects as "Group Work for Board Members," "Developments in American Jewish Life," "The Search for Jewish Identity." These active business and professional executives were not only spending part of their day on communal affairs, they were also studying evenings to enhance their understanding of current problems.

One course on Judaism for women, it was announced, had attracted a dozen non-Jews. They were not married or engaged to Jews, they were just curious.

Los Angeles has the most ambitious adult-education tradition of any community in the country. The Jewish community has not only participated in the general upsurge of interest in education, but has also taken advantage of the cultural climate—especially at the University of Judaism on Sunset Boulevard—to fashion an elaborate program of its own. Mrs. Hirsch referred to two unusual study groups: thirty-five Jewish center directors met regularly to study Talmud (inconceivable anywhere else in America); and 100 Hadassah leaders have been meeting once a month for more than fifteen years for Jewish study. (The Hadassah board used to meet for two-hour monthly meetings; the sessions were extended to four hours, to allow two for study!)

One California touch intruded into the report of the Committee Dealing with Senior Citizens, a major problem in Los Angeles. "Every twenty-four hours," reported the chairman, "in Los Angeles, a Jewish gentleman over seventy-five proposes to a Jewish woman over sixty whom he has met at one of our club gatherings. And she accepts!"

Despite the distance separating the West Coast community from the center of American Jewish life, the level of religious education has improved over the years, according to Dr. Samuel Dinin, director of the Bureau of Jewish Education. Every Reform temple teaches Hebrew (this is not true in many parts of the country), and several have Hebrew high-school departments—one of them the largest in the United States.

Religious education has one archenemy, the climate. The outdoors beckons. Jews have more swimming pools per capita than the general population. Sports loom large in their lives—fishing, skiing, boating. Who wants to read or study when it's tempting to relax in the seductive sunshine? Besides, many came West to escape from the old ways, including the burdens of ancestral religious ties.

Economic opportunity in a booming community has brought prosperity to a large number of Los Angeles Jews. Real estate and building have attracted many, and quite a few professionals—dentists, doctors, pharmacists, and lawyers—have left their fields of training to enter banking and real estate. Most southern Californian Jews are Democrats, whatever that means in a politically volatile state. Ninety per cent voted for John F. Kennedy in 1960.

What about the status of the Jews in the Gentile world? I received conflicting answers from men who were close observers of communal life. The optimists told of excellent rapport with the Protestant establishment, of their close relationship with Methodist Bishop Gerald Kennedy, a national religious leader. Jews were certainly the cultural pace setters in southern California. They had joined with Mrs. Norman Chandler in spearheading the campaign for the prodigious Art Center, one of the showplaces of the nation. Judge Isaac Pacht, chairman of the Jewish Community Relations Council, now in his seventies, has led the fight against the powerful John Birch Society, and is highly esteemed by the entire community.

One of Los Angeles Jewry's ablest leaders, Martin Gang, attorney for many Hollywood stars and film executives, is chairman of the Board of Regents of the Immaculate Heart College, a leading Catholic college. Many Jewish judges sit on the highest courts of the state: two of the seven Supreme Court justices are Jewish.

On the other hand, there are few Jews in the executive ranks of big business, the three most important downtown clubs are Judenrein, and on the whole Jews tend to segregate themselves protectively into their own ghettos.

I checked on the community's notoriously bad record for philanthropic contributions. Kansas City Jewry, for example, gives five times as much per capita as the Jews of southern California. Several explanations were offered: Californians spend too much on the abundant life, leave little for civic needs. And the general community has low standards of giving: write a check for a hundred dollars to any cause and they place you on the board of directors.

I studied the Book of Life of Federation: the list of donors and the amounts contributed. They included several famous Hollywood names, and occasionally the fluid state of marriage creates problems. There is a story told of one much-married star who was asked by a neighbor for a contribution to Federation. She asked the neighbor to wait while she called to her husband upstairs: "Honey, are we Jewish?"

The men at 590 Vermont bewailed the ungenerous spirit of many movie people. But I noted that by far the largest contribution was made by a violinist from Milwaukee whose stage character is based on stinginess—Jack Benny.

Optimism—Jewish-American style

A few years ago, I visited the offices of Prime Minister David Ben Gurion in Jerusalem, together with Dr. Norman Vincent Peale. The Israeli premier, an avid student of Oriental religions and an authority on Buddhism, admitted he was unfamiliar with the writing of the American preacher.

"Tell me," he asked Dr. Peale, "what is there in your books that have made you so successful?"

The author of *The Power of Positive Thinking* gave the white-haired statesman a brief summary of his optimistic philosophy.

The scholar-statesman waved his hand in a kind of benign impatience: "There's nothing new in your teaching, my dear doctor. We Jews have been thinking positively for thousands of years!"

The affinity of spirit between American optimism and Jewish messianism accounts, at least in part, for the feeling of at-homeness of experienced Jews in America, and the natural way in which the American has accepted, not only the Jew, but his philosophy and his faith. Every rabbi who has expounded the principles of his religion to a Gentile audience, on the college campus, or at a Sunday-night church supper, or at a luncheon club meeting, has sensed a warm response to his presentation. "I like your religion. It makes a lot of sense. I can buy nearly everything you told us."

Two of the basic ingredients of optimism are a faith, however irrational, that tomorrow will be better than today, and a self-perspective which equips us not to take ourselves too seriously. This probably explains why the Jewish humorist evokes such a sympathetic response in American audiences, Jewish and non-Jewish alike. When the hero of *Fiddler on the Roof* wryly proclaims, in the words of Sholom Aleichem, "it's no disgrace to be poor—but it isn't an honor either," he expounds a philosophy that is essentially Jewish and essentially American at the same time. Mark Twain's "I come from poor but dishonest parents" pokes the same fun at the reverse snobbishness of the unsuccessful who are able to find some redeeming virtue in their failures.

Who but confirmed and congenital optimists could have set out, as did thousands of Jewish immigrants, with less than a handful of English words on their tongues, and a packet of pins and assorted pots and pans to peddle along the highways of the South and the West? Did they dream that their grandchildren would own department stores in Richmond, Denver, and Seattle?

An Iowa Jew, born in Russia, described his arrival in the United States at the turn of the century. He told me that his passage from Europe had been underwritten by the Baron de Hirsch Fund but that no one had told him that his destination was not New York City, as he had assumed, but Galveston. When his boat pulled into the Texas port, in blazing summer heat, the docks were filled with Negro longshoremen.

"My God," he told a fellow passenger, "they've taken us to Africa!" At the dockside they were greeted by an agent of Union Pacific Railroad who offered them a free trip to the Middle West. Without really understanding the English spoken, they accepted his offer, and found themselves on a long train ride heading to the unknown North.

The cars were primitive, and the natives of Oklahoma and Arkansas used the spittoons with unerring accuracy. The immigrant travelers looked at one another in horror—they had never heard of chewing tobacco, especially red tobacco.

"Woe is us!" they cried to one another. "Not only are we in Africa, but everyone here seems to have consumption!"

All along the route of the Union Pacific, in the small towns of Illinois, Iowa, and Nebraska, three or four of the Jews from the

Russian pale were set down and told, "This is the place you are going to live." And in those towns they lived and they prospered, sending their children to the state universities, becoming mayors and presidents of Rotary Clubs, and blending into their Waterloos and Dubuques and Sioux Cities as though they had come over on the *Mayflower*.

Despite the years of travail and the struggle for a livelihood, there must have been a good deal of enthusiasm in the letters they dispatched from their "African" refuge to relatives in Poland, Rumania, and Czarist Russia, for many followed after them convinced that the streets of Iowa and Nebraska and the Dakotas were paved with gold.

Dakota Diaspora

In South Dakota there are thirty Indians for every Jew and one Jew for every 100 square miles of territory. I would venture the guess that most South Dakotans have never spoken to or even laid eyes on a Jew. But the Sovereign Grand Inspector General of the Scottish Rite for South Dakota is Harry Margolin, a Yankton Jewish merchant. And a number of years ago Ben Strool, a Jewish rancher, was elected and later re-elected Commissioner of School and Public Lands. Abe Pred, state senator from Aberdeen for two terms, is one of the beloved citizens of that city.

To the north, the mayor of Fargo, North Dakota, the state's largest city, was at the time of this writing Jewish attorney Herschel Laschkowitz. Laschkowitz had also been a state senator, and once ran for governor. Evidently his Jewish name was no handicap in a community whose ethnic stock is largely Scandinavian and German.

I spoke to Judge Mose Lindau, who has presided over the Juvenile and County Court of Brown County (Aberdeen) for the past fifteen years. Mose and I had been in the same army outfit in France during World War II, and we had a chance to renew acquaintances.

Mose Lindau was born in Sioux City, but he dislikes living in a large city and prefers semi-rural life. "We Jews have taken on the characteristics of our Gentile associates in dress, manner of speech, and activities and interests. Most of us are 32nd Degree Masons and Shriners and many belong to the local country club."

Judge Lindau was elected venerable master of his local Scottish

Rite bodies. He and his wife and son, a medical student at Minnesota, adhere firmly to Jewish practices, and many Jews, such as Judge Lindau, have kept their traditional ties.

"I feel that I bring my Judaism to my work on the bench. I'm conscious of the standards set down by the Torah for the guidance of judges, of the high valuation our religion places on the guidance of children, particularly those who have lost their way. Before I commence work every day, I spend fifteen to twenty minutes studying Torah, translations of the Talmud, or Jewish works that will give me insight or guidance. My English translation of the Torah rests on my desk at all times."

Like most of the Jews of South Dakota, Lindau's father had been a traveling salesman covering the North Midwest. Many of the forebears of today's residents were pack peddlers; their children and grandchildren are successful retail merchants in department stores and smaller establishments dealing in clothing, hides, and furs. A few are cattle buyers, as they are in Wyoming and Nebraska.

The early Jewish pioneers in the late nineteenth century were Ukrainian Jewish immigrants whose one ambition was to show the world that Jews could till the soil successfully. They began their homesteading on a former Indian reservation (South Dakota was not destined to become a state for another ten years). "The whole town of Mitchell turned out to stare at the immigrants brewing and drinking Russian tea in the middle of the street," report Bernard Postal and Lionel Koppman in their delightful book, *A Jewish Tourist Guide to the U.S.*

Ultimately the original colony grew to 200, but their inexperience with the soil, coupled with drought, hail, and blizzards, drove most of them back to New York, leaving behind the only grand piano in the Dakotas. Some of the colony remained, however, and retained their Jewish identity: Sioux Falls and Aberdeen now have synagogues, and, according to Postal and Koppman, six families remained in Deadwood, where the first Jewish prospectors had joined Wild Bill Hickok and Calamity Jane.

I am told that other Jews in the Northern plains states have melted into the general population. A Russian Jew who settled near an Indian reservation married an Indian girl, and from the union of the tribe of Israel and the tribe of Sioux came a son who took his Ph.D. at an Ivy League college and now represents his state in Congress.

EPILOGUE

"I am a Jew." In the fact that these four words are spoken today in the United States without self-consciousness or hesitancy lies the miracle of American Jewry.

The young American Jew, born after World War II, affirms his identity in a natural, unaccented way. The shadings of feeling that often plagued his parents have vanished. There is no tinge of furtiveness, no over-the-shoulder tones, no need to turn on his Jewish "radar" to discover whether his neighbor is for or against him. There is no suggestion of defensiveness, no apologizing for those fellow Jews whose dialect is neither Yankee, Oxford, nor west of the Mississippi. His may not be the Chosen People, but neither are they the Un-Chosen People.

Alfred Kazin once wrote of a couple he had met at Cape Cod. "Their voices resounded with the confident pleasure of their being English." The American Jew, for the most part, has not quite attained the "confident pleasure" of his own being.

But for the young Jew, at least, group memory has none of the taint of immigrant squalor, of doors slammed in one's face, of accusations of deicide. Although he knows that 6 million people were dispatched to an ignominious death, simply because they bore the same label he does, he is too far removed to share the humiliation of the poet, Bialik, who wrote, in the wake of a ghetto slaughter:

Forgive, ye shamed of the earth, yours is a pauper-Lord!
Poor was He during your life, and poorer still of late. . . .
Your dead were vainly dead; and neither I nor you
Know why you died or wherefore, for whom, nor by what
laws;
Your deaths are without reason; you lives are without cause.

Those Jews who have died violently as Jews in the 1960s have fallen in defense of Israel's frontiers. Their lives are not "without cause"; their deaths are not "without reason."

An American child born in the 1950s, lacking the traumas of past indignities, can say, as a Bar Mitzvah boy recently declared: "I like the sound of the word Jewish." Another teen-ager wrote to me not long ago: "It's a good feeling to belong to a minority group. In this day and age, when everything is done in masses, it's wonderful to be part of something small and good."

The fact that today's American can feel the goodness of being small, can belong to a minority without feeling embattled, marks a considerable transformation in America's self-image. I think there are many historians who would pinpoint the date of that change as Election Day, 1960, when John F. Kennedy, a Catholic and the grandson of an Irish immigrant, became a presidential symbol of the nation from a hitherto minority group.

Prof. Eli Ginzberg has observed that "all significant change in social life is the result of a believing minority which finally convinces an unbelieving majority of the wisdom of a particular approach." It is my conviction that Jewish values and Jewish communal effort played a vital role in moving America of the sixties in the direction of cultural pluralism.

True, the New-World Jew has not been American very long. He carried much of himself across the Atlantic and, like Tennyson's Ulysses, he is very much a part of all that he has met. He shares with the Italian, the Spaniard, and the Greek the zest for life and breezy abandon which characterize many Mediterranean people. His Semitic roots, although seemingly remote, are yet discernible, in the brooding pensiveness, the lack of discipline, and the heightened individualism so frequently ascribed to the Arabs.

Some Slavic qualities have rubbed off during his sojourn among the Russians, a bit of the melancholy, music in a minor, bitter-sweet key, an unembarrassed, gushing sentimentality, a preoccupation with the word.

But he is surely a creature of the West as well—the ordered intellectualism of the French, the British, and the Germans has blended well with his own *sechel,* honed fine in the ancient academies.

It is most of all in the free atmosphere of America that the Jew has experienced his greatest creativity—in the arts and sciences, in literature, and in the economic arena.

Does such freedom mark the end of Jewish distinctiveness? It is not an easy question to answer. In every other great country in the world Jewish citizens have made their imprint on the national fabric. But it is a design that is superimposed upon the cloth, not woven into the fabric as in the case of America. What happens to the Jewish strands? In such a setting, how long do they retain their individuality? The prize for Jewish involvement and participation in America is apparent: they feel totally at home in the United States. There is no "we" and "they" as there is everywhere else in the world. But the price is considerable.

American Jews, try as they may, find difficulty in feeling the peoplehood of Israel, the mystical bond that unites them with their coreligionists outside the United States. They cry for them when they are hurt, and are quick to reach out a helping hand; but they sense no kinship with those not in distress. The boundaries of America are the limits of their creative Jewish concerns.

I asked one of the world's foremost Jewish theologians, Rabbi Abraham Joshua Heschel, who was born in Warsaw, took his doctorate in Berlin, and is now very much an American, "What are the chances for Jewish survival in the United States?"

"It is more than a problem of survival. It is rather how to keep our people from vanishing in the abyss of drabness and vulgarity, how to resist being committed to the nationwide prisons of triviality.

"I think that the attitude of the Christian community in America has undergone a radical change. Instead of hostility, there is not only respect but an *expectation*—a belief that Jews have a message to convey, insights which others may share. *We mustn't disappoint them.* Our generation, especially our young people, have begun to cultivate a sophistication of the inner life. With their intellectual orientation, our youth wants to know something about Jewish religious thought. They just won't call it theology."

The fundamental question remains: How long can a value system survive which is not embodied in an institution devoted exclusively to the propagation and perpetuation of those values?

In the spirit of the prophets, as long as Jews continue to "seek justice and love mercy" the *tradition* of Judaism will survive. Will the pursuit of justice, the need for compassion and the matchless concern for the world of ideas that have been the special hallmark of the Judaic tradition long endure without a clear and uniquely distinctive *community* of Jews in the United States?

ABOUT THE AUTHOR

MORRIS N. KERTZER has been university teacher, preacher, pastor, military chaplain, and author on the "art" of his faith, for Jews and non-Jews. He is now rabbi of the Larchmont, New York, Temple.

Doctor Kertzer's reputation as a leader in world Jewry has taken him all around the world, and has won acclaim from several quarters. He received the Pro Deo Gold Medal in Rome for his work in promoting Jewish-Catholic understanding, and was awarded the George Washington Medal of 1956 for his analysis of anti-Semitism in Soviet Russia. In 1964 he was honored as "Rabbi of the Year" and given the Israel Cummings Award for his work between the rabbinate and the social-work profession.